THE
QUIET
GAME

G·K
Hall
&Cº

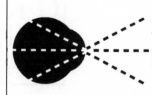

This Large Print Book carries the
Seal of Approval of N.A.V.H.

GREG ILES

THE

QUIET GAME

G.K. Hall & Co. • Thorndike, Maine

Published in 2000 by arrangement with Dutton, a division of Penguin Putnam Inc.

G.K. Hall Large Print Core Series.

The text of this Large Print edition is unabridged.
Other aspects of the book may vary from the original edition.

Set in 16 pt. Plantin by Anne Bradeen.

Printed in the United States on permanent paper.

Library of Congress Cataloging-in-Publication Data

Iles, Greg.
    The quiet game / Greg Iles.
      p. cm.
    ISBN 0-7838-9299-3 (lg. print : hc : alk. paper)
    ISBN 0-7838-9300-0 (lg. print : sc : alk. paper)
    1. Public prosecutors — Fiction. 2. Afro-Americans —
Crimes against — Fiction. 3. Natchez (Miss.) — Fiction.
4. Large type books. I. Title.
PS3559.L47 Q54 2000
  813'.54—dc21
                                          00-046115

For
Madeline and Mark
Who will always be my best work.

And
Anna Flowers
Who taught me about class in every sense.

ACKNOWLEDGMENTS

Aaron Priest, for taking me to the next level.

Phyllis Grann, for faith and vision.

David Highfill, for a wonderful editorial experience.

Clare Ferraro, Rich Hasselberger, and the gang at Dutton for first-rate work.

Courtney Aldridge, the best buddy a writer could have.

Senior Special Agent Ronald Baughan, BATF, Certified Explosives Specialist, retired.

Field research, weapons: Keith Benoist, force recon marine and budding writer.

Historical expertise: Ron Miller.

Legal advice: Michael Henry, District Attorney Ronnie Harper, Kevin Colbert, Chancery Judge George Ward, Circuit Judge Lillie Blackmon Sanders.

Medical advice: Dr. Jerry W. Iles, Dr. Michael Bourland.

Cultural perspective: Mildred Lyles, Georgia Ware, Peter Rinaldi.

Advance readers: Ed Stackler, Natasha Kern, Courtney Aldridge, Mary Lou England, Betty Iles, Michael Henry, Dianne Brown.

To those I omitted through oversight, my apologies.

All mistakes are mine.

Be not deceived; God is not mocked:
for whatsoever a man soweth,
that shall he also reap.
— GALATIANS 6:7

CHAPTER 1

I am standing in line for Walt Disney's It's a Small World ride, holding my four-year-old daughter in my arms, trying to entertain her as the serpentine line of parents and children moves slowly toward the flat-bottomed boats emerging from the grotto to the music of an endless audio loop. Suddenly Annie jerks taut in my arms and points into the crowd.

"Daddy! I saw Mama! Hurry!"

I do not look. I don't ask where. I don't because Annie's mother died seven months ago. I stand motionless in the line, looking just like everyone else except for the hot tears that have begun to sting my eyes.

Annie keeps pointing into the crowd, becoming more and more agitated. Even in Disney World, where periodic meltdowns are common, her fit draws stares. Clutching her struggling body against mine, I work my way back through the line, which sends her into outright panic. The green metal chutes double back upon themselves to create the illusion of a short queue for prospective riders. I push past countless staring families, finally reaching the relative openness between the Carousel and Dumbo.

Holding Annie tighter, I rock and turn in slow circles as I did to calm her when she was an infant. A streaming mass of teenagers breaks around us like a river around a rock and pays us about as much attention. A claustrophobic sense of futility envelops me, a feeling I never experienced prior to my wife's illness but which now dogs me like a malignant shadow. If I could summon a helicopter to whisk us back to the Polynesian Resort, I would pay ten thousand dollars to do it. But there is no helicopter. Only us. Or the less-than-us that we've been since Sarah died.

The vacation is over. And when the vacation is over, you go home. But where is home? Technically Houston, the suburb of Tanglewood. But Houston doesn't feel like home anymore. The Houston house has a hole in it now. A hole that moves from room to room.

The thought of Penn Cage helpless would shock most people who know me. At thirty-eight years old, I have sent sixteen men and women to death row. I watched seven of them die. I've killed in defense of my family. I've given up one successful career and made a greater success of another. I am admired by my friends, feared by my enemies, loved by those who matter. But in the face of my child's grief, I am powerless.

Taking a deep breath, I hitch Annie a little higher and begin the long trek back to the monorail. We came to Disney World because Sarah and I brought Annie here a year ago — before the diagnosis — and it turned out to be the best vacation of our lives. I hoped a return trip might give Annie some peace. But the opposite has happened. She rises in the middle of the night and pads into the bathroom in search of Sarah; she walks the theme parks with darting eyes, always alert for the vanished maternal profile. In the magical world of Disney, Annie believes Sarah might step around the next corner as easily as Cinderella. When I patiently explained that this could not happen, she reminded me that Snow White rose from the dead just like Jesus, which in her four-year-old brain is indisputable fact. All we have to do is *find* Mama, so that Daddy can kiss her and make her wake up.

I collapse onto a seat in the monorail with a half dozen Japanese tourists, Annie sobbing softly into my shoulder. The silver train accelerates to cruising speed, rushing through Tomorrowland, a grand anachronism replete with *Jetsons*-style rocket ships and Art Deco restaurants. A 1950s incarnation of man's glittering destiny, Tomorrowland was outstripped by reality more rapidly than old Walt could have imagined, transformed into a kitschy parody of the dreams of the Eisenhower era. It stands as mute but eloquent testimony to man's inability to predict what lies ahead.

I do not need to be reminded of this.

As the monorail swallows a long curve, I spy the crossed roof beams of the Polynesian Resort. Soon we will be back inside our suite, alone with the emptiness that haunts us every day. And all at once that is not good enough anymore. With shocking clarity a voice speaks in my mind. It is Sarah's voice.

You can't do this alone, she says.

I look down at Annie's face, angelic now in sleep.

11

"We need help," I say aloud, drawing odd glances from the Japanese tourists. Before the monorail hisses to a stop at the hotel, I know what I am going to do.

I call Delta Airlines first and book an afternoon flight to Baton Rouge — not our final destination, but the closest major airport to it. Simply making the call sets something thrumming in my chest. Annie awakens as I arrange for a rental car, perhaps even in sleep sensing the utter resolution in her father's voice. She sits quietly beside me on the bed, her left hand on my thigh, reassuring herself that I can go nowhere without her.

"Are we going on the airplane again, Daddy?"

"That's right, punkin," I answer, dialing a Houston number.

"Back home?"

"No, we're going to see Gram and Papa."

Her eyes widen with joyous expectation. "Gram and Papa? Now?"

"I hope so. Just a minute." My assistant, Cilla Daniels, is speaking in my ear. She obviously saw the name of the hotel on the caller-ID unit and started talking the moment she picked up. I break in before she can get rolling. "Listen to me, Cil. I want you to call a storage company and lease enough space for everything in the house."

"The house?" she echoes. "Your house? You mean 'everything' as in furniture?"

"Yes. I'm selling the house."

"Selling the house. Penn, what's happened? What's wrong?"

"Nothing. I've come to my senses, that's all. An-

12

nie's never going to get better in that house. And Sarah's parents are still grieving so deeply that they're making things worse. I'm moving back home for a while."

"Home?"

"To Natchez."

"Natchez."

"Mississippi. Where I lived before I married Sarah? Where I grew up?"

"I know that, but —"

"Don't worry about your salary. I'll need you now more than ever."

"I'm not worried about my salary. I'm worried about you. Have you talked to your parents? Your mother called yesterday and asked for your number down there. She sounded upset."

"I'm about to call them. After you get the storage space, call some movers and arrange transport. Let Sarah's parents have anything they want out of the house. Then call Jim Noble and tell him to sell the place. And I don't mean list it, I mean *sell* it."

"The housing market's pretty soft right now. Especially in your bracket."

"I don't care if I eat half the equity. Move it."

There's an odd silence. Then Cilla says, "Could I make you an offer on it? I won't if you never want to be reminded of the place."

"No . . . it's fine. You need to get out of that condo. Can you come anywhere close to a realistic price?"

"I've got quite a bit left from my divorce settlement. You know me."

"Don't make me an offer. I'll make you one. Get

the house appraised, then knock off twenty percent. No realtor fees, no down payment, nothing. Work out a payment schedule over twenty years at, say . . . six percent interest. That way we have an excuse to stay in touch."

"Oh, God, Penn, I can't take advantage like that."

"It's a done deal." I take a deep breath, feeling the invisible bands that have bound me loosening. "Well . . . that's it."

"Hold on. The world doesn't stop because you run off to Disney World."

"Do I want to hear this?"

"I've got bad news and news that could go either way."

"Give me the bad."

"Arthur Lee Hanratty's last request for a stay was just denied by the Supreme Court. It's leading on CNN every half hour. The execution is scheduled for midnight on Saturday. Five days from now."

"That's good news, as far as I'm concerned."

Cilla sighs in a way that tells me I'm wrong. "Mr. Givens called a few minutes ago." Mr. Givens and his wife are the closest relatives of the black family slaughtered by Hanratty and his psychotic brothers. "And Mr. Givens doesn't ever want to see Hanratty in person again. He and his wife want you to attend in their place. A witness they can trust. You know the drill."

"Too well." Lethal injection at the Texas State Prison at Huntsville, better known as the Walls. Seventy miles north of Houston, the seventh circle of Hell. "I really don't want to see this one, Cil."

14

"I know. I don't know what to tell you."

"What's this other news?"

"I just got off the phone with Peter." Peter Highsmith is my editor, a gentleman and scholar, but not the person I want to talk to just now. "He would never say anything, but I think the house is getting anxious about *Nothing But the Truth*. You're nearly a year past your deadline. Peter is more worried about you than about the book. He just wants to know you're okay."

"What did you tell him?"

"That you've had a tough time, but you're finally waking back up to life. You're nearly finished with the book, and it's by far the best you've ever written."

I laugh out loud.

"How close *are* you? You were only half done the last time I got up the nerve to ask you about it."

I start to lie, but there's no point. "I haven't written a decent page since Sarah died."

Cilla is silent.

"And I burned the first half of the manuscript the night before we left Houston."

She gasps. "You didn't!"

"Look in the fireplace."

"Penn . . . I think you need some help. I'm speaking as your friend. There are some good people here in town. Discreet."

"I don't need a shrink. I need to take care of my daughter."

"Well . . . whatever you do, be careful, okay?"

"A lot of good that does. Sarah was the most careful person I ever knew."

"I didn't mean —"

15

"I know. Look, I don't want a single journalist finding out where I am. I want no part of that deathwatch circus. It's Joe's problem now." Joe Cantor is the district attorney of Harris County, and my old boss. "As far as you know, I'm on vacation until the moment of the execution."

"Consider yourself incommunicado."

"I've got to run. We'll talk soon."

"Make sure we do."

When I hang up, Annie rises to her knees beside me, her eyes bright. "Are we really going to Gram and Papa's?"

"We'll know in a minute."

I dial the telephone number I memorized as a four-year-old and listen to it ring. The call is answered by a woman with a cigarette-parched Southern drawl no film producer would ever use, for fear that the audience would be unable to decode the words. She works for an answering service.

"Dr. Cage's residence."

"This is Penn Cage, his son. Can you ring through for me?"

"We sure can, honey. You hang on."

After five rings, I hear a click. Then a deep male voice speaks two words that somehow convey more emotional subtext than most men could in two paragraphs: reassurance, gravitas, a knowledge of ultimate things.

"Doctor Cage," it says.

My father's voice instantly steadies my heart. This voice has comforted thousands of people over the years, and told many others that their days on earth numbered far less than they'd hoped. "Dad, what are you doing home this time of day?"

"Penn? Is that you?"

"Yes."

"What's up, son?"

"I'm bringing Annie home to see you."

"Great. Are you coming straight from Florida?"

"You could say that. We're coming today."

"Today? Is she sick?"

"No. Not physically, anyway. Dad, I'm selling the house in Houston and moving back home for a while. What comes after that, I'll figure out later. Have you got room for us?"

"God almighty, son. Let me call your mother."

I hear my father shout, then the clicking of heels followed by my mother's voice. "Penn? Are you really coming home?"

"We'll be there tonight."

"Thank God. We'll pick you up at the airport."

"No, don't. I'll rent a car."

"Oh . . . all right. I just . . . I can't tell you how glad I am."

Something in my mother's voice triggers an alarm. I can't say what it is, because it's in the spaces, not the words, the way you hear things in families. Whatever it is, it's serious. Peggy Cage does not worry about little things.

"Mom? What's the matter?"

"Nothing. I'm just glad you're coming home."

There is no more inept liar than someone who has spent a lifetime telling the truth. "Mom, don't try to —"

"We'll talk when you get here. You just bring that little girl where she belongs."

I recall Cilla's opinion that my mother was upset

17

when she called yesterday. But there's no point in forcing the issue on the phone. I'll be face to face with her in a few hours. "We'll be there tonight. Bye."

My hand shakes as I set the receiver in its cradle. For a prodigal son, a journey home after eighteen years is a sacred one. I've been home for a few Christmases and Thanksgivings, but this is different. Looking down at Annie, I get one of the thousand-volt shocks of recognition that has hit me so many times since the funeral. Sometimes Sarah's face peers out from Annie's as surely as if her spirit has temporarily possessed the child. But if this is a possession, it is a benign one. Annie's hazel eyes transfix mine with a look that gave me much peace when it shone from Sarah's face: *This is the right thing,* it says.

"I love you, Daddy," she says softly.

"I love you more," I reply, completing our ritual. Then I catch her under the arms and lift her high into the air. "Let's pack! We've got a plane to catch!"

CHAPTER 2

One of the nice things about first-class air travel is immediate beverage service. Even before our connecting flight lifts out of Atlanta's Hartsfield Airport, a tumbler of single-malt Scotch sits half-empty on the tray before me. I never drink liquor in front of Annie, but she is conveniently asleep on the adjacent seat. Her little arm hangs over the padded divider, her hand touching my thigh, an early-warning system that operates even in sleep. What part of her brain keeps that hand in place? Did Neanderthal children sleep this way? I sip my whisky and stroke her hair, cautiously looking around the cabin.

One of the bad things about first-class air travel is being recognized. You get a lot of readers in first class. A lot of lawyers too. Today the cabin is virtually empty, but sitting across the aisle from us is a woman in her late twenties, wearing a lawyerly blue suit and reading a Penn Cage novel. It's just a matter of time before she recognizes me. Or maybe not, if my luck holds. I take another sip of Scotch, recline my seat, and close my eyes.

The first image that floats into my mind is the face of Arthur Lee Hanratty. I spent four months convicting that bastard, and I consider it time well spent. But even in Texas, where we are serious about the death penalty, it takes time to exhaust all avenues of appeal. Now, eight years after his conviction, it seems possible that he might actually die at the hands of the state.

I know prosecutors who will drive all day with smiles on their faces to see the execution of a man they convicted, avidly anticipating the political capital they will reap from the event. Others will not attend an execution even if asked. I always felt a responsibility to witness the punishment I had requested in the name of society. Also, in capital cases, I shepherded the victims' families through the long ordeal of trial. In every case family members asked me to witness the execution on their behalf. After the legislature changed the law, allowing victims' families to witness executions, I was asked to accompany them in the viewing room, and I was glad to be able to comfort them.

This time it's different. My relationship to death has fundamentally changed. I witnessed my wife's death from a much closer perspective than from the viewing room at the Walls, and as painful as it was, her passing was a sacred experience. I have no desire to taint that memory by watching yet another execution carried out with the institutional efficiency of a veterinarian putting down a rabid dog.

I drink off the remainder of my Scotch, savoring the peaty burn in my throat. As always, remembering Sarah's death makes me think of my father. Hearing his voice on the telephone earlier only intensifies the images. As the 727 ascends to cruising altitude, the whisky opens a neural switch in my brain, and memory begins overpowering thought like a salt tide flooding into an estuary. I know from experience that it is useless to resist. I close my eyes and let it come.

Sarah lies in the M.D. Anderson hospital in Houston, her bones turned to burning paper by a disease whose name she no longer speaks aloud. She is not superstitious, but to name the sickness seems to grant it more power than it deserves. Her doctors are puzzled. The end should have come long ago. The diagnosis was a late one, the prognosis poor. Sarah weighs only eighty-one pounds now, but she fights for life with a young mother's tenacity. It is a pitched battle, fought minute by minute against physical agony and emotional despair. Sometimes she speaks of suicide. It is a comfort on the worst nights.

Like many doctors, her oncologists are too wary of lawsuits and the DEA to adequately treat pain. In desperation I call my father, who advises me to check Sarah out of the hospital and go home. Six hours later, he arrives at our door, trailing the smell of cigars and a black bag containing enough Schedule Two narcotics to euthanize a grizzly bear. For two weeks he lives across the hall from Sarah, tending her like a nurse, shaming into silence any physician who questions his actions. He helps Sarah to sleep when she needs it, frees her from the demon long enough to smile at Annie when she feels strong enough for me to bring her in.

Then the drugs begin to fail. The fine line between consciousness and agony disappears. One evening Sarah asks everyone to leave, saying she sleeps better alone. Near midnight she calls me into the bedroom where we once lay with Annie between us, dreaming of the future. She can barely speak. I take her hand. For a moment the clouds in her eyes part, revealing a startling clarity. "You made me happy," she whispers. I believe I have no tears left, but they come now. "Take care of my baby," she says. I vow with absolute conviction to do so, but I am not sure she hears me. Then she surprises me by asking for my father. I cross the hall and wake him, then sit down on the warm covers from which he rose.

When I wake, Sarah is gone. She died in her sleep. Peacefully, my father says. He volunteers no more, and I do not ask. When Sarah's parents wake, he tells them she is dead. Each in turn goes to him and hugs him, their eyes wet with tears of gratitude and absolution. "She was a trooper," my father says in a cracked voice. This is the highest tribute my wife will ever receive.

"Excuse me, are you Penn Cage? The writer?"

I blink and rub my eyes against the light, then turn to my right. The young woman across the aisle is looking at me, a slight blush coloring her cheeks.

"I didn't want to bother you, but I saw you take a drink and realized you must be awake. I was reading this book and . . . well, you look just like the picture on the back."

She is speaking softly so as not to wake Annie. Part of my mind is still with Sarah and my father, chasing a strand of meaning down a dark spiral, but I force myself to concentrate as the woman introduces herself as Kate. She is quite striking, with fine black hair pulled up from her neck, fair skin, and sea green eyes, an unusual combination. Her navy suit looks tailored, and the pulled-back hair gives the impression that Kate is several years older than she probably is, a common affectation among young female attorneys. I smile awkwardly and confirm that I am indeed myself, then ask if she is a lawyer.

She smiles. "Am I that obvious?"

"To other members of the breed."

Another smile, this one different, as though at some private joke. "I'm a First Amendment specialist," she offers.

Her accent is an alloy of Ivy League Boston and something softer. A Brahmin who graduated Radcliffe but spent her summers far away. "That sounds interesting," I tell her.

"Sometimes. Not as interesting as what you do."

"I'm sure you're wrong about that."

"I doubt it. I just saw you on CNN in the airport. They were talking about the Hanratty execution. About you killing his brother."

So, the circus has started. "That's not exactly my daily routine. Not anymore, at least."

"It sounded like there were some unanswered questions about the shooting." Kate blushes again. "I'm sure you're sick of people asking about it, right?"

Yes, I am. "Maybe the execution will finally put it to rest."

"I'm sorry. I didn't mean to pry."

"Sure you did." On any other day I would brush her off. But she is reading one of my novels, and even thinking about *Texas* v. *Hanratty* is better than what I was thinking about when she disturbed me. "It's okay. We all want to know the inside of things."

"They said on *Burden of Proof* that the Hanratty

23

case is often cited as an example of jurisdictional disputes between federal and state authorities."

I nod but say nothing. "Disputes" is a rather mild word. Arthur Lee Hanratty was a white supremacist who testified against several former cronies in exchange for immunity and a plum spot in the Federal Witness Protection Program. Three months after he entered the program, he shot a black man in Compton over a traffic dispute. He fled Los Angeles, joined his two psychotic brothers, and wound up in Houston, where they murdered an entire black family. As they were being apprehended, Arthur Lee shot and killed a female cop, giving his brothers time to escape. None of this looked good on the resume of John Portman, the U.S. attorney who had granted Hanratty immunity, and Portman vowed to convict his former star witness in federal court in Los Angeles. My boss and I (with the help of then president and erstwhile Texas native George Bush) kept Hanratty in Texas, where he stood a real chance of dying for his crimes. Our jurisdictional victory deprived Portman of his revenge, but his career skyrocketed nevertheless, first into a federal judgeship and finally into the directorship of the FBI, where he now presides.

"I remember when it happened," Kate says. "The Compton shooting, I mean. I was working in Los Angeles for the summer, and it got a lot of play there. Half the media made you out to be a hero, the other half a monster. They said you — well, you know."

"What?" I ask, testing her nerve.

She hesitates, then takes the plunge. "They said

24

you shot him and then used your baby to justify killing him."

I've come to understand the combat veteran's frustration with this kind of curiosity, and I usually meet it with a stony stare, if not outright hostility. But today is different. Today I am in transition. The impending execution has resurrected old ghosts, and I find myself willing to talk, not to satisfy this woman's curiosity but to remind myself that I got through it. That I did the right thing. *The only thing,* I assure myself, looking down at Annie sleeping beside me. I drink the last of my Scotch and let myself remember it, this thing that always seems to have happened to someone else, a celebrity among lawyers, hailed by the right wing and excoriated by the left.

"Arthur Lee Hanratty vowed to kill me after his arrest. He said it a dozen times on television. I took his threats the way I took them all, *cum grano salis.* But Hanratty meant it. Four years later, the night the Supreme Court affirmed his death sentence, my wife and I were lying in bed watching the late news. She was dozing. I was going over my opening statement for another murder trial. My boss had put a deputy outside because of the Supreme Court ruling, but I didn't think there was any danger. When I heard the first noise, I thought it was nothing. The house settling. Then I heard something else. I asked Sarah if she'd heard it. She hadn't. She told me to turn out the light and go to sleep. And I almost did. That's how close it was. That's where my nightmares come from."

"What made you get up?"

As the flight attendant passes, I signal for another Scotch. "I don't know. Something had registered wrong, deep down. I took my thirty-eight down from the closet shelf and switched off my reading light. Then I opened the bedroom door and moved up the hall toward our daughter's room. Annie was only six months old, but she always slept through the night. When I pushed open her door, I didn't hear breathing, but that didn't worry me. Sometimes you have to get right down over them, you know? I walked to the crib and leaned over to listen."

Kate is spellbound, leaning across the aisle. I take my Scotch from the flight attendant's hand and gulp a swallow. "The crib was empty."

"Sweet Jesus."

"The deputy was out front, so I ran to the French doors at the back of the house. When I got there, I saw nothing but the empty patio. I felt like I was falling off a cliff. Then something made me turn to my left. There was a man standing by the French doors in the dining room. Twenty feet away. He had a tiny bundle in his arms, like a loaf of bread in a blanket. He looked at me as he reached for the door handle. I saw his teeth in the dark, and I knew he was smiling. I pointed my pistol at his head. He started backing through the door, using Annie as a shield. Holding her at center mass. In the dark, with shaking hands, every rational thought told me not to fire. But I had to."

I take another gulp of Scotch. The whites of Kate's eyes are completely visible around the green irises, giving her a hyperthyroid look. I reach down and lay a hand on Annie's shoulder. Parts of this story I still cannot voice. When I saw those teeth, I sensed the giddy superiority the kidnaper felt over me, the triumph of the predator. Nothing in my life ever hit me the way that fear did.

"He was halfway through the door when I pulled the trigger. The bullet knocked him onto the patio. When I got outside, Annie was lying on the cement, covered in blood. I snatched her up even before I looked at the guy, held her up in the moonlight and ripped off her pajamas, looking for a bullet wound. She didn't make a sound. Then she screamed like a banshee. An anger scream, you know? Not pain. I knew then that she was probably okay. Hanratty . . . the bullet had hit him in the eye. He was dying. And I didn't do a goddamn thing to help him."

Kate finally blinks, a series of rapid-fire clicks, like someone coming out of a trance. She points down at Annie. "She's that baby? She's Annie?"

"Yes."

"God." She taps the book in her lap. "I see why you quit."

"There's still one out there."

"What do you mean?"

"We never caught the third brother. I get postcards from him now and then. He says he's looking forward to spending some time with our family."

She shakes her head. "How do you live with that?"

I shrug and return to my drink.

"Your wife isn't traveling with you?" Kate asks.

They always have to ask. "No. She passed away recently."

Kate's face begins the subtle sequence of expressions I've seen a thousand times in the last seven months. Shock, embarrassment, sympathy, and just the slightest satisfaction that a seemingly perfect life is not so perfect after all.

"I'm sorry," she says. "The wedding ring. I just assumed —"

"It's okay. You couldn't know."

She looks down and takes a sip of her soft drink. When she looks up, her face is composed again. She asks what my next book is about, and I give her the usual fluff, but she isn't listening. I know this reaction too. The response of most women to a young widower, particularly one who is clearly solvent and not appallingly ugly, is as natural and predictable as the rising of the sun. The subtle glow of flirtation emanates from Kate like a medieval spell, but it is a spell to which I am presently immune.

Annie awakens as we talk, and Kate immediately brings her into the conversation, developing a surprising rapport. Time passes quickly, and before long we are shaking hands at the gate in Baton Rouge. Annie and I bump into her again at the baggage carousel, and as Kate squeaks outside in her sensible Reeboks to hail a taxi, I notice Annie's eyes solemnly tracking her. My daughter's attraction to young adult women is painful to see.

I scoop her up with forced merriment and trot to the Hertz counter, where I have to hassle with a clerk about why the car I reserved isn't available (although for ten dollars extra per day I can upgrade to a model that is) and how long I'll have to wait for a child-safety seat. I'm escalating from irritation to anger when a tall man with white hair and a neatly trimmed white beard walks through the glass doors through which Kate just departed.

"Papa!" Annie squeals. "Daddy! Papa's here!"

"Dad? What? What are you doing here?"

He laughs and veers toward us. "You think your mother's going to have her son renting a car to drive eighty miles to get home? God forbid." He catches Annie under the arms, lifts her high, and hugs her to his chest. "Hello, tadpole! What's shakin' down in Disney World?"

"I saw Ariel! And Snow White hugged me!"

"Of course she did! Who wouldn't want to hug an angel like you?" He looks over her shoulder at me. For a few uncomfortable moments I endure the penetrating gaze of a man who for forty years has searched for illness in reticent people. His perception is like the heat from a lamp. I nod slowly, hoping to communicate, *I'm okay, Dad,* at the same time searching his face for clues to the anxiety I heard in my mother's voice on the phone this morning. But he's too good at concealing his emotions. Another habit of the medical profession.

"Is Mom with you?" I ask.

"No, she's home cooking a supper you'll have to see to believe." He reaches out and squeezes my hand. "It's good to see you, son." For an instant I catch a glimpse of something unsettling behind his eyes, but it vanishes as he grins mischievously at Annie. "Let's move out, tadpole! We're burning daylight!"

CHAPTER 3

My father served as an army doctor in West Germany in the 1960s, and it was there he acquired a taste for dark beer and high-performance automobiles. He has been driving BMWs ever since he could afford them, and he drives fast. In four minutes we are away from the airport and roaring north on Highway 61. Annie sits in the middle of the backseat, lashed into a safety seat, marveling at the TV-sized computer display built into the dashboard while Dad runs through its functions again and again, delighting in every giggle that bursts from her lips.

Coronary problems severely reduced my father's income a few years ago, so last year — on his sixty-sixth birthday — I bought him a black BMW 740i with the royalties from my third novel. I felt a little like Elvis Presley when I wrote that check, and it was a good feeling. My parents started life with nothing, and in a single generation, through hard work and sacrifice, lived what was once unapologetically called the American Dream. They deserve some perks.

The flat brown fields of Louisiana quickly give way to green wooded hills, and somewhere to our left, beyond the lush forest, rolls the great brown river. I cannot smell it yet, but I feel it, a subtle disturbance in the earth's magnetic field, a fluid force that shapes the surrounding land and souls. I roll down the window and suck in the life smell of hardwood forest, creek water, kudzu, bush-hogged wildflowers, and baking earth. The competing aromas blend into a heady gestalt you couldn't find in Houston if you grid-searched every inch of it on your hands and knees.

"We're losing the air conditioning," Dad complains.

"Sorry." I roll up the window. "It's been a long time since I smelled this place."

"Too damn long."

"Papa said a bad word!" Annie cries, bursting into giggles.

Dad laughs, then reaches back between the seats and slaps her on the knee.

The old landmarks hurtle by like location shots from a film. St. Francisville, where John James Audubon painted his birds, now home to a nuclear station; the turnoff to Angola Penitentiary; and finally the state line, marked by a big blue billboard: WELCOME TO MISSISSIPPI! THE MAGNOLIA STATE.

"What's happening in Natchez these days?"

Dad whips into the left lane and zooms past a log truck loaded from bumper to red flag with pulpwood. "A lot, for a change. Looks like we've got a new factory coming in. Which is good, because the battery plant is about dead."

"What kind of factory?"

"Chemical plant. They want to put it in the new industrial park by the river. South of the paper mill."

31

"Is it a done deal?"

"I'll say it's done when I see smoke coming from the stacks. Till then it's all talk. It's like the casino boats. Every other month a new company talks about bringing another boat in, but there's still just the one."

"What else is happening?"

"Big election coming up."

"What kind?"

"Mayoral. For the first time in history there's a black candidate with a real chance to win."

"You're kidding. Who is it?"

"Shad Johnson. He's about your age. His parents are patients of mine. You never heard of him because they sent him north to prep school when he was a kid. After that he went to Howard University. Another damn lawyer, just like you."

"And he wants to be mayor of Natchez?"

"Badly. He moved down here just to run. And he may win."

"What's the black-white split now?"

"Registered voters? Fifty-one to forty-nine, in favor of whites. The blacks usually have a low turnout, but this election may be different. In any case, the key for Johnson is white votes, and he might actually get some. He's been invited to join the Rotary Club."

"The *Natchez* Rotary Club?"

"Times are changing. And Shad Johnson's smart enough to exploit that. I'm sure you'll meet him soon. The election's only five weeks away. Hell, he'll probably want an endorsement from you, seeing how you're a celebrity now."

"Papa said another bad word!" Annie chimes

in. "But not too bad."

"What did I say?"

"H-E-L-L. You're supposed to say *heck*."

Dad laughs and slaps her on the knee again.

"I want to stay low-profile," I say quietly. "This trip is strictly R-and-R."

"Not much chance of that. Somebody already called the house asking for you. Right before I left."

"Was it Cilla, my assistant?"

"No. A man. He asked if you'd got in yet. When I asked who was calling, he hung up. The caller-ID box said 'out of area.' "

"Probably a reporter. They're going to turn the South upside down trying to find me because of the Hanratty execution."

"We'll do what we can to keep you incognito, but the new newspaper publisher has called four times asking about getting an interview with you. Now that you're here, you won't be able to avoid things like that. Not without people saying you've gone Hollywood on us."

I sit back and assimilate this. Finding sanctuary in my old hometown might not be as easy as I thought. But it will still be better than Houston.

Natchez is unlike any place in America, existing almost outside time, which is exactly what Annie and I need. In some ways it isn't part of Mississippi at all. There's no town square with a lone Confederate soldier presiding over it, no flat, limitless Delta horizon or provincial blue laws. The oldest city on the Mississippi River, Natchez stands white and pristine atop a two-hundred-foot loess bluff, the jewel in the crown of nineteenth-century steamboat ports. For as long as I can remember, the population has been twenty-five thousand, but after being ruled in turn by Indians, French, British, Spanish, Confederates, and Americans, her character is more cosmopolitan than cities ten times her size. Parts of New Orleans remind me of Natchez, but only parts. Modern life long ago came to the Crescent City and changed it forever. Two hundred miles upriver, Natchez exists in a ripple of time that somehow eludes the homogenizing influences of the present.

In 1850 Natchez boasted more millionaires than any city in the United States save New York and Philadelphia. Their fortunes were made on the cotton that poured like white gold out of the district and into the mills of England. The plantations stretched for miles on both sides of the Mississippi River, and the planters who administered them built mansions that made Margaret Mitchell's Tara look like modest accommodations. While their slaves toiled in the fields, the princes of this new aristocracy sent their sons to Harvard and their daughters to the royal courts of Europe. Atop the bluff they held cotillions, opened libraries, and developed new strains of cotton; two hundred feet below, in the notorious Under the Hill district, they raced horses, traded slaves, drank, whored, and gambled, firmly establishing a tradition of libertinism that survives to the present, and cementing the city's black-sheep status in a state known for its dry counties.

By an accident of topography, the Civil War left Natchez untouched. Her bluff commanded a straightaway of the river rather than a bend, so

Vicksburg became the critical naval choke point, dooming that city to siege and destruction while undefended Natchez made the best of Union occupation. In this way she joined in a charmed historical trinity with Savannah and Charleston, the quintessentially Southern cities that survived the war with their beauty intact.

It took the boll weevil to accomplish what war could not, sending the city into depression after the turn of the century. She sat preserved like a city in amber, her mansions slowly deteriorating, until the 1930s, when her society ladies began opening their once great houses to the public in an annual ritual called the Pilgrimage. The money that poured in allowed them to restore the mansions to their antebellum splendor, and soon Yankees and Europeans traveled by thousands to this living museum of the Old South.

In 1948 oil was discovered practically beneath the city, and a second boom was on. Black gold replaced white, and overnight millionaires again walked the azalea-lined streets, as delirious with prosperity as if they had stepped from the pages of Scott Fitzgerald. I grew up in the midst of this boom, and benefited from the affluence it generated. But by the time I graduated law school, the oil industry was collapsing, leaving Natchez to survive on the revenues of tourism and federal welfare money. It was a hard adjustment for proud people who had never had to chase Northern factories or kowtow to the state of which they were nominally a part.

"What's that?" I ask, pointing at an upscale residential development far south of where I re-

35

member any homes.

"White flight," Dad replies. "Everything's moving south. Subdivisions, the country club. Look, there's another one."

Another grouping of homes materializes behind a thin screen of oak and pine, looking more like suburban Houston than the romantic town I remember. Then I catch sight of Mammy's Cupboard, and I feel a reassuring wave of familiarity in my chest. Mammy's is a restaurant built in the shape of a Negro mammy in a red hoop skirt and bandanna, painted to match Hattie McDaniel from *Gone With the Wind*. She stands atop her hill like a giant sculptured doll, beckoning travelers to dine in the cozy space beneath her domed skirts. Anyone who has never seen the place inevitably slows to gape; it makes the Brown Derby in L.A. look prosaic.

The car crests a high ridge and seems to teeter upon it as an ocean of treetops spreads out before us, stretching west to infinity. Beyond the river, the great alluvial plain of Louisiana lies so far below the high ground of Natchez that only the smoke plume from the paper mill betrays the presence of man in that direction. The car tips over on the long descent into town, passing St. Stephens, the all-white prep school I attended, and a dozen businesses that look just as they did twenty years ago. At the junction of Highways 61 and 84 stands the Jefferson Davis Memorial Hospital, now officially known by a more politically correct name, but for all time "the Jeff" to the doctors of my father's generation, and to the hundreds of other people, both black and white, who worked or were born there.

"It all looks the same," I murmur.
"It is and it isn't," Dad replies.
"What do you mean?"
"You'll see."

My parents still live in the same house in which they raised me. While other young professionals moved on to newer subdivisions, restored Victorian gingerbreads, or even antebellum palaces downtown, my father clung stubbornly to the ash-paneled library he'd appended to the suburban tract house he bought in 1963. Whenever my mother got the urge to move to more stately mansions, he added to the existing structure, giving her the space she claimed we needed and a decorating project on which to expend her fitful energies.

As the BMW pulls up to the house, I imagine my mother waiting inside. She always wanted me to succeed in the larger world, but it broke her heart when Sarah and I settled in Houston. Seven hours is too far to drive on a regular basis, and Mom dislikes flying. Still, the tie between us is such that distance means little. When I was a boy, people always told me I was like my father, that I'd "got my father's brain." But it is my mother who has the rare combination of quantitative aptitude and intuitive imagination that I was lucky enough to inherit.

Dad shuts off the engine and unstraps Annie from her safety seat. As I unload our luggage from the trunk, I see a shadow standing motionless against the closed curtain of the dining room. My mother. Then another shadow moves behind the curtain. Who else would be here? It can't be my sister. Jenny is a visiting professor at Trinity College in Dublin, Ireland.

"Who else is here?"

"Wait and see," Dad says cryptically.

I carry two suitcases to the porch, then go back for Annie's bag. The second time I reach the porch, my mother is standing in the open door. All I can see before she rises on tiptoe and pulls me into her arms is that she has stopped coloring her hair, and the gray is a bit of a shock.

"Welcome home," she whispers in my ear. She pulls back, her hands gripping my upper arms, and looks hard at me. "You're still not eating. Are you all right?"

"I don't know. Annie can't seem to get past what happened. And I don't know how to help her."

She squeezes my arms with a strength I have never seen fail. "That's what grandmothers are for. Everything's going to be all right. Starting right this minute."

At sixty-three my mother is still beautiful, but not with the delicate comeliness that fills so many musket-and-magnolia romances. Beneath the tanned skin and Donna Karan dress are the bone and sinew and humor of a girl who made the social journey from the 4-H Club to the Garden Club without forgetting her roots. She could take tea with royalty and commit no faux pas, yet just as easily twist the head off a banty hen, boil the bristles off a hog, or kill an angry copperhead with a hoe blade. It's that toughness that worries me now.

"Mom, what's wrong? On the phone —"

"Shh. We'll talk later." She blinks back tears,

then pushes me into the house and takes Annie from Dad's arms. "Here's my angel! Let's get some supper. And no yucky broccoli!"

Annie squeals with excitement.

"There's somebody waiting to see you, Penn," Mom says.

I pull the suitcases inside. A wide doorway in the foyer leads to the dining room, and I stop dead when I see who is there. Standing beside the long table is a black woman as tall as I and fifty years older. Her mouth is set in a tight smile, and her eyes twinkle with joy.

"Ruby!" I cry, setting the bags on the floor and walking toward her. "What in the world . . . ?"

"Today's her day off," Mom explains from behind me. "I called to check on her, and when she heard you were coming, she demanded that Tom come get her so she could see you."

"And that grandbaby," Ruby says, pointing at Annie in Peggy's arms.

I hug the old woman gently. It's like hugging a bundle of sticks. Ruby Flowers came to work for us in 1963 and, except for one life-threatening illness, never missed a single workday until arthritis forced her to slow down thirty years later. Even then she begged my father to give her steroid injections to allow her to keep doing her "heavy work" — the ironing and scrubbing — but he refused. Instead he kept her on at full pay but limited her to sorting socks, washing the odd load of clothes, and watching the soaps on television.

"I'm sorry about your wife," Ruby says. " 'Cept for losing a child, that the hardest thing."

I give her an extra squeeze.

39

"Now, let me see that baby. Come here, child!"

I wonder if Annie will remember Ruby, or be frightened by the old woman even if she does. I should have known better. Ruby Flowers radiates nothing to frighten a small child. She is like a benevolent witch from an African folk tale, and Annie goes to her without the slightest hesitation.

"I cooked your daddy his favorite dinner," Ruby says, hugging Annie tight. "And after tonight, it's gonna be your favorite too!"

At the center of the table sits a plate heaped with chicken shallow-fried to a peppered gold. I've watched Ruby make that chicken a thousand times and never once use more than salt, pepper, flour, and Crisco. With those four ingredients she creates a flavor and texture that Harland Sanders couldn't touch with his best pressure cooker. I snatch up a wing and take a bite of white meat. Crispy outside and moist within, it bursts in my mouth with intoxicating familiarity.

"Go slap your daddy's hand!" Ruby cries, and Annie quickly obeys. "Ya'll sit down and eat proper. I'll get the iced tea."

"I'll get the tea," Mom says, heading for the kitchen before Ruby can start. "Make your plate, Ruby. Tonight you're a guest."

Our family says grace only at Thanksgiving and Christmas, and then almost as a formality. But with Ruby present, no one dares reach for a fork.

"Would you like to return thanks, Ruby?" Dad asks.

The old woman shakes her head, her eyes shining with mischief. "I wish you'd do it, Dr. Cage. You give a *fine* blessing."

Thirty-eight years of practicing medicine has stripped my father of the stern religious carapace grafted onto him in the Baptist churches of his youth. But when pressed, he can deliver a blessing that vies with the longest-winded of deacons for flowery language and detail. He seems about to deliver one of these, with tongue-in-cheek overtones added for my benefit, but my mother halts him with a touch of her hand. She bows her head, and everyone at the table follows suit.

"Father," she says, "it's been far too long since we've given thanks to you in this house. Tonight we thank you for the return of our son, who has been away too long. We give thanks for Anna Louise Cage, our beautiful grandchild, and pray that we may bring her as much happiness as she brings to us each day." She pauses, a brief caesura that focuses everyone's concentration. "We also commend the soul of Sarah Louise Cage to your care, and pray that she abides in thy grace forever."

I take Annie's hand under the table and squeeze it.

"We don't pretend to understand death here," Mom continues softly. "We ask only that you let this young family heal, and be reconciled to their loss. This is a house of love, and we humbly ask grace in thy name's sake. Amen."

As we echo the "amen," Dad and I look at each other across the table, moved by my mother's passion but not its object. In matters religious I am my father's son, having no faith in a just God, or any god at all if you shake me awake at four A.M. and put the question to me. There have been times I would have given anything for such faith, for the belief that divine justice exists somewhere in the universe. Facing Sarah's death without it was an existential baptism of fire. The comfort that belief in an afterlife can provide was obvious in the hospital waiting rooms and chemo wards, where patients or family members often asked outright if I was saved. I always smiled and nodded so as to avoid a philosophical argument that would benefit no one, and wondered if the question was an eccentricity of Southern hospitals. In the Pacific Northwest they probably offer you crystals or lists of alternative healers. I have no regrets about letting Sarah raise Annie in a church, though. Sometimes the image of her mother in Heaven is all that keeps my daughter from despair.

As Dad passes around the mustard greens and cheese grits and beer biscuits, another memory rises unbidden. One cold hour before dawn, sitting beside Sarah's hospital bed, I fell to my knees and begged God to save her. The words formed in my mind without volition, strung together with strangely baroque formality: *I who have not believed since I was a child, who have not crossed a church threshold to worship since I was thirteen, who since the age of reason have admitted nothing greater than man or nature, ask in all humility that you spare the life of this woman. I ask not for myself, but for the child I am not qualified to raise alone.* As soon as I realized what I was thinking, I stopped and got to my feet. Who was I talking to? Faith is something you have or you don't, and to pretend you do in the hope of gaining some last-minute dispensation from a being whose existence you have denied all your life goes against everything I am. I have never placed myself above God. I simply cannot find within myself the capacity for belief.

Yet when Sarah finally died, a dark seed took root in my mind. As irrational as it is, a profoundly disturbing idea haunts me: that on the night that prayer blinked to life in my tortured mind, a chance beyond the realm of the temporal was granted me, and I did not take it. That I was tested and found wanting. My rational mind tells me I held true to myself and endured the pain as all pain must be endured — alone. But my heart says otherwise. Since that day I have been troubled by a primitive suspicion that in some cosmic account book, in some dusty ledger of karmic debits and credits, Sarah's life has been charged against my account.

"What's the matter, Daddy?" Annie asks.

"Nothing, punkin."

"You're crying."

"Penn?" my mother says, half rising from her chair.

"I'm all right," I assure her, wiping my eyes. "I'm just glad to be here, that's all."

Ruby reaches out and closes an arthritic hand over mine. "You should have come back months ago. You know where home is."

I nod and busy myself with my knife and fork.

"You think too much to be left alone," Ruby adds. "You always did."

"Amen," Dad agrees. "Now let's eat, before my beeper goes off."

"That beeper ain't gonna ring during this meal," Ruby says with quiet certainty. "Don't worry 'bout that none."

43

"Did you take out the batteries?" Dad asks, checking the pager.

"I just know," Ruby replies. "I just know."

I believe her.

My mother and I sit facing each other across the kitchen counter, drinking wine and listening for my father's car in the driveway. He left after dinner to take Ruby home to the black section north of town, but putting Annie to bed took up most of the time I expected him to be away.

"Mom, I sensed something on the phone. You've got to tell me what's wrong."

She looks at me over the rim of her glass. "I'm worried about your father."

A sliver of ice works its way into my heart. "Not more blockage in his coronary vessels?"

"No. I think Tom is being blackmailed."

I am dumbfounded. Nothing she could have said would have surprised me more. My father is a man of such integrity that the idea seems utterly ridiculous. Tom Cage is a modern-day Atticus Finch, or as close as a man can get to that Southern ideal in the dog days of the twentieth century.

"What has he done? I mean, that someone could blackmail him over?"

"He hasn't told me."

"Then how do you know that's what it is?"

She disposes of my question with a glance. Peggy Cage knows more about her husband and children than we know ourselves.

"Well, *who's* blackmailing him?"

"I think it might be Ray Presley. Do you remember him?"

44

The skin on my forearms tingles. Ray Presley was a patient of my father for years, and a more disturbing character I have never met, not even in the criminal courts of Houston. Born in Sullivan's Hollow, one of the toughest areas of Mississippi, Presley migrated to south Louisiana, where he reputedly worked as hired muscle for New Orleans crime boss Carlos Marcello. He later hired on as a police officer in Natchez and quickly put his old skills to use. Brutal and clever, his specialty was "vigorous interrogation." Off-duty, he haunted the fringes of Natchez's business community, doing favors of dubious legality for wealthy men around town, helping them deal with business or family troubles when conventional measures proved inadequate. When I was in grade school, Presley was busted for corruption and served time in Parchman prison, which to everyone's surprise he survived. Upon his release he focused exclusively on "private security work," and it was generally known that he had murdered at least three men for money, all out-of-town jobs.

"What could Ray Presley have on Dad?"

Mom looks away. "I'm not sure."

"You must have some idea."

"My suspicions have more to do with me than with your father. I think that's why Tom won't just tell Presley to go to hell. I think it involves my family."

My mother's parents both died years ago, and her sister — after two tempestuous marriages — recently married a wealthy surgeon in Florida. "What could Presley possibly know about your family?"

"I'm not sure. Even if I knew, Tom would have to be the one to tell you. If he won't —"

"How can I help if I don't know what's happening?"

"Your father has a lot of pride. You know that."

"How much is pride worth?"

"Over a hundred thousand dollars, apparently."

My stomach rolls like I'm falling through the dark. "Tell me you're kidding."

"I wish I were. Clearly, Tom would rather go broke than let us know what's going on."

"Mom, this is crazy. Why do you think it's Presley?"

"Tom talks in his sleep now. About five months ago he started eating less, losing weight. Then I got a call from Bill Hiatt at the bank. He hemmed and hawed, but he finally told me Tom had been making large withdrawals. Cashing in CDs and absorbing penalties."

"Well, it's going to stop. I don't care what he did, I'll get him out of it. And I'll get Presley thrown under a jail for extortion."

She laughs, her voice riding an undercurrent of hysteria.

"What is it?"

"Ray Presley doesn't care about *jail*. He's dying of cancer."

The word is like a cockroach crawling over my bare foot.

"Which is almost convenient," Mom goes on, "but not quite. He's taking his sweet time about it. I've seen him on the street, and he doesn't even look sick. Except for the hair. He's bald now. But he still looks like he could ride a bull ragged."

I jump at the sound of the garage door. Mom gives me a little wave, then crosses the kitchen as silently as if she were floating on a magic carpet and disappears down the hall. Moments later, my father walks through the kitchen door, his face drawn and tired.

"I figured you'd be waiting for me."

"Dad, we've got to talk."

Dread seems to seep from the pores in his face. "Let me get a drink. I'll meet you in the library."

CHAPTER 4

All my life, whenever problems of great import required discussion — health, family, money, marriage — the library was the place it was done. Yet my positive feelings about the room far out-weigh my anxieties. The ash-paneled library is so much a part of my father's identity that he carries its scent wherever he goes — an aroma of fine wood, cigar smoke, aging leather, and whiskey. Born to working-class parents, he spent the first real money he made to build this room and fill it with books: Aristotle to Zoroaster and everything in between, with a special emphasis on the military campaigns of the Civil War. I feel more at home here than anywhere in the world. In this room I educated myself, discovered my gift for language, learned that the larger world lay not across oceans but within the human mind and heart. Years spent in this room made law school relatively simple and becoming a writer possible, even necessary.

Dad enters through a different door, carrying a bourbon-and-water brown enough to worry me. We each take one of the leather recliners, which are arranged in the classic bourgeois style: side by side facing the television. He clips the end of a

Partagas, licks the end so that it won't peel, and lights it with a wooden match. A cloud of blue smoke wafts toward the beamed ceiling.

"Dad, I —"

"Let me start," he says, staring across the room at his biographies, most of them first editions. "Son, there comes a time in every man's life when he realizes that the people who raised him from infancy now require the favor to be returned, whether they know it or not." He stops to puff on the Partagas. "This is something you do not yet have to worry about."

"Dad —"

"I am kindly telling you to mind your own business. You and Annie are welcome here for the next fifty years if you want to stay, but you're not invited to pry into my private affairs."

I lean back in the recliner and consider whether I can honor my father's request. Given what my mother told me, I don't think so. "What's Ray Presley holding over you, Dad?"

"Your mother talks too much."

"You know that's not true. She thinks you're in trouble. And I can help you. Tell me what Presley has on you."

He picks up his drink and takes a long pull, closing his eyes against the anesthetic fire of the bourbon. "I won't have this," he says quietly.

I don't want to ask the next question — I'd hoped never to raise this subject again — but I must. "Is it something like what you did for Sarah? Helping somebody at the end?"

My father sighs like a man who has lived a thousand years. "That's a rare situation. And when things reach that point, the family's so desperate to have the horror and pain removed from the patient's last hours that they look at you like an instrument of God."

He drinks and stares at his books, lost in contemplation of something I cannot guess at. He has aged a lot in the eighteen years since I left home. His beard is no longer salt-and-pepper but silver white. His skin is pale and dotted by dermatitis, his joints eroded and swollen by psoriatic arthritis. He is sixteen years past his triple bypass (and counting) and he recently survived the implantation of two stents to keep his cardiac vessels open. All this — physical maladies more severe than those of most of his patients — he bears with the resignation of Job. The wound that aged him most, the one that has never quite healed, was a wound to the soul. And it came at the hands of another man.

When I was a freshman at Ole Miss, my father was sued for malpractice. The plaintiff had no case; his father had died unexpectedly while under the care of my father and five specialists. It was one of those inexplicable deaths that proved for the billionth time that medicine is an inexact science. Dad was as stunned as the rest of the medical community when "Judge" Leo Marston, the most prominent lawyer in town and a former state attorney general, took the man's case and pressed it to the limit. But no one was more shocked than I. Leo Marston was the father of a girl I had loved in high school, and whom I still think about more than is good for me. Why he should viciously attack my father was beyond my understanding, but

50

attack he did. In a marathon of legal maneuvering that dragged on for fourteen months, Marston hounded my father through the legal system with a vengeance that appalled the town. In the end Dad was unanimously exonerated by a jury, but by then the damage had been done.

For a physician of the old school, medical practice is not a profession or even an art, but the abiding passion of existence. A brilliant boy is born to poor parents during the Depression. From childhood he works to put food on the table. He witnesses privation and sickness not at a remove, but face to face. He earns a scholarship to college but must work additional jobs to cover his expenses. He contracts with the army to pay for his medical education in exchange for years of military service. After completing medical school with an exemplary record, he does not ask himself the question every medical student today asks himself: what do I wish to specialize in? He is ready to go to work. To begin treating patients. To begin living.

For twenty years he practices medicine as though his patients are members of his family. He makes small mistakes; he is human. But in twenty years of practice not one complaint is made to the state medical board, or any legal claim made against him. He is loved by his community, and that love is his life's bread. To be accused of criminal negligence in the death of a patient stuns him, like a war hero being charged with cowardice. Rumor runs through the community like a plague, and truth is the first casualty. His confidence in the rightness of his actions is absolute, but after months of endlessly repeated allegations, doubt begins to assail him. A lifetime of good works seems to weigh as nothing compared to one unsubstantiated charge. Smiles on the street appear forced to him, the greetings of neighbors cool. Stress works steadily and ruthlessly upon him, finally culminating in a myocardial infarction, which he barely survives.

Six weeks later the trial begins, and it's like stepping into the eye of a hurricane. Control rests in the hands of lawyers, men with murky motives and despicable tactics. Expert witnesses second-guess every medical decision. He sits alone in the witness box, condemned before family, friends, and community, cross-examined as though he were a child murderer. When the jury finds in his favor, he feels no joy. He feels like a man who has just lost both legs being told he is lucky to be alive.

Could the present-day blackmail somehow be tied to that calamitous case? I have never understood the reason for Leo Marston's attack, and I've always felt that my father — against his nature — must have been keeping the truth from me. My mother believes Ray Presley is behind the blackmail, and I recall that Judge Marston often hired Presley to do "security work" when I was in high school. This translated into acting as unofficial baby-sitter for Marston's teenage daughter, Olivia, who was also my lover. I remember nights when Presley's truck would swing by whatever hangout the kids happened to be frequenting, its hatchet-faced driver glaring from the window, making sure Livy didn't get into any serious trouble. One night Presley actually pulled up behind my car in the woods and rapped on the fogged windows, terrifying Livy and me. I still remember his face peering into the clear circle I rubbed on the window to look out, his eyes bright and ferretlike, searching the backseat for a sight of Livy unclothed. The hunger in those eyes . . .

"Does this have anything to do with Leo Marston?" I ask softly.

Dad flinches from his reverie. Even now the judge's name has the power to harm. "Marston?" he echoes, still staring at his books. "What makes you say that?"

"It's one of the only things I've never understood about your life. Why Marston went after you."

He shakes his head. "I've never known why he did it. I'd done nothing wrong. Any physician could see that. The jury saw it too, thank God."

"You've never heard anything since? About why he took the case or pressed it so hard?"

"To tell you the truth, son, I always had the feeling it had something to do with you. You and Olivia."

He turns to me, his eyes not accusatory but plainly questioning. I am too shocked to speak for a moment. "That . . . that's impossible," I stammer. "I mean, nothing really bad ever happened between Livy and me. It was the trial that drove the last nail into our relationship."

"Maybe that was Marston's goal all along. To drive you two apart."

This thought occurred to me nineteen years ago, but I discounted it. Livy abandoned me long before her father took on that malpractice case.

Dad shrugs as if it were all meaningless now.

"Who knows why people do anything?"

"I'm going to go see Presley," I tell him. "If that's what I have to do to —"

"You stay away from that son of a bitch! Any problems I have, I'll deal with my own way." He downs the remainder of his bourbon. "One way or another."

"What does that mean?"

His eyes are blurry with fatigue and alcohol, yet somehow sly beneath all that. "Don't worry about it."

I am suddenly afraid that my father is contemplating suicide. His death would nullify any leverage Presley has over him and also provide my mother with a generous life insurance settlement. To a desperate man, this might well seem like an elegant solution. "Dad —"

"Go to bed, son. Take care of your little girl. That's what being a father's all about. Sparing your kids what hell you can for as long as you can. And Annie's already endured her share."

We turn to the door at the same moment, each sensing a new presence in the room. A tiny shadow stands there. Annie. She seems conjured into existence by the mention of her name.

"I woke up by myself," she says, her voice tiny and fearful. "Why did you leave, Daddy?"

I go to the door and sweep her into my arms. She feels so light sometimes that it frightens me. Hollow-boned, like a bird. "I needed to talk to Papa, punkin. Everything's fine."

"Hello, sweet pea," Dad says from his chair. "You make Daddy take you to bed."

I linger in the doorway, hoping somehow to

draw out a confidence, but he gives me nothing. I leave the library with Annie in my arms, knowing I will not sleep, but knowing also that until my father opens up to me, there is little I can do to help him.

CHAPTER 5

My father's prediction about media attention proves prescient. Within forty-eight hours of my arrival, calls about interviews join the ceaseless ringing of patients calling my father. My mother has taken messages from the local newspaper publisher, radio talk-show hosts, even the TV station in Jackson, the state capital, two hours away. I decide to grant an interview to Caitlin Masters, the publisher of the Natchez *Examiner*, on two conditions: that she not ask questions about Arthur Lee Hanratty's execution, and that she print that I will be vacationing in New Orleans until after the execution has taken place. Leaving Annie with my mother — which delights them both — I drive Mom's Nissan downtown in search of Biscuits and Blues, a new restaurant owned by a friend of mine but which I have never seen.

It was once said of American cities that you could judge their character by their tallest buildings: were they offices or churches? At a mere seven stories, the Eola Hotel is the tallest commercial structure in Natchez. Its verdigris-encrusted roof peaks well below the graceful, copper-clad spire of St. Mary Minor Basilica. Natchez's "skyline" barely rises out of a green canopy of oak leaves: the silver dome of the synagogue, the steeple of the Presbyterian church, the roofs of antebellum mansions and stately public buildings. Below the canopy, a soft and filtered sunlight gives the sense of an enormous glassed-in garden.

Biscuits and Blues is a three-story building on Main, with a large second-floor balcony overlooking the street. A young woman stands talking on a cell phone just inside the door — where Caitlin Masters promised to meet me — but I don't think she's the newspaper publisher. She looks more like a French tourist. She's wearing a tailored black suit, cream silk blouse, and black sandals, and she is clearly on the sunny side of thirty. But as I check my watch, she turns face on to me and I spot a hardcover copy of *False Witness* cradled in her left arm. I also see that she's wearing nothing under the blouse, which is distractingly sheer. She smiles and signals that she'll be off the phone in a second, her eyes flashing with quick intelligence.

I acknowledge her wave and wait beside the door. I'm accustomed to young executives in book publishing, but I expected something more conventional in the newspaper business, especially in the South. Caitlin Masters stands with her head cocked slightly, her eyes focused in the middle distance, the edge of her lower lip pinned by a pointed canine. Her skin is as white as bone china and without blemish, shockingly white against her hair, which is black as her silk suit and lies against her neck like a gleaming veil. Her face is a study in planes and angles: high cheekbones, strong jawline, arched brows, and a straight nose, all uniting with almost architectural precision, yet somehow escaping hardness. She wears no makeup that I can see, but her green eyes provide all the accent she needs. They seem incongruous in a face that almost cries out for blue ones, making her striking and memorable rather than merely beautiful.

As she ends her call, she speaks three or four consecutive sentences, and a strange chill runs through me. Ivy League Boston alloyed with something softer, a Brahmin who spent her summers far away. On the telephone this morning I didn't catch it, but coupled with her face, that voice transforms my suspicion to certainty. Caitlin Masters is the woman I spoke to on the flight to Baton Rouge. Kate . . . *Caitlin*.

She holds out her hand to shake mine, and I step back. "You're the woman from the plane. Kate."

Her smile disappears, replaced by embarrassment. "I'm surprised you recognize me, dressed like I was that day."

"You lied to me. You told me you were a lawyer. Was that some kind of setup or what?"

"I didn't tell you I was a lawyer. You assumed I was. I told you I was a First Amendment specialist, and I am."

"You knew what I thought, and you let me think it. You lied, Ms. Masters. This interview is over."

As I turn to go, she takes hold of my arm. "Our meeting on that plane was a complete accident. I want an interview with you, but it wouldn't be worth that kind of trouble. I was flying from Atlanta to Baton Rouge, and I happened to be sitting across the aisle from you. End of story."

"And you *happened* to be reading one of my novels?"

"No. I've been trying to get your number from your parents for a couple of months. A lot of people in Mississippi are interested in you. When the Hanratty story broke, I picked up one of your books in the airport. It's that simple."

I step away from the door to let a pair of middle-aged women through. "Then why not tell me who you were?"

"Because when I was waiting to board, I was sitting by the pay phones. I heard you tell someone you didn't want to talk to reporters for any reason. I knew if I told you I was a newspaper publisher, you wouldn't talk to me."

"Well, I guess you got your inside scoop on how I killed Hanratty's brother."

She draws herself erect, offended now. "I haven't printed a word of what you told me, and I don't plan to. Despite appearances to the contrary, my journalistic ethics are beyond reproach."

"Why were you dressed so differently on the plane?"

She actually laughs at this. "I'd just given a seminar to a group of editors in Atlanta. My father was there, and I try to be a bit more conventional when he's around."

I can see her point. Not many fathers would approve of the blouse she's wearing today.

"Look," she says, "I could have had that story on the wire an hour after you told it to me. I didn't tell a soul. What better proof of trustworthiness could anyone give you?"

"Maybe you're saving it for one big article."

"You don't have to tell me anything you don't want to. In fact, we could just eat lunch, and you can decide if you want to do the interview another time or not."

Her candid manner strikes a chord in me. Perhaps she's manipulating me, but I don't think so. "We came to do an interview. Let's do it. The airplane thing threw me, that's all."

"Me too," she says with a smile. "I liked Annie, by the way."

"Thanks. She liked you too."

As we step into the main dining space of the restaurant, a smattering of applause starts, then fills the room. I look around to see whose birthday it is, then realize that the applause is for me. A little celebrity goes a long way in Mississippi. I recognize familiar faces in the crowd. Some belong to guys I went to school with, now carrying twenty or thirty extra pounds — as I did until Sarah's illness — others to friends of my parents or simply well-wishers. I smile awkwardly and give a little wave to cover the room.

"I told you," says Caitlin. "There's a lot of interest."

"It'll wear off. As soon as they realize I'm the same guy who left, they'll be yawning in my face."

When we arrive at our table, she stands stiffly behind her chair, her eyes twinkling with humor. "You're not going to pull my chair out for me?"

"You didn't look the type."

She laughs and takes her seat. "I wasn't before I got here. Pampering corrupts you fast."

While we study the menus, a collection of classic

60

Cajun dishes, I try to fathom how Caitlin Masters wound up in the job she has. The *Examiner* has always been a conservative paper, owned when I was a boy by a family that printed nothing that reflected negatively upon city worthies. Later it was sold to a family-owned newspaper chain which continued the tradition of offending as few citizens as possible, especially those who bought advertising space. In Natchez the gossip mills have always been a lot more accurate than anything you could find in the *Examiner*. Caitlin seems an improbable match, to say the least.

She closes her menu and smiles engagingly. "I'm younger than you thought I'd be, aren't I?"

"A little," I reply, trying not to look at her chest. In Mississippi, wearing a blouse that sheer without a bra is practically a request to be arrested.

"My father owns the chain. I'm doing a tour of duty down here to learn the ropes."

"Ah." *One mystery cleared up.*

"Okay if we go on the record now?"

"You have a tape recorder?"

"I never use them."

I take out a Sony microcassette recorder borrowed from my father. "The bitter fruit of experience."

Our waitress appears and takes our orders (crawfish beignets and iced tea for us both), then stands awkwardly beside the table as though waiting for something. She looks about twenty and, though not quite in Caitlin Masters's league, is quite lovely. Where Masters is angles and light, the waitress is round and brown and sultry, with the guarded look of the Cajun in her eyes.

"Yes?" Caitlin says, looking up at her.

"Um, I was wondering if Mr. Cage would sign a book for me."

"Sure," I tell her. "Do you have one with you?"

"Well — I live over the restaurant." Her voice is hesitant and terribly self-conscious. "Just temporarily, you know. I have all your books up there."

"Really? I'd be glad to sign them for you."

"Thanks a lot. Um, I'll get your iced tea now."

As she walks away, Caitlin gives me a wry smile. "What does a few years of that do for your ego?"

"Water off a duck's back. Let's start."

She gives me a look that says, *Yeah, right,* then picks up her notebook. "So, are you here for a visit, or is this something more permanent?"

"I honestly have no idea. Call it a visit."

"You've obviously been living a life of emotional extremes this past year. Your last book riding high on the best-seller list, your wife dying. How —"

"That subject's off limits," I say curtly, feeling a door slam somewhere in my soul.

"I'm sorry." Her eyes narrow like those of a surgeon judging the pain of a probe. "I didn't mean to upset you."

"Wait a minute. You asked on the plane if my wife was traveling with me. Did you know then that she was dead?"

Caitlin looks at the table. "I knew your wife had died. I didn't know how recently. I saw the ring. . . ." She folds her hands on the table, then looks up, her eyes vulnerable. "I didn't ask that question as a reporter. I asked it as a woman. If that makes me a terrible person, I apologize."

I find myself more intrigued than angered by

this confession. This woman asked about my wife to try to read how badly I miss her by my reaction. And I believe she asked out of her own curiosity, not for a story. "I'm not sure what that makes you. Are you going to focus on that sort of thing in your article?"

"Absolutely not."

"Let's go on, then."

"What made you stop practicing law and take up writing novels? The Hanratty case?"

I navigate this part of the interview on autopilot, probably learning more about Caitlin Masters than she learns about me. I guessed right about her education: Radcliffe as an undergrad, Columbia School of Journalism for her master's. Top of the line, all the way. She is well read and articulate, but her questions reveal that she knows next to nothing about the modern South. Like most transplants to Natchez, she is an outsider and always will be. It's a shame she holds a job that needs an insider's perspective. The lunch crowd thins as we talk, and our waitress gives such excellent service that our concentration never wavers. By the time we finish our crawfish, the restaurant is nearly empty and a busboy is setting the tables for dinner.

"Where did you get your ideas about the South?" I ask gently.

At last Caitlin adjusts the lapels of her black silk jacket, covering the shadowy edge of aureole that has been visible throughout lunch. "I was born in Virginia," she says with a hint of defensiveness. "My parents divorced when I was five, though. Mother got custody and spirited me back to Massachusetts. For the next twelve years, all I heard about the South was her trashing it."

"So the first chance you got, you headed south to see for yourself whether we were the cloven-hoofed, misogynistic degenerates your mother warned you about."

"Something like that."

"And?"

"I'm reserving my judgment."

"That's kind of you. Do you like Natchez?"

"I do. It's not sterilized or Disneyfied like Williamsburg. It's still funky. Gossip, sex, whisky, and eccentricity, all behind a gossamer veil of Southern gentility."

I chuckle. "A woman I grew up with decided to move back here after working ten years as a film producer in Los Angeles. When I asked why, she told me she was worried that she was losing her mind, and knew that if she did it in Natchez, no one would notice."

Caitlin laughs. "That's exactly it! What about you? Do you like it?"

"That's like asking someone if they like their mother. I've been away for years, but no one who grows up here ever really leaves this town behind."

She makes a note on her pad. "I was surprised it's such a haven for gays. But the contrasts are disturbing. You've got a real race problem here."

"So does Los Angeles."

"But this is a purely white-black race problem."

"And your paper contributes to it."

She reddens. "Would you care to elaborate on that?"

"Sure. The *Examiner* has never dug beneath the surface, never urged people toward their better natures. It was always too afraid to upset the white elite."

"You think I don't know that?"

"You talk like you don't."

"Trust me, I do. Let me ask you something. I've been following local politics pretty closely, and there's something funny going on."

"Like?"

"You'd think Shad Johnson, the black candidate, would be making race a major issue, trying to mobilize every black vote."

"How's he playing it?"

"He's not even mentioning race. He's in the former money capital of the slaveholding South, thirty percent of the black population receives some form of public assistance, and he acts like he's running for mayor of Utopia. Everything is New South, Brotherhood of Man. He's running as a *Republican,* for Christ's sake."

"Sounds like a shrewd guy."

"Will African Americans vote for him if he sucks up to the white vote like that?"

I can't help but laugh. "If Johnson is the only black man in the race, local blacks will vote for him if he buggers a mule at high noon on the courthouse lawn."

Two pink moons appear high on Caitlin's cheeks. "I can't believe you said that. And I can't believe Johnson would stand for the way things are. The things I hear around here . . . sitting in restaurants, riding in cars with people. I've heard the N-word a thousand times since I've been here."

"You'd hear it in Manhattan if you rode in the right cars. Look, I'd really rather not get into this. I spent eight years in the Houston courts listening to more bullshit about race than I ever want to hear."

She shakes her head with apparent disgust. "That's such a cop-out. Racism is the most important problem in America today."

"Caitlin, you are a very rich, very *white* girl preaching about black problems. You're not the first. Sometimes you have to let people save themselves."

"And you're a very white *guy* putting black men on death row for state-sanctioned murder."

"Only when they kill people."

"Only when they kill white people, you mean."

A surge of anger runs through me, but I force myself to stay silent. There's nothing to be gained by pointing out that Arthur Lee Hanratty is a white supremacist, or that I once freed a black man who had been mistakenly put on death row by a colleague of mine. You can't win an argument like this. We stare at each other like two fighters after a flurry of punches, deciding whether to wade in again or rest on the ropes.

"Hanratty's an exception," Caitlin says, as though reading my mind.

This lady is dangerous. It may be a cliché, but her anger has brought color to her cheeks and fire into her eyes, and I am suddenly sure that a string of broken hearts lie in the wake of this self-assured young woman.

"I want to understand this, Penn," she says with utter sincerity. "I need to. I've read a hundred books by Southern writers, Southern journalists, everything. And I still don't get it."

"That's because it's not a Southern problem."

"Don't you think the answer must be wrapped up in the South somehow?"

"No. Not the way you think, anyway. It's been thirty years since the last vestiges of segregation were remedied under the law. And there's a growing feeling that blacks have done damn little to take advantage of that. That they've been given special breaks and blown it every time. That they don't want an even playing field but their turn on top. White America looks at the Vietnamese, the Irish, the Jews, and they say, 'What's the problem with the blacks?' The resentment you hear around this town is based on that, not on old ideas of superiority."

"Do you feel that way?"

"I used to. I don't anymore."

"Why not?"

"The Indians."

"Indians? You mean Native Americans?"

"Think about it. Indians are the only minority that's had as much trouble as blacks. Why? Both races had their cultures shattered by the white man. All the other groups — Irish, Italians, Vietnamese, whatever — may have come here destitute, but they brought one thing with them. Their national identities. Their sense of self. They congregated together in the cities and on the plains, like with like. They maintained their cultural identities — religions, customs, names — until they were secure enough to assimilate. Blacks had no chance to do that. They were stolen from their country, brought here in chains, sold as property. Their families were split, their religion beaten out of them, their names changed. Nothing was left.

67

No identity. And they've never recovered."

"And you parallel that with Native Americans?"

"It's the same experience, only in reverse. The Indians weren't stolen from their land, their land was stolen from them. And their culture was systematically destroyed. They've never recovered either, despite a host of government programs to help them."

Caitlin stops writing. "That's an interesting analogy."

"If you don't know who you are, you can't find your way. There are exceptions, of course. Bright spots. But my point is that whites don't look at blacks with the right perspective. We look at them like an immigrant group that can't get its shit together."

She takes a sip of tea as she processes this perspective. "Does Shad Johnson have the right idea, then? Should Natchez simply sweep its past under the rug and push ahead?"

"For Johnson, it's the smart line to take. For the town . . . I don't know."

"Please try to answer. I think it's important."

"If I do, we go off the record."

She doesn't look happy, but she wants her answer. "Okay."

"Faulkner thought the land itself had been cursed by slavery. I don't agree." I pause, feeling the writer's special frustration at trying to embody moral complexities in words. "Have you ever read Karl Jung?"

"A little, in college. Synchronicity, all that?"

"Jung didn't try to separate good and evil. He knew that both exist in every human heart. He called the propensity to evil the Shadow. And he believed that trying to deny or repress the Shadow is dangerous. Because it can't be done. He believed you have to recognize your Shadow, come to grips with it, accept it, and integrate it."

"Make friends with the evil in yourself?"

"Basically. And the South has never done that. We've never truly acknowledged the crime of slavery — not in our collective soul. It's a bit like Germany and the Holocaust, only slavery is much further in the past. Modern generations feel no guilt over it, and it's easy to see why. There's no tangible connection. Slave owners were a tiny minority, and most Southerners see no larger complicity."

"How does the white South acknowledge the crime?"

"It'll never happen. *That's* what's scary about what Shad Johnson is doing. Because the day of reckoning always comes, when everything you've tried to repress rears up in the road to meet you. Whatever you bury deepest is always waiting for the moment of greatest stress to explode to the surface."

"You're the only white person in this town who's said anything like this to me. How did you turn out so different?"

"That's a story for another day. But I want you to be clear that I think the North is as guilty as the South when it comes to blacks."

"You don't really believe that."

"You're damn right I do. I may criticize the South when I'm in it, but when I'm in the North, I defend Mississippi to the point of blows. Prejudice in the North isn't as open, but it's just as destructive. Most Yankees have no concept of living in a town — I mean *in* a town — that is fifty percent black. No idea of the warmth that can exist between black and white on a daily basis, and has here for years."

"Oh, come *on*."

"What happened in Boston when they tried busing?"

"That's a different issue."

"Watts. Detroit. Skokie. Rodney King. O.J."

She sighs. "Are we going to refight the Civil War here?"

"How long have you lived here, Caitlin?"

"Sixteen months."

"You could live here sixteen years and you'd still be on the outside. And you can't understand this place until you see it from the inside."

"You're talking about the social cliques?"

"Not exactly. Society is different here. It's not just tiers of wealth. Old money may run out, but the power lingers. Blood still means something down here. Not to me, but to a lot of people."

"Sounds like Boston."

"I imagine it is. The structure is concentric circles, and as you move toward the center, the levels of knowledge increase."

"Were your parents born here?"

"No, but my father's a doctor, and doctors get a backstage pass. Probably because their profession puts them in a position to learn secrets anyway. And there are a thousand secrets in this town."

"Name one."

"Well . . . what about the Del Payton case?"

"Who's Del Payton?"

"Delano Payton was a black factory worker who got blown up in his car outside the Triton Battery plant in 1968. It was a race murder, like a dozen others in Mississippi, only it was never solved. I'm not sure anybody really tried to solve it. Payton was a decorated combat veteran of the Korean War. And I'll bet you a thousand dollars we're sitting within five miles of his murderers right now."

Excitement and awe fill her eyes. "Are you serious? Did the *Examiner* cover the murder?"

"I don't know. I was eight years old then. I do know Dan Rather came down with a half dozen network correspondents. The FBI was up in arms, and two of their agents were shot at on the road between here and Jackson."

"Why was Payton murdered?"

"He was about to be hired for a job that until then had been held exclusively by whites."

"The police must have had some idea who did it."

"Everybody knew who did it. Racist cowards motivated by the tacit encouragement of white leaders who knew better. A year before, they bombed another black guy at the same plant, but he survived. My father treated him. This guy was on the hospital phone with Bobby Kennedy every day, had guards all around his room, the works."

"This is great stuff. My aunt went to school with Bobby."

Her self-centered dilettantism finally puts me over the edge. "Caitlin, you're so transparent. You want to hear the same thing every other Northern journalist wants to hear: that the Klan is alive and well, that the South is as Gothic and demonic as it ever was. Terrible things did happen here in the sixties, and people who knew better turned a blind eye. As a boy I watched the Klan march robed on horseback right out there on Main Street. City police directed traffic for them. But that has nothing to do with Natchez as it is today."

"How can you say that?"

"You want to assign guilt? The *Examiner* printed the time of that Klan march but refused to print the time or location of a single civil rights meeting. Is the *Examiner* the same newspaper it was then?"

She ignores the question. "Why haven't I heard people talking about the Payton case before? Even the African Americans don't talk about it."

"Because if you live here, you want to make the best life you can. Stirring up the past doesn't help anybody."

"But cases like this are being reopened every day, right here in Mississippi. The Byron de la Beckwith case. The retrial of Sam Bowers, the Klan Wizard from Laurel. You must know that the state recently opened the secret files of the Mississippi Sovereignty Commission?"

"So?"

"The Sovereignty Commission was like a racist KGB. They kept files not only on African Americans but on hundreds of whites suspected of liberal sympathies."

"So?"

Caitlin looks at me in bewilderment. "So? *Newsweek* just ran a big piece on it, and Peter Jennings's people have been calling around the state, trolling for stories. The Payton case could be reopened at any time."

"Glad to hear it. Justice should be better served than it was in Natchez in 1968. But this isn't some old trial with an all-white hung jury. This is an unsolved murder. A capital murder. No defendant. No suspects, as far as I know. No crime scene. Old or dead witnesses —"

"Nobody said winning a Pulitzer is easy."

A light clicks on in my head. "Ah. That's the plan? Winning a Pulitzer before you're thirty?"

She gives me a sly smile. "Before I'm twenty-nine. *That's* the plan."

"God help this town."

Her laugh is full and throaty, one I'd expect from an older woman. "Did you know that some of the Sovereignty Commission files are going to remain sealed?"

"No."

"Forty-two of them. Some of them on major politicians. I heard Trent Lott's was one of them, but that turned out to be wrong."

"That's no surprise. A lot of the most sensitive files were destroyed years ago."

"Why haven't you explored any of this in your novels?"

"A sense of loyalty to the place that bore me, I suppose. A lot of people would have to die before I could write a book like that."

"So, until then you write fluff and take the easy money?"

"I don't write fluff."

She holds up her hands in contrition. "I know. I did a Nexis search on you. *Publishers Weekly* named

False Witness the fourth-best legal thriller ever written."

"After what?"

"*Anatomy of a Murder, The Caine Mutiny,* and *Presumed Innocent.*"

"That's pretty good company," I murmur, painfully aware that *False Witness* was four books ago.

"Yes, but it just seems so obvious that you should be writing about all this. Write what you know! You know?"

Caitlin picks up the check and walks over to the cash register, her movements fluid and graceful despite the phenomenal energy that animates her. The restaurant is empty now but for the cashier and our waitress, who chooses this moment to come forward with her copy of *False Witness.* I take the book, open it to the flyleaf, and accept the pen she offers.

"Would you like me to personalize it?"

"Wow, that would be great. Um, to Jenny. That's me."

"No last name?"

"Just Jenny would be cool."

I write: *Jenny, I enjoyed meeting you. Penn Cage.*

She blushes as she takes back the book, then glances at Caitlin, who stands waiting for me. "I'd love to talk to you sometime," she says in a quavering voice. "Ask you some questions, maybe."

I recognize the nervous tones of an aspiring writer. "I'll be in again. A friend of mine owns the place."

"Wow, okay. Thanks."

I join Caitlin as she walks out onto the brightly lit street.

74

"Did you get enough for your piece?"

"More than enough." She tucks her copy of *False Witness* under one arm and buttons her jacket. "AP will probably pick it up, and it'll be reprinted all over the South. They like fluff as much as anybody."

I sigh wearily.

"I'm joking, Penn. God, take it easy, would you?"

"I guess I'm a little tense."

"A little?" She takes *False Witness* in both hands, then bends at the waist and touches the book flat against the sidewalk, displaying a limberness that makes my back hurt and draws looks from several passersby. "Mmm, I needed that."

"If I tried that, they'd hear tendons popping across the river."

She smiles. "Not if you practiced. We should do this again. You can be deep background on Southern crime and psychology."

I start to decline, then surprise myself by saying, "I might be able to help you with that."

Her eyes sparkle with pleasure. "I'll call you. And I'm sorry again about the airplane. Tell Annie I said hello."

She holds out her hand and I take it, not thinking anything of it and so being all the more surprised by the shock I feel. When our eyes meet, we recognize something in each other that neither expects and both quickly look away from.

"The story will probably run Wednesday in the Southern Life section," she says in a flustered voice, and awkwardly releases my hand. "I'll mail some copies to your parents. I'm sure your mom still clips everything about you."

"Absolutely."

Caitlin Masters looks at me once more, then turns and walks quickly to a green Miata parked across the street with its top down. I am acutely aware of her physical presence, even across the street, and inexplicably glad that she suggested another lunch. With that gladness comes a rush of guilt so strong that it nauseates me. Seven months ago I was standing at my wife's deathbed, then her coffin. Seven seconds ago I felt something for another woman. This small and natural response causes me more guilt than sleeping with a woman out of physical necessity — which I have not yet done. Because what I felt was more than physical. A glacier consumes whole forests by inches. As small as it is, that glimmer of feeling is absolute proof that someone else will one day occupy the place Sarah held in my life.

I feel like a traitor.

CHAPTER 6

My father wakes me by slapping a newspaper against my forehead. After I rub the sleep from my eyes, I see my own face staring up from the front page of the Natchez *Examiner*, above the fold. They've scanned my most recent author photo and blown it up to "this man assassinated the president" size. The headline reads: *PRODIGAL SON RETURNS HOME.*

"The goddamn phone hasn't stopped ringing," Dad growls. "Everybody wants to know why my son is disparaging his hometown."

Beneath the author photo is a montage of smaller shots, like a family album: me as a lanky kid with Dad's arm around my shoulders, printed in a Father's Day issue in 1968; as a high school baseball player; as the flag runner in the annual Confederate pageant; my Ole Miss graduation photo. I quickly scan the columns, recognizing most of what I said yesterday, laid out in surprisingly faithful prose.

"I don't get it," I say. "What's wrong with this?"

"Have you been in Houston so long you've forgotten how things are here? Bill Humphreys said you set back thirty years of good race relations."

"I didn't say anything you haven't said a hundred times in our kitchen."

"The newspaper isn't our kitchen!"

"Come on, Dad. This is nothing."

He shakes his head in amazement. "Turn the page, hotshot. You'll see something."

When I turn the page, my breath catches in my throat.

The banner headline reads: *30 YEARS LATER "RACIST COWARDS" STILL WALK STREETS.* My stomach flips over. Underneath the headline is a photo of a scorched Ford Fairlane with a blackened corpse seated behind the wheel. That picture never ran in the Natchez *Examiner* in 1968. Caitlin Masters must have dug up an old crime-scene photo somewhere.

"Jesus," I whisper.

"Harvey Byrd at the Chamber of Commerce thinks you may have singlehandedly sabotaged the chemical-plant deal."

"Let me read the thing, okay?"

Dad plants himself in the corner, his arms folded.

The story opens like a true-crime novel.

On May 14, 1968, Frank Jones, a scheduling clerk at the Triton Battery plant, walked out to his car in the middle of the third shift to run an errand. Before he could start his engine, he heard a boom "like an artillery piece," and a black-wall tire slammed into his windshield. Thirty yards away, a black man named Delano Payton sat burning to death. Jones was the sole eyewitness to the worst race crime in the history of this city, in which a combat veteran of the Ko-

rean War was murdered to prevent his being promoted to a "white-only" job. No one was ever arrested for the crime, and many in the black community believe that law enforcement officials of the period gave less than their full efforts to the case. Best-selling author and Natchez native Penn Cage characterized the killers of Delano Payton as "racist cowards," and stated that justice should be better served than it was in Natchez in 1968.

Former police chief Hiram Wilkes contended that leads were nonexistent at the time, and said that despite exhaustive efforts by law enforcement, and a $15,000 reward offered by Payton's national labor union, no suspects were turned up. The FBI was called in to work the case but had no more success than local police. Former Natchez police officer Ray Presley, who assisted on the case in the spring of 1968, stated, "It was a tough murder case, and the FBI got in the way more than they helped, which was par for them in those days —"

I reread the last sentence, my heartbeat accelerating. I had no idea Ray Presley was involved in the Payton case. I want to ask my father about him, but with the blackmail issue — and my mother's suspicions about Presley — hanging like a cloud between us, I don't.

"You've been dealing with the media for twelve years," Dad grumbles. "That publisher must have shown you a little leg and puréed your brain. I've seen her around town. Face like a model, tits like two puppies in a sack. I know what happened. It took her about five seconds to get Penn Cage at his most sanctimonious." He grabs the newspaper out of my hands and wads it into a ball. "Did you have to dredge up the goddamn Payton case?"

"I just *mentioned* it, for God's sake. I thought we were off the record."

"She obviously didn't."

I try to remember the point at which I asked to go off the record. I can check my tape, of course, but I already know what Caitlin Masters will say: she thought I wanted the Jungian analysis and the comparison between Germany and the South off the record, but not the Del Payton remarks, which were an extension of our earlier conversation on racism. At least she honored my request not to mention the Hanratty execution.

"What about that Klan rally stuff?" Dad mutters.

"You took me to that rally!"

"I know, I know . . . damn it. I just wanted you to see that wasn't any way to be. But you didn't have to drag it all back up now, did you?"

"I made it clear that stuff was all in the past. And she printed my qualifications, I'll give her that."

"God almighty, what a mess. Do you think —"

The front doorbell rings, cutting him off.

"Who the hell could that be?" he asks. "It's only eight-thirty."

He walks out of the bedroom, taking the wadded-up newspaper with him.

My thoughts return to Caitlin Masters. Despite her assurances, I was foolish to say anything to her that I didn't want printed. Maybe she did show me a little leg and lull my usually vigilant defenses. Am

I that easy to manipulate?

"Get some clothes on," my father says from the door, his face grave. "You've got visitors."

"Who? You look almost scared."

He nods slowly. "I think I am."

Uncertain what to expect, I hover in the hall outside my mother's living room. The hushed sibilance of gracious women making polite conversation drifts from the wide doorway. I walk through the door and stop in my tracks. Two black women sit primly on the sofa, delicate Wedgwood cups steaming before them on the coffee table. One is in her eighties, if not older, and dressed in an ensemble the like of which I have not seen since the Sundays I drove past black churches as a teenager. The skirt is purple, the blouse green, the shoes a gleaming patent black. Her hat is a flowered concoction of black straw and varicolored silk. Beneath the hat is a shining black wig, beneath the wig a raisin of a face with watery eyes that glisten amid the wrinkles.

The woman beside her looks thirty years younger and wears a much more subdued outfit, a pleated navy skirt with a periwinkle blouse. She looks up, and her gaze disconcerts me. Most black people I grew up with rarely made direct eye contact, locking their feelings behind a veneer of humility. But this woman's gaze is unveiled, direct and self-confident.

"You keep a fine house, Mrs. Cage," the older woman says in a cracked voice. "A *fine* house."

"You're so kind to say so," my mother replies from a wing chair on the other side of the coffee table. She wears a housecoat and no makeup, yet even in this state radiates a quiet, stately beauty. She turns to me and smiles.

"Son, this is Mrs. Payton." She gestures toward the elderly woman, then nods at her younger companion. "And this is Mrs. Payton also. They've come to thank you for what you said in this morning's paper."

I flush from my neck to the crown of my head. I can only be looking at the widow and mother of Delano Payton, the man bombed and burned to death in 1968. Barefoot and unshaven, I make a vain attempt to straighten my hair, then advance into the living room. Without rising, the elder Mrs. Payton enfolds my right hand in both of hers like a dowager empress. Her palms feel like fine sandpaper. The younger Mrs. Payton stands and shakes my hand with exaggerated formality. Her hand is moist and warm. Up close, she looks older than I first guessed, perhaps sixty-five. Because she has not gone to fat, she projects an aura of youth that her eyes cannot match.

"Althea works in the nursery at St. Catherine's Hospital," Dad informs me from the door. "I see her all the time. And I've treated Miss Georgia for thirty-five years now."

"Yo' daddy a good doctor," the elder Mrs. Payton says from the sofa, pointing a bony finger at me. "A *good* doctor."

My father has heard this ten thousand times, but he smiles graciously. "Thank you, Miss Georgia."

"I remember you makin' house calls *late* at night," Georgia Payton goes on, her voice reedy and difficult to follow as it jumps up and down the scale. "Givin' shots and deliverin' babies. Had you a spotlight back then to see the house numbers."

"And a pistol in my black bag," Dad adds, chuckling.

"Sho' did. I seen it once. You ever have to use it?"

"No, ma'am, thank God."

"Might have to one of these days, with all this crack in the streets. I told the pastor last Sunday, you want to find Satan, just pull up to one of them crack houses. Sheriff ought to burn ever' one to the ground."

We all nod with enthusiasm, doing our best to foster a casual atmosphere. Blacks visiting socially in white homes — and vice versa — is still as rare as snowfall in Natchez, but this is not the reason for the general discomfort.

"Mr. Cage," Althea says, focusing her liquid brown eyes on me, "we really appreciate you speaking out like you did in the paper."

"Please call me Penn," I implore her, embarrassed by thanks for a few lines tossed off without any real feeling for the victims of the crime.

"Mr. Penn," says Georgia Payton, "ain't no white man in thirty years said what you said in the paper today. My boy was kilt outside his job in nineteen hundred and sixty-eight, and all the polices did was sweep it under the rug."

Her statement hangs suspended in crystalline silence. I sense my father's reflexive desire to answer her charge, to try to mitigate the behavior of the law enforcement figures of the period. But the murder remains unsolved, and he has no idea what efforts were made to solve it, if any, or how sincere they might have been. Althea Payton looks momentarily disconcerted by her mother-in-law's frankness, but then her eyes fill with calm resolution.

"Are you still a lawyer, Mr. Cage?" she asks. "I mean, I know you're a writer now. Can you still practice law?"

I incline my head. "I'm still a member of the bar."

"What that mean?" asks Georgia.

"I can still practice law, ma'am."

"Then we wants to hire you."

"For what?"

"I think I know," Dad says.

"To find out who murdered my baby," the old woman says. "The po-lice don't want to do it. FBI don't want to. The county lawyer neither."

"The district attorney," Althea corrects her.

"You've spoken to the district attorney about this?"

Althea nods. "Several times. He has no interest in the case."

Dad emits a sigh easily interpreted as, *Big surprise.*

"We hired us a detective too," Georgia says. "I even wrote to that man on *Unsolved Mysteries,* that good-looking white man from that old gangster TV show."

"Robert Stack?" asks my mother.

"Yes," Althea confirms. "We got back one letter from the show's producer expressing interest, but after that nothing."

"What about this detective?" I ask. "What happened with him?"

"We hired a man from Jackson first. He poked around downtown for an afternoon, then told us there was nothing to find."

"White man," Georgia barks. "A no-good."

"Then we hired a detective from Chicago," Althea says in a tense voice. "He flew down and spent a week in the Eola Hotel —"

"Colored man," the old woman cuts in. "A no-*count* no-good. He stole all our money and went back to Chicago."

"He was very expensive," Althea concedes. "And he said the same thing the first detective told us. The pertinent records had been destroyed and there was nothing to find."

"NAACP say the same thing," Georgia adds with venom. "They don't care about my baby none. He wasn't a big enough name. They cry about Martin and Medgar every year, got white folks makin' movies about Medgar. But my baby Del in the ground and nobody care. Nobody."

"Except you," Althea says quietly. "When I walked out in my driveway this morning and picked up that paper — when I read what you said — I cried. I cried like I haven't cried in thirty years."

Dad raises his eyebrows and sends me one of his telepathic messages: *You opened your damn mouth. See what it's got you.*

"I still gots some money, Mr. Penn," Georgia says, clutching at a black vinyl handbag the size of a small suitcase.

I envision a tidal wave of one-dollar bills spilling out of the purse, like money at a crack bust, but Mrs. Payton has clutched the bag only to emphasize her statement. I cannot let this go any further.

"Ladies, I appreciate your thanks, but I don't deserve them. As I said in the paper, I'm here for a vacation. I'm no longer involved in any criminal matters. What happened to your husband and son was a terrible tragedy, but I suspect that what the detectives told you is true. This crime happened thirty years ago. Nowadays, if the police don't solve a homicide in the first forty-eight hours, they know they probably never will."

"But sometimes they do," Althea says doggedly. "I've read about murder cases that were solved years after the fact."

"That's true, but it's rare. In all my years with the Houston D.A.'s office, we only had a couple of cases like that."

"But you had them."

"Yes. But what we had more of — a hundred times more of — was distraught relatives pleading with us to reopen old cases. Murder is a terrible thing, and no one knows that better than you. The repercussions reverberate through generations."

"But there's no statue of limitations on murder. Is there?"

Statue of limitations. I see no point in correcting her grammar; I've heard attorneys make the same mistake. Like congressmen referring to *nucular* war. "Everything hinges on evidence," I explain. "Has any new evidence come to light?"

Her desolate look is answer enough.

"That's what we were hoping you could do," Althea says. "Look back over what the police did. Maybe they missed something. Maybe they *buried* something. I read in a book that sixty percent of the Natchez police force was Klan back then. God knows what they did or didn't do. You might even get a book out of it. There's a lot nobody knows about those times. About what Del was doing for his people."

I fight the urge to glance at my parents for assistance. "I'm actually in the middle of a book now, and I'm behind. I —"

"I've read your books," Althea breaks in. "All of them. In paperback, of course. I read them on the late shift, when the babies are resting well."

I never know what to say in these moments. If you say, *Did you like them?* you're putting the person on the spot. But what else can you say?

"I liked the first one the best," Althea offers. "I liked the others too, but I couldn't help feeling. . . ."

"Be honest," I urge her, dreading what will follow.

"I always felt that your gift was bigger than the stories you were telling. I don't mean to be critical. But that first book was so real. I just think if you really understood what happened to Del, you'd have a story that would take all the gift you have to tell it."

Her words are like salt on my soul. "I truly wish I could help you. But I can't. If some new evidence were to come to light, the district attorney would be the proper man to see." I look at my father. "Is Austin Mackey still the D.A. here?"

He nods warily.

"I went to school with Mr. Mackey. He's a good man. I could —"

"He nothing but a politician!" scoffs Georgia Payton.

The old woman gets slowly to her feet, using her huge handbag as a counterweight. "He don't care none. We come here 'cause we thought *you* did. But maybe you don't. Maybe you was talking free in the paper 'cause you been gone so long you ain't worried 'bout what people thinks around here. I told Althea, you must be like your daddy, a hard-working man with a good heart. But maybe I told her wrong."

I flush again, suddenly certain that the men of the Payton family are intimately familiar with the guilt trip as a motivational tool.

Althea stands more slowly than her mother-in-law, as though lifting the weight of thirty years of grief. This time when she speaks, she looks only at the floor.

"I loved my husband," she says softly. "After he was killed, I never remarried. I never even went with another man. I raised my boy the best I could and tried to go on. I don't say it was hard, because everybody got it hard, some way. You know that, Dr. Cage. The world's full of misery. But my Del got took before his time." Her lower lip is quivering; she bites it to keep her composure. "He wanted us to wait to have children. So we'd be able to give them the things they needed. Del said our people hurt themselves by having too many children too quick. We just had one before he died. Del was a good boy who grew into a good man, and he never got to see his own baby grow up."

The mournful undertone in her voice pierces

my heart. All I can see is Sarah lying in her casket at age thirty-seven, her future ripped away like a cruel mirage. Althea Payton breaks the image by reaching into her purse and taking out a folded piece of paper, which she hands to me. I have little choice but to unfold it.

It's a death certificate.

"When the ambulance men got to Del, he was already burned up. But they couldn't get him out of the seat. The springs from the seat had blown up through his thighs and pinned him there. That's why he couldn't get out, even though he was still alive after that bomb went off."

I stare at the brittle yellowed paper, a simple form dated 5-14-68.

"Look in the middle," Althea says. "Under cause of death."

I push down a hot wave of nausea. Thirty years ago, on the line beside the printed words CAUSE OF DEATH, some callous or easily cowed bureaucrat had scrawled the word *Accidental*.

"As long as I live and breathe," Althea whispers, "I'll do what I can to find out the truth."

I want to speak, to try to communicate the empathy I feel, but I don't. Sarah's death taught me this. In the face of grief, words have no power.

I watch the Payton women follow my mother into the hall. I hear Georgia repeat her compliment about the fine house my mother keeps, then the soft shutting of the front door. I sit on the sofa where Althea sat. The cushion is still warm. My mother's slippers hiss across the slate floor of the foyer, the sound like a nun moving through a convent.

"The neighbors are standing out in their yards," she says.

Wondering at the sight of black people who aren't yard men or maids, I reflect. *And tomorrow the maids and the yard men will return, while the two Mrs. Paytons sit or work in silent grief, mourning a man whose murder caused no more ripples than a stone dropped into a pond.*

"I know that was hard," my father says, laying a hand on my shoulder. "But you did the right thing."

I shake my head. "I don't know."

"That boy's long dead and gone. Nothing anybody can do will help him now. But it could hurt a lot of people. Those two poor women. The town. Your mother. You and Annie most of all. You did the right thing, son."

I look up at my father, searching for the man Georgia Payton said he is.

"You did," my mother insists. "Don't dwell on it. Go wake Annie up. I'm going to make French toast."

CHAPTER 7

The couch in my father's medical office has heard many terrible truths: revelations by the doctor (you're sick; you're dying; they couldn't get it all), confessions by the patient (my husband beats me; my father raped me; I want to die), but always — always — truths about the patient.

Today the truth about the doctor will be told.

I can imagine no other reason for the sudden summons to his office. It requires a conscious effort to control my anxiety as I sit on that worn leather couch, waiting for him to finish with his last patient of the day.

After the Payton women left our house this morning, Dad took his old pickup truck to work so that Annie and I would have the BMW. Having no desire to endure the glares of the local citizenry, I spent the morning in the pool with Annie, marveling at how well she moved in the water and fighting a losing battle to keep her skin covered with sun block. Mom and I had tuna sandwiches for lunch, Annie a bowl of SpaghettiOs. When the two of them drove downtown to buy Annie new shoes, I retired to the library and read T. Harry Williams's *Huey Long* on the sofa until I fell asleep.

The telephone woke me at four-thirty P.M. I hated to chance answering it myself, but I thought it might be my mother.

"Penn?" said my father. "Can you drop by my office about five? Alone?"

"Sure. What's up?"

"I think it's time we had a talk."

"Okay," I said, trying to sound casual. "I'll see you at five."

I went to the bathroom and showered off the chlorine from the pool, then dressed in chinos and a polo shirt. Dad's office is only a couple of miles from the house, so I read another twenty minutes in *Huey Long*. When I fell asleep, the Grand Imperial Wizard of the Ku Klux Klan, speaking from the "imperial klonvocation" in Atlanta, had just announced that he was going to Louisiana to campaign against Huey because of his pro-Negro policies. The Kingfish stormed into the press gallery of the state senate while the legislature was in session and announced that if that "Imperial bastard" crossed the Louisiana state line, he would shortly depart "with his toes turned up." The Klan leader wisely elected not to test the Kingfish's sincerity. As humorous as it seemed in retrospect, Long could all too easily have backed up his threat. I could see how dictatorial power might be an asset in solving sticky problems like racism. Of course, that road also leads to the crematorium ovens.

When I got to my father's office building, I used his private door. I'd known Anna, his chief nurse — an attractive black woman — for most of my life, but I was too curious to spend even ten minutes reminiscing about old times. I sat on the couch opposite his desk and waited in the lingering haze of cigar smoke.

During his first fifteen years in Natchez, Dad practiced in a sprawling downtown house. This was the era of separate waiting rooms for "colored" and white, but his only nod to this convention was a flimsy wooden partition set up in the middle of the room. On any day you could find whole families — white and black — camped out in that great room, kids playing on the floor, parents eating from bag lunches and waiting to see the doctor on a first-come, first-served basis. His new office, convenient to both hospitals and sterile as a hypodermic needle, runs like any other doctor's — almost. He has rigidly scheduled appointments, a gleaming laboratory, and modern X-ray facilities, but he still routinely brings everything to a standstill by spending whatever time he feels a patient needs for examination, commiseration, or just plain conversation.

At last his strong baritone filters around the door. The volume tells me he is bidding farewell to a geriatric patient. Old people comprise the bulk of his practice now, as his "patient base" has aged with him. Anna leans in and gives me a smile, then closes the door behind Dad. He squeezes my shoulder as he walks past and sits in the big chair behind his desk.

This is how I picture him in memory: white lab coat, stethoscope hanging loosely around his neck, ensconced behind mountains of incomplete medical records, drug samples, and junk mail. He reaches into a small refrigerator behind his desk and takes out a Dr Pepper, which he offers to me.

When I decline, he pops the top and takes a long pull from it, his eyes watering from the sudden shot of carbonation.

"I'm in a bad spot, Penn," he says in a frank voice. "I apologize for being an ass the other night. It's not easy for a father to admit weakness to his son."

I nod awkwardly, imagining a future when I am certain to fall short of Annie's idealized image of me. "Dad, there's nothing you can tell me that will change my opinion of you. Just tell me what's going on so we can deal with it."

He clearly doubts my statement, but he's made up his mind to talk. "Twenty-five years ago," he says, "your Aunt Ellen got into some trouble."

My mind is spinning. When he said "twenty-five years ago," I thought he was going to start talking about Del Payton. But Payton was killed thirty years ago. The shift to my mother's younger sister, Ellen, throws me completely.

"She was divorced and living in Mobile, Alabama. Ellen was about your age now, I guess. Dating a guy there. He was a year or two younger than she was. Name was Hillman. Don Hillman. Your mother and I didn't know it at the time — at least I didn't — but Hillman was abusing Ellen. Beating her, controlling every word and action. Your mother finally convinced her that the relationship was going to end badly no matter what she did, and Ellen tried to break it off. Hillman didn't take it well. I advised Ellen to go to the police. Then I found out Hillman was the brother of a cop over in Mobile. A detective. This was 1973. Nobody'd heard of stalking laws."

"I hope you brought her here."

"Of course. She stayed with us for a summer. You remember, don't you?"

I do. For most of one summer our hall bathroom became an exotic world of hanging stockings, lacy underwear, cut-glass perfume bottles, and blue Noxema jars.

"Hillman called the house a few times after the breakup. Late, drunk out of his mind and railing, or else hanging up. One night when he didn't hang up, I told him if he came to Natchez making trouble, he'd be a long time getting back to Mobile. The calls stopped. After a while Ellen wanted her own place, so I rented her an apartment at the Windsor Arms and got her a job at the Jeff Davis."

He takes another slug of Dr Pepper. "As soon as she got her own place, strange things started happening. Slashed tires, eggs on her door, more juvenile crap. One morning she found her cat at her door with its throat cut. I called the Natchez police, but they couldn't find Hillman anywhere in town." He closes his eyes and sighs. "Then he raped her."

A shudder of horror accompanies my amazement. Families are mazes of secrets, and none of us ever knows them all.

"Hillman was waiting inside her apartment when she got home from a date. He beat the hell out of her, raped her, sodomized her. Then he disappeared. Ellen was too shaken up to swear out charges. I had to sedate her. I got the Natchez D.A. to call the Mobile D.A. and make a lot of noise, but Ellen would have been a shaky witness at best, even if I could have gotten her to press charges. And Hillman's brother was a cop, remember? The Mobile D.A. didn't sound excited about making trouble for him."

I nod in sympathy. The old-timers in Houston told me a thousand times how tough it was to get rape convictions before feminists changed public perception of the crime. And the cop angle was a serious complication. Nothing is more incestuous than Southern law enforcement. Everything is personal relationships.

"Needless to say, things were pretty bad at home," Dad goes on. "We tried to keep it from you and your sister, but your mother and Ellen were at the end of their rope. Peggy was driving her to Jackson every three days to see a psychiatrist."

I remember this too. Mom taking Aunt Ellen to the doctor all the time. "We thought it was her ovaries or something."

"That's what we told you. Anyway, two weeks after the rape, Hillman started calling again." Dad is clenching and unclenching his right fist on the desk. "I never felt so goddamn impotent in my life."

I don't know what's coming, but the hair on my forearms is standing up.

"About this time, Ray Presley happened to come see me about his blood pressure. You know how I get to talking to patients, and Presley always had a good story. He saw that I wasn't myself. He asked what was bothering me, and I told him. He'd been a cop, after all. I thought he might have a suggestion."

He'd also done a hitch in Parchman prison, I think,

but now does not seem the best time to bring that up.

"Ray heard me out, and he didn't say much. Grunted a couple of times in the right places. You never know what he's thinking. So we're both just sitting there, saying nothing. After a while he says, 'So what's this shitbird's name, Doc?' I didn't say anything for a minute. Then I told him. We shot the bull for a few more minutes, and Ray left. Three weeks later, the Natchez D.A. called and told me Hillman was dead. Somebody'd shot him in the head and taken his wallet outside a topless bar in Mobile."

"Jesus Christ."

"At first I was relieved. But somewhere in the back of my mind I was worried about Ray. He'd always appreciated me taking care of his mother, and some part of me wondered if he hadn't taken it into his head to get rid of my problem for me."

"Oh, man."

"A month later he came back in to get his pressure checked. I told the girls I was too busy to talk, but he slipped into my office and waited for me. When I went in, I asked him point blank if he knew anything about Hillman's death."

"And?"

"He told me right out he'd killed the guy."

"Shit."

Dad shakes his head. "Just like saying, 'I fixed that flat for you, Doc.' He gave me this funny smile and told me not to give it another thought. Said I didn't owe him anything. Just get back to doctoring and living. Those were his exact words."

"Tell me you reported this to the police."

"I didn't."

Having watched my father make moral choices that cost him money and friendships for years, I am stunned by this answer. "That's accessory after the fact, Dad. Five years in the pen."

"I realize that. But the situation was more complicated than you know."

"You hadn't committed any crime until you kept Presley's confession from the police."

"Listen, damn it! Ray must have seen how he upset me. Because twenty minutes after he walked out, he came back and handed me a zipper pouch. Inside it was a pistol I'd lent him about six months before, a forty-five."

My heart slaps against my chest wall. "He killed Hillman with that pistol?"

"No. But he was always borrowing things from me back then. Guns, books, my Nikon for a stakeout, that kind of thing. You know I can't say no to anybody. Anyhow, I'd lent him another pistol about a year before, a little featherweight thirty-eight. So, when he handed me the forty-five, I asked about the thirty-eight." Dad takes a deep breath and exhales slowly. "He told me it had been stolen."

I close my eyes as though to shield myself from what is coming.

"He told me not to worry about it, that he'd get me another thirty-eight. But he was really telling me that reporting the murder wasn't an option. He'd killed Hillman with my thirty-eight, and he still had the gun. If I tried to report him, he could tell the police that I'd asked him to commit the crime and had given him the gun to do it."

"How soon did he start blackmailing you?"

"He didn't mention it again for twenty-five years."

"What?"

"He had no intention of blackmailing me, Penn. Ray Presley idolized me back then. Still does, I think. But last year he got prostate cancer, and he doesn't have health insurance. He needed money, so he started getting it wherever he could. For all I know, he's blackmailing ten other people besides me. The point is, he had me over a barrel. I couldn't see any option but to pay him."

"Why didn't you call me when he first came to you?"

"Do you really have to ask? I was ashamed. Because of me, a man was murdered."

"You had nothing to do with that! You didn't solicit the thing, for God's sake. You couldn't know Presley would kill the guy."

Dad dismisses this rationalization with a wave of his hand. "Do you remember *Becket*?"

"The movie or the historical archbishop?"

"The movie. After Becket makes his moral stand against King Henry, the king is alone in the palace with his nobles. These so-called nobles are a nasty bunch, greedy, violent, and drunk. And though King Henry loves Becket, he says out loud: 'Will no one rid me of this meddlesome priest?' And of course they do. They go to Canterbury and murder him with swords."

Sometimes I wish my father had less rigorous moral standards.

"Henry knew what he was saying, Penn. He

99

knew the company he was in. And that made him guilty of murder. That's why he submitted to the lashing by Becket's monks."

"You're not a king. You couldn't know what Presley would do."

Dad is too wracked by guilt for me to get through to him. "I've spent years thinking about this. I didn't know Presley would kill the man, but when he asked for the name, I knew he might do *something*. I'd treated his parents for free, and he felt indebted to me. He'd just gotten out of prison. From the moment I told Presley that name, Hillman was bound to get hurt, maybe killed. There's no getting around that."

I know what it has cost my father to admit this. He may even be right. But that's not my primary concern at this point. "That's not how the law would see it. Technically, your only crime was accessory after the fact. And the statute of limitations ran out on that in 1975."

"What about the gun?"

"That's another story. If Presley will lie to the D.A. and say you asked him to kill Hillman, and that you gave him the gun — and if he still *has* the gun — that adds up to capital murder. It puts you in line for what I've got to witness in two days. Lethal injection."

"That's what I thought."

"Why did you decide to tell me this today?"

"You want to find out who killed Del Payton. I know you do, and you're right. Maybe you even have an obligation to do it. But the road to Payton's killers runs right through Ray Presley, because he worked on the case. I knew you'd eventually go see him, and if you did, you'd probably find out about this. He might even hit you up for money. I wanted you to hear the truth from me."

"The hell with Del Payton. There's only one thing to do."

"What?"

"Go to the D.A. before Presley can. Tomorrow morning we're going to walk in there, tell the whole story, and demand that Presley be arrested for murder and extortion."

Dad raises both hands like a supplicant. "I've thought of doing that a hundred times. But why should the D.A. believe me?"

I think of Austin Mackey, district attorney and former schoolmate of mine. Not my first choice for a sympathetic confessor, but we go back a lot of years. "The D.A. has a lot of discretion in a case like this. And it's possible we could sting Presley. Wire you before meeting with him. Videotape a blackmail payment."

"You're underestimating Ray. Since he started this, he's talked and acted as though we were partners from the beginning."

"Damn."

"Mackey would probably insist that you drop the Payton business, Penn."

"I dropped it the second you told me about this. We don't have any options. We've got to come clean, and Mackey's the man we have to see."

Dad seems to sag behind his desk. "If that's what you think, I'm prepared to do it. It'll be a relief, no matter what happens. But even if Mackey decided not to prosecute, wouldn't I still be subject to prosecution in Alabama?"

He has a point. "Yes. Anywhere that an element of the crime took place. But I can get Mackey to talk to the Mobile D.A. for us."

"Hillman's brother still lives in Mobile. The cop. I checked two months ago."

Wonderful. Even if Mackey does his best to convince the Mobile D.A. to lay off, my father's life will be in the hands of the Alabama authorities. And that comes pretty close to unacceptable risk. That's why Dad has not come forward before now.

"Presley has cancer," I say, thinking aloud. "How long does he have to live?"

Dad shrugs. "His oncologist thought he'd be dead before now. But he's still ambulatory. Ray is one tough son of a bitch. One of those I always say is too damn stubborn to die. He could live another year."

"A year isn't so long. We could keep paying him till he dies. Pay his medical bills."

"That's what I've been doing so far. It's getting damned expensive."

"How much have you paid him?"

"A hundred and sixteen thousand dollars to date."

I shake my head, still unable to believe the situation. "Over how long?"

"Seven or eight months. But he wants more. He's talking about needing to provide for his kids now."

"That's the way it is with blackmail. It never stops. There's no guarantee it would stop with his death. He could give the gun to one of his kids. He could leave documentary evidence. A videotape, for example. A dying declaration. You know, 'I've got cancer, and I've got something to get off my chest before I stand before my maker.' That kind of thing is taken very seriously by the courts."

My father has turned pale. "Good God."

"That leaves us only one option."

Something in my voice must have sounded more sinister than I intended, because Dad's eyes are wide with shock. "You don't mean kill him?"

"God, no. I just told you his death wasn't necessarily a solution."

Relief washes over his face.

"Everything depends on that gun."

"What are you suggesting? That we steal it?"

"No. We buy it."

Dad shakes his head. "Ray will never sell it."

"Everybody has a price. And we know Presley needs money."

"You just said it could be a meal ticket for his kids for years."

"Presley knows me. By reputation, at least. I'm a nationally known prosecutor, a famous author. If I stand for anything, it's integrity. Same as you. I'll show Presley a carrot and a stick. He can sell me the gun, or he can watch me go to the D.A. and stake my reputation on convincing the authorities that you're innocent. I have contacts from Houston to Washington. You and I are pillars of our communities. Ray Presley's a convicted felon. At various times he's probably been suspected of several murders. He'll sell me the gun."

A spark of hope has entered Dad's eyes, but fear still masks it, dull and gray and alien to my image of him. "Buying evidence with intent to . . . to destroy it," he says. "What kind of crime is that?"

"It's a felony. Major-league."

"You can't do it, Penn."

His hands are shaking. This thing has been eating at him every day for twenty-five years. Long before Presley's blackmail began. God, how he must have sweated during the malpractice trial, worrying that Leo Marston would learn about Hillman's murder from Presley, his paid lackey. I saw this situation a hundred times as a prosecutor. A man lives morally all his life, then in one weak moment commits an act that damns him in his own eyes and threatens his liberty, even his life. Seeing my father in this trap unnerves me. And yet, to get him out of it, I am contemplating committing a felony myself.

"You're right," I tell him. "We've got to take the high road."

"Talk to Mackey?"

"Yes. But I want to feel him out first. I'll call him tonight. Maybe stop by his house."

"He won't be home. There's a party tonight, a fund-raiser for Wiley Warren." Riley Warren — nickname "Wiley" — is the incumbent mayor. "Your mother and I were invited, but we weren't going to go."

"Mackey will be there?"

"He's a big supporter of Warren's. You're invited, by the way."

"By you?"

"No. By Don Perry, the surgeon hosting the party. He stopped me at the hospital after lunch and asked me to bring you along."

"Why would he do that? Especially after the story in the paper?"

"Why do you think? It's a fund-raising party, and he thinks you're loaded."

"That's it, then. I'll talk to Mackey there. If he sounds amenable, I'll set up a formal meeting, and we'll figure a way to sting Presley."

Dad lays his hands on his desk to steady them. "I can't believe it. After all this time . . . to finally *do* something about it."

"We've got to do something about it. Life's too short to live like this."

He closes his eyes, then opens them and stands up. "I feel bad about the Paytons. I feel like we're buying me out of trouble by burying the truth about Del."

This is true enough. But weighed against my father's freedom, Del Payton means nothing to me. Blood is a hell of a lot thicker than sympathy. "You can't carry that around on your shoulders."

"Back during the sixties," he says, hanging his stethoscope on a coat rack, "I was tempted to ask some of those Northern college kids over to the house. Give them some decent food, a little encouragement. But I never did. I knew what the risks were, and I was afraid to take them."

"You had a wife and two kids. Don't beat yourself up over it."

"I don't. But Del Payton had a wife and child too."

"Mom told me you patched up two civil rights workers from Homewood after the doctor over there refused to do it. They were beaten half to death, she said."

He looks disgusted. "I did take the Hippocratic oath, goddamn it."

105

"I guess that Homewood doctor forgot it."

Anger and shame fill his eyes. "It wasn't enough. What I did was not enough."

I stand and take my keys out of my pocket. "Nobody white did enough. Payton's killers will pay sooner or later. It just won't be me who makes them do it."

Dad takes off his lab coat and hangs it on the rack. "If you don't, Penn, I don't think anybody else will."

"So be it."

CHAPTER 8

Dad and I are dressing for the Perry party — me in a sport jacket borrowed from his closet — when the phone rings beside his bed. He reaches for it without looking, the movement as automatic as scratching an itch.

"Dr. Cage," he says, waiting for a description of symptoms or a plea for narcotics. His face goes slack, and he presses the phone against his undershirt. "It's Shad Johnson."

"Who's that?"

"The black candidate for mayor."

"What does he want?"

"You. Want me to say you're not here?"

I reach for the receiver. "This is Penn Cage."

"Well, well," says a precise male voice in the middle register, a voice more white than black. "The prodigal son himself."

I don't know how to respond. Then a fragment of Dad's thumbnail sketch of local politics comes to me: Shad Johnson moved home to Natchez from Chicago specifically to run for mayor. "I hear the same could be said of you, Mr. Johnson."

He laughs. "Call me Shad."

"How can I help you, Shad?"

"I'd like you to come see me for a few minutes.

I'd come to you, but you might not want the neighbors thinking we're any closer than we are. News travels fast in this town. Like those Payton women coming to see you this morning."

A wave of heat rolls up the back of my neck. "I have no intention of getting involved in local politics, Mr. Johnson."

"You got involved the second you talked to the newspaper about Del Payton."

"Consider me uninvolved."

"I'd like nothing better. But we still need to talk."

"We're talking now."

"Face to face. I'm over at my campaign headquarters. You're not afraid to come to the north side of town, are you?"

"No." My father is straining hard to hear both sides of the conversation. "But I've got to be somewhere in an hour."

"Not that fund-raiser for Wiley Warren, I hope?"

Shad Johnson obviously has the town wired. I'm about to beg off when he says, "You and your family are in danger."

I fight the impulse to overreact. "What are you talking about?"

"I'll tell you when you get here."

"Give me your address."

"Martin Luther King Drive. It's a storefront setup, in a little strip mall."

"Where's Martin Luther King Drive?"

"Pine Street," Dad says, looking concerned.

"That old shopping center by the Brick House?" I ask, recalling a shadowy cinder-block bar I went to once with two black guys I spent a summer laying sewer pipe with.

"That's right. But it's not the Brick House anymore, just like it's not Pine Street anymore. Times change, counselor. You on your way?"

"Give me fifteen minutes."

"What the hell did he want?" Dad asks, taking the phone from me and hanging it up.

"He said our family's in danger."

"What?"

I tie my tie and walk to the bedroom door. "Don't worry. I'll be back in forty-five minutes. We'll make the party in plenty of time."

He gives me his trademark stern-father look. "You'd better take a pistol with you."

The north side looks nicer than it did when I was a boy. Back then it was a warren of shotgun shacks and dilapidated houses separated by vacant lots and condemned buildings, their walls patched with tin or even cardboard. Juke clubs operated out of private houses surrounded by men drinking from paper bags, and paint-and-body shops sagged amid herds of junk cars, looking like sets for *The Road Warrior.* Now there are rows of well-kept houses, a sparkling video store, a state-of-the-art Texaco station, good streetlights, smooth roads.

I swing into the parking lot of the strip mall and scan the storefronts: a styling salon, a fish market, an NAACP voter-registration center, a Sno-Cone stand thronged by black kids, and one newly painted front hung with a bright banner that reads, SHAD JOHNSON — THE FUTURE IS NOW.

An open-air barbecue pit built from a

sawn-in-half fifty-five-gallon drum smokes like a barn fire outside the NAACP center, sending the aroma of chicken and pork ribs into the air. A knot of middle-aged black men stands around the pit drinking Colt .45 from quart bottles. They fall silent and watch with sullen suspicion as I get out of the BMW and approach Johnson's building. I nod to them and go inside.

A skinny young man wearing a three-piece suit that must be smothering him sits behind a metal desk, talking on a telephone. Behind the desk stands a wall-to-wall partition of whitewashed plywood with a closed door set in it. The young man looks up and motions me toward a battered church pew. I nod but remain standing, studying the partition, which is plastered with posters exhorting the public to vote for Shad Johnson. Half show him wearing a dark suit and sitting behind a large desk, a model of conservatism and rectitude; the other half show a much younger-looking Johnson sporting a Malcolm X-style goatee and handing out pamphlets to teenagers on an urban playground. It isn't hard to guess which posters hang in which parts of town.

A voice rises over the partition. It has anger in it, but anger communicated with the perfect diction of a BBC news reader. As I try to get a fix on the words, the young assistant hangs up and disappears through the door. He returns almost instantly and signals me to follow him.

My first impression of Shad Johnson is of a man in motion. Before I can adequately focus on the figure sitting behind the desk, he is rising and coming around it, right hand extended. A few inches shorter than I, Johnson carries himself with the brash assurance of a personal-injury lawyer. He is light-skinned — not to a degree that would hurt him with the majority of black voters, but light enough that certain whites can reassure themselves about his achievements and aspirations by noting the presence of Caucasian blood. He shakes my hand with a natural politician's grip, firm and confident and augmented by a megawatt of eye contact.

"I'm glad you came," he says in a measured tenor. "Take a seat."

He leads me to a folding chair across from his spartan metal desk, then sits atop the desk like a college professor and smiles. "This is a long way from my office at Goldstein, Henry in Chicago."

"Up or down?"

He laughs. "Up, if I win."

"And if you lose? Back to white-shoe law in Chicago?"

His smile slips for a nanosecond.

"You said my family is in danger, Mr. Johnson."

"Shad, please. Short for Shadrach."

"All right, Shad. Why is my family in danger?"

"Because of your sudden interest in a thirty-year-old murder."

"I have no interest in the murder of Del Payton. And I intend to make a public statement to that effect as soon as possible."

"I'm relieved to hear you say that. I must have taken fifty calls today asking what I'm doing to help you get to the bottom of it."

"What did you tell them?"

"That I'm in the process of putting together the facts."

"You didn't know the facts already?"

Johnson examines his fingernails, which look professionally manicured. "I was born here, Mr. Cage, but I was sent north to prep school when I was eleven. Let's focus on the present, shall we? The Payton case is a sleeping dog. Best to let it lie."

The situation is quickly clarifying itself. "What if new evidence was to come to light that pointed to Payton's killer? Or killers?"

"That would be unfortunate."

His candor surprises me. "For local politicians, maybe. What about justice?"

"That kind of justice doesn't help my people."

"And the Payton family? They're not your people?"

Johnson sighs like a man trying to hold an intelligent conversation with a two-year-old. "If this case was dragged through the newspapers, it would whip white resentment in this town to a fever pitch. Black people can't afford that. Race relations isn't about laws and courts anymore. It's about attitudes. Perceptions. A lot of whites in Mississippi want to do the right thing. They felt the same way in the sixties. But every group has the instinct to protect its own. Liberals keep silent and protect rednecks for the same reason good doctors protect bad ones. It's a tribal reaction. You've got to let those whites find their way to the good place. Suddenly Del Payton is the biggest obstacle I can see to that."

"I suppose whites get to that good place by voting for Shad Johnson?"

"You think Wiley Warren's helping anybody but himself?"

"I'm not Warren's biggest fan, but I've heard some good things about his tenure."

"You hear he's a drunk? That he can't keep his dick in his pants? That he's in the pocket of the casino companies?"

"You have evidence?"

"It's tough to get evidence when he controls the police."

"There are plenty of black cops on the force."

Johnson's phone buzzes. He frowns, then hits a button and picks up the receiver. "Shad Johnson," he says in his clipped Northern accent. Five seconds later he cries "My brother!" and begins chattering in the frenetic musical patois of a Pine Street juke, half words and grunts and wild bursts of laughter. Noticing my stare, he winks as if to say: *Look how smoothly I handle these fools.*

As he hangs up, his assistant sticks his head in the door. "Line two."

"No more calls, Henry."

"It's Julian Bond."

Johnson sniffs and shoots his cuffs. "I've got to take this."

Now he's the urbane attorney again, sanguine and self-effacing. He and Bond discuss the coordination of black celebrity appearances during the final weeks of Johnson's mayoral campaign. Stratospheric names are shuffled like charms on a bracelet. Jesse. Denzel. Whitney. General Powell. Kweisi Mfume. When the candidate hangs up, I shake my head.

"You're obviously a man of many talents. And faces."

"I'm a chameleon," Johnson admits. "I've got to

113

be. You know you have to play to your jury, counselor, and I've got a pretty damn diverse one here."

"I guess running for office in this town is like fighting a two-front war."

"*Two*-front war? Man, this town has more factions than the Knesset. Redneck Baptists, rich liberals, yellow dog Democrats, middle-class blacks, young fire eaters, Uncle Toms, and bone-dumb bluegums working the bottomland north of town. It's like conducting a symphony with musicians who hate each other."

"I'm a little surprised by your language. You sound like winning is a lot more important to you than helping your people."

"Who can I help if I lose?"

"How long do you figure on sticking around city hall if you win?"

A bemused smile touches Johnson's lips. "Off the record? Just long enough to build a statewide base for the gubernatorial race."

"You want to be governor?"

"I want to be president. But governor is a start. When a nigger sits in the governor's mansion in Jackson, Mississippi, the Civil War will truly have been won. The sacrifices of the Movement will have been validated. Those bubbas in the legislature won't know whether to shit or go blind. This whole country will shake on its foundations!"

Johnson's opportunistic style puts me off, but I see the logic in it. "I suppose the black man who could turn Mississippi around would be a natural presidential candidate."

"You can thank Bill Clinton for pointing the way. Arkansas? Shit. Mississippi is fiftieth in education, fiftieth in economic output, highest in illegitimate births, second highest in welfare payments, the list is endless. Hell, we're fifty-*first* in some things — behind Puerto Rico! I turn that around — just a *little* — I could whip Colin Powell hands down."

"How can you turn this town around? Much less the state?"

"Factories! Industry! A four-year college. Four-lane highways linking us to Jackson and Baton Rouge."

"Everybody wants that. What makes you think you can get it?"

Johnson laughs like I'm the original sucker. "You think the white elite that runs this town wants industry? The money here likes things just the way they are. They've got their private golf course, segregated neighborhoods, private schools, no traffic problem, black maids and yard men working minimum wage, and just one smokestack dirtying up their sunset. This place is on its way to being a retirement community. The Boca Raton of Mississippi."

"Boca Raton is a rich city."

"Well, this is a mostly poor one. One factory closed down and two working half capacity. Oil business all but dead, and every well in the county drilled by a white man. Tourism doesn't help my people. Rich whites or segregated garden clubs own the antebellum mansions. That tableau they have every year, where the little white kids dance around in hoop skirts for the Yankees? You got a couple of old mammies selling pralines outside and black cops directing traffic. You see any people

115

of color at the balls they have afterward? The biggest social events in town, and not a single black face except the bartenders."

"Most whites aren't invited to those balls either."

"Don't think I'm not pointing that out in the appropriate quarters."

"Mayor Warren doesn't pursue industry?"

"Wiley Warren thinks riverboat gambling is our salvation. The city takes in just over a million dollars from that steamboat under the hill, while the boat drains away thirty million to Las Vegas. With that kind of prosperity, this town will be dead in five years."

I glance at my watch. "I thought you brought me here to warn me."

"I'm trying to. For the first time in fifty years we've got a major corporation ready to locate a world-class factory here. And you're trying to flush that deal right down the toilet."

"What I said in the paper won't stop any company serious about locating here."

"You're wrong. BASF is a German company. They may be racists themselves, but they're very sensitive to racial issues in foreign countries."

"And?"

"They have concerns about the school system here."

"The school system?"

"The public school is eighty percent black. The population's only fifty percent black. BASF's management won't put their employees into a situation where they have to send their kids to expensive and segregated private schools for a decent education.

They have to be convinced that the public schools are safe and of excellent quality."

"And is that the case?"

"They're safe enough, but the quality's not the best. We've established a fragile consensus and convinced BASF that the public school is viable. We've developed all sorts of pilot programs. Those Germans are damn near committed to build here. But if the Payton case explodes in the media, BASF will crawfish so fast we'll finally hear that giant sucking sound Ross Perot always whined about."

I hold up my hands. "I have no interest in the case. I made a couple of comments and attracted the attention of Payton's family. End of story."

As Johnson smiles with satisfaction, my defensive tone suddenly disgusts me. "But I'll tell you this. The harder people try to push me away from something, the more I feel like maybe I ought to take a look at it."

He leans back and eyes me with cold detachment. "I'd think long and hard before I did that. Your little girl has already lost one parent."

The words hit me like a slap. "Why do I get the feeling *you* might be the danger you warned me about?"

He gives me a taut smile. "I'm just trying to do you a favor, brother. This town looks placid, but it's a powder keg. Drop by McDonald's or the Wal-Mart deli and watch the black workers serve blacks before whites who got there first. Blacks are angry here, but they don't know how to channel their frustration. What you've got here are blacks descended from those who were too dumb to head north after the Civil War or the world wars. No self-awareness. They take things out on whitey however they can. A while back, some black kids started shooting at white people's cars. Killed a young father. There's a white backlash coming, and when it comes, there's enough resentment among black teenagers to start a war. That's what you're playing with. Not to mention whoever killed Del Payton. You know those cracker bastards are still out there somewhere."

"Sounds to me like Del Payton died in vain."

"Payton was a paving stone in the road to freedom. No more, no less. And right now he's best honored by leaving him lie."

I stand, my face hot. "I've got to be somewhere."

"When you get to your party, tell Wiley Warren I'm going to whip his lily-white ass."

I pause at the door and look back. Johnson already has the phone in his hand.

"I think you're underestimating blacks in this town," I tell him. "They're smarter than you give them credit for. They see more than you think."

"Such as?"

"They can see you're not one of them."

"Don't kid yourself, Cage. I'm Moses, cast onto the waters as a child and raised by the enemy. I *prospered* among the mighty and now return to *show my people the way!*"

In an instant the candidate's voice has taken on the Old Testament cadence and power of a young Martin Luther King.

As I gape, he adds in his mincing lawyer's voice: "Next time come over to campaign headquarters south. It's on Main Street. The atmosphere's more

118

your style. Genteel and Republican, the way the old white ladies like it. Over there I'm a house nigger made good."

Johnson is still laughing when I leave the building.

The sky is deep purple, the warm night falling to a soundtrack of kicked cans, honking horns, shouting children, and squealing tires. The smell of chicken sizzling on the open pit pulls my head in that direction. Two black teenagers on banana bikes whiz toward me as I stand beside the BMW. I'm about to wave when one spits on the hood of my car and zips past, disappearing into a cloud of dark laughter. I start to yell after them, then think better of it. I did not bring the pistol my father advised me to, and I don't need to start the riot Shad Johnson just warned me about. I get into the BMW, start it, and head south toward the white section of town.

I've hardly begun to reflect on Johnson's words when I notice the silhouette of a police car behind me. Blinding headlights obscure its driver, but the light bar on the roof leaves no doubt that it's a cop. As he pulls to within fifteen yards of my rear bumper and hangs there, it hits me. I'm driving a seventy-five-thousand-dollar car in the black section of town. Some eager white cop is probably running my father's plate right now, checking to see whether the BMW has been reported stolen. As we pass in tandem under a street lamp, I notice that the vehicle is not a police car but a sheriff's cruiser. A sickening wave of adrenaline pulses through me as I wait for the flare of red lights, the scream of a siren.

Somewhere along here, this road becomes Linda Lee Mead Drive, named for Natchez's Miss America. As I top the hill leading down to the junction with Highway 61, the cruiser pulls out and roars past me. I glance to my left, hoping to get a look at the driver.

The man behind the wheel is black.

He is fifty yards past me when both front windows of the BMW explode out of their frames, shattering into a thousand pieces. I whip my head to the right, trying to shield my eyes. My eardrums throb from sudden depressurization, and I instinctively slam on the brakes. As the back end of the car skids around, something hammers my door, sending a shock wave up my left thigh. The car comes to rest facing the right shoulder, blocking both lanes of the road. In the silence of the dead engine, the reality of my situation hits me.

Someone is shooting at me.

Frantically cranking the car, I notice the brake lights of the sheriff's cruiser glowing red at the bottom of the hill, a hundred yards away.

It's just sitting there.

As my engine catches, two bullets smash through the rear windshield, turning it to starred chaos. I throw the BMW into gear, stomp the accelerator, whip around, and start down the hill. Before I've gone thirty yards, the sheriff's cruiser pulls onto the highway and races off toward town.

"*Stop!*" I shout, honking my horn. "*Stop, goddamn it!*"

But he doesn't stop. The rifle must have made a tremendous noise, though I don't remember hearing it. Maybe the exploding glass distracted me. But the black deputy in the cruiser *must* have heard it. Unless the weapon was silenced. This thought is too chilling to dwell on for long, since silenced weapons are much rarer in life than in movies, and indicate a high level of determination on the part of the shooter. But if the deputy didn't hear the shots, why did he stop so long? There was no traffic at the intersection. For a moment I wonder if he could have fired the shots himself, but physics rules that out. The first bullet came through the driver's window, while the deputy was fifty yards in front of me. The last two smashed the back windshield after the skid exposed it to the same side of the road.

My heart still tripping like an air hammer, I turn onto Highway 61, grab the cell phone, and dial 911. Before the first ring fades, I click End. Anything I say on a cell phone could be all over town within hours. The odds of catching the shooter are zero by now, and my father's blackmail situation makes me more than a little reluctant to bring the police into our lives at this point.

Shad Johnson's words echo in my head like a prophecy: *A while back, some black kids started shooting at white people's cars. Killed a father of three.* But this shooting was not random. This morning's newspaper article upset a lot of people — white people exclusively, I would have thought, until Shad Johnson disabused me of that notion. What the hell is going on? Johnson warns me that my family is in danger but gives no specifics, and ten minutes later I'm shot at on the highway? *After* being followed by a black deputy who doesn't stop to check out the shooting?

121

Whoever was behind that rifle meant to kill me. But I can do nothing about it now. I'm less than a mile from my parents' house, and my priority is clear: within an hour I will be talking to the district attorney about my father's involvement in a murder case, and deciding how best to sting Ray Presley, a known killer.

CHAPTER 9

"Tom Cage, you dog! I can't believe you came!"

In small towns the most beautiful women are married, and Lucy Perry proves the rule. Ten years younger than her husband — the surgeon hosting the party — Lucy has large brown eyes and a high-maintenance muscularity shown to perfection in a black silk dress that drapes just below her shapely knees. She also has suspiciously high cleavage for a forty-year-old mother of three, which I know she is, having been given a social update by my father on the way over to the party. Lucy uses the sorority squeal mode of greeting, which is always a danger in Mississippi. She flashes one of the brightest smiles I've seen off a magazine cover and throws her arm around my father.

"I'm here for the free liquor," Dad says. "Not for Wiley Warren to pick my pocket."

Lucy has a contagious laugh, and Dad has drawn it out. He's one of the few people honest enough to use the mayor's nickname within earshot of the man himself. Now Lucy looks at me as though she's just set eyes on me.

"So *this* is the famous author."

I offer my hand. "Pleased to meet you, Mrs. Perry."

"Mrs. Perry? For God's sake, *Lucy*." She steps inside my proffered hand and draws me to her in a one-armed hug that lasts long enough for me to learn that she's been drinking gin without much tonic and that her breasts are not original architecture. "I've *forbidden* anyone to mention that awful newspaper story. No one believes anything they read in the *Examiner* anyway."

The house is full of people, and it's some house. Though not one of Natchez's premier mansions, it would easily fetch nine or ten million dollars in Los Angeles. A brass plaque announces that it is on the National Register of Historic Places. The interior has been meticulously restored at a cost of countless gall bladders and appendices. A wide hallway bisects the ground floor, with arched doorways leading to capacious rooms on both sides. Of the fifty or so faces in the hallway I recognize about a quarter. People I went to school with, friends of my parents, a half dozen doctors I know. I give a broad wave to cover the group. Many nod or smile in acknowledgment, but no one approaches. Caitlin Masters's article has done its work. I stick close to Dad as we work our way toward the bar table at the end of the hall.

As Shad Johnson predicted, the only black faces in the house belong to white-jacketed bartenders and maids, who circulate with heaping platters of hors d'oeuvres.

"Bourbon and water, Roosevelt," Dad tells the bartender. "Easy on the water. Penn?"

"Gin and tonic."

The bartender grins. "Good to see you, Dr. Cage."

Dad and I jump as a boom rattles the window-panes behind the bar table. Terror grips me until a trombone, trumpet, and double bass join the thundering drum kit and reorient me to normalcy. A black Dixieland jazz band is performing on the patio. There are no dancers. It's too damned hot to dance on a patio. It's too damned hot to be playing music out there too, but Lucy and her hubby aren't worried about the musicians.

Dad squeezes my arm and leans toward me. "Think they were gunning for you again?"

I try to laugh it off, but both of us are nervous as cats. He agreed with my decision not to report the shooting to the police, but he insisted on bringing a pistol to the party. He's wearing it in an ankle holster.

I turn and pan the hall again. At the far end, beyond the talking heads, Lucy Perry opens the front door and pulls a young woman inside. I feel a little jolt when I recognize Caitlin Masters. She's wearing a strapless jade dress with sandals, and her black hair is swept up from her neck. As she steps aside for Lucy to close the door, I spy the rebellious flash of a gold anklet above one sandal. How do I feel about her? Angry that she printed something I considered off the record. But I can't help admiring her for shaking up our complacent town a little.

A blustering male voice pulls my attention to the staircase, where Wiley Warren stands dispensing political wisdom to seven or eight smiling listeners. Warren is a natural bullshitter, an ex-jock with enough brains to indulge his prodigious appetites within a younger group that admires his excesses

125

and keeps his secrets like JFK's press corps. Dad says he's done a fairly good job as mayor, but nothing he's accomplished thus far would compare to getting the BASF plant, a deal which would secure his political future.

"The reason Shad Johnson isn't making race an issue," Warren crows, "is that he's damn near white as I am."

This is vintage Wiley. The crowd chuckles encouragement.

"Ol' Shadrach went off to prep school with the Yankees when he was eleven, and didn't come back till he was forty and ready to run for mayor. He's no more a representative of his people than Bryant Gumbel!"

"Who *does* he represent?" someone calls.

"Himself, of course."

"So he's just like you," says a gastroenterologist whose name I can't recall.

Warren laughs louder than anyone, tacitly admitting the self-interest that drives all politicians and which Southern voters prefer to see in the open rather than cloaked in hypocrisy. Brutal honesty in such matters is part of the mayor's charm.

I am about to go in search of Austin Mackey, the district attorney, when I spot him at the edge of the group listening to the mayor. He motions for me to follow him to some chairs in an empty corner. Mackey was a year ahead of me in school from kindergarten through college. A perennial middle-of-the-class kid, he managed to make most athletic teams but never the first string. His grades were unremarkable, and I'm pretty sure he chose Ole Miss Law School so he wouldn't have to pass the bar exam in order to practice in Mississippi, a rule they changed the year after he went into practice.

"Any particular reason you came home and shat in our little sandbox?" he asks as we sit.

This is not a fortuitous beginning. "Good to see you again, Austin."

"Skip the sentiment, Cage." He keeps his eyes on the mayor.

Watching Austin Mackey play the tough throws me a little. But Natchez is his legal fiefdom now, and if he chooses to behave like George Raft in a bad film noir, he can.

"Look, Austin, about that article. Caitlin Masters didn't exactly —"

"Earth to Cage, give me a fucking break. By now every jig in this town is bitching about how Austin Mackey never lifted a finger to help Mrs. Payton find out who killed her poor baby."

I don't know how to segue from this to warm reminiscences of our shared history. Mackey seems to have forgotten we have one. "I just mentioned the Payton case as an example of a local mystery. Because it was an unsolved murder."

Mackey's eyes glint with superiority. "Don't be so sure about that."

"What do you mean?"

"The FBI worked the Payton case. You think they tanked it? Just because no one went to jail for that particular crime doesn't mean the perp didn't go down for something."

"If that's the case, why not tell the family? Give them some peace."

"I can't tell them what I don't know for sure. Listen, when I ran for D.A., I knew the blacks might ask me about past civil rights cases. So I asked the Bureau for their files on the Payton murder. I was assistant D.A. then, and I requisitioned them in the name of the office."

"And?"

"They said that unless we'd developed a suspect and had new evidence, they wouldn't be showing our office any files."

"Why would they say that?"

"Can I read the mind of J. Edgar Hoover?"

"Hoover? He's been dead twenty-five years."

"Well, his spirit's alive and well. Hoover made the final decisions on the disposition of those civil rights cases. And he worked them hard, especially the murders up in Neshoba County. But it's no secret that his personal agenda had nothing to do with advancing civil rights. He hated Martin Luther King and the Kennedys. Cases like Payton's were nothing to him but chips in a political game."

"What about your office file?"

"There isn't one. No one was ever charged with the crime."

"Have you looked?"

"I don't need to." He finally meets my eyes. "Let's get this straight right now. Unless you're the attorney of record for a member of the Payton family, you'll receive zero assistance from my office. And since you're not licensed in this state, that pretty much settles things."

Actually, I am licensed to practice in Mississippi, but I see no reason to point this out now. And though my combative instincts urge me to tell Mackey that a single phone call could secure my position as attorney for the Payton family, concern for my father stops me.

"You really get to me, Cage," Mackey goes on before I can change the subject. "Mr. St. Stephens, law review at Texas, big-time author. You've got nothing better to do than come back here and make your old schoolmates look like assholes?"

Bitterness and envy literally crackle off the man. I am so surprised that I can do little but apologize. "That wasn't my intention, Austin."

"I'd hate to see what would happen if you really meant some harm."

"What would you say if I told you I was shot at by a sniper less than an hour ago?"

His head snaps up. "Were you?"

"Yes."

"Did you report it?"

"Not yet."

His eyes are like signs reading, *Thank God for small favors.* "Where did this happen?"

"The black section, Linda Lee Drive."

"What the hell were you doing over there?"

"Shad Johnson wanted to talk to me."

"Jesus." The muscles in Mackey's jaw tighten. "What did he say?"

"He warned me off the Payton case."

An ironic smile. "Shad's no fool. The election's five weeks off, and the polls have him and Warren neck and neck."

"That's all you have to say about an attempt on my life?"

"You're back in Mississippi, bubba. You piss people off, they're going to hit back. Anyway, it's pretty obvious which side you're on."

I sip my drink. Melting ice has drowned the gin.

129

"I'm not on any side."

"Then you've forgotten the primary political reality of your home state."

"Which is?"

"There's no middle ground. Whatever's there gets crushed to powder by the sides. I'd pick one quick if I were you."

Mackey stands abruptly and drifts back into watchful orbit around his candidate. The conversation couldn't have gone any worse if I'd set out to make him hate my guts. This is the man upon whose mercy I advised my father to throw himself?

I stand and walk into the hallway, half looking for Dad and half aiming for the bar. I'm almost to the alcohol when a powerful hand closes on my shoulder and a voice whispers in my ear: *"Don't move, you outside agitatin' son of a bitch."*

I whirl, ready for anything, only to find the laughing bearded face of Sam Jacobs, whom I've known since we were five years old.

"A little nervous, are we?" Sam wiggles his black eyebrows up and down. "Wishing we'd been a little less candid with the fourth estate?"

I punch him in the chest, then hug him hard.

When Sam and I were tenth-graders at St. Stephens, an assistant football coach invited the varsity football team to establish a chapter of the Brotherhood of Christian Athletes at the school. While the rest of the team lined up to get the necessary applications, two boys remained in the otherwise empty bleachers: Penn Cage and Sam Jacobs. As a Jew, Sam was barred from membership. And I — ever since walking out of Episcopal communion at age thirteen — was a devout agnostic. Under the suspicious gaze of teammates and coaches, Sam and I left that meeting joined in a way that had more to do with manhood than football ever would. Now a petroleum geologist, Jacobs is one of only three non-family members who flew to Houston for Sarah's funeral.

"It's great to see you, Sam. What are you doing at this tight-ass function?"

He grins. "I've sold Don Perry enough Wilcox production to qualify him as a certified oil maggot."

"So, that's how he paid for this palace. You must be doing well."

"I ain't complaining. When the bottom dropped out of the drilling business, I slid over into production. Bought up old wells, worked them over, got them running full bore, and sold out at an obscene profit. It's getting harder to find wells, though. Everybody's into it now."

"I'm sure whatever happens, you'll be the guy sitting on top of the pile."

"The last guy clinging to the limb, more like." Sam sips his drink. "How does it feel?"

"What?"

"Having everybody in the place stare at you."

"I'm pretty used to the fishbowl lifestyle now."

"Natchez is a lot smaller bowl than Houston. Even small waves seem big here."

"Come off it. A week from now, who'll give a damn about that article?"

"Everybody, ace. How much do you know about the BASF deal?"

I shrug. "A little."

"That chemical plant means salvation to a lot of

131

people. Not just blue-collar either. These doctors need patients with private insurance to keep the gravy train running. Everybody's on their best behavior, trying to sell Natchez as a Southern utopia. We're pushing our opera festival, the literary celebration, the hot-air balloon race. And this morning you tossed a toad right into the punch bowl."

I glance around the room and instantly find what I'm looking for: Caitlin Masters, deep in conversation with two older men. "You see that girl?"

Sam cranes his neck. "Caitlin Masters?"

"You know her?"

"I know she's fine as wine and worth a few million bucks."

"She printed a little more than I intended her to."

"Fess up, man. You were just being you. At your pompous best."

"That's what Dad said."

"Speaking of your old man, I'm surprised he came."

Before I can ask what Sam means, someone taps me on the shoulder. Sam hides a smile behind his drink. I turn and look into the luminous green eyes of Caitlin Masters.

"Are you going to slug me?" she asks.

"If you were male, I might consider it."

"I know I angled that story in a way you didn't expect."

"*Angled* it? Try sensationalized it. Remember the words 'off-the-record'?"

Her lips part slightly in surprise. "I honored that request."

"About the Hanratty execution. But as for Del

Payton —" I force myself to shut up, not wanting to argue the point in front of a crowd.

"Why don't we have lunch tomorrow?" she suggests. "I'd like to help you understand why I did what I did."

I want to say no, but just as yesterday, something about Caitlin Masters makes me want to see her again. The jade dress is linen, and it lies against her skin like powder. She is a study in elegance and self-possession.

"Is that a no?" she asks.

"Once burned, twice shy," Sam chimes in.

"I like Wilde's quote better," Caitlin rejoins.

"What's that?" I ask.

"The burnt child loves the fire."

She winks at me, then turns on her heel and walks away, ignoring the gazes of half the people in the room, who have watched our exchange with intense interest.

"You sure know how to liven up a town," Sam says, his eyes glued to her retreating form. "And she knows how to fill out a dress. A *shiksa* from dreamland, that one."

I step hard on his toe. "You already married one of those, remember? What were you saying about my dad?"

"I'm surprised he came, is all."

"Why?"

"Because I'm pretty sure Judge Marston is on the guest list."

I feel a sliding sensation in my stomach. A quick survey of the room yields no sign of either Marston or my father. Squeezing Sam's shoulder, I push off through the crowd. Natchez is a funny town.

People involved in running feuds frequently socialize together. Men who've gutted each other in business disputes leave their rancor at the doors of certain seasonal soirées, and it's not unheard of to see a woman who has caught her husband in bed with someone else pouring punch for that woman — or man — at a party.

Leo Marston and Tom Cage are different. The judge once made it his mission to try to ruin my father's medical career, and Dad hates him with a fury that will brook no false bonhomie. He behaves, in fact, as though the judge were dead. Since Dad rarely goes anywhere other than his office or the hospitals, he rarely crosses paths with Marston, making that illusion easy to maintain. But if Sam Jacobs is correct, that might change tonight. Dad has already drunk one bourbon, probably two by now. If Marston provokes him, Dad is capable of swinging on him. With that thought my blood pressure plummets, because with it comes the memory that my father is carrying a gun tonight.

Catching sight of a silver head a few inches taller than the others near the bar, I move quickly forward, take Dad's arm, and pull him into the kitchen. It's empty save for a black maid, who smiles and nods when she sees us.

"What's going on?" He takes a sip of his bourbon and water *sans* water.

"Judge Marston's on the guest list. He may already be here."

Dad blinks. Then his cheeks turn red. "Where is he?"

"Dad, this isn't the time or the place."

"Why not? I've avoided that SOB too many

years already." His breathing is shallow, and his motions have a jerky quality that might be the result of anger or alcohol.

"That's the whisky talking. You're a hundred percent right about Marston, but if you talk to him now, you're going to hit him." *Or shoot him.* "And I'll have to spend all my time at home defending you on a battery charge. That's after I bail you out."

"What do you want me to do? Leave?"

"Considering what we have to do in the next few days, I think you should."

That brutal reminder of the blackmail situation gets his attention.

"What about talking to Mackey?" he asks.

"I already did. And this isn't the place to discuss it."

His eyes flit back and forth; then he dashes his plastic cup against the stainless steel sink. "Goddamn it. Let's go."

"Stay close to me."

I take his forearm, lead him into the hallway, and freeze. Twenty yards away, in the open front door, stand Judge Marston and his wife, Maude. The odds of getting through that door without anyone making a smart remark are zero. I drag Dad back toward the kitchen.

"Where the hell are we going now?"

"The back door's closer to where I parked."

"You saw Marston, didn't you?"

He tries to pull free. I tighten my grip and hustle him toward the back door, knowing that if he really tries to resist me, I won't be able to stop him.

"Goddamn it, I'm not running!"

"That's right, you're not. You're taking the advice of your lawyer."

"You're not licensed in this state."

"Actually, I took the Mississippi bar exam when I graduated, and I've paid the licensing fee every year."

He is so distracted by this information that he allows himself to be pulled through a side garden to the street.

"Here's the car." I unlock my mother's Maxima — the damaged BMW having been consigned to the garage — and practically push him into the driver's seat.

He looks up at me, eyes anxious. "You felt Mackey out?"

"Yes. It was like feeling out a porcupine. We're going to have to go the other way."

"What other way?"

"We're going to have to buy the gun."

He blinks in disbelief. "Christ. Are you sure?"

"It's the only way. I want you to call Ray Presley at ten in the morning. Tell him I'll be at his place at ten-thirty. That doesn't give him enough time to get the police involved."

Dad looks down at the steering wheel. "Goddamn it, if anyone has to do this, it should be me."

"You've been under Presley's thumb too long. He'd never buy your bluff. Do you have a hundred thousand dollars liquid?"

He looks up, helpless with rage. "It'll cost a fortune in penalties, but I can get it. And I won't have a damn cent to pay the IRS in January."

"Don't worry, I'll pay you back. But there's no point in creating a paper trail to me yet. Have the money at your office as early as you can. I'll pick it up. I may not offer Presley the whole hundred grand, but I need to be able to go up to that."

He looks too dazed to keep track of this. "Well . . . get in. We'll get it all figured out."

"I'm not coming, Dad."

"What?"

"I want to talk to Sam Jacobs about Presley. Sam knows everything that goes on in this town. Have you got everything straight?"

He takes a deep breath and nods slowly. "I'll have the money waiting. Ray too."

"Good. Now, go home and get some sleep. And don't speed. The last thing you need tonight is a DWI."

He gives me a somber salute, then shuts the door, starts the engine, and pulls slowly away. I stand at the curb and watch the taillights wink out as he hooks around the block to get headed home on the downtown streets, which are all one-way.

After years of putting men into prison — even into their graves — for committing crimes, I am about to cross the legal line myself. Tomorrow morning I am going to risk prison, forced separation from my child, to try to spare my father the same fate. That knowledge simmers in my stomach like a bad meal, acid and portentous. Is it the right thing to do? Is it stupid? Ultimately, it does not matter.

It's the only thing I can do.

CHAPTER 10

As I pass through the wrought-iron gate of the Perry garden, I see a figure standing at the foot of the steps leading to the side door of the mansion, and the orange eye of a cigarette burning in the dark.

The shrubs and trees in the garden are lighted with white Christmas lights, like little stars. Nearing the steps, I realize that the figure is Caitlin Masters. She's rocking slightly to the rhythm of "Don't Get Around Much Anymore" wafting from the back of the house. I stop a few feet from her.

"I didn't know you smoked."

She blows a stream of smoke away from me. "I don't. You're hallucinating. Is your father okay?"

"He had an emergency call. So, you only smoke at parties?"

"Only when I'm bored."

She doesn't look bored. She looks like she's been waiting for me. "Are there many people in town your age?"

She cuts her eyes at me. "You mean men?"

"I guess I did."

"*Nada.* It's a desert." She stubs out the cigarette with her sandal and takes a sip of her drink. It looks

138

like white wine, but it's not in a wineglass, and in the dim light has a tinge of green.

"Is that Mountain Dew?"

"God, no. It's a gimlet. Gin and Rose's lime juice. Raymond Chandler turned me on to them."

The Chandler reference surprises me. I'm starting to suspect that Caitlin Masters is full of surprises.

"You know the book?" she asks.

"*The Long Goodbye.*"

"Very good. For that, I'll tell you a little secret I learned today. Interested?"

"Sure."

"Remember I told you about the Sovereignty Commission files? How forty-two of them are sealed for security reasons?"

"Yes."

"One of my reporters requested a Sovereignty Commission file today, and I was more than a little surprised to learn that it was one of the forty-two."

I think for a minute. "Not Del Payton?"

She nods. "I thought you'd be interested."

"Surprised, anyway."

"I saw you talking to the D.A. inside. Anything I should know about?"

"He's just an old school friend."

"He didn't look too friendly."

Caitlin Masters doesn't miss anything. I wonder what she would do if she knew her story had got me shot at tonight. Probably tear into the story like a bulldog.

"You're dangerous, aren't you?"

She laughs softly and pulls a loose thread of linen from the front of her strapless dress. Her shoulders are lean and ghostly white in the shadows, accenting the long, graceful lines of her neck.

"I try to be. You're sure you won't reconsider lunch tomorrow? I promise to show a little remorse about the articles."

Her tone is casual enough, but there is more in it than hunger for a story. Her steady gaze has nothing to do with the words she spoke. Whatever I felt when we touched after the interview yesterday, she felt too. Between us floats a curious longing to feel that shock again, that aliveness. Without preamble she reaches out with her free hand and takes my right, her eyes unwavering. Her hand is cool, but a rush of warmth runs up my arm.

She smiles. "Feels good, doesn't it?"

It's only her hand, but the intimacy of her touch is undeniable. It's been so long since I've had any physical contact with a woman that it almost paralyzes me. Sarah's illness made it impossible at the end, and in the months since her death I've felt no response at all to the flirtations of the women I've met. It's as though the sexual component of my personality, once dominant, has been wrapped in so many layers of guilt and grief that the prospect of having to work through them with someone new discourages me from even trying. But with one simple gesture Caitlin Masters has cut through all of that.

"I suppose I'm being forward," she says. "By Southern standards anyway."

The urge to kiss her is a living thing inside my chest, and with it returns the guilt I felt yesterday, magnified a hundredfold. I close my eyes and squeeze her hand, fighting and savoring the pleasure at the same time. As though bidden by my thoughts, her lips brush mine.

When I open my eyes, hers are only inches away, green and wide, full of curiosity. She closes them, rises on tiptoe, and presses her lips to mine, sending another thrill of heat through me. From the first moment it is a knowing kiss, not the timid tasting of strangers, but the self-assured encounter of lovers who recognize each other. Her tongue is warm against mine, her lips cool. My senses read every curve and valley beneath the linen, and my arousal is immediate. Immediate and obvious. I slip my hand into the small of her back and for a moment kiss her as I truly want to, and the passion of her response explodes the boundaries I had perceived around us. As she kisses me, I feel something shift deep in my soul, a heavy door, and whatever stirs behind that door is too powerful to set free here, in this place. I break the kiss.

"Well," she says with a laugh, "I guess that answers that question."

"Which question?"

"Did we really feel something yesterday."

Her cheeks are flushed, and part of her hair has fallen around her neck. She points at the edge of the flower bed beside us, where her gimlet glass lies in the monkey grass. "I dropped my drink."

"I'm sorry, Caitlin."

"I can get another one."

"I meant for getting so . . . you know."

She shakes her head. "I liked it. Hey, you didn't break any laws here. You look like you saw a ghost." Her smile vanishes. "You did see a ghost. God, I'm such an ass sometimes."

"It's all right."

She takes my hand again. "This just happened, okay? Nobody's fault. We'll just be friends, if you want."

"This is unfamiliar territory for me."

"We're the only ones out here, Penn. Everything's fine." She reaches behind her neck to pin her hair back up. "Do you need a ride home?"

"No. I need to talk to Sam Jacobs. He'll give me a ride. Thanks, though."

She releases my hand and gives me the kind of encouraging smile you give a sick friend, then walks up the steps ahead of me. As she turns the doorknob, I reach out and touch her elbow. "I do think that lunch would be nice, though."

She turns and smiles. "Same place?"

"Works for me. Twelve?"

"I'll meet you there."

She opens the veneered door and goes inside, and I follow, watching her wend her way through the crowd in the hall, drawing looks from most of the women and all of the men. A woman that beautiful and perceptive hasn't been seen in these precincts for quite some time. Not since Livy Marston came back from the University of Virginia to serve as Queen of the Confederate Pageant.

As Caitlin disappears into one of the great rooms, I detour out of the hallway to search for Sam. The first room I enter is relatively empty, but the arched proscenium leading to the next is completely blocked by a semicircle of men and women.

I move closer to the line of backs, then freeze.

The focus of their attention is Judge Leo Marston.

The mere sight of him raises my temperature a couple of degrees, from anger mostly, but also — though I hate to admit it — from a residue of fear. Most of the men I knew as a boy I outgrew during high school, and they seem small to me now. Leo Marston still has three inches on me, and age has not diminished his physical presence. He must be nearly seventy by now, but he looks as though he could outfight any man here. With bulk in proportion to his height, he dwarfs the men standing in his audience. He masks his rawboned body in bespoke suits shipped to him once a year from London, but his outsized hands betray the power beneath. Like my father, Marston has kept his hair through the years, and he wears it in a steel-gray brush cut reminiscent of the leading men of the 1950s. When I was younger, I thought of him as an oversized Lee Marvin with a patina of Southern refinement. But no amount of refinement can conceal the animal alertness of his eyes. The irises are ice blue with gray rims, giving him a wolfish aspect, and they never settle anywhere for long. In moments they will pick me from the crowd.

I step behind a tall man to my right, removing myself from Leo's line of sight. Still, his mellifluous basso carries to me without losing any volume to distance. It's one of his most formidable weapons as an attorney, second only to his intellect. The timbre of that voice is graven forever in the circuits of my brain. Twenty years ago I listened to it accuse my father of negligence bordering on murder, first indirectly, as Marston tried to draw out testimony from reluctant nurses and technicians, then directly, like an inquisitor, as he cross-examined Dad on the stand. I took two weeks off from college to attend the trial, and by the second Friday I was ready to confront Marston on his way home from court and put a bullet through his heart.

"My point," Marston is saying, "is that the Germans are either at your feet or at your throat. We have to let BASF know that while we *want* them to locate here, we won't grovel."

"But we will," someone says. "And they know it."

Everyone laughs, then stops abruptly when they see that Marston does not share their humor.

"It all comes down to dollars," he says in a cold voice. "That's when you find out who needs whom. And that remains to be settled."

He continues in this line, tantalizing the men with his inside knowledge and the women with his references to money. When people speak of "old Natchez families," they mean the Marstons. Leo's great-great-grandfather, Albert Marston, owned a massive cotton plantation in Louisiana, which he administered from an Italianate mansion in Natchez called Tuscany. During the Civil War, Albert paid lip service to the Confederate cause while lavishly entertaining the Union officers occupying the city. He was the first Natchez planter to sign the loyalty oath to the Union, which enabled him to maintain his assets and continue to do business while prouder men lost everything. Many called Marston a traitor, but he laughed all the way to the bank.

144

People say Leo is the reincarnation of Albert, and they're right. I often saw the grim ancestral portrait in the hall at Tuscany when I picked up Olivia in high school, a canvas enshrining a virtual twin of the man who warned me without subtlety to have "his angel" home by eleven "or else." By the time Leo graduated law school nearly a century after Albert's death, the family appetites for power and profit had expressed themselves as forcefully as the genes for those chilling blue eyes. Leo Marston knew the secret and immutable laws of Mississippi politics the way a farmer knows his fields. The state's eighty-two counties function more or less as feudal domains, each with its closed circle of power, and Leo was born into one of the richest. Yet despite the relative wealth of Adams County, its elected officials cannot help but be swayed by admiration, envy, or outright fear of men like Leo Marston. Add to these the appointees whose hirings Marston has assured, and the result is a local political network that allows the judge to grant or quash things like building permits and zoning variances with a single phone call.

And Marston's power is not limited to the city. During his judicial career — first as a circuit judge, then a justice of the state supreme court — he did so many favors for so many people that his capital reserves of influence are impossible to estimate. Nor did he idly spend his time as state attorney general or chairman of the Agriculture Board. He has like-minded friends in every corner of Mississippi, and owns financial stakes in businesses all over the state, including the two biggest banks. He can sway the trials of friends and enemies from Tupelo to Biloxi, and put fear into newspaper editors as far away as Memphis and New Orleans. He is a vindictive son of a bitch, and everybody knows it.

On the other hand, he is easy to like. A man doesn't attain that kind of power without being able to play the social game with flair. Marston can discuss the finer points of obscure wines with vintners vacationing in Natchez, and an hour later put a crew of roughnecks on the floor of an oil rig with jokes that would make a sailor blush. In the company of women he becomes whatever the mood and situation require. With a priggish society wife he fancies, he tells off-color stories in a quiet, bourbon-laced voice, flustering her with the idea that a man in the judge's exalted position could be so down-to-earth. With a buxom barmaid he plays the cultured Southern aristocrat for all he is worth. I've seen Leo Marston play so many roles that I'm not sure anything lies at the center of the man other than a burning compulsion to increase his dominion over people, land, and money.

As I contemplate him, his words begin to lose their rhythm, then falter altogether. He has spotted me. The blue-gray eyes hold mine, unblinking, searching, revealing nothing. A few heads in the audience turn to me, wondering who could possibly have upset the equilibrium of the judge. Noticing this, Leo resumes speaking, though without the ease he earlier displayed.

He focuses on the women in his audience, lingering upon the prettiest. That his weakness was women I discovered in high school, when his sexual escapades almost destroyed his family. Leo's wife found a way to live with his flagrant infidelities, but his youngest daughter could not. When Olivia Marston learned at sixteen that her father had left a wake of brokenhearted and pregnant women behind him (which clarified the mystery of her mother's chronic alcoholism), she turned the strength she'd inherited from Leo against him, shaming and threatening him into changing his ways. It worked for a while, but appetites on that scale can't be suppressed long. What I found fascinating — and Livy disgusting — was that she was the only woman who ever challenged him. Not one of Leo's cast-off paramours ever tried to bring him down. The single ones he paid off with abortion money and more, frequently enough to send them back to college or get them started in a new town. The married ones nursed their broken hearts in silence, or, if they confessed to their husbands, were surprised by the nonviolence of the reaction. Such male passivity was unheard of in the South, but by virtue of his power, Leo Marston enjoyed a sort of modern-day droit du signeur, and he used it. As far as I know, he's paid only one price for his sexual adventures. Though his name has been floated more than once as a potential candidate for governor, each time party officials quietly let the suggestion die. No one feels confident about exposing Leo Marston's past to the scrutiny of a modern election.

"You're not carrying a gun, are you?"

Startled from my reverie, I find Sam Jacobs standing beside me. He looks as though he's only half joking.

"Am I that obvious?"

"You look like you're ready to tear Leo a new one."

"I can dream, can't I? Look, I need to talk to you. Can you give me a ride home?"

"I'm ready now. Let's hit the bar before we go. Don's got a bottle of Laphroig over there."

Sam leads the way. I shake hands with several people as we move through the crowd, accepting compliments on my books and answering polite questions about Annie. The alcohol has loosened everybody up, though thankfully not too much. As Lucy Perry promised, no one mentions the newspaper article. When I catch up to Sam at the bar, he's chatting with two other men waiting for drinks.

"Hell's bells!" cries a gravelly female voice behind me. "If it ain't the Houston representative of the *N-Double-A-See-P.*"

Dread fills me as I turn, certain that I'm about to endure a public dressing-down for my comments in the paper. The speaker is Maude Marston. Leo's wife is obviously drunk, as she has been for as long as I can remember. In response to the judge's amorous adventures, Maude developed a sort of battleship manner, charging through her daily social round with prow thrust forward and guns primed for combat. Anyone who whispers malicious comments within her hearing risks a withering broadside salvo or, worse, depth charges dropped with stealth and unerring aim, that detonate days or weeks later, leaving the offender shattered and forever outside the inner social circle. I hate to guess what she has in store for me.

"Whassa matter, hotshot?" she drawls. "Cat got your tongue?"

I force myself to smile. "Good evening, Maude. It's nice to see you."

She stares with blank rage, as though the synapses behind her eyes have stopped firing. Maude was once a great beauty, but her two daughters are the only remaining testament to that fact. Her hair should be gray, but it has been bleached and hennaed and sprayed so often that it has acquired a sort of lacquered-armor look. The cumulative effect of that hair, the gin-glazed eyes, combative stance, and scowling avian face stretched taut by various plastic surgeries is enough to send any but the most stalwart running for the exits.

She pokes a grossly bejeweled finger into my chest. "I'm *talking* to you."

"You're drunk," I say quietly.

She blanches, then pokes me again, harder. "That's assault."

"You gonna have me arrested, hotshot?"

Over Maude's shoulder I see Caitlin watching from the hall, her eyes flickering with curiosity. "No. I'm going to ask your husband to take you home."

A harsh cackle bursts from Maude's lips, and she wobbles on her feet. "You appointed yourself special protector of the nigras in this town or what?"

Sam Jacobs reaches between us and takes hold of my forearm. "Got the drinks! Let's roll! Great to see you, Maude!"

As Sam pulls me away, Maude speaks softly but with a venom that makes me pause. *"You ruined my*

149

daughter's life, you bastard."

Then she throws her drink in my face.

A collective gasp goes up from the nearby guests. The drink is mostly ice. It's Maude's words that have stunned me. I have no idea what she's talking about. It has to be Livy, but that makes no sense at all. Before I can gather my thoughts for a question, Lucy Perry appears and gentles Maude away from the bar the way a trainer gentles a wild mare.

"Let's blow this joint before somebody gets killed," Sam whispers.

As we depart, Caitlin leans toward me. "I can't wait to hear the story behind that."

Perfect.

CHAPTER 11

Sam Jacobs drives a royal blue Hummer, the civilian version of the military Humvee. He claims it's the only way to travel in the oil fields. I cling to the window frame as the huge vehicle rumbles like a tank down State Street.

"Talk about a babe magnet!" he says, trying to hold his drink steady with his left hand. "More women come on to me in this thing than when I had my Mercedes."

I nod absently. Maude Marston has popped the cork on a dark vintage of memory.

"Did you give Caitlin Masters a tour of the garden?" Sam asks, giving me a bemused smile. "You two had that *couple* look when you came in."

"Did you hear what Maude said before she threw the drink in my face?"

"About ruining her daughter's life?"

"Yes. She had to be talking about Olivia, right?"

"Had to be."

"When did Livy's life get ruined? Isn't she still married to that sports lawyer in Atlanta?"

"Definitely fartin' through silk, on the money side."

I laugh, wondering whether the Jewish crowd in Manhattan would believe the Southern accent coming from Sam Jacobs's mouth.

"How*ever*," Sam adds, cutting his eyes at me. "My wife's sister was in Atlanta last month for some kind of Tri-Delt alumni ball, and Livy showed up without her husband."

"So?"

"The gossip of the party was trouble in paradise."

"Not exactly a reliable source. Do they have any kids?"

"Don't think so." He glances at me again. "It would be pretty strange, the two of you being available at the same time. It's like fate. Maybe history's reversing itself."

Not wanting to continue in this line, I stick my head out of the window as the Hummer roars up the bypass toward my parents' neighborhood. The wind is warm and wet in my hair. The downtown bars and riverboat casino will still be going great guns, but this part of town looks like Mayberry, R.F.D.

"Have you seen anybody?" Sam asks. "You know . . . since Sarah died?"

I pull my head back inside and look him in the eye. "Lunch with Caitlin Masters tomorrow is my first date since the funeral. If you call that a date."

"Shit. I know it's tough, Penn. I joke about fooling around, but if I ever lost Jenny, I wouldn't know what to do."

I take his cup from his hand and gulp a sweat-inducing shot of Laphroig.

"That's the ticket," he says, slapping me on the knee.

The Hummer jerks as Sam hits the brakes, then

152

lets off slowly. "Would you fucking look at this?"

"What?"

"A cop. Looks like a sheriff's deputy."

I turn slowly. A sheriff's department cruiser just like the one that tailed me from Shad Johnson's headquarters has settled in twenty yards behind the Hummer. The sight throws me back to the shooting, glass exploding inches from my face.

"Sam, what do you know about Ray Presley?"

"Ray Presley? He's sick, I heard. Bad sick."

"What's he been up to the last few years?"

"Same thing he was always up to. Being a sleazy coonass who'll do anything for money."

"Presley's no coonass. He's from Jones County. Who did he work for?"

"Old Natchez people, mostly." Sam's eyes keep flicking to the rearview mirror. "He did some things for a driller I know. Strong-arm stuff. I think Marston kept him on his payroll as a security consultant, if you believe that." Sam accelerates, as if daring the deputy to pull him over. "You know what? I'll bet the BASF deal is what set Maude off on you."

"What does Maude Marston care about a chemical plant? She has more money than God."

"But does she have *enough?* That chemical plant means more to the Marstons than anybody. Short term, anyway."

"Why?"

"The industrial park isn't big enough for the projected facility. You want to guess who owns the land contiguous to the park site?"

"Leo?"

"Yep. He'll squeeze blood out of BASF for every

square foot of land, or kill them on usage and access fees."

"But that's got nothing to do with Livy."

Sam nods, then turns and looks hard at me. "Caitlin Masters's article said Ray Presley worked the Payton murder when he was a cop. Is that what this is about?"

"It's nothing to do with that."

Sam slams his hand against the Hummer's steering wheel. "*Look* at this asshole! I hate it when they follow you like that." He cranes his neck around and looks through the back windscreen. "You gonna stop me or what!"

"I don't think he is. I think it's the same guy who followed me from Shad Johnson's headquarters earlier tonight."

"Shad Johnson's headquarters?" Sam shakes his head. "I'm riding with a crazy man."

"Ten seconds after he passed me, somebody shot up my car with a rifle."

"*What?*"

"I'm just saying that if this guy passes us, watch him close."

Sam reaches under the seat, pulls out a holstered Colt .45, and sets it in my lap. "He's fucking with the wrong vehicle if that's his plan. This Hummer will drive right *over* that Crown Vic he's in."

"Take it easy. He's just tailing us."

"Why the sudden interest in Ray Presley?"

"I'll tell you in a couple of days. Do you think we could find anybody who could testify that Presley has committed murder for money?"

"A lot of people could. *Would* is another question."

Sam turns into my parents' neighborhood, watching his rearview mirror through the turn. "There goes our shadow. Bye, bye."

A minute later he pulls the Hummer into our driveway and leaves it idling. "I feel bad about mentioning Sarah. I guess time is the only thing that can get you past something like that."

I swallow the last of the Scotch. "I'll never get past it, Sam. I'm a different person now. Part of me is lying in that grave in Houston."

"Yeah, well. Most of you is sitting right here. And your daughter needs that part."

"I know. I keep thinking about Del Payton's widow. Race doesn't even come into it for me. For thirty years part of her has been buried wherever her husband is. We're both wounded the same way. You know?"

Sam shuts off the engine. "Listen to me, Penn. Whoever blew up Del Payton was in their twenties then, thirties max. Kluckers full of piss and vinegar. Those guys have got wives and grown kids now. And if you think they're gonna let some hotshit, nigger-lovin' *writer* take all that away, you're nuts. That's who shot at you tonight. And if you keep pushing, they'll kill you."

Sam has the Jew's special fear of fanatics. During the civil rights era this anxiety caused many Mississippi Jews to keep as low a profile as possible. Some gave heroic support to the Movement; others, primarily in the Delta, actually joined the White Citizens' Councils, for fear of the consequences if they didn't. Sam's parents chose the difficult middle ground.

"Don't worry, Sam. Caitlin Masters has given

everybody the idea I'm a crusading liberal, ready to drag the town through the mud. Nothing could be further from the truth."

"Bullshit. I know you when you sound like this. You'll pull down the temple to find the truth."

"I remember you sounding like this once. That time in junior high, when your dad hired us to clean out his attic?"

Sam gives no sign that he's heard, but I know he has.

"Going through all those boxes," I remind him. "We found that list. Two hundred names, all hand-written."

He reaches out and toys with the Hummer's ignition key. The papers we found had listed most members of Natchez's Ku Klux Klan and White Citizens' Council. The Jewish community had maintained the list as a security measure, and more than a few names on it belonged to fathers of kids we went to school with.

"You remember how you felt when you saw those names?"

He picks up the drink cup and nervously shakes the ice. "Scared."

"Me too. But it pissed me off more. I wanted to expose those assholes for what they were. So did you. Have you ever done business with anybody on that list?"

He looks up, his eyes hard as agates. "Not a fucking one. And I spiked them where I could."

A side spill of headlights washes across my parents' house.

"Would you look at this?" Sam mutters, looking over his shoulder. "It's the same car."

156

The sheriff's cruiser sits idling in the street, fifteen yards behind us.

Bolstered by the confidence of being on my father's property, I set the .45 in Sam's lap, climb out of the Hummer, and walk toward the car. The passenger window whirs down into the door frame. It's the black deputy who followed me before. I put my hands on the door and lean into the window.

"Can I help you?"

The deputy says nothing. He has a bald, bullet-shaped head dominated by black eyes set in yellow sclera shot with blood. He's at least fifty, but he fills out his brown uniform like an NFL cornerback. Even at rest he radiates coiled energy.

"You were following me earlier tonight, right?"

The black eyes burn into mine with unsettling intensity. "Could have been," he says in a gravelly voice.

"Ten seconds after you passed me, somebody shot up my car. You stopped. Why didn't you help me?"

"I didn't hear no shots. I saw you stop. I waited to make sure you started again. Why didn't you report it if you was shot at?"

"What the hell is this about, Deputy? Why are you following me?"

He purses his lips and taps the steering wheel. "Get rid of your friend. Tell him I warned you off the Payton case, then go inside. After he leaves, meet me back out here."

"Look, if this is about Del Payton —"

"This is about *you*, Penn Cage." He spears me with a chilling stare. "And unfinished business."

Unfinished business? A needle of fear pushes

157

through my gut. Could he be talking about Ray Presley? Could he know something about what happened in Mobile in 1973? "Do you know a man named Ray Presley, Deputy?"

His jaw muscles flex into knots. "I know that motherfucker."

"Does this have anything to do with him?"

"It might. You just be out here when I get back."

He presses the accelerator, spinning me away from the car. After regaining my balance, I watch the cruiser disappear, then walk back to the driver's window of the Hummer.

"What the hell was that about?" Sam asks.

"How many black sheriff's deputies are there?"

"Nine or ten, I think. That was one of them?"

"Yeah. Fiftyish, but tough. Bald-headed."

"Had to be Ike Ransom. You know him."

"I do?"

"Ike the Spike. Remember?"

I do remember. Ike "the Spike" Ransom was a legendary football star at Thompson, the black high school, in the mid-sixties. He was so good that his exploits were trumpeted in the pages of the *Examiner* despite his skin color, and the records he set had held until Sam and I played ball ten years later.

"What the hell did Ike Ransom want here?" Sam asks.

"Same as everybody else. Warned me off the Payton case. I can't believe Ike the Spike is a deputy. I figured he played pro football or something."

Sam shrugs. "He was a cop first. After he put in his twenty there, he went to the sheriff's department. He's a bad son of a bitch, Penn. Even the blacks don't like him."

"What do you mean? He was a hero."

"Ransom was one of the first black cops. I heard those guys had to prove they'd be tough on their own people to keep their jobs. Some people say Ransom was worse than white cops."

"Great."

Sam cranks the Hummer. "Forget Del Payton. Take care of your own. And if somebody fucks with you, give me a call. I can still pull your slack if you need me."

I squeeze his shoulder. "Sounds like a plan. Thanks."

He backs out of the driveway and roars away, the echoes reverberating off the houses on the silent street.

I walk into the garage and lean against the trunk of my mother's Maxima. The high whistling *cheeep* of crickets rises to a manic drone, overpowering the buzz of the streetlight overhead and giving me a strange sense of peace. Our street looks almost exactly as it did thirty-five years ago, when we moved in. A few houses have changed color, some trees have disappeared, others have grown. But for the most part it's the same.

In the corner of our yard stands a huge oak. When I was a boy, a wisteria vine grew around its trunk, spiraling around and around until it reached the high branches. My friends and I used to splay our bare feet on that vine, spread our arms wide around the trunk, and see how high we could work our way up and around the tree before we fell. I never won those contests; I had too much imagination to successfully block out my fear. Back then the vine was the thickness of a boy's wrist. Now it's thicker than my thigh and looks as though it will soon strangle the old oak like a boa constrictor.

The drone of an engine cuts through the hot night air. As promised, Ike the Spike's cruiser turns the corner and rolls to a stop at the end of our driveway.

I push off the Maxima and walk toward the street.

CHAPTER 12

The inside of the cruiser smells like a black man sweating. I know the odor from summer jobs digging ditches and riding in trucks with men who gave off a different scent than I did — no worse but harder somehow, distinctive enough for me to know it forever. I pull the door shut, closing myself into an oppressive square completed by the dashboard, a wire mesh screen, and Deputy Ike Ransom.

"Let's take a ride," he says.

"How about you tell me what I'm doing here?"

"You want the neighbors asking everybody what the sheriff's department was doing at your folks' house?"

I look up the street. There are still lights in a few windows. "How do I know you're not in with whoever shot at me tonight?"

"If I wanted you dead, your mama would be at the funeral home right now."

This is easy enough to believe. "Okay. Ride."

Ike Ransom drives up to the bypass and heads south. Most of the traffic is eighteen-wheelers bound north for the interstate junction sixty miles away, or west for the bridge over the Mississippi.

"What's this about, Ike?"

He glances at me. "You know me?"

"My friend did. What's the big secret?"

"It's about Del Payton."

"I told you I didn't want to hear about that."

"It's about you and Del both."

"Me and Del? I was only eight years old when the guy died."

He looks at me again, the yellow sclera of his eyes washed white by oncoming headlights. "He didn't *die*, college boy. He was murdered. There's a difference. You and him tied together, though. Ain't no doubt about that."

"How do you figure that?"

"First tell me why you said what you said in the paper."

"I was talking through my hat. I wasn't thinking."

"That newspaper bitch didn't pick Del's name out of the blue."

"I mentioned him."

"There you go."

I sigh in frustration. "I'm lost, Ike."

"That's for damn sure. Can't you see? Del died thirty years ago and nobody paid for it. His soul ain't never been at rest. It's been wandering 'round here all this time, looking for peace. But it can't *get* no peace. Not while his killers walk free."

Maybe Ike the Spike is some kind of religious nut.

"Now, here you come, thirty years later, and in one day you got more people talking about Del's killing than they was the day he died."

"That wasn't my intent."

"*That* don't matter. Don't you see? What goes

162

around comes around! You just an instrument. An instrument of a higher power."

"I'm a guy with a big mouth. I'm not an instrument of anything."

Ransom shakes his head and laughs with eerie certainty. "You just sit tight. You gonna understand everything in a minute. You gonna thank old Ike for this one."

He turns right at the Ford dealership and crosses Lower Woodville Road near the paper mill, which glows fluorescent in the dark like a small city, churning white smoke into the night sky.

"Where are we going? The river?"

"Battery plant."

"The battery plant? What for?"

"Privacy. They closed right now. Asian market's down. They crank back up in thirty-six hours."

There are few lights on this road. Beneath the sulfurous odor of the paper mill drifts the thick, ripe smell of kudzu, sweetened by a breath of honeysuckle. The river is only six hundred yards away, and just a few feet below our present elevation.

The dark skeleton of the Triton Battery plant materializes to our right as Ike turns onto Gate Street, then right again into a parking lot lighted by the pink glow of mercury vapor. The Triton Battery Company came to Natchez in 1936 to build batteries for Pullman rail cars. In 1940 they retooled the line to manufacture batteries for diesel submarines. After the war it was truck batteries, marine batteries, whatever fit the changing market. The last I heard, Triton was using its ancient equipment to produce motorcycle batteries for European manufacturers.

163

Ike stops the cruiser on the far side of the parking lot. We're sitting on an acre of gravel packed into dirt by years of hard use, bordered on three sides by trees and unkempt grass. The west side faces the main gate of the battery plant, with Gate Street running between. I used to bring girls out here in high school.

"Is this where Del Payton died?"

"This it," Ransom says. "Come on."

"Where?"

He laughs harshly. "You a nervous son of a bitch, ain't you? Come on."

I get out of the cruiser and follow him across the gravel. A massive old pecan tree grows out of a clump of grass at the center of the lot. The spaces in its shade are probably coveted by everyone who uses the lot.

Ransom stops ten yards short of the tree, his back to me.

"Thirty years," he says. "Thirty years ago Del Payton parked his Fairlane right in this spot. When he came out of the plant, the bomb was in his car." He half turns to me and spits on the gravel. "I seen car bombs go off, man. It's a motherfucker. That fire burned forty minutes before they got it out. Del was sitting behind the wheel all that time."

I stand silent in the buzzing of the lights, wondering where Ike Ransom has seen car bombs go off. He squats on his haunches and picks up a piece of gravel.

"A man's soul left this earth right here."

I walk a few steps closer. "Look, Ike . . . I know what happened that night. And I'm damn sorry it did. But I don't see any connection to me."

164

He stands and points at me, his black eyes smoldering. "I'm gonna say two words, college boy. After that you gonna be in this thing up to your neck."

"Okay."

"Leo Marston."

He watches me as though waiting for me to guess a riddle.

"Leo Marston? I don't get it. What —"

"*Judge . . . Leo . . . Marston.*"

My palms tingle. "Are you saying Marston was somehow involved in the Payton murder?"

"Involved?" Ike the Spike laughs quietly in the dark. "Oh, yeah."

"That's impossible. What could Leo Marston possibly have had to do with Del Payton?"

"He was D.A. back then, wasn't he?"

My head is swimming. "Leo Marston was district attorney in 1968?"

"You didn't know that? It was in the article this morning."

I see my father jerking the paper from my hands and wadding it up. "I didn't read the whole thing."

"That wasn't too smart, was it?"

"You're saying Marston covered something up? Buried evidence while he was D.A.?"

Ike fires his rock across the street like a major league outfielder. It flies over the cyclone fence bordering the plant and strikes something metal, silencing the crickets for a few seconds. "I'm saying all these years that motherfucker been handing out jail time and making millions, he should have been rotting at Parchman Farm."

A dark thrill ripples through my chest. "You're

saying Marston was involved in the actual *crime?*"

"I done said all I got to say."

"You can't drop a bomb like that and then shut up! How do you know any of this?"

"You a cop in this town for twenty years, even a black cop, you get to know some things."

The hair on my arms is standing erect. I cannot interpret my emotions. Fear? Excitement? I walk the ten yards to the pecan tree, unzip my pants, and urinate on its trunk as I try to get my mind around what Ransom has told me.

"Shook you up, huh?" he says, laughing.

I zip up and turn back to him. "You've known for thirty years that Leo Marston was guilty of a felony and you've done nothing about it?"

"What says I knew for thirty years? I wasn't on the job thirty years ago. What I'm gonna do anyway, man? A nigger cop on the bottle gonna go up against the judge? That's why you here, man. Takes somebody like you to do it."

"Like me?"

"You're white, famous, and you make your money someplace else. They can't hurt you much here."

"Who's they?"

"That's what you got to find out."

"Christ. Just tell me what you know. I'll take it and run with it."

Ike gives me a knowing smile. "You want Marston's ass bad, don't you?"

"Tell me, goddamn it!"

"That don't play, college boy. You gotta work your way to it. Then you'll understand."

"Why tell me this, Ike?"

"Why me, Ike?" he mocks in a woman's voice. "Don't play that shit with me! Everybody knows the judge went after your old man. Damn near got him too."

This stings me to the quick. "That's bullshit. My father was unanimously exonerated by a jury."

"I ain't talking 'bout that. I'm talking about *damage.* Doc Cage had a heart attack while he was waiting for that trial, didn't he?"

I nod slowly.

"Hey, I love your daddy, man. He took care of me when I was a kid. Took care of my mama till she died. That's why I'm telling you this. It's what the hippies used to call karma. What goes around comes around. That's what brought you back here. You the chicken coming home to roost. Right on Marston's ass."

"So give me what I need to nail him."

Ike shakes his head. "Gimme, gimme, gimme. I told you, it don't play that way. I can point you in the right direction. But that's it."

"I don't like playing games."

Ransom snickers. "That's what they do here, college boy. You ain't been gone so long you forgot that yet. Right now they playing their favorite game of all."

"What's that?"

"The quiet game."

"The quiet game?" Memories of Sarah flood into my brain, of her trying to trick Annie into being silent long enough for us to eat dinner in peace, by seeing who could go the longest without talking. "Who's playing the quiet game, Ike?"

"Everybody, man. White and black both. Everybody keeping quiet, making like things is sweet and easy, trying to fish that new plant in here. Nobody wants nobody digging into Del's killing. Nobody 'cept you. You got a reason."

"What about you? What's your reason?"

His grin vanishes as though it never existed. Hatred comes off him like steam. He extends his forefinger and taps his powerful chest with it. "That's between me and me. Del's killers is playing the quiet game too. They been playing it thirty years. Not even sweatin'. You got to make people *nervous* to win the quiet game. And I got a feeling you pretty good at that."

Something is coiling within my chest, something I have not felt for years. It's the hunter's tension, wrapped like the armature of an electric motor, tight and copper-cored, charged with current and aching for resolution, for the frantic discharge of retribution.

"A lot of people think poking into this case would be damned dangerous," I tell him.

Ike the Spike closes the distance between us and squeezes my right shoulder, his grip like the claw of a wild animal, like he could close his hand a little tighter and snap the bone.

"That's where I come in. Boy, you lookin' at dangerous. Ask anybody."

We do not speak as Ransom drives back to my parents' house. I watch the dark streets drift by, lost in memory. I think mostly of the malpractice trial, of Marston's savage cross-examination of my father just five weeks after his triple coronary bypass surgery. It required a supreme concentration of will on my part not to jump up in the courtroom and attack the man. In all my years as a prosecutor, I never stooped to the tactics Marston used that day.

"You got any FBI contacts?" Ike asks.

"A few. Why?"

"You might not want to use them on this."

"Why not?"

"Free advice. Take it or leave it."

"You know Ray Presley worked the Payton case, don't you?"

Ike glances away from the road long enough to give me a warning look. "Presley was dirty from the day he was born. That motherfucker crazy as a wall-eyed bull and mean as a snake. You don't talk to him unless I'm somewhere close."

This does not bode well for my meeting tomorrow morning.

The radio chatters over a low background of static. There's a domestic-violence call in the southern part of the county, followed by a disturbance at the gangplank of the riverboat casino. As we roll into my parents' neighborhood, I glance over at Ransom. The man is too old to be doing the job he has.

"Can I ask you a question, Ike?"

He takes a Kool Menthol from his shirt pocket, lights up, and blows a stream of smoke at the windshield.

"How'd you wind up a cop?"

"That's what college boys ask whores. How'd a girl like you end up here?"

"I remember the stories about you playing ball. Ike the Spike. You were a hero around here."

He sniffs and takes another drag. "Like the man said, that was my fifteen minutes."

"You must have played college ball."

"Oh, yeah, I was the BNOC."

"What's that?"

"The Big Nigger On Campus." His voice is laced with bitterness. "I got a full scholarship to Ohio State, but I went to Jackson State instead. First quarter of the first game, a guy took out my shoulder. Back then doctors couldn't do shit for that."

"You lost your scholarship?"

"They gave me my walking papers before I even caught my breath. I was good enough for the army, though. I'd been drafted in early sixty-six, but I had a college deferment. When I lost my scholarship, I couldn't afford to stay in school. Next thing I knew, I was landing at Tan Son Nhut air base in DaNang."

I am starting to perceive the twisted road that led Ike Ransom to this job. "I'd like to hear about it sometime."

Another drag on the Kool. "You one of them war junkies?"

"No."

"You get off on other people's pain, though. That's what writers do, ain't it? Sell other people's pain?"

"Some do, I guess."

"Well, this is your big chance. There's a heap of fucking pain at the bottom of this story."

I try to gauge Ransom's temper, but it's impossible. "Sam says you've got a bad rep. Even with black people."

He stubs out his cigarette and flips it out the window. "I was the third black cop on the Natchez P.D. Back then a lot of the force was Klan. I didn't take that job to make no civil rights statement. I'd been an M.P. in Saigon, and that was the only thing I knew how to do. The first time I got called to a black juke, I had to go alone. When I walked in the door, everybody thought it was a big joke. Patting me on the back and laughing, handing me beer. But this big field nigger named Moon had a machete in there. He'd already cut the guy who was dicking his old lady, plus the first nigger who said something about it. He was sitting by hisself at a corner table. I'd seen lots of guys lose it overseas, and this guy was like that. *Gone.* I told him he had to give up the blade. He wouldn't do it. When I held out my hand, he jumped up and charged me. I shot him through the throat."

"Jesus."

"I didn't want to waste that brother. But I didn't have no backup. And that pretty much set the tone for the next twenty years. I had the white department on one side watching me like a hawk, making sure I was tough enough, and my people on the other, always fucking up, always begging for a break. I cut slack where I could, but goddamn, it seemed like they never learned. It got to where I hated to pull a nigger over, knowing he'd be drunk or high. Hated to answer a domestic call. Couple years of that, I was an outsider. It fucked with me, man. That's what got me on the bottle."

"Why didn't you resign?"

Ransom rolls down his window, hawks and spits. "I didn't come here to give you no Jerry Springer show." He pulls something out of his shirt and hands it to me. It's a card. On it are printed Ransom's name and rank, and the phone numbers of the sheriff's department. "My cell phone's on the back. When you call, don't use names. I'll know you, and I'll pick a place for a meet."

"You're the only person not named Payton who seems to want the truth told."

The radio crackles again, this time about a theft of guns from a hunting camp in Anna's Bottom. Ike picks up the transmitter and says he'll respond to the call.

"You gonna do this thing?" he asks, putting the transmitter back in its cradle.

I think of my father and his trouble, of Ray Presley and the gun I hope to have in my possession by tomorrow. "I don't know yet."

His eyes flash with dark knowledge. "You know you lying. Get out of my fucking car."

Before I can close the door, the cruiser screeches off into the night.

My father is waiting in the kitchen with a bowl of melted ice cream in front of him, smoking the last of a cigar in his boxer shorts and a tank T-shirt. Beside the ice cream lies the pistol he wore to the party, a 9mm Beretta.

"Everything okay?" I ask.

"Are you sure you want to try to buy that gun from Ray? I'd rather throw myself on the mercy of the court than get you involved in this."

I shake my head. "It's the only way. You just call Presley in the morning and set up the meeting."

"You'll have to go to his trailer. He lives out toward Church Hill, past the Indian mound. It won't be pretty. He's a bitter son of a bitch."

"You say he gets around okay?"

"Yeah. The home-health people see him a good bit. And I hear he's got a private nurse now. I've made a couple of house calls to give him shots for pain. Trailer calls, I should say."

"Fifteen-mile house calls for Ray Presley?"

"I've treated the man for thirty years, Penn. He doesn't call unless he's hurting bad. And if Ray says it's bad, it's bad."

This is vintage Tom Cage, making house calls on a man who is blackmailing him, not out of fear but because he feels he should.

"Prostate cancer was about the worst thing for Ray to get," he reflects. "He's got the biggest dick I ever saw on a white man, and he likes to brag about it. I think the surgery probably made him impotent. He says no, but he's twice as surly as he ever was. More dangerous, if anything."

"Worrying won't help. Come on. We both need some sleep."

He stubs out his cigar, then stands looking at me, his eyes unreadable. I long to tell him what Ike Ransom said about Leo Marston, but this isn't the time. *Get the gun first.* Without quite meaning to, I step forward and put my arms around him. The embrace surprises him, and he stiffens. Age has changed the shape of him, this body that once lifted me as though I weighed nothing.

"Dad, tomorrow you're going to find out what being born again really means."

He pulls back and looks me in the eye. "I'll let you go see Ray. But by God, you're going armed."

He picks up the Beretta. "And if he gets squirrelly, you shoot first and ask questions after. Okay?"

"Okay."

My mother is curled up in bed beside the smaller lump of Annie in my old room. My old baseball trophies gleam in the dark on the shelves above them, like little watchmen. I creep in and touch Mom on the shoulder, and she stirs in the shadows.

"Tom?"

"It's Penn, Mom. Go on to bed. I'll sleep with her."

She rubs her eyes. "All right, honey."

I reach out and stroke Annie's hair. Mom is already asleep again. I gently push her leg with my knee. "Mom?"

She opens her eyes again and smiles blankly, then gets up and sleepwalks toward the hall.

I quickly brush my teeth, strip to my shorts, and climb into bed beside Annie, who is already stirring. In seconds her hand finds my shoulder, re-establishing her early-warning system.

As I lie in the dark, her shallow breathing troubles rather than soothes my heart. Sleeping with Annie always brings memories of Sarah. After the funeral I had to move Annie's bed into my room because she couldn't fall asleep alone, and still she wound up in my bed most nights. The pulse of her life so near always stirs my dreams. I dream of Sarah before the diagnosis, before fear entered our lives and took away the most precious gift, which is not hope but youth. Immortality. The sense of unlimited possibility. It's an illusion, of course, the most precious illusion of life.

Sometimes my dreams are linear, like movies, other times disconnected, like fragments of film snatched at random from an editing room floor. As Annie breathes steadily beside me, fatigue deadens the signals flashing through my brain, the anxiety about meeting Presley, the delicious prospect of revenge on Leo Marston. Consciousness tries to hold me with the terrifying jerk of a perceived fall, but I catch myself. Soon the darkness above me tunnels into light, and I see the silver surface of a pool surrounded by lush ferns and massive cypress trees. The wind-rippled surface slowly stills to glass, opening the water to my gaze. There are plants below the surface, green fronds reaching up from unknown depths, gently waving in an invisible current. Among the fronds something moves, pale against the green. A person. A woman. She turns lazily, gracefully among the water plants, like a swimmer synchronized to unheard music. Her hair floats around her head in a bright corona, obscuring what must be extraordinary beauty. Ceasing her languid motion, she lifts her arms and pulls toward the surface. I recall the Lady of the Lake, who gave Excalibur to Arthur. This woman is like that. She has something to give me. But even as she fights her way to the surface, she somehow recedes, like reality rewinding. I reach down to help her, but I am far too high. Slowly the storm of hair parts and reveals her face, and she opens her mouth to speak. I cannot hear her words, but her face nearly stops my heart. Something pure and cold courses through me as the translucent eyes seek mine in mute desperation. That face once haunted me like an inner shadow, a secret sharer watching, judging, holding me in thrall until at last the light of Sarah and Annie shone into the hidden chambers of my heart, and it receded into memory. Receded but did not die. Once, long ago, that face taught me what it was to be alive.

That face. . . .

Olivia Marston.

CHAPTER 13

Driving through rural Mississippi with a hundred thousand dollars' cash in your trunk can make you nervous. Ray Presley's trailer is fourteen miles north of town, situated between Emerald Mound and the tiny rural community of Church Hill. The second-highest ceremonial mound in North America, Emerald Mound rises from the forest like a Mayan temple of earth. When I was a boy, we sledded down its great slope on pizza pans, on those biannual occasions when Natchez got its inch of snow. As teenagers we gathered there to watch the sun rise while we drank beer and cheap wine and howled over the treetops in the ecstatic tongues of adolescence.

The wooded road between Emerald Mound and Church Hill is dotted with trailers and small houses, but as I near the two-hundred-year-old Episcopal church that marks the settlement, the woods recede, and the landscaped grounds of splendid plantations stretch away from both sides of the road. Beyond moss-hung cedar trees and white fences, swans glide majestically across ponds that might be in England. But the only cathedrals near these estates are cathedrals of kudzu, arsenical green spires and buttresses which construct themselves at a terrifying rate, using oaks and pecans and elms as scaffolding, encroaching upon the old cotton fields with the stealth of new jungle.

The history here is not all antebellum. Andrew Jackson married Rachel Robards at the end of this road in 1791, but of late the neighborhood has entertained more eccentric visitors. When I was in high school, the actor George Hamilton purchased one of these homes and lived there for a while in opulent planter style. The fall of the Marcos regime in the Philippines brought to light the strange revelation that the "Hamilton" house was actually owned by Imelda Marcos. It then passed for a time into the hands of Hare Krishnas, a separatist faction which morphed into the Southern Vedic Life Association, stirring up the country with fears of brainwashing. Even in rural Mississippi nothing is what it seems.

Ray Presley's trailer is set a little way back from the highway, beneath a stand of pine trees, and beside an algae-covered pond that might be an oil sump. The trailer has seen better years, but there's a gleaming new satellite dish hammered onto the southwest eave, like a ribbon on a pig's ear. A shining Ford pickup and a rusted Chevy Vega sit out front.

I pull my mother's Maxima beside the Vega, set the burglar alarm, and walk up to the door, leaving the Wal-Mart briefcase holding the extortion money in the trunk. Before I can press the bell, the door is opened by a thin young woman I assume is Presley's nurse, though she is wearing a denim work shirt, not a uniform. Blonde and lank-haired, she could be twenty-five or thirty-five. She has the indeterminate look of hill people everywhere: sallow skin and hard angles, though she is pretty in the way waitresses at the Waffle House can be pretty at four A.M. She doesn't speak but leads me into the den of the trailer, which is a time capsule of blue shag carpet and dark, seventies-era paneling.

Presley himself sits on a sofa opposite a large color television tuned to a soap opera, a TV tray before him and a stainless steel intravenous drug caddy standing beside. He looks surprisingly fit for a fifty-six-year-old man with metastatic carcinoma. He has the stringy toughness of a laborer, the long, ropy muscles you see on men working shirtless on highways, shrimp boats, and oil rigs. He wears blue cotton pajama pants and a white tank T-shirt. A grease-stained John Deere cap covers his head, which has been burned bald by chemotherapy, the green bill shading browless eyes that smolder in their sockets.

I glance around the room so that he won't feel I'm staring. The walls are decorated with plaques and photos commemorating a career in law enforcement: certificates from various police societies, a couple of trophies sporting a man aiming a pistol. There's also the usual complement of stuffed deer heads and mounted largemouth bass, along with a fearsome compound bow hanging from a hook. Sliding glass doors open onto a small deck behind the sofa, where a gas grill and a smoker stand rusting in the sun.

"So you're Doc Cage's boy," Presley says. His voice is deep and rough as a wood rasp. "I recognize you from the paper. Excuse me if I don't get up."

"Please don't." It's odd how we revert to the basic courtesies, even when talking to killers, especially if they are ill. My seating choices are a cracked Naugahyde recliner and a pillowy velour monstrosity that looks like a Kmart special.

"Take the La-Z-Boy," Presley advises.

I sit on the edge of the chair so that I can keep my forward attitude. With men like Ray Presley, the critical subtext of any conversation is animal. Even in the silences, everything is territory and dominance, a battle for advantage.

"So you're the one shot his mouth off about Del Payton in the paper," he says, a half-humorous light in his eyes.

"That's right."

"You looking to make a name for yourself?"

"I already have that."

He leans back and regards me with disdain. "I guess you do. But you'd have to go a long way to outdo your daddy." He reaches down and eats a crust of toast from the egg-stained plate on the TV tray. "How come you didn't go to medical school? Grades not good enough?"

This is the ultimate baiting question for any doctor's son who didn't follow his father into the profession. "They were too good. The medical school thought I'd be bored there."

I let Presley chew on this a minute, and it takes him about that to finally decide I am joking. His primitive instincts are finely honed, but his grasp of the larger world is limited.

"I remember you in high school," he says. "You was porking Livy Marston."

I keep my face impassive.

180

"That was one fine bitch," he goes on, watching my reaction. "Had too much of everything, that was her trouble."

The skin of my face seems to stretch and burn, but I say nothing, unwilling to be drawn into this game. After an interminable wait, he says, "You here to ask me about Del Payton?"

"I'm here because I heard you had a gun for sale."

He picks up a remote control and flips through several channels, finally settling on a fishing program. "You heard wrong."

"I don't think so."

"What kind of gun did you hear it was?" His eyes remain on the screen. "This gun you're talking about, I mean."

"A featherweight thirty-eight. Smith and Wesson."

"That's a damn good piece. Good for close work. How much would you be looking to spend on a gun like that?"

I take a piece of paper from my wallet, write *50,000* on it, then lean forward and pass it to him.

He studies it for a few seconds. "That's a piece of money."

"Cash."

He hands the paper back to me. "Too bad I don't have what you're looking for. I could use a piece of money like that."

"I think you need some air. Why don't we step outside?"

"I don't get around so good anymore."

"I didn't realize you'd lost so much strength."

His pride thus goaded, Presley puts down the remote and stands almost as easily as he must have at age twenty. He walks to the double glass doors, slides one open, and steps onto the little square redwood deck.

I follow.

Presley stops at the rail, surveying the modest lot left him in life: a few weed-choked rows of exposed earth where a garden once grew; a small barn stripped of its walls, rotted, and collapsed inward, leaving a modernist sculpture of rafters and tin. The wall boards were probably bought by some itinerant New England artist. Beyond the barn the land falls abruptly into the woods.

"Take your shirt off," Presley says in a peremptory tone he probably used with prisoners in the days before he was one himself.

Had he not demanded this ritual, I would have, but it irks me that he beat me to it. "I'll show you mine if you show me yours," I reply.

He actually grins at this. We pull off our shirts and turn in a circle. My body is lean but smooth as a lamb's, the legacy of my generation, which was never shipped overseas to do battle, and has done less manual labor than any generation before it. Presley's torso is marked by multiple knife scars, at least two bullet wounds, and what might be the scar of a central venous line for chemotherapy.

"Pants too," I tell him.

We both strip our pants halfway down our thighs. Like me Presley still wears jockey briefs, and my father's comment about his anatomy is readily borne out. Satisfied that neither of us is wired, we button and zip back up.

"I don't like bullshit," I tell him. "So I'll get right

to it. You killed a man named Don Hillman in 1973 in Mobile, Alabama. You did that on your own hook, no matter what you thought. I'm prepared to offer you a substantial price for the pistol used in that crime, but it's a one-time offer. An outright purchase. You can take what I'm offering, or we can go to Plan B."

"You fixing to threaten me, sonny?" Presley sounds more amused than angry.

"If we don't come to terms over this, I'm going to go straight to the district attorney — whom I went to school with — and use every bit of influence at my disposal to have you indicted for capital murder and extortion. That's a risk for my father, but it's one he's prepared to take. He's been more than generous with you, and he's tired of living in fear."

Presley looks off into the trees.

"He deserves better. And you know it."

"I can't help the way things turned out," Presley says bitterly. "Fact is, Doc has money and I don't. And I need some."

"My father treated your family free for years, just like he did a lot of others. What he's got now is patients who think he's a saint and not much else. He's in bad health himself. He deserves to retire in peace."

Presley scratches his ratty pajamas. "The way I figure, that gun's worth a lot more than fifty thousand."

"Or nothing. It could simply be evidence sitting in the D.A.'s office."

"A hundred grand. Cash money."

Relief trickles through my veins like cool water.

"You've committed other murders in the past. I suspect you're blackmailing other people as we speak. Right now I haven't the slightest bit of interest in those crimes. But that could change. You could spend what little time you have left in jail. And you know what that's like, Ray." I spit off the deck. "Sixty-five thousand."

He doesn't like me using his first name. And though he hasn't moved, something changed in him at the mention of prison. "Eighty," he says in a taut voice.

"Is the gun here?"

"Could be."

"If you get it now, I'll go seventy-five. That's all I brought with me."

Presley's facial muscles flex. He's grinding his teeth. He wants that money. But as badly as he does, he hates to give up the gun. He's like a miser sitting on his last nickel. His eyes burn beneath the bill of the cap, hating me for who I am, for the life I've had. He rolls his tongue around his inner cheek, wanting to tell me to fuck myself. But at last he breaks eye contact and walks toward the glass doors of the trailer. His growl floats back to me on the humid air.

"Get your money, boy."

I hurry down the dry-rotted stairs of the deck and around the trailer to the Maxima. I parked so that I could open the briefcase in the trunk without being seen from the trailer. Popping the trunk, I move the sack of quick-setting cement behind which I concealed the case and count out twenty-five thousand dollars, which I stuff into the spare tire well. Then I snap the case and shut the trunk.

Before going back to the trailer, I get in the car. Inside the glove box is Dad's 9mm Beretta. I slip the automatic into my waistband at the small of my back, tuck my shirt over it, and head up the front steps.

Presley is waiting for me on the sofa. The sallow blonde is attaching a plastic saline bag to the IV stand, and her back is to me. Her motions are quick and efficient. Presley points at the TV set. Lying atop it in a Ziploc bag is a small .38-caliber revolver, Smith & Wesson. I take a card from my wallet. On it is written the serial number of the pistol my father has not seen for twenty-five years. I remove the .38 from the Ziploc and compare its serial number to the one on the card.

They match.

Resealing the pistol in the bag, I slide it into my trouser pocket and toss the case containing the money onto the sofa. Presley tugs it onto his lap, unsnaps it, and counts the packets with methodical care. As the blonde waits, she glances over her shoulder at me, her eyes vaguely accusatory. Presley finally snaps the case shut, drops it on the floor, leans back on the sofa, and extends his right wrist toward the blonde woman, dorsal side up.

"Time for my poison," he says, the corners of his mouth turned up with black humor.

The girl removes a heparin-lock catheter from its packaging, swabs Presley's wrist with Betadine, and pops it through the skin in the time it would take most lab techs to locate a vein. As she tears off some white tape and fixes the catheter in place, Presley leans up and slaps her on the rump with the familiarity of a lover. The blonde does not complain or make any move to stop him. She doesn't even look embarrassed.

"You'd best get going, sonny," he says. "Crystal's gonna take the edge off the nausea for me."

The girl half turns to me, a resentful gleam in her eye. The top three buttons of her work shirt are unbuttoned, revealing the clasp of a black bra beneath it. She's at least twenty years Presley's junior — probably thirty — and for some reason this offends me. My Puritan morals, I suppose. I'm not one to deny a dying man what pleasure he can get, but something about this arrangement seems wrong. The woman doesn't strike me as a hooker, but Presley is paying her in some way. Probably not much either. When you're poor, a little money looks like a lot. Or maybe he's not paying her. Maybe she's here because she wants to be here — or needs to be. That bothers me even more.

"I didn't know nurses could administer chemotherapy at home."

Presley laughs darkly. "This is my Mexican cocktail. They UPS it up here from Tijuana. My New Orleans cancer doc says it'll kill me, but I've outlived that bastard's prediction by a year already."

Bootleg chemotherapy. Is that what's keeping him alive? Or is it just brute redneck stubbornness?

"They cut out my damn prostate," he mutters, "but I made 'em leave the nerves in. I can still go like a Brahma bull."

The blonde sits on the floor at his feet, waiting for me to leave.

"Just remember something, Ray. You've got all

you're going to get from this particular well."

"Nice doing business with you, son. Let me give you a piece of advice before you go."

"What's that?"

"Leave Del Payton in the ground. You start messing with business that old — especially nigger — business, it makes a lot of people nervous."

"I figured that out already."

"You're a smart boy, ain't you?"

The blonde checks Presley's IV line for bubbles, then leans back against his legs.

I walk to the door, but something makes me turn. "Let me ask you something, Ray. How did Judge Marston get involved in Payton's murder?"

Presley goes as still as a snake poised to strike, his eyes locked on mine. "Maybe you ain't so smart after all."

"There's a lot of guys on death row who think different."

I shut the door, leaving him to his bootleg chemo and his blonde. My stomach is fluttering like the wings of a hummingbird, but the Smith & Wesson is a hard bulge in my left front pocket. I have the gun. *I have the gun.* Seventy-five thousand dollars is a small price to pay to have a spike removed from your heart.

CHAPTER 14

As soon as I hit the highway, I dial my father's office and wait for him to come to the phone.

"Dr. Cage," he says finally.

"It's me."

"What happened?"

"I have the package."

A long exhalation. An expression of relief I can only guess at. He's been waiting with the same anxiety his patients suffer through when awaiting a call from him about test results. "Jesus," he breathes. "Son, you don't know —"

"Forget it, Dad. It's all over. We'll talk tonight, okay?"

"I can't believe it."

"Believe it. It's a new world. I'll see you tonight."

I punch off and zoom south toward Natchez, profoundly aware of the gun in my pocket. I feel like a character from Poe, the symbol of guilt attached to my body and screaming for atonement. But there's no danger. Ray Presley is happy with his seventy-five grand. He isn't calling anybody about that gun. Not today, anyway. With every mile I put between myself and his trailer, the burden of my father's anxiety falls away, and my mind returns to its own selfish concerns.

Ike Ransom awakened a sleeping giant within me. The giant is anger. Anger so profound, complex, and deeply buried that I have never fully plumbed it. I have, in fact, spent years not thinking about it, which required that a constant portion of my life energy be devoted to denial. Yet the anger was always there, pulsing quietly beneath my surface life, affecting my judgment, my decisions, my very concept of justice and morality. For years I thought it was based on Leo Marston's attack on my father, but this was self-delusion. My anguish was not for my father's pain but for my own. The most devastating result of Marston's merciless legal persecution of my father was the end of any possibility that Olivia Marston and I would have a future together. And that altered *my* life in ways beyond measuring. Ultimately, it weakened my character, like a crack in the steel of a bridge. Because always, at the periphery of my existence, the unwalked road of my life with Livy stretched tangentially to infinity, to be reflected upon only in sadness, frustration, and regret. Last night Ike Ransom offered me a chance I never thought I would get: a chance to settle up with Leo Marston for all he did to me and my family. To put paid to two decades of resentment and confusion.

The sheer power of my desire to destroy the man disturbs me. As a prosecutor I tried to divorce myself from the concept of revenge. Justice, not punishment, was my ideal. I didn't always succeed, but I tried. This is different. I have no idea *how* Leo Marston could be involved in Payton's murder, but he is a complex man of vast appetites, and he has rarely been thwarted in his desires. I can easily envision a situation in which he let his temper get the best of him. Great wealth does not confer immunity to violent impulses.

I lift the cell phone and punch in the number of my Houston office, which occupies nine hundred square feet of our house. At least it did until I instructed my assistant to store my furniture and sell the place.

"Penn Cage's office," says Cilla Daniels.

Relief floods through me. "I'm glad to know I still have one."

She laughs. "I let the movers take everything but the office furniture and equipment."

"Good instinct. Leave it all set up for now." I swing the Maxima into the left lane and goose it around a pulpwood truck.

"What about the Hanratty execution?" Cilla asks. "Mrs. Givens called this morning. She's decided to witness the execution without her husband, and she wants you there."

"Any last-minute filings? Likely stays?"

"The usual desperation tactics, but they won't stop it this time. And George W. Bush isn't about to grant a pardon. Midnight tomorrow night, Hanratty gets the needle."

"Damn. Tell Mrs. Givens . . . tell her I don't know yet whether I can make it."

"Please try, Penn. That woman needs you. You walked her family through the whole trial."

"Message received. Listen, do you remember Peter Lutjens?"

"Sure. The FBI analyst who helped on *Presumption of Guilt*."

"I need his phone number at the Bureau."

"Hang on. . . . I think the FBI switchboard is the best I can do on Lutjens."

"That'll do." I scrawl the number on my wrist. "Thanks, Cil. I've got to go."

"Not so fast. What are you up to? Have you resurrected the manuscript?"

"Just some research."

"That's what you always say when you're on to something."

"Bye, Cil."

I hang up, dial the Hoover Building, and ask for Peter Lutjens, giving my name as Special Agent Jim Gates. During my time with the D.A.'s office, I became friends with several Houston-based field agents, one of whom was Jim Gates. Most of those friends are now stationed around the country and globe, and occasionally prove excellent sources for my books, despite a standing order from FBI Director Portman to give me no assistance. Peter Lutjens is better at research and analysis than chasing bank robbers, and because the FBI knows this as well as I do, they keep him buried in the massive archive of past Bureau case files.

"Gates?" asks a surprised voice. "What are you doing in Mississippi?"

Lutjens is obviously looking at some sort of caller-ID readout. "This isn't Jim Gates, Peter. It's Penn Cage."

"Penn Cage? Jesus, you've got some nerve. What kind of trouble do you want to get me into now?"

"Did I get you into trouble before?"

"Well . . . the acknowledgment in your book made me semi-famous up here. And the new director is no fan of yours, as you well know."

"The new director's an asshole, Peter, as you well know."

"No comment. What's going on?"

"I need a favor. It's right up your alley, historical stuff."

"Save the Vaseline. What is it?"

"I'm looking into a thirty-year-old murder case in my old hometown. A civil rights murder. I know the Bureau worked the case. Somebody took a shot at a couple of your agents on Highway 61 during the same time frame."

"You've sure got piss-poor timing."

"Why?"

"Since the opening of the Mississippi Sovereignty Commission files, we've been deluged with requests for records from that period. I'm talking about requests by law enforcement, i.e., *legitimate* requests."

"I really need this, Peter. It's personal."

Lutjens doesn't reply. There's no reason for him to bend any rules on my account — other than the goodwill resulting from a few enjoyable lunches, the easy rapport of kindred spirits — and all the reason in the world for him not to. "I know a guy who's processing those requests," he says in a cautious voice. "We worked together on the internal history of the Bureau."

"Peter —"

"Give me the victim's name."

"Delano Payton. Killed Natchez, Mississippi, fourteen May 1968."

"Was anyone convicted of the crime?"

"No one even arrested."

192

Lutjens clucks his tongue in admonishment. "You'll never get a file on a case that's technically open. Not under the Freedom of Information Act."

"I just want names. The agents who originally worked the case."

"These guys worked for J. Edgar Hoover, Penn. They're not the talkative type."

"Somebody always wants to talk. Nobody'll ever know how I found them."

"Portman would boil my balls for this." He hesitates a moment longer. "Stay by your phone. I'll know all I'm ever going to know within five minutes."

"I'm at —"

"I've got the number."

I hang up and hit the accelerator, feeling a burst of adrenaline as I eat up the miles between Emerald Mound and the city limits. Lutjens's willingness to help me says a lot about the success — or lack of it — that John Portman has had since taking over the Bureau. When he was appointed to the directorship seven months ago, great things were expected from the former field agent, both within the Bureau and without. But according to the reports I've heard, Portman has displayed the same traits in the Hoover Building that brought him into conflict with me when he was a U.S. attorney. He masks coldness as competence, manipulation as management, and megalomania as superachievement. The simple fact that he still carries a grudge against an ex-assistant district attorney from Houston tells me that he is a pygmy in his soul.

Lutjens calls back as I pull into the drive-through line at Hardee's Hamburgers for some breakfast.

"Call me back from a land line," he says.

Two pay phones stand at the edge of the gas station lot next to Hardee's. "Give me thirty seconds."

I pull out of the line of cars and use my credit card to call Lutjens back. He answers his line in a near whisper.

"This is the only conversation we're going to have on this matter. Don't use names."

"Okay."

"You're not the only interested party. A request for the same file came in forty-five minutes before you called. From your local D.A.'s office. An A.M. made the request. You know him?"

Austin Mackey. "Yes. This case is political dynamite down here. He's probably got the mayor pushing him, trying to cover their asses. Is there any way you can —"

"No copy of the file. No way, no how. Anyway, it's forty-four volumes."

"Forty-four volumes! How many pages in each?"

"Two to three hundred."

"Jesus, I wish I could get a look at that."

"You're not alone in your disappointment. A.M. won't be seeing the file either."

"Why not?"

"It's sealed."

"Sealed how?"

"There are several exceptions to the Freedom of Information Act. Reasons we can refuse to release

194

documents. The most common ones exist to safe-guard the lives of informants or to protect the privacy of citizens involved in investigations —"

"I know all that. But A.M. is a law enforcement official."

"We can also refuse to release documents that pose a risk to national security. Under this exception we can refuse to release documents to *anyone*, even other law enforcement agencies."

"This is a thirty-year-old Mississippi murder. It's got nothing to do with national security."

"Nevertheless, the file was sealed on grounds of national security in May 1968. The order was signed personally by the director."

A faint buzzing has started in my head. "J. Edgar Hoover?"

"The man himself. The file can't be opened for nine more years. Not without a vote by Congress. There's no telling what you've stepped into. Hoover used the rubric of Vietnam to conceal a multitude of sins during the sixties."

I'm so lost that I don't even know what questions to ask. "What about the names? The agents."

"I'm going to send a fax to your office. A list of agents working out of the Jackson, Mississippi, field office in the summer of sixty-eight. I don't know how complete it is, but it's the best I can do. Personal memoirs from the period might help you narrow it down."

"I owe you big-time for this."

"Yes, you do. Listen, the Bureau has been very supportive of Mississippi prosecutors this year, providing files on these old civil rights cases. Even if the files embarrassed us a bit. This file is obviously different. I'd think long and hard about pursuing it."

"I will."

"Watch your back, buddy."

And with that he is gone.

I pull back onto the highway, heading toward my parents' house. I suddenly have a lot to do today, but I can't do it with a murder weapon in my car. Accelerating through the bypass traffic, I punch in my office number and get Cilla, who tells me Lutjens's fax is already coming through.

"No cover page. It looks like a list of some kind. Sixty or seventy names. Social Security numbers too."

I say a silent thank-you to Peter Lutjens.

"There's a handwritten note at the bottom. It says, 'If you telephone anyone on this list, you've announced your interest to Washington.' Penn, what's going on?"

"You don't want to know. Those names belong to FBI agents, probably all retired. Find phone numbers for every one you can. Then start calling them. Give them the usual line: you're working for me, researching a novel. I need to know which agents worked in Natchez, Mississippi, in the summer of 1968. Particularly on the Delano Payton case. Okay?"

"Delano Payton. No problem."

"Fax a copy of the list to my father's medical office."

"Right."

"And, Cil?"

"Yes?"

"Use a fake name on these calls."

"I will. I'll — My God, a KHOU truck just pulled into the driveway. Got to be about the Hanratty execution."

"You can handle them."

"You got that right. I'll call you."

She rings off.

As I punch End on the cell phone, I see my hand shaking. I am crossing a line I have crossed only a few times previously, and always with a sense of euphoria mingled with dread. In the great train of cases that crossed my desk as a prosecutor, a few engaged not merely my mind or my talents or even my heart. A few penetrated the deepest springs of my being: my fears, my prejudices, and my desires. When that happened, I became more than a lawyer. I became a personification of justice. And not justice as the law defined it, but as *I* did.

That is how I feel now.

Last night, when Ike Ransom told me Leo Marston was involved in a thirty-year-old capital murder, I wanted to believe it, but some part of me refused. I could see no possible connection between Marston and his supposed victim. But when Peter Lutjens said the words "J. Edgar Hoover" and "national security," a circuit closed somewhere in my brain, sparking the faintest glimmer of understanding. Leo Marston is a political man from a political family, and if the Delano Payton murder had a political angle sensitive enough for the file to be hidden from public view, then a connection to Leo Marston no longer seems impossible.

Twenty years ago, that ruthless bastard wronged my father, hurt my mother, and stole my future.

He did not suffer one moment for doing that. He lived as men of his kind always have: exempt from justice, untouchable. But now, far in the distance, he has come into sight, like a buck on a high ridge line. And this time I have a weapon in my hands. That weapon is a dead man.

Del Payton.

CHAPTER 15

The district attorney's office is in a three-story building near the courthouse, and there are open parking spaces out front. I take one, then trot up the stairs beside the brass plaque with Mackey's name on it. There is no receptionist, only a long hall with offices on both sides and a black custodian working in a broom closet at the far end. I walk past partly open doors until I see Mackey sitting behind a desk, wearing one of those striped oxford shirts with a white collar that I always found a little too precious.

Pushing open the door, I see a heavyset woman sitting across from Mackey's desk. "I'm sorry. I'll wait."

As I close the door, I hear Mackey say, "Excuse me just a moment, ma'am." He steps into the hall, looking put upon by the unannounced visit. "What do you want, Cage?"

"I came to see if you have any files on the Del Payton murder."

His fair-skinned face goes red, making him look like a pissed-off fraternity boy. "Do you have wax in your ears? I told you last night there was no file. I also said I'd give you no assistance unless you're the attorney of record for a member of the Payton family."

"Let's say I am."

He swallows, brought up short. "Are you or aren't you? I checked with the bar association this morning. They told me you're licensed to practice in Mississippi."

"Put it this way, Austin. If you insist on being a pain in the ass, I'm a lot more likely to be."

His lips disappear into a tight seam.

"What about the file?"

"There *is* no file. After the party last night I stopped by here and checked, just to be sure. All the records from 1966 through 1968 were destroyed in a fire when you and I were still in grade school."

This throws me. My first instinct is to ask whether Leo Marston was still district attorney during that fire, but I don't. Mackey isn't Clarence Darrow, but if I appear too interested in Marston, he'll zero in on my real motive quickly enough. And Marston will instantly hear about it.

"What about the police department?"

"The chief won't show you files on an unsolved murder case."

"Is he actually investigating the case?"

"What do you think?"

"I think he may be investigating it before the week is out, whether he wants to or not. What about the sheriff?"

Mackey reaches backward and pulls his door completely shut. "Why do you have a bug up your ass about this? I don't remember you as a flaming liberal."

"I'm not. I'm a flaming humanist. I happen to

care that some poor son of a bitch was blown to pieces and his family never saw justice done."

A strange light comes into Mackey's eyes. "I've got it now. You don't give two shits about Del Payton or his family. You want a best-seller out of this. Maybe get yourself on Oprah's book club? Penn Cage, whitebread crusader for justice."

"Yeah, that's it."

Mackey draws himself to his full height, positive that he's divined my true motive. Greed is something he can understand. "You may be willing to drag this town through the mud for a dollar. I've got more loyalty than that. Don't come back here unless you've got new evidence in your hands."

He goes back into his office and softly closes the door.

As I turn toward the stairs, I hear footsteps closing quickly on me from behind. I whirl and find myself staring at the black custodian who was standing at the broom closet before. He's over sixty, with bluish skin and pink blemishes like freckles below his eyes, and he reeks of cigarettes.

"Keep walking," he says.

I move toward the staircase, the custodian on my heels.

"I heard you ask about Del Payton. Mackey tell you all them files burned up in a fire?"

"Yes."

"Some did, some didn't. Everything that's left is down in the basement. Five, six boxes."

I stop on the landing. "Is the basement locked?"

"Yep." He looks up and down the empty stairwell. "The door's out back. If you was to check there in about five minutes, you might find a key.

When you done, leave it where you found it."

He shuffles down the stairs without another word.

I wait a few moments, then walk out onto the street and stare across at the oak-shaded courthouse. Sifting through old legal files could take some time. I need to move my father's car in case Mackey comes out before I'm done. When I stopped at my parents' house to take care of the Smith & Wesson, I found that the glass in the BMW had been repaired. I gave the Maxima back to Mom, so that if anyone targeted the BMW again, it would be me, and not my mother and daughter, who took the risk. I also transferred the remaining $25,000 into the trunk of the BMW, meaning to get it back to my father before the end of the day. Climbing inside the car, I pull around the corner, call directory assistance for the number of the *Examiner*, and have them connect me.

"Caitlin Masters, please."

"Ms. Masters is in a meeting. Would you like me to transfer you to her voice mail?"

"Tell her Penn Cage is on the phone."

"Sir —"

"Please just do it."

Thirty seconds later, Caitlin says, "You'd better not be standing me up for lunch."

"I do need to postpone. Something's come up."

"What could be more important than me?"

"Actually, I was going to suggest dinner tonight."

"Who says change is bad? Does eight o'clock work for you?"

"Yes. Thanks, Caitlin."

"You can repay me with information."

I hang up laughing, then lock the car and hurry into the inner square of the block. It harbors parked cars, dumpsters, and fire escapes, but thankfully no people. At the rear of Mackey's building, eight concrete steps and a green handrail descend to a steel door. There's no key in the lock. I go down the steps and feel beneath the crack of the door. Nothing. In the lee of the bottom step lies a broken, rust-colored brick. I bend and lift it.

The key is there.

The basement is lighted by bare hanging bulbs, and it stinks of mildew. I feel like I'm breathing fungus. What I first perceived as walls are stacks of boxes, hundreds of them, old bellied cardboard things that look like they were stolen from a grocery store trash pile. Thankfully, there are dates scrawled on them in black magic marker.

There seems to be no organizing concept. Files from the 1920s have been stacked next to files from the 1970s. I scan the wall of dates as though searching for my size in a display of blue jeans. No luck. But after twenty minutes of digging through rat droppings and dust, I find a short stack of boxes labeled '73 FIRE.

Dragging the stack into the nearest pool of light, I open the top box and riffle through its contents. The files inside are charred, stained, and mildewed, and all date from 1966. I set that box aside and open the next one. My pulse quickens. The files inside are dated 1968.

Starting at the front of the box, I examine the first page inside each folder. Marston's name is all over the files, but none deals with Delano Payton.

When I get to the end of the box, I go back to the beginning and flip through every sheet in every folder, but again I find nothing. One by one I go through each folder in the boxes dating from the fire with painstaking care, but I find nothing related to Del Payton.

It looks like Mackey was telling the truth.

After restacking the boxes, I lock the door, put the key back under the brick, and climb back into the sunlight. The custodian is standing thirty yards away, smoking a cigarette in the shadow of a nearby building. I walk straight up to him like a tourist asking for directions.

"Mackey was right."

He spits on the concrete. "Shit."

"You don't happen to clean the police station, do you?"

He shakes his head.

"I guess that's it, then. I appreciate your help." I start to leave, but he reaches out and touches my elbow.

"You know, we had a couple of black police chiefs. The first one was back in 'eighty-one. I knew him pretty good. He didn't mind stepping on toes to get the job done, so they fired him after a few months. He might know something."

"What was his name?"

"Willie Pinder."

"Does he still live in town?"

"He stay over to Gaylor Street. Blue house. Drives a old Dodge pickup."

"Would he be home during the day?"

"I believe he 'tired. You could see."

"I'll call him. Hey, I never got your name."

"That's right. You watch your ass, Penn Cage. And tell your daddy Zoot say hello."

He grinds his cigarette beneath the heel of a cheap work boot and walks back toward the D.A.'s office.

As soon as I reach the car, I dial directory assistance again. There's a listing for a Willie Pinder on Gaylor Street. This time I dial the number myself.

"Yeah?" says a coarse voice.

"Is Willie there?"

"This Willie."

I hang up.

Gaylor Street is in a black neighborhood off the road that leads up to the city cemetery. It takes several trips through blocks of small, brightly colored houses, but I finally find the ex-chief's Dodge pickup parked on the street. A cracked pad of cement leads to the rear of the house. I drive around and park near Pinder's back porch. It's fully screened, with rust eating the black wire in big orange patches.

"Who the hell are you?" shouts a hostile voice. "You just call me on the telephone?"

I wave broadly at the dark screen. For all I know, I'm looking into the barrel of a shotgun. "I'm Penn Cage. I'm looking for the former chief of police, Willie Pinder."

"Who you work for, chump?"

The screen door opens with a screech of protesting springs, and a big black head appears in the opening. The sleepy-eyed face says late fifties, with some rough years on the back end.

"Car like that, you ain't no process server. Must

be a lawyer. You work for my ex-old lady?"

"No. My name's Penn Cage. If you're Willie Pinder, I want to ask you about the Del Payton murder."

At the words "Del Payton" the sleepy eyes wake up. "I'm Willie," he says, looking closely at me.

"You got my name, right?"

"Trouble. That's your name."

"Will you talk to me?"

"Sure." Pinder laughs. "I might be hearing your last words. Come on up."

He holds the door open for me. Three steps lead up to the porch, the kind of weed-grown slat steps that snakes like to lie under in the heat. In one bound I am up and through the door, which slaps shut behind me with a bang like a pistol shot.

"Porch is far enough," says Pinder. "Hotter inside anyway. AC's busted. You want a beer?"

"Sure." I try not to glance at my watch; it can't be eleven A.M. yet.

Pinder goes inside and returns with two sweating cans of Schaeffer. He hands me one, then sits beside me in a green iron lawn chair, pops the top off his can, and drinks.

"So you're retired now?" I say, opening my beer.

He laughs again. "That don't quite seem to say it. I'm fucked now. How about that?"

I'm not sure how to proceed. I don't want the man's life story, but neither do I want to offend him. Thankfully, Pinder spares me.

"You the crazy man who popped off about Del Payton in the paper?"

"I mentioned the case."

"Case? Ain't no *case* on Del Payton."

"What about a file, then? There must have been a police file."

He takes another long swig of Schaeffer. "I was pretty busy back then. It was all I could do to hold the goddamn place together."

"I'm sure. Still, I'd think you might have wanted to check some things the white chiefs had let slide for too long."

Pinder sniffs and looks through the rusted screen. "I worked in that department eleven years, and I never saw no Payton file. Didn't think there was one. But when the old chief gave me the combination to the station safe, and I opened it up, there it was. Sitting on the bottom of a stack of insurance policies. Just like that. First day on the job."

"Did the police seriously investigate the case in sixty-eight?"

He smiles. "In 1968 the city slogan was 'Natchez, Where the Old South Still Lives.' It *looked* like they investigated. There was lots of confidential-informant reports, rumors tracked down, stuff like that."

"Any suspects?"

"A couple."

"Who?"

He smiles enigmatically. "You know, I might ought to check the file. My memory ain't what it used to be."

Something quivers in my chest. "How can you check the file?"

"Easy. I got it inside."

Jesus. "You made a copy?"

"Nope. I got the original. Took it when they

207

screwed me out of my job."

I feel like hugging him. "May I see it?"

"I ain't no loan library, boy. I think we're talking about a rental situation here."

"How much?"

Pinder's face goes blank as he computes a price. "Five hundred," he says finally, a note of challenge in his voice. "And you read it right here in front of me."

When I think of what I just paid Ray Presley for my father's .38, I feel like laughing. "A thousand," I counter. "But I take the file with me. I'll photocopy it and get the original back to you within twenty-four hours."

Pinder has lost a little of his studied calm. "How 'bout two thousand?"

"What's in the file? How long is it?"

"About twenty-five pages. Plenty of names in there, if that's what you're after."

"Any mention of Judge Marston in it? He was D.A. back then."

Something ticks in the ex-chief's face. "That motherfucker in there."

"Two thousand it is."

His head slides back on his neck, his eyes full of suspicion. "I don't want no check, now."

"You get the file, I'll get the cash."

"You got it here?"

"Oh, yeah. Get the file."

While Pinder goes inside, I go to the car and open the spare tire well, count two thousand dollars from the remaining twenty-five, and return to the porch. Shuffling and sliding sounds come from inside the house, as though Pinder is moving furniture. Then the door bangs open and he reappears with a worn manila folder in his hand. I hand him the cash, and he takes it, but he doesn't pass me the file. He sits down again and drinks from his beer can.

"You ain't asked me if I solved the case or not."

"Did you?"

"No." He looks at me out of the corner of his eye. "But not because it ain't solvable. I kept that file close to my vest, man. Didn't tell no white officers nothin' 'bout it. Told a couple of black ones I trusted I was gonna be working the case real quiet. One week later somebody sent me a message."

"What kind of message?"

"They sent a man to talk to me. A man I hated but wasn't about to ignore."

"Who was he?"

"Ray Presley."

I try to keep my composure, but Pinder cannot fail to notice the thunderous effect the name has on me. "I know Presley," I say carefully. "He was somehow involved in the original case."

"That's right. And that son of a bitch'll kill a man like picking off a scab. He's killed for less than what you just give me."

"Did he threaten you over the Payton case?"

"Not the way I expected. If he had, I'd have thrown him in a cell. He'd been to Parchman by then, and I was still riding my high horse. He didn't say, 'Stay out of this or you might wind up dead.' No, he said, 'I hear you're thinking about looking into the Del Payton murder, Willie. I worked that case myself in sixty-eight, worked it hard, and just about the time I thought we was getting somewhere, somebody told me to leave it alone. And I did. I left it alone. I was white and I wanted to solve that bombing, but I let it go. You ought to think about that.' "

"What do you think he meant? Who was he talking about?"

"Don't know." Pinder's voice softens, becomes vulnerable. "But anybody who could put fear into Ray Presley scared me plenty. My kids was still living with me then, and I wasn't about to watch them die for my pride. Or black pride, or whatever you want to call it. I couldn't even trust the brothers in my own department. How far was I gonna get? Del Payton was gonna be just as dead either way."

"Was it the Klan, you think?"

"The Klan? Shit. Klan wouldn't scare Ray Presley. Those kluckers scared of *him*. He did shit them crackers only talked about."

"Could it have been the FBI?" I ask, recalling Lutjens's story of the sealed file.

A funny gleam comes into Pinder's eyes. "Why you ask that?"

"Is it possible?"

"Anything's possible. The feds and the local cops didn't get on too good then. Not much better now, really. But why they'd warn Presley off . . . don't make no sense. Hoover hated Martin Luther King. But Del didn't have nothing to do with no big-time peoples like that." Pinder stands suddenly and drops the file in my lap. "We finished here."

Despite this strong hint to leave, I open the file. The first page is headed: SUPPLEMENTARY INVESTIGATION REPORT, and dated 5-15-68. Beneath

210

this is typed: *Delano Payton Murder Bombing*. Then come four handwritten paragraphs that appear to detail an anonymous phone call. The signature beneath them reads, *Patrolman Ray Presley*.

"You can do your reading at home," Pinder says. "I'm goin' fishin'. Gonna spend the afternoon forgettin' I ever saw you."

I stand and shake his hand. "I appreciate the help, Chief. Don't spend it all in one place."

He chuckles. "Hey, I got an old bulletproof vest I can sell you. Wanna take a look?"

"I don't plan to need it." I push open the screen door and walk quickly down the steps. "I'll drop the original back tomorrow."

"Keep it. I don't want no part of that no more."

"I never saw you." I put one leg into the BMW. "Hey . . . if you really gave up on the case, why'd you steal the file when you left?"

Pinder stands motionless in the open doorway. "Get a little of my own back, I guess. I knew I'd be the last black chief for a long time." He smiles oddly, as though he has just seen something in a new light. "Maybe that file's been waiting here for you all this time. Mysterious ways, right? Maybe the bastards won't get you after all."

I give Pinder a salute. "Hope they're biting today, Chief."

He winks at me. "They biting every day, if you know where to look."

CHAPTER 16

The Payton house is a typical rural home, built with cheap materials on concrete blocks, but better maintained than most. Lovingly tended flower beds border the front, concealing the dark crawl space beneath the structure. The cars in the driveway are probably worth more than the house, but at least the nearest neighbor is fifty yards up the road.

Georgia Payton sits beneath a large pin oak, rocking slowly in a white cotton dress. She lifts a hand as I pull into the driveway, but she does not get up.

I walk over to say hello before going to the front door. "Hot one, isn't it?"

She cackles at me. "I lived three-quarters of my life without no air conditioning. The Lord's breeze be good enough for me."

"Mr. Cage?"

Althea Payton is beckoning to me from the door. She wears navy shorts and a red blouse tied at the waist. She looks like she's been gardening.

"Come in out of that heat!" she calls. "Georgia's fine out there."

I smile at the old woman, then cross the drive and follow Althea into the house.

"Georgia's like an old loggerhead turtle sunning itself on a rock," she says. "I asked her to stay outside while we talk. She can be a little hard to handle. Have a seat."

I sit on a flame-print love seat, and Althea takes a cloth-covered easy chair to my right. The living room holds old but clean furniture, all of it arranged around a new television set. Dozens of framed family photos hang on the wall behind the TV. I look away when I realize I'm staring at a wedding photo of Del and Althea. They look young and happy, destined for anything but what happened to them in the spring of 1968.

"On the phone," she says hesitantly, "you said it was about my husband."

"Yes, ma'am." My next words are an irrevocable step. "I've decided to look into Del's death after all. I've already taken some steps in that direction."

She seems not to have understood. Then her eyes well up and her voice spills out in a reverent tone. "Sweet Lord Jesus, I can't believe it."

"I don't want us to get ahead of ourselves. There may not be anything to find out."

She nods, her hands clasped over her chest. "I realize that. I just . . . it's been so many years. Do you have any idea what you need to charge me?"

"Yes. I'm going to need a retainer of one dollar. And I'll bill you for my time at the rate of one dollar per day."

She shakes her head in confusion. "You can't be serious."

"I'm deadly serious, Althea. Don't give it another thought."

She wipes tears from her eyes, and I look away.

The wall to her left holds the sacred trinity of photographs I've seen in the homes of many black families: Martin Luther King, JFK, and Abraham Lincoln. Sometimes you see Bobby, or FDR. But the Paytons have only the big three. A plastic clock hangs above the photographs, its face painted with a rather bloated likeness of Dr. King. The words *I HAVE A DREAM* appear in quotes beneath him.

"Georgia bought that clock from some traveling salesman in May of 1968," Althea says. "It stopped running before that Christmas, but she never let me get rid of it."

"Maybe it's a collector's item."

"I don't care. Those clocks probably put a million dollars in some sharpie's pocket." She grips her knees with her palms and fixes her eyes on me. "Could I ask you one thing?"

"Why did I change my mind?"

"Yes."

"I have a personal stake in the case now. I want to be honest with you about that."

"Are you going to write a book about Del? Is that it?"

"No. But if anybody asks you what I was doing here, that's what you tell them. And I mean anybody, police included. Okay?"

"Whatever you say. But what is your personal interest, if not a book?"

"I'd prefer to keep that to myself, Althea."

She looks puzzled, then relieved. "I'm glad you've got a stake in it. You having a child like you do. It would be too hard if I thought you were taking this risk only for me."

"I'm not. Rest assured of that."

"Thank you." She leans back in her chair and looks at me with apprehension. "What can you tell me? Have you learned anything yet?"

"We won't be getting any help from the district attorney. The police either, if my guess is right. I've managed to obtain some documentary information dating back to 1968 that could be helpful, but that's between us and God."

"Can you tell me what it is?"

"No. I won't expose you to potential criminal charges."

She nods soberly. "Just tell me this. Do you think there's any hope? Of finding out the truth, I mean."

I fight the urge to be optimistic. A lawyer has to make that mistake only once to learn what it costs. You give people hope; then the pendulum swings the wrong way and they're left shattered, as much by false hope as by misfortune.

"I wouldn't take the case if there wasn't hope. But I want to proceed cautiously. I promise to contact you if and when I learn anything of value. I understand that you've waited a long time for justice."

Althea's hands are clenched in her lap, the knuckles white.

"If you feel up to it, I'd like you to tell me what you can about what Del was doing at the battery plant before he died. For civil rights, I mean."

She takes a deep breath and closes her eyes, as though striving to remember with perfect accuracy. "Del wasn't any big civil rights worker. He was a workingman. He just saw things he thought were wrong and did what he could to change them.

When he was a young man, he was carefree. You never saw a smile so full and happy. When he went to Korea, something changed in him. He still had that smile, but it didn't fill up his eyes the way it used to. He was different inside. He got shot over there, and I think he saw some pretty bad things. When he got back, he told me life was too short to spend it standing at the back of the line."

"When did he go to work at Triton Battery?"

"A couple of years after the war. He put in his time and saved his money back then. Said he didn't want to marry me till he could afford to take care of me like I deserved." Althea's voice cracks a little, but she smiles. "I sure got tired of waiting. Del bought this house in 1959, for cash money. Not many black men could do that back then."

"You got married in fifty-nine?"

She nods. "It was right around then that Del met Medgar."

"Medgar Evers?"

"Yes. Medgar heard how good Del was doing at the plant, and wanted to meet him. Medgar was building up the NAACP back then, pushing voter registration. Del *loved* Medgar. Loved his quiet way. Said he'd known men like Medgar in the army. Quiet men who worked hard and wouldn't back down for anything. Medgar took to Del too. He saw that Del didn't hate the white man. Del believed if we could help white people see inside us, see past the color, their hearts would change."

"So Medgar got Del into civil rights work?"

"Lord, yes. Medgar ate right in this house whenever he came through town." Althea shakes her head sadly. "When Beckwith killed Medgar in

June of sixty-three, Del changed again. He said the war had come home to America. Then President Kennedy was shot that November. Del had joined the NAACP by then, of course, and by 1965 he was in charge of voter registration for this area. Del was the highest-ranking black man at the battery plant. Even the white men liked him. They knew he knew his job."

"Who do you think planted that bomb, Althea?"

"Well . . . the Klan, I guess. There were a lot of beatings out at the paper mill around then, Klan workers beating black workers. You know. Scaring them off. There was some Klan at the tire plant, and at the battery plant too."

"A car bomb is quite an escalation from a beating. Did Del have any personal enemies you know of?"

"Del didn't have an enemy in this world."

He had at least one, I say silently. But it's certainly possible that Payton was chosen at random, to send a warning to someone. "Did he seem any more worried than usual about going to work near the time of his death?"

She shakes her head. "We had some death threats, but we got those with every promotion Del had. He just kept on keeping on. He'd say, 'Thea, we can't let 'em get us down.' "

I remember the nightmarish weeks of the Hanratty trial, when death threats arrived almost daily. What courage it must have taken for Del Payton to get up every morning of his life and go to work with men he knew wanted him dead.

"He was depressed," Althea adds. "Over Dr. King's death. Martin was assassinated just five

217

weeks before Del was killed. And Del was so saddened by that, because already he saw the Movement being taken over by advocates of violence. Men with bitterness in their hearts. Stokely Carmichael and the rest. Black racists, he called them."

The more I learn about Del Payton, the more I feel that his murder was a terrible loss to the community in which I grew up. "Does anything else stand out?"

"No. The FBI asked me all this back when it happened, and I told them the same thing. One day Del went to work and just didn't come home."

I looked helplessly around the room. Del Payton has been dead for thirty years, but he is as alive here as a dead man can be. When Annie is a grown woman, will this large a piece of my heart still be reserved for Sarah?

"Do you remember the names of any of the FBI agents who talked to you?"

"I remember one, very well. Agent Stone. He was about Del's age, and he'd served in Korea too. Agent Stone really tried to help me. But he was the only one. He had a younger man with him who never said much. He didn't care nothing about us. Like all the rest."

"Do you remember his name?"

"No. Just a stuck-up Yankee. Agent Stone came by the house before he left town the last time. He apologized for not having gotten justice for Del. He was a good man, and I got the feeling he knew there was some dirty work at the crossroads on Del's case."

"Did he say anything specific?"

"No. He just seemed like he wanted to say more than he could."

"Do you know a deputy named Ike Ransom? Some people used to call him Ike the Spike."

A strange stillness comes over Althea. "They still call him that. Ike was a good boy who turned out bad. He got on that dope over in Vietnam and drank all the years after that. He hurt a lot of black people to impress his bosses. Why you asking about Ike Ransom?"

"It's not important." I stand. "I think that's enough questions for now."

Althea studies me for a few moments, then stands and presses her shorts flat against her thighs. "Come out to the garden and let me get you some tomatoes."

"Oh, no. But thank you."

"Nonsense. Your daddy *loves* my tomatoes. I been paying him in tomatoes for years."

I follow her to the kitchen, where she picks up a Piggly Wiggly sack and goes out the back door.

The backyard is bordered by woods, and most of the yard is taken up by a vegetable garden laid out with architectural precision. The vines along the ground are bursting with squash and rattlesnake watermelons, and the tomato plants stand four feet tall. Toward the back rows I see butter beans, corn, collards, and pole beans. The only eyesore is a rusted, weed-grown husk of a car sitting up on blocks on the near side of the garden.

Althea pulls a red bandanna from her back pocket, ties it around her head, and walks between two rows of tomato plants. I check the junker for obvious wasp nests, then climb onto its trunk and watch Althea pick prize specimens for her sack.

"This is some garden," I call after her.

"Daddy always had a garden. Drove Mama crazy. We had mason jars stacked to the ceiling at canning time."

The low rumble of a truck passing on the road breaks the stillness, then fades. I wish Annie were here to see the garden.

"I don't know why I keep that old wreck," Althea says from among the plants. "It makes me sad more than anything. But sometimes it reminds me of the times me and Del went riding out by the river, when we were young. We'd roll down the windows and cruise up the levee road, listening to Nat Cole. Del would have his arm around me, and it was like nobody could touch us. We could do anything we wanted, you know? Go anywhere. It was just a dream, but it was a good one."

I feel a strange heat at the back of my neck. For the first time I really look at the car I am sitting on. It's a Ford Fairlane. A white sedan, maybe a '61. I slide off it slowly.

"Is this . . . ?"

"I thought you recognized it when you first saw it," Althea says, stepping out of the rows. "From the newspaper picture."

"I guess it's the rust," I say distractedly.

The Fairlane's hood is lying crossways over the engine compartment. I put my hands under the hot metal and flip the hood off the car. Several dessicated wasp nests cling to the fender wells, but it's not the wasp nests that send a chill through me. The Ford's engine is a mass of mangled metal. The bomb that killed Del Payton was set between the engine block and the firewall. The explosion blew the motor forward, breaking the mounts, tore the transmission away from the bell housing, and cut a fissure through the lower part of the firewall. I can't believe Payton survived two seconds after that blast. Even the engine block shows signs of shearing, and the whole compartment is littered with tiny metal fragments. The exhaust manifold was sliced in two like a length of salami. This image tickles something at the back of my mind.

"It sat rusting behind the jail for a year," Althea says. "I thought they were keeping it in case they got a clue about the bombing, but they'd just forgot about it. So I had my father tow it out here. Nothing but a home for birds and wasps now."

As I bend over the wrecked engine, something else strikes me. This car burned. I knew that, of course, from Caitlin's article, and also from the picture, but it never really registered. Rust has eaten away the charring on the exterior of the car, but the passenger compartment is a nightmare of blackened metal and melted plastic. This too has hidden significance.

"What do you see?" Althea asks.

"I'm not sure."

Alarms are ringing now. I don't know the significance of what I am seeing, but I know with utter certainty that it *is* significant. And I know a man who can tell me why. While researching my third novel, I spent two days with a BATF explosives expert named Huey Moak. Huey showed me a lot of photographs and even more pieces of stretched and twisted metal. What I'm seeing now, I saw in some of those photos.

"Do you mind if I borrow a piece of this engine?"

"Take the whole car if it will help."

Reaching down into the mass of metal debris, I pull out a flat piece about two inches square, sheared off as cleanly as if it had been cut by a blowtorch. I slip this into my pocket, then rake a handful of tiny shrapnel off the top of a smashed and corroded Triton battery. Like his coworkers, Del Payton got his batteries at a sixty percent discount from the company.

"May I borrow your bandanna?"

Althea unties the red cloth from her head and hands it to me. I lay it on the roof of the Fairlane, set the shrapnel in it, and tie the cloth into a tight sack.

"Thanks. I'd better get going."

"You've seen something," she says. "You're excited. I can tell."

"Yes, but I don't know what it means. I'll let you know as soon as I do."

She looks into my eyes, then nods. "All right. I'll walk you to your car."

As we round the house, a battered pickup pulls into the drive. Three black kids stand in back, looking over the roof of the cab. Two girls and a boy. The truck wheezes to a stop, and a black man a few years younger than I gets out wearing a grease-stained jumpsuit. As he approaches, I see a white patch on his breast pocket. The word DEL is stenciled on it in red. Over his shoulder, Georgia Payton continues her purposeful rocking.

"Penn," says Althea, "this is my son, Del Junior. Del, this is Mr. Penn Cage."

I offer my hand, but the man makes no move to shake it.

"You shake this man's hand," Althea snaps in a voice crackling with maternal authority. "This the man who's going to find out who killed your daddy."

Del Jr. grudgingly holds out his hand, and I shake it. You'd have to cut a quarter inch into his palm to draw blood.

"Take the kids inside," Althea tells him.

Del Jr. jerks his head toward the house, and the children walk backward to the front door, staring at me as they go. Del looks at my father's BMW, and it's painfully easy to read his face. The money that car cost would keep his family fed and sheltered for five years. He turns and follows his kids into the house.

"He's got a lot of bitterness in his heart," Althea says.

"He's got reason to. I sure thank you for the tomatoes."

"Any time, Penn."

I get into the car and lay the bandanna on top of the police file, then wave at Georgia Payton as I drive away. She doesn't respond.

As I clear the first turn, the significance of what I saw in Del Payton's charred Fairlane bursts into my conscious mind with the brilliance of a flare. I pull onto the shoulder, park, and with shaking hands pick up the file I bought from Willie Pinder. Caitlin's article said Del's car was destroyed by dynamite. That fit with the story I'd heard all my life. But if I remember Huey Moak's drawled lectures correctly, much of what I saw five minutes ago contradicts that version of events.

For one thing, dynamited cars almost never burn. Payton's did. But it's the shearing that's important. Whatever exploded in that Fairlane attacked both engine and firewall with tremendous cutting force, like an acetylene torch completing its job in a fraction of a second. It left shrapnel no bigger than thumbtacks. And it created a flash hot enough to set fire to a car constructed with only a fraction of the plastic used in modern vehicles. I can still hear Huey's voice in my mind: *Those are characteristics of a uniquely stable, versatile, and powerful explosive that the Army calls C-4. The Russians call it Semtex. The French, plastique.* Civilians call it good old plastic explosive. . . .

Fifteen pages into the Payton file, I find the crime-scene report. Near the middle of the page a handwritten sentence reads "Bomb constructed of unknown material" in black ink. But a blue line has been drawn through the words "unknown material" and the words "commercial-grade dynamite" written above them. At the bottom of the page, a note in blue reads, "One day following the initial scene investigation, Patrolman Ray Presley discovered fragments of civilian blasting caps and wire fragments in the wooded area one hundred feet from the vehicle. Subsequent lab analysis showed traces of nitroglycerine." Nitroglycerine is one of the main ingredients in dynamite. Beneath that final note are two signatures: *Detective First Grade Henry Creel* and *Detective Ronnie Temple.*

One day after a bomb destroyed Del Payton's Fairlane, Ray Presley discovered "proof" that the bomb was made of dynamite. Thirty years later I glance into the same car and find evidence that seems to indicate something quite different. I could be wrong, of course. I know of no reason why Presley should lie about the type of bomb that destroyed Del Payton's car. And speculation is pointless until I know that he did. But that's the beauty of physical evidence. I'll get my answer. All I have to do is get that sheared fragment and sack of shrapnel to Huey Moak, then convince the BATF agent that it's in his interest to help me. And the surest way to do that is to let him know that a quick analysis could put a great deal of egg on the face of the FBI.

Though I can't see how, I am strangely certain that I've taken one step closer to Leo Marston.

CHAPTER 17

"Daddy, look at the crawdads! They've got humongous claws!"

Annie races across the patio and leaps into my arms like a thirty-pound bullet. Though petite for her age, she is wiry and strong, like her mother.

"You'd better not let one get your nose!" I warn her. "It'll thunder seven times before he turns loose."

"Your daddy's lying to you, girl," Ruby calls from beside the pool. "That's a snapping turtle he talking 'bout. Crawfish can't hurt you none."

"One already pinched my finger!" Annie cries. "It didn't even hurt."

Dad is tending a five-gallon boiler near the house, and the roar of burning propane makes my stomach rumble, a Pavlovian response that remains automatic even after twenty years away. A cooler full of live crawfish sits beside the boiling water.

"Sam Jacobs brought these by," he explains. "He went over to Catahoula Parish to look at a stripper well and brought them back. They're good-sized. Pretty too."

"Did you ask him to stay?"

"He said he had to get home, but that you

should call him one night and go get a beer."

"I could use one now."

"There's a six-pack of Corona in the fridge. Limes too. Bring me a Heineken while you're at it."

"On the way."

I walk over and hug Ruby, then go inside. My mother's in the kitchen, washing corn and potatoes for the crawfish pot. She asks how my day went, and I say something inane about how little the town has changed. During the past hour I photocopied the Del Payton police file, rented a safe deposit box and stored the original inside, bought packaging material at Fred's Dollar Store, and delivered the fragments of Del's engine to the UPS office five minutes before they closed. I also spoke to Huey Moak, whom Cilla tracked down in Lexington, Kentucky, where he is investigating an explosion at the university. Huey could not conceal his pleasure at the prospect of solving a bombing case the FBI had bungled, even if it was thirty years old. The engine fragments will arrive before noon tomorrow at the Holiday Inn where he and his BATF team are staying. All that activity left me only one task to complete: the felony I started this morning.

I carry a Heineken out to my father and sit in a lawn chair at the edge of the pool. Annie has taken two crawfish from the cooler and is trying to make them race across the patio. She quickly learns that the only direction crawfish will move under duress is backward. I sip the Corona and watch the crustacean derby while Dad purges the mudbugs in the cooler by dumping salt water over them. Mom brings out a huge bowl of new potatoes, corn, and onions, which she dumps into the steaming pot along with three bags of Zatarain's crab boil. The sharp aroma of spices fills the air, making my mouth water, and Annie stares with saucer eyes as Dad loads the wire-mesh inner boiler with brown crawfish and submerges them in the boiling water. When he hauls them out twenty minutes later, they are a flaming red-orange.

"Wow!" Annie marvels.

"Time to eat 'em!" Dad says.

Mom covers the wrought-iron patio table with newspaper, and Dad dumps the steaming crawfish onto the center, making a small mountain. I spear some potatoes and corn with a fork and make a plate for Annie, assuming she likes the look of crawfish better than she'll like the taste. But I'm wrong. She isn't strong enough to crack the tails efficiently, but with Dad peeling for her, she goes through a half pound of tails before she's done. As I watch her joyful eyes, the Payton case recedes in my mind. I should have brought Annie here right after the funeral. My mother's matter-of-fact attitude toward the mysteries of life has already brought her out of her melancholia. When Annie announces that her tummy is full, Mom leads her over to the faucet to wash the hot spices from her hands.

"Annie wants ice cream," Mom calls from the faucet. "Anybody else?"

"Y'all go ahead," Dad shouts back. "We'll clean up this mess and be inside in a minute."

He slides a cigar from his pocket and puts it in his mouth, but doesn't begin the ritual of lighting it. "You want another beer?"

"I'd better skip it. We need to take a ride."

He raises an eyebrow. "We do?"

I raise my hand and make a mock pistol with my thumb and forefinger, then drop my thumb like a hammer.

"I see. Let's clean this mess up for your mother first."

As he begins wrapping the crawfish shells in newspaper, I carry the heavy boiler to the edge of the yard to dump the water. The gun is only twenty feet away from me, in the pool house, preparing for its final journey.

I am standing in the stern of a rusty green johnboat, poling it across a cypress swamp south of town. The sky is aflame with orange and purple light, the dying sun turning the hanging moss into long black beards on the cypress limbs. The johnboat belongs to a pumper who monitors an oil well that stays underwater for much of the year. The well has been pumping for over twenty years, and the johnboat has been sitting in a thicket nearby for most of that time. Sam Jacobs pointed it out to me one summer during college.

Dad sits forward, facing me, smoking his cigar and keeping watch on the receding shoreline. Between us stands a five-gallon plastic paint bucket filled with rock-hard cement. Embedded somewhere inside it is the Smith & Wesson .38 I bought from Ray Presley this morning. Dad flips some ash into the water and speaks in a casual voice.

"A patient told me she saw my car over at Willie Pinder's house today. She asked if the ex-chief was having heart trouble again."

"God can take a rest from watching sparrows fall in Natchez," I reply. "Nothing gets by anybody here."

He laughs mirthlessly. "And a rather strange fax arrived at my office this morning. A list of names with a note at the bottom saying something about Washington."

I forgot all about the fax. "I'm sorry about that. Where is it now?"

He takes a folded piece of fax paper from his pocket. "What's it about? This list?"

"Those are FBI agents who worked out of the Jackson field office in 1968. Did you see the name Stone on it?"

He unfolds the paper and scans it, then shakes his head. "No Stone. Where'd you get that name?"

"Althea Payton remembered a sympathetic FBI man."

"And the visit to Willie Pinder?"

"Pinder had the original police file on the Payton murder. He stole it when he lost his job as chief. I bought it from him."

My father looks out over the dark water. Already the ranks of cypress trunks screen us from anyone on shore. "I know what I said yesterday. About how justice needs to be done. God knows black people have had a shitty deal for a long time. I saw things growing up in Louisiana that I'd never want to say out loud. I understand why your blood is up. You and Althea Payton have experienced one of the worst tragedies there is. Losing a spouse, I mean. But I don't think you fully appreciate the danger of what you're doing."

"I think I do. Everybody I talk to tells me to watch my back."

"That's not what I'm talking about. I'm going to be candid, son. You're not my main concern here. If a man wants to risk his life for something noble, that's his lookout. But Annie's life is something else."

The undercurrent of fear in his voice gives me pause. "Do you really think whoever killed Payton would hurt Annie or Mom?"

"Anybody who'll hide in the shadows and bomb a man is capable of anything. They're scum. Dogs. And they have the dog's pack mentality." He gives me the cold eye. "You've already been shot at. You put these people at risk for the death house at Parchman, they'll come for you the way they're surest to get you. And that's through your family."

"Who is this 'they' you're talking about? Do you have any idea?"

My father sighs and looks at the bottom of the boat, then picks up a red and white plastic fishing bob and starts working the line mechanism with his thumb. "Natchez is a good town. I've practiced here thirty-five years, and I know. But towns are like people. Even the best of us has dark places in his soul. Fears, prejudices, appetites. The capacity for sin, I suppose. Whoever's behind this Payton business is an expression of that. It could be some white-trash asshole, or our next-door neighbor. The point is, you'll never see them coming."

"Dad, if you'll listen to me for one minute, I think you'll understand why I have to do this."

"Nothing to do out here *but* listen."

"Do you know a deputy named Ike Ransom?"

"Sure. Ike the Spike. I treated his mother for years."

"He followed me home last night after the party. He wants Payton's killer punished. And he knows who it is."

"Why doesn't he do something about it, then? He was a cop for twenty years."

"He's scared."

Dad shakes his head wearily. "Over the years at least three men I know of have claimed they killed Delano Payton. Drunk rednecks like to take credit for that kind of thing. Ransom probably overheard something like that and believed it. Who does he say did it?"

"Leo Marston."

Dad's mouth drops open. "Leo Marston? That's crazy. Marston's a lot of things, but he's no racist."

"That's what I thought too. But how do you know he's not?"

"Well . . . I've seen pictures of him with Bobby Kennedy, for one thing. With Charles and Medgar Evers too. I think I even saw a shot of him with Martin Luther King."

"How do you know that wasn't just public relations?"

"In the sixties? A white man posing with the Evers boys and King?" Dad shakes his head again. "Is Livy Marston a racist?"

"No. But that doesn't prove anything."

"Sure it does. Apples don't fall far from the tree." He draws thoughtfully on his cigar. "Ike Ransom's a bad alcoholic, son. Has been for years. I think he's playing you. He knows Marston hurt our family, so that makes Marston the best way to suck you into the Payton case. He figures once you're into it, you'll go for the throat of whoever turns out to be guilty. That's what the blacks in this town want, and I don't blame them."

"I don't think blacks want that at all. Shad Johnson sure doesn't. They want that new chemical plant in here as much as anybody. I can't believe you're defending Marston."

He slaps himself like a madman as a horsefly the size of a small fighter plane attacks him, refusing to give quarter. Fearing that this battle will overturn the boat, I scramble forward and smash the insect against his shoulder.

"Thanks," he mutters. "I'm not defending that bastard. But Leo Marston destroys people. He doesn't murder them."

"You're thinking in a business context. What if it was personal? Maybe Payton and Marston had business dealings of some kind. Or maybe Payton was in a position to know something about Marston's personal affairs."

He dismisses this with a flip of his hand. "No way, no how. Different universes."

"Ike's anger felt personal to me. He *hates* Marston."

"That's a big club. Look, for all we know, Marston sent Ike Ransom's brother to jail. He could have any kind of grudge against Marston, and we wouldn't know it."

"But if Marston's *not* involved in the Payton case, how would putting me on it hurt Marston? You see? You can't have it both ways."

He groans in exasperation.

"You're looking for logic," I continue. "But

233

Marston went after you for malpractice in 1979, and we never learned why. Motives aren't always obvious."

Now he's listening.

"Leo Marston was D.A. when Payton was killed. I think that's how he's tied into it. When Willie Pinder became police chief, he started looking into Payton's murder. Very quietly, using only black officers. But before he got far, somebody warned him off the case."

"Who?"

"Ray Presley."

Dad tosses his cigar into the water, where it hisses and sputters out. "Why am I not surprised?"

"Ray told Willie that he'd tried to solve the case in sixty-eight, but that *he'd* been warned off too. He wouldn't say by whom, but it was enough to scare him off."

"That would take some doing."

"That's what Willie said. He dropped it. Didn't Presley do a lot of work for Marston in the seventies?"

"I believe he did."

"Think about it. We've got Ray Presley, a blatant racist, investigating a politically sensitive race murder while Leo Marston is D.A. I don't think it's outside the realm of possibility that Marston could have committed criminal acts under those circumstances."

"But *why?* That's what I can't see."

"I don't know."

"Wouldn't the statute of limitations have run out on anything short of murder?"

"That's right. Anything short of murder."

He looks like a sculpture in the bow of the boat, frozen in contemplation. We're two hundred yards from shore now, far enough that even a severe drought would be unlikely to uncover the swamp bottom. Even if it did, there would only be the cement-filled pail lying in the baking mud among the dead fish and loggerhead turtles. A lost anchor. Nothing else.

I lift the long pole out of the water and lay it along the gunwale of the boat. Dad starts to get up, but I motion for him to stay seated. The last thing we need is to capsize in water teeming with water moccasins, and perhaps even alligators.

I drag the heavy bucket toward the stern and lift it onto my seat, then sit beside it, flex my arms, and roll it over between my legs. After a deep breath, I slip my hands under it and stand up, using my legs for power. In seconds my arms are quivering from the weight.

"Throw it!" Dad cries.

I heave the bucket to my left and into the black water, heeling the boat hard to starboard and almost losing my balance. The splash sounds like a cannonball and showers both of us with slimy water.

"God almighty!" Dad exults. "I thought we were going over!"

"That gun is history," I say quietly. "Let's go to the house."

I pick up the pole, plunge it to the muddy bottom, and work the bow back around until it points to the dirt road where we parked Dad's pickup. High above us, a hawk circles over unseen prey. As it sails through the falling dusk, Dad says:

"Could it have been the feds who warned Ray off the Payton case?"

Despite the heat, I feel a shiver deep in my chest. Willie Pinder's remarks are playing in my head. "What makes you ask that?"

"I remember a picture from somewhere. It showed Marston and J. Edgar Hoover together. Both of them glaring into the camera like junior G-men. Marston always claimed to be a personal friend of Hoover's. That's not fashionable now, of course. But thirty years ago it was quite a coup."

I had thought I might be able to keep my father on the periphery of this case, but that's simply not practical. The fact is, I need his help. "Dad, the guy who sent me that list of FBI agents is Bureau himself. He told me a couple of disturbing things."

"Like?"

"This morning Austin Mackey requested the FBI file on Del Payton, and he was turned down. The Payton file was sealed by J. Edgar Hoover in 1968 on grounds of national security."

His eyes narrow in disbelief. *"What?"*

"Now you tell me Marston was a personal friend of Hoover's. I've already determined that Presley probably lied about the bomb that blew up Payton's car. The FBI had to know that. I don't know how it all adds up, but as district attorney, Marston had to be right in the middle of all this."

He looks toward the shore, as though trying to spot his truck against the darkness of the trees. When he answers, his voice is so soft it seems to drift out of the lap of water against the bow.

"Leo Marston put our family through hell for a year and a half. The stress damn near killed me, and it changed your mother forever."

I say nothing, wondering if he's talking to me or himself.

"The things he's done to other people . . . compromised them, bullied them. You don't know half of what he's done. I'm not a vindictive man. But to make that bastard pay for some of that . . . God, that would be justice."

He is taking himself where I wanted to take him all along.

"We'd have to find a way to protect Annie and Peggy," he says. "Around the clock."

"We can do that."

He looks back at me. "You're not in Houston anymore. You have no authority here. You can't investigate secretly. Half the town already knows what you're doing."

"The more people who know, the safer we'll be."

"Marston can apply pressure from angles you never dreamed of. But physical safety is the first priority. I know a couple of good men. Cops. Patients of mine."

"Do you really think you can trust them? Cops, I mean. Ray Presley was a cop."

Dad chuckles softly in the shadows. "They're both black. What do you think?"

CHAPTER 18

Caitlin Masters has the corner booth in Biscuits & Blues. She smiles and waves when she sees me walking through the tables. I speak to a couple of people I know, but there's no applause tonight. The restaurant is packed with diners absorbed in their own affairs.

"I'm sorry," Caitlin says, pointing at a shrimp cocktail before her. "I was starved. I couldn't wait. Have one."

"No, thanks," I reply, sitting down opposite her. She's wearing a white button-down oxford shirt and emerald drop earrings that bring out the color in her eyes. Each time I see her, I'm shocked by the way those green eyes are almost wrong for her face. The fine black hair and porcelain skin seem to call for something else. Yet the final result is a remarkable beauty.

The young waitress who asked me to sign *False Witness* the other day hurries over and asks if she can get me something to drink.

"Jenny, right?"

She blushes and nods.

"What happened to my waiter?" Caitlin asks.

"I switched tables with him. I'll take much better care of you guys."

Caitlin gives her a sidelong glance. "I'll bet you will."

"Jenny, I'd love a Corona with a lime."

"On the way." She disappears like a dark-complected elf.

"Jenny has the hots for you."

"A little starstruck, maybe. She's probably got a novel in progress upstairs."

"I don't think that's it. She watches you in a strange way." Caitlin drinks from a sweating martini glass. "Trust me. I have lethal instincts."

"You're not drinking gimlets tonight?"

"They're out of Rose's lime. So, how'd you spend this lovely day?"

"I'll tell you later. First, you owe me an explanation."

She gives me a wry look. "Why did I make such a big thing of Del Payton?"

"Yes."

"It's simple, really. My father."

"The one you grew up without?"

"That's him. When he took over the chain from *his* father, it was five dailies, all in Virginia. In twelve years he built that into thirty-four papers across the Southeast."

"I'm impressed."

She raises a cynical eyebrow. "Do you know how he did that? He went into small cities that had only one or two newspapers. If there were two, he'd buy the dominant one, then institute John Masters's Commandments, the cardinal one being, 'Don't piss off the advertisers.' He printed every detail of little league games, weddings, society parties, high school graduations — everything but controversy.

It didn't make for very informative newspapers, but it kicked profits into the stratosphere."

"Is it a public company now?"

Caitlin makes a fist and thrusts it toward the ceiling with mock fervor. "Never! Family-owned, down the line. Starting to get the picture?"

"You want to shake up Daddy's world."

"Yes. But not for some Freudian reason. Hard news is going unreported in every town where we have a newspaper. I'm instituting a new policy. At *one* paper, anyway." She takes another swallow of her martini, and her eyes flash with conviction. "From now on, hard news leads."

"The Payton murder wasn't news until you made it news."

"So, sue me. My gut tells me it's a big story, and I'm going with it."

"Good for you. It is a big story."

She freezes with a shrimp in midair.

I take my Corona from Jenny the waitress before she can set it down. "How would you like an exclusive on the solution?"

"Is that a trick question?"

"There's one condition. You print absolutely nothing until I give you the okay."

"You know who killed him?"

"Maybe. But even if I do, proving it could be difficult."

She pops the shrimp into her mouth and chews for a few moments. "I don't get it. If you don't want me to print anything, why bring me in at all?"

"Because I need your help."

"For what?"

"Research that I don't have the time or resources to do."

"What do you need to know?"

"You haven't agreed to my condition yet."

She mulls it over some more. "Why should I muzzle my paper to help you? How do I know you'll solve the case any faster than I could?"

"Do you have a copy of the original police file?"

"No. But I'm working on a request for his FBI file under the Freedom of Information Act."

"Don't bother. You won't get it. J. Edgar Hoover sealed the Payton file in 1968 for reasons of national security."

She shakes her head in disbelief. "I smelled a Pulitzer the minute you told me about this case. Okay, deal. Tell me what you want, I'll get it. Fast. But I want in on everything."

"Fair enough," I say, wondering if I mean it. A half hour ago Cilla called from Houston. After spending hours tracing the names on Peter Lutjens's list, and finding most retired or dead, she lucked into a fan of mine. He hadn't worked the Payton murder, but he remembered it. More important, he numbered Special Agent Dwight Stone, the field agent Althea Payton recalled so fondly, among his old friends. Stone is retired and living outside Crested Butte, Colorado. Cilla called him and found him friendly enough until she mentioned Del Payton, at which time Stone bluntly stated that he would not discuss the Payton case with me or anyone. I intend to test his resolution very soon.

"So, what do you want to know?" Caitlin asks.

"I need everything you can get on Leo Marston.

241

You know who he is?"

"Sure. A big-time attorney everybody calls Judge because he served on the state supreme court. I tried to get a comment from him for my Payton story, but I couldn't get through. His secretary's a cast-iron bitch."

"You should meet his wife."

"The woman who baptized you at the cocktail party?"

"That's her."

"No, thanks. Why Marston?"

"You don't need to know that yet."

She doesn't like this response. "Who else?"

I'd like a detailed bio of Ray Presley, but Caitlin can't access the kind of information I need on him. "Just start with Marston. Companies he owns, whole or in part. Personal and political connections. His tax returns if you can get them."

Jenny reappears at our table, her dark eyes watching me with a disconcerting intensity. "Have you decided?"

"I'm not really hungry," I confess, handing her my unopened menu. "I had to eat before I came. My daughter helped cook."

"How old is she?"

"Four."

"That's a fun age."

"Are they working on my ribs back there?" Caitlin asks.

"They'll be out in a minute." Jenny gives her a curt smile and heads back to her station.

"You owe me an answer too, remember?" says Caitlin. "You're the most liberal person I've met here, as far as race goes. You're a fascist on the death penalty, of course, but we'll skip that for now. How did you wind up so different from other people here?"

"It's simple, really. My father."

She puts her last shrimp in her mouth and chews slowly, her green eyes luminescent in the soft light. "Let's hear it."

"This never sees print. It's no big deal, but it's personal. That's something we need to get straight right now. If we're going to work together, some things *never* see print."

"No problem. It's in the vault."

"I remember three defining moments with my father when I was growing up. The first had to do with race. Most kids I grew up around used the word 'nigger' the same way they used 'apple' or 'Chevrolet.' So did their parents and grandparents before them. One night, at home, I used it the same way. My father got out of his chair, turned off the television, and came and sat beside me. He said, 'Son, I grew up working in a creosote plant right alongside colored people. And they're just like you and me. No better, no worse. We don't say that word in this house.' Then he turned the TV back on. And I stopped saying nigger.

"A couple of years later, the thing to be was a hippie, and I tried my best. Grew my hair down my back, smoked grass, the whole bit. I heard hippies on TV saying the 'pigs' this, the 'pigs' that. The cops, you know? So, one day, riding in the car, I said something about the pigs. My father pulled onto the shoulder, turned around, and said, 'Son, if we had to go three days in this country without police, it wouldn't be a place you'd want to live. We don't use that word.' And I never used it again."

Caitlin's eyes shine with fascination. "And the third moment?"

"I was fifteen, and I'd been sleeping with this older girl from the public school who went off to junior college. I stole the family car a couple of times to go see her. In the kitchen one night my mother told me I couldn't do that anymore. In my hormone-intoxicated state, I said, 'Mom, why are you being such a bitch about this?' "

"Oh, my God."

"My dad clocked me. This man of reason who had never lifted a finger to me slapped me an open-handed blow that damn near blacked me out. I was spiritually stunned. But it was the right blow at the right moment. The only one I ever needed. It drew the line for me."

Caitlin nods slowly, a smile on her lips. "Thank you for telling me that. You're lucky to have a father like that."

I wonder what she'd say if she knew that an hour ago my wonderful father and I sank a murder weapon in a swamp.

Her barbecued ribs finally arrive, and we run through a half dozen other subjects while she eats. Journalism, my law career, publishing. She grew up with money but worked hard to make her own mark. She did internships with the *New York Times* and the *Washington Post*, traveled extensively overseas, and worked a year for the *Los Angeles Times*. When she asks obliquely about the Hanratty execution, I change the subject.

"Where do you live? I don't picture you in an apartment."

She smiles and wipes her mouth with a napkin, knowing I'm evading her question. "I pretty much live at the paper. But I did buy a house on Washington Street."

"Roughing it, huh?" Washington Street is old Natchez; most of the town houses there sell for over three hundred thousand dollars.

"I need my space," she says frankly. "You should come see it. It was completely restored just before I bought it."

A wave of warmth passes over my face. Is she hinting that I should go to her house after dinner? I've been out of circulation for years, and she's only twenty-eight. In the realm of dating, she is the expert, not me.

"Do you need to get home?" she asks. "I'll bet Annie's waiting up for you."

That is what she's suggesting. I look at my watch to conceal the fact that I'm blushing. "Annie's falling asleep about now. I'm okay for a bit."

"Well . . . would you like to see it? We could have some tea and talk. Or we could just take a ride. You could show me the real Natchez."

In the dark? But the automatic rejections I've practiced since Sarah's death don't come to me. "A ride might be fun."

My answer surprises her. More than that, it makes her happy. With a smile of anticipation she signals Jenny over, asks for two go-cups, and passes her a company credit card. Jenny meets us at the front door with the ticket, and while Caitlin signs it, I say hello to a couple of people at the bar. It's strange to be back in a place where I know someone every place I go.

Stepping from the air-conditioned restaurant to the street is like putting on a mildewed coat in the jungle. October in Mississippi. In Crested Butte they're skiing right now.

"We could take my Miata," Caitlin says, "but I don't advise it. I thought a convertible would be perfect for the South, but it's too damn hot down here to use it."

"My car's right down there."

I lead her across the street, then turn right on the sidewalk, heading toward the small parking lot where I left Dad's BMW. A country dance bar is going strong on this side, and knots of people line the sidewalk for the length of the block. The club draws mainly from the Louisiana farmland across the river, hard-shell Baptist country that birthed Jimmy Swaggart and Jerry Lee Lewis. Caitlin and I weave carefully through boots and hats and clouds of cigarette smoke.

As we near the parking lot, I see four men who look a little rougher than the rest, passing around a bottle of Jack Daniel's. They're wearing oil-stained denim and caps instead of hats. Roughnecks who drove straight from the oil field to the bar, most likely. Lean, hard-muscled, burned brick red by the sun, they wear thin mustaches and suck dips of snuff while they drink. As Caitlin and I approach, one points at me.

"You oughta keep your goddamn mouth shut about the niggers in this town, Cage."

The use of my name surprises me, but I have no intention of stopping to discuss the issue. Feeling Caitlin slow down, I squeeze her arm and keep walking.

"You're fucking up the chemical plant deal," says another.

Now that we're closer, I recognize the man who spoke first. His name is Spurling. A year older than I, he attended the White Citizens' Council school on the north side of town. Spurling has the sullen expression of a man for whom life holds few happy surprises. He will fight me on the slightest provocation, and probably on none. These guys have never gotten past the emotional age of fifteen. They brawl over disputed calls at little league games, beat up homosexuals for fun, and shoot each other over marital infidelities.

"Keep walking," I whisper to Caitlin, and we pass them with only a brush on the shoulder.

"I'm talking to you, cocksucker," Spurling calls after me.

"That was the newspaper chick," says a slurred voice. "That stuck-up Yankee bitch."

Caitlin stops and turns. "Why don't you dickless Neanderthals find a gun to play with? Maybe you'll do the world a favor and shoot each other."

They hoot and run after us. This is exactly what they wanted. I admire Caitlin's courage, but she is writing verbal checks that I might have to cash with blood. In seconds the four of them have formed a line between us and the parking lot.

"She's a bitch," says the one with the slurry voice. "But she's a fine bitch." He jabs a finger toward Caitlin's crotch. "I'd sure like to get in those pants."

"I already have one asshole in my pants," she retorts in a voice like a saber's edge. "Why would I want another?"

247

The roughneck blinks, thrown off balance by the ricochet comeback. But Spurling has his Academy Award–winning line ready. "How about sitting on my face when you say that?"

"If I thought you'd know what to do once I sat down, I might."

Spurling sticks out his tongue and flicks it up and down like a snake. He's trying to force me to throw a punch, which I do not especially want to do, considering the odds. Chivalry is a wonderful concept, but just now it doesn't seem the most prudent of options.

Spurling is still wiggling his tongue when Caitlin pops him across the mouth with a closed fist. He's more surprised than hurt, but he must have bitten his tongue, because he's spitting blood on the concrete.

"You thucking cunt!" he gurgles.

"Let's all take it easy!" I say, holding up my hands. "We were minding our business, walking along a public street —"

"Nobody wants you on this fucking street!" yells the one with the Jack Daniel's bottle. "Go back to Beverly Hills or wherever the fuck you live. We gotta make a living here, unlike you."

A few club patrons have noticed our exchange and are moving toward us, but they don't look like ready sources of aid. I take Caitlin's arm, spin her around, and walk her toward the BMW. She hisses something indignant, but I'm not listening to her. I'm listening for the scuff of boots on gravel.

Soon enough, I hear it.

I shove her to my right and dart left, feeling a breeze as the whiskey bottle arcs through the space my head occupied a split second ago and smashes on the gravel of the parking lot. Guessing that someone will follow the bottle forward, I whirl and throw a blind punch.

Luck is always better than skill. I hear bone crack, or maybe nasal cartilage, then a strangled scream of agony as someone hits the gravel. Throwing the car keys at Caitlin, I yell, "The black BMW!" then whirl to face the other three, who jump me simultaneously.

We're wrestling more than fighting, but once they get me on the ground, they'll remove my teeth two at a time.

"She bit me!" someone screams. *"She bit my fucking ear off!"*

I would probably laugh had not serious blows begun landing on my skull. My thoughts instantly evaporate into survival instinct as I cover my head and try to keep my feet.

A wallop to my right temple obliterates my sense of balance, and I drop to my knees, glimpsing the silver toe cap of a boot just before it savages my ribs. Another head blow puts me on my back, and the fists come down in a steady hail. I see white flashes of light, and my ears are roaring. You hope you black out at a time like this, but I'm not that lucky. Every fist feels like I walked into a steel pole.

Suddenly a new sound breaks through the fog in my jiggling brain. A brief, percussive *pock*. Again: *pock-pock*. At first I think it's the sound of something hitting my skull, but no one is hitting me anymore, yet the sound goes on. *Pock! Pock-pock!*

Rolling onto my side, I see three men cowering against a brick wall. A large uniformed man stands over them, hammering them mercilessly with a stick.

Deputy Ike Ransom.

Ike the Spike is beating Spurling and his redneck posse like willful dogs, his baton cracking shins, shoulders, elbows, and skulls with surgical precision. The flashing lights I saw must have been the arrival of his squad car.

"Penn? Penn, can you hear me?"

It's Caitlin. Soft hands try to pull me to my feet, but they haven't the strength to lift my frame.

"Count to five!" she orders, her voice electrified by fear.

"Is that what they teach you at Radcliffe?" I croak, wobbling to my feet. "I'm surprised you're not over there screaming about police brutality."

"Screw them. They need to learn some respect for women."

Two roughnecks have fallen facedown, but Ike shows no inclination to stop what he's doing. Spurling makes the mistake of lunging at the deputy and screaming "nigger," which earns him a sweeping baseball-style lick that lays him out flat on the ground.

"Ike!" I yell. "Stop it, man!"

Caitlin and I run toward him, but I'm not about to try to grab his baton. In his present state he might not be able to distinguish between white faces quickly enough to spare me a concussion. Caitlin isn't so timid. She steps between Ike and his targets and holds up both hands, creating a sight arresting enough to paralyze the deputy. Ike lowers his baton and turns to me, his eyes filled with sweat.

"You'd best get out of here quick. Police won't be long."

Now isn't the time for extended thank-yous. I take Caitlin's arm and hobble toward the driver's door of the BMW.

"You're not driving," she says. "Give me the keys."

"I'm fine."

"You took at least ten blows to the head. Your nose is bleeding. I'm driving you to the hospital."

"My father can check me out when I get home. Get in the car!"

She scrambles over the driver's seat to the other side. I crank the car and pull slowly out of the lot. Ike's cruiser is already gone.

One circuit of the block takes me to Caitlin's green Miata, and I park in the street beside it. Double-parking is an old Natchez tradition.

"I can't believe you bit that guy," I tell her, rubbing the back of my skull. "You fight more like a bar girl from Breaux Bridge than a blueblood from Boston."

"When in Rome, right?" She slaps her thighs and yells, "*Whooooooo,* what a rush! That's the most fun I've had with my clothes on in a long time."

"Yeah, loads of fun," I mutter, but her excitement is contagious. Her face is flushed like a sprinter's, and her breath comes in short gasps.

"I assume that deputy was a friend of yours?"

"I'd say he's a friend of ours." I give her a hard look. "We still have a deal, right? No story about that little altercation in tomorrow's paper?"

"Absolutely. No story." She pokes me in the shoulder. "I told you I could hold my own."

251

"I'm afraid that was just the first round. It'll get a lot worse."

Her smile doesn't waver. "We can handle it." She gets out of the car and closes the door, then leans into the open passenger window. "Would you be furious if I asked a personal question?"

"Go ahead."

"Have you thought much about our kiss since last night?"

I'm glad for the dark. The black veil of her hair gleams in the window, framing her porcelain face, setting off her lips and eyes.

"Please tell me to drop dead if I'm out of line," she says quickly. "It's just . . . I've been thinking about it. It literally curled my toes. And I wanted you to know that."

A pulse of pure pleasure spreads outward from my heart. How do I answer? *Yes, I've thought about it a hundred times, in a way that's not even thought but a constant awareness of how your mouth opened to mine, the coolness and knowingness of it —*

"Would you like to go to Colorado with me tomorrow?"

She opens her mouth but makes no sound.

"I'm flying up to talk to the lead FBI agent on the Del Payton case in 1968. But part of your job will be baby-sitting Annie. She's coming along."

Caitlin is shaking her head in confusion. "Is this trip business or pleasure? Or a baby-sitting job?"

"I'm sorry — I didn't put that very well. It's business, but I'm taking Annie along for her safety, and we have a stop to make on the way. A place I can't take her."

"Where?"

252

"Huntsville, Texas. The Hanratty execution."

Her eyes go wide. "Are you serious?"

"Yes. You can be there when I interview the agent, but I need you to stay at the hotel with Annie during the execution."

"The hottest ticket in journalism this week, and I'm going to be baby-sitting?"

"They wouldn't let you in the witness room anyway. It's your call."

She purses her lips in thought. "I'm still not sure how to think of this. Do you *want* me to come?"

"Very much."

"Then I will. But what if Annie won't stay in the hotel without you there?"

"Then I'll skip the execution. I don't really want to see it anyway."

"She'll be fine with me. We got along great on the plane. Hey, what's this FBI agent's name?"

Caitlin's mention of that flight makes me remember her deception about her identity, and this makes me hesitant to confide Stone's name. I wipe my bloody nose on my shirtsleeve and look through the windshield.

"Penn, I could have the guy's life story before we ever talk to him."

She has a point. "Dwight Stone. Crested Butte, Colorado."

"That wasn't so hard, was it?" Her eyes are almost mocking, but they hold more understanding than I have seen in a long time.

"The answer to your earlier question is yes. I've thought about it since last night."

A serene smile lights Caitlin's face.

"And I'd like to kiss you again."

Her smile broadens.

"May I?"

She leans through the window and across the passenger seat, her eyes not closed like last night but open, inviting me into them. Our lips touch, and a perfect echo of the warmth I felt last night rolls through me. This kiss is passionate but more intimate, the crossing of another boundary together. She pulls back and peers into my eyes, then closes hers and kisses me once more.

When she pulls away this time, she has a Charlie Chaplin mustache.

"You've got blood on your lip."

"My first war wound," she laughs. "It'll wash off. What time do we leave?"

"Seven-thirty for the drive to Baton Rouge Airport."

She touches her forefinger to my nose, then pulls back through the window. "Pick me up at the paper. I'll be ready."

CHAPTER 19

The trip to Baton Rouge airport takes eighty minutes, just enough time for Annie to adopt Caitlin as a big sister. Caitlin seems to know every TV character Annie does, outlandish names I can never keep up with but which Caitlin rattles off like the names of old friends. When I asked my mother if she thought Annie was ready for a trip to Colorado with Caitlin and me, she said, "Annie's ready. Just make sure you are." When I asked what this meant, she gave me one of her looks and said, "Am I wrong, or is this the first extended time you've spent with a woman since Sarah died?" I told her she wasn't wrong. "Just don't rush it," she advised. "Even chitlins smell good to a starving man." Caitlin Masters is a long way from chitterlings, but there's no point in trying to explain this to my mother.

The short-term parking lot is easy walking distance from the Baton Rouge terminal. I carry the suitcases, Caitlin the carry-ons, and Annie her pink backpack. We check our bags at the door and go straight to our gate, only to find that our plane, which is parked at the gate, is running twenty minutes behind schedule. As irate passengers begin to deplane, Annie announces that she has to tee-tee, and Caitlin escorts her off to the ladies' room. I'm absently watching the gate when Olivia Marston walks through it.

I know it's Livy because of the sudden tightness in my chest. Also because the plane just flew in from Atlanta, her home for the past thirteen years. As soon as she clears the gate, she steps out of line and starts past the other passengers, not rushing but somehow overtaking businessmen who have five inches on her. Southern belles are notorious for traveling heavy; Livy travels light. Yet the single overhead-sized suitcase rolling behind her will contain a color-coordinated ensemble versatile enough to get her through every social event from a luau to a formal ball.

A belle by birth, Livy matured into something altogether different. The beauty of belles is a soft beauty: pliant curves and shapely baby fat. Livy is leaner, with enough sculpted cheekbone to separate her utterly from the peach-skinned debutantes who fill the ranks of the Junior League below the Mason-Dixon line. Her eyes are a deep and brilliant blue, and the tailored jacket and skirt she's wearing bring out their color just as she intended.

Her name is actually Livy Sutter now, but I live in such denial about her marriage that the name Sutter never really registered. I remember it only on those rare occasions when I pass through Atlanta on business and in the tipsy midnight of a lonely hotel room pick up the phone book and flirt with the idea of calling. Of course, I never have. *Oh, John, that was Penn Cage, the writer. He's an old friend from Natchez. . . .* I'd rather die than be another "old friend" of Livy Marston's. Have good old John think of me with pity, knowing that every heterosexual man who ever met his wife fell in love with her to some degree. As far afield as Montreal and Los Angeles, I've had lawyers — upon learning that I'm originally from Natchez — come alive with questions about the fantastic Livy Sutter. Do I know her? Isn't she remarkable? Unique? Different somehow? That was certainly the opinion of the Pulitzer prize–winning writer-in-residence who made a fool of himself (in his sixties, no less) and ruined his marriage over Livy when she was a junior at UVA.

Twenty yards away from me, Livy slows and pans the concourse. She has her father's survival instincts. Her eyes pass over me, then return.

"Penn Cage," she says, without the slightest doubt that it's me.

"Hello, Livy."

She walks toward me with a smile that cuts right through resentment and regret. Her hair is the color of winter wheat in summer and just touches her shoulders, looking much as it did during high school. The last time I saw her (at Sarah's funeral) she had a short, severe, lady-lawyer cut. She must have been growing it out ever since. I like it much better this way. Probably because it fits the images that haunt my dreams.

"My God, what happened to you?" she asks.

For a moment I'm confused, but it's the bruises she's noticed. Last night's altercation left me looking quite a bit worse for wear.

"I ran into the welcome wagon."

She shakes her head as though this is about what

she would expect from me, then leans forward. Livy is a big hugger, but I have never submitted to this. Her hugs somehow put you at a remove even as they seem to pull you in. Remembering my aversion, she drops one hand and squeezes my wrist with an intimate pressure, her eyes already working their subversive spell upon me, blurring my critical faculties, creating a juvenile desire in me to please her, to make those blue eyes shine.

"What are you doing here?" I ask.

"I'm on my way home. To Natchez, I mean. My mother's having health problems. Dad's been after me to come visit, so when he called this time, I decided to spend a few days with them."

Her health was good enough to toss a drink in my face two nights ago, I think. Maybe "health" is a euphemism for alcoholism. If they intend to try an intervention with Maude, I don't want to be within a hundred miles of it. In fact, I'd recommend Kevlar body armor to the participants.

"What about you?" Livy asks.

"I'm on my way to Huntsville Prison."

"Oh, God, the Hanratty thing. It's all over the news. Midnight tonight, right? Are you required to be there?"

"No. The victim's family wants me there."

She shakes her head. "You always were one for duty." In a lighter voice she says, "I still see your books in all the airports. And it still makes me jealous."

"Come on."

"I mean it. I make great money, but I'm compromising every day for it. You're living the life you always talked about."

"You talked about that kind of life too."

She blushes, but before she can reply Annie is tugging my trouser leg. I reach down and scoop her into my arms. "Hey, punkin! You remember Miss Livy?"

Annie solemnly moves her head from side to side. I was stupid to think she'd remember anyone from the funeral.

"My hair was shorter then," Livy tells her. Like Caitlin, she makes no attempt to talk baby talk. "I sure remember *you*, Anna Louise."

I can't believe she remembers Annie's full name. The female memory defies explanation.

Suddenly something brushes my shoulder. It's Caitlin, holding out her hand to Livy.

"Caitlin Masters," she says, cutting her eyes at me as she gives Livy a professional smile.

"I'm sorry," I apologize, far too late.

"Liv Sutter," Livy says, giving Caitlin's hand a firm shake.

Liv Sutter. Another thing I'd forgotten: Livy's name metamorphosed as she progressed through life. She wasn't like a Matt who suddenly insisted on being called Matthew to be taken more seriously. Her name actually got shorter with each incarnation: "Olivia" in grade school; "Livy" in high school; and just plain "Liv" in college and law school. And there was never any question of people not taking her seriously — Livy Marston Sutter is as serious as a garrote.

"You two obviously know each other," says Caitlin.

"Oh, we go way back," Livy explains, laughing. "Too far back to think about."

"We only go back a couple of days," Caitlin replies. "But we're looking forward to Colorado."

There's nothing quite like the meeting of two beautiful women of the same class. I would never have guessed that Caitlin had a catty side. Livy is ten years older but gives up nothing in any department. The friction is automatic.

"How's John?" I ask as Livy studies me with new interest. "Her husband," I add for Caitlin's benefit.

"We're separated. Six weeks now."

So, Sam Jacobs's gossip was accurate. "I'm sorry."

"Don't be. I should have gotten out of it five years ago."

This bombshell leaves me tingling with a sense of unreality. We all stand around feeling awkward until Caitlin takes Annie from my arms, points at the broad picture window, and says, "Let's go look at those big airplanes!"

They're quickly swallowed by the crowd, but not before Caitlin gives me a reproving look over her shoulder.

"Who was that?" Livy asks.

"The new publisher of the *Examiner*."

"You're kidding."

"Her father owns the chain."

"Ah." Livy feels comfortably superior again. "Nepotism run amok. She doesn't seem your type."

And what's my type? Dead saints and ghosts from my youth? "I think my type is changing. Rich heiresses seem like a good place to start."

Livy gives me a look intended to make me feel

guilty, but we share too much history for me to be taken in by that.

"How long will you be in Colorado?"

"A couple of days."

"Call me when you get back. We should get together and talk."

We should? "Why don't you call me? Then I can skip speaking to your father."

She lets this pass. "I will. Wait and see."

"I'd better find Annie. We'll be boarding soon."

She reaches out and takes my hand. "It's strange, isn't it?"

"What?"

"Twenty years after high school, and suddenly we're both free."

I can't believe she said it. Gave voice to something I would not even allow myself to think. "There's a difference, Livy. I didn't want to be free."

She pales, but quickly recovers and squeezes my hand. "I know you didn't. I'm sorry. I didn't mean to put it that way."

I take back my hand. "I know. I'm sorry too. I've got to run."

I turn to go in search of Annie and Caitlin, but after ten steps I stop and look back. I don't want to. I have to.

Livy hasn't moved. She's looking right at me with a provocative expression of both regret and hope. She holds up her right hand in farewell, then turns and disappears into the crowd.

"Daddy, was that lady a movie star?"

Annie and Caitlin have reappeared at my side.

"No, punkin. Just someone I went to school with."

"She looks like somebody on TV."

She probably does. Livy is a living archetype of American good looks: not a Mary Tyler Moore but a warmer, more accessible Grace Kelly. A *Southern* Grace Kelly.

"*I* didn't think she looked like a movie star," Caitlin announces.

"What do you think she looks like?" I ask, not sure I want to hear the answer.

"A self-important B-I-T-C-H."

"Hey," Annie complains. "What's that spell?"

"*Witch*," says Caitlin, tickling her under the arms, which triggers explosive giggles. "The Masters intuition never fails," she adds, looking up at me. "You've got it bad for her, don't you?"

"What? Hell, no."

"Daddy said a bad word!" Annie cries.

"Daddy told a fib," says Caitlin. "And that's worse."

"I think I need a drink."

The ticket agent announces that first class will begin boarding immediately.

"First love?" Caitlin asks in a casual voice as we move through the mass of passengers funneling toward the gate.

"It's a long story."

She nods, her eyes knowing. "If short stuff here goes to sleep on the plane, that's a story I wouldn't mind hearing."

Perfect.

Airplanes work like a sedative on Annie. After drinking a Sprite and eating a bag of honey-roasted peanuts, she curls up next to Caitlin and zonks out. At Caitlin's suggestion, I move her across the aisle to my seat and, when she begins to snore again, move back across the aisle beside Caitlin.

"You're going to make me drag it out of you?" she says.

I say nothing for a moment. Certain relationships do not lend themselves to conversational description. Emotions are by nature amorphous. When confined to words, our longings and passions, our rebellions and humiliations often seem melodramatic, trivial, or even pathetic. But if Caitlin is going to help me destroy Leo Marston, she needs to know the history.

"Every high school class has a Livy Marston," I begin. "But Livy was special. Everyone who ever met her knew that."

"Marston? She said her name was Sutter."

"Her maiden name was Marston."

"Marston . . . *Marston*. The guy you asked me to check out? The D.A. when Payton was killed? Judge Marston?"

"He's Livy's father."

"God, it's so incestuous down here."

"Like Boston?"

"Worse."

Caitlin calls the flight attendant and orders a gimlet, but this is beyond the resources of the galley. There seems to be a nationwide shortage of Rose's Lime Juice. She orders a martini instead.

"So," she says, "what made her so special?"

"How many people were in your graduating class?"

"About three hundred."

263

"Mine had thirty-two. And most of those had been together since nursery school. It was like an extended family. We watched each other grow up for fourteen years. And those thirty-two people did some extraordinary things."

"Such as?"

"Well, there's high school, and then there's life. Out of thirty-two people we had six doctors, ten lawyers, a photographer who won the Pulitzer last year —"

"And you," she finishes. "Best-selling novelist and legal eagle."

"Every class thinks it's special, of course. But in a town as small as Natchez, and a school as small as St. Stephens, you have to have something like a genetic accident to get a class like ours. Our football team had eighteen people on it. Everyone played both ways. And we were ranked in the top ten in the state in the rankings of public schools. That's ranked against schools like yours, with seventy players on the squad. Our baseball team was the first single-A team in the history of Mississippi to win the overall state title."

She rolls her eyes. "So you were big-time in Mississippi sports. Let's call CNN."

"Sports means a lot in high school."

"What about academics?"

"Second-highest SATs in the state."

"When do we get to Miss Perfect?"

"Livy was the center of all that. The star everyone revolved around. Homecoming queen, head cheerleader, valedictorian . . . you name it, she was it."

Caitlin groans. "Gag me with a soup ladle."

"If you plop most high school queens down at a major university, they'll disappear like daisies at a flower show. Not Livy. She was head cheerleader at Virginia, president of the Tri-Delts, *and* made law review at the UVA law school."

"She sounds schizophrenic."

"She probably is. She was born to a man who wanted sons, in a decade when the cultural dynamic of the fifties was still alive and kicking in the South. She was a brilliant and beautiful girl with a mother who thought in terms of her marrying well and a father who wanted her to be president. She killed a ten-point buck when she was eleven years old, just to prove she could do anything a boy could."

"Spare me the body count. I suppose she graduated, won the Nobel prize, and raised two-point-five perfect kids?"

I can't help but laugh at the animosity Livy has inspired in Caitlin; it can only be based on the degree to which Livy has intimidated her. "Actually, she sold out."

Caitlin cringes in mock horror. "Not the head cheerleader of the law review?"

"She took the biggest offer right out of law school and never looked back. Chased money and power all the way."

"Who did she marry?"

"This is the part I like. She had this Howard Roark fixation. You know, the architect from Ayn Rand's *The Fountainhead*? She wanted the absolute alpha male, an artist-logician who wouldn't take any shit off her or compromise once in his life."

"Did she find him?"

"She married an entertainment lawyer in Atlanta. He represents athletes and rap singers."

"There is justice," Caitlin says, laughing. "Though I guess he made a lot more money than a Houston prosecutor."

"Twenty times more, at least."

"Why did you stay in the D.A.'s office so long? I thought most lawyers only did that for a couple of years to prep themselves for private defense work."

"That's true. Most people who stay are very different from me. Zealots, moralists. Jesuits, I call them. Military types who like to punish criminals. My boss was a lot like that."

"So, why did you stay?"

"I was accomplishing something. I felt I was a moral counterweight to those people. Some liberals even said I had an overdeveloped sense of justice. And that may be true. I convicted a lot of killers, and I don't apologize for it. I believe evil should be held accountable."

"Whoa, that was *Evil* with a capital E."

"It's out there. Take my word for it."

"An overdeveloped sense of justice. Is that why you're investigating the Payton case?"

"No. I'm doing that because of Livy Marston."

Caitlin looks like I hit her in the head with a hammer. "What the hell are you talking about?"

I lean into the aisle and signal the flight attendant; it's time for a Scotch. "Twenty years ago Livy's father used every bit of his power to try to destroy my father. He didn't succeed, but he separated Livy and me forever. And I never knew why."

"And you think Marston is involved in the Payton murder?"

"Yes."

"God, I'm trapped in a Southern gothic novel."

"You asked for it."

She finishes off her martini in a gulp. "I hope nobody's going to ask me to squeal like a pig."

I laugh as she orders another martini, amazed by how quickly the age difference between us has become irrelevant. I wonder how far apart we really are. Does she know that John Lennon and Paul McCartney were the greatest songwriters who ever lived? That the pseudo-nihilism of Generation X was merely frustrated narcissism? That I, at thirty-eight years old, am as trapped in my own era as a septuagenarian humming "Don't Sit Under the Apple Tree With Anyone Else But Me" and dreaming of the agony of Anzio is trapped in his?

"Back up," Caitlin says. "You and Livy were high school sweethearts?"

"No. For most of high school we were competitors. She only dated older guys, and no one steadily. She was her own person. She never wore a boy's letter jacket or class ring. She needed nothing external to define her or make her feel accepted. But at some point we both realized we were destined for bigger futures than most people we knew. We were going to leave that town far behind. That awareness inevitably pulled us together. We both loved literature and music, both excelled in all our classes. We dated for four months at the end of our senior year. We were both going to Ole Miss in the fall, but she was going to Radcliffe for the summer —"

"Oh, my God," Caitlin exclaims. "That magnolia blossom actually darkened the door of Radcliffe?"

"Aced every class, I'm sure. She wouldn't let Yankees feel superior to her for a second."

Caitlin makes a wry face, then sips her martini and looks out her window. "Was she good in bed?"

"A gentleman never tells."

She turns and punches my shoulder. "Jerk."

"What would you guess?"

"Probably. She has the intensity for it."

Yes . . .

"How did her father split you up?"

"He took a malpractice case against my father and pressed it to the wall. My dad was exonerated, but the trial was so brutal it nearly broke him. There was no way Livy and I could work through that."

Caitlin is watching me intently. "You're leaving a lot out, aren't you?"

Of course I am. How do we explain the abiding mysteries of our lives? "Livy never showed up at Ole Miss," I say softly. "She disappeared. Fell off the face of the planet. Her parents told people she'd gone to Paris to study at the Sorbonne, but I called to check, and they had no record of her. A year later word filtered out that she'd just entered the University of Virginia as a freshman. I have no idea where she spent the previous year, and neither does anyone else."

"Maybe she got pregnant. Went off and had the baby somewhere."

"I thought about that. But this was the late seventies, not the fifties. Her older sister had gotten pregnant a few years before, and she had an abortion, even though they were Catholic. Livy would have done the same thing. She wouldn't have let

268

anything slow down her career." There's another reason I'm sure pregnancy is not the answer, but there's no point in getting clinical about it.

"Why did she go to the University of Virginia?"

"I think because it was far from Mississippi but still the South. She got an unlisted number, cut herself off from her old friends. By the time my father's trial got going, I didn't care anymore."

"You didn't ask her why her father was going after yours?"

This memory is one of my worst. "I flew up to Charlottesville a week before the trial, to try to get her to make Leo drop the case. My dad had already had a heart attack from the stress. She said she thought it was just a normal case, and that her father wouldn't listen to her opinion anyway. She was back in her high school queen mode, winning hearts and minds at UVA. It was like talking to a stranger." I take a burning sip of Scotch. "I wanted to kill her."

"Yes, but you loved her. You're still in love with her."

"No."

Caitlin smiles, not without empathy. "You are. You always will be."

"That's a depressing thought."

"No. Just recognize it and move on. Livy's not the person you think she is. Nobody could be. And you'd better be careful. She just separated from her husband, and you're still grieving over your wife. She could really mess you up."

"I'm no babe in the woods, Caitlin."

Her smile is timeless. All men are babes in the woods, it says. "You're trying to destroy *her* father now. How do you think she'll react to that?"

"I don't know. She has a love-hate relationship with him. It's like something out of Aeschylus. She knows he's done terrible things, but in some ways she's just like him."

"You should try very hard to keep that in mind."

"Why?"

She takes a pair of headphones from her lap, plugs them into the seat jack, and starts flipping through her channel guide. "How long has it been since you've seen her?"

"She came to my wife's funeral. We only spoke for a moment, though."

"Before that."

"A long time. Maybe seventeen years."

"You pull the lid off something that might get her father charged with capital murder, and suddenly she shows up like magic?"

"What are you saying? That her father called her to Natchez to . . . to influence me somehow? Because of your newspaper story?"

Caitlin shrugs. "I don't want to upset you, but that's what I'm saying."

She gives me a sad smile and puts on the headphones.

CHAPTER 20

I thought I was the last person to arrive in the witness room at Huntsville Prison until FBI Director John Portman walked in, flanked by two field agents who shadowed him like centurions guarding an emperor. Up to that point the preparations for the execution had proceeded with the tense banality that characterizes them all.

I had arrived to find the room nearly full. My old boss, Joe Cantor, motioned me to the empty chair beside Mrs. Givens, the closest relative of the victims. The curtain was drawn over the window of the extermination chamber, but I knew Arthur Lee Hanratty was already strapped to the gurney behind it, while a technician searched for veins good enough to take large-bore IV lines.

I hadn't seen Mrs. Givens for eight years, but the smell of cigarettes on her clothes brought back everything, a nervous woman who chain-smoked through every pretrial meeting and rushed for the courthouse door at every recess. She had a Bible in her lap tonight, open to Job. When I touched her hand, she clenched my wrist and asked if I'd seen many executions before, and if they were difficult to watch. In a quiet voice, I explained the procedure: sodium thiopental to shut down Hanratty's brain; Pavulon to paralyze him and stop his breathing; potassium chloride to stop his heart.

"You mean they put him to sleep before they give the bad chemicals?"

"Yes, ma'am."

"Will he be able to say anything?"

"I'm afraid so. He'll be allowed to make a final statement for the record."

She patted the leather-bound book in her lap. "I'm not going to listen. I'm going to read the Good Book then."

"That sounds like a good idea." Killers often asked forgiveness at the end, but that wasn't Hanratty's style.

That was the moment that the door at the back of the room opened. Some reporters in front of me turned around, and recognition and amazement lit their faces. I turned and froze, confronted by the most unlikely vision I thought I would see at midnight in Texas.

John Portman looks like a walking advertisement for Brooks Brothers: thin and strong but a bit stiff, handsome with a longish face framed by hair gone gracefully gray. He was fifty-five when he and I crossed swords over Arthur Lee Hanratty, but he looked forty. He scarcely looks older now. I've always sensed a Dorian Gray aura about him, as though he were committing secret sins that never registered on his countenance.

I can't imagine what he's doing here. There's no upside for him. None that I can see, anyway. Maybe it's as simple as revenge. His experience with Hanratty almost derailed his juggernaut career, and Portman definitely knows how to carry a grudge. Watching Hanratty die might give him a great deal of satisfaction.

While his guards take up positions against the wall, he walks straight to the front row and sits in the empty chair next to Joe Cantor, who looks as surprised as the rest of us. I half expect Portman to turn and give me a grim smile, but he stares straight ahead at the curtain beyond which Arthur Lee Hanratty will soon take his last breath.

As we wait in silence, I realize I'm listening for the ring of a telephone. Conditioned by movies — and by a couple of real-life experiences — I run through the dramatic possibilities: the last-minute pardon, the hard-won stay courtesy of some crusading young lawyer from the ACLU. But that won't happen tonight. Even the mob of placard-bearing demonstrators outside the walls looked smaller and more subdued than usual as I passed through it. A few hundred people chanting dispiritedly in the Texas rain. Arthur Lee Hanratty is a poster boy for capital punishment.

Suddenly the curtain is drawn back, revealing a man in an orange jumpsuit on an execution gurney, which looks like a medical exam table that has been welded to the floor. Strapped to the gurney with IV lines running saline into his arms, Hanratty doesn't look much like the madman I remember — a killer with the bunched and corded muscles of the convict weightlifter — but like every other man I've seen on that table. Helpless. Doomed. He reminds me of Ray Presley, though Hanratty has the lamplike eyes of the fanatic, not the cold rattlesnake beads of Presley.

The warden retained a good venipuncturist tonight — or else Hanratty has good veins — because the execution is proceeding on schedule. The warden stands with two guards against the wall behind the gurney. At 11:58 he steps forward and asks Hanratty if he has any final words. I once watched a man sing "Jesus Loves Me" with tears in his eyes at this point, and die with the song on his lips. But I don't think that's what's coming now.

Hanratty cranks his neck around and searches our eyes one witness at a time, like a brimstone preacher trying to put the fear of Hell into his congregation. I've always felt that the window here should be one-way glass, to prevent the killer from making eye contact with the spectators. But the families of murder victims don't want it that way. Many of them want their faces to be the last thing the condemned sees before he dies. When Hanratty finds my eyes, I give him nothing.

"Well, well, *well*," he croons from the gurney, "*everybody's* here tonight. We got Mr. Penn Cage, who got famous killing my brother and convicting my ass. We got Joe Cantor, who got reelected off Mr. Cage convicting my ass. And we got former U.S. Attorney Portman, head of the FBI. I'm flattered you came to see me off, Port. Ironic, ain't it? If you could have covered up me killing that Compton nigger like you wanted to, none of us would have to be here tonight."

The reporters devour this unexpected windfall like starving jackals. Surely, Portman must have known something like this could happen. The warden takes a step closer to the gurney. The word "nigger" has got him thinking about gagging

Hanratty, though legally the condemned man is allowed to speak freely.

"After tonight," Hanratty goes on, "there'll only be one of us Hanrattys left. But that's all right. My brother knows what to do. Some of you folks are gonna get a visit real soon. Some warm night when you least expect it, a deer slug's gonna plow right through your brain. Or maybe through your kid's brain —"

The warden motions to his guards.

"I got a right to speak!" Hanratty shouts, neck muscles straining.

The warden raises his hand, stopping the guards. He'd like to avoid being branded a fascist by the media if he can avoid it.

"*Evening,* Mrs. Givens," Hanratty says in a syrupy voice. "I'll be thinking 'bout your sister and your niece when they send me off to Jesus. I've thought about them many a night when I'm falling asleep. Yes, ma'am."

Mrs. Givens's shivering hand clenches my wrist like a claw.

"The black man is a mongrel creature," Hanratty says with a tone of regret. "But the good Lord knows a nigger wench is heaven between the sheets."

"Gag the prisoner," orders the warden.

"*All you motherfuckers gonna die worse than me!*" Hanratty shouts. "*This ain't nothing! Nothing!*"

Two guards seize Hanratty's head and fasten a black leather restraining device over his mouth and chin. The warden checks his watch and motions for the guards to follow him out of the room. Mrs. Givens isn't reading her Bible anymore. She's grip-

275

ping my left wrist like it is the handrail on a cliff, her eyes riveted to the gurney.

"Are the chemicals going in?" she asks.

"Yes, ma'am. He's got about five minutes to live."

Mrs. Givens says something under her breath.

"I beg your pardon?"

"I said, he ought to be *awake* while it happens. My people was."

Mrs. Givens doesn't notice when I lift the Bible from her lap with my free hand and take up reading where her bookmark lies.

> *Now, there was a day when the sons of God came to present themselves before the Lord, and Satan came also among them. And the Lord said to Satan, Whence comest thou? Then Satan answered the Lord and said, From going to and fro in the earth, and from walking up and down in it. And the Lord said unto Satan, Hast thou considered my servant Job, that there is none like him in the earth, a perfect and upright man, one that feareth God, and escheweth evil? Then Satan answered the Lord, and said, Doth Job fear God for nought? Hast Thou not made an hedge about him, and about his house, and about all that he hath on every side? Thou hast blessed the work of his hands, and his substance is increased in the land. But put forth thine hand now, and touch all that he hath, and he will curse thee to thy face. . . .*

As God takes Satan's suggestion and puts forth his hand, I recall with soul-searing clarity the feeling of being singled out for suffering, of sitting

276

in a plastic chair in the oncologist's office and hearing the white-coated doctor say to my wife that most terrible of words: *malignant.* Later I would learn more arcane terms, like *daughter cells* and *highly refractory* —

Suddenly everyone in the witness room is standing around me, shuffling, speaking in hushed tones. The prison doctor stands beside the gurney, listening to Hanratty's chest through a stethoscope, double-checking the leads that run to the EKG monitor. The reporters are wired — they always are at this point — unsure of their reactions even as they try to record them. No first-timer is ever ready for the banality of execution. Only we functionaries of the justice system know how depressing it really is. The doctor nods to the warden, and the warden motions for the curtain to be closed.

Mrs. Givens thanks me for coming, then moves purposefully toward the door.

"You switched to prizefighting for a living?" Joe Cantor is standing beside me, a glint of humor in his eyes.

My hand instinctively goes to my bruised eye. "I fell."

"We still miss you at the office," he says, shaking my hand with a grip reminiscent of Shad Johnson's. "Nobody works a jury the way you did, Penn."

"I wasn't working them, Joe. I was speaking from the heart."

"That's what I'm talking about. They don't teach that in school. You were also the only assistant with the balls to argue with me. I kind of miss that too, believe it or not." He leans closer. "Watch out for Portman. That prick's had a hard-on for you ever since Hanratty's trial. And call me if you ever get tired of writing books."

Then he is past me, shaking hands with someone else, working the crowd even here.

As I pass into the hall beyond the door, I find myself face to face with John Portman. His guards stand two feet behind him, their jackets unbuttoned to provide easy access to their weapons. Portman studies me with gray eyes set in his windburned face, a badge of privilege he has cultivated since youth. I decide to fire the first shot in this skirmish.

"I can't figure out what you're doing here, Portman. You must have known you were exposing yourself to something like what just happened."

"I can absorb what just happened," he replies, his voice edgier than I remember. "It was worth it to see that genetic debris put down."

A couple of reporters stop to question the FBI director, but the guards hustle them through the door.

"You're friends with Special Agent Peter Lutjens, aren't you?" Portman says.

A cold wind blows through my soul. "Just tell me."

"He's being transferred to Fargo, North Dakota. Lovely winters, I hear."

"The guy is blameless, John."

"Internal security is one of the hallmarks of the new Bureau," he replies in a PR voice. "Agent Lutjens didn't understand that."

As I wonder how Portman learned of my contact

with Lutjens, he says, "Stick your nose into Bureau business, you get rhinoplasty. It's that simple."

I usually try to avoid confrontations like this. They profit no one. But John Portman has a special place in my pantheon of dark spirits, and my guilt for what happened to Lutjens already weighs on me like a heavy stone.

"I go where the cases take me," I tell him. "And you'd do well to remember what happened the last time you went up against me."

After years of near omnipotence as a federal judge, a man becomes unused to resistance. FBI directors must enjoy similar insulation from unpleasantness, because Portman's thin lips narrow to a white line, and his eyes blaze. Before he can threaten me further, I simply walk past him and down the hall. A rush of footsteps comes after me, and a hand jerks me around.

It's Portman, his face livid. "You fucking dilettante —"

"You're not a judge anymore, Portman. You're a civil servant, serving at the pleasure of the President. And presidents are pretty sensitive to negative publicity."

His grimace morphs into a twisted smile. "You don't know what power is, Cage. But if you keep pushing, you're going to find out."

"All this over a little Mississippi murder," I murmur. "I push in Natchez, you feel it in Washington. I find that very interesting. I think a lot of people will."

This time when I walk away, Portman doesn't follow.

As I descend the staircase and cross the dark pavement outside the death house, I feel my pulse pounding in my temples. There's nothing quite like threatening the director of the FBI to get the blood circulating. I quicken my steps toward the parking lot, wanting to get out of the prison as swiftly as I can. Life is back at the hotel with Annie and Caitlin, not here at the Walls.

But Portman won't leave my thoughts. I can't shake the feeling that he came to Huntsville specifically to see me, and not Arthur Lee Hanratty. He knew he could speak to me here without appearing to have sought me out. His ruthless punishment of Peter Lutjens proves that my interest in the Payton murder has touched a bureaucratic nerve, at the very least. And at worst? I can't even guess. Anything is possible.

As I near my rental car, a couple of reporters from the witness room start shouting questions at me. Do I really believe the death penalty is a deterrent? Am I absolutely convinced of Hanratty's guilt? What were John Portman and I talking about? What was the FBI director doing here at all? I climb into the car, resisting the temptation to pour gasoline onto the fire of the Payton case. I need to think. I need to see Annie and Caitlin.

As I drive through the gate of the Walls, passing the now silent crowd standing their candlelight vigil in the rain-swept darkness, one thing comes clear to me. This is the last trip I will make to this prison. The yellow glow of the candles grows smaller in my rearview mirror. Three more men pass their days on death row because I put them here.

They will die without me present.

CHAPTER 21

When I reach the hotel, Caitlin is waiting for me with a cold can of Dr Pepper and a chicken sandwich. I'm starving. It took two hours to get back to Houston through the rain and traffic, but knowing that Annie might not go to sleep without me close kept me from stopping for food. I shouldn't have worried. She is sound asleep in one of the double beds, while the television plays CNN in muted tones. Caitlin is wearing silk pajamas that somehow look demure and sexy at the same time. I collapse at the table by the window and devour the sandwich, then drink the Dr Pepper in a few gulps. Her instincts are as accurate as always; she says nothing while I eat.

"Thank you," I tell her, tossing the sandwich wrapper into the wastepaper can. "Really."

"I saw a clip of you coming out of the prison. Was it bad?"

"Bad enough. That's the last one I go to."

"Let's change the subject, then. Annie only woke up once, and I rubbed her back till she fell asleep again."

"I really appreciate you staying with her."

"No problem. She's great." Caitlin reaches out and touches my knee. "You really look tired. You want me to go to my room so you can crash? Our flight to Gunnison leaves at eight-thirty."

We're renting a Cherokee in Gunnison for the drive up to Crested Butte. "I don't think I can get to sleep yet."

"Okay." She scoots back in her chair and folds her legs beneath her. "Let's talk business, then. Your assistant called. Your ATF friend called her and confirmed that Payton's car was destroyed by C-4 plastic explosive. They found traces of something called RDX in the shrapnel. He said there should be plenty more embedded in the metal of Payton's car. No problem to prove in court."

Half my fatigue disappears in the shot of adrenaline this produces. "So, Ray Presley planted the blasting caps and dynamite. And someone falsified the lab report."

She nods. "I've been studying your copy of the police report. It's mostly gossip, really. Wild theories. The interesting thing is that there were rumored suspects the detectives never talked to, local guys who had done other race crimes. Almost as if Creel and Temple knew those suspects weren't guilty."

"Presley may well have planted that C-4 himself. He's killed before. But for money usually. If he killed Payton, it wasn't on his own hook."

"You think he killed Payton for Leo Marston?"

"Yes."

"Where did you first get the idea Marston was involved?"

"From the deputy who saved us the other night. Ike Ransom."

"Well . . . I hope you can trust him. Because I've

282

got to tell you, everything my people have found on Marston indicates that he's a liberal, as far as race goes, anyway."

"I know. I think the murder might not have been about race at all."

Her mouth opens slightly. "What else could it have been about?"

"I don't know yet. Have your people learned anything about Dwight Stone?"

"Yes. One of our reporters in Alexandria, Virginia, says Stone was dismissed from the FBI in 1972 for alcohol-related problems."

"Anything else?"

"He was second-generation law enforcement. His father was a state trooper in Colorado. Stone himself served with the marines in Korea and won a handful of medals I don't know the significance of. He went to law school after he got out of the service, and joined the Bureau in 1956. He spent sixteen years in, and received several commendations before being dismissed."

"Althea Payton told me Stone was sympathetic to her, that he really wanted to solve the case. I wonder if the fact that they both served in Korea was the root of that?"

"I guess it could be."

"Something strange happened at the prison tonight, Caitlin."

"What?"

"The director of the FBI showed up."

"John Portman? Why would he show up at the Hanratty execution?"

"To warn me to stay out of the Del Payton case."

"*What?*"

283

"Portman and I have a history. When you asked about the Hanratty case on the plane, I left out some details. When Hanratty committed that first murder in Compton, he was seen by a dozen witnesses before he fled the scene, and they ID'd him from photographs under his real name. An LAPD detective remembered that Hanratty had been the star witness in a federal hate-crime trial a while back. His testimony put a half dozen white supremacists in jail and made a star out of the U.S. attorney of Los Angeles."

"Portman," Caitlin says softly.

"Exactly. The LAPD went to Portman, who told them Hanratty was under witness protection and couldn't have committed the crime. Political pressure started building. The next day Hanratty 'escaped' from the program and wound up in Houston with his brothers. The rumor was, Portman tried to cover up the murder to keep his reputation clean. I'm pretty sure now that it's true. Hanratty referred to it tonight in his deathbed statement. Anyway, Portman wanted to neutralize the rumor by throwing the book at Hanratty in the L.A. courts."

"And you stopped him."

"Exactly. The guy hates my guts."

"But what does that have to do with the Del Payton case?"

"I'm not sure. But Portman just killed the career of an FBI agent who gave me a little help on the phone. He's transferring him to Fargo, North Dakota. I don't think there's even a field office there. Just a resident agency. Whatever's in the Del Payton file must be embarrassing as hell to the Bureau. I want you to get your people working on Portman immediately. I want to know everything there is to know about him."

"I'll call our Alexandria guy before we fly out in the morning."

"I'm going to call that FBI agent right now. I owe him an apology."

"It's the middle of the night. And it's later in Washington."

"I doubt he's sleeping."

I pull the phone over from between the beds, dial directory assistance, then use my credit card to call Peter Lutjens at his home in Washington. His phone rings five times before he answers, but his voice is wide awake.

"Peter, this is Penn Cage."

Silence.

"I had no idea this thing would boomerang on you like this. I am so sorry."

"Shit. I don't blame you. I gave you the list, didn't I?"

"Peter, if there's anything I can do —"

"Can you get Portman fired?"

"I don't —" Suddenly an idea hits me. "Maybe I can."

"What?"

"Peter, have you wondered why Portman would punish you so severely for what you did?"

"He hates you, that's why."

"It's the Payton file. Portman flew to Huntsville, Texas, tonight to warn me off the Payton case. And asking about the Payton file is what got you into trouble. Right?"

"Yes."

"I think Portman is concealing some illegality about that case. If he is, and you can find out *what* it is —"

"Stop right there. Are you suggesting that I go back and try to look at that file myself?"

"Have they barred you from the building?"

"No, but —"

"When do you leave for Fargo?"

"Don't even say that word, goddamn it. And I'm not losing my pension for you. Cowboy time is over."

"Peter, if that file is damaging enough, it might get Portman thrown out of the directorship. It might buy your old job back."

"I've got a wife and kids. And I'm not out to trash the Bureau."

"I'll shut up, then. I really called to apologize anyway."

"That makes me feel so much better."

The phone goes dead in my hand.

Caitlin puts the phone back between the beds for me. "He wouldn't try it?"

"No."

"Let's just forget it all for tonight, then."

She picks up the remote control and flips through the channels, finally settling on a showing of *To Catch a Thief.* Grace Kelly and Cary Grant zoom across the screen in a vintage sports car.

"Okay with you?"

Staring at Grace Kelly, the coolly luminous Princess Grace, I recall my earlier thought that she and Livy Marston look more than a little alike. The similarities go deeper than looks too, for despite her cool exterior, Grace Kelly had a dark and promiscuous sexual history.

"It's fine," I say absently.

Caitlin turns up the sound, and we watch from our chairs while Annie snores away on the bed. My mind is so full I cannot think clearly, but one image is predominant: Livy Marston in the Baton Rouge airport, seemingly as beautiful and untouched as she looked at seventeen. But when is anything ever what it seems? As beautiful as Livy was, she was not untouched. No girl that radiant survives adolescence without attracting the attention of every male in the three grades above her. And nature being what it is (and the seventies what they were), sex usually follows. I didn't understand this so clearly then, of course. At sixteen, though I was as perpetually and mindlessly horny as the rest of my compatriots, I was also ready to place some lucky (or unlucky) girl on a pedestal of mythic proportions. When, after a showing of *Looking for Mr. Goodbar*, Livy tearfully confessed to me how she'd lost her virginity — a date rape by a senior with whom I played football — she installed herself on that pedestal with the permanence of a pietà.

Once she occupied this place of reverence in my psyche, it became impossible for me to see her clearly. Her public image was flawless. Queen of the elite private school in a city with five high schools, she was wanted by every male student in the city — not merely lusted after, but actually worshiped — and thus floated above the usual tortured angst of high school life. What I didn't understand then was that, to a girl like that, the most exciting company would be guys who didn't care what she said or thought, and

287

who treated her accordingly.

Everyone knew Livy Marston occasionally went out with boys from the public schools — rough, handsome guys who straddled the line between "hoods" and outright criminals — some of whom were so dumb as to boggle the mind. It was hard to imagine what Livy could find to talk about with these guys. What I didn't understand then — or was too afraid to admit — was that she was not interested in talking to them.

It was something of a tradition for St. Stephens boys to sleep with girls from the public schools, who we thought to be "looser" than the ones we saw in class every day. Whether this was true or not, I'm still not sure. Some public school girls defended their virtue like Roman vestals, while many St. Stephens girls led active romantic lives, to say the least. In any case, it was understood, according to a time-honored double standard, that boys slept around as a rite of passage into adulthood. When girls did it, they entered that unjustified but unforgiving territory known as sluthood. When Livy Marston did it, she confused everybody. To the point that no one really believed she was doing it. Everyone thought she was putting on a show. Acting wild. Driving her uptight father crazy. Now, of course, I understand it perfectly. In the time-honored tradition of Southern women of a certain class, Livy was taking her pleasures downward.

When she opened to me like a flower in the spring of our senior year, I accepted her attentions like a divine gift. For girls that age, having sex is usually so tied up in the desire to be accepted by peers that true motives are impossible to fathom. But for Livy Marston acceptance was not an issue. When she gave herself, it was because she wanted to, and that knowledge immeasurably dilated the experience. That her skills did not seem virginal I wrote off to her being as gifted sexually as she was in so many other ways. I submerged my self into hers, basked in the glow of being seen with her, of being known to be loved by her. I cared as little for what lay ahead of me as for what lay behind, and so set myself up for the fall of my life.

"Penn? Are you awake?"

I blink and look over at Caitlin. She's watching me from her chair, her face flickering in the television light.

"What are you thinking about?"

"Nothing. Everything."

An enigmatic smile. "Livy Marston?"

"God, no," I lie, thinking that Caitlin was absolutely right when she told me she had lethal instincts.

"I'm going to bed," she says, rising from her chair. "Tomorrow's a big day."

I get up to walk her to her room, amazed by how tired I feel. Witnessing death up close saps you like a day under the sun. It also stokes the sexual fires, urging toward procreation. As we stand outside her door, Caitlin looks up at me, her face tilted perfectly for a kiss, and I realize again how beautiful she is. But I no longer see her as I did last night in the restaurant. I'm looking through the distorting memory of Livy Marston. Caitlin lowers her chin, and the moment passes.

"What do you think Dwight Stone knows?" she asks.

"More than we do. Maybe he knows everything."

She opens the door and slips through without looking back, leaving me alone with my ghosts.

CHAPTER 22

Crested Butte, Colorado, is a tiny village nestled nine thousand feet in the Rocky Mountains, twenty-five miles from Aspen as the crow flies, three hours by car. The easiest way to get there is to fly into Gunnison and drive north up the valley for half an hour. But to get to former special agent Dwight Stone's cabin, you must leave the pastel storefronts of Crested Butte's old town behind and drive northwest into the mountains on a forest service road, past the summer homes of the rich, until the road turns into a jeep trail that follows the Slate River upstream between Anthracite Mesa and Schuylkill Mountain. A few hundred yards north of an eight-foot vertical drop in the river, situated in the thick fir and spruce between the jeep track and the narrow blue-black span of the Slate, stands a small but well-built cabin, facing southwest to catch the sun.

Dwight Stone likes his solitude.

When I called Stone from the Gunnison airport and asked if I could speak to him about the Payton case, he politely declined. I did not tell him where I was calling from.

That was an hour ago.

Now Caitlin and Annie and I approach his front porch like a lost family asking for directions. I'm glad we brought coats. When we left Natchez it was ninety degrees. Here it's less than fifty, and there are dark clouds glowering over the summit of Gothic Mountain to the east.

Before I can knock, a tall, fit-looking man in his late sixties clumps around the side of the cabin wearing hip waders, a Black Watch flannel shirt, and carrying a fly rod.

"You folks lost?" he asks in a deep, resonant voice.

"That depends on where we are." I've already recognized the voice, but I say, "Are you former special agent Dwight Stone?"

Stone has the eyes of a combat veteran, and they narrow instantly, assessing threat. A man with a woman and a little girl can't seem like much danger, but I don't know what his anxieties are.

"You're on my property," he points out, quite reasonably. "Why don't you introduce yourself first?"

"Fair enough. I'm Penn Cage."

His eyes relax, but he sighs wearily. "You've wasted your time, son. Flying up here to get told no to your face instead of over the phone."

"I hoped you might soften up a little when you saw us."

He shakes his head, climbs onto the porch, and leans the fly rod against the cabin wall.

"I'm not a journalist. I have no interest in sensationalizing this story."

"You're a writer, aren't you?"

"Yes, but that's not why I'm looking into this case."

"Why are you?"

My gut feeling about Dwight Stone is that if you want to get anywhere with him, honesty is the best policy. "I could say it was to help the victim's family. Althea Payton and her mother-in-law. And I do want to help them. But I also have a selfish reason. I'm trying to nail a man who hurt my father a long time ago."

Stone studies me for several seconds. "Who would that be?"

"Leo Marston. Judge Leo Marston. He was the district attorney back —"

"I know who he was." Stone eyes Caitlin. "This your wife?"

"No, a friend. Caitlin Masters. But this is my daughter. Say hello, Annie."

Annie waves her right hand while clinging to Caitlin's leg with her left.

"You bring her along for the sympathy factor?"

"I brought her to keep her out of harm's way. I've already been shot at. Not many people want the Payton case reopened."

A flicker of something in Stone's eyes. "You convicted Arthur Lee Hanratty, didn't you?"

"That's right."

"I saw you on CNN last night, at the Walls."

I nod but say nothing.

"That'll buy you a half hour of my time, Mr. Penn Cage. How about some coffee?"

"Coffee would be wonderful," Caitlin says, lifting Annie into her arms.

Stone takes a trout bag from his shoulder, then

wipes his hands on his shirt and reaches for the cabin door. "I don't get much company up here, but I think maybe we could rustle up some hot chocolate too."

Annie breaks into a wide grin.

Stone settles Caitlin and me on a sand-colored leather sofa with Annie between us. Before us is a huge fieldstone fireplace, and Stone quickly builds a roaring blaze in it. The cabin is full of hunting and fishing gear, snowshoes hanging on the walls, rifles over the mantel, a fly-tying bench littered with bright feathers. A large double-paned window faces the Slate, which runs flat and smooth thirty yards from the cabin's back door. Only a large white propane tank mars the illusion of virgin wilderness, and when there's snow it's probably invisible.

After putting the trout in his sink, Stone brings us mugs of coffee and chocolate heated on an old woodstove, then sits opposite us in a rough hand-made chair. His waders hang on a hook by the door, dripping into a brass bucket with the sound of men making use of a spittoon.

"You've got a nice place," I tell him. "No neighbors at all. How'd you manage that?"

He smiles. "Everything you see around this place is government land. But this cabin sits on a mining claim that's been in my family for three generations. Grandfathered down to the present. The federal government can't do a thing about me."

"I love it," Caitlin says.

"Thank you. Now, I heard the story Mr. Cage

told me on the telephone. Tell me what you really know about the Payton case. And why you care."

"We've read the original police file," I begin. "Informant reports, interviews, interrogations, theories."

"What did you learn from that?"

"The report was wrong about the bomb that blew up Payton's Fairlane."

If this rings a bell, Stone has one hell of a poker face. "Wrong how?"

"It said the bomb was made of dynamite, based on a patrolman discovering fragments of blasting caps, plus lab analysis."

"So?"

"I located Payton's car. It's still in decent shape, believe it or not. The damage looked more characteristic of C-4 to me. A lot of metal shearing, small shrapnel. I sent a fragment of the engine to an expert for analysis. Last night he confirmed it. C-4."

Stone nods thoughtfully. "C-4 was damn hard to come by in 1968. And your Klan boys didn't know shit about using it."

He has not directly refuted my assertion. "You're saying the expert is wrong?"

"It's happened before. But that's not what I'm saying."

"Then you're saying the Klan wasn't behind the murder."

"I didn't say that either. What kind of theories were in the report?"

"Mostly rumors. I thought one story was plausible. Someone thought Payton's death was a mistake. That the real target was the president of the local NAACP. He apparently rode to and from work with Payton a good bit."

Stone nods with familiarity. "What about the one where a black button man was hired from New Orleans to come up and pop Payton? Strictly a money hit."

This scenario had been reported to the police by a Louisiana woman. Her story was given credence because she turned down the full fifteen-thousand-dollar reward rather than give more details. She claimed she'd never live to spend the money. No further information was recorded in the file.

"Is that what you think happened?" I ask.

Stone smiles. "It *could* have happened. How old are you, Mr. Cage? Thirty-five?"

"Thirty-eight."

"Do you have any idea what things were like in 1968?"

"In Mississippi?"

"In America."

"Well . . . the country was turning against Vietnam. LBJ was being ground down by the war. Civil rights hit its high-water mark, with Martin Luther King at his peak before he —"

"I'm glad you passed your civics course," he interrupts. "I'm talking about reality, son. Behind the scenes. In 1968 a few powerful and paranoid men were trying to hold their vision of this country together in the face of social revolution. It was a tide they had no prayer of stopping, but they didn't understand that, and they used every method at their disposal to try."

As Stone speaks, I glimpse a furnace of anger seething behind his eyes. He has tight control over it, but he's been holding in that anger for years.

"The Constitution meant nothing to these men. Richard Nixon was one of them, but he was bush league compared to them."

"You're talking about J. Edgar Hoover?"

"Hoover was one of the more visible."

"How does this tie in with Del Payton?"

Stone looks from my face to Caitlin's, as though deciding whether we have earned the right to any of his hard-won knowledge. Now that I think of it, he's probably seventy years old, but his tanned, weathered face and soldier's eyes convey the strength of a much younger man.

"A lot of blacks were killed in Mississippi in the nineteen-sixties," he says in a deliberate voice. "Del Payton was one. But he was killed later than most. Have you thought about that? A lot of the race murders happened around sixty-four. Payton came later."

"What's the significance of that?"

"Just something for you to think about."

Everything's riddles with this guy. "Martin Luther King was assassinated in 1968," I point out.

He shakes his head. "I'm talking about grass-roots murders."

Caitlin looks ready to pop; she obviously has a hundred questions, but I hope she won't ask them. The harder we push Stone, the more he'll resist us. From lawyerly instinct, I move away from Del Payton and ask a question to which I already know the answer.

"Did you serve your full term of service with the Bureau? That is to say, did you retire at full pension?"

297

He takes a deep breath, and a little more anger spills through his eyes. "I'm going to answer that because you're going to find it out anyway, if you don't already know. And because I'm not ashamed to answer. I was asked to resign in 1972. Officially for alcoholism."

Caitlin nods with empathy. "Did your drinking have anything to do with the Del Payton case?"

"That I won't answer. But I'll tell you this. If every alcoholic in the Bureau in 1972 had been asked to resign, Hoover couldn't have mounted a raid on a cathouse. You had to drink just to stomach what was going on back then."

"What kind of things are you talking about?" I ask.

"You ever read *American Tabloid*, by James Ellroy?"

"No."

"Give it a look. Things weren't quite that crazy, but they were damn close."

"How did you earn a living after leaving the Bureau?"

A sour look wrinkles his face. "Worked as a private dick for a while. Big firm. That was sleazier than Hoover's Bureau, so I quit. Worked as an insurance investigator. I drank professionally for a few years. I was close to dying when my daughter pulled me back up to the light. I finally hung out my shingle here and started helping the locals fight the government and the mining companies. That suited my temperament."

"Were you in charge of the Payton investigation?"

"I was."

298

"How did you like Natchez?"

"It wasn't much like the rest of Mississippi. Better in a lot of ways. More liberal, the people more educated. But in a way that made the things that happened there worse. You know? Because there were people there who knew better."

Stone goes to the stove and returns with the coffeepot, talking as he refills our cups. "When I was assigned to that case, I was only a couple of years younger than Payton was when he died. I had a wife and two kids, and I still had a few illusions. That case knocked them right out of me."

He sets the empty pot on the stone hearth of his fireplace and takes his chair. "Do you have any illusions left, Mr. Cage?"

"Not many."

He studies me as if judging the truth of my statement.

Caitlin takes this chance to jump in. "How do you feel personally about J. Edgar Hoover?"

Stone examines his fingernails, a seemingly casual gesture calculated to hide inner turmoil. "I don't care if the man wore Frederick's of Hollywood to bed every night. I don't care if he wanted to *marry* Clyde Tolson, that pompous ground squirrel. But the man presented himself to this nation as a paragon of law and order. A champion of right. And the son of a —" Stone winces like Humphrey Bogart — "the *man* didn't know the meaning of the words. He stole from the government, misused agents for personal gain, colluded with mobsters, broke the securities laws. . . . Human beings just weren't meant to have that much power. Jesus, I need a drink."

"Go right ahead." It's barely two P.M., but I feel like I could use one too.

Stone shakes his head. "Four months sober. It's a daily battle."

Watching him get control of his craving is like watching a man fight a malarial fever. As a younger man Dwight Stone did what most Americans never do — peered behind the curtain at the men running the machine — and he is a different man because of it. America isn't the same country now, of course. It's better in a lot of ways. But I can see how this wouldn't matter to Stone. We are, all of us, men of our own eras.

"You want to destroy Leo Marston?" he asks, his eyes hard.

The name flows easily from his lips. He has thought about Marston since 1968. "Do you think that's possible?"

"Put it this way. I think it's a noble goal."

Caitlin presses her knee hard against mine. I can feel her excitement, but I don't look at her. It's suddenly as clear to me as the mountain air outside Stone's cabin: the man sitting across from us knows who killed Del Payton, and why, and probably why that knowledge was never made public.

"But it won't be easy," he adds.

"That's what someone else told me."

"Who?"

Stone is playing it so close to the vest that I decide to keep Ike Ransom's name to myself. "You wouldn't know him. He came along after your time. But he's interested in the case, and he hates Leo Marston. What can you tell us about

300

Marston's involvement?"

"Nothing more than I have already."

"Will you help us with this case?"

A deep conflict is playing itself out behind the old agent's eyes, one only hinted at by the tension in his muscles and the tightness of his lips. "I can't," he says finally.

"Why not?"

"Because despite what you see here, I'm not alone in the world. There are people I care about. I'm thinking of getting married, believe it or not. And I won't put innocent lives at risk for something that can't make any difference now."

"Do you really think there's that much danger?" asks Caitlin.

Stone rakes a hand along his jaw. "Make no mistake about it. You are already swimming with sharks."

His baleful eyes linger on mine, trying to impress his seriousness upon me. He reminds me of an old homicide cop I knew in Houston, a guy who'd been shot twice in the line of duty. When he told you to start worrying, it was time to put on the Kevlar.

"What about the Mississippi Sovereignty Commission files?" Caitlin asks. "Payton's is sealed. Do you think we could learn anything significant from it?"

"Those were state files. I never saw them."

"The FBI file is sealed as well. Does that surprise you?"

He barks a laugh. "I'd be surprised if the damn thing exists at all."

"It exists, all right," I tell him. "Forty-four vol-

301

umes. The question is, what's in it?"

"Forty-three volumes of nothing, and my final report."

"What was in your final report?"

He sighs and looks past us, to the front windows of his cabin. "I can't tell you that."

Caitlin glances at me, her lower lip pinned by her teeth, her gesture of concentration. "The file was ostensibly sealed for reasons of national security," she says. "Can you give us any hint as to what the Payton case could have to do with national security?"

Stone taps his fingers nervously on the arm of his chair. "Del Payton was killed five weeks after Martin Luther King was assassinated, and three weeks before Robert Kennedy. Have you considered that?"

Caitlin and I share a look.

"Are you saying Payton's death was somehow connected to those assassinations?" I ask.

"Kings climb to eminence over men's graves, Mr. Cage."

"Who said that?"

"A very wise man."

"Who is the king you're referring to?"

"I'm just quoting an old poet, son."

"Last night I was threatened by the present director of the FBI. Why should John Portman be concerned with a thirty-year-old civil rights murder?"

"Why do you assume Payton's death was a civil rights murder?"

At this echo of Ike Ransom, my heart twitches in my chest. "You're saying it wasn't?"

"I'm just thinking aloud."

"Have you ever met Portman?" I ask, my pulse racing.

"I met him." Stone's distaste is plain. "He joined the Bureau a few years before I got out."

"What did you think of him as an FBI agent?"

"He was a brown-nosing, manipulative, Ivy League rich boy with the moral sense of a cat. A good little German with obsessive ambition. After seven years in the field they promoted him to the Puzzle Palace."

"The Puzzle Palace?" Caitlin asks.

"The Hoover Building. FBI Headquarters. The guys who work there call it SOG. For 'Seat of Government.' It's the perfect environment for devious, back-stabbing sons of bitches. I apologize for the profanity. I forgot about your little girl."

Annie didn't hear him. She's busy examining a rock collection displayed in a glass-box end table. If she had heard him, she would have yelled, *Mr. Stone said a bad word!*

"Did you keep any personal notes from the Payton investigation?" I ask, recalling the habits of that cop Stone brought to mind a moment ago. "Something you didn't turn in to your superiors, maybe?"

His gaze wanders to the rear window, where the stream rushes along the rocks. "You want to learn what I learned back in 1968?" He looks back at me, his eyes burning into mine as though striving to communicate something he cannot say aloud. "Do what I did. Talk to the eyewitnesses. Have you done that? Have you talked to the eyewitnesses?"

I admit that I haven't.

"You didn't convict Arthur Lee Hanratty by sitting in your office, did you? Pound the bricks. Talk to everybody who'll talk and pressure those who won't. That's what we did back then. And we learned the truth."

This statement hangs in the air like a volatile gas.

"Then why didn't anyone go to jail?" Caitlin asks softly.

Stone's jaw muscles clench in an effort to control his rage. "For the same reason this country is going to hell in a handbasket. And don't ask me that again."

"What was your partner's name?"

"We didn't have partners," he says, his eyes still on me. "Not like municipal police. I worked a lot with Henry Bookbinder. He died of cirrhosis back in seventy-four."

"I know you're fond of quotes. Have you heard this one? 'You yourself are guilty of a crime when you do not punish crime.' "

Stone's right hand squeezes into a fist. "I think your half hour's up, pardner."

"May I ask you one more question?"

He stands and stretches his back muscles. "What is it?"

"Do you remember a cop named Ray Presley?"

Just before Stone's eyes glass over, I glimpse an anger even more personal than that which I have seen to this point.

"I remember him," he says in a flat voice.

"Do you think the police made an honest attempt to investigate the case?"

"That's two questions." Stone turns to Annie, who's now touching a clay pot that looks like

Pueblo work. "How'd you like that hot chocolate, little darling?"

"Mmmm. It was great!"

He walks to the door, leaving us little choice but to follow. I take Annie's hand and lead her after him.

"Sorry you folks had to come all this way for nothing," he says, opening the door to the dark vista of Gothic Mountain rising above the mesa. "Rain coming. That's October for you."

We're on the porch now. The sibilant sound of the Slate beckons from the edges of the cabin.

"I don't think it was for nothing," Caitlin says, turning to Stone with a look of absolute frankness. "I think something evil happened in Natchez in 1968. I think you know what it was. I realize we sort of ambushed you here, and I apologize for that. But we want justice for Del Payton. I think you do too." She takes a card from her pocket and passes it to Stone. "You're going to do a lot of thinking after we leave. You can reach us at this number."

His jaw tightens as he examines the card. "You're a goddamn reporter?"

"A publisher. An honest one."

He looks at me, his eyes brimming with outrage.

"She won't print a word you said," I assure him. "She won't even print your name. She prints nothing at all until this whole mess is resolved."

Stone shifts his gaze to Caitlin.

"I want the truth," she says. "The truth, and justice. Nothing else. Thank you for your time, Agent Stone."

As we walk to the Cherokee, he stands in his doorway looking — for the first time since we've seen him — a little unsure of himself. It strikes me that he liked Caitlin using his old rank. Despite all his deep-rooted anger, Stone is still proud to have been an FBI agent.

Unlocking the door, I hear the scuff of boots behind me. Stone has come down off the porch. He puts his right arm on my shoulder in a fatherly way and looks into my eyes.

"You've got too much to lose to dig into this mess, son. The world has already changed too much for it to make any difference."

"I don't agree."

A strange recognition lights his eyes, and I am suddenly sure that in me he sees a shadow of the man he was years ago. "I'd like to give you one more quote," he says. "If you don't mind."

"Whatever."

"The hour of justice does not strike on the dials of this world."

I look away from his sad eyes, wondering what could possibly have driven a man of his strength and experience into such a miasma of defeatism. "No offense, Agent Stone, but I think you've been doing too much reading and not enough soul-searching."

To my surprise, this does not anger him. He squeezes my shoulder. "You have more illusions than you think. I wish you luck."

"I wouldn't need it if you'd tell me what you know."

He shakes his head and takes a step back. "Whatever you do, you send that little girl someplace safe before you take another step. You hear?"

"That I'll do."

As he retreats to his porch, I buckle Annie into her safety seat and join Caitlin in the front. She looks at me with fire in her eyes.

"Did you catch what he said inside?"

"About Payton's murder not being about civil rights?"

"No. When you asked him if he had any personal notes he kept from his superiors."

Stone is still watching us from the porch.

"He said if we wanted to learn what he did, we should do what he did."

She nods excitedly. "Talk to the eyewitnesses, right? That was the first thing he said. He looked at you real hard. Remember?"

"Yes. Like he was trying to communicate something nonverbally. Do you know what it was?"

She gives me an almost taunting smile. *"Talk to the eyewitnesses."*

"What is it, for God's sake?"

"Penn . . . he used the plural. According to all accounts, there was only one eyewitness to the Payton bombing."

She's right. Frank Jones, the scheduling clerk. Had Dwight Stone tried to tell me — without telling me — that there was more than one witness in the Triton parking lot on the day Del Payton died?

"I told you I was good at this," she says, smiling with triumph. "Let's get out of here."

I start the Cherokee and wheel it around until we're pointed back toward the jeep track. "What did you think of Stone?"

"I think he's scared."

"Me too."

We spent the night in Gunnison. We might have rushed and made our flight, but none of us really wanted to race back to the heat of Mississippi. We took a suite at the Best Western and ate a long meal in a local steak house. Caitlin and I tried to list every possible reason Del Payton could have been murdered besides civil rights work, but Annie didn't cooperate with this effort, which made it virtually impossible.

Back in the suite, we rented *The Parent Trap* on the in-house movie channel and watched it from the big bed. Annie lay between Caitlin and me, facing the TV, while we leaned back against the headboard, the pillows from both beds padding our backs. When Annie allowed it, which wasn't often, we speculated about Stone and his cryptic statements. But watching TV with a four-year-old means *watching* it.

Lying in bed with Annie and Caitlin catapulted me back to a time so innocent and wonderful that I could hardly bear to think about it. Before Sarah got sick. Before the hospitals. Just us and our baby, laid up on Sunday mornings watching *Barney* with no fear of the future. When our biggest problem was deciding where we wanted to go for dinner.

When *The Parent Trap* ended, Annie said she wanted another movie. As I punched in the code for *Beauty and the Beast* and Caitlin called room service for ice cream, I wondered if Annie was experiencing the same memories I was, or at least the safe warm feeling she once knew with her mother and me. I thought perhaps she was, because two minutes after she finished her ice cream, she began snoring at the foot of the bed.

With this background of Disney music and snores, Caitlin asked me about Sarah. I sat silent for a while, but Caitlin didn't apologize or ask if I was all right. When she interviewed me, I had told her this subject was off limits. But that interview seemed a long time ago. As I sat there watching Belle confront her beast, I felt Caitlin's hand close around mine, tentative at first, then firm and warm. After a few moments I looked over at her. She gave me a smile that asked nothing, assumed nothing. A sense of pure goodness flowed from her.

Sarah would like this woman, I thought. For the first time since the previous day, the ghost of Livy Marston receded in my mind. I began to speak, and I did not stop until I had told Caitlin all of it, the pleasure and the pain, the joy and the grief, the beginning and the end. She asked to see a picture of Sarah, and I showed her the snapshot I carry in my wallet. It could have been an awkward moment, but it wasn't. Caitlin made it natural.

After I put the picture away, I tried to be as natural as she but found it impossible. The sadness that had been accreting in my soul for the past seven months began to break loose, and I found myself doing what I never allowed myself to do in front of Annie. I remember Caitlin holding my head against her breast, speaking soft words that escape me now. I must have fallen asleep that way, for I awakened to find light streaming through the curtains and Annie lying beside me, with no idea how we got beneath the covers. Caitlin was not in the bed, but she had taken good care of us before she left it.

CHAPTER 23

When we reached Natchez the next afternoon, I found a fax waiting for me on my parents' kitchen table. It had been sent to my father's office just before lunch. There was no originating number at the head of the page, but the fax itself was a copy of a newspaper story clipped from the Leesville *Daily Leader*. Leesville, Louisiana, is a community located next to Fort Polk, a huge army training base, and a hundred and fifty miles from Natchez. Above the article was a copy of the paper's masthead, and it showed the date as May 19, 1968. Five days after Del Payton died.

The article recounted the capture of two men — a supply sergeant and a civilian — who one month previous had stolen armaments from a military arsenal at Fort Polk. While the troops were on maneuvers and the marching band was parading around the base in full dress uniforms, these two enterprising souls had filled a two-ton truck with M-16s, Claymore mines, hand grenades, and C-4 plastic explosive, then had driven off the base and sold most of the ordnance piecemeal throughout the southeast. The civilian half of this duo was named Lester Hinson. I noticed because his name had been circled, probably by whoever sent the fax.

There was also a note for me to call Althea Payton at St. Catherine's hospital. I tried, but someone in the nursery told me she couldn't come to the phone. I called Caitlin at the newspaper, explained the mystery fax, and gave her Lester Hinson's name so she could begin tracing him. She asked if I thought Dwight Stone had sent the fax. My guess was Peter Lutjens, but I didn't say his name on the telephone. I did make a mental note to call him again and make a pitch for him to take a run at Payton's FBI file before he woke up in North Dakota. Caitlin asked if I'd gotten started doing what Stone had told me to do: talk to the eyewitnesses of the Payton bombing. She recalled from her research that Frank Jones — the "sole" witness to the bombing — worked as a salesman at the local Pontiac dealership. Jones didn't know it yet, but he was about to take me for a test drive.

The Pontiac dealership is festooned with balloons and strips of colored foil, but the only customers are clustered around the service bay. The salesmen hover in a loose knot inside the air-conditioned showroom, watching for customers through the huge glass window like predators scanning a drought-burned plain. The sight of my father's BMW 740i brings them all to their feet, albeit with feigned aloofness. They probably know the car on sight, but hope that old Doc Cage has temporarily taken leave of his senses and decided to buy American for once.

After parking at the end of the main display line,

I make a show of looking at price stickers as I walk toward the showroom door. I search the salesmen's faces through the glass, gambling that the oldest will be Frank Jones. It stands to reason, although in a tough economy retirees might be working jobs like this to supplement their Social Security. When I open the door, everyone is suddenly busy, as though I've blundered into a Labor Day blowout sale.

I nod to the nearest salesman, then walk over to a Trans-Am sitting on the display floor and study the price sticker. Twenty seconds of silence is all it takes.

"She's a beaut, ain't she?" A head has suddenly materialized from behind a wooden partition near the back wall. "You want two, or just the one?"

The face on the head is over seventy, and it splits into the forced grin of a man who always supplies the laughs for his own jokes. He comes out from behind the partition, right hand extended in greeting, revealing a baby blue polyester sports coat over a blue plaid shirt and brown tie.

"Frank Jones, sales manager!" he barks, pumping my hand. "What can we do you for today?"

"I want to take a test drive."

"That's why we're here. Which car?"

I drop the flat of my hand on the roof of the Trans-Am. "How about this one?"

"You bet." He looks vaguely to his left. "Open the big door, Jimmy Mac."

"Sure," says a young salesman by the window. "Can I talk to you a second first?"

"I got a customer here, son."

Jones has the gleam of money in his eye. He hasn't yet spotted the BMW, and he seems to have sized me up as an all-cash type. I sit in the passenger seat as he guides the Trans-Am out of the showroom and stops so we can trade seats. Once behind the wheel, I adjust the seat for my longer frame, then pull out to the edge of the highway.

"That looks like Doc Cage's car," he says, finally noticing the BMW.

"It is." I merge into traffic, make a U-turn, and head for the Mississippi River bridge. "I'm driving it."

He looks at me and starts to speak but doesn't.

"I'm Penn Cage."

"Shit. You're the book writer." He stares straight through the windshield for half a minute, then turns to me. "Did you say all that crap they printed in the paper?"

"Some of it. They didn't exactly stick to what I said."

Jones snorts. "Don't I know it. You can't trust a damn thing you read in that rag. They did the same to me back in sixty-eight."

"About your account of the bombing?"

"Not so much that. It was the little things. Hell, they misspelled my name. How the hell can you misspell *Jones?* By God, that takes some doing."

When we top the hill that runs down to the cut in the bluff, I remember that there are two bridges spanning the Mississippi now. Throughout my childhood there was only one, and I can't seem to keep the new one in my mind. As the Trans-Am ramps onto the main span of the westbound bridge, the mile-wide tide of brown river opens

313

seventy feet below us. The vistas to the north and south look much as they did to Sam Clemens a hundred years ago: muddy water swollen into the forest and sandbars on both banks, pale blue sky blanked out at the center by a relentless sun. Ahead of us, Vidalia, Louisiana, is laid out like a toy town behind its levee, some buildings no higher than the river itself, the personification of provisional existence.

"You want to ask me about that killing, don't you? Hell, I've told the story a thousand times. A dozen times a day since that article ran."

"Did the police question you a lot about what you saw?"

Jones squints, his rather dull version of a cagey look. "Everybody questioned me a lot. I was the only person who saw that Fairlane blow."

This isn't the time to contradict him. "Did you get the feeling the police really wanted to solve the case?"

"What do you mean?"

I let the silence speak for me.

He licks his lips and looks out his window. "You writing a book about this?"

"No."

"Well, if you was . . . it seems like my story might be pretty valuable to you."

"I'm not. I just want to know about the police. Do you remember who investigated the case?"

"Henry Creel and Ronnie Temple. And you're goddamn right they tried to solve it. Those guys had a hundred-percent clearance rate back then."

"They must be the only detectives in the world with that record."

314

"These days maybe. Back then they didn't have the goddamn ACLU breathing down their necks."

"But they didn't solve the case."

Jones rolls down the window and spits into the wind. "Somebody killed a nigger. Case closed."

"What do you know about Ray Presley?"

"Enough not to say a word about him."

I turn onto Deer Park Road, which follows the river south on the Louisiana side. Soon we're driving past cotton and soybean fields, the levee on our left, the monotony broken only by shotgun churches, house trailers, and tar-paper shacks.

"You seem to know a lot about Creel and Temple."

"Creel was my wife's cousin."

"Was?"

"Lou Gehrig's disease, over to Shreveport. Temple's dead too. Heart attack."

I swing the car up onto the road that runs atop the levee. Between the levee and the river lie the perpetually flooded "borrow pits" created by the dredging that built the levee. The blackwater pits teem with catfish, crawfish, gar, water moccasins, alligators, abandoned cars, and the occasional corpse.

"Good fishing down there this month," Jones offers.

"Do you think Payton was killed for doing civil rights work?"

He shrugs. "I don't know nothing from civil rights work. He was stirring up a pile of shit, I know that. He used the national union to get himself promoted to quality-control inspector, which was a white job up till then. That pissed off a lot of

315

people. Then he started bucking for injection-mold foreman. What the hell did he expect? Wasn't nobody out there gonna tolerate a nigger foreman in sixty-eight. Next thing they'd be wanting the front office. Too far, too fast. It's that simple."

"Did the Klan kill him?"

Jones's cheeks redden. "I don't know nothing about no Klan. Payton just pissed off too many people. Anybody coulda killed him." He snaps his fingers nervously. "Turn this damn thing around. I gotta get back to work."

"I noticed you guys were pretty busy."

"Kiss my sanctified ass."

He turns on the radio, selects a country station, and adjusts the volume so that further conversation will be impossible. I make a U-turn and head back toward the twin bridges. A couple of minutes later, he surprises me by yelling over the roar of the stereo: "I can't stand this shit!"

"What?" I ask, turning down the volume.

"All this happy-ass, fake-rock, slicky-boy country shit. They don't play nothing good no more."

"What's good? Hank Williams?"

"Hank's all right, sure. But Jim Reeves, boy, that's the prime stuff."

I almost laugh. I'm no Jim Reeves fan, but whatever differences separate me from this redneck, he and I are bound together by manner, rites, and traditions imprinted deep beneath the skin. That's why Caitlin's newspaper story didn't stop him from talking to me. I am white and Mississippi-born, and at bottom Jones perceives me as a member of his tribe. I wonder how wrong he is. If push comes to shove, and I'm forced to choose between white and black, will I realize there is no choice at all?

"Did the FBI question you?"

"Shit. Federal Bureau of Integration, we called 'em back then." Now that we're headed back, Jones has regained some of his old swagger. "Had 'em an office up in the City Bank building. A dozen Yankees with blue suits and ramrods up their butts. Agents came down from Jackson special just to question me. I think Bobby Kennedy sent 'em. Hoover wouldna sent assholes like these were."

"They were tough on you?"

"A pack of pussies, more like. They didn't do no better with the case than Creel and Temple did. And Kennedy got what he deserved a couple weeks later."

Robert Kennedy deserved a bullet in the head? "What about an agent named Stone? Special Agent Dwight Stone?"

Jones's face goes as dead as though someone zipped it shut. "Never heard of him."

"He was lead agent on the Payton murder."

The ex-Triton man sets his jaw and stares straight ahead like an obstinate mule. He remembers Agent Stone, all right. And not fondly.

We're approaching the arched midpoint of the eastbound bridge. Above us, Natchez stretches across the horizon like a Cecil B. De Mille movie set, sweeping up from the cotton-rich bottomland to the spires and mansions on the great bluff, then back down again to the Triton plant and the sandbars where the river rolls on toward New Orleans

317

and the Gulf. It's the first time in years that I've seen the city from this aspect, and it's breathtaking. Below us, two steamboats are docked at Under-the-Hill, grand anachronisms that now carry tourists rather than cotton merchants and gamblers. As we roll off the bridge and top the first long incline, the Pontiac sign appears in the distance. Jones's posture instantly relaxes. This will be my last chance to speak to the man with any hope of a candid answer.

"What were you doing out there in the parking lot by yourself at eight o'clock that night?"

Something in his reaction telegraphs that he is about to lie. He does not squirm in his seat or make a sharp exclamation. Rather, a new stillness settles over him, one that sits heavily on a man unaccustomed to it.

"My wife called me," he says. "She wanted me to get some bread and eggs and such. I was on night shift and the Pik Quick was about to close."

This is the story recorded in the police report. But hearing Jones repeat it aloud, I sense the wrongness of it. "You were coming back from getting groceries when you saw the explosion?"

"I never got to leave." He shifts in his seat, finally giving release to his nervous energy. "Had a problem with my battery. Or I thought it was my battery. Turned out to be my solenoid."

A strange elation takes hold of me. Eight years of questioning hostile witnesses honed my intuition to a pretty fine point. Frank Jones is lying. He's been lying for thirty years. And any cop worth a damn would have seen it as easily in 1968 as I saw it today. Dwight Stone would have

318

seen it a damn sight quicker.

I pull onto the edge of the Pontiac lot and stop, then catch Jones's left wrist and hold it tight. "Who else was in that parking lot that night?"

His eyes go wide with surprise. "What? Nobody."

I squeeze harder. He tries to pull away, but he hasn't the strength.

"Nobody, I tell you!"

"You saw the killer."

"That's a goddamn lie!"

"Then who was it? Who else was there that night?"

Jones jerks his arm free and rubs his wrist. "You don't know shit!"

"I'm going to blow this case wide open, my friend. And the longer you lie, the harder it's going to go on you."

He glances nervously at the showroom window. He actually looks like he wants to talk, but he has stuck with a lie for thirty years, and he won't abandon it easily now. He grabs the key from the ignition, killing the engine. "Get out of this goddamn car."

I start to get out, then stop. "You don't mind if I call your wife to confirm that story, do you? About her calling you to go get groceries?"

"Do what you want. I divorced that bitch thirty years ago. Just get the hell out of this ride."

I climb out and walk to my father's car. The other salesmen are lined up against the showroom window, staring openly now. As Jones switches seats and pulls the Trans-Am toward the building, I start the BMW and drive quickly off the lot.

One cell phone call to my mother tells me all I need to know. Frank Jones's ex-wife still lives in Natchez. After a messy divorce she married the president of a local oil company, quite a trade up from Frank Jones. The "messiness" involved affairs Jones had trailed with several secretaries at the battery plant. I dial the oilman's home and ask for the ex-wife by her new name: Little.

"This is Mrs. Little," says a rather prim voice.

"Mrs. Little, this is Penn Cage."

"Dr. Cage's boy?"

"That's right. I —"

"I remember when you used to take the blood and X rays at your daddy's office."

At least she didn't hang up. "Yes, ma'am. I wanted to ask you a couple of questions, if you don't mind."

"What about?"

"The day Del Payton died."

A hesitation. "What about it?"

"I just talked to your ex-husband, and —"

"Sweet Jesus. What did that no-count say about me?"

Her anger sounds fresh, even after thirty years. "He used you for an alibi, Mrs. Little. He said he went out to the Triton parking lot on the night Del Payton died because you asked him to pick up some groceries."

"That's a damn lie, pardon my French. He was in that parking lot because he was diddling one of his floozies."

This remarkable statement stops me for a moment. "Are you . . . you're saying you think someone was in the lot with him that night?"

"Are you hard of hearing? That no-good tomcat came home that night and asked me to tell the police same story he told you. And I did, numbskull that I was."

I'm not sure I'm breathing.

"The next morning I took the car to the grocery store — for real that time — and as I was loading the bags into the backseat, I found a pair of stockings. They weren't mine, and they were not in pristine condition — *if* you know what I mean. When I got home, I kicked that sorry sack right out of the house. For good."

"Have you ever told this to anyone before today?"

"Sure. The police. I called them back and told them I hadn't been straight with them. That my husband made me lie."

A car horn honks behind me. I pull into the right lane and accelerate to the speed of the cars around me. "What did the police say?"

"Not to worry. That I wouldn't get into any trouble. Everything was under control."

Under control. "Do you remember which officer you told?"

"Yes. He came out to the house. It was that cop they sent to Parchman later on. Ray Presley."

No account of this meeting made it into the case report. "Was Presley alone when he came to see you?"

"Yes. He gave me the creeps, that Presley. Always did."

"Did anyone from the FBI question you about this?"

Mrs. Little says nothing, but not because she

has nothing to tell.

"Mrs. Little, do you remember an FBI agent named Dwight Stone?"

"Well, actually . . . I do, yes. But that's all I have to say. Good—"

"Please wait! Do you have any idea who your husband was with on that day? Which floozie, I mean? I know this is painful, but it's terribly important. The faster I get to the bottom of this, the less chance anyone is going to get hurt."

"I don't like talking about this." Her breaths are shallow, anxious. "If you get to the bottom of it, my ex-husband is going to come out of it smelling like a cowpie, isn't he?"

"Probably."

"Betty Lou Jackson."

"Ma'am?"

"That's the slut's name. She's married to some electrical contractor now. Beckham, her name is. Acts like she's as good as anybody, but she's a tramp through and through."

"Thank you, Mrs. Little."

"Don't thank me, because I never told you anything."

The phone goes dead.

The nice thing about small towns is that it's easy to find people. Directory assistance has only one Beckham listed. I'm starting to feel like I might solve the Payton case without ever leaving the car.

"Hello?" A woman's voice.

"Is this Betty Lou Beckham?"

"Yes. I don't use the 'Lou' anymore, though. It's just Betty. Betty Beckham. Who is this?"

"This is Penn Cage, Mrs. Beckham."

Deafening silence.

"Mrs. Beckham?"

"I'm real busy right now, Mr. —"

"I just wanted to ask you a couple of quick questions."

"I can't help you. I'm sorry."

"You don't know what I'm going to ask you." *Or do you?*

"I saw the paper the other day." Her voice is so tight that her vocal cords must be near to snapping. "It's about that, isn't it?"

"Mrs. Beckham, I realize this might be a delicate matter. I'd be glad to speak to you in person if you'd feel more comfortable."

"Don't you come around here! Somebody might see you."

"Who are you worried would see me?"

"Anybody! Are you crazy?"

"Mrs. Beckham, I really only have one question. Were you in that parking lot when Del Payton's car exploded?"

"Oh, my God. Oh, dear Jesus. . . ."

"I have absolutely no interest in what you might have been doing there, Mrs. Beckham. I just want to know about the bombing."

How stupid did that sound? If Betty Lou was doing what Mrs. Little suspected she was doing in that parking lot, it might end up on the network news.

"Don't call back," she pleads. "You'll get me in bad trouble. Yourself too. You don't know. You just don't know!"

She's hung up, but the fear in her voice was real enough to raise the hair on the back of my neck. She is afraid of more than memories. She's been living in dread ever since Caitlin's story ran in the paper.

As I turn into my parents' neighborhood, the cell phone rings. It's Althea Payton.

"I tried to call you earlier, Althea, at the hospital. But you were busy."

"I know. I got this number from your father." She sounds out of breath. "I think I've remembered something important."

"Take it easy. I'm not going anywhere. What is it?"

"I was visiting an adult patient this morning, and his TV was tuned to CNN. I really wasn't paying attention, but then I heard your name. They were talking about that execution in Texas. How you were the lawyer who convicted that man."

"Right. . . ."

"They showed you walking into the prison. And then, right after that, they showed another man. They said he was the head of the FBI. I didn't hear his name, but I watched again an hour later to see if they'd run the same thing, and they did."

"I don't understand, Althea. What did you remember?"

"I knew that man. Mr. Portman. John Portman."

"You knew him? From where?"

"From here. Right here in Natchez."

"You've seen John Portman in Natchez?"

"That's what I'm trying to tell you. Remember I told you about Agent Stone? How he was nice and really wanted to help us?"

"Yes."

"And I told you some of them didn't. How Mr.

Stone had another man with him, a young Yankee man, who was cold and never said anything?"

My chest feels hollow. "Yes. . . ."

"That was him. That John Portman on the TV was him."

"Althea, you must be mistaken. John Portman would have been very young in 1968."

"It's him, I tell you. His hair's a little grayer, but that's the only difference. The second time they ran the story, I watched close. Ain't no doubt about it. It was him. A young Yankee man, cold as February. Chilled me right to the bone."

Somewhere in my mind Dwight Stone is saying, *I knew Portman. He came into the Bureau a few years before I got out. . . .*

"Don't say anything else, Althea. I'm on a cell phone. I'm going to check on this and get back to you."

"What do you think it means?"

"I don't want to speculate. Don't talk to anyone about this. I'll get back to you."

"I'll be waiting."

I hit End, then turn into my parents' driveway and park, leaving the engine running. Of all the things I could possibly have learned about this case, this is the most astonishing. If John Portman was in Natchez in 1968, a lot of things suddenly make sense. Dwight Stone's personal hatred of him. Stone's unwillingness to talk about the case. Maybe even the national security seal on the Payton file, although this is probably going too far. No one could have known in 1968 that Special Agent John Portman would wind up director of the FBI thirty years later. So that wasn't the reason

Hoover sealed the file. But Portman almost certainly knows *why* the file was sealed, as does Stone. Given Stone's hatred of Portman — and Stone's dismissal from the Bureau while Portman rose through its ranks — that reason must have been something Stone could not stomach but which Portman went along with. *He was a good little German,* Stone had said of Portman. *He followed orders.* The question is, what was he ordered to do?

As I get out of the car, a middle-aged black cop in uniform walks around the corner of the house, one hand on the gun at his hip.

"Are you Penn Cage?"

"Yes, sir."

He smiles and nods. He has the sad, drooping eyes of a beagle. "I'm James Ervin. Just keeping an eye on things for you and your daddy."

"I'm glad to see you, Officer Ervin." I reach out and shake his hand. "That gun loaded?"

He taps the automatic on his hip. "You bet."

"Good man."

"You sure got a pretty little girl in there. Reminds me of my girls when they was little."

"Thank you. Do you know what all this is about?"

Ervin sucks in his upper lip and looks at the ground. "You trying to get whoever killed Del Payton, ain't you?"

"That's right. Did you know Del?"

"My daddy knew him." He raises the beagle eyes to mine, and they are full of quiet conviction. "Don't you worry none. You ain't gonna have no trouble. Somebody come messin' 'round here, they on the *wrong side.*"

CHAPTER 24

It takes less than ten minutes on my mother's computer to verify what Althea Payton told me on the cell phone. The FBI's official web page features a thumbnail biography of its new director. The bio boasts of Portman's first year as a field agent, one which he spent investigating race murders in Mississippi and Alabama. That year was 1968. A *Time* magazine writer hailed Portman's "year in the trenches" and stated that his "sterling civil rights credentials" were one of the major reasons the President had tapped the Republican federal judge to lead the FBI in a bipartisan gesture that shocked most Democrats. The Bureau had been wracked by racial problems for the past decade, and had been successfully sued by both African-American and Hispanic agents. Portman's Deep South experience sat well with minority political interests.

By my calculations, Portman was twenty-five when he visited Althea Payton's house with Dwight Stone. Fresh out of Yale Law. Stone was probably ten years older. Beyond this my facts are few. Portman rose swiftly through the Bureau's ranks while Stone was fired five years later. In Crested Butte I sensed that Stone felt his dismissal was related to the Payton case. But if that was true, why would Hoover wait five years to terminate him? Or had whatever happened in 1968 haunted Stone, fueling his alcoholism, until Hoover was finally left no choice but to fire him?

Unable to answer this question, I list the names of main players on the computer and stare at them a while. *Payton. Presley. Marston. Stone. Portman. Hinson.* One of the first things a writer learns is that the best way to solve a problem is to get out of the way of his subconscious and let it work. Following this dictum, I begin playing with the screen fonts and point sizes, switching from Courier to Bookman, from flowing Gothic to a tortured Algerian. As the fonts swirl and transform themselves before my eyes, it strikes me that men like Leo Marston and John Portman cannot be investigated by normal means, especially by a private citizen. Caitlin's status as a reporter lends us some theoretical authority under the First Amendment, but this means next to nothing in the real world. What is required is some creative thinking.

Kings and presidents can be brought down with the right weapons. The trick is to find their vulnerabilities. Men like Portman and Marston live for power. They hunger for it even as they wield more than most men will ever know. They act with certainty and dispatch, rarely allowing themselves the luxury of doubt. And so long as they operate from this fortress of psychological security, they are untouchable. Perhaps the way to bring them down is to breach that fortress, to turn their worlds upside down and force them into a *re*active mode. The way to do that seems obvious

328

enough. Re-introduce them to an emotion they have not felt in a great while.

Fear.

My first thought when my father comes through the pantry door is that he looks ten years older than he did two days ago. He kisses my mother and Annie, then motions for me to follow him into the library. I shrug at my mother and follow.

He sits in his leather recliner and switches on the television, apparently to mask our conversation.

"Somebody just tried to kill Ray Presley."

"What?" I exclaim, dropping onto the sofa to his left.

"His girlfriend was giving him the first few cc's of that Mexican chemotherapy he takes. He started complaining of angina and ripped the catheter out of his wrist. The girl called 911 and gave him CPR until the paramedics got there. He was having a coronary. He just checked himself out of the CCU against my orders."

"What makes you think it was attempted murder?"

"The girl brought in the IV bag, and one of our lab techs ran a few tests. He thinks there's some potassium chloride mixed in with the cocktail."

"Jesus. Did you call the police?"

"Ray told me not to. He was so goddamn mad he wouldn't let anybody but me close to him. He said he'd handle it himself."

"I'll bet he will. How much damage did his heart sustain?"

"I don't have enough enzyme tests back to tell." Dad drums his hands on the arms of the chair.

"We've got another problem."

"What?"

"You talked to Betty Lou Beckham today?"

"How do you know that?"

"She showed up at my office at four o'clock, half in the bag. Said she had to talk to me."

I should have expected this. For years my father has acted as a confessor to countless souls, particularly women, who have no outlet for their sorrows and anxieties other than their ministers or local psychologists, as Natchez has attracted only one or two psychiatrists over the past two decades, and none has stayed. In this vacuum, a compassionate M.D. fills the void as no one else can.

"Was she in that parking lot when Del Payton died?"

"Yes. She and Frank Jones were having sex in his car when the bomb went off, if you can believe it. She saw Payton walk out to his car. She actually saw the damned thing explode."

"Christ. What else did she see?"

"When the bomb went off, Jones panicked. He started to take off, but Betty Lou reminded him that he was supposed to be working inside the plant. She was off that day, so she got into her VW to leave. When she was almost out of the lot, she looked up and saw somebody watching her from a pickup truck."

"Who?"

"Ray Presley."

A fist closes around my heart. "Presley was there *when* the bomb went off?"

Dad nods once, very slowly.

"So . . . he was involved in the actual murder."

"It looks that way."

"Did Betty Lou tell anybody she'd seen him there?"

"Not at first. Presley came to see her and explained that might not be good for her health."

This scene is all too easy to imagine.

"Then Frank Jones's wife found Betty Lou's stockings in his car and kicked Jones out of the house. I gather that Mrs. Jones then told the police her husband had lied about why he was in the parking lot, because Presley came to see Betty Lou again. Gave her a harsher warning."

"But she told the FBI, didn't she? Special Agent Dwight Stone."

"Not at first. When Agent Stone found out Jones's wife had kicked him out the morning after the murder, he talked to the wife, and she led him to Betty Lou. Stone offered her money, but Betty Lou wouldn't talk. She was too scared of Ray. Then somebody shot at those FBI agents on the highway. Stone came back and told Betty that if she withheld evidence, he'd make sure she did time in federal prison. He convinced her. She's basically a good girl. She wanted to tell the truth all along."

"She gave up Presley to Stone."

"Yes."

"Then what happened?"

"Nothing. Betty Lou kept waiting for Presley to be arrested, but he never was. Then the FBI pulled Stone out of town. Presley showed up again, beat the hell out of her, forced her to give him oral sex . . . she was a basket case. She was about to skip town when Presley was arrested on the drug-trafficking charges that sent him to Parchman."

I sit back on the sofa, trying to process it all.

"She's still scared to death of Ray. She's been working herself toward a nervous breakdown since Caitlin Masters's article came out. When you called this afternoon, she lost it. I gave her a shot of Ativan and drove her home."

"Ray is the problem you were talking about. He's directly involved in the murder, but if I push him, he'll push back. He doesn't have your gun anymore, but he could still raise a hell of a stink if he wanted to."

Dad sighs and leans back in his chair.

"It doesn't matter," I decide. "Presley wasn't solely responsible for Payton's death. The fact that someone just tried to kill him proves that. Somebody's afraid he'll talk."

We both look up as my mother slides open the library door. I assume she is summoning us to supper, but she says, "You've got a visitor, Penn."

"Who is it?"

"Caitlin Masters."

I wasn't expecting Caitlin, so she must have news. "Bring her in."

"She's playing with Annie."

When Mom disappears, Dad says, "How much does Masters know?"

"Nothing about the blackmail."

"Don't tell her what happened to Ray. Not yet."

Caitlin comes to the door carrying Annie in her arms, then passes her off to my mother and promises to be back in the kitchen in a few minutes. She's wearing black jeans, sandals, and a white pinpoint button-down with her sable hair spilling around the collar. She looks harried but also ready to burst with excitement.

Dad stands as I make the introductions, and as soon as Mom closes the door, Caitlin says: "I just hit the jackpot."

"What are you talking about?"

"I traced Lester Hinson. The guy in the article from the Leesville *Daily Leader*?"

"What's his story?"

"He's a small-time crook who spent most of his life in Angola Prison. He lives in New Orleans now."

"You talked to him?"

Too excited to remain in one place, Caitlin begins pacing. "More than that. I found out exactly how he ties in to the Payton case. In April of 1968 Lester Hinson and a supply sergeant named Earl Wheeler ripped off an arms depot at Fort Polk and started selling the stuff on the black market. A month later they were busted by the Army CID. That's what the article was about, right? Well, Hinson was a civilian, and he got a visit in jail from Special Agent Dwight Stone. Stone wanted to know if the pair had sold C-4 to anyone from Mississippi, particularly Natchez. They had. Stone had to get the charges pled down to find out who the buyer was, but he didn't mind that at all."

"The buyer was Ray Presley," I say in a monotone.

Her mouth drops open. "You're not guessing, are you?"

"No. We just placed Presley at the crime scene when the bomb went off."

"How did you do that?"

"You finish first. I can't believe Hinson just

333

spilled his guts to you."

"He didn't. I did what cops do."

"What's that?"

She grins. "I paid him. I told him what I wanted, then wired five hundred dollars to a Western Union office in New Orleans. I told him I'd wire him another five hundred if he told me what I wanted to know. He would have talked all day for that money."

Dad gives Caitlin an admiring look.

"Forget that," she says. "How did you put Presley at the scene?"

"You were right about what Stone was trying to tell us. There was another witness to the murder. One who never made it into the police report."

"Who?"

"Her identity isn't important right now. What matters —"

"Not important!"

Caitlin isn't going to like this. "This witness can only implicate Ray Presley. Presley probably killed Payton, but he almost certainly did it for someone else. That's how he worked. And I don't want to move on Presley until we have the man who ordered the crime."

Caitlin is shaking her head. "But that's how you get to the top guy, isn't it? You squeeze the little fish until they talk."

"Usually, yes. But Presley's a special case. He's never scared easy, and now he has terminal cancer. He doesn't have a lot of fear of earthly punishment. So, he bought some plastic explosive in 1968. The statute ran out on that long ago. The witness who saw him in the Triton parking lot is a

334

terrified woman who's now married and respectable, but who happened to be committing adultery in a car when the bomb exploded. I seriously doubt she would make a statement to the police, much less testify in open court."

"Penn, I can't believe I'm hearing this. We now have means and opportunity for Presley to have committed homicide. The motive could be racial prejudice. He's a lock for it. If we don't squeeze Presley, how can we get any further?"

"We've just been discussing that."

She looks from one to the other of us, her green eyes probing. "You guys know something I don't. Right? Something about Presley. Something that's keeping you from going after him."

"Yes."

"What is it?"

"I can't tell you. Not at this point."

The familiar pink moons appear high on her cheeks. "What kind of bullshit answer is that? Are we partners or not?"

I trust Caitlin implicitly, but I cannot trust her with my father's secret. "If I could tell you, I would. But I have to ask you to trust me for now."

"You ask me to trust you, but you don't trust me." She looks at my father, who is staring pointedly at the floor, then back at me. "You think Leo Marston hired Presley?"

"Don't you?"

"There's no evidence of that."

"Ike Ransom says it's Marston, and Dwight Stone said the same thing in so many words."

"But neither of them will go public."

"There's been another development as well."

335

She sighs and looks at the floor. "I'm afraid to ask."

"Stone lied to us in Colorado. He knew John Portman a hell of a lot better than he led us to believe."

"How do you know that?"

I quickly explain Althea Payton's call about seeing Portman on CNN, and my subsequent verification that he worked in Mississippi in 1968.

Caitlin gropes backward for her chair and falls into it. "Holy shit. Do you realize what this means?"

"Tell me."

"This story just went national. This story is *huge*."

"Remember our deal. You print nothing until I say so."

"When I made that promise, I didn't know you were going to obstruct the investigation for reasons you don't see fit to tell me."

"There were no conditions on the promise. And I expect you to abide by it."

She purses her lips. "Could I please point out a couple of things? One, we have no real investigative power. Two, the files we need are under government seal, and we're unlikely to get that changed without a protracted court battle. Three, the Payton case somehow involves the director of the FBI, who has practically unlimited power to interfere with us. Four, the case also involves Leo Marston, the single most powerful man in this county, possibly in the state. Five, no one directly involved in the case wants to talk to us." She holds up her hands in desperation. "What do you want to *do?* I think the media is the only weapon we have."

"I agree."

"You do?"

"I simply want to use it in a different way than you."

"How?"

"To scare the shit out of Portman and Marston, and see which way they jump."

Now I have her attention. "How can you do that?"

"By making them think we can prove they're guilty of Payton's murder."

"And how do you propose to do that?"

"Simple. I state publicly that Leo Marston was responsible for the murder of Del Payton."

"What?" my father cries.

"With no evidence?" asks Caitlin. "Just slander him?"

"Exactly. I slander him."

"But why?"

"Because by doing that, I leave Marston no option but to sue me."

Dad snorts in amazement. "What the hell does that accomplish?"

"The minute Marston sues me, I'll answer his charge by stating that truth will be my defense. I will then be free under the rules of discovery to request Marston's business records, personal papers, tax returns — all kinds of things from the years surrounding the crime."

"A fishing expedition?" asks Caitlin. "You think you'll find some documentary proof that Marston ordered Payton's murder?"

"Not really. My primary goal is psychological. Ike Ransom says everyone around here is playing the quiet game. He says the way you win that game is by making people nervous. So, that's what I'm going to do. Marston won't believe I'd make a public charge like that without hard evidence. He'll panic. His first thought will probably be Ray Presley. After Presley, who knows? Portman maybe. We don't know who else was involved. But Marston does."

"You *think* he does. What if you're wrong? What if you have no evidence by the time the slander case comes to trial?"

"Then I'll lose a great deal of money. Maybe everything I have."

"How long would that be? From the time of the slander till the trial?"

"Hard to say with someone like Marston. The deck would be stacked against me from the start. He'd want a quick trial, and he'd get one. Everybody in this town owes him favors, especially in the judicial system."

"He's got his share of enemies too," Dad points out. "You might get some unexpected help."

"I'll tell you what would scare the shit out of him," I think aloud, feeling excitement building inside me. "A jury trial. In this town the jury might be fifty percent black. We might even get a black judge."

Dad actually cackles. "Marston would be apoplectic! After a lifetime of moderation on race, he gets hauled before a black jury on a case like this?"

"How would you do it?" Caitlin asks. "The slander, I mean. Walk into a bar, pound on a table, and accuse him of murder?"

"No. I'd have to make it impossible for him not to sue."

"Talk radio?"

"Maybe. But the ideal medium is print. It carries the most authority."

She blanches. "You mean *my* newspaper? Not a chance in hell."

I smile. "Hey, are we partners or what?"

She stands and jabs her forefinger at me. "Marston would sue the paper for libel. He'd sue my father!" She shakes her head violently. "My father will tolerate a lot. But a libel suit? Do you know what kind of damages people have been awarded in libel cases? *Tens of millions of dollars.* He'd jerk my butt out of here so fast my feet wouldn't touch the ground."

"Caitlin —"

She shakes her head again and walks quickly to the door. "I'm going to forget I ever heard this. And I suggest you think long and hard before you put everything you have up for grabs. You have a daughter to raise."

"Not a word in the paper about any of this," I remind her.

She closes her eyes and sighs angrily.

"Unless you want to print my accusations of Marston's guilt. Then you can blow the story wide open. You can take it national tomorrow morning. The more noise, the better."

She stands in the door with her hands on her hips, nostrils flared, eyes burning. "Damn you, Penn Cage." She glares at my father. "If I were you, I'd try to talk some sense into my son."

Then she steps through the sliding door and shuts it with a bang.

Dad looks at me with a glint in his eye. "That's some woman." He takes a cigar from his shirt pocket, unwraps it, and sticks it between his back teeth. "Desperate times call for desperate measures?"

"What choice do we have? Even if Betty Lou would go public, she might never get the chance. Presley could kill her. And even if we somehow turned Presley, Marston could have him killed. But as soon as I go public, any suspicious accidents make Marston look guilty."

"I agree. Not only that, I like it."

"There's only one problem," I murmur, fighting the fear germinating in my gut.

"What's that?"

"Leo is one cool customer. What if I can't spook him?"

By nine P.M. I've pretty much decided to go forward without Caitlin's help. Finding a newspaper reporter or radio talk-show host who will let me spout off about Leo Marston and a race crime shouldn't be too difficult. In the current media climate, where celebrity and controversy are the benchmarks of ratings, they'll probably fight over the story. But Caitlin's apprehension still worries me. What I need now is positive confirmation that I'm right to go after Marston.

Dwight Stone answers his phone after five rings, but as soon as I identify myself, he hangs up. I try once more, in case he made a mistake, but the result is the same. More curious than discouraged, I take out my wallet and fish out the card with Ike Ransom's cell phone number. The deputy answers instantly.

"This is your buddy from the Triton plant," I tell him.

He asks if I'm home, then says he'll call back from a land line. A minute later, he tells me to meet him at an abandoned warehouse by the river, in the industrial park. This doesn't strike me as a good way to spend the evening, so I suggest that he pick me up in the Wal-Mart parking lot. He reluctantly agrees.

Fifteen minutes later, I climb into his cruiser, the claustrophobic little world of anger and guns and cigarettes. He looks just as he did the other night, only more nervous. He looks, in fact, like he might be wired on speed.

"Where the hell have you been?" he demands.

"Colorado. I talked to an FBI agent who worked the case in sixty-eight."

Ransom hits the brake, then catches himself and continues up the bypass. "I thought I told you to stay away from the FBI."

"You did. And I'm curious as to why."

He ignores the comment. "What's this guy's name?"

"Stone."

He taps the wheel impatiently. "Couple of people I talked to remembered him. They said it seemed like he really tried to solve the case."

"He did more than try. He solved it."

Ransom looks over at me, his speed-pinned eyes distant. "He tell you that?"

"In so many words."

"No details?"

341

"He won't talk about it."

Ike laughs humorlessly. "What did I tell you? The quiet game. Everybody's playing it."

"What are they so scared of? Marston?"

"Judge Leo got some serious juice, man."

"Is that all?"

"What you mean?"

"Did you know John Portman was here in 1968?"

"John who?"

I hesitate before answering. I have a feeling Ike knows exactly who I'm talking about. "The director of the FBI," I say, watching him.

He accelerates and whips around the car ahead of us, but I can't tell whether he did it to buy time or not.

"What you mean, he was here?"

"It was his first year as an FBI agent. He was working the Payton case with Stone."

Ike shrugs. "That's the first I heard of it. But I told you to stay away from the FBI, didn't I? You can't trust no Feds, man."

"Never mind. Look, I've thought of a way to go after Marston. But it's risky. I've got to know more than I know now. You understand? You've got to give me something more."

"Like what?"

"How about some evidence?"

"Shit, man, if I had evidence, I'd get that motherfucker my own self. Finding evidence is your job."

"Why do you think he was behind Del's murder?"

"I just know, okay?"

"It's not okay, damn it. It doesn't make sense. Why would Marston want Del Payton dead?"

"That's what you're supposed to find out."

My father's original doubts about Ike's motives are coming back to me. "Why do you hate Marston so much, Ike?"

He turns to me, his eyes smoldering. "I done told you once. It's personal."

"That's not good enough anymore."

"Fuck you, then!"

I say nothing for the next mile. Ike's respiration is heavy and erratic, as though so much energy is consumed by his anger that he has to remind himself to breathe.

"Were you and Ray Presley cops at the same time?"

He keeps his eyes on the road. "Presley was in Parchman when I joined the force. But I knew that motherfucker later on. We were like two bad dogs on a street. We always stayed on different sides. Still do."

"Well, somebody just tried to kill him."

An eerie stillness comes over Ike. Then he turns his head toward me, and the intensity in his eyes is frightening. "Tried to kill him how?"

"Poison."

"Take more than poison to kill that bastard."

"I think Presley planted the bomb that killed Del Payton."

Ike rolls his tongue around his cheek, his eyes moving on and off me. "Why you think that?"

"I've got reasons. What do you think?"

"I think all the evidence in the world against Ray Presley ain't gonna get you no closer to Marston."

343

"Why not?"

" 'Cause Presley don't know shit about the *reason*. You got to find the *why* of it."

"Take me back to my car. You want me to fight your battles for you, but you don't give me shit for help."

He spins the wheel and turns the cruiser back toward Wal-Mart, his anger making his knuckles pale. "Marston fucked up my family," he says through clenched teeth. "Fucked up my whole life. That's all I'm gonna tell you. It's got nothing to do with Del Payton, but I knew you could bring Marston down behind the Payton thing. That's why I went that way. I want that bastard destroyed. In *public*. That's what'll hurt him the most. If it wasn't for that, I'd have killed his ass a long time ago."

I settle back on the seat and let my eyes go out of focus, which turns the oncoming headlights into slow white meteors. "Ike . . . I want you to swear on the soul of your mother that Marston ordered Del Payton's death."

He doesn't hesitate. "On the soul of my mother. If it wasn't for Leo Marston, Del Payton would be alive today."

I guess that's all the certainty I'm going to get.

When I get home, Caitlin's Miata is parked in the driveway. She is standing in the garage, talking to Officer Ervin.

"What's the matter?" I ask as she walks out to meet me.

"Dwight Stone just called me at the newspaper. He thinks his phone is tapped. He gave me the number of a pay phone and told me to get you to call him back. He said you should use a pay phone too. One far from your house."

"Let's go."

I drive us up to the bypass, then north to Highway 61. There's a pay phone at a convenience store, but I go a little farther to a grocery store parking lot, where there won't be so much noise. Caitlin stands beside me as I dial the number.

"Yes?" Stone says in a gruff voice.

"It's Penn Cage."

"Listen to me, Cage. My phone is tapped. So are the phones at your father's house and medical office. Probably the lines at the newspaper as well. You should also assume physical surveillance. I'm being watched right now."

"Jesus. Someone just tried to kill Ray Presley."

Caitlin tenses beside me, but I ignore her.

"How?" asks Stone.

"Poisoned his IV bag. He had a coronary, but he's still ambulatory and mad as hell."

Stone says nothing, but I can sense the conflict raging within him. "I know you worked with Portman on the Payton case in sixty-eight," I tell him. "Why did you lie about that?"

"I was trying to protect people."

"Who?"

"You, for one. Others too."

"Well, I took your advice. I talked to the eyewitnesses, and I've placed Presley at the crime scene."

"And?"

"I want Leo Marston, not Presley."

"Squeeze Presley."

"That's easier said than done."

Stone laughs softly. "Ray's not very squeezable,

is he? Son of a bitch tried to kill us on the highway to Jackson."

"You're the agent who got shot at on Highway 61?"

"Portman and me, if you can believe it. The world would be a lot nicer place if Presley had hit Portman that day."

"Why? Goddamn it, what's the big secret? What was so terrible that Hoover had to bury it under a national security seal? What's Portman hiding? What could still scare you after thirty years?"

"Do you really expect me to answer that?"

"You're damn right I do. It's time you listened to your conscience, Stone."

"Don't preach to me, son. You haven't earned the right."

"If Ray Presley shot at you, why didn't he go to jail for it?"

"He did."

"Presley went to Parchman for drug trafficking. That's a state prison."

"Justice doesn't always happen in a straight line. You should know that."

I grip the phone with exasperation. "I've thought of a way to go after Marston without Presley's help, but it's a gamble. A big one. I can't afford to be wrong."

"What are you asking me, counselor?"

"Am I wrong about Leo Marston being behind the murder of Del Payton?"

Just as I decide Stone is not going to answer, he says, "You're not wrong."

A wave of triumph surges through me.

"But that doesn't mean there's evidence lying

around waiting to be picked up," he adds. "I don't know how much I'd gamble on being able to prove it."

"Did you prove it in sixty-eight?"

"Yes."

"Then why wasn't the son of a bitch prosecuted?"

"Oldest reason in the world. You just be damn sure about every step you take. This road doesn't end where you think it does."

"Hold on. Why are you willing to warn me, but not to help me?"

"I thought I just did. Good hunting, counselor."

When I hang up, Caitlin grabs my arm, her eyes furious. "Why didn't you tell me someone tried to kill Presley?"

"No one knew but my father, and he asked me not to tell."

She takes a deep breath and expels it slowly. "What did Stone say?"

I glance around the dark parking lot, searching for suspicious vehicles. Would I even see surveillance if it was there? Surely the FBI is better than that. I pull Caitlin to me and put my mouth to her ear. She stiffens.

"What are you doing?"

"Stone says we're probably under surveillance. Act like we're lovers."

After a moment her arms slip around me and her breasts flatten against my chest, but her eyes are anything but romantic.

"We've got to go with my slander plan," I whisper. "We don't have time for anything else, and the more public this is, the safer we are."

She slides her cheek past mine and answers in my ear. "I won't do that. Don't ask me to."

"It's the only way."

She pulls away from me, her eyes bright. "Take me back to my car."

"You told me you wanted to shake up your father's business."

"Not like that. I have no right to put him in jeopardy that way."

We get into the car, and I cross the highway to 61 South. "You think Marston's going to stand on ethics?" I ask her. "He'd kill us in a second if he thought he had to."

She turns to me with a defiant look. "As far as I know, the worst thing Leo Marston has ever done is sabotage your love life. And that's not against the law."

"The danger is real, Caitlin."

"Give me a break. Nobody killed Woodward and Bernstein."

"They weren't working in Mississippi."

CHAPTER 25

Einstein said the arrow of time flies in only one direction. Faulkner, being from Mississippi, understood the matter differently. He said the past is never dead; it's not even past. All of us labor in webs spun long before we were born, webs of heredity and environment, of desire and consequence, of history and eternity. Haunted by wrong turns and roads not taken, we pursue images perceived as new but whose provenance dates to the dim dramas of childhood, which are themselves but ripples of consequence echoing down the generations. The quotidian demands of life distract from this resonance of images and events, but some of us feel it always.

And who among us, offered the chance, would not relive the day or hour in which we first knew love, or ecstasy, or made a choice that forever altered our future, negating a life we might have had? Such chances are rarely granted. Memory and grief prove Faulkner right enough, but Einstein knew the finality of action. If I cannot change what I had for lunch yesterday, I certainly cannot unmake a marriage, erase the betrayal of a friend, or board a ship that left port twenty years ago.

And yet . . . today I am granted such a chance.

Livy Marston does not call as she promised she would. She shows up at our front door at nine A.M. wearing faded Levi's and a white blouse tied at the waist, sapphire earrings one shade darker than her eyes, a silk scarf in her hair. On the street behind her, a midnight blue Fiat Spyder convertible idles like a resting cat.

"I'm kidnaping you," she says. "If it's all right with Annie."

It takes a moment to center myself in the present. "Kidnaping me to where?"

She smiles. "It's a surprise. If you thought about it, you'd know. But don't think. Today is a right-brain day."

Five minutes after I clear it with Mom and Annie, I'm clinging to the passenger door of the Spyder as Livy races up the highway, cutting in and out of traffic like a Grand Prix driver. She borrowed the car from a friend of her mother's, and we both know why. Our senior year in high school, after she received some honor or other, Livy was given a Fiat convertible much like this one by her father. The night they brought it back from the dealership in New Orleans, she and I drove across half the state with the top down, drinking beer and reveling in the promise of futures unbound by visible limits. We spent many of our best moments in that car, and she has apparently decided to relive some of them. I've fantasized about scenes like this more than once, but there is something eerie about tearing up the sun-drenched highway toward the edge of town twenty years after we did it the first time, and in the same car.

As the Spyder crosses the westbound bridge into

Louisiana, Maude Marston's words echo in my mind: *You ruined my daughter's life, you bastard.* I want to ask Livy outright what her mother was referring to, but Livy always had a way of being elliptical where serious matters were concerned.

"What did you mean, today is a right-brain day?" I ask.

She laughs. "I mean today everything is off limits." Her voice has deepened slightly over the years. "Everything except experience."

"Livy, I have some questions."

"You mean like why are my husband and I separated? Why did you and I really split up in college? Why did my father try to destroy yours?"

"Yes. Little things like that."

"We'll get to all that. I have questions too. But first we give ourselves a little of the past. A little innocence." She grants me a brilliant smile. "We owe ourselves that."

At the foot of the bridge she pulls into the parking lot of the liquor store we patronized during high school. Joking that it's finally legal for us to shop here, she goes inside and returns with two chilled bottles of Pouilly Fuisse. Handing them to me, she takes a small ice chest from the trunk and sets it on the backseat. Inside, I see French bread, cheese, grapes, peeled shrimp, and chocolate chip cookies.

She crosses the four-lane and whips the Spyder onto Deer Park Road, the same route I drove yesterday with Frank Jones. Only Livy takes the gently curving blacktop at ninety miles per hour. She was always an excellent driver, aggressive but in control. When the road jumps onto the levee, she has

351

to slow to seventy, but the wind still whips through our hair, keeping the sun from frying us. I serve her wine in a styrofoam cup, and when she drinks, the wine clings to the same fine golden down that dusted her upper lip when she was seventeen. But she is not seventeen now. And the questions hanging between us cannot be ignored.

She pulls a pair of Ray-Bans down from the visor and slips them on, snapping me straight back to Sarah's funeral. I didn't notice Livy at the church service, but later, at the graveside, I saw her standing at the edge of the crowd, a hauntingly beautiful apparition in a black dress and sunglasses, unmistakable even after twenty years.

"It meant a lot that you came to the funeral," I say above the whine of the engine. "I'm sorry I couldn't do more than say hello."

She shakes her head and touches my arm. "I had to come. And I didn't expect any more than that."

At the end of the levee she stops, and we switch seats for the return leg. Somewhere in the middle of the empty cotton fields, she intertwines the fingers of her left hand in my right. I don't look at her, but I feel a sudden tingling, as though I've put my hand through a portal in time and felt a charge of energy pour through. On some level, acceding to this intimacy seems a betrayal of myself, but it also presages a deeper connection, one that might lead to meaningful conversation, so I leave my hand in hers.

As we climb the eastbound bridge, the Cecil B. De Mille panorama of Natchez rises above us as it did yesterday when I crossed the bridge with Frank Jones. The whole grand stage seems laid out with such dramatic intent that I ask myself the question Caitlin asked at our first meeting: why haven't I written about this place?

"What are you thinking?" Livy asks.

"I thought questions were prohibited."

She ignores this remark. "I was thinking about this place. The town. The fact that it *is* a place, with a unique identity. Atlanta is so sterile that I literally can't stand being in it sometimes."

"I've felt the same thing in Houston."

Looking up from the bridge, I see Natchez as the tourist sees it: the high bluff where sun-worshiping Natchez Indians massacred the French soldiers of Fort Rosalie in 1729; where Aaron Burr was arrested as a traitor and set free to the cheers of crowds; where an African prince labored twenty years as a slave; where Jefferson Davis wedded Varina Howell in the halcyon days before the Civil War. But I see so much more. I see the city Livy Marston captivated with a beauty and poise not seen since P. T. Barnum brought Jenny Lind down the river in 1851. I see the thin edge of a universe of vibrant life and mysterious death, of shadowy secrets and bright facades, and of races inextricably bound by blood and tears, geography and religion, and above all, time.

"This is a good place to be from," I murmur.

"Could you ever live here again?" Livy asks in a strange voice.

I sense a deeper question beneath the one she's asked. "I don't know. Could you?"

She doesn't take her eyes from the bluff. From this place she left to conquer the world. How does it look to her now?

"Not while my parents are alive," she says, so softly that I'm not sure she knows she spoke aloud.

Before I can ponder what she meant, she turns to me, her eyes languid, and says, "Let's go to the Cold Hole."

The tingling in my hand spreads up my arm and across my neck and shoulders. *The Cold Hole.* One mile from the spot where my father and I sank the pistol I bought from Ray Presley — in the midst of that slimy, sulfurous swamp — a cold spring bubbles up through the green water, creating a pool as clear as Arctic snowmelt. It is the pool from my dream, the one I had the night Ike Ransom first told me about Leo Marston's involvement in the Payton murder. The woman in my dream was Livy Marston, and she sits beside me now, asking me to take her to that pool. Only in the dream she had something to tell me. Today she says the past is off limits.

Her presumption offends me. The Cold Hole was the geographic center of our intimate life, the name alone a talisman of spiritual and sexual exploration. Does she really believe that the passage of twenty years has somehow deactivated the mines that lie between us? Surely not. But perhaps she feels that in that hidden place, surrounded by our secret past, we can speak of things too painful to broach anywhere else. If that's what it takes to get her to solve the riddle of our truncated history, I'm willing. As I point the Spyder south and let the motor out, she lays her head back on the seat and smiles into the sky.

This is not the first time since my father's trial that Livy has tried to bridge the gulf it opened be-

354

tween us. Three years after she disappeared from Natchez, she was asked to be Queen of the Confederate Pageant, the apogee of social recognition by old Natchez standards. She was at UVA then, and everyone who was anyone waited on pins and needles to see whether she would accept. No one had ever declined the invitation to be queen, but all her life Livy had vowed that, if asked, she would be the first. That she *would* be asked was never in doubt. Her grandmother had been queen in the nineteen-thirties, her mother in the fifties, and if Livy accepted, she would be the first third-generation queen in history. Yet for years she had denigrated the Confederate Pageant (the nightly highlight of the pilgrimage to Natchez's antebellum mansions) as a hobby for garden club ladies with nothing better to do, a celebration of the Old South without a trace of irony or racial awareness. A lot of "new Natchez" people thought she was mostly right, and she earned points with them for flouting tradition. So, in the spring of my junior year, when it was announced to great fanfare that Livy Marston had agreed to sacrifice two weeks of college to serve as queen, I was stunned. For nine nights she would preside over the very pageant she had scorned, playing a generic Scarlett O'Hara for those Yankees and Europeans who journeyed thousands of miles to see the Old South reincarnated. This was vintage Livy Marston, the girl who liked to have things both ways.

The Pilgrimage season sparkles with evening parties, culminating in formal balls — the Queen's and King's — where liquor and champagne flow like water, and guests spanning four generations dance deep into the night. Nowadays the king's and queen's balls are often compressed into a single event, a telling commentary on the reduced fortunes of the city. But twenty years ago they were Gatsby-like orgies of conspicuous consumption, competitive arenas for the proud parents of young royalty. Livy's ball was the grandest in recent memory, and no one expected anything less. I was not invited, of course. But my date was: an "old Natchez" girl with a wicked sense of humor and no great love for the Marstons. I initially declined her invitation, but she finally convinced me that it would be a crime to skip such a historic display of excess.

Fifteen hundred invitations were mailed, and more than two thousand people chose to attend. Leo chartered a jet to fly Livy's sorority sisters down from UVA, a plane packed with Tri-Delts that — had it crashed — would have sent the Virginia marriage market into an irrecoverable tailspin. Ice sculptures were trucked down from Memphis in refrigerated vans, wondrous fantasy figures that melted so fast they drew solemn crowds of matrons who looked near tears that such extravagant beauty would be allowed to perish. Livy herself wore an eighteen-thousand-dollar gown hand-sewn by the woman who crafted the dresses for the Mardi Gras queens in New Orleans. It was made of candlelight silk, white brocade, and imported satin gathered tightly at the waist and spreading to a veritable landscape of snowy fabric embellished with alençon lace, pearls, iridescent paillettes, and jewels, and trailed by a seven-foot, three-paneled fan train to be carried by toddler pages during the pageant.

Traditionally queens never wore their pageant dresses to the balls, but Livy Marston, as ever, decided to make her own rules. When she appeared in the entrance of the hotel ballroom — escorted by the quarterback of the University of Virginia football team — a thousand women sighed together, making a sound like a soft wind. All I could think of was Audrey Hepburn at the head of the staircase in *My Fair Lady*, a shimmering chrysalis transformed into the most beautiful creature in the world. Even when the ball began in earnest, you could sense where Livy was at all times, a center of social gravity around which everyone whirled in attentive, almost worshipful fascination.

My date and I danced at the periphery of the crowd. She knew that, were I to come face to face with Leo Marston so soon after the trial, sparks would fly. I occasionally glimpsed Livy near me, spinning in the arms of her quarterback or her father, or passing in a glittering flock of Tri-Delts. But our eyes never met.

In the third hour of the ball, she suddenly appeared at my shoulder, touched my date on the arm, and said, "May I borrow him for one dance?"

I don't know why I went with her, but I did. Livy led me off without even pretending to dance, whisking me through the crowd as though pursued by paparazzi. She stopped long enough to hug a sorority sister, who giggled and glanced at me during a strange flurry of arms and handbags. Then Livy pulled me on again, nodding regally to anyone who tried to stop her, floating through the tuxedos and store-bought gowns like the daughter of a tsar in the Winter Palace.

Suddenly we were outside, moving along a row of blue doors. In a brick alcove she stopped and pressed her lips to mine, her eyes flashing in the dark. She tasted like champagne. When we pulled apart to breathe, she said, "I can't believe you came. My parents are livid." Before I could answer, we were off again, passing door after numbered door until she stopped and opened one with a key. *That's what she hugged her sorority sister for,* I thought as she pulled me inside the room.

That was the last coherent thought I had for some time. Livy sat on the edge of the bed and held me before her, working at my belt, then freed me with an exhalation of satisfaction and enclosed me again in an infinitely warmer place. Receiving this sort of attention from a woman wearing an eighteen-thousand-dollar gown is quite an experience, enough to obliterate consciousness. As I felt myself crossing the point of no return, she drew back and said, "My turn," then pulled me down to my knees, kissed me, lifted the jeweled hem of that dress, and lay back on the bed.

Her undergarments were surprisingly simple considering the dress worn over them, and I removed them with a surreal sense of wonder. She tasted as she always had — clean and coppery — and climaxed almost instantly, as though she'd been poised on a cliff, preparing for a long dive, with only a slight push needed to send her over. The ululations that escaped her throat drove me into a state of primitive arousal. I reared up over her, but she held me away and said, "No. The dress." While I stared in amazement, she stood, turned around, and guided my fingers to an invisible line of eyelets that ran along her spine. There must have been two hundred of them, and each had to be unhooked before the dress would free her. While I worked at the hooks, Livy reached back and worked at me, and after a seeming eternity, eighteen thousand dollars of Leo Marston's money hit the cheap hotel carpet with a haughty rustle.

She lifted the dress off the floor and laid it carefully across the table by the window. Then she stood before me with a pride I have seen in no other woman, supremely secure, elegant even without clothes. The bitterness that had tortured our families was nowhere in her eyes. There was only us. She reached past me and pulled the coverlet off the bed, then took both my hands and pulled me onto the sheet, kissed me deeply, and lay back, pulling me across her. I supported my weight on my arms and peered into her eyes, which were wide open and glowing with desire. She caressed my nipples with her fingers, the hint of a smile on her lips. When my breath went shallow, she slid her hands down to my waist, pulled me between her legs, and whispered, "Make love to me."

In that moment I became almost preternaturally aware of the ball in the next building, missing its queen now, the guests like hundreds of planets and moons whirling through space without their sun. I could feel the anxiety of the quarterback, the puzzlement of Livy's parents, the confusion of her sorority sisters. Their sun was here, in this dark room, unclothed, aroused, wanting me.

But she didn't, really. Not the way I wanted her

to. She wanted me, yes, but she also wanted Virginia and her quarterback and her parents' admiration and a thousand things besides. She wanted me for those few minutes, in that context, while I filled some discomfiting space in the puzzle of how she saw herself in her sheltered little universe. The first glimmer of this knowledge cut me to the bone. Despite all that had happened between our fathers, I loved her. I wanted her in the way most women dream of being wanted. Till death do us part. She wanted me *for the night*. The way I'd wanted girls before. Utterly and completely until my passion was spent, and then not at all. She wanted me to fill her with myself, and by so doing, make myself less. She would own me then, in a way, without ever having to bother with me again. She would nullify the past and move on. She should have whispered "Fuck me" — not "Make love to me" — because that was what she meant. This realization terrified me, and it taught me more about what it was to be female than I would learn in all the rest of my life.

"I can't," I said, looking down at her with secret horror.

She reached between us and squeezed the rigid evidence to the contrary, pressed me against her sex, her eyes triumphant. For an instant — for the only time in my life — I felt the urge to rape, to plunge inside her with all the violence I could muster and pound against her womb until she could stand no more. But even that would have been her victory. She would, I suspect, have enthusiastically endured my most violent onslaught, reached a slightly more intense orgasm than usual, and then subsumed my rage and sadness into her with my seed, leaving her serene and content. That is the superiority of a woman unencumbered by love.

I could do only one thing to save myself, and I did it. I climbed off of her and began to dress. From the expression on her face, I was the only man who had ever done this, at least for any reason other than performance anxiety. And I was doing it because I loved her. She stared wordlessly at me, unable to believe I was doing what her eyes told her I was, even when I buttoned my tuxedo trousers and walked to the door.

"What are you *doing?*" she asked finally, her voice hoarse with confusion.

I couldn't see her clearly at that distance, so I focused instead on the white dress, which lay across the table like a fallen battle flag in the darkness, an artifact of a secret engagement no one would ever record. "Saving my soul," I said.

"What about my dress?" she asked, hysteria creeping into her voice. "I can't put it on by myself."

"You'll think of something."

And she did. She reappeared at the ball a half hour later, looking no worse for wear, and I'm certain that the UVA quarterback got the lay of his life later that night, without ever knowing why. I didn't tell my date what had happened, but when I took her home, she kissed me fervently and pushed my hands into her dress. I resisted at first, but she pressed me against her until I gave in to the moment. We spilled out of the car onto the grass and made love recklessly and fiercely beside her par-

361

ents' house, until all I had withheld from Livy sluiced from me in an annihilating rush. I did not love that girl, but that was all right. She knew I didn't, and she wanted me anyway.

"Where are you, Penn?"

I blink myself to the reality of Liberty Road, startled to find Livy beside me, her hand in mine. She looks scarcely older than she did on the night of that ball.

"Nowhere good," I reply, steering the Fiat around a hairpin turn. This road was old when Mississippi became a territory in 1798, and it has settled deep into the earth over the centuries. The dirt banks rise higher than the car, and in some places the limbs of oaks meet high above our heads.

"What are you really doing in Natchez?" Livy asks.

"I thought you said no questions."

She refills my styrofoam cup and passes it to me. "You don't have to answer if you don't want to."

"Annie's having a tough time getting over Sarah's death. I couldn't help her. My mother has already worked wonders with her." I sweep around another turn, passing a cement truck like it's standing still. "What are *you* really doing here?"

"Visiting my mother. I told you that." Livy points to our right. "There's the turn."

I swing the Spyder off the pavement and into deep gravel that quickly shallows to ruts as thick pine forest closes around us.

"The next turn's easy to miss," she reminds me.

Twenty years ago, a dirt oil-field road led to the Cold Hole. Some lucky wildcatter hit a well not fifty yards from the pool, and while this damaged the aesthetic of the place, the pool itself remained pure and clear. Surrounded by a jungle of cypress trees, dense fern, and a carpet of lily pads, it remained an essentially secret place, where time and society held no sway. Summer after summer adolescents reenacted the eternal rites there, clothed and naked, drunk and sober, but always defiantly, totally alive. A plank walkway led across the lily pads to the edge of the clear water, and high in a tall cypress a diving platform had been built. Livy and I spent the most perfect day of our lives on that perch, lost in each other's eyes, talking of God and time and other imponderables, poised in that blessed state of awareness that has yet to comprehend its own mortality.

We were drinking white wine that day too, but we also had one bottle of red. The sun was so hot that we wanted to keep even the red cold. To this end, I climbed down the platform and swam to the bottom of the pool, into the waving fronds, so deep that my eardrums ached in the cold current welling up from the spring below. I wedged the bottle tightly among the stems of the water plants, then fought my way back to the surface and climbed up to the platform.

Hours later, when the sun began to fall, we carefully negotiated our way back down to the water, and I dove for the bottle of red that I'd cached at the bottom. I could not find it. Livy joined me, but we searched in vain, though we stayed until night descended over the swamp, and snakes and alligators became a real concern.

Many times since, I've thought of that bottle.

Once I even considered donning scuba gear to salvage it, so that I could ship it to Livy as a gift. (I'm pretty sure I conceived this madness on the night I heard she was getting married.) I'm not much for symbolism, but that unopened bottle of red wine fills the bill if ever anything did. Inside it is a road unwalked, a life unlived. And today, I suspect, Livy means to find it. An impossible task, probably. But impossible is a word she never paid much attention to. Her attitude is simple: where Livy Marston goes, the rules do not apply.

"Stop!" she cries. "I think you passed it."

I hit the brakes, skid a few yards through the gravel, then back up until Livy says stop. An autumnal sadness suffuses me when I see the overgrown track, a desolate path through the trees that none would take but a killer looking for a place to dump his victim.

"Pull in," orders Livy.

I nose the Spyder into the trees, and she climbs out without opening the door and starts through the waist-high weeds. I put up the top of the convertible as quickly as I can and follow.

Five minutes' hard walking brings us to the edge of the swamp. The old pumping unit is still here, its great black arm frozen in place like a broken limb, the oil-bearing sands beneath the swamp long since depleted. The smell of stale crude permeates the air, and the cypress trees have no tops, casualties of salt water leaking from the well. The swamp itself is a scummy greenish-brown, swarming with breeding mosquitoes and obscured by a head-high wall of swamp grass. Our enchanted pool is gone.

"Well," I say philosophically. "I guess it's true."

"What?"

"You can't go home again."

Livy stares at the mess as though willing it back to its former beauty. I stand mute, waiting for her to face reality. But she won't. Why should she? Reality never stopped her before. She strips off her shirt and jeans, revealing a white one-piece bathing suit underneath. Then she hops onto a fallen tree that angles off through the hissing grass and walks like a gymnast down the rotting trunk. I call out for her to stop, but she pays no attention.

I have little choice but to follow.

When I get to the end of the trunk, I find myself stranded in a snaky morass with Livy nowhere in sight.

"Penn?" she calls from a jungle of foliage to my left. "Come here."

"Where are you?"

"There's a stump just below the surface of the water. That will take you to the next trunk."

Sighting the half-submerged stump, I leap onto it, catching myself just before I tumble headfirst into the slime. From here I can jump to the next fallen tree. Landing on the end of that one, I find myself peering down a green tunnel of leaves.

Livy stands at the other end, a motionless figure silhouetted by dazzling sunlight. Her body is still remarkable, not in the willowy way of a model or the lush way of a pinup girl, but somewhere in between. Her breasts are small but beautifully shaped, her wrists and ankles slim, her hands graceful. Yet the predominant impression she projects is of strength. She could be Artemis, more at home in the forest than among people. In this moment I cannot imagine her in a courtroom.

"Here," she beckons, stretching out her hand, her voice laced with mystery.

I teeter out to the end of the trunk like a drunken riveter working high steel, then perform the tightly pleasant maneuver of edging around Livy. She holds my waist from behind and whispers: "Oh, ye of little faith."

The Cold Hole sparkles like a diamond on brown velvet, a pristine world in the midst of decay. The swamp must have risen over the years, its edge creeping ever nearer the oil well, but our spring-fed pool is where it always was. You just have to work a little harder to find it. Livy points high into the trees, and I follow her line of sight. Even the diving platform has survived, though damaged by the growth of the cypress. Once we spent hours kissing and touching each other up there, quivering like dryads in the high branches.

Without warning, Livy dives off the tree trunk and swims to the foot of the ladder. She climbs four planks high, then turns and motions for me to follow. I strip to my underwear and dive after her. The climb requires the negotiation of many rotten and missing steps, but before long we are perched forty feet above the water, breathing hard and laughing. From here the pool looks translucent, bottomless, like a hole in the floor of the world.

"Do you think it's still there?" she asks.

"It can't be."

"The pool is."

"Storms . . . the current from the spring . . . that bottle could be a mile away by now."

She shakes her head. "It's down there in the mud and the plants. And I'm going to find it."

"Livy —"

Before I can argue, she arcs down to the pool like a falling arrow, lands dead center with scarcely a splash, and surfaces laughing. She waves and submerges again. I consider going down to help her, but I don't think she wants that. She wants to prove to me that she can find the bottle alone.

She searches with systematic diligence, diving to the bottom and probing the mud and plants in ever widening circles, surfacing for air, then diving again, her movements supple and efficient. It's like watching a Japanese pearl diver, except that Livy looks as unlike a Japanese woman as one can get. She is archetypally Western — Aryan even — like a hawk that has plummeted a thousand feet to penetrate the water and seize its prey. After fifty minutes by my watch, she surfaces and begins treading water, her face lifted to mine.

"I can't find it!"

I hold up my hands in commiseration and call down to her. "It doesn't matter. You can't resurrect the past with a bottle of wine."

She gives me an insouciant smile and dives again, so deeply that I lose sight of her. When she surfaces, she is at the edge of the pool, holding something in her hand. Not the wine. Her bathing suit. She drapes the white lycra over a cypress knee, then with a graceful roll pushes away from the stump and, floating effortlessly on her back, drifts to the center of the pool. This vision is more potent than any wine; it is my dream made flesh: Livy's hair floating in a corona around her face, her

367

arms loose at her sides, her breasts little rose-tipped islands, her abdomen a submerged reef stretching to the rise of her pubis with its twist of burnished gold. The sight of her heats the backs of my eyes. As I gaze down, she raises a hand to block the sun and calls out:

"Don't you swim anymore?"

I scoot to the edge of the platform and drop forty feet through space, plunging deep into the pool. When I float to the surface, I find Livy treading water beside me. She splashes me playfully and says: "I really thought I could find it."

"Even if you had, it wouldn't make things like they were before. We have to talk about what happened."

She looks off through the silver cypress trunks. "I can't. Not yet." She stops treading and lies back, half floating, gazing into the hazy blue sky. "I've thought about that bottle sometimes. Over the years."

"Me too. During low times. Four o'clock in the morning, wondering if I ever made a single right choice in my life."

She seems amused by this. "Not me. I thought about it during good times. Or times that were supposed to be good. I thought about it on my wedding night."

"Your wedding night?"

She turns her head slightly, watching me as she floats. "There I was, supposed to feel some profound completion as a woman, and all I could think was that I was closing off forever an option I'd always thought I had."

"And you did."

Her eyes narrow. "You hadn't exactly made me feel wanted the last time we'd seen each other."

I look away, unwilling to explain my actions on the night of the ball without reciprocal explanations from her.

"We should have drunk that bottle twenty years ago," she says. "The extra time it would have taken might have changed everything that came after."

I shake my head, unwilling to grant her this easy revision of history. "Then I wouldn't have Annie."

For a moment she looks as though she might make some cruel remark, but her face softens. "I didn't mean it like that. We're here now. I'm not complaining." She brings herself upright in the water, flips a wet strand of hair from her eyes, then reaches out and touches my nose. "Will you do one thing?"

"What?"

"Kiss me."

Livy has given me nothing that I need, not a single answer. But I want to kiss her. Between the fatigue of treading cold water and the proximity of her naked body, I feel as though every capillary in my skin has dilated, magnifying sensation. She swims closer and slips a hand behind my neck. I lean forward and press my lips to hers, gently at first, then harder in response to her passion. Treading water is impossible now. I take a quick breath through my nose as we slide beneath the surface.

Undulating in the slow current of the spring, time is the oxygen remaining in our lungs and blood, but there is enough to remember her taste, the pressure of her breasts against me as we sink like a single creature, an incarnation of salt water, only slightly denser than the fluid surrounding us. As my chest begins to burn, I feel the soft roughness between her legs, pressing against my thigh, seeking more complete union, and I swell with unthinking eagerness. Then my lungs betray me, sending me fighting toward the shimmering surface. I smash through gasping for air, resenting the fact that I need it. Livy gently breaks the surface beside me, her neck and shoulders flushed the color of broken seashells. She pulls back her hair, then treads easily as her clear blue eyes search mine.

"I want you inside me."

I shake my head.

"I love you, Penn. I always have. I just didn't have the courage to choose you."

Her words are like needles thrust into my heart, triggering emotions too intense to withstand, much less interpret. Caitlin's warning on the plane sounds in my head: *She could really mess you up* —

"You don't have any right to say that, Livy."

"I know. I won't say it again. But I had to let you know."

I roll away from her and swim back to the fallen tree that leads to the shore. As I climb onto it, I turn and see her perched on the cypress knee where she left her bathing suit, slipping on the white lycra as gracefully as she does everything else.

"Where next?" she calls across the water, making no attempt to cover herself.

"I think it's time we got back."

"Home? But the day's not half over."

"I need to check on Annie."

She nods somberly. "I understand."

I turn and make my way carefully along the slippery log. For any other woman I would wait, but Livy Marston can take care of herself.

As I swing the Fiat back onto Highway 61, I realize with a dull shock that guilt is not among the torrent of emotions rushing through me. A moment's thought tells me why: my past with Livy predates my life with Sarah. Intimacy with Livy is not a new experience. It's like walking through a checkpoint to a country I visited long ago and to which I now return, older and — hopefully — wiser.

She doesn't speak as the Spyder thrums northward in the afternoon sun, but I feel her eyes upon me, trying to penetrate my thoughts. What really brought her back to Natchez? Caitlin's belief that Livy has returned to persuade me to leave her father alone is not impossible. But Livy would not declare her love for such a cynical reason. That is the one gift she's reserved through the years, if indeed she has given love to anyone. She certainly must have said the words more than a few times, probably while trying to believe them herself. But why did she want this reprise of a perfect day twenty years past? And why does she think she loves me? Is it some strange analogue of a man wanting to marry the only girl who wouldn't sleep with him?

As we pass St. Stephens Preparatory School and join the traffic heading into town, Livy touches my knee and says, "After you check on Annie, let's do something else. We still have our picnic."

Her voice is calm enough, but I sense anxiety be-

371

neath it. She is reluctant to let this day end. To-morrow things will not be so simple. It's one thing to pretend for a few hours that we can evade the past, as this town somehow evades the future. But it will be quite another when I insist on asking the questions she didn't want to hear today. And what will happen after I tell the world that her father ordered the murder of Delano Payton? When I commence my campaign of attrition against him? How will she feel then?

"I think we've done a lot to think about already," I say evenly.

She bites her lower lip and looks away.

The whine of a siren overtakes us from behind, and I glance at the rearview mirror. Traffic is parting on the highway behind us. We're at the turn for my parents' neighborhood, so I swing right off the bypass, clearing the way.

"Penn?" Livy says, her voice tinged with fear. "Look."

A column of gray smoke is roiling out of the treetops in the distance.

"Penn, that's a fire."

I hit the accelerator hard, knowing that a neighbor could be in trouble. Most of them are older now, and it doesn't matter whose house it is: I've probably known the family all my life.

"Where is it?" she asks, her voice tight.

"Close to my parents."

I press harder on the gas, roaring up the street, with every yard becoming more afraid of something my brain does not want to consider. It couldn't be our house burning. It couldn't be.

Fifty yards from the corner, I see that it is.

CHAPTER 26

I drive the Fiat right into the yard, where my mother stands with Annie and a dozen neighbors, all pointing helplessly at the burning house, all in various stages of shock. I jump out of the car, run to my mother, and take Annie from her arms.

"Daddy, the house is on fire!" she cries, more amazed than frightened.

"The fire engine's right behind me," I tell Mom. "Is everybody okay?"

She grabs my arms, her eyes wide with terror. "Ruby's in there! We heard a boom and then smelled smoke . . . when we saw the flames we ran but Ruby fell. Penn, I think she broke her hip. I couldn't drag her out. I brought Annie out, and by then it was too bad to get back in. But that off-duty policeman — Officer Ervin — he went in anyway. He went after Ruby, but he never came out!"

"How long ago was this?"

My mother is close to hyperventilating. I put my hands on her shoulders and squeeze hard enough for her to feel pain.

"Five minutes . . . maybe more. I don't know."

As I stare at the house, a runner of flame races up the roof shingles. That's no kitchen fire. The whole house is burning. The house I grew up in.

"Where was Ruby when she fell?"

"By the back bathroom."

There's no exterior door anywhere near that bathroom. And going through the front door would be suicide. I wouldn't even make it to the bedrooms before being overcome by smoke. I hug Annie and pass her to Mom, then kiss them both.

"When the firemen get here, tell them to look for Ervin."

My mother blanches. "Penn, you can't go in there."

"I'm not leaving Ruby in there to die."

Livy grabs my arm from behind. "Penn, it's too late. Wait for the fire truck."

I yank my arm free and sprint toward the garage before either of them can say more. In the garage I grab a shovel, then race around to the back of the house. As I near it, I begin smashing windows, trying to give the trapped smoke as many outlets as possible. I may be feeding oxygen to the blaze, but if I don't get some smoke out of there, I'll never reach Ruby alive.

The back bathroom has no window, but the adjacent bedroom does. A high, horizontal one about five feet wide and eighteen inches tall. I smash the glass with the shovel and stand back as thick gray smoke explodes through the opening. After thirty seconds, the plume thins a little, and I put my hand through the window. The heat is intense, but when I stand on tiptoe and put my face to the opening, I see no flames.

Taking off my shirt, I soak it in water at the outdoor faucet, then tie it around my face. I am

374

scraping the window sill clean of glass shards when the scream comes. The sound is an alloy of animal terror and human agony, a child's wail from the throat of an eighty-year-old woman. An eighty-year-old woman who showed me more love and kindness than anyone but my mother. I feel like someone stuck my fingers into a 220-volt socket.

"Ruby! Ruby, it's Penn! I'm coming to get you!"

Hooking both hands over the sill, I swing my right leg up into the window and pull myself into the frame. The smoke that looked thin from out-side instantly scorches my eyes, throat, and lungs. Breathing is pointless until I get my face down to the floor. I roll off the window frame and drop to the carpet.

There's air here, but the smoke is still too thick to see through. Before I lose my nerve, I shut my eyes and crawl around the bed toward the door that leads to the hallway. If I hadn't lived in this house for fourteen years — and stayed here for the past few nights — I wouldn't have a chance of finding Ruby. That's why Officer Ervin didn't get out. He's probably lying unconscious in the hall, if he even made it past the den furniture.

At the doorway I pause and shout again.

"Ruby! *Rubeee!*"

All I hear is a living roar, the sound of fire de-vouring wood and carpet, curtains and glass, photos and china, silver and books — *Books.* My father's library is burning. If Ruby was not some-where in this house, I would probably risk my life to save those books.

The bathroom, I remember. *Ruby fell by the bath-room.*

375

Thankfully, the heat is more intense to my right, toward the central hall. I put my nose to the carpet, take a breath, and crawl to my left, toward the bathroom. It's two rooms, really, a narrow dressing room and linen closet with the commode and bathtub in a smaller cubicle beyond. I go through the door on my belly, groping forward like a soldier clearing a minefield.

The dressing room is empty. As I crawl toward the commode, my nostrils start to whistle with each breath. Panic ambushes me, like a wild thing tearing around in my chest. *Maybe Ruby isn't here at all. Maybe Ervin got her out. Maybe the scream I heard was the sound she made as he dragged her out.* I can't search the whole house. That's how firemen get killed, trying to save people who aren't there. I grope around the commode and inside the bathtub, then scramble back to the bathroom door.

The roar is closer.

"Ruby! It's Penn! Are you here?"

At first there is only the roar. Then a whimper floats out of the noise like a leaf from a bonfire. It came from the central hall. My lungs feel near to bursting, but I alligator along the carpet toward the corner, my eyes shut tight. The heat is nearly unendurable. Forcing my stinging eyes open, I look down the hall.

Dancing tongues of red and orange caper out of the black smoke like laughing demons. Primal terror seizes my muscles, paralyzing me long enough to fully comprehend the danger. Then my reptile brain shrieks: *Death! Run!*

But I don't run. I can't. When I was six years old,

a German shepherd got out of a neighbor's back-yard and trapped me in a corner of our carport. That dog weighed ninety pounds, and when it bared its teeth and lunged at my face, all I could do was throw up my arms. When its teeth ripped into my flesh, I was too panic-stricken even to yell for help. After a seeming eternity of gnashing teeth and blood, I heard a sound like a hatchet hitting a watermelon, and saw a black woman as tall as our house swinging a shovel like a broadsword, blud-geoning that monstrous animal within an inch of its life. Ruby Flowers was terrified of dogs, but when she saw "her baby" in danger, she pressed down her fear and charged out of our house like the wrath of God.

Fixing that image in my mind, I shut my eyes and crawl toward the flames. The frantic reptile voice whispers that the orange demons are flanking me, racing across the roof to close off my escape. But I hold Ruby's face in my mind, keep inching forward.

My hand touches flesh.

Bone.

An ankle.

The smell of cooked meat fills my nose and lungs, and I vomit up the wine I drank with Livy. Retching in the darkness, I take hold of the ankle and pull with all my strength. Something gives, and Ruby screams. At least she's alive. A broken hip can kill an old woman, but not as quickly as fire.

Switching ankles, I pull with both hands, drag-ging her far enough to get clear of the flames. She's moaning now, the sound like that of a wounded animal. I press my nose to the floor, take another breath of smoke, then get to my knees and heave her over my shoulder. As I struggle to my feet, dizziness pitches me against the wall, but somehow I right myself and stagger back toward the bedrooms.

The smoke is dense here too, but at the center of it is a dim, cool flicker of blue. I lean toward that blueness, trying to keep Ruby on my shoulder as I go forward. *Move your feet,* I yell silently. *Move . . .* It's as though my nerve fibers are shorting out one by one, attenuating the signals firing from my brain. Again the stench of scorched meat gags me, but I'm almost to the light. With a last heave I lift Ruby onto the windowsill and hold her there.

I don't want to drop her, but I can barely stand, much less lower her the six feet to the ground.

Suddenly two bright yellow gloves appear and pull her from my grasp. Male voices are shouting through the window, but I can't make out the words. The world outside the window seems part of some other universe. More yellow hands reach out of the brightness, reaching for me, but they are too far away.

I am falling.

The sun is in my eyes, and the skin of my face is burning.

A teenager wearing a black fireman's hat is holding something over my mouth and nose, and something like cool ambrosia is laving the burning walls of my lungs. I try to suck in more of it, but the effort triggers a coughing fit, great wracking spasms like blades tearing at my ribs and trachea as smoke pours from my nose and throat.

"Penn, I'm here," says a woman's voice.

"Mom?"

"Livy."

I see her face beside the fireman's now, her hair still damp from the Cold Hole. She takes my hand and squeezes gently.

"Ruby?" I ask.

"She's right over there. Look to your left."

As I turn, I see two paramedics rolling a gurney across the lawn. A third is holding an IV bag at shoulder level as it drains fluid into Ruby's arm.

"I want to see her," I croak, rolling over and getting to my knees.

"Easy, sir," says the fireman. "You've been through a little hell in the past few minutes."

He's not really a teenager. He's probably in his mid-twenties, with a thin blond mustache and a hank of straight hair spilling from under his helmet.

"The cop?" I ask, recalling Officer Ervin's droopy beagle eyes. "The cop who went in after her?"

"We got him out. Take it easy."

"I'm okay . . . really."

Livy slides under my right arm as I get to my feet, supporting me with surprising strength. I've never felt so jittery in my life. All my muscles are quivering and jerking as though exhausted by an overexpenditure of adrenaline, and my heart is laboring noticeably in my chest.

"The library," I remember. "My dad's books."

Livy shakes her head. "It's too late. The whole house is going up. It's a miracle you got out alive."

"That's a fact," says the fireman. "We pulled you out just as the flames came through the bedroom door."

"Thank you. I know I could have died in there."

He smiles and gives me a salute. "You done pretty good yourself, buddy."

With Livy's help I make my way around to the front yard.

It looks as though every neighbor for a square mile has come to watch the fire. The crowd fills the surrounding yards and much of the street. Two fire trucks have their hoses trained on the house, and a third on the old oak with the creeper vine.

My mother runs up to me, her face ashen. "Penn! I can't find Annie!"

I jerk erect and shake my head clear. "Where did you see her last?"

"After you went in. It was taking so long — I was looking for you. I just put her down for a second!"

"How long ago?"

"Three or four minutes!"

The area is so choked with people that Annie could be ten feet away and we'd still miss her. The only thing in our favor is that we know most of the people in the crowd. Within five minutes, everyone on the street is looking for her.

As I run shirtless through the throng, fighting down panic, all I can think is that this fire was no accident. The "boom" my mother heard had to be some kind of fire bomb. This whole disaster was staged to draw the attention of the cop watching the house. And it did. Officer Ervin bravely charged into the inferno to save Ruby's life, and in the process left my mother and daughter unprotected. My similar effort completed the kidnaper's work, by breaking my mother's concentration.

After five minutes of searching in vain, I realize I have to call the police. I prosecuted several kidnaping cases in Houston, and I learned one thing from the FBI agents who worked them. The first hour is the best chance of finding the victim, and every lost minute can mean disaster.

As I run across the street to use our neighbor's phone, a ripple of noise like the roar at a football stadium rolls through the crowd. I turn back to our house, expecting to see the roof collapsing, the spectacular climax of residential fires. But it's not the roof. The crowd parts like the Red Sea, and my mother comes running through the open space.

She's carrying Annie in her arms.

Relief surges through me with such force that I nearly faint for the second time. But I run forward and hug them both as tightly as I dare. Annie's face is white with terror, and her chin is quivering.

"Someone dropped her off at Edna Hensley's," Mom gasps. "Edna answered her door and saw Annie standing there crying."

A heavyset, blue-haired woman I faintly recognize has appeared behind my mother, wheezing from her exertions. Edna Hensley.

"Where do you live?" I ask her.

"About a half mile away. You've been there before, Penn. When you were a little boy."

"Who dropped her off?"

Edna shakes her head. "I didn't see anyone. Not a car, not anything." Her gaze darkens. She reaches into her pocket, pulls out a folded sheet of construction paper, and hands it to me.

I unfold the paper with shaking hands. Printed on it in magic marker are the words: *THIS IS HOW EASY IT IS. LAY OFF, ASSHOLE.*

Livy braces me from the side, making sure I keep my feet.

I am back in Houston, watching Arthur Lee Hanratty's brother carry Annie out of the house, a tiny bundle about to disappear forever. It's as though I missed him that night, and he has returned to try again. But he can't. He's been dead for four years. His youngest brother is alive, but this isn't his work. Whoever kidnaped Annie today could easily have killed her, and the last surviving Hanratty would have done so, taking his revenge for his two brothers. This is something else entirely. This is a warning. This is the Del Payton case.

"Mom, take this piece of paper to the Lewises' house and put it in a Ziploc bag. I'll take care of Annie."

She is reluctant to go, but she does. I thank Edna Hensley, then carry Annie through the crowd to Livy's borrowed Fiat and sit in the passenger seat, hugging her against me, rocking slowly, murmuring reassurances in her ear. She is still shivering, and her skin is frighteningly cold. I need to find out everything she can remember about her kidnaper before she starts blocking out the trauma, but I don't want to upset her any more than she already is.

"Annie?" I whisper, lifting her away from me enough to look into her hazel eyes. "It's Daddy, punkin."

Tears spill down her cheeks.

"Everything's all right now. I love you, punkin."

She opens her mouth to speak, but her quivering chin ruins the words before they emerge.

"Honey, who took you to the lady's house? Did you see?"

She nods hesitantly.

"Who was it? Did you know them?"

"Fuh . . . fire. Fire man," she stammers. "Fire man."

"A fireman? With a red hat?"

She shakes her head. "A black and yellow hat."

"That's good, punkin. He was just making sure you were all right. Did you see his face?"

"He had a mask. Like a swimming mask."

A respirator. "That's good. Did he say anything to you?"

"He said he had to get me away. Get me safe."

"That's right, that's right. He was just getting you away from the fire. Everything's fine now."

Her face seems to crumple in on itself. "Daddy, I'm scared."

I crush her to my chest, as though to protect her from the threat that has already passed. "I love you, punkin. I love you."

She shudders against me.

"I said, I love you, punkin." I pull her back and look into her eyes, waiting.

"I love you more," she says softly, completing our ritual, and my anxiety lessens a little.

Livy climbs into the driver's seat, squeezes Annie's shoulder, then takes her silk scarf from the glove compartment and begins wiping soot from my face.

"Where do you want to go?" she asks.

"Let's just sit for a minute."

"Do you think it's safe here? Your mom told me about the note."

Instead of answering her question, I lift the Fiat's cell phone, call Information, and ask for the number of Ray Presley. Livy takes her hand from my knee and watches me with apprehension. Presley's phone rings twenty times. No one answers.

"Is he there?" she asks in a quiet voice.

"No."

Her face is strangely slack. "Penn, why did you call Ray Presley?"

"There's no time to go into it now."

"Penn? Where are you, son?"

It's my father. "Over here, Dad!"

Livy looks back over the trunk of the convertible. "He's seen us. He's coming."

"Olivia!" Dad cries, rushing up to the car. "Are you all right?"

"I'm fine, it's Penn and Annie who need help. I'm so sorry about this, Dr. Cage. It's just unbelievable."

Dad leans over the passenger door and hugs Annie and me. Annie keeps her head buried in my neck.

"Is she all right?"

"I think so. Considering what just happened. Somebody —"

"I already heard. The story's spreading like —" He laughs bitterly. "Like wildfire. Where's your mother?"

"I told her to go across the street and put the note in a Ziploc. There might be fingerprints." I reach up and take his hand. "I should have listened to you. You told me they'd stoop this low."

He squeezes my hand hard. "It's just a house. We'll build another one."

"I was crazy to get involved in this case."

He shakes his head, his eyes on the great column of smoke rising into the sky. "Gutless sons of bitches . . . laid hands on my granddaughter. If I find the man who did this, I'll flay him alive."

"Do you know anything about Ruby's condition?"

He sighs heavily. "They carried her to St. Catherine's Hospital. Peter Carelli's in the ER with her now. It doesn't look good. Massive third-degree burns, a broken hip. The helicopter's on its way from Jackson. I'm about to go over there."

"We'll follow you as soon as Mom gets back."

He nods absently, watching the water pour onto the ruin that sheltered our family for thirty-five years.

"Dad, the library —"

"I know. No point thinking about it now. Right now we worry about the living." He looks down at me, his eyes flinty and cold. "This is the crossroads, son. We back off or we go forward. It's your call. I'll back you either way."

Go forward? After this? "Let's just find Mom and get to the hospital."

He nods. "I'll see you there."

The treatment room in the ER is crowded but quiet. The muted beeps of monitors punctuate the hushed voices like metronomes. Ruby lies at the center of the room, a technological still life surrounded by doctors, nurses, a respiratory therapist, and my father. I move closer, straightening the scrub shirt a nurse brought me to replace the shirt I lost in the fire. Two large-bore IV lines are pouring fluids into Ruby's arms, and oxygen is being pumped into her lungs through a mask. Her mostly nude body is exposed to the air, the parts ravaged by fire — her right arm, shoulder, trunk, and both legs — bathed in Silvadene ointment. She was apparently wearing some sort of synthetic dress that caught fire and melted into her skin. The helicopter ambulance summoned from Jackson is under orders to whisk her to the burn center in Greenville as soon as it arrives, but my father doubts she'll survive to make the flight.

"Let my son in here," Dad says, and the white coats part for me.

My first reaction is horror. Ruby's dentures have been removed and this makes her face look like a sunken death mask. Her black wig is also gone, leaving a thin snowy frizz atop her head. Her eyes are closed, her respiration labored. She looks like a dying woman photographed in some plague-stricken African village.

"Is she conscious?"

"She was until a minute ago," Dad replies. "She's in and out now. Mostly out. In her condition, it's a blessing."

One of Ruby's hands is undamaged, and I move around the table and take it, squeezing softly. "Did Mom talk to her?"

"A little. Ruby had a panic attack, and Peggy calmed her down."

The thought of Ruby in terror makes it difficult for me to breathe. As I look down at her, her lips tremble, then move with purpose. She's trying to speak. But what comes from behind the mask is only a ragged passage of air. I lean closer and speak into her ear.

"Ruby? It's Penn, Ruby. I hear you."

At last the rasps form words. *"...fine blessing. You ...give a fine blessing, Dr. Cage. You go on ...go on, now."*

A chill races over my neck and arms. "Dad? I think she wants you to say something religious."

"She's obtunded, son. She doesn't really know what she's saying."

"She knows. She wants you to say something over her."

My father looks around at the ring of expectant faces. "Jesus. I don't remember much."

"Anything. It doesn't matter."

He takes Ruby's hand and leans over her.

"Ruby, this is Dr. Cage. *Tom,* by God, though you refused to call me that for thirty-five years." He chuckles softly. "You're the only one in the world who could get me reciting from the Bible. Haven't done it since I was a boy."

Ruby's lips move again, but no sound emerges.

"The Lord is my shepherd," Dad says quietly. "I shall not want. He maketh me to lie down in green pastures. He leadeth me beside the still waters. He restoreth my soul. He leadeth me ... he —" Dad stops and picks up further on. "Yea, though I walk through the shadow of ... through the *valley* of the shadow of death, I will fear no evil. For thou art with me. Thy rod and thy staff they comfort me.

Thy . . ." He looks over at me. "Damn it, what's the rest of it?"

I lean down beside Ruby's ear and continue for him. "Thou preparest a table for me in the presence of mine enemies. Thou anointest my head with oil. My cup runneth over. Surely goodness and mercy will follow me all the days of my life, and I shall dwell in the house of the Lord forever."

Ruby has stopped trying to speak. Her face is placid.

Dad lays a hand on my shoulder. "Well, between us we managed it. She's got two atheists praying over her. Pretty pathetic, I guess."

"It was good enough."

Looking around, I notice expressions of shock and awe on the faces of the assembled doctors and nurses. "What's the matter?"

"They've never seen me do anything like that before."

"She's trying to speak," says a nurse.

Ruby's jaw is quivering with effort, her wrinkled, toothless mouth opening and closing behind the mask like that of a landed fish. Dad and I lean over her and strain to hear. At first there is only a lisping sound. Then three words coalesce from the shapeless sounds.

"Thank you . . . Tom."

Ruby's eyes flutter open, revealing big brown irises full of awareness. She seems to see not only us but beyond us. I suppose this is the look of faith.

"Lord Jesus," she says, as clearly as if she were talking to me across the breakfast table. "Ruby going home today. Home to glory."

Seconds later her eyes close, and the monitors

that were so muted before begin clanging alarms.

"She's coding," Dad says.

"Crash cart!" cries one of the other doctors.

A hurricane of activity erupts around us, everyone rushing to his appointed task.

"Cardiac arrest," Dad says in a calm voice.

"Tom?" says Dr. Carelli, a lean dark man in his late forties. "Clear, Tom."

Dad holds up his right hand. "Everyone listen to me. This case is DNR."

The alarms go on ringing with relentless insistence.

"Do you know that for a fact?" asks Carelli, standing anxiously over the cart with a laryngoscope in his hand. "Tom, you know the rules."

"This woman is eighty years old, she's got third-degree burns over sixty percent of her body, and a broken hip."

"Tom, for a DNR we need it on paper."

"She also has carcinoma of the lung," Dad says softly. "No one knows that but me. There's nothing on paper, but she's discussed it with me on several occasions. No extraordinary measures. Do not resuscitate. Turn off those alarms."

The whole apparatus of technology stands poised on the edge of action, and my father has ordered it to stand down.

"Tom, are you sure?" asks Carelli.

"I take full responsibility. Turn off those goddamned alarms."

One by one the alarms go off. Dad looks at me, his eyes weary. "Go on out, Penn. Check on Annie and your mother. You don't want to see this."

"Not until she's gone."

He nods slowly. "All right." He turns to the assembled staff. "Thanks for the effort, everybody. We'd like to be alone with her."

I squeeze Ruby's good hand, kiss her forehead, and wait for the end. Looking at this ravaged shell of a woman, I find it hard to believe that she was the towering figure who saved me from that German shepherd. But she was. She is. As the last nurse files out, the drumbeat of rotor blades descends over the hospital, announcing the helicopter that will return to Jackson without its scheduled passenger.

Ruby Flowers is leaving Natchez by another route.

Our family has gathered in the small chapel provided by the hospital for patients and their families. It's a small, dim room, with electric candles, two pews, an altar, and some "new" Bibles full of undistinguished prose. I'm not a believer myself, but in time of death you can do a lot worse than the King James Bible for comfort.

My mother is praying quietly at the altar. Dad sits beside me in the front pew, with Annie on his lap. This is the first time we have been together in anything like a church since Sarah's funeral. My older sister was with us for that, but she's been teaching in Ireland ever since. Today was a good day to be there and not here.

I have never seen my father this angry. Not even during the malpractice trial. He is by nature a gentle and even-tempered man, and his medical experience has taught him to be calmer as situations deteriorate. But right this minute he has blood in his eye, and I understand the feeling. If I knew with certainty that Ray Presley set that fire, or that Leo Marston had ordered it, I would shoot them both without a second thought.

Mom rises to her feet, then walks over and takes Annie from Dad. "We'd better check into a motel," she says. "And we need to think about getting some clothes. I'm sure everything is ruined."

"The insurance will cover most of it," Dad replies. "The police are waiting to talk to me in the ER."

Mom looks at him and shakes her head. "The things I cared about in that house, no insurance can replace."

"I know that, Peggy."

"Mom, I'm sorry," I say uselessly. "I know this happened because of me."

She reaches out with her free hand and squeezes my arm. "Let's just get checked in somewhere. We need to take care of this little girl."

Dad follows her to the door, then shuts it and comes back to me. "We're going to need some protection, son. Real protection. Off-duty cops aren't up to this. Who do we call?"

"I know some people in Houston. Serious people. An international security company. I'll call the CEO right now."

"I want them here tonight. I don't care what it costs."

"They'll be here. And I'm paying."

He sighs and looks at the altar. "Who do you think set that fire?"

"First guess? Ray Presley. I called his trailer while the house was burning. He wasn't home.

Could he have managed it after that poisoning attempt? After his heart attack or whatever?"

Dad nods. "Physically, he could do it. He's a lot more able than I am. What about Marston?"

"Leo Marston knows everything that goes on in this town. He wouldn't dirty his hands with the actual deed, but he'd order someone to do it."

"I hate to think Ray would go that far. kidnaping Annie . . . my God. What do you want to do?"

"Let's get settled somewhere first, get the security in place. Then we'll talk about it."

He opens the chapel door and nearly walks over Livy, who's standing in the hall. She backs up so that we can exit, and as we do I see my mother and Annie waiting at the end of the hall, by the wide ER doors.

"Tell me what I can do," Livy says. "Your mother said you're going to a motel."

"For now. We need to get Annie settled. She —"

Suddenly the ER doors swing open, and Caitlin Masters runs up the corridor with a camera swinging around her neck and her black hair flying behind her.

"I just came from your house," she says. "Penn, I'm so sorry."

"Caitlin —"

"I need to talk you and your father. Right now."

"What is it?"

She looks at Livy. "Could you excuse us for a moment, Mrs. Sutter?"

Livy bristles and looks at me, expecting me to tell Caitlin she can stay.

"Why don't we go in the chapel?" I suggest.

"We'll just be a minute, Livy."

Livy starts to say something to Caitlin but doesn't. Instead she bites her bottom lip and watches us walk into the chapel.

Caitlin's energy is like a flame inside the little room. She can't remain still, and her eyes simmer with anger. "Someone kidnaped Annie?" she asks. "Is that right?"

"Yes."

"And they brought her back? With a warning note?"

"Yes."

"The same person who set the fire?"

"Almost certainly."

"Okay . . . okay." She nods furiously, then paces out a tight circle. "That's all I wanted to know."

"Caitlin, what's going on? Why are you so worked up?"

"I'll print the story."

"The story. About the fire?"

She blinks in confusion. "The fire? Hell, no. The slander. Marston being behind the Payton murder. You say it, I'll print it. In type big enough to give him a coronary over breakfast."

I simply stare at her.

"Maybe that's the answer," Dad says. "Last night we thought it was."

"Last night you had a house," I remind him. "What changed your mind?"

Caitlin stops pacing and looks me dead in the eye. "Annie, for one thing."

"This girl is good people," Dad says, squeezing her shoulder.

"For another, my instincts have started hum-

393

ming. Don't ask me why, because I don't know. Maybe because this happened two days after we went to see Stone, and Stone says Marston was behind Payton's death. Maybe because John Portman threatened you, and we know he worked the Payton case in sixty-eight. And we know Marston and J. Edgar Hoover were friends. Maybe it's because I get a funny vibe from Marston's daughter. All I know is that I'm not sitting still while these bastards go after people I care about. They want to play hardball? They're going to get the game of their goddamn lives."

My father looks like he wants to kiss her.

"What time is your deadline?" I ask.

"Just call me after you guys get settled somewhere. I'll come to you."

"I don't know what to say. Just . . . thank you."

When we leave the chapel, Caitlin walks past Livy without a word. She hugs my mother by the ER doors, kisses Annie, then slips through the doors and disappears.

Livy keeps pace with Dad and me as we walk down the hall and join my mother and Annie.

"Where do you think we should go, Tom?" Mom asks.

"The Prentiss Motel is right up on the highway. Let's stay there tonight. We'll worry about the long term tomorrow."

As Dad opens the ER doors, Mom follows him through with Annie on her hip, leaving Livy and me alone on this side. The awkwardness between us is palpable. Two hours ago we were in each other's arms. Now . . .

"What can I do?" she asks. "I'll help with Annie,

go out for food. Whatever you need."

"I think it better just be family tonight," I say gently. "Thanks for offering, though. Thanks for today too."

Her eyes cloud with frustration and confusion. "Penn, for God's sake . . . what's happening here?"

"Maybe you should ask your father."

CHAPTER 27

When the *Examiner* hit the driveways at four this morning, it polarized the town. Caitlin's words entered the public consciousness like electrodes dipped into water, ionizing opinion to positive or negative with no neutral between, the opinions predictable in most cases by the simple indicator of skin color. The process took about three hours: from the time the insomniacs, farmers, and shift workers walked outside to read the front page by street lamp until the last Washington Street matrons toddled downstairs to read what the maid had laid out beside their morning coffee. By seven A.M. telephones were ringing all over town, and by eight every conversation from the sewer ditches and oil fields to the paper mill and the hospitals was centered on two men: Leo Marston and Penn Cage.

My only contributions to Caitlin's story were the actual accusations against Marston, slander per se if I ever heard it. Of course, my slanderous charges became libel per se — meaning that the libeled party would not have to prove damages — the moment Caitlin printed and distributed them. My phrases, preserved for the ages, ran as follows:

There is no doubt that Delano Payton was murdered on May 14, 1968. It is just as certain that former State Attorney General Leo Marston, known locally as "Judge" Marston because of his stint on the state supreme court, was the man behind the conspiracy that resulted in Payton's murder. Under Mississippi law, that makes Marston as guilty of murder as the man who planted the bomb. Murder by explosive device is a capital crime in this state, and there is no statute of limitations. I urge the local district attorney to reopen the Payton case. If he does, he will quickly find enough proof to send Leo Marston to death row at Parchman.

Asked by "the publisher" to describe the evidence on which I based my accusations, I stated:

I am in contact with certain members of the Justice Department who have long known of Marston's involvement in the crime. Conscientious citizens and law enforcement officers have also come forward with previously unknown facts about the Payton murder. I believe we would already have seen a prosecution of Judge Marston but for the fact that John Portman, the present director of the FBI and a former federal judge, was involved in the original Payton investigation in 1968. Some former FBI agents believe the Bureau itself may have been involved in a cover-up of certain facts of Payton's death, but this will be difficult to prove without the original FBI file

397

on the Payton case, which is sealed until the year 2007, ostensibly for reasons of national security.

I was purposefully vague about Marston's possible motives for the crime, but on Caitlin's advice I hinted that Marston, heretofore considered a moderate on race, might secretly have been working in concert with members of the Mississippi Sovereignty Commission to prevent black workers from rising into "white jobs."

Because of my reference to John Portman, the wire services picked up the story before noon, and just before one Caitlin received a call from CNN in Atlanta. There were already two network stringers in town to cover the "black-white" mayoral election, and they spent the morning outside my family's motel rooms, pleading for comment on the story.

But the morning paper had far more tragic consequences. Caitlin had written a separate piece about the fire and kidnaping. In it she vividly described the rescues of Ruby Flowers and Officer Ervin, and also Ruby's death in the ER. She quoted several citizens on Ruby's character, in particular the pastor of the Mandamus Baptist Church, of which Ruby had been a devoted member. She also quoted the fire chief, who pronounced the fire arson, based on the discovery of an incendiary device in the collapsed attic of our house. Caitlin concluded by saying that the arson and kidnaping were clearly attempts to stop my investigation into the Delano Payton murder. It was yellow journalism at its finest, and the consequences were immediate.

At a little after one, a seventy-four-year-old white man named Billy Earl Whitestone walked down his sidewalk to get his mail from the box. He got both barrels of a twelve-gauge shotgun instead, fired from a red Monte Carlo driven by two unidentified black youths. The gunmen stopped long enough to drop a copy of the *Examiner* on Mr. Whitestone's shattered skull, but even if they hadn't, the shooting would have been recognized as a reprisal for Ruby's death. In his younger days Billy Earl Whitestone had achieved national notoriety as a Grand Wizard of the White Knights of the Imperial Ku Klux Klan. He had also enjoyed a brief renaissance of fame during the 1980s when, Wallace-like, he marched at the head of some black civil rights parades, but apparently this belated conversion had not sufficiently impressed certain members of the African-American community. At least not the two young men in the Monte Carlo.

A drive-by shooting in Natchez is the equivalent of a race riot in Los Angeles. Within the hour Mayor Warren went on the local country radio station to appeal for calm and to condemn the "reckless and irresponsible charges" made against "one of the city's finest citizens" by former Natchezian Penn Cage. He also blasted the "Yankee editor" of the local newspaper. Shad Johnson also took to the airwaves — the black AM station — to urge restraint in the face of "the deteriorating racial situation." Unlike Wiley Warren, Shad urged the city authorities to look into the charges printed in the morning paper and, if they were found to be substantive, to reopen the investigation into Del

Payton's murder. Despite his wish that the Payton murder remain a non-issue, Shad could not in the aftermath of the fire and shooting afford to be seen as anything but a champion of the black community, his core of electoral support.

Three hours after Whitestone's death, I was invited to the police station to discuss the statements I'd made in the newspaper, particularly my reference to "local law enforcement officers." The police chief conducted the interview, and he seemed to labor under the misapprehension that I was subject to arrest if I didn't answer his questions. I calmly and courteously enumerated my rights under the Constitution, then explained that I had first contacted the district attorney about my suspicions and found him apathetic. I refused to answer any questions, and suggested that the chief talk to Austin Mackey instead. As I departed, he told me he considered the death of Billy Earl Whitestone my responsibility, and I didn't argue. He was mostly right.

I left my bodyguard outside during this interview. He and his three associates from Argus Security had arrived from Houston just after midnight, flying into Baton Rouge via Argus's Gulfstream V and driving up to Natchez in four separate rental cars. They checked into the Prentiss Motel, and by two A.M. my family was being protected by some of the finest bodyguards in the world. The total cost of this protection was staggering, but my memory of Annie's quivering chin was enough to make me ashamed for even thinking of money.

Three of the four guards were former FBI agents, and fit exactly the mental image I'd had before they arrived. Lean and tight-lipped. Late forties. Economical movements. Nine-hundred-dollar business suits specially tailored to conceal the bulges of various firearms. The fact that they were former FBI agents concerned me a little, but their boss had assured me that none of his men had worked under John Portman. The fourth Argus man was about thirty-five and blond, with the lean, confident look of a professional mountain guide. He wore jeans, a sweatshirt, and hiking boots. Daniel Kelly was a veteran of the army's Delta Force, and like the others, was billed at eight hundred dollars per day.

After hearing the details of our situation, the senior member of the detail suggested the following plan. One operative should remain with my mother and Annie at all times, another with my father, and one with me. The fourth would sleep at the hotel for six hours, then relieve one of the other men, beginning a continuous rotation. I agreed, and chose Daniel Kelly as my guard.

After my interview at the police station, Kelly and I stopped by the offices of the *Examiner,* where we found Caitlin doing her best to handle a barrage of phone calls from other newspapers. She stopped working long enough to tell me that her father had called from Richmond and demanded to know what the hell she thought she was up to, then ordered her aboard the first Virginia-bound aircraft leaving Mississippi. Caitlin told him he had better get ready to mount a libel defense, because she was sticking by her story, and if he fired her, he should prepare to read further installments of the Payton story in the *Washington Post.* I didn't envy Mr. Masters. Caitlin had been preparing for this day for a long time.

Thirty minutes before the courthouse closed, Leo Marston filed suit against myself and the Natchez *Examiner* for a grand total of five million dollars, his complaint drafted in record time by his junior law partner, Blake Sims. Actually, they filed two separate suits — one for slander and one for libel — neatly severing my fate from that of the *Examiner*, which, as part of a media group, will have a battery of attorneys on retainer, many of them First Amendment specialists. A deputy served me with the papers just as our family was leaving the motel for dinner at the Shoney's Restaurant across the street.

I invited the Argus men to eat with us, but they took their jobs too seriously for that. Two stood in the front parking lot near their cars, like businessmen shooting the breeze after an early dinner, while Daniel Kelly covered the rear entrance. I hadn't felt that safe in a long time. The Argus men made quite an impression on Annie too. She'd spent most of her waking hours since the fire on my mother's lap, but during dinner she began to loosen up, using the Shoney's crayons to play each of us in games of tic-tac-toe.

Ruby's death hung over the adults like a pall, but we tried to focus on the good times we'd had with her, which were countless, as they spanned thirty-five years. My father had stopped by Ruby's house earlier to give her husband, Mose — a retired pulpwood cutter — a substantial check and a gallon of Wild Turkey. They talked for half an hour, shared some whisky, and Dad left the house wondering how long the old man would survive without Ruby around to take care of him.

Caitlin's articles had upset my mother, but Marston's lawsuit terrified her. I tried to reassure her by explaining that my intent had been to force just such a lawsuit, but she refused to be mollified. Like most people who have lived any length of time in Natchez, my mother believes that Leo Marston is untouchable, and that anyone who tries to hurt him is doomed to failure or worse.

I kept the good news of the day to myself. Just after noon Special Agent Peter Lutjens had called the motel from a pay phone in McLean, Virginia, and asked me to call him back from a pay phone. When I did, he told me he'd been stewing about the Payton case and had decided to try to photocopy the sealed FBI file. He still had his security pass to the proper archive. The problem was the staff. The "friend" who had reported his initial inquiry to Portman worked every day but Sunday, so Sunday was Lutjens's only shot. And he was due to report in Fargo on Monday. I thanked him profusely and tried to reassure him that what he was doing would ultimately serve the Bureau, not undermine it. He told me he'd call me Sunday if he wasn't in jail, and hung up.

When we got back to the motel after supper, I found two old-fashioned handwritten messages waiting: "Call Livy" and "Call Ike." I had no idea what Livy could want, other than to curse me for vilifying her father in the newspaper, but I called Tuscany anyway. The number of the Marston mansion hadn't changed since we were kids, but the fact that it had remained in my memory for twenty years probably said something about my buried feelings for Livy. Butterflies fluttered in my stomach as the phone rang, but I resolved to tell Leo to kiss my ass if he answered.

"Marston residence." A maid.

"Yes, could I speak to Liv, please?"

"Who's calling?"

"Her husband."

"Just a moment, Mr. Sutter."

After a few moments Livy came on the line and said, "John?"

"It's Penn."

"Oh. Just a minute." Her voice was under tight control. I heard the clacking of heels on hardwood, then her voice again, more relaxed. "I'm glad you called back. How's Annie doing?"

"Better. Look, I know you must be upset about the paper."

A strange laugh. "Things are pretty crazy around here. I don't know what you're trying to do. But I know *why* you're doing it."

I said nothing.

"Penn . . . hurting my father won't make up for the years we lost."

"I know that."

"I hope so. Because I called to tell you that, as bad as all this is, I don't want to let him come between us again."

We both waited in the vacuum of the open line, each hoping the other could somehow bridge the chasm my accusations had opened between us. I imagined her sitting alone in the Italianate palace that had sheltered her throughout her childhood. She had often portrayed it to me as a prison, but I

404

never bought into this. She wouldn't have traded Tuscany for anything.

"Livy?"

"I'm here."

"You haven't asked where I got my information about your father. You haven't protested his innocence."

"Of course I haven't. It's ridiculous. My father murdering a black man? He's probably the least prejudiced man in this town."

"Del Payton's death may not have been a race murder. Tell me something, Livy. What would you do if you found out your father had ordered the burning of my parents' house?"

"That's insane."

"Just pretend it was true. What would you do?"

"Well, obviously, I'd be the first one to call the police."

Maybe she didn't even know she was lying. "I need to go, Livy."

"Can we see each other tonight?"

I couldn't believe she wanted to be within ten miles of me after the newspaper story. "Not tonight."

"Tomorrow, then?"

Images from the day before filled my mind: Livy floating naked in the pool, kissing me passionately as we sank slowly through the green water, her thigh pressing against me. "We'd better play it by ear. There's a lot going on right now."

"That's all the more reason to stay close. Just remember what I said about my father. I meant it."

"I will."

I hung up and dialed Ike's cell phone before thoughts of Livy could overwhelm me. I wanted to call her back and say, "Pick me up in twenty minutes." But the past had finally caught up with us, and Ike the Spike was growling in my ear.

"Meet me where I wanted to last night," he said, meaning the warehouse in the industrial park by the river. "One hour."

"What about?"

"What *about*? About whatever the fuck it is you think you're doing, man. This town's going crazy. One hour."

"I'll be there."

"Damn straight you will."

I've been sweating in the dark warehouse for twenty minutes, breathing the stink of fertilizer and wondering what could be keeping Ike. It's fully dark now, and the spotlight of a tugboat pushing barges upriver arcs through the night like a Hollywood klieg light, searching for sandbars and unexpected traffic. A slight breeze off the Mississippi penetrates the twenty-foot-wide warehouse door, where I stand watching the dark line of the levee, waiting for the headlights of Ike's cruiser.

I am unarmed but not unprotected. Daniel Kelly is covering me. After asking four times if I really trust Ike Ransom, Kelly parked his rental car behind the warehouse and told me to forget he was there. I parked the BMW out front so that Ike would see it when he drove up.

What I take for the sound of another tugboat suddenly resolves into a car engine. A set of headlights descends the levee, pulls into the parking lot of the warehouse, and stops beside my car.

It's Ike's cruiser.

He gets out, his brown uniform looking black under the single security light, and walks toward the warehouse door. Halfway there he stops, turns, and watches the levee for nearly a minute. Maybe he senses Kelly's presence. Whatever the reason, he resumes walking toward me. When he's ten yards away, I step into the light, holding both hands in plain view.

Ike draws his pistol faster than I would have believed possible, recognizing me just as the barrel lines up with my chest. He quickens his step and shoves me back into the shadows.

"You ought to know better than that," he mutters.

"Why are you so jumpy?"

The whites of his eyes flick left and right in the darkness. "You ain't jumpy? After somebody burned down your house and took your kid?"

"Who set that fire, Ike? Who took my daughter? Ray Presley?"

"Could have been." He holsters his pistol. "But I don't know for sure. Not yet."

"Why are we here?"

"So you can tell me what the hell you think you're doing in the paper. You crazy? Making statements like that?"

"You're the one who told me Marston was guilty."

"Jesus. Is that the way you did it in Houston? Shoutin' shit in the papers before you got any proof?"

"Take it easy. Everything's under control."

407

"Under control? Shooting your mouth off about local law enforcement coming forward?"

"I'm pursuing this the way I think best. As far as the newspaper story goes, I wanted Marston to sue me, and the story accomplished that."

"You what?"

"I wanted the right to request everything from personal papers to phone records from Marston under the rules of discovery."

A gleam of recognition. "That lawsuit means you can ask for Marston's personal shit? And *get it?*"

"That's right."

"Okay . . . maybe you ain't crazy. You get the judge's legal files, you're liable to find all kinds of illegal shit."

"Marston's legal files are protected under client confidentiality rules. But everything else is fair game."

"How long you got to answer his suit? At least thirty days, right? That should give you plenty of time for fishing."

"I'm going to file my answer tomorrow."

His mouth drops open. "Why you gonna do that?"

"By proceeding aggressively, I force Marston to conclude that I either have evidence in my possession, or that I know people willing to come forward and testify against him."

"But you don't."

"Don't be so sure. I'm building a case."

Ike's eyes narrow to slits. "What you talking about? What kind of case? You holding back on me?"

408

"What if I am? You've been holding back on me from the start."

He raises a warning finger but says nothing, and instead begins a staring contest. His bloodshot eyes are so jerky that he can't focus in one direction long, and he soon looks away.

"What are you taking, Ike? Speed? What?"

"I take me a drink now and then. So what? Have you talked to Stone again?"

"Yes, but he's just like you. Scared to tell what he knows."

"I told you, man, I know Marston done it, but I don't know why."

"*How* do you know, Ike? How can you know he did it if you don't know why?"

He grunts in the dark. "I know what I know. Why'd you slam Portman in the paper? You go pissing off the head of the FBI, you're asking for some serious payback."

"I did it to protect myself and my family. That newspaper story threw a lot of light on Portman. On me too. It makes it harder for him to retaliate."

"Yeah? I heard somebody tried to poison Ray Presley. Who the hell you think did that?"

"I figured Marston ordered it. You think it was Portman?"

"Sure as hell wasn't the tooth fairy." Ike scrapes the tip of a boot along the cement floor of the warehouse. "Stone say anything about surveillance?"

"Why?"

"There's somebody watching me."

A shiver runs along my forearms. "How long?"

"I picked him up today, but he could have been there longer."

"Stone's under FBI surveillance himself. He thinks Caitlin and I are too. Phones, the works. But why would the FBI be watching you?"

"Maybe 'cause of your damn newspaper article."

"I didn't mention your name. Why did you warn me away from the FBI, Ike? Have you tried to talk to them about the Payton case before?"

"Say what?" He takes out a cigarette and taps it against his palm but does not light it. "Why don't you focus on some shit that'll get you somewhere? Like Marston's papers. There's bound to be something in there to prosecute him on. He's had his hands in all kinds of shit for years. I mean, who cares what he goes down for, 'long as he rots in Parchman."

"*I* care. To get out from under this slander charge, I've got to prove Marston guilty of murder. Not campaign finance fraud or any other bullshit. *Murder.* Do you comprehend that?"

Instead of answering, Ike flips open his lighter, ignites it, and puts the flame to the tip of his cigarette. As the orange glow illuminates his face, something incomprehensible happens. The flame reaches toward me as though sucked by a wind, and Ike slams his shoulder into my chest, punching the air out of my lungs and knocking me to the cement floor.

As he lands on top of me, gunfire erupts outside the warehouse and echoes through the metal building. Two shots, I think. Then a third, the sound quick and flat.

"Get *off*," I grunt, unable to draw breath with Ike on top of me.

He rolls off and up into a kneeling position, his pistol pointed through the warehouse door.

"What happened?" I ask.

"There's two guns out there. One silenced."

"I've got a man out there, Ike. Maybe one of the guns was his."

He whips his head around. "What man?"

"A private security guy. From Houston."

He peers into the darkness the way he must have done in Vietnam, with absolute concentration. "I can't see shit," he hisses. "But some lardass ex-cop ain't gonna help us one bit, I know that."

"He's not what you think."

After a minute of silence, he works his way toward the edge of the door.

"What do you see?"

"Shut the fuck up."

A boom like a cannon shot shatters the silence, reverberating through the warehouse for at least four seconds. Ike hits the floor with his pistol still aimed at the door.

"That's a deer gun," he says. "Stay down. We got serious shit going down out there, and it ain't all got to do with us."

"How do you know?"

"Ain't but one bullet come into this warehouse."

As I lie facedown on the floor, breathing accumulated dust and oil, the seconds drag past. There are no more shots, but the instinctual voice that warned me during the fire that killed Ruby is not comforted by this fact. It knows that silence is the cloak of the approaching enemy.

"How long we gonna lie here?" I whisper.

"Till I tell you to get up."

Another five minutes pass.

"Penn Cage!" yells a man from beyond the warehouse door. "It's Kelly! Daniel Kelly."

"That your guy?" asks Ike.

"It's Kelly," shouts the voice again. "Come out! And bring your friend. We need some law out here."

I scramble to my feet and trot to the edge of the door.

Daniel Kelly stands forty feet away, an MP-5 submachine gun slung over his shoulder.

"What happened?" I ask, walking into the parking lot.

"Somebody tried to whack you. Or the cop. I couldn't tell which."

Ike steps into the light, his pistol aimed at Kelly. "Who shot who out here?"

Kelly holds up his hands. "Take it easy, Deputy. I'm a friendly. I was out here covering your meeting when I saw a muzzle flash from over there." He points at the levee, a dark silhouette fifty yards away. "It was a silenced rifle, and it was firing subsonic rounds, because I didn't hear the bullet crack. I started running toward the flash, whipping out a spotter scope as I ran, trying to get within range and see at the same time. The shooter was firing from the prone position, already setting up for his second shot. I yelled just as he pulled the trigger, and as he swung around to deal with me, I double-tapped him on the run."

"Is he dead?" Ike asks.

"Definitely. I put one through his head to be sure, and it's a good thing, because he was wearing a vest."

"What about that deer gun I heard?"

Kelly points into the darkness south of the warehouse. "The deer gun belonged to the guy over there. Who is also dead. The shooter on the levee took him out. That was the first muzzle flash I saw. He fired across my line of sight, at a right angle to you guys. The other guy must have fired off that deer slug as he was dying. Pure reflex, probably."

"I don't get it," I say. "Why would they shoot at each other? A falling-out among hit men?"

Kelly shakes his head. "I don't think these guys were together. They're dressed different, and their equipment's different. I think the guy with the deer gun was just in the way."

"Who knew you were coming to this meeting?" Ike asks.

"My father and Kelly. That's it."

"What about you?" Kelly asks Ike.

"Nobody knows where I'm at. How did these guys get so close if you were covering the meeting?"

Kelly scratches the side of his nose, as though to emphasize his calmness. "First of all, they're not that close. Second, the curve of the levee blocked my line of sight to the guy with the deer gun, but not his line to you. Third, the sniper on the levee followed *you* in. He probably drove with his lights off and parked well back, then moved up on foot." Kelly pauses, his cool blue eyes level with Ike's. "And fourth, if I was in with those guys, you'd be bagged and tagged right now."

413

Ike snorts and turns toward the levee. "Show me the dead guys."

Kelly unslings his MP-5 and starts jogging toward the levee. We follow him across the lot, trying to stay with him as he pounds up the spongy grass on the side of the levee. The odors of cow manure and bush-hogged grass weight the humid air. At the crest, Kelly points at a black shape lying at the edge of the gravel road that runs atop the levee.

"No wallet," he says. "No ID at all. Car's clean too. A rental."

"That's risky," Ike remarks. "He gets stopped at random without ID, he's gonna get run in."

"Unless he's willing to do the cop."

Ike walks to the corpse, bends over, and takes a long look. "Never seen him. Take a look, Cage."

I walk over and glance at the dead sniper. He's dressed from head to toe in black, and looks like he stepped off a film set. His face is pale and placid in the dark, as though he were shot while sleeping. A dead face can be difficult to identify, so I give it long enough to be sure.

"I don't know him."

"Here's his weapon." Kelly holds out a long, bolt-action rifle to Ike. "Rank-Pullin starlight scope. Fourth-generation passive amplification. Expensive toy."

"Guy's definitely out of town," Ike declares. "Nobody around here uses shit like this. Caliber looks awful small."

"It's a special twenty-two magnum. Chambers subsonic rounds. An assassin's gun."

"Christ," I whisper. "Where's the other guy?"

Kelly points into the darkness south of the ware-

414

house, then starts down the slope.

The second corpse is lying facedown in a thicket of weeds, dressed in jeans and a plaid flannel shirt. There's a red bandanna knotted around its head.

Ike bends down and pulls a rifle from the dead hand. "An old Remington thirty-aught-six. Seen better days too."

Kelly says, "The shooter on the levee probably saw him moving up to get a shot. Poor bastard didn't have a chance."

Ike puts both hands under the corpse and rolls it over. Below the dead man's left eye is a small black hole. Small but obviously fatal.

"I've seen a hundred shitkickers just like him," says Ike. "But I don't know this one."

As I stare, the slack features suddenly coalesce into a coherent whole, and a feverish heat shoots through me. The dead man is a nightmare made flesh, a physical echo of the most terrifying night of my life.

"I know him," I say, grabbing Ike's arm.

"Who is he?"

"His name's Hanratty. I convicted his brother of capital murder. He was just executed."

"I'll be damned. That Aryan Brotherhood bastard?"

"Right. I also shot his other brother four years ago."

"No shit," says Kelly, with respect mingled with surprise.

"This one was the last." The fever heat has disappeared, leaving a chill in its wake. "The youngest."

Ike kicks the corpse's leg. "No more boom-

boom for this Aryan *papasan*."

He kneels and starts going through the dead man's pockets, quickly turning up a wallet. "Hanratty, Clovis Dee," he says, reading the driver's license.

"Brother of Arthur Lee," I say absurdly.

"And white people make fun of African names," Ike mutters, getting to his feet. " 'Least we know what happened now. This shitkicker was out for revenge, and he picked the wrong night to try it. He was crowding that ninja assassin up on the levee, and he paid for it. The question is, who sent the assassin?"

"Portman?" I suggest. "The hardware looked pretty sophisticated."

"John Portman would definitely have access to people like that," Kelly says quietly. "Retired Bureau. Agency. Former CT operators." He looks at Ike. "In any case, I hope you appreciate this enough to take care of any problems that might arise."

"Don't sweat it," Ike replies. "We're in the county here. Me and the sheriff understand each other. Although three killings in one day is big-time trouble for this town."

"The district attorney could be a problem," I tell them, thinking of Austin Mackey.

"Fuck that tightass," Ike mutters. "We got three witnesses telling it one way, dead guys got nobody. Mackey got no choice."

"I was thinking of Kelly's submachine gun. It's illegal."

Kelly smiles and draws a pistol from his holster.

"What you gonna do with that?" Ike asks, dropping his hand to his own gun.

Kelly fires three quick rounds into the night sky, then holsters the pistol. "Browning Hi-Power," he says with a smile. "Chambers the same nine-millimeter cartridge as the MP-5. Very convenient, as long as they don't do a ballistics analysis."

Ike nods as if noting this for future use. "Well, let's get this over with. Let me call the sheriff."

He starts back toward the warehouse, but I take his arm and stop him. "Who sent the sniper, Ike? Who's trying to kill me?"

He looks back, his face indignant. "How you know he was shooting at *you?*"

He pulls his arm free and walks on, but I stay where I am, breathing the cooler air blowing off the river. The stars are bright here, the water close. A few minutes ago a silent bullet passed within inches of my face. But I am still alive. And the last Hanratty brother is finally dead. My daughter is a lot safer than she was before Daniel Kelly did something not many men could have done.

"Thanks, Kelly," I say softly.

He gives me a self-deprecating smile. "Just doing my job, boss."

Right.

CHAPTER 28

The sheriff's office looks like an armed camp when we arrive. It's a modern, fortress-like building, with a state-of-the-art jail occupying its upper floors. Uniformed deputies swagger through the halls like cowboys in a western, stoked by the air of incipient violence blowing through the city. Ike disappears for a few moments, leaving Kelly and me in the entrance hall.

Five minutes later, he returns and escorts us into the sheriff's office. I sense immediately that we're going to benefit from the jurisdictional rivalry that exists between the police department and the sheriff's office. Had we reported the levee shootings to the police, the chief would have kept Kelly and me all night, mercilessly grilling me as payback for the constitutional lesson I gave him earlier in the day.

The sheriff is tan and fit-looking, with the watchful eyes of a hunter. He seems to view the death of the youngest Hanratty as a fortuitous event, though the timing could have been better.

"When those black kids shot Billy Earl Whitestone," he says, leaning back in his chair and folding his hands behind his neck, "they turned this town into a powder keg. The Sports Center sold out of ammunition at four o'clock. They sold

418

mostly to whites. Wal-Mart sold out of everything but paintball rounds. They sold mostly to blacks. We may have a world of trouble coming down on our heads tonight. And all because of that newspaper story." He looks at me like a wise poker player. "You think going after Leo Marston is worth all this trouble?"

"The built-up resentment in this town is none of my doing, Sheriff. What's happening now would have happened eventually, whatever the cause."

"Maybe," he allows. "I sure hope you've got some evidence, though. Messing with Judge Leo ain't generally good for your health."

"Any leads on the Whitestone shooters?" Ike asks.

"The P.D. has an informer working it. They're not telling me squat, of course, but the word is, it's some kids from the Concord Apartments. Nobody's been arrested yet, though. And we need an arrest. Jailing those two might go a long way toward calming people down. Maybe you ought to take a ride over to those apartments, Ike. See if you can shake something loose."

"I'll do it."

The sheriff smooths his thinning hair. "Think you can give me some overtime tonight?"

"Glad to get it."

"I want you to stick to the north side, try to keep everybody indoors."

The sheriff is telling Ike to keep the black population inside their houses.

"I've given the white deputies the same orders for their parts of town," he adds for my benefit. "It's fear that drives all this nonsense. If we can get

419

through this first night, we might just make it okay."

The sheriff's phone starts ringing, and he leans forward to shake our hands. "You boys try not to shoot anybody else, okay?"

Ike leads us out to the front steps of the building, where he takes a pack of Kool Menthols from the pocket of his uniform. He offers Kelly one, but Kelly declines. As Ike holds his lighter flame to the tip of his cigarette, his hand trembles, and Kelly shoots me a quick glance.

"You sleep with this boy if you have to," Ike tells Kelly, exhaling a long stream of smoke. "He's doing some good, even if he is doing it the hard way."

Kelly winks at Ike. "No sweat, Sergeant."

"How'd you know I was a sergeant?"

"It's like a sign around your neck, brother."

Ike's laugh is good to hear, but as we move down the steps toward our cars, Kelly leans toward me and says, "He's speeding like a racehorse, with bourbon underneath. Something's eating him. Bad. None of my business, of course."

I slap him on the shoulder. "You say whatever pops into your head, Kelly."

"Will do."

Since my mother's computer was destroyed in the fire, I planned to draft my answer to Marston's suit at the offices of the *Examiner*. They occupy an entire building in an old section of downtown, a long one-story structure with inadequate parking.

Even at this late hour the door is open, and we find Caitlin in the newsroom, sitting before a twenty-one-inch monitor, commanding her staff with a cell phone in one hand and a computer trackball in the other. She's dressed in jeans and a teal pinpoint button-down, which gives her the look of a college yearbook editor. She waves when she sees me but continues her phone conversation. The newsroom is forty feet long and twenty wide, with a half dozen computer workstations — all in use — and photos of distinguished Natchezians decorating the walls.

"Who's this?" Caitlin asks, sliding her cell phone into a belt holster as we approach.

"Daniel Kelly. Part of the security from Houston. Kelly, this is Caitlin Masters, fledgling muckraker."

Caitlin sizes Kelly up as she leads us down a hall, noting his average size and easy demeanor. Falling back beside me, she whispers, *"Is he qualified?"*

Kelly chuckles softly.

"He just saved my life," I say in a normal voice. "I'm sold. Have you put tomorrow's issue to bed?"

Her eyes flash with excitement. "Are you kidding? This town's about to pop."

She pushes us into a glass-walled conference room screened with venetian blinds for privacy. "We're pushing back the deadline as far as we can. Two in the morning if we have to."

"Can you do that?"

"With computers we can reformat the whole paper and go to plate in thirty minutes. There's a rumor that the police are close to an arrest in the Whitestone killing. And we must have gotten a dozen calls about people carrying guns in and out of their houses. They're saying it's just like it was before the riot in sixty-eight."

"That wasn't much of a riot. Everybody was scared to death, but nobody got killed. Just a bunch of broken store windows."

"Let's hope that's all that happens this time."

"I'm glad to hear you say that."

She gives me an icy look. "You think I want the town to explode so I can sell papers?"

"No."

She doesn't look convinced. "Three hours ago a CNN crew yelled a question at John Portman as he was leaving the Hoover Building. He walked over and told them on camera that the Del Payton case involved matters of national security, and that the FBI was looking into the question of whether you or I had violated any laws in our pursuit of the case."

"The best defense is a good offense, I guess. Anything else I should know?"

"Leo Marston's attorney gave me a phone interview. He said your charges are ridiculous and they're going to cost both of us seven figures. I'm running it tomorrow."

"I expected that."

Caitlin smiles like a child hiding a cookie. "I also have some good news. My father called back and told me that if I was sticking by my story, there must be something to it. He's going to help."

"How?"

"By committing the full resources of the media group to investigating Marston and Portman. He's already spoken to Senator Harris from Virginia. Tomorrow, Harris is going to the Senate Intelligence Committee to ask for a special resolution authorizing the opening of the Payton file. Failing that, he'll ask that it be moved from FBI custody to a place where it can't be tampered with, at least until Director Portman's involvement in the case can be clarified. If that doesn't work, he'll stand up on the Senate floor and ask the same things on C-Span."

I feel the relief of a man trying to push a car uphill when four strong backs join him in his effort. But the feeling vanishes quickly. "Asking that the file be opened is good. But if he can't get that, it's best that the file stay where it is. At least until Sunday."

For a moment Caitlin looks confused. Then she grabs my wrist. "Lutjens is going to try for the file?"

"Sunday."

"I'll tell my dad to call the senator back."

"It's nice to have powerful friends."

Her eyes twinkle with irony. "Isn't it?"

Kelly laughs. He's not sure what he's gotten into, but he's clearly enjoying it.

"How did Mr. Kelly here save your life?" Caitlin asks.

"He killed two guys who were trying to kill me. One was Arthur Lee Hanratty's brother."

"Jesus. Did this happen near the river? We heard some kind of call on the scanner, but it was coded."

"That was it."

"Can I print this story?"

"Absolutely. The more public this thing gets, the safer we are."

"We ought to be very safe, then. I'm getting nonstop calls from the major papers, the networks, everybody."

There's a sharp knock at the door, and Caitlin walks into the hall for a hurried conference. When she returns, her face is flushed pink with excitement. "The police just trapped the Whitestone suspects in the Concord Apartments. I'm going over to cover the arrest."

The Concord Apartments are a low-income housing development, and a center of drug and gang activity in Natchez. "The residents over there aren't big fans of the police," I warn her. "They're probably as volatile as old dynamite right now."

"That's why I'm going. You want to come along?"

"I can't take the time. I've got to file my interrogatories and requests for production along with my answer. That'll keep Marston off balance, make him think I'm ready to go to court on a moment's notice."

"Speaking of Marston, where's your other friend?"

"My other friend?"

She gives me a sidelong glance. She means Livy.

"Oh. I have no idea. With her father, I guess."

Caitlin obviously wants to say more, but she's unwilling to do so in front of Kelly. "I've got to get going, guys."

"Wait. Go with her, Kelly."

Kelly looks at Caitlin, then back at me. "I think you're the one who needs protection, boss."

"I'll have a photographer with me," she protests. "I'll be fine."

"Kelly's worth ten photographers. I'll be here

for at least two hours, then I'm going straight back to the motel. He can tell you how he saved my life on the way."

Caitlin is wavering.

Kelly bends over, lifts a cuff of his jeans, and pulls out a small automatic, which he passes to me. "Safety's on."

I slip the gun into my pocket and look at Caitlin. "Satisfied?"

"Okay, I'll take him. But you go straight to the motel from here. No side trips."

"I need a computer. And coffee. Lots of coffee."

"We've got plenty of both."

Kelly and Caitlin still haven't returned when I leave for the motel. While typing my discovery requests, I overheard enough newsroom conversation to follow the situation unfolding at the Concord Apartments. The two teenagers who allegedly shot Billy Earl Whitestone had holed up in the apartment of their grandmother. Somehow, Caitlin managed to get them on the telephone, and during that conversation one of the boys admitted to the shooting. He claimed he'd shot Whitestone because Ruby Flowers's death had so upset his grandmother that he had to do *something*. He chose Whitestone as his victim because he'd often heard an uncle talk about how Whitestone had run the Klan during the "bad times." An hour after this confession, the grandmother talked the boys into giving themselves up, on the condition that Caitlin be allowed to accompany them to the police station to ensure their safety. I assume Caitlin is still at the station now, running the police crazy and keeping Kelly jumping.

Kelly's pistol is on my lap as I drive toward the motel. There's no traffic on the streets, or even the highway. Fear has worked its way into the fabric of the town.

A police car screams out of the empty darkness, siren blaring, going in the opposite direction. Halfway to the motel, a jacked-up pickup filled with white teenagers roars alongside me, pauses as its occupants peer in at me, then roars off again. Night riders looking for a fight? Or kids trying to figure out what all the excitement's about? I won't know until I read tomorrow's paper.

The single-story buildings of the Prentiss Motel remind me of the motor courts of my childhood vacations. But viewed without the kaleidoscopic lens of wonder, they are a mean and depressing sight. The thought of my parents forced to live here because of my actions is hard to bear. Yet they have not uttered one word of complaint since the fire, not even my mother, who urged me to avoid the Payton case from the beginning. Now that events have proved her right, what is she doing? Making the best of things. I feel like dragging some realtor out of bed and buying her the biggest god-damn house in the city.

Orienting myself by the greenish glow of the swimming pool, I park and start walking toward our rooms with Kelly's gun held along my leg. Halfway there, I feel a sudden chill.

There's someone sitting in one of the pool chairs. Fifty feet away, a dark silhouette against the wavering light of the water. As I walk down the long row of doors, the figure rises from the chair. I

426

put my finger on the trigger of the pistol and quicken my steps.

"Penn?"

The voice stops me cold. It's Livy.

I slip Kelly's gun into my waistband and jog toward the pool fence. Livy opens the gate and waits just beyond it. She's wearing a strapless white evening dress that looks strangely formal beside the deserted swimming pool. The moonlight falls lustrous upon her shoulders but is somehow lost in her eyes, which look more gray than blue tonight.

"What are you doing here? What's the matter?"

"I wanted to see you," she says. "That's all. I had to see you."

"Is everything all right?"

"That depends on what you mean by all right. Things are a bit tense at our house. More than a bit, really. But I'm sure your house was like that when my father went after yours."

She has no idea how bad things got at our house during the year leading up to that trial. But soon she might. Before she can say anything else, I ask what I've been wanting to ask since I saw her at the airport in Baton Rouge.

"Livy, a few nights ago, at a party . . . your mother threw a drink in my face."

"She *what?*"

"She told me I'd ruined your life."

Livy's expression does not change. She holds her eyes on mine, attentive as a spectator at the opera. But I sense that she's expending tremendous effort to maintain this illusion of normalcy.

"What was she talking about?" I ask.

"I have no idea." She looks away from me.

"Mom probably doesn't either. She's a hair-breadth from the DTs by five o'clock every day. Daddy's talking about sending her to Betty Ford."

"She was referring to something specific. I saw her eyes."

Livy turns and peers into the cloudy water. "My divorce has upset her quite a bit. Divorce isn't part of the fairy tale. If it were, she'd have left my father long ago."

"I thought you were only separated."

"Pending divorce, then. It's just semantics." She looks at me over her bare shoulder, an injured look in her eyes. "You think I'd ask you to make love to me if there was a chance my husband and I would get back together?"

This is one of those moments where we make a heaven or hell of the future, by choosing honesty or deception. "I don't know. You weren't that discriminating in the past."

She flinches, but she can endure much worse than this. "The past, the past," she says. "The damned sacred past. Can't we try living in the present for once?"

"Yesterday was the only free ride we're going to get."

She looks back into the depths of the pool. "I have a room," she says in a deliberate voice. "It's two doors down from yours. Why don't we talk there?"

A room. Part of me wants to slap her for assuming so much. I move sideways so that I can see her face. "Will you really talk?"

She pulls her hair back into a thick ponytail, as though to feel the breeze on her neck. Her collarbones are sculpted ivory, creating shadowy hollows at the base of her throat.

"About what?"

"About what? Everything. Why you did what you did twenty years ago."

"What do you mean?"

This is Kafkaesque. Can she really have edited the past so completely that she no longer remembers how badly she betrayed our dreams? "Why you disappeared for a year. Where you went. Why you ran off to Virginia. Why you treated me like a stranger when I flew up to ask you to get your father to drop the suit."

She turns to me and lets her hair fall, and whatever mask she was maintaining falls with it. She looks more vulnerable than I have ever seen her, and when she speaks, her voice is stripped of all affect. "Penn, I can't do it."

"Livy, if I understood some of those things, I might . . . well — things might not have to happen the way they are."

"What do you mean? If I answer your questions, you'll withdraw the charges you made against my father?"

I don't know what I mean. I started into the Del Payton case to destroy Leo Marston, but compared to understanding the mysteries that shaped my life, revenge seems meaningless. Of course, there is still Del Payton. And Althea. And the small matter of justice —

"I can't pull out of the Payton case now. It's too late for that. But I can pursue it a different way. If your father's part was only —"

"Stop," she says, shaking her head. "I can't talk

about twenty years ago. Not even to make things easier on my father."

She takes a step toward me. I want her to stay back, because the closer she gets, the more I want to go to her room with her. She is achingly beautiful in the moonlight.

"How did I ruin your life?" I ask.

She shakes her head, absolving me of any possible sin. "You didn't." Another step. "But you can save it."

"Livy, listen —"

"Come with me," she pleads. "Right now."

If she had kissed me then, I would have walked away. But she didn't. She picked up her purse from the pool chair, took my hand, and led me across the parking lot toward the motel, a purposeful urgency in her stride.

The déjà vu of walking beside the numbered doors is powerful enough to dislocate time. If I were to close my eyes and open them again, I would see the eighteen-thousand-dollar gown flowing behind her like a trail of mist. The lifetimes of water that have passed under the bridge since that night have all flowed back in a span of moments.

When she opens the door and closes us inside, I pull her to me and kiss her with the thirst of a binge drinker returning to the bottle. My questions fade to dying sparks, made irrelevant by the absolute connection of our lips and hands. I don't even know I am backing her toward the door until she collides with it, the unyielding wooden face holding her as I continue forward, pressing against her, my hands groping at her dress, searching for the hem.

"That's right," she says hoarsely. "That's right . . . that's —"

The moment my hand finds her sex, she is breathing like a sprinter in the last few yards of a race. She kisses me with almost desperate passion, then pushes down the front of the strapless dress and pulls my mouth to a breast. In seconds both her arms are outstretched, fingers splayed and quivering, discharging the frantic energy pouring from her core. Touching her this way is rapture, at once within her and without, needing no other thing, no friend, no thought —

The knock at the door reverberates through our bodies, stunning us from our trance. Yet still Livy presses herself down against my hand, unwilling to let the world back in. I jerk her away from the door and onto the bed, fearing someone might shoot through the thin metal.

The knocking comes again. This time, with the distance to the bed and with half my faculties restored, it sounds reasonably discreet.

"Who is it?" I call, digging in my pocket for Kelly's gun, hating the ragged edge of fear in my voice.

"Kelly."

Relief cascades through me. I turn to tell Livy everything's all right and find her standing with both hands pointed rigidly at the door, a pistol clenched between them. She must have taken it from her purse.

"Whoa!" I say, holding up my hands. "I know this guy. He's with me."

She lowers the gun slowly, as though unsure whether to trust my judgment. I turn back to the

431

door and open it a crack.

Daniel Kelly's sandy blond head leans toward mine.

"I saw you go in here as I pulled up. I just wanted you to know I'm back."

I nod. "I heard about what happened at the apartments. You must be tired. You can go ahead and get some sleep."

"I'm fine. Wired, really."

I hesitate to ask the next question, but I want to know. "Is Caitlin with you?"

An ironic smile, there and gone. "She's back at the paper, writing the story. She's a tough lady, man."

Coming from Daniel Kelly, this is high praise indeed. "Thanks for looking out for her. And thanks again for the levee thing."

He nods, but there's a curious hesitancy in his face.

"What is it, Kelly?"

"Well, I thought maybe you and Caitlin were . . . you know." He looks past me, through the crack in the door. "I guess not, huh?"

"I guess not," I reply, feeling a strange hollowness in my chest.

He makes a clicking sound with his tongue. "I'm gonna get some eggs over at Shoney's. One of the other guys'll be watching this door."

"Thanks."

"Oh, and your little girl is fine. No worries."

His words hit me like a blow. Maybe he meant for them to. My cheeks burn with self-disgust.

" 'Night, boss," he says, and disappears from the crack.

432

I shut the door and bolt it.

Livy is sitting on the bed, her face composed, the gun nowhere in evidence. Only her tousled hair hints at our brief encounter at the door.

"Why are you carrying a gun?"

She shrugs. "The town's gone crazy, hasn't it? And Daddy insisted."

Leo would.

Livy's shoes, hose, and panties lie on the floor beside her bare feet. She looks at me like she can't understand why I'm still standing where I am. Like what happened against the door was the opening movement of a symphony.

I glance at my watch. Twelve-twenty. Annie is almost certainly asleep, but Kelly's words have left me with a guilty longing, like an unresolved chord. I need to see my daughter sleeping.

"I need to check on Annie."

Livy stands and takes my hand, pulls me toward her. "I know."

"I mean it."

"I know." She puts her arms around my waist and pulls me against her.

"Livy —"

She kisses my nipple through my shirt. The sharp edges of her teeth pull at flesh and wet cloth, sending a delicious current of pain through me.

"It'll only take a minute," I tell her. "I'll be right —"

With three or four quick movements she unbuckles my pants and pushes them far enough down to free me, then entwines her fingers behind my neck. When I try to speak, she takes my right hand and lifts it to my mouth, cutting off my

433

words. Her scent on my fingers is overpowering.

"Me first," she whispers.

Even as I despise myself for it, in one violent motion I reach beneath her dress, lift her into the air, and set her down upon me.

CHAPTER 29

I am parked in the alley between Wall and Pearl Streets, the legal center of the city. It's nearly dark and raining steadily, a drizzle with a breath of fall in it. The courthouse towers above me on its pedestal of earth, grayish-white and imposing amid the windblown oaks that surround it. Across the street, running down the block in a line, stand the offices of various law firms, all of them small, most very profitable. The most prestigious among them is Marston, Sims. Founded in 1887 by Ambrose Marston, Leo's great-grandfather, the firm has handled everything from high-profile criminal cases to corporate litigation involving tens of millions of dollars. And I am parked in this alley to see whether the senior partner of the firm will commit a felony tonight.

I filed my requests for production this morning, and if Leo plans to hide or destroy any documentary evidence, the sooner he does it the better, at least from his point of view. I would like to be there when he tries. I've staked out his office because Tuscany — his fenced estate — does not lend itself to surveillance. Daniel Kelly is covering the back entrance for me, and we're in contact via handheld radios, which were among the toys he and his associates brought from Houston. Also among those toys was a Hi-8 video camera with a night-vision lens, which rests on the seat beside me. The rear entrance of the office is well lighted by a security lamp, so Kelly is using a standard camcorder borrowed from Caitlin Masters. The pistol he lent me last night lies on the seat beside the Hi-8 camera, its safety off.

"One-Adam-twelve, one-Adam-twelve." Kelly's voice crackles out of the radio. *"Sitrep, please."*

I laugh and press Send on my walkie-talkie. "Nothing out here but rain."

"It's like fishing. That's what my butt's telling me, anyway."

"Yeah. Maybe we'll catch something."

As I set the radio back on the passenger seat, something bangs against my window, nearly stopping my heart. I grab for the gun, knowing I'll never bring it up in time to save myself if the person outside the car means me harm.

When my eyes focus through the rivulets of water on the window, I see Caitlin Masters, her hair soaked from the rain. I let out my breath with a sigh of relief and motion for her to come around to the passenger side.

"I'm glad I wasn't trying to kill you," she says, sliding into the passenger seat. "You'd be dead."

She's wearing a windbreaker with *Los Angeles Times* stenciled on the chest. From the pocket she takes a barrette and puts the end in her mouth, then flips down the visor mirror above her seat. "Nothing yet?" she asks through her teeth.

"Nope."

She gathers her fine black hair and pins it in a

loose bun behind her head. "There. I should have done that before I left."

She turns and gives me a dazzling smile. "Well, are you up on the day's events?"

"I'm up on *my* events. The rest of the world I know nothing about."

"Four TV vans covered the Whitestone suspects' walk to their arraignment. Jackson, Baton Rouge, Alexandria, and a Gulf Coast station. The courthouse looked like it was under siege. The wire services picked up all three of my stories, and they're being rerun in dozens of papers."

"That Pulitzer's getting closer every day. Which judge did the kids get?" Natchez has two criminal court judges, a white woman and a black man.

"The black one. And he gave them bail."

"On first-degree murder?"

"With a confession, no less. He set it at a million apiece, which is like a billion to those kids' families. But I heard the NAACP may put up the cash bond. Two hundred thousand."

"They might as well paint targets on the kids' backs."

Caitlin picks up the video camera, switches it on, and trains it on the polished mahogany door of Marston, Sims. It's set deep in a deep brick alcove; a brass plate on the street announces the presence of the office to the public.

"Night vision," she murmurs. "Nice. Where's Kelly?"

"Watching the back door."

She zooms in on the door, then pans the rain-slickened street. "How much are those body-guards costing you?"

437

"Let's just say I'm going to have to hurry up and finish another book."

She laughs. "It's money well spent. That Kelly's been all over and done some wild things. He's cute too."

An irrational prick of jealousy irritates me. "I wouldn't know about that."

"Don't get all homophobic on me." She pokes my knee as she scans the street. "Well . . . here comes a familiar face."

"Where?" I turn the ignition key and flip on the windshield wipers.

"Our side of the street."

Now I see. A woman is jogging up the sidewalk in tight lycra warm-up pants and a TULANE T-shirt.

"It's the waitress with the crush on you," says Caitlin.

"Jenny?" I lean forward and watch the dark-haired young woman approaching through the rain. It is Jenny. "Give me a break."

"I mean it. That chick is fixated on you."

Jenny jogs past the car at a good clip, not paying us the slightest bit of attention. The rain has soaked her T-shirt, leaving absolutely nothing to the imagination.

"She ought to wear a sign," Caitlin says drily. "Please stare at my tits."

"I'm surprised you'd comment, after the blouse you wore the day you interviewed me."

Caitlin takes her eye away from the viewfinder and gives me an elfin smile. "That was different. I was trying to distract you."

"It worked."

"It always does. I'm really rather modest."

"Modesty isn't what comes to mind when I think of you."

Her smile changes subtly. "You don't really know me very well, do you?"

She reaches over and switches off the engine, killing the windshield wipers. "Any word on when Ruby Flowers's funeral will take place?"

Her quick segues are hard for me to follow. "Mose — Mr. Flowers — is thinking of Sunday, but that's not set in stone."

"Sunday? But that's . . . five days after she died."

"That's how the blacks do it. Haven't you read your own paper's obituary column?"

"Why do they wait so long?"

"Well, they usually have to wait days for relatives who live up North to get back to Mississippi. Sometimes they have to ride the bus. Ruby has two sons in Detroit, a daughter in Chicago, and another boy in Los Angeles."

"Can't you fly them in?"

"I'll do anything Mr. Flowers asks me to do, but he hasn't asked. My father already bought Ruby's coffin and headstone, which probably cost more than the church the funeral will be held in. Personally, I think he overdid it. Ruby never wanted to stand out from her own people in life, and I don't think she'd want to in death. Why do you care when the funeral is, anyway?"

"I hate to be the bearer of bad tidings, Penn, but Ruby's funeral is going to be the epicenter of a media hurricane."

"What?"

"Shad Johnson is going to speak, and there are bound to be TV trucks there —"

"Damn it, that's all wrong."

"You should thank God for small miracles. Al Sharpton called Shad this morning and offered to come down and 'help out with the Movement.' Shad told him to stay in New York."

Even as I say a silent thank-you to Shadrach Johnson, bitter gall rises into my throat.

"Take it easy," Caitlin says, touching my arm. "Tell me what you did today."

"What I did? It isn't what I did. It's what the judge did."

"Which judge?"

"The white one. Franklin. Two hours ago she set our trial date."

Caitlin goes still. "*Our* trial date? The libel trial?"

"Just my part of it. You don't have to worry. But my slander trial is set for next Wednesday."

"Next *Wednesday?* That's only" — she counts swiftly on her fingers — "six days from now!"

"Yep."

"That's ridiculous."

"I expected a quick trial date, but I thought I'd get at least a month. Simply going through the materials I've requested under discovery could take a month."

"How can the judge set a date like that?"

"Easily. She's in Marston's pocket. Why do you think he picked her?"

"Picked her? I thought they assigned judges by drawing lots or something."

"In this district they match cases to judges by simple rotation. Theoretically, whichever judge's name is up when a suit is filed gets that case. But all the clerk has to do to steer a case to a particular judge is hold on to it until that judge's turn comes up. One phone call from Marston to the clerk would do it."

"How do you know he has Franklin in his pocket? Maybe he just has the clerk."

"I talked to a local lawyer I went to school with. Marston was the heavy hand in getting Franklin elected. Big contributions, an endorsement, words in the right ears. That was eight years ago, but she won't have forgotten who put her on the bench."

"But how can she possibly defend that trial date? No one could build a defense that fast."

"In my answer to Marston's complaint, I stated that my defense would be truth. Truth is the oldest defense against a slander charge. By definition, truth cannot be slanderous. If Franklin is challenged about the trial date, she'll say, 'The defendant doesn't dispute that he uttered the alleged slander. He claims that his statements are true. Therefore, let him prove that without delay. Leo Marston's reputation should not suffer any more than it already has while Mr. Cage goes on a fishing expedition.' She can also cite the racial violence in the community resulting from my charges."

Caitlin is shaking her head. "Shit. You're in a deep hole."

"Will you help me wade through the materials I've requested in discovery?"

"Absolutely. I'll get my reporters and interns going through the stuff as soon as you get it."

She digs into her windbreaker pocket, pulls out a Snickers bar, and tears open the wrapper. After two bites she freezes and looks guiltily at me.

"Sorry." She offers me what's left.

"That's okay. You eat it."

"Come on. It's not like we haven't already exchanged germs. Though that seems quite a while ago."

I take it from her hand. "Thanks. I haven't eaten for hours."

The chocolate seems to be absorbed directly though the lining of my mouth, giving me an instant sugar buzz.

"Stakeouts are the worst," Caitlin grumbles. She glances toward the law office, then looks back at me. "Was your wife from a wealthy family?"

"Sarah? No. Why?"

"Well . . . Livy Marston is from a wealthy family."

"So?"

"And *I'm* from a wealthy family. And I felt that you were attracted to me. Until Livy showed up, anyway. I just wondered if something about that background draws you in some way."

"No. Sarah's father was a carpenter. That's probably how she stood the years when I was an assistant D.A. When we got rich, she wasn't sure how to react. At first she insisted that I put every penny in the bank, not spend any of it. Save it for the kids. But after my third book hit the list, she loosened up. When we bought our house in Tanglewood, she thought she'd died and gone to heaven."

Caitlin is watching me with a strange intensity. I reach out and touch her wrist. "Hey. I'm still attracted to you."

She looks vulnerable, yet ready to withstand a hard truth. "But you're sleeping with Livy Marston. Right?"

I know it's a mistake to look away, but I can't meet her eyes in this moment. "Did Kelly tell you that?"

"No. I just felt it. I shouldn't say anything about it. I don't have any right to. But I care about you. And Livy is just trying to keep you from hurting her father."

"She hasn't asked me to do anything like that. You don't really know her. In some ways she hates her father."

"Some ways. But not all." Caitlin's eyes hold wisdom far beyond her years. "And she's too smart to be overt. Maybe she just wants to distract you. Maybe she doesn't even admit her real motives to herself. But that's what she's doing. Protecting her father."

"Message received, okay?"

"May I ask one more question?"

"All right."

"Did your wife like her?"

A hollow feeling spreads from the pit of my stomach. "No."

Caitlin looks away as though embarrassed by forcing me to admit this. I am about to speak when she grabs the video camera, zooms in on the office door, and begins recording.

"What is it?"

"The object of your obsession is parking in front of her father's office."

Peering through the rain, I see a silver Lincoln Town Car parked in front of Marston, Sims. A woman with shoulder-length hair sits behind the wheel. She could be Livy, but I'm not sure. Until she gets out. She walks briskly through the rain to the mahogany door, her regal carriage as distinctive as a fingerprint.

After Livy unlocks the door, Leo's huge frame emerges from the passenger door of the Town Car, his close-cropped hair gleaming silver under the light of the street lamp.

"What the hell are they doing?" Caitlin whispers.

"Let's wait and see."

Livy holds the door open for Leo, scanning the dark street as she waits. I want to believe the best of her, but even from this distance her eyes look full of purpose. She lays a hand on Leo's shoulder as he passes through the door, then takes one more look up the street, seeing us but not seeing. I am suddenly back in the motel room last night, being led through a carnal labyrinth with Livy as my guide, dissolving and reforming inside her until I lay inert, my mouth dry as sand, my skin too sore to touch—

"*Shit,*" Caitlin hisses. "We can't see anything now. We should call Judge Franklin."

"Calm down. They could be doing legitimate work. Preparing his case. Livy is an attorney, you know."

"I'll bet they're shredding the files you asked for right this minute."

"Let's just sit tight, okay? See what happens."

The seconds pass in tense silence, with Caitlin tapping the door the entire time. My walkie-talkie crackles from the edge of Caitlin's seat.

"I've got lights in the building," Kelly says.

444

"We've got visitors. We're not sure what they're up to. Just stay put."

"I'm here if you need me."

Suddenly the mahogany door opens, and Leo backs out of the alcove with two large file boxes in his arms.

"Would you look at that?" Caitlin breathes. "The son of a bitch *is* guilty."

"Is the time-date stamp working?"

"I think so. It's displayed in the viewfinder."

As Leo loads his boxes into the backseat of the Town Car, Livy emerges from the office carrying another one.

"She's helping him!" Caitlin cries. "You've got to call the judge."

"We don't know what's in the boxes. They could be using those records to prepare Leo's case."

She shakes her head with manic exasperation as Leo returns with another box. Livy soon does the same, and one more trip by Leo makes six. Livy locks the door behind them.

Caitlin takes her cell phone from the holster on her belt and shoves it at me. I push it back at her.

"No. Let's see where they're going first."

"Jesus. She's got you wrapped around her little finger."

"Enough!"

I start the car and wait for Livy to pull out.

"What about Kelly?" Caitlin asks.

I pick up the walkie-talkie and press Send. "I'm following Livy Marston, Kelly. You keep watching the back. I'll call if I need you." I drop the radio on the floor and glance at Caitlin. "Less for them to notice."

I stay several car lengths behind the Town Car, but I needn't have worried. Livy drives straight to Tuscany. The mansion is set far back from the road, with eight acres of trees shielding it from sight and sound of passing traffic. A motorized gate closes after the Lincoln passes through, leaving us locked outside.

Caitlin jumps out of the car even before I've stopped, video camera in hand. I shut off the engine and follow her, which requires some fast footwork, as she has already scaled the gate and run on by the time I reach it. My feet crunch on the wet pea gravel as I race after her up the long, curving drive.

Tuscany was built in 1850 by a retired English general who imported the Italianate craze to Natchez from London. Three stories tall, the mansion is a splendor of northern Italian design, with an entrance tower, front and side galleries, marble corner quoins, huge roundheaded windows with marble hood moldings, and balustrade balconies on the second floor. Yet despite its grandeur, the overall effect of this transplanted villa is surprisingly tasteful.

The great door of the mansion closes just as Caitlin and I come within sight of it. From where we stand — beneath a dripping oak with a trunk as thick as ten men — Tuscany looks like an epic film set, floodlit, surrounded by trimmed hedges, azaleas, moss-hung Southern hardwoods, and luxurious magnolias. The broad, waxy leaves of the magnolias glisten with beads of rainwater.

"Do you know your way around the house?" Caitlin whispers.

"I used to."

"I'll bet. Come on."

She starts toward the house in a running crouch. Soon our faces are pressed to the panes of a ten-foot-tall window, with spiky hedges pricking our backs. The window glass is more than a century old, full of waves and imperfections, but Caitlin is videotaping through it anyway. Through the distorting medium I see Leo Marston standing before an enormous marble fireplace. Above the fireplace is a portrait of Livy as a teenager, or perhaps Maude. Leo bends, obscuring part of the fireplace, then straightens up and puts his hands on his hips. Beyond his knees, yellow flames billow up from a gas jet.

"He's building a fire," Caitlin says in a tone of disbelief. "It's seventy-five degrees and he's building an effing fire."

My last resistance crumbles. "Give me your cell phone."

I call directory assistance for Judge's Franklin's number, then let the computer connect me. The judge herself answers, and it sounds like cocktail hour at her house.

"Penn *Cage,* Judge Franklin. The lawyer Leo Marston is suing for slander."

"Oh. Why are you calling me at home?"

Leo lifts one of the file boxes and sets it squarely on the andirons. The flames lick their way up the sides of the cardboard, burning it black.

"Judge, at this moment I am watching Leo Marston destroy what I believe is the evidence I requested today in my requests for production."

A stunned pause. "Is he in the room with you?"

"No, ma'am. A few minutes ago I observed him

447

removing file boxes from his office in a surreptitious manner. I followed him home, and I am now watching him burn those file boxes in his fireplace. Watching through a window."

"You mean you're trespassing on his property?"

"Is that really the point, Judge?"

I hear the clink of ice against glass, a hurried swallow.

"Judge, I have the publisher of the Natchez *Examiner* with me, and the events I described are all on videotape. She's taping right this minute."

"Christ on a crutch. What do you want me to do, counselor?"

"Call the police and have them come straight to Marston's house and confiscate those files. And I'd like you to come with them. You might just prevent bloodshed."

"I'll do it, Mr. Cage. But you get your tail off Leo Marston's property right this minute, before he puts a load of rock salt in your butt. Or worse."

"Yes, ma'am."

I click End and touch Caitlin's arm. "She's sending the police."

"They won't make it in time. The gate's closed, and they won't be able to get through."

"What do you want to do?"

"Make Marston *want* them to get here."

She pulls free of my grip and bulls her way through the hedge. Seconds later, the sound of shattering glass reverberates across the floodlit lawn.

Leo goes rigid before the fireplace, his ears pricked. Caitlin's rock smashed the window of another room, and he is unsure of what he heard.

448

Then another hundred-fifty-year-old pane smashes, this one less than ten feet from Marston. He stares at the broken window, looks back at the fireplace, then hurries out of the room.

Caitlin is standing in the drive like a pitcher on the mound, right arm cocked, a rock in her hand. She may not know what Leo is going after, but I do. And from the gallery Marston could pick her off firing from the waist.

I charge through the prickly hedge and run onto the lawn. "Get your ass under cover!"

Her cocked arm fires, and another pane shatters into irreparable shards. I sprint the last few yards and grab her arm, dragging her toward a thicket of azaleas. Just as we plow into the bushes, the front door of Tuscany crashes open and Leo bellows into the night:

"Where are you, you gutless sons of bitches? Come out and fight like goddamn men!"

I have to give him credit. At this moment most Natchezians are huddled in their houses, terrified of a race war. For all Leo knows, a gang of crazed rioters smashed his windows and is now waiting to pick him off from the bushes. Yet there he stands, shotgun in hand, defending his castle like Horatius at the bridge. He shouts twice more, then fires blindly into the night. I cover Caitlin with my body as the shotgun booms through the trees like a cannon. After five shots Leo shouts a final curse, then goes back inside, slamming the door behind him.

God only knows what Maude and Livy are thinking. Surely one of them must have called the police and opened the gate by now.

"Get off," Caitlin groans from beneath me. *"I can't breathe."*

I roll off and scrabble to my knees in the azaleas.

She smiles up at me, breathing fast and shallow. "That wasn't exactly how I've pictured us getting horizontal together."

"Me either."

The smile vanishes. "Marston can still burn those files before the cops get here."

"There's nothing we can do to stop him."

"Give me your gun."

"No way, no how. You're a menace."

She sighs in frustration and rolls over to watch the mansion while we wait for the police.

Before long, three uniformed cops come racing up the driveway on foot. They rap on the great door, which Leo answers shouting at full volume, condemning the police department as a useless bunch of fools and high school dropouts. From their body language, the responding officers do not appear to be reacting favorably to his words. As he continues his tirade, two squad cars roar up the drive and stop before the front steps, which are bookended by Negro lawn jockey hitching posts. A black patrolman gets out of the first cruiser and opens his passenger door.

Circuit Judge Eunice B. Franklin emerges, looking like hell warmed over. She's wearing boxy blue jeans, an Ole Miss sweatshirt, hair curlers tied beneath a blue scarf, and she looks pissed. I pull Caitlin to her feet and hurry toward the gallery. When we arrive, Leo is lambasting Judge Franklin in the same superior tone he used with the police.

Franklin seems to be enduring it with remarkable equanimity.

When Leo recognizes me standing behind the judge, his face flushes bright red. There's murder in his eyes, and everyone on the gallery sees it.

"Did you smash my windows, Cage?" he yells.

"Don't say anything, counselor," Judge Franklin orders me. She turns back to Marston. "Leo, the issue tonight is files. Did you remove any files from your office tonight and attempt to burn them?"

At last comprehension dawns in Marston's eyes. "Did that bastard tell you that?"

Caitlin aims the video camera at Leo's face. "I have it all on tape, Judge Franklin. You can watch it right now, if you'd like."

Franklin looks back at Marston. "You want to rethink your answer, Leo?"

Marston draws himself up like a feudal lord being forced by a priest to deal civilly with serfs. "I brought some files home from my office. Old junk. Tax records, bad-debt files."

Franklin nods patiently, but her jaw is set. "Then you won't mind if these officers take them down to my chambers for safekeeping. I'm sure this is all a misunderstanding, but it'll save you the trouble of hauling away the ashes."

Leo blocks the door with his considerable bulk, his arms outstretched from post to post. "Eunice, I think you and I should have a private word."

Franklin glances at the video camera. "Turn that off, Ms. Masters."

"I'm sorry, Judge, but the First Amendment of the Constitution guarantees my right to do what I am doing now."

Judges do not react well to defiance. Eunice Franklin reddens a shade, and for a moment I fear she is about to order Caitlin's arrest. To my surprise, she turns to Marston and says, "Clear that door, Leo."

Marston's hard blue eyes lock onto Franklin's. "Eunice, you'd better think about what —"

"Officer Washington," she cuts in, "go in there and confiscate whatever files you find. Take them straight to my chambers."

Two cops push past Marston, whose only choices are to stand aside or defy the orders of a judge by assaulting police officers. He stands aside, his face red with fury. Eunice Franklin will pay a heavy price for this, but my sympathy is limited. Dilemmas like these are the price of backroom politics. With a final savage glare in my direction, Marston stomps back into the dark reaches of his mansion.

Judge Franklin pokes me in the chest, her eyes cold. "I want you in my chambers at nine A.M., mister." She points to Caitlin. "I want that videotape there as well."

"Will Marston be there?" I ask.

"That's not your concern."

"Destroying evidence is a felony, Judge."

Franklin's lips tighten until all I can see is the spiderwork of lines around her mouth, the result of years of smoking cigarettes. As we stare at each other, a patrolwoman carries a charred box of files through the front door.

"Go home, Mr. Cage," orders Judge Franklin. "And you will pay restitution for any physical damage to this property."

I am about to follow her advice when Livy walks through the front door of Tuscany. In a voice that could shave a peach, she says, "Judge, my name is Livy Marston Sutter. I'm here as counsel for my father, Leo Marston. Those boxes contain files of Marston, Sims clients, and thus enjoy the protection of attorney-client privilege."

Judge Franklin is momentarily taken aback, but she recovers quickly. "They'll be as safe in my chambers as they will anywhere."

Livy looks past her to me. "Penn? Would you please tell me what's going on here?"

I stand mute before her. Tonight's events have cast us as enemies, but even at this awkward moment part of me remains inside her, linking us in the most primitive way.

"You tell me, Livy."

"Who broke our windows?"

"I did," Caitlin says, as though she would welcome another lawsuit.

Livy gives her a glance of disdain. "What's Lois Lane doing here?"

Caitlin holds up the video camera. "Making home movies, sweet cheeks. I don't think you're going to like them."

"That's it," says Franklin. "Get out of here, both of you. Go back inside, Ms. Sutter."

"Your father was trying to destroy evidence, Livy. I couldn't let that happen."

"Evidence? You mean those old tax records? Daddy told me the day I got back that he needed to clean out his old files. I helped him because of his bad back."

Is she really trying to convince me that her motives are pure? Or is she using my presence as an opportunity to try to mitigate her culpability in the presence of Judge Franklin?

"I said this meeting is over," snaps Franklin.

I take Caitlin's arm above the elbow and lead her away from the house. Soon we're in darkness, surrounded by the smells of wet grass and decaying leaves. The pulse in her brachial artery is pounding like a tom-tom.

"What do you think?" she asks.

Instead of answering, I turn back and gaze through the dripping trees at Tuscany. What was once a temple of memory is now alien to me. The gallery that once hosted so many lawn parties now creaks under the tramp of police boots, and the sweet air of the grounds carries the tang of gunpowder. After five generations of seclusion, the world outside the gates has crashed through to Tuscany with a vengeance.

My gaze drifts upward, to the third floor, where a solitary light glows in a high window. Framed in that window is an amorphous shape that confuses me at first, but at last resolves into something human. It's the harridan head of Maude Marston, once a celebrated beauty, now a wreck, ravaged by emotional pain and by the alcohol she uses to blunt it. As Caitlin takes my arm and pulls me along the drive, I remember Dwight Stone's penchant for quotes, and I think, *What havoc hath he wrought in this great house?*

CHAPTER 30

The two days after Judge Marston's attempt to destroy the files pass in a blur of work that reminds me what it is to be a working lawyer. At nine o'clock Friday morning, Judge Franklin and I agree to an unconventional compromise worthy of Solomon. Without giving reasons, she makes it clear that she prefers not to charge Leo with obstruction of justice or contempt of court. Before I can argue this point, she tells me she considered recusing herself from the case but rejected the idea because Marston played as big a part in getting the black circuit judge elected as he did Judge Franklin. We both know I can go to the judicial oversight committee to plead for relief, but I sense that Eunice Franklin intends to offer me something.

What she offers is the boxes Marston tried to destroy, one of which contains three legal files, as Livy indicated. Marston's blatant attempt to destroy them has convinced Judge Franklin that he was attempting to hide evidence of criminal activity. She feels that a case can be made to the court of appeal that Marston's act justifies giving me access to these records. Moreover, Leo himself has agreed to this arrangement rather than be charged with obstruction or contempt. This tells me that the files, while probably damaging to Marston's reputation, will not contain proof of complicity in Del Payton's murder.

This agreement accomplished, the judge and I spend a few minutes getting to know each other. Eunice Franklin is fifty-six years old, and graduated from the Ole Miss Law School a year before Del Payton was killed. I can only imagine what she must have endured during her three years at that temple of Southern male traditionalism. She is a bit defensive about her court, and my "big-time" experience in Houston seems to be the cause of this. She warns me that she will run her courtroom with at least as much discipline as I am accustomed to in "the big city," and perhaps more. She will tolerate no antics or theatrics, either from myself or from Marston's attorney.

Leo will be represented by Blake Sims, the son of Creswell Sims, his partner of forty years. Judge Franklin has already instructed Sims that, considering the early trial date his client requested and got, they should have all discovery materials in my hands by the close of the business day.

She expresses strong misgivings about my intention to represent myself at trial, but says she cannot stop me from sabotaging my case if that is my intent. She defends the trial date along the lines I predicted to Caitlin, and adds that the recent racial tensions and violence played a part in her decision. With the mayoral election only four weeks away, she wants my inflammatory statements about the Payton murder resolved and hopefully forgotten by the time the voters walk into the polling booths on November 3.

Leaving her chambers, I feel a little better about the situation than I did walking in. Judge Franklin owes Marston some favors, but Leo's attempt to destroy evidence has made her angry. Under the blaze of scrutiny this trial will draw, Eunice may stiffen her backbone and run a relatively impartial court.

The media frenzy is already underway. Tying men like John Portman and Leo Marston to a dead black man is like waving a red cape in front of a herd of bulls. Twenty-four hours after my accusations hit the paper, Mississippi resumed its role as whipping boy for the nation on race. Celebrated authors and academics weighed in with windy and self-righteous op-ed pieces in every major paper from New York to Los Angeles. At the close of last night's newscast, a somber-faced Dan Rather recalled his days covering civil rights in Mississippi. Black media stars roundly condemned the state, speaking as though the lynchings of the distant past were still daily occurrences.

Contrary opinions were few, and the battle was becoming embarrassingly one-sided until this morning, when into the fray charged my old friend Sam Jacobs, the self-styled Mississippi Jew, who in a half-humorous letter to the *New York Times* pointed out that while Mississippi might seem behind the times to outsiders, it actually had its collective finger on the pulse of America. The Magnolia State, Sam opined, had given the world William Faulkner, Elvis Presley, and Tennessee Williams. And while that holy trinity of American culture ought to be enough for anybody, for skep-

457

tics there were also Robert Johnson, Richard Wright, Jimmy Rodgers, and Muddy Waters; Leontyne Price, Charley Pride, Tammy Wynette, and John Grisham; Howlin' Wolf, B. B. King, four Miss Americas, and Oprah Winfrey. And while boneheaded nuisances like the Ku Klux Klan had committed atrocities to shame the South Africans, and slavery had come near to breaking an entire people, you couldn't by God refine gold without a fire. The state of Israel was created from the ashes of the Holocaust, and Mississippi was on its way to redemption. Why, the legacy of blues music alone, declared Sam, which was jazz and rock 'n' roll, had done more to end the Cold War than all the thin-blooded diplomats ever minted at Harvard and Yale.

How the *Times* selected Sam's letter I'll never know, but it prompted my editor to telephone and read it aloud to me over breakfast, claiming that the list of artists only bolstered his theory that great suffering produces great art, and since I'd had my share of the former, I should now move north to more civilized environs. I declared myself a loyal Southerner to the last and headed out for Judge Franklin's office. I forgot the article during our conference, but after I loaded Marston's charred file boxes into my trunk, I heard a Jackson disc jockey reading Sam's letter on the air as I drove to the Natchez *Examiner* building. Sam Jacobs will be a household name throughout the South by nightfall.

Caitlin has offered me her glass-walled conference room as a work space, plus staff volunteers to help me wade through the files. After I lug

Marston's boxes into the conference room, she gathers her reporters, photographers, and interns for a brief orientation. The *Examiner* is used as a training ground for the Masters media group; thus the staff hails from all points of the compass. Not one among them is over thirty, and all are rabid liberals. I view this as a positive, for when the Marston camp discovers I'm using these kids against them, they'll almost certainly try to bribe a few for inside information. Youth and left-wing politics may give my team an immunity to filthy lucre that I couldn't hope to find elsewhere.

Caitlin's speech is modeled on those given by army officers requesting volunteers for particularly dirty missions. She succinctly summarizes my reasons for provoking the slander suit, then in broad strokes describes what we'll be looking for in the mountain of paper that will arrive later in the day.

"This is an unusual situation," she concludes. "Some of you may think I'm stepping over an ethical line by involving the paper in a legal proceeding that we'll be reporting on. That's true enough. But I stepped over a harder line when I printed Mr. Cage's charges. We'll be reporting this story the way papers reported stories in the good old bad old days. We're throwing the full weight of our media group behind a cause."

A buzz of approval runs through her audience.

"We are seeking the truth about a terrible crime, and I'll publish the truth as I find it, whether it conforms to my preconceptions or not. I think that lives up to the truest spirit of objectivity."

A burst of applause follows this. Two of the male reporters, whose goatees make them look like anarchists in a Sergei Eisenstein film, pump their fists in the air.

Caitlin brushes an errant strand of hair from her eyes and goes on. "Anyone who feels uncomfortable about this, see me in my office. You'll be excused with no questions asked and no negative consequences."

A blond guy in the back says, "And go back to covering board of supervisors meetings?"

"At least there's comedy at the supervisor meetings," squawks a dark-haired girl with a Brooklyn accent. "Try covering the flower shows."

Caitlin holds up her hands. "Before we disperse, I want Mr. Cage to say a few words."

Facing the ring of expectant young faces, I feel as I did addressing new assistant district attorneys in Houston, smart kids who concealed their idealism behind shells of aggressive cynicism. "First of all, everyone here calls me Penn. No exceptions. Second, when I made those charges against Leo Marston, I had no intention of setting foot in a courtroom. But Marston is a powerful man, and there is going to be a trial. That trial is five days from now. I have *five days* to prove Leo Marston guilty of murder."

Skeptical sighs blow through the conference room.

"The good news is, he's guilty. The bad news is, the people who know that won't testify. Your job is to wade through documentary evidence. You're looking for several things. First, illegal activity. You're not lawyers, but if it looks or smells dirty to you, it probably is. Second, any correspondence mentioning Ray Presley or the Triton Battery

Company. Third, any reference to or correspondence with the federal government, particularly with FBI Director John Portman or former director J. Edgar Hoover."

"*Whoa,*" says one of the anarchists. "This is like *X-Files*, man."

A ripple of laughter sweeps through the group.

"This case may be more like the *X-Files* than any of us wants to believe," I tell him. "Just remember that none of you are Fox Mulder or Agent Scully, okay? People are dying in this town, and they're dying because of this case. I don't want anybody in this room trying to win a Pulitzer by going after Ray Presley. He's killed before, and he probably set the fire that killed Ruby Flowers. He wouldn't hesitate to kill any of you if he felt you were a threat to him. Is that clear?"

Grim nods around the room.

"Are there any questions?"

One of the goateed reporters raises his hand. "This murder happened thirty years ago. It's gone unsolved all that time. Do we have a hope in hell of solving it in a week?"

"You're assuming that someone has been trying to solve it. This is a small town. In small towns there are sometimes truths that everyone knows but no one mentions. Open secrets, if you will. No one really wants to probe the details, because it forces us to face too many uncomfortable realities. We'd rather turn away than acknowledge the primitive forces working beneath the surface of society."

"Amen," someone murmurs.

"In the case of Del Payton, no one knew exactly who planted the bomb that killed him, but ev-

461

eryone believed they understood what had happened. An uppity nigger got out of line, so somebody stepped in and reminded the rest of them where the line was. Unpleasant but inevitable." My easy use of the "N-word" obviously shocks some members of the audience. "I believe this crime was misunderstood from the beginning. Del Payton's death may have had nothing to do with civil rights. Or only peripherally to do with it. His death may be old-fashioned murder masquerading as a race crime. And understanding that could be the key to solving this case."

Caitlin steps up beside me. "Any other questions? We've got work to do."

No more hands go up.

She sends everyone back to work with a two-handed "scoot" gesture. After they've gone, she sits at the head of the conference table, a skeptical look on her face.

"Penn, do we have any hope of tying Marston to Ray Presley or the crime scene in time for the trial?"

"That depends on what we find in the discovery material."

"Do you really believe Marston would send you anything incriminating?"

"I've found some pretty big surprises during discovery in my career. People make blunders." I motion toward the boxes the police saved from the fireplace at Tuscany last night. "And then there's that stuff. Maybe we'll get lucky."

Caitlin nods, but she doesn't look hopeful. "Do you realize that almost every witness who knows anything you need to tell the jury would have to embarrass themselves terribly by testifying? Frank Jones . . . Betty Lou Jackson. Not only that, they'll be putting themselves in the killers' sights. Your ATF pal will testify, and maybe Lester Hinson, if you pay him enough. But the rest? No way."

"That's what subpoenas are for."

"You're not that naive. Portman, Marston, and Presley know about all these people, or soon will. And they'll try everything from bribes to murder to keep them quiet."

"That's why we have to crack Marston's nerve between now and next Wednesday."

"And if you can't?"

"Then we pray our long shots come through."

"And those are?"

"Peter Lutjens, for one. He's going for the Payton file in two days."

"I've been thinking about that. What exactly is he going to try to do? The file is forty-four volumes long. He can't walk out with it under his coat. He can't even photocopy it unless he has all night."

"He won't have to. Remember what Stone told us in Colorado? The file is forty-three volumes of nothing and his final report. That's all we need. Stone's final report."

"Lutjens knows that?"

"I talked to him this morning."

"What's the other long shot?"

"Stone himself."

She shakes her head. "Never happen. He's too scared. They've got something on that guy. Stone's not going to talk."

"I disagree. Whatever dirt Portman has on Stone is a two-edged sword. And Stone's conscience is working on him. It's been working on him for thirty years. Guilt is a powerful thing, Caitlin. Stone needs to unburden himself, and I think he'll come through for us. Or for himself, rather."

"What about Ike Ransom? What's his story?"

"I think Ike's got a personal grudge against Marston that has nothing to do with Payton. He knew I'd go after Marston if I had any kind of weapon, so he gave me the Payton case."

"But has he given you any real information? Any idea of Marston's motive for the crime?"

"Not really."

She drums her fingers on the table. "Motive, means, and opportunity, right? The means and opportunity are Ray Presley, but we're stuck on motive. Marston actually made public statements supporting civil rights in the sixties. I found them in the morgue here."

"I think it's money. Somehow Payton's death increased Marston's fortune or power."

"I can't see that. Financially, Payton was a nonentity."

"Maybe he was an obstacle to something. Some deal."

"What about sex?" suggests Caitlin. "Sexual jealousy. That's a common motive for murder."

The photo shrine in Althea Payton's house flits through my mind, followed by images of Del Payton huddled over his dinner table with Medgar Evers, talking about changing the white man's heart. "That's not it. Payton was a family man all the way."

"That's what they all say until they're caught

with their wee-wees in the wrong cookie jar."

"It's not sex, Caitlin. It's money or power. That's what Marston lives for."

She sighs and gets up, then drops her left hand on the charred box of files. "I hope there's something in here."

"You've got to remember one thing. I'm treating this like a murder case, but it's not. It's a civil case."

"So?"

"So the standard of proof is lower. I don't have to prove Marston's guilt to twelve people beyond a reasonable doubt. I have to convince nine jurors that it was *more likely than not* that Marston was involved in the Payton murder. That means a fifty-one percent certainty. And the jury won't have to agonize over their decision the way a criminal jury would. Because their verdict won't send Marston to jail or to a gurney for lethal injection. Another jury will get that job."

Caitlin moves toward the door. "I think you're going to have a hell of a job convincing those nine people unless you figure out *why* Marston would want Payton dead. And prove it."

When she opens the door, the goateed anarchists pop through it with their sleeves rolled up and smirks on their faces.

"Mulder and Scully reporting for duty," says one.

Caitlin shakes her head and walks out, leaving me to deal with my new assistants.

In the forty hours between the end of my lecture on Friday and dawn on Sunday, we built a circumstantial case against Leo Marston. The only sleep I got was brief naps on the couch in Caitlin's office, taken while reporters, photographers, and interns worked in shifts over the boxes of Marston papers that arrived in desultory waves from storage rooms unknown. Only my anarchists — who did have actual names, Peter and Ed, prosaically enough — kept pace with me during this marathon. They seemed to see it as a holy mission, one in which iconoclasts could cheerfully take part.

Daniel Kelly moved through the building like the ghost at the feast, making wry observations, delivering coffee, and disappearing for brief reconnaissance patrols, which he called "checking the perimeter." Whenever Caitlin left the building to cover a story, Kelly went with her. The police scanner in her office enabled her to reach the scene of several racial altercations before the cops did. Most of these involved two or three individuals, and broke out in stores or restaurants, where inflammatory language was easily overheard. On two occasions these fights escalated into brawls, and Kelly proved his value both times by protecting Caitlin with his rather alarming skills.

Saturday morning, Ed the anarchist decided we needed fresh inspiration, so he sat down with a computer and inkjet printer and went to work. An hour later, he walked into the conference room wearing a T-shirt with NAIL BOSS HOG emblazoned across the chest in red. I found it hard to believe that Ed had ever watched an episode of *The Dukes of Hazzard*, but he assured me he'd followed it religiously as a child growing up in Michigan, and that most of his ideas about the South had been formed by this grotesque television show. By that afternoon, half the *Examiner* staff was wearing NAIL BOSS HOG shirts, and their galvanizing effect was undeniable. Even Caitlin popped into the conference room wearing one.

But the work itself was tedious and exhausting. The master map that guided us on our paper journey into Marston's past was his 1997 tax return. It listed most of his business holdings (the number of Schedule C's and E's was astounding), and I immediately began drafting a supplemental request for production, using these as a guide. His form 1040 showed an adjusted gross income of over two million dollars for 1997, and the sheer variety of his holdings was staggering. Real estate, manufacturing, banking, timber. And despite the moribund oil business, he had recently struck a significant gas field in south Texas. What fascinated me was the variety of small enterprises in which he participated. Several fast-food franchises around town. A steam laundry. A Christmas tree farm. Hunting camps. Apartment buildings in the black sections of town. We even found a scrawled note listing income he had realized from arranging private adoptions over a period of twenty-five years.

In short, Leo Marston appeared to administer an empire of great and small dominions, all entirely aboveboard. On closer examination, however, a dark underside began to show itself. One of the boxes Leo had planned to burn contained records of a collection agency wholly owned by him. Listed as an officer of that company was one Raymond Aucoin Presley. This was the first tangible proof of a connection between Marston and

467

Presley. We found copies of letters sent to hundreds of local citizens, demanding payment of debts on everything from materials bought through Marston companies to personal loans made by the judge. It wasn't hard to guess what function Presley served when these letters failed to bring payment of the outstanding balances. Most important, he was operating in this capacity during 1968, while serving as a Natchez police officer and in the month Del Payton was murdered. Closer inspection of Marston's other companies revealed that Presley was listed as a paid "security consultant" to several of them.

Another of the "burn boxes" contained records of land transfers made to Marston or his business partners. I noted the disturbing frequency with which the parcels of land had been sold by recent widows whose estates Marston's firm had handled. Many other sellers could be cross-indexed to debtors listed in the "collection-agency" box. It was a letter from this box that gave me my first glimmer of a possible motive for Payton's murder.

The letter pertained to a large parcel of land south of town, near the present industrial park. It was written in an oblique style, but from it I inferred that Marston had used a secret intermediary to buy this parcel of land. Thus, while Marston was not legally the owner, he controlled the parcel's future use and would receive all monies from such use, without anyone but the intermediary knowing about it. A related letter — this one from one Zebulon Hickson, the owner of several carpet factories in Georgia and Alabama — expressed interest in purchasing this land for use as a site for a new factory. Hickson also expressed concern about labor conditions in Adams County. He was aware that Natchez had long been a "union" town, but what concerned him more was the "wave of racial unrest" sweeping through Southern factories. This was clearly a euphemism for "nigger trouble." What made all this interesting was that the letters had changed hands in January 1968, a few months before Del Payton died. The situation was oddly similar to the present one, in which Leo Marston owns the land BASF needs to have adequate space for its projected facility.

On Saturday night, things began to turn our way. I had requested Marston's telephone records, but with the trial only a week away, I had little hope of getting them. Technically, phone records can be had at the touch of a computer key, but the phone company is a hidebound bureaucracy, and in actuality it can take weeks to get them. I'd put in a call to a Bell South executive in Jackson, who promised to try to expedite the process, and apparently he did. A local Bell South technician arrived Saturday night with a manila envelope containing Marston's phone records, logging all calls beginning the day before Caitlin's "libelous" article ran.

I hurried to Caitlin's office, and we pored over the printouts together. On the day the article ran, there was a call from Marston's law office to a number in Washington, D.C., at 1:45 P.M. Caitlin quickly confirmed this number as the main switchboard at the Hoover Building, headquarters of the FBI. The call lasted eighteen minutes. One hour later Marston's office had received a call from

469

D.C., this one from a different number, which turned out to be John Portman's office in the Hoover Building. In all, six calls passed between Marston's office and the Hoover Building that day, and several more had since. We could now prove that a link existed between Leo Marston and the director of the FBI, who had worked the Del Payton murder as a field agent in 1968, when Marston was district attorney. And while we could not know what was said during those calls, their timing indicated that they were almost certainly related to the Payton case.

Caitlin's father faxed us a steady stream of information on both Marston and Portman. Marston's Mississippi history was familiar to me, but his national political activities weren't. He is not only a powerful force in the Mississippi Republican Party, but he also has major influence in the national GOP. Like many Mississippians, Marston was a nominal Democrat for most of his life, voting Democratic in local elections and Republican in presidential races. But in the Reagan era he jumped ship and voted GOP straight down the line. A close friend and adviser of Senators John Stennis and "Big" Jim Eastland — Mississippi Democrats whose seniority gave them unparalleled power on Capitol Hill for decades — Marston became a major supporter of Senator Trent Lott, who eventually rose to the position of Senate majority leader.

John Portman's thumbnail biography fascinated me. Born to old money in Connecticut while his father "patrolled the coast" of Rhode Island for German U-boats in his yacht, Portman was raised

470

in a cloistered world of governesses and squash courts. He attended Choate, then Yale, where he was tapped for Skull-and-Bones and graduated second in his class at Yale Law. He was the right age for Vietnam but did not serve (perhaps owing to a dearth of yacht units). And while the FBI seemed an odd choice for a blue-blooded lawyer, during the Reagan era these "street" credentials fueled Portman's meteoric rise into the upper ranks of the Justice Department. His stellar legal career as a U.S. attorney and federal judge was crowned by the poetic symmetry of returning to the fields where he'd begun, no longer a foot soldier but a general, and the media ate this up. The Hanratty affair provided the only bump in the road to his confirmation as FBI director, and since nothing could be proved, that came to naught. Portman sailed through the hearings without further trouble, and he has ruled the Bureau without a public misstep ever since.

In short, John Portman appeared to be a Teflon-coated bureaucrat with no visible weaknesses. His evasion of Vietnam service might be fertile ground for tabloids, but that wouldn't help my case any, and there was probably nothing to it anyway, or it would have exploded during his confirmation hearings. The more I learned about him, the more I became certain that the only way I would uncover his secrets would be if Dwight Stone decided to break his silence, or if Peter Lutjens succeeded in stealing Stone's final report from the Payton file in the FBI archive.

As I waded through the mountains of paper, eyes blurring, pulse skipping from caffeine, the tragedies of the past few days began to weigh heavily upon me. I'd involved myself in the Del Payton case for essentially selfish reasons, and because of my actions my parents' house had been destroyed, my daughter terrorized, and Ruby Flowers murdered. The sad irony was that I had returned to Natchez to help heal my daughter, yet she had not received my full attention for many days, and had not even seen me for the past two. Yet something drove me on. Despite the selfishness that had initiated my quest, I sensed a new, yet familiar energy stirring inside me. As I pored over the yellowed documents and musty ledgers, doing the sort of work I had done as a young lawyer, the sterile hollowness and free-floating anxiety I had felt in the months after Sarah's death began to fall away. I felt alive again. And I knew this: Annie would fare far better with a father who was fully engaged with the world than with one grasping at meaning while clinging to the past.

I was not laboring in a vacuum. I was surrounded by idealistic kids who had no doubt they were on the right side of a noble quest for justice. During the forty-hour marathon, rumors and snippets of information filtered into the *Examiner* building that opinions in Natchez were not as clear-cut or one-sided as I had imagined. Many whites interviewed about the Payton case stated on the record that if Del Payton's killer could be found, he should pay the maximum price, no matter who he might be or how much time had passed. They regretted that the battle between myself and Marston had generated such bad publicity for the town, but justice, they said, had to be served. A consensus was building that the rest of the nation had to be shown that Mississippi was not afraid to confront its old demons, if and when they could be dragged into the light.

The rumored riot of a few nights ago never materialized. On Saturday afternoon local black leaders staged a silent march to commemorate Ruby's death, and the hushed procession walked without incident from the bandstand on the bluff to the crossroads of St. Catherine Street and Liberty Road, where slaves had been auctioned before the Civil War. The symbolism of this destination was not lost on whites, but black restraint in the face of Ruby's murder was seen as a signal of black faith in Natchez's justice system.

The real whirlwind was taking place outside Mississippi. We stood in the eye of a media storm, quietly going about the business of justice while national figures raged and pontificated about our backwardness. I soon began to see this as a metaphor for the Payton case itself. Yes, Ray Presley was probably the man who planted the bomb that killed Del Payton. And perhaps Leo Marston had ordered him to do it. But it was clear to me that they had not acted alone. J. Edgar Hoover had not sealed the Payton file because it could potentially embarrass the state of Mississippi. And John Portman was not threatening me or punishing Peter Lutjens because of the local implications of this case. Nor was the fearsomely equipped sniper who shot at me from the levee the type of hit man an angry Southern businessman like Leo Marston would typically hire. Still more disturbing, I had begun to recall Dwight Stone's comment about the timing of Payton's slaying. Del was killed five weeks after Martin Luther King and three weeks before Robert Kennedy. Could there possibly have been some connection between a black factory worker in Natchez, Mississippi, and the explosive national politics of 1968?

As I pondered this question, my motive, which had begun as a quest for revenge and evolved with Livy's arrival into an exorcism of my past, began to change again. Like a stubborn coal lying dormant in the ashes, a desire for truth flickered awake in my brain. Fanned to life, this glowing ember dimmed the baser motives that had brought me thus far. Revenge against Leo Marston is a hollow and perhaps even self-destructive goal. For by destroying him, would I not also destroy the second chance I've been granted for a life with Livy? And what of my hunger for explanations from Livy? Is it her fault that I've carried confusion and bitterness inside me for twenty years like shrapnel from some undecided war, a war that a more mature man would have put behind him long ago?

Ten years before Livy disappeared from my life, Del Payton was brutally murdered. That's what's important. That's what has brought death back to this quiet town, and put the lives of those I love in mortal danger. I have but one riddle to answer. Ike the Spike told me that from the beginning. Not *who* killed Del Payton, but *why*. Because the why of it is as alive today as it was in 1968, and therein lies the answer to all my other questions. The relief that accompanied this liberating insight put me into a dead sleep on the couch in Caitlin's office late Saturday night.

When Sunday dawned, this was the sum of our knowledge: a potential land deal in 1968 that involved Marston and a Georgia industrialist concerned with "racial" labor problems in Natchez (a deal that, as far as we could determine, was never consummated); phone records proving suspicious contact between Marston and John Portman; and proof that Ray Presley had worked as a "security consultant" for Marston at the time of the Payton murder and while employed by the police department. It was a good harvest for forty hours' work, but with the trial only three days away, it wasn't nearly enough. All the NAIL BOSS HOG T-shirts in the world wouldn't put me one step closer to proving Marston's complicity in the murder. And without that I would never unravel the tangled skein of lies, corruption, and official silence that made Del Payton's unpunished murder such a travesty, and forced my native state to bear the sole guilt which by rights should have been shared with others.

I needed a witness.

A star witness.

I needed Peter Lutjens or Dwight Stone.

At eleven A.M. on Sunday, I was about to call Stone to set up a secure call when Caitlin stuck a cup of scalding coffee in my hand and told me to go home and get dressed for Ruby's funeral, which was scheduled to begin in three hours.

CHAPTER 31

There is no more moving religious spectacle than a black funeral. If you've been to one, you know. If you haven't, you don't. Grief and remembrance are not sacrificed to the false gods of propriety and decorum but released into the air like primal music, channeled through the congregation in a collective discharge of pain. Ruby's funeral should be like that, but it isn't. It's a ritual struggling under the weight of a political circus.

The church itself is under siege when I arrive, Annie in the backseat with my parents, Kelly in front with me, the other Argus men in a second car behind us. Sited on a hill in a stand of oak and cedar trees, the one-room white structure stands at the center of an army of vehicles, including a half dozen television trucks parked in a cluster beside the small cemetery. Lines of parked cars stretched down both sides of the church drive to Kingston Road, the winding old two-lane blacktop leading to the southern part of the county, where the Cold Hole bubbles up from the swamp.

A black-suited deacon waves us away from the drive, but Kelly ignores him and accelerates up the chute created by the parked cars, stopping only

476

when he reaches the church steps. Camera crews instantly surround the BMW.

An old white-haired black man appears on the steps and jabs a finger at the human feeding frenzy around us. A wave of young men in their Sunday best rolls into the reporters, pushing them bodily away from the car, assisted by the three Argus men who drove up behind us. The old man comes down the steps and opens the back door of our car.

"I'm so sorry about this, Dr. Cage. Afternoon, Mrs. Cage. I'm Reverend Nightingale. Y'all come inside. One of these young mens will park your car for you."

Annie climbs between the seats into my arms, and I hurry up the steps with her as the camera crews close around us. A cacophony of shouted questions fills the air, but all I can distinguish are names: *Marston, Portman, Mackey, Mayor Warren. . . .* As soon as we clear the church door, I turn and see my mother and father fighting their way through. A deacon slams the door behind them, leaving Kelly outside to help defend the entrance.

Two hundred black faces are turned toward the rear of the church, staring at us. People are jammed into the pews and packed along the walls like cordwood. The building seems to have more flesh in it than air. Only the center aisle is clear. Reverend Nightingale takes my mother's arm and leads her along it, through the silent staring faces. Dad and I follow, me carrying Annie in my arms. The rear pews hold a bright sea of color, oscillating waves of blue, orange, yellow, and green (but no red, never red) and, like proud sails above the waves, the most stunning array of hats I have seen

477

outside of a 1940s film. All the children are dressed in white, like angels in training. As I follow my mother, Ruby's voice sounds in my mind: *You never wear red to no funeral; red says the dead person was a fool.* The nearer we get to the altar, the darker the dresses get, until finally all are black.

At the end of the aisle Reverend Nightingale pulls my mother to the left, and I see our destination: a special box of pews standing against the wall, protected by a wooden rail. Despite the throng in the church, this box is empty. It's the Mothers' Bench, seats reserved for "sisters" who have reached a certain age (eighty, I think) and accepted "mother" status. Today it has been reserved for us. As we take our seats behind the rail, I see an identical box against the other wall. The Deacons' Bench. Behind its rail sits Ruby's immediate family: her husband, Mose; her three sons (all tall men with gray in their beards); her daughter, Elizabeth, wiping her eyes with a handkerchief; a handful of grandchildren (all in their twenties) and two infants.

A single camera crew has been allowed inside the church to tape the ceremony. The logo on the camera reads WLBT, the call letters of the black-owned station in Jackson. As I pan across the crowd, I see several familiar faces. In the first row sits Shad Johnson, wearing a suit that cost enough to buy any ten suits behind him. A few feet down the same pew sits the Payton family: Althea, Georgia, Del Jr., and his children. Althea nods to me, her brown eyes full of sympathy. In the second row sits the Gates family, the most powerful force in black politics in Natchez for forty years, now upstaged by the urban prodigal from Chicago. Several pews beyond them sits Willie Pinder, the former police chief. Pinder winks as I catch his eye. And in the last pew, sitting restlessly in the aisle seat as though prepared to make a quick exit, sits a man who looks very much like Charles Evers. The former mayor of Fayette and brother of Medgar looks like a man who does not intend to be bothered by anyone.

Suddenly the back door opens and two white faces float through it, Caitlin Masters and one of her photographers, escorted by Deputy Ike Ransom in his uniform. Ike remains just inside the back door, like a sentry, while Caitlin and her photographer slip through the crowd at the back wall and stop beside the WLBT camera.

In the shuffling, sweating silence the organist begins to play, and the purple-robed choir rises to its feet, beginning a restrained rendition of "Jesus, Keep Me Near the Cross." The rich vibrato of two dozen voices fills the building, making the church reverberate like the soundboard of a grand piano. The whole congregation knows the words, and they join in softly.

As the last chorus fades, Reverend Nightingale makes his way slowly down the aisle and ascends to the pulpit. He is a small man, with fine white hair and frail limbs, but his voice has the deep, resonant timbre of the best black preachers.

"Brothers and sisters. Mothers. Deacons and officers. Visitors and friends. We are gathered here today to mourn the passing of Sister Ruby Flowers."

A collective *Mm-hm* ripples through the church,

punctuated by a couple of soft *Amens*. Reverend Nightingale touches the rim of his spectacles and continues.

"Everyone in this room knows how loyally Sister Flowers supported this church. She was born in 1917, and came to Jesus when she was nine years old. Reverend Early was pastor then. He was a godly man, but sparing with his praise. Yet as a boy I often heard him speak of how lucky he was to have womenfolk like Sister Flowers in his flock."

Yes, Lord, comes the reply. *Yes, sir.*

"In the last few days a lot of reporters been asking me what Sister Flowers was like. Do you know what I tell them?"

Tell it.

"I say, 'You know how when you got two people, and you got to carry something heavy for a ways? Like a big chest of drawers? There's different ways you can pick up on it. You can pick up on it straight and level, with your legs and your back, and take your share of the weight' — Reverend Nightingale pauses, letting the image sink in — 'or you can kind of *fudge* it. Pick up with just your arms, or pick up a little *high*, puttin' most of the weight on the other person.' "

Soft laughter, guilty recognition. But Reverend Nightingale's face is set in stone.

"That was *not* Sister Flowers," he thunders.

No, Jesus, comes the chorus. *I know that's right.*

"Sister Flowers picked up square and straight," he declares. "She picked up whenever she was asked to. And more than that, she picked up when she *wasn't* asked to."

Praise Jesus.

"Sister Flowers was not a rich woman," the reverend says in a conversational tone. "But she gave unstintingly of the money she made. She had a generous heart. She bought flour and sugar and butter, and she baked cakes deep into the night to sell to raise money for the poor." Nightingale raises his right hand, forefinger extended toward Heaven. "During the Depression? Sister Flowers visited white families, collecting old coats and sweaters, hats, shoes, and mittens for the wintertime, bringing them out here to kids who didn't have *nothing* between them and the cold." The finger descends, admonitory now. "You children today smirk and turn up your nose when I say *old* coats and *old* shoes. But what you don't know — and you better thank God you don't know — is that when you're *cold,* you'll take what*ever* coat you can get, and praise Jesus for it."

Lord, yes! Praise Jesus!

Reverend Nightingale turns to the Deacons' Bench and remarks on what fine children Ruby raised. My parents always felt Ruby's children didn't do enough for her after they were grown, considering the sacrifices she'd made for them. But they did what Ruby most desired that they do, went North and found good jobs, raised families. Part of the price of their success may have been embarrassment at their mother's humble position, or confusion at her unwillingness to leave Mississippi, a place they regarded as backward and evil.

"Sister Flowers was not seriously ill or afflicted," Reverend Nightingale says soberly. "She was taken before her time, by the hand of a stranger. The po-

481

lice don't know who set that terrible fire. But *I* know who it was."

A gasp of shock from the pews.

"It was a man cut off from the Lord. That man is suffering right now. Today. And I hope he'll soon see the only way to wash his soul is to come forward, confess his sins, and pay the price of justice."

Reverend Nightingale grips the forward edge of the podium with both hands. "And I know *why* this man killed Sister Flowers. Because he wanted to stop Mr. Penn Cage from finding out who killed Brother Delano Payton."

Silence blankets the room. Every eye focuses on me.

"Now, some of you may feel anger toward Mr. Cage because of what happened to Sister Flowers. But not one soul in this room should blame him. Because Penn Cage is doing what no man — white or black — has done in the last thirty years. He is putting himself and his family on the line to find out who murdered Brother Del.

"And why was Del killed?" Reverend Nightingale slams a hand against the podium with a report like a pistol shot. "To keep the black man in this community down! To keep honest black men from getting a leg up. To keep us from making a working wage at a good job. A job with some *dignity*."

He removes a white cotton handkerchief from his coat pocket and wipes his forehead. The mass of bodies is turning the little building into a convection oven.

"You may wonder why Mr. Cage, a white man, is doing what he's doing. He must be gonna make some money some way, right? He must want to get

482

on *Oprah* with a book or something. But that's not it. No, sir. I'll tell you why Mr. Cage is doing what he's doing. He's doing it because he was *raised* by Sister Flowers."

My mother's hand closes around mine.

"And he wasn't raised by Sister Flowers alone. He was raised by Dr. Tom Cage. And Dr. Cage been takin' care of black people in this town for nigh on forty years. If you couldn't pay, did Dr. Cage turn you away from the door?"

A great tide of *No, sir! Lord, no!* issues forth from the congregation and rolls through the church, accompanied by shaking heads and murmurs of gratitude. When I turn to my left, I see a sight I have never seen in my life: my father sitting with his head bowed, staring resolutely at the floor, his jaw muscles clenched as tears run down his face.

"And *Mrs.* Cage," says Reverend Nightingale. "Mrs. Cage was one of the ladies who helped Sister Flowers gather up them old coats in the wintertime, and made sure they got where they needed to get." He smiles at my mother and goes on. "Thursday last, after that newspaper story ran about Del, I asked Sister Flowers about Penn Cage. You know what she said? She said, 'Pastor, that boy was raised right, and he'll do whatever he's got to do to make things right about Del.' "

Ruby and I never discussed the Payton case. But the realization that she knew I was working on it, and approved, eases my conscience in a way nothing else could.

"Some of you older members may remember," says Nightingale, "that Del Payton visited this church several times when he was a boy. Del was a member of Beulah Baptist, out to Pine Ridge. But that boy had too fine a voice to confine it to one house of worship. Several Sundays we were blessed to have Del solo here at Mandamus. And many a family" — Reverend Nightingale says *fambly* — "requested Del for solos at funerals. I know right now Del is beatifying Heaven with that sweet voice, preparing the host of angels to receive Sister Flowers."

"Praise Jesus," answers the chorus.

"Right now we're going to have a solo by Sister Lillian Lilly. Sister Lilly is a gospel recording artist from Jackson, and she's come down to bless us with her talents. Afterwards, Brother Shadrach Johnson wants to speak to you for a few minutes. You all know Brother Johnson is running for mayor, and the election's getting close. He believes what's happened in the past few days is important to us all, and he's gonna talk to you about that. Sister Winans?"

From the midst of the choir a woman in a flowing blue gown rises, folds her hands before her, and begins singing "Precious Lord" with such raw power and authentic faith that the initial cries of *Sing it! Sing it!* fade to awed silence, and many of the elderly members of the congregation weep openly. When she takes her seat again, the air is brittle with expectation, and it is then that Shad Johnson stands and walks up to the podium. How must he look to this audience, in his two-thousand-dollar suit that shines like a deuce-and-a-quarter on Saturday night? He must look, I believe, like a savior.

"Brothers and sisters," he begins in a gentle

voice. "When I came into this church, I thought I was a stranger to Sister Ruby Flowers. But when I heard Reverend Nightingale's impassioned eulogy, I knew I was wrong. I knew a hundred women like Sister Flowers when I was growing up here in Natchez. Five hundred, probably. Strong black women who sacrificed everything so that their children could climb one step higher up the ladder to a better life."

Yes, Lord. . . .

Shad nods to his left, and the assistant I saw at his headquarters hurries toward the back of the church. He stops beside the WLBT cameraman and says a few words. The cameraman looks confused, but a moment later he shrugs and touches the controls on the tripod-mounted camera.

"Brothers and sisters," Shad resumes, "I've asked that the camera be turned off, so that I can speak frankly to you. We all know what's happening in this town. Why there's so much agony in our hearts today. Sister Flowers died hard. She died scarred and in terrible pain. She died at the hands of a murderer. Undoubtedly at the hands of a *white* murderer. And the consequences of that act are tearing this community apart. At this moment two of our children are sitting in jail for taking the life of a man who once ordered the beatings and murders of African Americans. You feel anger over this. You feel *rage*. And that's only natural."

Shad holds up his hands and brings them softly together. "But I've come here today to ask you to set aside that rage. Because we are poised on the brink of a great victory. The plantation mentality that has paralyzed this town for so long is finally eroding from the inside out. Significant numbers of white people have grown tired of the self-aggrandizement and profiteering of men like Riley Warren. And those are the people who can put me into the mayor's office. Not you, my good friends. Lord knows, I need every one of you. But without those good white people, all our work will have been for naught. The sacrifices of Ruby Flowers and Del Payton? All for nothing. Think about that. Del Payton died thirty years ago. He died for civil rights. But how much better off are you, really, than you were in 1968? You can drink from the public water fountain. You can go into a restaurant and eat next to white people. But can you afford to pay the check? How good a job can you get? If this violence escalates any more, I don't think we'll ever see those men from BASF in town again. There are too many towns where things are peaceful to put a good plant like that in a trouble spot.

"So." Johnson lays his hands on the podium. "What am I asking you to do? Only the same thing Jesus asked. It's the hardest thing in the world, brothers and sisters. Especially for you younger men. I want you to turn the other cheek. Keep cool. Because if you do, the meek are going to start inheriting a little of this Mississippi earth."

Shad turns slowly, giving every person in the room a chance to look him in the eye, then stops, facing me. "And I'm asking Penn Cage, right here and now, to withdraw his charges against Judge Leo Marston."

A low murmur moves through the congregation.

Even Reverend Nightingale looks caught by surprise.

"After the election," Shad goes on, "there'll be plenty of time to probe the death of Del Payton. And with me running the city, you can rest assured that will happen. But further pressure on Marston at this point could keep Riley Warren in the mayor's office for another four years. And we simply cannot afford that."

Shad is staring at me as though he expects me to rise and answer him, here, at the funeral of a woman I loved like a second mother. Every eye in the church is upon me. As though pulled by the collective will of the congregation, I start to stand, but my mother's hand flattens on my thigh, pushing me back onto the bench. At that moment Althea Payton rises from the first pew and looks around the church. She speaks softly, but in the silent room every word rings with conviction.

"Thirty years ago my husband was taken from me. Murdered. For thirty years I've waited for justice. And no man alive has lifted a finger to help me get it, without I paid him money. Last week I went to Mr. Penn Cage and asked him to help me. And he *did*."

Althea raises her eyes to the pulpit, from which Shad stares like an attorney facing a dangerously unpredictable witness, and points at him. "That man there wants to be our mayor. He's come down from Chicago special to do it. And he might be a good one. He sure talks a good game. But I know this. He never came to my house and offered to help me find out who killed my man. And to stand up here like this . . . to use this poor lady's funeral to tell a good man to stop trying to do good so *he* can get elected . . . well, it don't sit right with me."

"Mrs. Payton, I think you've misunderstood my motives," Shad says in an unctuous voice.

"I understand more than you think," Althea replies. "Get me elected, you say. *Then* I'll do good. But like the man said a long time ago, 'If not now, when?' "

"Tell him!" comes a shout from the back pews.

"Yes, Lord!" from the choir stand. *"If not now, when?"*

Shad is about to respond when Reverend Nightingale eases him away from the pulpit with a forced smile. Althea retakes her pew as the reverend smooths his jacket and says, "I thank Brother Johnson for that thoughtful comment. We sure have a lot to think about these days. Now, the service is almost over, but I think I'd be remiss if I didn't give our white friends a chance to speak today."

This is unexpected, but in the silence that follows, my mother stands and turns to the congregation. Her voice is softer than Althea's, but it too carries in the church.

"Ruby worked for our family for thirty-five years," she says. "We considered her part of our family, and we always will."

And she sits down.

The expression on Shad Johnson's face makes it clear that he views this statement as white paternalism at its worst, but the faces in the pews say something different.

Reverend Nightingale closes the funeral with a

prayer, then directs the choir to sing "Amazing Grace."

The pallbearers carry Ruby's casket down the aisle and out the front door, preceded by the deacons, who act as an informal security force, hustling reporters away from the door with the help of Daniel Kelly and the Argus men. The congregation waits for our family to depart, then follows us out, and soon we are all gathered in the small graveyard beside the church, while five camera crews film steadily from the perimeter of the crowd.

Ruby's coffin lies above the freshly turned earth, on straps that will lower her into the ground when the graveside service is done. As Reverend Nightingale begins his prayer, a horn honks loudly from Kingston Road, blaring again and again but thankfully dropping in pitch as the vehicle goes on down the road. While a cameraman runs off to try to get a shot of the heckler, Reverend Nightingale increases his volume and pushes right through the twenty-third psalm. When he finishes, he turns to the gathered mourners.

"The family will remain seated. The members will please turn away from the body."

Though unfamiliar with this custom, I obey. From the air, this would look strange indeed, two hundred people gathered in a circle around a hole in the ground, facing away from it. I'm not sure of the significance of this ritual, but turning away from death is sometimes the best thing we can do. Reverend Nightingale recites another brief prayer, including the words, "Ashes to ashes, dust to dust," and the congregation walks away from the grave as one.

A half dozen younger black men remain behind, beside a loose stack of shovels, and I remain with them. After Ruby's children drop flowers into the grave, they start toward their cars with their own children. I shake hands with them as they pass, and express my condolences. I sense different reactions in each, but all are courteous.

When Ruby's casket reaches the bottom of the grave, I pick up one of the shovels and spade it into the soft pile of earth. Dad starts to join me, but I touch his chest, reminding him of his heart trouble, and he rejoins my mother and Annie at the edge of the little cemetery.

I feel like it should be raining, but the sun is hot on the back of my suit jacket. As we shovel the diminishing pile of dirt over the gleaming casket, I think of the white funerals I have attended, how everyone walks away at the end of the graveside service, leaving the coffin to be covered by a backhoe or by a couple of unknown gravediggers. This way is better. We should be covered into the earth by people who loved us.

After the grave is full and tamped down, and the camera crews have shot all the footage they want, only a few people remain on the hill. My parents stand with Annie and Reverend Nightingale beside the BMW, which someone has brought from wherever it was parked. Kelly and his associates drift around the edge of the hill, looking for possible threats. Caitlin and the photographer sit on the church steps, fiddling with a camera as Ike Ransom watches.

After Reverend Nightingale toddles off toward his baby blue Cadillac, Ike beckons me to the side of the church, out of earshot of Caitlin and the photographer. I walk over and speak to my parents, then join Ike.

"What you got?" he growls, stepping around me so that I can see no one but him. The blood vessels in his eyes form a red network around the dark irises, and the smell of cheap whisky blows past me with every word. "You got enough to nail Marston on Wednesday?"

"I'm working on it."

"Working? The trial's three days from now!"

"You think I don't know that?"

"So, tell me what you got."

I quickly summarize my case, from Frank Jones to Betty Lou Beckham and everyone in between.

"Will that bitch testify in open court?" Ike asks, loudly enough to be heard across the hill. "Betty Lou?"

"I don't know. She's scared of Presley, and her husband doesn't want her to testify. I've got my father working on her."

"What about tying Presley to Marston?"

"I've got something working," I say grudgingly, thinking of Peter Lutjens, who at this moment may be risking prison to get a copy of Stone's original FBI report.

Ike grabs my wrist, his grip like a claw. "What you talking about?"

I jerk my hand free. "I'll let you know if it works out."

His glare is disquieting. "Is Stone helping you?"

"No."

"You ask him to testify?"

"He won't. Look, I need to go. My family's waiting."

"You ain't telling me shit, man!"

"You need to get some sleep, Ike."

"Sleep? Let me tell you something. I been thinking. I been thinking I messed up coming to you. You may put Presley in jail, but that ain't nothing. He's dying anyway. Marston's laughing at you, man. Old Shad may be right about you leaving this alone, even though the nigger be a little *bright* for my taste."

"I'm going now, Ike."

He grabs my arm. "You keep me posted, right?"

I nod slowly. "Let go of my wrist."

He looks down at the junction of our limbs as though unaware he has hold of me. As the hand relaxes, a question comes to me. "Are you a member of this church, Ike?"

"Me? Baptist? I'm Catholic, man. Holy Family."

"You've known more than you've told me from the start. Whatever you have, now's the time to tell me."

His head moves forward, then back, like a man falling asleep at the wheel of a car. "You think I'm playing the quiet game too?" A faint smile, as though at a private joke. "I told you, man, everybody keeps something back. It's the only way to stay safe."

"I'm gone, Ike. Be careful, okay?"

When I come around the corner of the church, everyone is waiting in the cars but Caitlin and Kelly. Caitlin says something to him, then breaks away and meets me halfway.

492

"What was all that about?" she asks. "It sounded like he was yelling at you."

"He's drunk. He's losing his nerve as the trial gets closer."

"What about you?"

"Solid as a rock."

She smiles. "I couldn't believe Shad put you on the spot like that."

"Are you going to report what he said?"

"He said it, he's responsible for it."

"Good."

"Have you heard anything from Peter Lutjens?"

"Not yet."

"You think he really has the nerve to try for that file?"

"If he doesn't, he's going to spend a lot of winters shoveling snow in North Dakota."

"God, I hope he gets it. If he doesn't —"

"There's still Stone."

"Don't hold your breath. You want to come back to the paper and wade through some files? I'll help."

"Not yet. I'm going to take a drive. My parents and Annie are riding back with the Argus guys."

Caitlin takes my hand. "Want some company?"

"Not this time." I squeeze her hand. "But thanks for offering."

She looks off toward Kingston Road. "You're taking Kelly on this ride, right?"

"No."

She looks back at me, her eyes worried, then suspicious. She drops my hand. "Tell Livy I said hello."

"Livy? I have no intention of seeing Livy. Kelly can come if he wants, but in his own car. I just want to be alone for a while."

Her eyes soften. "I'm sorry. I understand. I'll tell him." She rises on tiptoe and kisses me on the cheek. "Keep your eyes open."

"I will."

CHAPTER 32

Sometimes we think we are moving randomly. But random behavior is rare in humans. We are always spiraling around something, whether we see it or not, a secret center of gravity with the invisible power of a black hole. As a teenager, most of my "aimless" rides led me past Tuscany. Usually I would drive past the entrance, hoping to catch sight of Livy entering or leaving in her car. But a few times, at night, I would idle up the long driveway (it wasn't gated then) and look up at her lighted window, staring at it like a caveman at a fire, then turn around and continue my endless orbit, a ritual that left me perpetually unsatisfied but which I was powerless to stop.

After Ruby's funeral, I circumnavigate the county on its back roads, hurtling along gravel lanes with Kelly in my wake, driving his rented Taurus. Like a planet and its moon, we circle the town and the mystery that lies at the heart of it. Often the act of driving acts as a catalyst that allows the information banging around in my subconscious to order itself in a new way.

Today is different.

Today the emotional fallout from the funeral will not dissipate. Reverend Nightingale's portrayal of my "unselfish" motives shamed me in a way I've never felt before. As he stood there praising me, I felt like a soldier who ran from battle being mistakenly awarded a Silver Star. At the other extreme was my anger at Shad Johnson, who hijacked Ruby's funeral for his own political ends. And yet, if I were black, his suggestion that I retract my charges against Marston would make sense. My public statements may already have frightened liberal whites who might have voted for Shad into casting their ballots for Wiley Warren and the status quo.

After an hour of driving, the secret heart of my troubled orbit finally reveals itself. For the past week I've been acting like a writer. I was a prosecutor for twice as long as I've been a novelist, and I should have been thinking like one. At least my hands know where to take me, if my brain doesn't. I'm on the Church Hill road, less than a mile from Ray Presley's trailer. When I pull off beside the dilapidated structure, Kelly parks behind me, gets out, and jogs up to my window.

"What's up, boss? Who lives here?"

"The man who killed Del Payton. I think he killed Ruby too."

Kelly winces. "And what are we doing here?"

"What I should have done days ago."

He squints and looks up the two-lane road. "I didn't sign on to kill anybody. Or to watch it done."

"I'm just going to talk to him."

He gives me a skeptical look. "That sounds an awful lot like, 'I'm just going to put it in a little way.'"

"I mean it. I'm here to talk. But this asshole is

496

dangerous. I assume you won't stand on ceremony if he tries to kill me."

"He makes the first move, I got no problem punching his ticket."

"Come on, then."

I get out and walk toward the trailer, Kelly on my heels. We're ten feet from the concrete steps when the front door bangs open and Presley yells from inside.

"That's far enough! What the hell you doing here, Cage?"

"I want to talk to you."

"Who's that hippie?"

"A friend."

"Is he carrying?"

"You bet your ass."

A long pause. "I got nothing to say to you. Except you're playing mighty fast and loose with your daddy's future, all that shit you're saying in the papers."

"You haven't heard my proposition, Ray. You might just save your life by listening. However much you've got left, anyway."

"Yeah? Fuck you. You could save your daddy from going to jail by shutting the hell up and going back to Houston."

"My father will never go to jail for the Mobile thing, Ray. But *you* will if you open your mouth."

A bluejay cries raucously in the silence, the sound like a rusty gate closing.

"You got two minutes," calls Presley. "But the hippie stays out there."

I look back at Kelly, who walks casually past me and up to the open door, his hands held out to his sides. I can't hear what he says, but when he's done, he walks back to me and gives me the OK sign.

"What did you say to him?"

"I made sure he understood that hurting you would be a bad idea. He understands. Watch the girl in the corner, though. She looks shaky."

Holding my hands in plain view, I walk up the three steps and into the trailer.

The stink of mildew and rotting food hits me in a wave, as though the trailer hasn't been opened for days. As my eyes adjust to the dimness, I see Ray standing by his wall of police memorabilia. He's dressed just as he was the other day: pajama pants, tank-top wife-beater T-shirt, and the John Deere cap pressed over his naked skull. He's also holding a shotgun, which is aimed in my general direction, and wearing a shoulder holster with the butt of a large handgun protruding from it. Deeper in the gloom, on the couch by the IV caddy, sits the pallid blonde I saw on my first visit. Her legs are folded beneath her, and she's clenching a rifle in her hands. She looks nervous enough to pull the trigger without provocation.

"So talk," says Presley.

"I've got three days to prove Leo Marston conspired to kill Del Payton."

He snorts. "Maybe you can find out who killed the Kennedys before Wednesday too."

"I know you killed Del, Ray."

Not even a tremor in the narrow face.

"I know you lied about the dynamite. You planted those blasting caps. I also know the murder wasn't your idea."

The eyes blink slowly in the shadows, like a snake's. "You don't know shit."

"You'll find out different on Wednesday."

The shotgun barrel moves closer to me. "You can't prove I killed that nigger, because I didn't kill him."

"Come on, Ray. What's the point in lying now?"

He chuckles softly. "You know how people say, 'That boy don't know nothing'? Well, you don't even *suspect* nothing."

"If you'll tell the D.A. how the Payton murder really went down — if you'll give up Marston — I'll get the D.A. to grant you full immunity."

"Immunity for murder."

"Your testimony would force Marston to plead guilty. If Leo cuts a deal, it saves the city the embarrassment of a public trial for a race murder. That's what the powers-that-be want."

"Rat out Judge Marston."

"And John Portman."

A short bark of a laugh. "Boy, you're so goddamn stupid I'm surprised you made it through law school. What you think Portman had to do with anything?"

"I don't know. But I know he's scared enough to try to kill you to keep you quiet."

The nerve in Presley's left cheek twitches. "That weasel. He wasn't shit in sixty-eight."

"He is now. And he'll try again. He's got too much to lose. Cut a deal, you short-circuit the whole trial. It'll all be over before Portman knows what hit him."

Presley waves the shotgun furiously. "You think I give a fuck if that trial happens? What do I care if

499

the niggers run wild in the streets? Let the god-damn bleeding hearts see what happens when there ain't nobody like me around to keep the jungle bunnies in line."

He turns his head and spits through a narrow door, which I hope is the bathroom. Then he says, "You're working with a nigger on this, ain't you?"

"You mean Althea Payton?"

"Shit, no. That nigger deputy. Ransom."

"Don't know him."

"Don't try to lie, boy. You ain't had the practice. That Ransom ain't right in the head. Never has been, since the army. He did dope and turned on his own people. He sucked that bottle like a tit for twenty years. The boy can't hardly function without a football in his hand. You ever ask yourself why he wants Marston so bad?"

I say nothing.

"I knew Ike when he was with the P.D. His old shit will drag him down quick as it will me."

"You're not listening, Ray. If I'm forced to put on my case, you'll be indicted for murder before sundown Wednesday. I guarantee it."

Presley squints at me as though measuring me for a shroud. "You keep pushing for that trial, you won't live to see Wednesday. And that fag body-guard you got out there won't be able to help you none."

"Who's going to kill me? You?"

"Me? I ain't leaving this trailer."

"Do the deal, Ray. It's your only chance."

"Me and the judge go back thirty years. I ain't no punk to roll over on my friends."

"You think Leo Marston is your friend?"

500

He jabs the shotgun at me. "I know *you* ain't."

The blonde's eyes track me over the sights of her rifle, all the way to the door. I shouldn't say another word, but Ruby's blood is calling to me from the ground.

"Where were you Tuesday afternoon, Ray?"

He cuts his eyes at the blonde, then looks back at me, a smug light in his eyes. "I believe I was delivering a message in town."

"A message," I repeat, recalling the flames eating through the roof of our house, the smell of Ruby's cooking flesh. My hands ball into fists at my sides.

"I don't think it got received, though," he says.

I step within two feet of him. "I'm going to settle that score, you piece of shit. You're going to die in the Parchman infirmary. They don't stock your Mexican cocktail there. And there aren't any blondes to take the edge off, as you like to put it. Not girls, anyway."

His thin lips part in a predatory smile, revealing small white teeth. "You'll be dead before I will. It's coming now, and you don't even see it."

When I open the door, the sun hits my eyes like a flashbulb, but it feels good to get out of the stinking trailer.

Kelly is standing by the cars. "Accomplish anything?" he asks.

"No."

When I reach the cars, he pats me on the shoulder. "Let's go back to town, boss."

One of the things that has always separated Natchez from other Mississippi towns is that if you want a drink you can get it, no matter the day or hour.

Kelly suggests the Under the Hill Saloon (a national treasure of a bar), but a big crowd gathers there on Sundays to watch the sun set over the river, and they start celebrating early.

A crowd is not what I want right now.

The bar at Biscuits and Blues is oak and runs a good thirty feet down one wall, with a mirror behind it and glittering bottles and glasses stacked in front. The restaurant is empty but for a couple eating in a booth against the wall opposite the bar. Clanks and clatters filter through the heavy kitchen doors, but otherwise the atmosphere is perfect.

I order Scotch, Kelly the same. Our reflections watch us from the mirror behind the bar like solemn relatives visiting from a cold northern country. When the whisky comes, I swallow a shot big enough to steal my breath, then wipe my mouth on my jacket sleeve. Kelly sips with a deep centeredness, like a man who has known life without luxuries and wants to savor them while he can. He doesn't talk. He doesn't look at me. He stares through the bottom of his glass, as though pondering the grain of the wood beneath. Yet I am certain that every movement in the restaurant — even on the street outside — registers on his mental radar. Kelly is covering me even now.

"Kelly?"

"Mm?"

"Did you have a maid when you grew up?"

His head bobs once. Then I hear soft laughter, an ironic chuckle.

"Did you?"

"My mother was a maid."

He glances at me from the corner of his eye, then looks back into his glass. Embarrassment is not exactly what I feel. It's more like mortification. I'm trying to think of how to apologize when he says, "Nothing wrong with being a maid. It's honest work. Like soldiering."

I want to hug him for that.

"How long did Ruby work for your family?"

"Thirty-five years. She came when I was three."

"That's a long time."

"And she burned to death. Because of what I'm doing, she burned to death."

Kelly rotates his stool and puts his foot on a crosspiece of mine. "Can I ask you something?"

"Sure."

"Why are you doing what you're doing?"

"The truth? I don't know. In the beginning I wanted to nail a guy who hurt my father a long time ago. And me." I take another shot of Scotch, and this one brings sweat to my skin. "That's a bad reason, I guess."

"Not so bad."

"It's not worth Ruby's life."

"No. But that's not the only reason you're doing it. You're trying to set a murder right. And from what I can tell, it needs setting right. I've watched you these last few days. You're a crusader. I knew some in the service, and you're one of them. I've got a feeling you saw some horrible atrocity when you were young. A race murder or something. Something that's weighed you down a long time."

"No. I never saw anything like that. Not much of that happened around here, to tell you the truth."

I swallow the remainder of my Scotch and signal the bartender for a refill. "What I do remember . . . it probably won't sound like anything. I was in the fourth grade when integration started here. I was in the public school then. The first semester they sent twenty black kids into our school. Twenty. Into an all-white school. The black kid in my grade was named Noble Jackson. Nobody was horrible to those kids. Not overtly. But every day at recess, we'd be out there playing ball or whatever, and Noble Jackson would be standing off at the edge of the playground by himself. Just standing there watching us. Excluded. I guess he tried to play the first couple of days, and nobody picked him for anything. Every day he just stood there by himself. Staring, kicking rocks, not understanding. The next semester my parents moved me to St. Stephens."

The Scotch has soured in my stomach. "Now that I'm older, I know that kid's parents made a conscious decision to do something very hard. Something my parents wouldn't do. They risked their child's education, maybe even his life, put him into a situation where it would be almost impossible for him to learn because of the pressure. They did that because somebody had to do it. When I think of that kid, I don't feel very good. Because exclusion is the worst thing for a child. It's a kind of violence. And the effects last a long time. I think maybe Noble Jackson is part of the reason I'm doing this."

"What happened to him? Where'd he end up?"

"I have no idea. I've often wondered. Wherever he is, I'll bet he got the hell out of the South

504

as soon as he could."

We return to our drinks, both lost in our own thoughts. As the bartender returns to refill his glass, Kelly says, "Got a phone book, chief?"

The bartender turns around and takes one from beneath the telephone. The Natchez phone book is only a half-inch thick, including the yellow pages. Kelly flips through it, then runs his finger down a page. "Here's your man. Noble Jackson."

A strange tightness constricts my chest. "That's probably his father."

"Let me borrow that phone," Kelly says to the bartender.

"Local call?"

"You bet." Kelly takes the phone and dials the number, watching me in the mirror. "Hello, I'm calling for Noble. . . . It is? This is Sergeant Kelly, Noble. *Daniel* Kelly . . . You don't recognize my voice? From Bragg? . . . Fort Bragg. I'm trying to track down some members of our old unit. . . . You're kidding me, right? . . . Never been in the service? You're *shining* me, man. Well, Noble always said he was going to get out of Mississippi as soon as he could. . . . Yeah? How old are you? . . . Well, that's the right age. What you do for a living? . . . Ha. Noble sure didn't know nothing about engines. You married? . . . No kidding. Man, I'm sorry I bothered you. My mistake all the way. You have a good Sunday, chief."

Kelly hangs up, and the bartender puts the phone back in front of the mirror.

"Noble Jackson works as a mechanic for Goodyear. He's thirty-eight years old, married with four kids, and he's lived in Natchez his whole life. He

505

sounds happier about it than a lot of people would be."

This knowledge, mundane as it sounds, somehow eases my grief over Ruby. "Kelly, you're a funny guy."

His eyes twinkle. "That has been said."

He looks past me, and I hear the restaurant door open behind me. His expression tells me that whoever came in is a woman, an attractive one. I find myself hoping it's Caitlin.

"Female inbound on your six," he says. "You know her?"

I rotate my stool and watch a tanned brunette walk toward me. It's Jenny, the waitress. She's wearing black jeans and a T-shirt that says LILITH FAIR. Her dark hair is swept back from her neck, and her large brown eyes are shining. She gives me a shy wave as she reaches us.

"Jenny, this is Daniel Kelly."

She smiles and shakes Kelly's hand, then looks back at me. "I'm surprised to see you here. Isn't the funeral today?"

"We just came from there."

"Oh. Um, could I talk to you for a minute?"

"Sure."

She looks furtively at Kelly. "Alone, I mean?"

Kelly starts to slide off his stool, but Jenny takes his arm and holds him there. "I didn't mean for you to leave."

"How about one of those booths?" I suggest.

"Well . . . I was hoping you'd come upstairs. To my apartment. Just for a minute."

My mental alarm is ringing now, soft but steady. Even modest fame can attract some strange people and propositions, and legal complications often follow. Caitlin pegged Jenny as having a fixation on me the first time she saw her. Maybe she's right.

"It's practically deserted in here," I say. "Let's just grab a booth."

Jenny suddenly looks on the verge of tears. "It's nothing weird, I promise. It's . . . personal. It has to do with what you're working on. Your case."

Curiosity muffles the alarm in my head. "The Payton case? What do you know about that?"

She glances at the bartender, who's totaling numbers on a calculator a few feet away. "It has to do with the Marston family."

I'm convinced. "Okay. Upstairs it is. Have another on me, Kelly."

"Glad to, boss. Keep your pants on."

Jenny leads me to the rear of the restaurant, where a spiral staircase winds up to the second floor. We pass some long tables set up for a party, then climb a short flight of stairs to a small landing and a red door. Jenny takes a key from her pocket, opens the door, and waits for me to go through.

Her apartment is as spartan as the cell of a lifer. You could bounce a quarter off the bed, and the linens are surprisingly masculine. A tall set of shelves stands against the wall to my right, and it's filled from top to bottom with books. Literary novels mostly, though the familiar spines of my books are among them, along with Martin Cruz Smith, Donna Tartt, and Peter Hoeg. There's no television, but a boom box sits beside the bed, an Indigo Girls concert flyer tacked to the wall above

507

it. Caitlin's suspicion that Jenny has a crush on me is looking less accurate by the second.

With careful steps Jenny crosses the room to the far corner, where a microwave oven and coffeemaker stand on a table beside a lavatory. She pours water from a Kentwood bottle into the coffee carafe, then from the carafe to the coffeemaker. Her back is to me, but she appears to be concentrating on her movements.

"Is green tea okay?" she asks.

"It's fine."

A spoon jangles loudly in a cup. Jenny's hands are shaking.

"Are you okay?" I ask.

She nods quickly, still facing away from me. "Just nervous."

"How do you know the Marston family? Are you originally from Natchez?"

"No." She turns and faces me, revealing the anxiety in her eyes. I have a sudden intuition that she's about to tell me Leo Marston forced her to commit some sexual act, or perhaps got her pregnant. She's far too young for him, but if an impoverished killer like Ray Presley can rob the cradle, why can't Leo Marston?

"But you know the Marstons," I press her.

"I know Olivia."

Olivia. "Does Livy have something to do with the Payton case?"

"I don't know."

"Jenny, why don't you just tell me what you know? Start at the beginning, and let me decide how important it is."

She shakes her head. "You've got the wrong

idea. I mean — I misled you a little. This isn't about your case."

My alarm is ringing again, full volume now. "Then what's it about?"

"This is so hard for me." She wrings her hands and looks at the ceiling, then focuses her glistening eyes on mine. "I think — I mean, I'm pretty sure — Mr. Cage, I'm pretty sure you're my father."

CHAPTER 33

I'm pretty sure you're my father.

Jenny's words hang in the air like ozone after a lightning strike. My discomfort escalates to panic in a fraction of a second. This is the root of the strange fascination Caitlin picked up that first night. It's something I've heard about my whole life, orphaned or adopted children convincing themselves that the father who abandoned them is some famous man.

"Look, miss —" I grope for her last name, then realize I never knew it.

"Doe," she says. "Isn't that pathetic? That's my last name. Jennifer Doe. It's on my birth certificate."

I'm backing toward the door, which leads to the stairs and the second floor and the spiral staircase and the restaurant and sanity. "I think we'd better go back down."

She holds up her hands in supplication, pleading for my attention. "I don't want anything from you. And I'm not crazy. Please believe me. I'm scared to death right now. I'm so scared. I just want to know who I am!"

Hot, clear water bubbles out of the coffeemaker, for tea that will never be made.

"I can't help you with that question, Jenny."

"If you'd listen to me for two minutes, you'll know you can."

My hand is on the doorknob.

"Livy Marston is my mother!"

This stops me.

"I was born in February of 1979."

My brain is working backward to the point of conception. February, January, December — oh hell, just go back twelve months and add three. If Jenny is telling the truth, she was conceived in May of 1978. The month Livy and I graduated high school.

"My birth certificate proves it," she says in a defensive voice.

I drop my hand from the knob. "Let me see."

She goes to the bookshelf, takes down my second novel, and opens it to the flyleaf. From there she removes a white sheet of paper, which she holds out to me. I don't look at her face as I reach for it. If I did, I know I would be searching for similarities to my own.

The birth certificate looks authentic. Issued by the state of Louisiana, the city of New Orleans. The child's name is listed as *Jennifer Doe*. What nearly stops my heart is what is printed on the line for *Mother*. Right there in black and white is the name *Olivia Linsford Marston*.

The line beside *Father* is blank.

"Jesus God," I murmur.

"It was a privately arranged adoption," Jenny says. "Set up before I was ever born. The adopting parents wanted the name Jennifer on the birth certificate."

511

My heart is skipping beats.

She rushes on, her voice shaky. "I didn't know any of this until a year ago. I spent most of my life in foster homes. I wanted to know where I'd come from. Who my birth parents were. I didn't have anybody —"

"Jenny, slow down." I hold up my hands. "I'm going to listen, okay? Just calm down and tell me your story."

She looks frozen, like a strip of film stopped in mid-motion. The relief in her eyes is heart-breaking. If she wasn't so caught up in her own emotions, she might realize that after seeing that birth certificate, it would take a winch to pull me out of her apartment. Already thoughts that haven't meshed for twenty years are falling into place. Livy was pregnant our senior year. Or the summer following it, rather. And she carried the child to term. That *is* why she disappeared. I guess the assumptions I made about female reproductive biology in 1978 were about as accurate as my judgments of Livy's true nature.

"Pour the tea," I say dazedly. "That'll calm you down."

"I don't want it."

"Okay . . . you said you wanted to find out who your birth parents were. How did you go about doing that?"

"Well, like I said, it was a private adoption, which is big business in Louisiana, if you don't know. It took a lot of work, but I finally learned the name of the lawyer who handled the adoption. Clayton Lacour, from New Orleans. I did some checking on him, and I found out he was well connected. Mafia connected. I was afraid that if I just walked in and asked, Lacour wouldn't tell me anything about my birth parents. All the law required was that he ask my mother whether or not she wanted to be found by me. And I was pretty sure that whoever she was, she wouldn't be too happy about me showing up on her doorstep after twenty years."

Jenny's voice is leveling out; the act of telling her story has distracted her from the fears bubbling inside her.

"I'd been around a little. I knew the street. So instead of marching in and asking my questions, I applied for a job at Lacour's office. P.A., gofer, answering the phone, whatever. I dressed like a college girl — a loose one — and I made sure Lacour saw me when I went in. He practically licked me from head to toe. Took me into his office for a personal interview and hired me on the spot."

Jenny would have made a good D.A.'s investigator.

"It was a race between finding out what I wanted to know and Lacour getting up the nerve to jump me right there in the office. Whenever I was alone, I'd search the place. I brought my lunch every day, told them I was dieting. File room, computers, his personal cabinets, closets, everything. A lot of the stuff had combination locks. It took five weeks to find out where everything was, and another week to copy it all."

"What did you find?"

"Lacour handled a lot of adoptions. All privately arranged, always white babies. And for real money. Thirty-five thousand dollars changed hands when

513

I was adopted. You believe that? I went through all his records and finally found the Jennifer Doe birth certificate. I'd always been called Jenny, every home I went to. So I copied the file and studied it at home. I found out I'd been adopted on the day I was born, by a childless rich couple from New Orleans. Lacour had made notes in the file. He thought the couple was trying save their marriage by adopting a baby. He turned out to be right. They divorced when I was two, and neither one wanted custody. I went into the state system. I was adopted by another family, but . . ." Her eyes glaze to opacity as she trails off. "I don't really want to go into that. It was . . . an abuse situation. I ended up in the foster care system, and that's where I stayed until I was eighteen."

She doesn't have to go into it. As a young assistant district attorney in Houston, I handled cases arising out of foster care that are still burned into my heart.

"All that mattered," she says, "was that the file contained the name of my birth mother. Olivia Marston. It also contained the name of another lawyer, the one who'd brought me to Lacour's attention."

"Leo Marston," I say softly.

"Yes. Judge Marston and Clayton Lacour went way back. They'd done a lot of deals together. Oil leases, real estate, you name it. What had happened was obvious. Marston's daughter got pregnant when she was eighteen, and he arranged to get rid of the baby for her. I was that baby. What I couldn't figure out is why she didn't just have an abortion."

"The Marstons are big Catholics."

Jenny gives me the jaded stare of a runaway who has seen it all. "What's your point?"

She's right, of course. Livy's sister had an abortion when she was in college.

"What did you do after you found that out?"

"I quit Lacour. But before I did, I stole everything pertaining to Marston. Most of it was files. The rest were tapes."

"Tapes?"

"Lacour taped everything. He was connected, like I said. And totally paranoid. He'd worked for the Marcello family when he was younger. Carlos Marcello, the Mob guy? Anyway, he saved these phone tapes just like files. Sometimes when he was drinking, he'd talk about his 'insurance.' That was the tapes. There were twelve tapes coded for Marston's name. I took them all on the day I split."

"What did Lacour say about you quitting?"

"I didn't stick around to talk. I'm sure he thought I left because he couldn't keep his hands off me. I'd used a fake name, so he couldn't trace me. He's bound to have noticed the missing files, but so what? I stole some other files related to Judge Marston just to confuse the trail."

"What did you do next?"

"I went to Atlanta to find my mother."

"And?"

"She refused to see me."

"At all?"

"When I called her at home, she hung up on me. So, one day at her office, I sort of ambushed her. It's a big law firm. She was so afraid I'd make a scene that she took me into her private office.

Acted like I was a client. She told me she didn't want anything to do with me. She had no interest in my life, nothing. She wrote me a check for twenty-five thousand dollars and told me to go away."

Jenny is crying now, but she wipes away the tears with fierce determination. "She broke my heart that day. I'd been through a lot in my life. I thought I was tough. But to have the woman who'd given birth to me offer me money to disappear . . . to pretend that I'd never even been born. I just couldn't stand it."

She closes her eyes, takes a very deep breath, and holds it.

"Why don't you sit down?" I suggest.

She expels the air in a long, steady exhalation. "No, this is better. Really."

"What did you do next?"

"I tore up her check. I probably should have kept it, because I really needed the money. But I couldn't. I tore it up and asked her to tell me my father's name. She turned white, Mr. Cage. That question scared her to death. I begged her to tell me, but she wouldn't. I told her I would never do anything to hurt her, and asked her to please reconsider. Then I left."

"I'm so sorry, Jenny."

"After that I got stoned for about three weeks. From the file, I worked out that my mother must have gotten pregnant at the end of her senior year of high school. Which meant she was probably living here at the time, right? And her father still lived here. I figured if I hung around here awhile, I might be able to find out who she was dating back then. Maybe figure out my birth father that way. So I got on a Trailways and came to Natchez. When I got here, I found out Livy Marston was practically a celebrity. Everybody remembered her. They talked about her like she was like a princess or something."

"She was, in a way. Did you tell anybody that she was your mother?"

"No. I played it very cool. I'd hear people talking about her sometimes, waiting tables or hanging out, and I'd ask about her. It didn't take long to find out that you were her boyfriend during her senior year. I even saw an old yearbook with a picture of you together. And you *were* a celebrity. I mean, you are. A real one. It freaked me out, honestly. I knew so many foster kids who made up those kinds of fantasies. But this fantasy was *real*."

I am past the point of being able to respond.

"People said Olivia disappeared for nearly a year after she graduated, that she'd gone to Europe or something. That's when she was pregnant with me."

The beginnings of nausea are welling in my stomach. The logic of Jenny's story — and its accordance with the known facts — is unassailable. In five minutes a waitress has supplied the missing piece of a puzzle that has haunted me for twenty years. Leo Marston went after my father because I got his daughter pregnant. Because I changed the course of her life and shattered the dreams he'd had for her. His dream that she would go to Ole Miss. That she would attend the same law school he'd gone to. Marry some suitable Mississippi boy and move back to Natchez to practice with her father. *That* was what Maude was talking about the night she threw the drink in my face. What I can't understand is why Livy wouldn't tell me she was pregnant at the time. Why keep it from me? And why hadn't her father called mine in a rage and demanded that I marry her?

But in that question lies the answer to the others. Livy's parents weren't white trash from the wrong side of the tracks, a family for whom a marriage to a doctor's son — even a shotgun marriage — would be a step up the social ladder. They were *Marstons.* Natchez royalty. The worst thing Leo and Maude could possibly imagine would be anything that might slow the momentum of their perfect daughter's perfect life. Marriage would never have entered their minds. They wouldn't want a single soul to discover that Livy was pregnant, and they would want the resulting child to disappear from the face of the earth. I can't believe Leo let Livy carry the child to term.

As for Livy keeping the pregnancy from me, her psychology was simple enough. She had ambitions, and marriage at eighteen wasn't one of them. When she thought of marriage, she envisioned someone who could not possibly be found in the backward and somnolent state of her birth. Yet for the past few days she has acted as though she'd like nothing better than to spend the rest of her life with me.

"She never told you anything about me?" Jenny asks in a small voice.

"Not a word. I never suspected that Livy had a child. No one did."

"Well, she does. She may not want me, but she's my mother."

"Jenny, I know this sounds pathetic, but . . . I don't know what to say."

"I know I sprang this on you at a terrible time. I'm so sorry about your maid."

"It's all right."

She takes a tentative step toward me. "Will you do me a huge favor, Mr. Cage?"

"If I can. What is it?"

"Will you get a blood test?"

My stomach flips over. "A paternity test?"

"It's just one tube of blood. For a DNA test."

"Jenny —"

"I know you feel like you've been hit with a ton of bricks. I don't want to creep you out or anything. But when I saw you sitting down there today, you looked so vulnerable. The way I feel all the time. I just knew you were more compassionate than — *her*. Even if you didn't want anything to do with me, I knew you'd be nicer about it."

My mind has slipped away again. Livy's reaction to Jenny's appearance in Atlanta seems incomprehensible. I can understand her being shocked, or afraid of what her husband might think. But to be so cruel . . .

"It is possible, right?" Jenny asks. "I mean, you were sleeping with Livy Marston in high school?"

"Yes."

She shakes her head as though she still can't believe we're talking face to face. "This is so scary. But it's liberating too. I really thought you were going to just run out of here. Straight to a judge to get a restraining order against me."

"Jenny —"

519

"And you have a little girl," she says excitedly. "I mean, I could have a *sister.*"

Primal fear grips my heart. "Jenny, we've got to take this one step at a time. You —"

"I know. I didn't mean to be pushy. I don't want to crash in on your life or anything. I'd never do that. I've just felt so alone my whole life." In an instant her face seems to collapse in upon itself. "You don't know the things that have happened to me, Mr. Cage."

"I can guess. Look, the first thing I should do is talk to Livy."

"She won't talk about it."

"She'll talk to me."

Jenny is wringing her hands again. "I heard a rumor last night. Someone in the restaurant said you were seeing her again. They saw you out driving. I've been so weirded out by that. I thought you had a thing for the publisher of the newspaper."

"Jenny . . . Livy may have been cruel to you, but she's not a monster."

"I'm telling you, she's not rational about this."

"Does Leo Marston know about you?"

"Oh, yeah." She nods slowly. "I talked to him once. He heard me out, then told me that he had to honor his daughter's wishes regarding me, and he expected me to do the same."

"I'll bet he offered you fifty grand to disappear."

"Ha. He told me it probably would have been better if I hadn't been born, but that I had been, so I had to do the best I could. Life is tough, he said. You believe that? Like his life was ever tough. That son of a bitch. But he scared me. He told me if I tried to make any public scandal, he'd have to take steps to 'resolve the situation.' And he wasn't talking about legal steps. God, I wish I'd taped that conversation. I'd seen mob guys in Lacour's office in New Orleans. They were basically okay guys, most of them. But Leo Marston . . . he's not a nice guy. He made me feel like I'd be doing the world a service if I slit my wrists."

"I'm sorry, Jenny. That's all I can say right now." Though I probably shouldn't, I walk to her and take her hands in mine. They're alarmingly cold. "I don't know what the truth is. I honestly don't. But if I am your father, I'll take care of you. It's too late for me to be a father in the real sense. But you won't want for anything, and you won't be alone."

To see a grown woman break into a child is a terrible thing, and I will not speak of it here.

The *Examiner* building is humming like a beehive, but I see no sign of Caitlin as I pass through the newsroom. I go straight to the conference room, which at the moment contains two female reporters poring over the Marston files, patiently separating wheat from chaff.

"Ladies, could I have the room for a few minutes?"

They look up at me like graduate students disturbed in their library carrels, then blink and look at each other.

"Uh, sure," says the one wearing glasses.

As soon as the door closes, I tear through the stacks of paper on the table, looking for something that seemed trivial only two days ago: the scrawled note listing the income Marston realized from private adoptions. Yesterday it was just another scrap of paper among thousands. Now it's my personal Rosetta stone.

It's not on the table.

I drop to my knees and start working through the carefully stacked piles on the floor, shoving aside page after page, letting them fall where they will. In five minutes the room is awash in paper, and sweat is running down my face. In ten I am trying to suppress the furious panic of an Alzheimer's patient who sets down his car keys and can't find them five seconds later.

And then I am holding the damn thing.

One sheet of yellow legal paper, with a column of years beginning in 1972 and continuing to the present. Some years aren't listed, but beside each that is, an amount of money is noted. The highest figures correspond to the 1980s, and some of these are followed by a one-digit number in parentheses, which probably indicates the number of adoptions handled in that year. Beside the year 1978 is written the figure $35,000.

Jenny Doe is telling the truth.

The weight of this knowledge is staggering, but before I can begin to absorb it, the door to the conference room opens a crack, and Caitlin walks in, her face flushed with excitement.

"I just heard you were here. Listen to this. My father called twenty minutes ago. He found out why Dwight Stone won't testify for us."

I fold the scrap of legal paper and slip it into my pocket. "Why?"

"Stone has a daughter."

"So? I have a daughter too." *Maybe two.*

"Your daughter's not an FBI agent."

The scrap of paper is momentarily forgotten. "Dwight Stone has a daughter in the FBI?"

A triumphant smile lights Caitlin's face. "Ten years in. John Portman can ruin her career with a single reassignment, and he can make it the same way."

It had to be something like this. In Colorado I had gotten such an impression of integrity from Dwight Stone that I couldn't fathom what would keep him from helping me expose the truth of what happened here in 1968. But children make us all vulnerable. They're hostages to fortune, as the poet said.

"Hostages to fortune?" says Caitlin.

I must have spoken aloud. "Nothing. It doesn't matter."

"Penn, what's the matter? You looked zoned out."

"I'm fine."

"Bullshit. You look terrible." She glances around the room, which is strewn with loose pages like leaves on a forest floor. "What happened in here? What are you looking for?"

"I already found it."

"What?"

"Something personal. Nothing to do with our case."

Caitlin goes to the table and picks up a few pages, straightens them into a stack, and sets them back down. Then she turns those remarkable green eyes on me and speaks in a voice raw with hurt. "It's Livy Marston, isn't it? Nothing else would get you so worked up."

"It has to do with Livy, yes."

"You can't tell me what it is?"

"Not yet. Not until I know something for sure. Right now I need a telephone."

She waves her hand with disgust. "Take any one you want."

"It has to be private."

"You can use my office." There is something like pity in her eyes.

She escorts me through the newsroom, shrugging at Kelly on the way. As soon as she shuts the door behind me, I dial Tuscany. Thankfully, Livy answers.

"This is Penn."

"What do you want?"

"We need to talk."

"You haven't thought so for the past three days."

"I do now. It's important."

"Important." There's a long pause, but I don't jump to fill it. "All right," she says finally. "Where?"

I close my eyes. "I haven't eaten. I was thinking of getting a bite at Biscuits and Blues. That sound okay to you?"

Silence.

"Livy?"

"I'm not really hungry."

"You could watch me eat," I say, pushing it.

"Why don't we take a ride instead? It's nice outside."

Sure, and why don't we ask our daughter to come along? "Is your father home?"

"No. He's at his office with Blake Sims, preparing for the trial."

524

"I'll pick you up in five minutes."

"Five minutes?"

"It's important."

"All right. I may look ghastly, but I'll be waiting on the gallery."

Livy Marston has never looked ghastly in her life. "Just have the gate open."

I hang up and start through the newsroom, heading for the front of the building. Caitlin and Kelly are talking quietly in a corner. When she sees me, she breaks away from him and physically bars the door.

"Penn, you've got to tell me what's going on."

"It's nothing to do with you. It's personal."

She looks around the newsroom and realizes that her employees are staring at her. Taking my wrist, she speaks in a quieter voice. "I consider your personal life personal to me."

I have no response to this. Caitlin matters to me, but right now there is a motor spinning in my chest, driving me irresistibly toward Tuscany, the only place where the truth of my life can be found. "It could be, someday. But it's not now. Let me by, Caitlin."

She hesitates, then drops my wrist and moves aside.

Kelly starts to fall into step with me.

"Stay here," I tell him. "I don't need you for this."

He stops, but before the main door closes behind me, I hear Caitlin say, "Go with him."

Tuscany is a magnificent mansion, but it would look incomplete without the indelible image of

Livy standing on the gallery. She's wearing a royal blue sun dress, belted at the waist and falling just below her knees. The air is cool beneath the trees, and the freshly fallen leaves have been gathered into random piles by the wind. The scene looks staged, like a rich color shot from an ad in *Architectural Digest. Who is that beauty waiting for?* you wonder as you flip past it. *If only she was waiting for me.*

This beauty is waiting for me. Only she has no idea what a dreadful gift I bring. The last thing she wants to receive. A demand for the truth, and the means to compel her to speak it.

I park beside the Negro lawn jockeys and remain in the car. Livy comes down the steps, her tread light, her movements graceful. Her eyes are curious as they take me in. She walks around to the passenger door, clearly wondering why I haven't scurried around to open it for her. Unable to wait for the pretense of a drive to speak to her, I get out and address her over the gleaming black roof of the car.

"Do you know a girl named Jenny Doe?"

She freezes with her hand on the passenger door. Behind those eyes I know so well, have dreamed of for years, another pair of eyes is looking out. Frightened, hunted eyes.

"Who have you been talking to?" she asks, her voice oddly devoid of emotion.

"Does it matter? I want to know if you were pregnant in 1978."

"That's none of your business."

"Not my business. Is that girl our daughter, Livy?"

She takes a deep breath, recovering her composure with remarkable resilience. "No," she says simply.

"No, she's not my daughter? Or no, she's not yours either?"

She purses her lips, as though calculating the impact of various replies. "Stay out of this, Penn. It's none of your affair."

"Were you sleeping with someone besides me in the spring of seventy-eight?"

Her eyes flash. "Weren't you?"

My heart feels suddenly cold. "No. But if you were, how do you know for certain who the father was?"

"Maybe I don't care who it was."

The steel in her voice cannot mask the fear and anguish in her face. "Livy —"

"Listen to me, Penn. *You are not that girl's father.* I know that with absolute certainty. And if you thought hard about it, you would too."

"What the hell does that mean? I worked out the months from her birth certificate. I could easily be her father. You got pregnant right before you disappeared."

She studies me with cold objectivity, as though taking some life-altering decision. "If you ever mention what I'm about to say, I'll deny I said it. Jenny Doe is my daughter. But she is not yours. She's twenty years old now, and I have no legal responsibility to care for her. As far as I'm concerned, she doesn't exist. Since she's not your child, you have no say whatever in the matter, and you should never mention it to me again."

"Livy, where is this coming from? How can you

be so cruel to this girl?"

"You're so naive. You don't know anything. You —"

She stops as the low purr of an engine murmurs through the trees. I assume it's Kelly until Leo Marston's silver Lincoln Town Car rounds the bend by the azalea bushes.

"Get out of here," Livy says in a taut voice. "Go. And don't come back. I was stupid to think we could ever make it work."

I don't move. I can't.

Leo's face is masked by the glare of the sun on his windshield as he parks behind the BMW. When he gets out, his face is not mottled red with fury, as I expect, but calm. A smug smile curls his lips as he walks toward me. When he stops three feet away, I see that his upper cheeks are flushed, and when he speaks I smell the sweet odor of bourbon.

"Livy?" he drawls, glancing at her over the roof of the BMW. "Does this person have your permission to be on our property?"

"He was just leaving."

"That doesn't answer my question. I asked if he's a guest, or if he's a *trespasser*, like the other night."

Livy looks at me with pleading eyes, the familiar eyes I once knew. "He's my guest, but he's leaving. Let's go inside."

"In a minute, in a minute." Leo is grinning like a six-year-old boy with a secret. "I'm glad I ran into you, Cage. I've got some news you'll be interested in."

"Is that right?"

"You're damn right that's right. A friend of

yours was just arrested in the Hoover Building in Washington, D.C."

Fear and guilt for Peter Lutjens clench my stomach.

"Seems this fellow was attempting to steal a file," Leo drones on. "A file sealed on national security grounds. He had a funny name. Foreign name. Dutch maybe. There's some question of treason, I believe. John Portman is personally investigating the situation."

He turns to Livy. "This boy's got no case, Livy. None at all." He turns back to me, laughter rumbling low and deep in his chest. "When Wednesday gets here, you're gonna wish you never opened your mouth about me. You're gonna *rue the goddamn day* you decided to fuck with Leo Marston."

Confused images fire through the synapses of my brain. My father on the floor of his bedroom, felled by a heart attack. My mother in tears, unable to cope with the stress of the malpractice trial. Jenny Doe describing her meeting with the man who stands before me now, the man who made her feel she'd be doing the world a favor by committing suicide. Peter Lutjens being handcuffed while his wife and children wait for him at home in a clutter of U-Haul boxes.

Victory is written on Leo's face like blood after a hunt, and the wolfish blue eyes are laughing. I have not struck another human being in anger since I was fifteen years old, but my knee rises into his groin with preternatural speed and force. The air explodes from his lungs. As he doubles over, my elbow crashes into the side of his head, just the way a Houston police detective once taught me.

"Stop it!" Livy screams. *"Penn, stop!"*

She is running around the car to get between us. Some part of my brain knows I should stop, but I'm still moving forward, pursuing Leo as he staggers back. He shakes his head and raises his big left hand to his jaw. I draw back my fist, then freeze as a silver derringer appears before my nose as though by magic. He must have had it palmed all along, a little nickel-plated gambler's special.

"Go ahead, you little pissant," he snarls. "Go ahead."

"Daddy?" Livy stands two feet behind her father, her voice riding a current of hysteria.

"Go inside, baby. You don't want to see this."

"Daddy, I love him."

This simple declaration hits Leo like an arrow. He actually flinches, like a bear struck between the ribs, and an expression of pure hatred comes over his face. "Go inside, Livy! This boy's forgotten his place. He assaulted me on my property."

But Livy doesn't go. The three of us remain locked in our positions, a pathetic standoff on the edge of tragedy that lasts until Daniel Kelly's rented Taurus rolls slowly up the drive.

Kelly parks alongside the cars, five feet from us, and rolls down his window like a tourist asking for directions. But what comes through his window is not a map but a Browning Hi-Power pistol, which he points at Leo's head.

"Please go inside the house, sir," he says.

"Who the hell are you?" Leo asks, keeping the derringer in my face.

Kelly's suntanned face remains calm, as though he were listening to a soothing piece of music. "I'm the man who's going to end your life unless you take that gun in the house."

"Bullshit," Leo grunts. "Get the fuck off my property."

"I'm here to do a job, sir," Kelly says in the same lazy voice. "Don't make yourself part of it."

At last Leo really looks at Kelly, and the muscles in his jaw tighten. He has vastly multiplied his family fortune by accurately judging men's characters. And whatever he sees in Daniel Kelly's eyes convinces him that today is the wrong day to tempt fate. He lowers the derringer.

"You just made yourself part of *my* job, sonny." He raises two fingers in a little toodle-loo gesture, then turns and walks up the broad steps of his mansion.

"Livy," he says without turning around. "Your mother needs you."

"I'm coming." She steps toward me and tries to take my hand, but I pull it away. "Make a public apology, Penn," she pleads. "Please. Do that, and I'll convince Daddy to drop the suit."

"It's too late for that."

She looks at me sadly. "You can't play my father's game and win. Not in this town. Not in this *state*. Nobody can. You could lose everything you have."

"You've got a short memory, Livy. Your father lost his case against mine twenty years ago, and he's going to lose this one."

"That was different. It was a weak case to start with."

"Then why did he take it?"

Unreadable emotion flares in her eyes. "I don't

know. But I do know you nearly fainted when he told you that man had been arrested. He was your last hope, wasn't he? He was your case. If you walk into that courtroom Wednesday, you'll be like a lamb going to slaughter."

I step back from her, trying not to think of Peter Lutjens. "That's my problem. Your problem is a lot bigger than that. Your whole life is built around some secret tragedy whose real victim is a girl crying alone in a room three miles from here. What are you going to do about that?"

Her eyes go cold again. "Nothing. And you'd better not either." She turns and walks up three steps, then looks back to me. "Don't say I didn't warn you about the trial."

This time she goes all the way up and through the massive door.

I get into the BMW and start to leave, but Kelly pulls his Taurus in front of it, blocking my way. Then he gets out and comes around to my window.

"Boss? To an objective observer, it looks like you're trying awful hard to get killed."

"I've learned some upsetting things in the past half hour. I haven't even begun to understand them yet. All I know is that I want to nail that son of a bitch more than anything I've ever wanted in my life, other than to save my wife from dying. And that was beyond my power."

"Maybe this is too," Kelly says gently. "I wouldn't mind bringing that bastard down a peg myself. But things seem pretty seriously stacked against you. Sometimes you've got to pull back. Regroup. Fight another day."

"No," I say doggedly, perhaps stupidly. "If I let the momentum die, Marston and Portman will never pay for whatever they did. Any evidence that exists will disappear." Althea Payton's words sound in my head like a ghostly refrain. "If not now, when. You know?"

A skeptical grunt. "Yeah, maybe."

"I've got one shot left, Kelly."

"What?"

"Dwight Stone. He knows the truth. He could bring down the whole damn temple."

"Caitlin says he won't testify."

"He wants to help me. I know he does. But he's got a daughter in the FBI. That gives Portman total control of her life, and by extension, Stone's."

"So, what can you do?"

"I'm going back to Colorado."

The old Kelly smile returns to his lips. "Well . . . I was ready for a change of scenery anyway."

"Do we still have FBI surveillance covering us?"

"I've seen them three times today. They're good."

"That's okay. You're going to keep them nice and busy for me."

"Yeah, and . . . ? How do we lose them?"

"We don't. This time I'm going alone."

CHAPTER 34

The American Eagle ATR plows into a trough of turbulence, drops like a stone, then catches an updraft from the Rocky Mountains below and settles out again. I and my fellow passengers are thirty miles from Crested Butte, Colorado, and I can't wait for the wheels to hit the runway. When I flew out of Baton Rouge, it was ninety degrees. When I changed planes in Dallas, it was sixty-eight. In Colorado there's two feet of snow on the ground, my plane is three hours behind schedule because of the unexpected storm, and the only thing I know about ATR aircraft is that they fly like hogs with ice on the wings. But that isn't the only reason for my anxiety. In less than an hour I will be face to face with former special agent Dwight Stone, the only man on earth who can give me what I need.

The desire for revenge I felt when I attacked Leo Marston at Tuscany yesterday seems trivial now. I am a different man than I was yesterday. The past I thought I knew is dead. Because last night I faced a truth so terrible I can hardly accept it even now.

After Kelly and I left Tuscany, we drove straight to the motel. I felt an overwhelming desire to hug Annie, the daughter I knew beyond any shadow of doubt to be mine. After spending the evening watching television with her, I put her to bed and sent Kelly out for a bottle of Absolut. For the first time in years I drank with the sole purpose of getting drunk. It didn't take long, and drunkenness brought with it the blessed inability to ponder clearly the events of twenty years before. Who was sleeping with whom. And when. And why, if I "really thought about it," as Livy had told me to do, I would know that I could not possibly be Jenny Doe's father. I passed out in a chair, and if my mother hadn't knocked on my door to check on me, I might not have fathomed the truth until much later. As it was, I awakened in the midst of a nightmare, tortured by images I could not have conceived of the day before.

Livy told me the truth.

I am not Jenny's father.

I know this because the last time Livy and I ever made love — prior to this week — was one week after graduation, and she was just starting her period. She had been a couple of weeks late at the time, and we were both terrified she was pregnant. When her cycle resumed, we celebrated by going to a hotel — which we almost never did — and making love. At that point Livy had two weeks left in Natchez before leaving for the summer program at Radcliffe. I was miserable because earlier in the spring I had promised my father I would go to Shiloh with him after graduation. Of my two remaining weeks with Livy, I was going to give up one to tromp over a Civil War battlefield. I consoled myself with the knowledge that we would both be at Ole Miss in the fall, but when I got back from Shiloh, Livy had already left for Cambridge, and I did not see her again for more than a year.

During that time, I naturally considered the possibility that Livy could be pregnant. But I was fairly certain that, while it was possible for a woman to conceive while having her period, the odds against it were high. I later learned that a woman can have a period *while* she's pregnant, but by then I'd written off the possibility altogether. Given that Livy's sister had had an abortion, I was certain that Livy would have done the same in the event of pregnancy, and certainly not run off for a year like some "girl in trouble" from *Peyton Place*. But clearly I had been wrong to assume that. The question was, why?

At Tuscany, Livy had told me in no uncertain terms that I was not Jenny's father. If I wasn't, who was? Livy delivered Jenny nine months after leaving Natchez. The father had to be someone she'd slept with immediately after that last period. Given Livy's shadowy sexual history, that could easily be someone I did not know. But when I jerked awake last night in a clammy sweat of panic, I knew that Jenny's father was not unknown to me. This knowledge came to me even before I consciously apprehended it, announcing itself with a wave of horror that sent me running to the bathroom.

Jenny's father is Leo Marston.

As sickening as this idea was, I could not push it from my mind. Only this conclusion made sense of every incomprehensible action and statement that had followed, right up to the present. Livy's inexplicable promiscuity during high school. Her mother's chronic alcoholism. Not telling me about her pregnancy, then disappearing for a year, cutting herself off from family and friends. Starting life in Virginia as though her life in Mississippi had never existed. Settling in Atlanta. And most telling, her unwillingness to speak to Jenny even twenty years after her birth. What had seemed so cruel hours before suddenly made sense. Jenny was a living reminder of something so terrible that Livy simply could not face it. What had Livy said on the bridge, when I asked if she could ever live in Natchez again?

Not while my parents are alive . . .

The idea that Leo had sexually abused his daughter from childhood on left me feeling hollowed out, like a wasting disease. Everyone in Natchez thought Livy Marston had enjoyed the most privileged and perfect childhood anyone could, free from want, full of love and adoration. But how many times had she told me that Tuscany was a prison, not a palace? How many times did I discount her laments as the whining of a spoiled rich girl? The night we first began to get close, when she confessed the date rape by an older boy at school . . . had that been a fictionalized version of rapes by her father? Were they still going on even then? It was difficult to imagine Livy submitting to Leo's advances at that age. He outweighed her by more than a hundred pounds, but by eighteen Livy was a strong, athletic girl. Yet I know very little about abuse, and so much human strength springs from the mind, not the body. Was Livy's entire childhood a lie? Were her stellar performances in every facet of high school and college life part of

537

some elaborate coping mechanism designed to conceal the awful reality she lived behind the walls of Tuscany?

Only two things argued against this interpretation of the facts. The first was Leo's persecution of my father. If I had gotten Livy pregnant, Leo's attack would be easy to understand: a quest for vicarious revenge. But if Leo had impregnated Livy, the malpractice case made no sense. The second was Livy's decision to carry the child to term. If her pregnancy had resulted from a rape by her father, her decision to keep the baby seemed unfathomable. Even the most dogmatic Catholic might consider abortion in those circumstances, and Livy wasn't dogmatic.

I reflected upon Marston's persecution of my father as I splashed water in my face from the motel lavatory and ate a handful of animal crackers Annie had left on the television. As soon as the sugar hit my bloodstream, I saw straight through to the truth of the malpractice lawsuit.

It was blindingly simple.

Maude Marston must have learned of her daughter's pregnancy. And that pregnancy somehow had to be explained. What more likely candidate for fatherhood could there have been than Penn Cage, Livy's most recent boyfriend? Whether Leo actually told Maude this lie or let her think of it herself did not matter. When the chance to persecute my father came, he jumped at it — his sole goal being to reinforce the initial lie about Livy's pregnancy. The question of whether Maude might — at some level — have known of the incestuous relationship was something I didn't even want to think about. But by trying to destroy my father as an act of "vengeance," Leo more deeply concealed his mortal sin from his wife, and perhaps even from himself. I suppose it's even possible that after twenty years of denial, he has convinced himself that I *am* Jenny's father, the man who "ruined" Livy's life.

Truth always clarifies, but with clarification comes a whirlwind of emotions no one can predict. My initial reaction was horror mixed with outrage. Suddenly even the murder of Del Payton seemed trivial. Payton burned to death in a few agonizing minutes. If I was right about Jenny Doe's parentage, Livy had died a thousand times before she reached adulthood. She has been burning alive for more than thirty years.

I sat alone in the dark well of the night, pondering what to do with this terrible knowledge. After an hour I made some long-distance calls, irritating more than a few people. When dawn broke, I woke Kelly and spoke to him, and a few hours later we executed a ruse which left him surrounded by our FBI watchers at the Natchez Mall Cinema while Sam Jacobs drove me to the Baton Rouge airport in his Hummer. In Baton Rouge, I paid cash for a ticket to Dallas, where I changed planes for Albuquerque, and there boarded the ATR bound for the tiny airport at Crested Butte.

The pilot has begun his descent, plowing up the long mountain valley from the southeast. The snowy majesty of the Rockies leaves me unaffected. At my core, in the moist and primitive darkness, a malevolent seed is germinating. A desire not to publicly humiliate Leo Marston, not even to destroy his career as a lawyer and judge by sending him to Parchman prison, but to end his very life. To remove him from the world. Not in Del Payton's name, but in Livy's. And in mine. For the life he stole from us.

I will soon be listening to former special agent Dwight Stone explain why he cannot tell a jury what he knows about Leo Marston and John Portman. He will soberly tell me about his daughter, the FBI agent. And he will expect me, as a father, to understand his position.

But I will not understand.

I have a surprise for Dwight Stone.

The snow has stopped when we touch down at Crested Butte, but thankfully the car rental company has fitted the tires of my Ford Explorer with chains. I am unaccustomed to icy roads, but it doesn't take me long to get the hang of it. The problem is that only the main roads have been plowed. The forest service road leading up into the mountains (and Stone's cabin) is plowed only to the summer houses by Nicholson Lake. The jeep track that breaks off from that is impassable, at least for someone of my limited mountain skills, so I have no choice but to abandon the Explorer near a large gravel pit and trek up between the mountains on foot.

It takes less than twenty yards to understand the necessity for snowshoes, a type of footwear I have never worn in my life. In my thinly padded windbreaker and tennis shoes, I am practically begging for frostbite, but Stone's cabin can't be more than three miles away. It's after three o'clock, but I should have plenty of light to make it. I rang Stone's phone from the airport to make sure he was there, and hung up as soon as he answered. I don't want him or anyone tapping his phone to know I'm coming until I arrive.

The jeep track is invisible in the snow, but by roughly following the course of the Slate River upstream, I must eventually strike on Stone's cabin, which is situated practically on top of it. Today the Slate, which was only ten or fifteen feet wide on my last trip, is a roaring flood of blue-black water sluicing down the valley like a logging flume. After a seeming eternity of slipping, falling, digging through drifts, and cracking my elbows and butt, I make my way past the entrance of an old mine, along the base of Anthracite Mesa, and up to the edge of a slot canyon, where the Slate is compressed into a raging chute that rockets over an eight-foot vertical drop. I pick my way along the edge of the canyon with care, knowing that a tumble into that water could easily kill me.

At last Stone's cabin comes into sight, nestled among the tall spruce and fir trees between the jeep track and the river. There's a welcome column of smoke rising from its chimney. I have not been this cold for many years. I stop to catch my breath and marshal my strength, then push on for the last two hundred yards like a climber going for the summit of Everest.

Stone answers his door with a pistol on his hip. The first words out of his mouth are, "You damn fool." Then he jerks me inside, slams the door, and darts to the front window, where he stands peering through the curtains.

A fearsome array of weapons lies on the coffee table before the sofa — a hunting rifle, two shotguns, several automatic pistols — and a huge fire crackles in the fieldstone fireplace. The curtains over the back windows are shut, blocking the view toward the Slate and the trees beyond.

Stone must be close to seventy, but his vitality is intimidating. He's one of those leathery guys who'll still be jogging six miles a day when he's eighty. The last time we met, he seemed charged with repressed anger. Now the whole interior of the cabin crackles with his fury, as though my first visit opened some channel to the past that made it impossible for him to hold in his rage any longer.

"What's out there?" I ask.

He keeps staring through the window, his eyes narrowed like those of a marksman. "You didn't see them when you came in?"

"All I saw was mountains and snow. No cars. No skiers. Nothing."

"They've been out there all day. Four of them."

"Who are they?"

"FBI, I hope."

"And if not?"

He glances at me. "Then they only let you come in here for one reason."

"Which is?"

"To make it easier to kill both of us."

"Shit. Why are we standing here, then?"

"We'd be sitting ducks if we tried to make it out."

"Call the police."

Stone's taciturn face hardly moves when he answers. "There's only the sheriff and a couple of deputies. If those men are here to kill us, they'll kill anyone who tries to interfere as well. And I happen to like the sheriff."

"But they could be legitimate FBI agents. Right?"

"They could. But they don't *feel* legitimate."

"What about the state police?"

"Take 'em too long to get here in the snow. And my phone's tapped. I have a cell phone, but whoever's out there will have those frequencies covered. If they mean to kill us, they'll move in the second I call for help."

"Isn't it early for snow? It's ninety degrees in Mississippi."

"Anything can happen in October. It rained four days up-country before it turned to snow. That's why the river's up like it is."

I edge up to the other front window and peer out. I see nothing but spruce, firs, and snow. "Why don't they move in now?"

"They're waiting for dark."

"So, we just sit here?"

Stone takes one more look out the window, then walks over to the table holding his weapons. "Look, you started all this. Now you've got to live with it. So just sit tight. I've been in spots like this before. It's a game of nerves."

I came to Colorado alone knowing that I would be walking right into the men watching Stone. I did this believing that Stone — a good man with a guilty conscience — would be unwilling to add my death to that conscience by sending me back to Mississippi alone. I was sure that my obvious vulnerability would convince him that the only decent thing to do would be to accompany me back to Natchez to testify. I didn't reckon with the possibility that the men watching him would attempt to kill him outright — and me with him.

He lifts a cordless phone from the coffee table, punches a button on it, listens, then hangs up and slips the phone into his pocket. "You killed Arthur Lee Hanratty's brother, right?"

I nod.

"That makes me feel a little better." He removes a pistol from the small of his back (I hadn't even noticed it), then takes the cordless phone from his pocket and sits on the sofa with both gun and phone in his lap. "Well, what'd you come back for?"

"The truth. You know it, I need it. It's that simple."

An ironic smile flickers over Stone's features. "I suppose since you and I may die together soon, I could make you aware of a few facts. But I'm not going to testify for you. Voluntarily or any other way. And first you'd better show me you're not wearing a wire."

It's a repeat of my visit to Ray Presley's trailer. I strip off my khakis and shirt, and Stone motions for me to remove my shorts and socks as well.

"Come over here," he says.

"I'm not submitting to a rectal exam," I tell him, walking toward the couch.

He chuckles, then stands and runs his fingers through my hair, following the line of my skull. He sticks a finger in each of my ears. "Sorry, but the transmitters are damnably small these days."

"Now that we've got that over with," I say,

pulling on my pants, "let's hear what really happened in Natchez in 1968."

"How far have you gotten on your own?"

"I've got Presley nailed down for the actual murder. My witnesses are Frank Jones, his ex-wife, and Betty Lou Beckham. An ATF bomb expert will confirm C-4 as the explosive, proving Presley planted evidence at the scene. And one of the Fort Polk thieves will put stolen military C-4 in Presley's hands."

Stone smiles. "So, you got my fax."

"Thanks."

"How do you link Presley to Marston?"

"You."

He raises his eyebrows. "I hope you've got something else."

"Well . . . I did have an FBI agent trying to copy your original report for me. But he was arrested yesterday."

Stone gives a somber nod. "I heard."

Of course. His daughter told him.

"So," he says. "Marston orders Presley to do the hit. That's how you see it?"

"Well . . . there's Portman, of course. But I don't know what his role was. Are there more people involved?"

"Conspiracies are always complicated. But in this case, Presley and Marston make a nice package, so why complicate it? Of course, you don't even have Marston yet."

"But you did."

"Yes."

"Tell me how."

He picks up the cordless phone again, presses a

button, listens, then hangs up and begins speaking to me in a low, clear voice, his right hand thumbing the gun in his lap.

"First of all, Portman wasn't my partner. Hoover foisted him on me, fresh out of Yale Law and the Academy. His father was a Wall Street lawyer with Washington connections. He thought the Bureau would be a good political incubator for his son. Like military service without the risk. So pal Edgar throws the kid into a high-profile assignment, safely under the wing of veteran agent Dwight Stone."

Stone stops speaking for a few moments and simply listens. I hear only the crackle of the fire and, perhaps, the rush of the swollen Slate behind the cabin.

"Portman didn't give a shit about the Payton case," he says finally. "All he cared about was kissing ass and getting promoted to the Puzzle Palace."

"But you cared. Althea Payton told me you did."

He nods thoughtfully. "Cage, in all the mountains of shit, sometimes one case gets to you. You know? For me, it was that one. Payton was a good guy who basically minded his own business and tried to better his lot in life. And he got killed for it. When I found out he'd served in Korea, it got personal. I'd known some black noncoms over there, and they were okay. Payton survived Chosin Reservoir only to get blown to shit by some gutless rednecks in his home town." Stone slaps the cordless phone against his thigh with a percussive pop. "Man, I wanted to nail those sons of bitches.

"My first steps were the same ones you've been

taking. Frank Jones, his wife, then Betty Lou Jackson. Beckham now, I guess. Betty Lou knew something, but she wouldn't talk. Then Portman and me got shot at out on Highway 61. Hoover got irritated after that incident. Scumbags shooting at the FBI and getting away with it didn't fit his PR plan. He authorized a lot more money and muscle. I cracked Betty Lou, and that put Presley at the scene. Portman and I braced Presley at home, and he told us to stick it. That bastard didn't rattle easy, I'll give him that. Even when we got the Fork Polk thieves to admit selling him the C-4, Presley told us to go to hell.

"We put on the full-court press. On my request, Hoover authorized illegal wiretaps on Presley's home, plus all the nearby pay phones. We bribed local Klansmen, but they couldn't find out a thing about Payton's death. Whoever killed Payton had acted without Klan authority. We put intermittent surveillance on Presley, tight enough to annoy him but loose enough for him to shake. After a week he called Leo Marston from a pay phone near his house."

"What did he say?"

"Nothing incriminating. Said he wanted to talk, somewhere private. Marston was the D.A. then, of course. Nothing illegal about wanting to talk to the district attorney. I thought Presley might be trying to cut a deal with the state authorities to avoid any sort of federal prosecution. The Klan had a lot of influence in Parchman in those days, and they could have assured him an easy stretch. They also had influence over pardons."

"But making a deal wasn't Presley's style."

"No," Stone agrees. "Anyway, the second Hoover heard Leo Marston's name in connection with the case, the whole case changed. The director assumed personal control."

"Why?"

"Hoover was a creature of politics. He demanded total control over every case that involved anyone who could do him good or harm down the road."

"What happened next?"

"We did a black bag job on Marston's mansion. Bugged it top to bottom. Phones, the house, the garden, gazebo, the works. It was a beautiful job."

"You and Portman?"

"Hell, no. Henry Bookbinder and me. The technology was primitive, but Henry was an artist with it, God rest his soul."

"What did you pick up?"

Stone smiles with satisfaction. "The mother lode. One day Presley drove up to the mansion and knocked on the door. Then he and the judge went out to the gazebo and had a long chat. They said enough in thirty minutes to put Marston in the gas chamber."

I hear a faint ringing in my ears. "Jesus. What did they say?"

Stone shakes his head. "You haven't got anywhere on a motive for Marston?"

"That's been my problem all along. I know Leo secretly owned some property that an out-of-town company was thinking of buying. There was some kind of race angle to that. Labor problems. Beyond that, I don't have anything."

"You were right on target, and you didn't know

it. It was a carpet company from Georgia. Zebulon Hickson, the owner, was about a mile to the right of Attila the Hun. He thought slavery was the finest and most misunderstood institution this country ever had. When he opened new factories, he went into communities where what he called 'the nigger problem' didn't exist. Of course, by 1968 towns like that were hard to find. Especially along the Mississippi River, which was where he wanted to be.

"Leo Marston stood to make a lot of money off that land. But the labor situation wasn't as stable as Hickson wanted it. Blacks were using the unions to push into white jobs. Hickson had the idea that if an example was made, it would calm the blacks down. Apparently he'd done this somewhere in Georgia, and it had worked."

Marston's plan seems so obvious now. All it takes is a few facts.

"I honestly doubt Marston ever thought it would work," muses Stone. "He was too smart for that. But he didn't *care* whether it worked. He just wanted to sell Hickson his land."

"So, he went to Ray Presley," I fill in. "He said, 'We need to make an example of somebody.'"

"You got it. Marston didn't care who died. It was just business."

"Why didn't he use the local Klan? Put a word into the right ear and let the Klan take care of Payton? Why use a cop?"

"Marston was the D.A. He knew the Klan was riddled with federal informants. He wanted zero risk of the murder being traced back to him. He also despised the White Citizens' Council. He

549

called them illiterate Baptist sons of bitches several times on the phone."

"But he trusted Presley."

"Yes. And he was right to. It's ironic as hell, really."

"Why?"

"You'll see in a minute. So, Presley chose Del Payton as the victim. Why, I don't know. He was in charge of voter-registration drives for the local NAACP, but he was a quiet guy. Had a nice house and a pretty wife. Saved his money. He had a nicer house than Presley did, really. That by itself could have been the reason. Anyway, Zeb Hickson was all set to announce his plans for a Natchez carpet factory —"

"But you had Marston by the short hairs."

"Yep."

"But you didn't make any arrests."

Stone sighs deeply. "Right."

"Why not?"

"As soon as Hoover heard the tape of Marston and Presley, he ordered me to forward every case note, transcript, surveillance report, witness interview, photograph, and audiotape to Washington. After he reviewed all that, he scheduled a visit to the Jackson field office. Good PR for the troops, he said. But the real reason for that trip was to meet Leo Marston."

The ringing in my head is an alarm bell now. "About what?"

"Politics. Clyde Tolson, Hoover's assistant, made the call. I still had the wiretap running, and I heard it. Marston thought he was going up to Jackson for a pat on the back for his performance as D.A. When he got there, Edgar read him the riot act, then laid the classic Hoover pitch on him."

"Which was?"

"Work for me, or endure the punishment you so richly deserve for your sins."

"Work for him how?"

A cynical smile thins Stone's lips. "This is where it gets interesting. And dirty. Del Payton died in May 1968, five weeks after Martin Luther King. What else was going on then?"

"The Vietnam War?"

He waves his hand dismissively. "The presidential primaries. Bobby Kennedy had jumped into the race as soon as Eugene McCarthy proved LBJ was vulnerable. After Kennedy came in, Johnson announced he wouldn't run for reelection. Del Payton was killed on the day Bobby won the Nebraska primary, and he'd won Indiana the week before. Kennedy was shaping up as the likely Democratic candidate in November."

"I'm not following you. What's the connection?"

"*Hoover,* Cage. Compared to the presidential race, Hoover didn't give a damn what happened to some black factory worker in Mississippi. Why? Because the FBI director has always served at the pleasure of the President. Hoover had been director since 1924, and he meant to stay director until he died. Two of his least favorite people in the world were Robert Kennedy and Martin Luther King. King's assassination had thrilled him, literally. But Bobby's presidential campaign was giving him ulcers. Can you guess what Hoover's mission in life was in 1968?"

551

"Not to kill Robert Kennedy?"

"No, no. Forget that crap. He wanted to put Richard Nixon in office. And he was willing to do whatever was required to accomplish that. Hoover and Nixon went way back, to the 1960 election when Nixon lost to JFK. Bobby Kennedy, on the other hand, had treated Hoover like shit when he was attorney general. So, in May 1968 Nixon is making sober speeches about law and order to middle America, while Bobby Kennedy runs from ghetto to college campus preaching about racial equality, poverty in Mississippi, the evils of the Vietnam War, and reaching out to the Soviet Union."

"I still don't see the relevance to Del Payton."

Stone looks exasperated by my slowness. "The relevance is to Leo Marston. And more important, to his father. Leo's father was a major Mississippi power broker, a former state attorney general, just like Leo turned out to be. He was close friends with Big Jim Eastland, a well-known segregationist, head of the Senate Judiciary Committee, and J. Edgar Hoover's number one cheerleader on Capitol Hill."

At last the picture is coming clear.

"The sixty-eight presidential election was the second closest in history, Cage, after Nixon and JFK in 1960. In sixty-eight Nixon won by less than one percent of the vote. That's how close it was in November. Back in May, when Del Payton was murdered, anything was possible. Mississippi was a Democratic state, but it voted strangely in presidential elections. In 1960 her electors didn't vote for JFK or Nixon, but some guy named Byrd. In sixty-four they voted for Goldwater. In 1968 they were leaning toward —"

"Wallace," I finish. "George Wallace."

Stone nods. "The racist firecracker from Alabama. Wallace was running as an Independent. Leo and his father were Democrats, but they thought Bobby Kennedy was a communist. Wallace was too racist for them, and more important, they didn't think he could win. So, they cast their lot with Nixon. Old man Marston was doing all he could to sway the movers and shakers in Mississippi to forget Wallace and vote Republican."

"Jesus."

"You see it now? Into this mess rides Special Agent Dwight Stone, telling J. Edgar Hoover that the son of one of Nixon's biggest supporters is responsible for a race murder in Mississippi. Did that make the director happy? No, sir. Do you think Hoover wanted to tell his buddy Senator Eastland that the son of an old crony was going to jail for killing a nigger who got out of line? No, sir. And the thought of what Bobby Kennedy would do with that information was enough to give Hoover a heart attack. So . . . what do you think Hoover said to Leo at that meeting in Jackson?"

"I have no idea."

"Sonny boy, you fucked up. You had the right idea, but you got caught. It's just a good thing you got caught by my people, or life would be getting very uncomfortable right now. In fact, it still could. Then Hoover talked to Leo's papa. It's a lot like *The Godfather*. Nothing formal, but everything understood. Fealty. Absolute loyalty." Stone modulates his voice into a scratchy Marlon Brando impersonation: " *'Someday, I may ask you to perform a difficult service, but until that day, accept this favor as a gift.'* From that day forward, Hoover owned the Marston family. All their influence, everything."

"Hoover buried your evidence?"

"All of it. Leo went back to his job and his future. The Payton investigation was allowed to die. Only Ray Presley paid a price."

"Presley?"

"He'd shot at us on the highway, remember? Hoover wouldn't let that pass. It was part of the price he demanded from Marston. Presley had to go down for something. Didn't matter what."

"Marston gave him up?"

"Didn't even hesitate. Presley had a dozen sidelines for making money. His police job was just a fulcrum for the rest of it. He fenced stuff, collected protection money —"

"And sold dope."

"Right. Amphetamines mostly, for truckers. Interstate transportation of federally regulated narcotics. Marston gave us everything we needed to nail him, and we fed it to the state police. They busted him on possession with intent to distribute. I showed up at the arrest, just so Presley would know it was payback."

"Did he find out it was Marston who gave him up?"

"Not as far as I know. That's the irony. Marston was right to trust Presley, but Presley was a fool to trust Marston. Presley's like a dog that way."

"A pit bull maybe."

Stone goes through his little phone ritual again.

"You waiting for a call?"

"No." He picks up his pistol, stands, and walks back to the front window.

"They still out there?"

"Still there."

"So, the national security seal was completely bogus?"

Stone chuckles dryly. "Completely. Think about the Payton case. The Bureau had been tasked with destroying violent opposition to civil rights in the South. Instead, Hoover purposefully protected a race murderer for his own political ends. Normally, he would have added the Payton evidence to his personal files. The infamous blackmail files. But Payton's file was too big for that. We had agents in Natchez generating reams of useless crap. The national security seal was an impenetrable shield."

"Do you think the audiotape of Marston and Presley is still with the main file?"

"I doubt it. That was the critical evidence. It was probably taken to Hoover's home when he died, with the other blackmail material. Shelves of books have been written about what might have happened to that stuff. You'll never find that tape."

"So, Marston's motive was just —"

"Money," Stone finishes. "Greed. Bastards like him only care about one thing: grabbing everything within their reach. They think every dollar they get takes them one step closer to immortality, and every person they step on puts them one step above everyone else. I don't think other people really exist for people like Marston.

555

They're just a means to an end."

Including his daughter, I think with a shiver. "When you had the bugs in his mansion," I say hesitantly, "did you ever pick up anything . . . unsavory?"

"Murder is pretty unsavory."

"I'm talking about sexual stuff."

"We heard him banging his wife's best friend one day."

"I'm talking about abuse. Child abuse."

He turns away from the window and looks at me. "No. I had a daughter myself. If I'd heard anything like that, I would have gone in there and thrashed him within an inch of his life." The corner of Stone's mouth twitches. "The mikes were only in for a couple of weeks, though. And I can't remember if Henry covered the little girl's room."

I force myself to push Livy from my mind. "I need you to tell this story to a jury."

"It'll never happen, son."

"I think it will. I know about your daughter."

In the midst of turning back to the window, he whips his whole head toward me, his eyes burning with anger.

I hold up both hands. "I'm just telling you I know she's what's been keeping you from helping me."

"Then you know it's pointless to ask me to testify."

"Is it? I talked to her today, and she thinks different."

Stone takes a step toward me. "You talked to my daughter today?"

"Yes. Caitlin Masters found her for me."

"You idiot. If you've put her life in danger —"

"She's all right! She's fine. And she agrees with me. Portman started playing carrot and stick with her days ago. I didn't even have to tell her you could bring him down. She knew."

"You had no right to put her in jeopardy, Cage."

"I want justice. That's all."

"You want revenge."

"You're right. But I used to want it for myself. Now I want it for someone else. Marston has done things he should die for, Stone. Take my word for that."

The old agent fingers the pistol in his hand. "My daughter told me two days ago that I should testify. She thinks getting this thing off my chest would save my damned soul or something." His face hardens. "She's got no right to sacrifice her career for my guilty conscience. She doesn't know how things really work."

"She knows."

"It's not her choice, damn it!" His eyes flick around the interior of the cabin. "God, I wish I had a bottle." He paces over to the fireplace and pokes the logs, sending a storm of sparks up the chimney. "You don't want me as a witness, Cage."

"Why not?"

"I'm damaged goods."

"Because of your drinking?"

"Drinking isn't one problem. It's a whole constellation."

"Why were you fired five years after the Payton murder? It wasn't for drinking."

He stirs the fire some more. "No. Though I was

drinking like a fish at the time. When Hoover cut the deal with Marston, I couldn't believe it. I don't know why. I'd seen him do it enough times before. But usually it was cases that were dirty all the way around. This murder had a real victim. An *innocent* victim. And the Korea angle really weighed on me. I started drinking to forget about it. Things were turning to shit in the Bureau. Hoover was using us to harass antiwar protesters, all kinds of unconstitutional stuff. Then we got Nixon. Parts of the Bureau started to function like the goddamn KGB. It made me sick. The booze made it tolerable. For a while, anyway. It also made me impossible to live with. I drove my wife and baby away. I screwed up a dozen different ways. Then I topped them all. You'll get a kick out of this, because it involves your friend Marston."

"What?"

"In 1972 I was in Washington, doing some shit work Nixon had requested from Hoover. Something too boring for Liddy and his plumbers. I was walking through the lobby of the Watergate office complex, and there, bigger than life, stood Leo Marston. He was in town lobbying John Stennis for something or other. I was soused when I saw him, and I snapped. The Payton thing had been eating at me for four years. When Marston saw me, that smug bastard tried to make out like we were buddies from way back, in on the big joke. The dead nigger. I straightened him out quick. And everybody in the Watergate lobby heard me. Marston lost it. He took a swing at me, and I pulled my gun."

I almost laugh, remembering the way I snapped

and went after Marston yesterday.

"Henry Bookbinder had been outside parking the car," Stone recalls. "He ran in and backed me down. Nobody died, but Marston screamed blue murder to Hoover. One of Hoover's last acts before he died in seventy-two was firing me. I guess that's a distinction of sorts."

"Where was Portman then?"

Stone goes still, the poker hovering above the crackling logs. "Climbing the Bureau ladder. I didn't tell you everything before. When Hoover took over the Payton case, I started making copies of my case notes. I also copied the audiotape that incriminated Marston."

The hair on my forearms is standing up. "Do you still have that copy?"

He shakes his head. "Portman saw what I was doing. He started spying on me, reporting to Hoover as the case progressed. I can just imagine his reports. May be *ideologically unsound*, blah, blah, blah. Anyway, everything was stolen out of my apartment two days before I was fired. That was Portman, I guarantee it. On Hoover's orders."

My heart sinks.

"You don't want me as a witness. They'd make me look pathetic on cross. Too many sins of my own."

"What's Portman so afraid of now? From the story you told, his involvement was peripheral."

"The Bureau's been under siege for ten years, in the public-relations sense. Its big Achilles' heel is racism. The FBI has been sued by black agents, Hispanics, women, all claiming systematic discrimination. And these groups have *won*. Portman

559

was appointed to correct these problems, to polish the image, and he was appointed by a Democratic president. If it was to come out that his 'heroic civil rights work' in Mississippi consisted of helping to cover up a race murder, he'd be out on his ass in an hour. The President would have no choice."

"So, let's make it known. Do the Bureau and the country a favor."

Stone sets the poker in its rack and sits on the hearth, his face weary. "I wish I could. Every trial decision Portman ever made as a federal judge would come into question, every decision as a U.S. attorney. He'd never work in the public sector again. And once the media got its nose into his past, God knows what they'd find. A guy like Portman doesn't cross the line once or twice. It's a management style with him."

"Why didn't the media discover anything during his confirmation hearings?"

"The Bureau is a closed culture. It outlives presidential administrations, judges, even Supreme Court justices. If the leadership of that culture wants to keep Portman's secrets so he can be appointed FBI director, that's the way it'll be."

Stone takes out his phone and checks the line again. "I'd like to help you, Cage. But they've held my daughter over me for a long time. Since she was a kid."

"What?"

"Oh, yeah. After he fired me, Hoover sent me a message. Portman delivered it. If I tried to air any dirty Bureau laundry, my kid wouldn't live to watch me on *Meet the Press*."

"That's pretty hard to believe."

He laughs bitterly. "This was 1972. Worse things were happening every day, and the government was right in the middle of it."

I pull the curtains away from the front window and squint through the gathering dusk. Beyond what must be the jeep track, the snow-covered wall of Anthracite Mesa climbs toward the sky, with spruce and fir trees marching up it in dark ranks. What I do not see is human beings.

"What did you mean about Presley and Marston making a nice package? You said, 'Why complicate it?' "

Stone stands and walks toward me, telephone in hand. "I didn't mean anything. Forget it."

"You're holding something back, aren't you?"

He has the phone to his ear now, and his face has gone white. He throws down the phone and rushes me, holding out his pistol. "Take it!"

"What?"

"The phone's dead! Take the gun!"

I take the gun, which looks like a Colt .45, and Stone snatches the hunting rifle up from the table. A Winchester 300, with a scope.

"Open the back door for me!" he orders. "There's a sniper out there."

As I run to the back door, I decide that not bringing Daniel Kelly with me was about the stupidest idea I've ever had.

Stone kneels six feet back from the door, shoulders the Winchester, and puts his right eye to the scope, as though preparing to shoot right through the door.

"Open it," he says. "Slowly. Then get clear, fast."

I slowly turn the handle, then stretch as far away

561

as I can from the door and pull it halfway open.

Stone quickly adjusts his aim, then fires. The report of the rifle inside the cabin is like a detonation.

"He's down!" shouts Stone. "Follow me!"

"Where to?"

Before he can answer, the front window of the cabin explodes inward and a bullet ricochets off the hearth. Stone whirls, draws a small automatic from his belt, and empties half a clip through the broken window.

"Move!" he yells, grabbing my arm and jerking me toward the door.

"*Where?*" I ask, my throat dry as sand.

"Somewhere they can't follow!"

"Where's that?"

"The river."

"The *river?* In what?"

"You'll see. Move your ass!"

CHAPTER 35

As Stone pulls me through the back door of the cabin, something explodes behind us. We fall facedown on the snow, stunned like cattle after being hit with an electric prod, but we scramble blindly backward for the cover of the cabin wall, knowing instinctively that exposure means death.

Hunched against the side of the cabin, I scan the swollen river and its banks in the dying light. I see no way to use that flooded stream as a means of escape. Stone's lips are moving, but I hear nothing. He turns and begins tugging at something beneath his cabin. It's some sort of inflatable boat, a long red plastic thing, like a cross between a canoe and kayak. Seeing that I can't hear his orders, Stone takes back the pistol he gave me, then motions for me to drag the kayak to the water, a distance of about eighty feet. He obviously means to cover me while I do this, but I'm not going to drag anything. If I have to cross that open space, I'm going to do it as fast as I can.

Dropping to my knees, I turn the kayak upside down and crawl under it, sliding it onto my back like an elongated turtle shell. Its coated fabric skin probably wouldn't stop a pellet gun, but at least I'll be able to run with the thing.

As I start toward the river, my Reebok-clad feet slip and crunch over the snow. The bow of the kayak bobs forward and back as I rush forward, obscuring my vision, making my gauntlet longer than it needs to be. I cringe at the stutter of an automatic weapon somewhere behind me, but the reassuring bellow of Stone's .45 pushes me on. At least I haven't completely lost my hearing.

The last half of my dash to the river has the terrible dreamlike quality of pursuing a receding horizon, the shock of my feet hitting rocks under the snow the only tangible proof that I'm awake. The swiftly falling darkness is probably providing more protection than Stone's pistol, but it can't be long before someone sprays a clip at the fleeing kayak.

When my feet kick up the first splash, I leap forward and land in a bone-chilling current that pulls at the kayak like a giant hand. Fighting to my knees in the current, I flip the kayak upright and lie down in the shallows beside it, leaving only my head exposed. Muzzle flashes in the cabin windows punctuate the flashes below them, where Stone must be firing. There's a brief lull, and then Stone comes charging out of the darkness toward the water, a two-bladed kayak paddle in one hand and his Winchester in the other.

He whirls and fires twice on the run, then breaks in my direction, using the white propane tank for concealment. He's halfway to the water when another flash lights up the interior of the cabin. Stone grabs his buttocks, lurches forward, then spins and returns fire as he goes down in the snow.

I start pulling the kayak toward the bank, but the bottom shallows quickly beneath me, forcing me into an exposed position. The water feels like glacial runoff, stealing my breath, making my teeth chatter uncontrollably. But it's better than what Stone is enduring. Every five seconds or so he lets off a .45 round back at the cabin windows, but he can't keep that up forever. Panic scrambles around in my chest like a crazed animal, urging me to flight. It wouldn't take anything, just a surrender to the current. I could float downstream for fifty yards, then climb into the kayak and be on my way.

As though sensing my panic, Stone holds the paddle and rifle along the length of his body and begins rolling across the snow toward the river. The old agent looks like a kid playing a game. Bullets kick up white powder in front of him, but he doesn't even slow down. When he is five yards away, I yell: "Th-throw me the pistol!"

The .45 skids across the snow, but I manage to get my fingers around it before it disappears in the river. The steel feels warm compared to the water. It's too dark to aim accurately at the cabin from here, but two more muzzle flashes obligingly appear, and I let off three shots at the afterimage on my retinas.

"Into the current!" shouts Stone.

"What about the kayak?"

"Too easy to hit! Just hang onto the rope!"

He rolls into the shallows, then hangs up on the rocks somehow. I fire twice more at the cabin, then grab his belt and drag him into the current while bullets spray water against my knees. The muzzle flashes are between the cabin and the river now.

They're coming for us.

As I grope helplessly for the kayak, Stone rises to his knees in the water, the big Winchester braced against his shoulder. He fires once, then cycles the bolt, waits three seconds, and fires again.

A fireball the size of the cabin itself explodes out of the darkness, sucking up all the air around us. I feel the pull in my lungs and sinuses as a millisecond's image of a blazing man is seared into my brain and I tumble backward into the freezing water. *The propane tank,* marvels a voice in my head. *One shot to pierce its skin, the second to ignite the gas . . .*

Stone is already in the main channel of the river, trying to keep his head and the rifle above the surface. Wrapping the kayak's bow rope tightly around my wrist, I leap into the black water where the current is strongest and give myself to it. A couple of desultory shots ring out, but they could be loose rounds in the pistols of dead men, cooking off in the inferno Stone has made of his home. The river has us in its power now, and the assassins are but a burning memory falling behind us in the dark.

"Stone? Stone!"

"Ahead of you," comes a faint reply. "Did they hit the kayak?"

"I don't think so."

"It's got three cells. Check it out."

Since I'm hanging onto the kayak for dear life, it's not difficult to obey Stone's order. The strange craft seems intact, though its cells don't seem as fully inflated as they might be. Stone's two-bladed paddle is wedged between the seats and the starboard gunwale.

"It's okay."

The water here is swift and smooth. The moon and stars shine with white brilliance, reflecting off the deep water like diamonds flung onto its surface. I kick with the current, hoping to ease my fear and aloneness by overtaking Stone.

A sharp cry comes from up ahead. I'm trying to place its direction when something smashes into my ribs, knocking the wind out of me. A rock. Stone must have hit the same one.

A white hand appears in the current. I grab it and pull, then wind the bow rope tightly around the wrist. Now at least we are riding the river together, and will share the same fate.

"Thanks," says Stone, his face a gray blur beside mine.

"Are you h-hit bad?" I ask, trying to control my voice.

"Bad enough. I don't think it hit bone, though."

"Shouldn't we get in the kayak?"

He shakes his head. "We'll have to beach it to get in. Another forty yards or so."

It's tough to judge distance in the dark, so I count to ten before I start kicking toward the left bank, watching for a suitable place to land. My kicks seem futile against the power of the river; we're like cars trapped in the center lane of an interstate, slaves to the main current.

"Get over!" Stone commands. "Hurry!"

At last a broad shelf of rock rises out of the river like a ramp, and it's simple enough to float the kayak up onto it. Stone lets the current wash him up onto his back, then lies there, wheezing for air.

"What do we do?" I ask.

"G-get in. Keep going."

"Where?"

"Town. Six miles south."

"Six miles!"

"Listen, Cage. The river's at flood. We're moving faster than you think. And it's a good thing, because we've got to beat those bastards back to town."

"But they can *drive*." I clench my arms over my chest in a vain effort to stop shivering.

"They had to abandon their vehicles just like you. They've got to cover three miles on foot before they can drive. In the snow. We can beat them if we hurry. You ever been on white water?"

It's been ten years since I've been in a raft, and on that trip my guide went overboard and got crushed between the raft bottom and some rocks, breaking his leg in three places.

"A long time ago."

"The Slate is easier to run at flood than at low water. But we've got two trouble spots. Both slot canyons. The first one's up ahead. It's a class-five vertical drop, but the floodwater should shoot us right over it."

An image of an eight-foot waterfall flashes into my head, the one I saw while trudging up to the cabin this afternoon. In my desperation to escape the guns, I somehow suppressed this memory. But that's what Stone is talking about. Going over that falls in a plastic boat.

"Just grab the sides of the kayak," he says, "lean back, and pray. I'll handle the paddle. A mile farther on is the second one. Walls higher than you can reach, ending in a tight chute that's like a piledriver. People drive their four-wheelers out there to watch the kayakers crash."

Jesus . . .

He grabs my windbreaker with a weak grip. "If I was covering the river, that's where I'd wait. It'd be tough shooting, though. We'll come through that second chute like a runaway freight train, and if we clear it, we'll be okay all the way to town. They won't be able to find us in the dark."

"This river goes through town?"

He grins. "Right through it. Let's get this bus on the road."

I slide the kayak down the rock ramp until the current is tugging it, then grab Stone by the belt buckle and manhandle him over the side near the stern. He goes rigid with pain when his buttocks hit the rock through the air-filled floor of the boat, but there's nothing to be done. I drag the kayak the rest of the way clear, then roll over the side and into the bow.

Immediately the main current has us, pulling us to its center, gathering speed as the rising banks constrict the water in its headlong flight to the first canyon. I get to my knees and try to obey Stone's barked orders — *Lean left! Lean right! Right again!* — as he expertly handles the paddle. Every twenty yards or so the bow lifts out of the water and slaps back down with a combative *thunk*.

"I hear the drop," Stone says from the stern. "Lean left. We've got to stay in the channel."

I don't hear what Stone hears, but the black trough beneath us bears steadily left, and my forward line of sight has gone black. Then, slowly, the sound registers on my traumatized eardrums, like holding my ear to the biggest conch shell in the world. Fear balloons in my chest, pressing my heart into my throat.

I don't think Stone's paddle is affecting the course of the boat anymore. I feel like I'm trapped in a roller coaster as it tops its highest incline and tips slowly forward, headed for the long vertiginous fall. On both sides, walls loom out of the dark, near enough to touch.

Then we are airborne.

"Lean back!" yells Stone as the kayak is hurled forward into space. I obey out of pure instinct, my stomach flying up my throat as the bow plummets down a thundering pipeline of water and smashes into something I cannot see, then bounces up into a roiling mass of foam and spray.

"We're clear!" he cries. "One down!"

We're back in the main current, riding as smoothly as a subway car on a scheduled run. The walls of the canyon have fallen away, and the sky above us has widened into a starry blanket that gives the snowy riverbanks a silver sheen.

For ten minutes we slide along as though on a Nile cruise, but every so often a stand of spruce near the river's edge reminds me just how fast we are moving. The farther we go, the more the valley widens around us, until it seems we are floating across a vast desert of snow. On another night this might seem an ideal time for Stone and me to talk, for him to tell me what to watch for ahead, or to discuss the eternal subjects like women and time. But tonight all we can do is shiver in the wind, chilled so deeply that if we don't find warmth and shelter soon, we could die from exposure.

Almost without our noticing, the banks begin to rise again. It feels like the river is cutting its way into the earth, carrying us with it on its darkening journey. The sound of the turbulent water grows as the walls rise, like the sound of a great beast waking from a long sleep.

"It's coming," Stone says from behind me. "Listen."

Only the center of the stream is smooth now, a black torrent rushing through the narrow canyon, throwing off a mist of silver froth and spray. The kayak hurtles down this black tunnel like it's on rails, but of course it's not. If the bow gets turned around, we could spin out of control and be smashed on a rock, or capsize and be pinned by an inescapable hydraulic.

"Lean right!" Stone yells.

The kayak's nose pulls left, then slingshots around a bend, its fabric skin scraping the rock wall with a resilient wail.

"Shit! They're covering the chute!"

It's difficult to judge distance in the dark, but about a hundred yards ahead of us, a pair of head-lights slices downward and across the narrow river, bright as a bonfire in the dark. And where those lights wait, guns are waiting too.

"We can't make it past that!" I shout toward the stern. "We've got to get out!"

"Too late. We're in the canyon."

A jet of fear flushes through my system. I feel like a steer being driven into a slaughter chute. "We've got to get out of the kayak, then!"

"We can't run the chute without it."

I turn in disbelief, but all I see is Stone's solemn face as he expertly wields the paddle.

The current continues to accelerate as the river is forced into an ever narrowing channel. The lights are only seventy yards away now.

"They won't see us until we're right on top of them," Stone assures me. "We'll be moving so fast, they'll only have a couple of seconds to fire."

"What if they have automatic weapons?"

"We need suppressing fire. Can you handle a rifle?"

I don't bother to answer him. If we go through that chute in this kayak, we'll be cut to pieces by anyone sighting down the beams of those headlights.

"Cage? Are you listening?"

As the lights loom closer, a bowel-churning roar reverberates between the walls. One thing I remember my raft guide telling me — just before he broke his leg — was that some white-water guides train by floating rivers wearing only life vests. If they can do that in preparation for making a living, Stone and I can do it without vests to save our lives.

"*I said, take this rifle!*" he yells.

Without hesitation, I throw myself onto the right gunwale of the kayak and press down with all my weight. Stone screams like a madman, but I ignore him, leaning harder and farther forward until the first rush of water surges over the side.

"*Stop it, you damn fool!*"

And then it is done. The inflatable tube that forms the right gunwale digs beyond the point of no return, and the river pours into the boat, swamping us in seconds. The shock of the cold water steals my breath again, but I roll over the side and into the main current.

The kayak is still floating upright — if mostly submerged — but Stone won't be able to get it above water without my help. At last he heaves himself over the rear gunwale and into the river. As soon as he's clear, the inflatable rises in the water. With a powerful wrenching move I flip it upside down in the current. When I let go, the buoyant craft rights itself as though nothing had happened.

"You stupid son of a bitch!" Stone appears beside me like a man in the last stages of drowning, his eyes furious points of light in the darkness.

I don't reply. The water is driving toward the chute with the momentum of a locomotive, Stone and me and the kayak bobbing along in it like fishing corks. I've got to slow us down a little, put us a few seconds behind the kayak —

A sledgehammer blow to the chest stops me dead in the water. Purely out of instinct, I grab whatever hit me and reach out for Stone with my legs. An explosive grunt sounds beside me as Stone collides with the object, and I lock my legs around his waist.

It's a tree trunk. A trunk the width of a man's thigh and smooth as glass, wedged into a crack in the ledge from which it fell. The river is trying to rip Stone's body from between my knees, but I hold him fast. With a supreme effort, I flex my stomach muscles and pull him higher in the water.

"Grab the tree!" I gasp. "Grab the tree!"

He drapes one arm over it, loses his grip, then at last manages to get both arms over the trunk.

"Can you hold yourself?" I ask, my legs burning from exertion.

He nods weakly, his face white.

As soon as I relax my leg muscles, the river sweeps both our bodies up onto the surface, holding us in near-horizontal positions. Forty yards away, halogen headlights illuminate a thirty-foot stretch of the chute like searchlights.

"Boat! Boat!" screams a voice from the roar at the end of the little canyon. A voice from the lights.

The illuminated water in the chute churns into boiling chaos as hundreds of bullets shred its surface. The kayak materializes in the headlights as though by magic and instantly explodes into confetti that sails through the bluish beams like the remnants of a child's balloon.

"Christ," Stone coughs.

"Listen," I hiss in his ear, hoping my raft guide knew what he was talking about. "You go through feet first. On your back, feet first, okay? That cushions the rocks."

He nods, his face looking bloodless in the dark.

"How long can you hold on?"

"Twenty seconds . . . maybe thirty."

"Then we might as well go now. Save our strength."

Stone nods, his eyes closed.

"Have you still got your pistol?" I ask.

"In my waistband."

"Let's do it. On three. One . . . two . . . *three*—"

Letting go of the tree trunk is like surrendering to a god, so mighty is the force carrying us down the chute. Yet the water around us seems placid. At the center of the channel there is no white water, no churning froth or spray, just a great black mass of fluid driving forward with unstoppable power. Stone falls slowly behind me as we hurtle toward the headlights, but I can't worry about him now. I can't worry about anything. I suppose I should pray or vomit from fear or see my life pass before my eyes, but I do none of these things. At some point, terror becomes so total and control so minimal that you simply shed fear like a coat.

I lie back in the water as though going to sleep, only my face above the surface, my arms held out from my sides like Christ on the cross as I rush feet first toward the great black door at the end of the chute. The inverted bowl of sky sparkles with more stars than I have seen in years, and I feel a sudden and absurd certainty that whatever is about to happen happened a long time ago.

As the headlights white out the sky above me, I expel all my air and let my head sink beneath the torrent. I am nothing to those above me, a ripple of water sweeping beneath them, a piece of driftwood borne on the flood.

Suddenly, the black tide swells beneath me, lifting me toward the sky like a magic carpet. Thunder roars around me, atomizing the water to mist. There is no air here, only different states of water. I am suspended long enough to hear bursts of gunfire behind me. Then a great fist slams me to the bottom of a well and holds me there, trying with all its power to bludgeon me unconscious. My lungs scream as they did the day I dragged Ruby from our burning house, but I dare not breathe. To breathe here is to join the hammering darkness.

As suddenly as before, the great hand hurls me

up out of the well and onto the surface, which feels land solid after the vaporous thunder of the chute. I feel as though some great beast had sucked me into its maw, chewed me for a few moments, and, finding me distasteful, spat me out whole.

The air feels warm against my face. I probe my arms and legs, searching for broken bones. Remarkably, I seem intact. Turning back toward the thundering mist, I watch the exit of the chute, a white mouth spitting foam between two rock walls like the jet of a great hose. Surely Stone has passed through by now, though not, I fear, as invisibly as I did. The gunfire I heard must have been directed at him.

I try to tread water, but my strength is gone. I can only lie back and float, nose and mouth above the surface, waiting for some sign that Stone survived. An image of his bullet-riddled body bobbing up beside me flits through my head, but I quickly banish it. My odds of surviving the night up here without him are very low.

Stone will come. If anything, the ex-FBI man is tougher than I. He is nearly seventy, yes. And he's wounded. But it's not as though physical prowess of any degree could affect one's fate while passing through that cataract. Stone's fate is in the lap of the gods.

"Swim, goddamn it."

For a dazed moment I think I am talking to myself, but I'm not. Stone has kicked up beside me like a shipwrecked sailor, looking more dead than alive.

"Did they hit you again?"

His eyes are only half open. "Kick your feet,

Cage. We've got another half mile to go."

"Why not get out here?"

"Too close . . . kick, damn you."

I start kicking, and soon enough the current is carrying us along as steadily as it did behind Stone's cabin, though more slowly. The river has spread out here. Shrubs and boulders sail past us in the moonlight, while smaller rocks abrade our knees and elbows. Stone grips my windbreaker and speaks as we drift along.

"Crested Butte is three miles south. We can't stay in the river without the boat . . . too cold. And I can't run. I'm not dying, but I can't run. There's a campground up here. When we get close, you're going to get out on the south bank. Right now they're stuck north of the river. Follow the river south, running as fast as you can, hugging the bluff for cover. When you see the lights of town, circle to your right and come in from the south, in case they're waiting for you."

"I'm not leaving you here. You —"

"We haven't got time for this! You want a bar called the Silver Bell. It's just off the main street, Elk Avenue. The bartender is a mountain of a guy called Tiny McSwain. In my drinking days we got pretty tight. Tell Tiny to take you to an airport. Any airport but the one you flew into. Still got your wallet?"

I grab my hip pocket. "Still there."

"Cash?"

I nod. I brought two thousand dollars in hundred-dollar bills for just this reason, so I couldn't be traced by credit card charges.

"You may have to hide out until you get a

morning flight. Denver maybe. Do whatever you have to do, but stay out of sight."

A yellow light appears from the darkness ahead, hovering in the air to my right, about fifty yards away.

"That's the campground," Stone says. "Come on."

We separate and fight our way to the south bank. As my hands collide with cold rock, I hear a screech of brakes ahead. Crawling out of the water, I realize my legs are nearly numb.

"They must have driven like banshees to get here that fast," Stone says through rattling teeth. "Tear off a piece of your shirttail."

"What?"

"Your *shirttail*."

In my weakened state, tearing the soaked cotton is like trying to rip a phone book in half. As I struggle with the hem, Stone jabs a stick through a stretched-taut place and rips off a long piece.

"What do you want me to do? Make a surrender flag?"

He hands me the fabric and rolls over on his stomach. "Wad up a hunk of that and jam it into my wound."

I tear off most of the shirttail and squeeze it into a tight wet tennis ball of cloth, then crouch over Stone's back. Garbled voices float to us from the direction of the campground.

"Where are you hit?"

"Left cheek of my ass. Took out a plug of muscle, I think."

I feel along his left buttock until my fingers mush into a warm opening. Stone doesn't even flinch.

The hole is ragged, but it runs across the buttock at an angle, like a deep grazing wound. The swelling below it is considerable, though, and it's bound to get worse now that he's out of the cold water.

"Hurry!" he grunts.

I squeeze the cloth into a tighter ball and hold it against the opening. "Ready?"

"Do it."

In one hard stroke I depress the cloth into the hole as he tenses beneath me. It reminds me of helping my father pack a decubitus ulcer when I worked for him in high school. Now I need something to hold the packing in the wound. Removing my soaked windbreaker, I pull off what's left of my shirt and slide it under Stone's left leg, then tie it over the hole.

"That's the best I can do for now," I tell him, pulling my jacket back on.

"What's the name of the bar?" he asks, rolling over. His face is even whiter than before.

"The Silver Bell. Bartender's Tiny McSwain."

"Good. Move your ass, kid."

"What are you going to do?"

He drops one hand to his waist, where the butt of his .45 glints dully in the dark. "Slow those bastards down for you."

"I'll stay and help you, damn it."

"You *can't* help me. You don't have a gun. You'll help me by getting your ass back to Mississippi and nailing Portman's hide to the barn wall."

"Stone —"

The old agent grips my arm with more strength than I thought he could possibly have left. "No matter what you hear, keep running. I mean that. If it sounds like the goddamn O.K. Corral up here, you keep running until you reach that bar."

"There's only one way I'll go."

"How's that?"

"If you promise to testify."

His laughter is full of irony. "Boy, if I survive this night, wild horses couldn't stop me from testifying. Portman gave the order for these sons of bitches to kill us because he thought I was going to testify. Well, now he's right. If I'm alive, I'll get to Mississippi. I'll drag Portman's ass down from the mountaintop if I have to tear the whole mountain down with him. Marston too. Now, get your ass out of here."

I get to my knees and look through the trees to the south.

"Don't come back," Stone says quietly. "Not with Tiny or the sheriff. After you leave, everybody up here but me is a target. That's how I want it. The whole thing'll be over by the time anybody could get here, and if I don't come out on top, whoever came would die for nothing. If you come back, I'll shoot you myself."

I grab his upper arm. "The trial starts in thirty-six hours. You get your ass back to Mississippi. You owe it to Del Payton."

He nods in the dark. "That I do, Cage. That I do."

My run to the town is a benumbed nightmare of falls and slides and collisions with trees, an endless march into a killing wind, but I never consider resting. Dwight Stone is offering up his life to cover my escape.

The first gunshot echoes down the valley behind me as the glow of Crested Butte appears like a mirage in the distance. All my instincts say, turn around, go back, and help Stone. But the old soldier's tone of his last order keeps me going. Over rock. Through snowdrifts. Past a black mirror of a lake. Through thickets, thorns. Plodding forward into the relentless wind, ever forward, until at last I am sliding down a white slope toward a geometric heaven of lights and warmth.

When I reach the level of the buildings, I circle to my right in a broad arc that takes me around to the south entrance of town. Muted television dialogue drifts on the air, and the occasional sound of a car motor rumbles from between the buildings.

Crested Butte looks less like a cowboy town than a nineteenth century New England village plopped down in the mountains. The buildings along Elk Avenue have Victorian facades, and flowers line every street and window box. The windows are mostly dark, but as I move along the street, a shopkeeper backs out of a doorway, gives me a furtive glance, then locks his door and hurries to a truck parked across the street.

Twenty yards farther on, a yellow funnel of light appears down a side street to my left, illuminating a wooden bell painted silver. I turn down the alley and crunch through the snow as fast as my tingling feet will carry me.

The Silver Bell has old-fashioned swinging doors. It's a rustic place that caters to locals, not a "ski bar" fluffed up for the tourist trade. There are three people sitting at the bar and two loners at the tables. All look like serious drinkers. Behind the bar stands a giant of a man with a gray-flecked black beard.

He has to be Tiny McSwain.

As soon as he sees me, he moves around the bar as though to throw me out. Before he can, I hold up my hands and croak:

"If you're Tiny McSwain, Dwight Stone sent me."

He stops, his eyes narrowed. "Who are you?"

"Better for you if you don't know. Stone told me you'd help me."

"Somebody heard shots up near the mesa," he says suspiciously. "Was that Dwight?"

"It was the people trying to kill him. Him and me both."

"I'll call the sheriff. Where's Dwight?"

"He's back by the creek. He told me not to call anybody. He said everything would be over by the time anybody could get to him, and if not, they'd get killed for nothing."

"Those his words?"

"Near enough."

Tiny nods. "Then we don't call anybody."

"There are at least two men up there, probably more."

"Stone's a tough old boy. What did he tell you to do?"

"He said tell you to take me to an airport."

"Which airport?"

"Denver. And he said do it quick."

Tiny motions for a T-shirt–clad woman at a table to get behind the bar, then takes a set of keys from his pocket. "Let's go, friend."

582

"Hey," calls the woman. "Where are you going, if anybody asks?"

"If anybody asks, me and this guy went back up the Slate to help Dwight." Tiny McSwain looks at his customers, who are staring indifferently at me. "Nobody else says different."

Blank nods from the drinkers.

"My Bronco's parked out back," he says. "Let's go."

CHAPTER 36

I am standing at the Continental Airlines gate in Baton Rouge, searching the crowds of travelers for Daniel Kelly as fear slowly devours me from the inside. A week ago I stood a few yards from here, entranced by the sight of Livy Marston. Now I stand shaking from adrenaline and lack of sleep, wondering whether Dwight Stone survived the night, and whether I will live to defend myself at my slander trial, which is scheduled to begin in less than twenty-four hours.

Kelly should have been here hours ago, but I've seen no sight of him. A dozen businessmen who could be FBI agents have passed me, stared at me, even bumped into me, but none has tried to stop me. So far, anyway. If Kelly doesn't show in the next five minutes, I'm going to try to reach Natchez on my own.

Last night Tiny McSwain drove me all the way to Denver and dropped me at an airport motel. I paid cash and checked in under a false name, then lay in the chilly darkness, unable to sleep. Twice I lifted the phone to call the Colorado state police and send them up the mesa after Stone. I had visions of him lying wounded beside the Slate River, his attackers dead, him dying but savable if he reached a surgeon in time. But Stone's orders came back to me, and each time I set the phone down.

Instead I called Sam Jacobs in Natchez, being fairly sure that his phone would not be tapped. The geologist promised to visit Caitlin Masters first thing in the morning and, through her, instruct Kelly to be at the Baton Rouge airport by ten A.M. and to meet every plane arriving from Dallas after that time. I know Jacobs well enough to know he followed through.

But Kelly isn't here.

When I did finally close my eyes last night, I saw nightmarish images of Leo Marston raping Livy as a child, forcing her into a conspiracy of silence, raising her in a schizophrenic world of material bounty and spiritual agony, somehow maintaining such a hold on her that she still allowed him sexual access at the age of eighteen. When I pondered the nature of that hold, I felt the dread and horror I felt the first time I saw Roman Polanski's *Chinatown*. The dread came when Faye Dunaway told Jack Nicholson that the young woman she had been hiding was her daughter *and* her sister. The horror arrived with the next line when Jack, reaching for a thread of sanity, asked about her father: "He raped you?" and Dunaway looked up and slowly shook her head. All sanity spun away with this terrible confession. I remember something similar from reading Anais Nin in college, that Nin had seduced her father several times; but Nin had been profligate in her sexual adventures, and besides, she was French. The idea of Livy Marston voluntarily having sex with her father simply would not set in

585

my mind as reality.

"Continental Airlines passenger Penn Cage, please pick up the nearest white courtesy phone."

It takes a moment for my name to sink in, but when it does, my fear escalates to alarm. The caller could be Kelly or Caitlin, but it could also be someone who means me great harm.

"Continental Airlines passenger Penn Cage, please pick up the nearest white courtesy phone."

There's a white phone across the concourse from me, near a bank of pay phones, but I can't make myself walk over to it. What if Portman's people are waiting to snatch whoever walks up to answer that call? On the other hand, what choice do I have? The caller could be Daniel Kelly.

"This is Penn," I say, picking up the phone.

"It's Kelly."

"Jesus, are you in the airport?"

"Yes, but we can't meet. Listen to me, Penn, we only have a few seconds."

Kelly's use of my first name rather than the facetious "boss" brings my inner self to attention. "What is it?"

"Portman's men are in the airport right now. You're going to have to get home on your own. I'm going to divert these guys, but you have to move fast."

"I'm listening."

"My Taurus is parked in sight of the terminal, in the short-term lot, space A-27. The keys are under the mat, and there's a cell phone under the seat. You got that?"

"A-27."

"Right. Next: downstairs, near the baggage

carousels, there's an Infiniti Q45 on display. I left a gun sitting on the left inside lip of the rear bumper."

"Jesus —"

"*Listen.* You get that gun, get to the car, and haul your ass back to Natchez."

"What are you going to do?"

"Buy you some time. But you've got another problem. I haven't been straight with you. Nobody at the company has. They've reported every move you've made to Portman."

My chest goes hollow. "How do you know that?"

"Because *we're* reporting every move you make back to the office. And we don't usually do that. Our CEO is former FBI, you know. And John Portman could swing a lot of corporate business to Argus any time he feels like it."

The implications of Kelly's revelation ricochet through my mind. "Is my family safe?"

"Argus doesn't kill people. Other than in defense of a client, like the other night. But I'd find myself some new security, just to be on the safe side. Local boys maybe. Buddies are good, family's better."

"Kelly . . . how do I know I can trust you?"

"Because you're alive. And because I'm telling you this."

"Why are you telling me?"

A brief silence. "I think it's got something to do with the way you buried your maid. Now, get your ass out of here. Walk fast, but don't run. And if you hear shooting, don't look back."

His order is an exact echo of Stone's. "Kelly —"

"We'll be sharing a Scotch again before you

know it. Move out."

Reluctantly hanging up the phone, I scan the concourse like a tailback picking holes in an offensive line, then start through the crowds at a rapid walk, looking back frequently for signs of pursuit. After clearing the metal detectors, I dodge a golf cart carrying a handicapped woman, then bound down the escalator to the baggage-collection point where Annie and I said goodbye to Caitlin Masters, before we knew who she was.

Parked in the middle of the floor is the Infiniti Q45. Midnight blue. I look around once, then crouch down and reach under the bumper, feeling along the inside lip for Kelly's gun. My fingers collide with something hard, but as I try to close them around it, the gun clatters to the floor. Glancing around at the people waiting for luggage, I drop to my stomach and sweep my hand across the tile, and the gun skitters into my chest.

It's Kelly's Browning Hi-Power.

I jam the pistol into my waistband beneath my shirt and trot past the rental car desks to the glass doors leading to the outdoor parking lot. I've heard no shots or even shouts since my conversation with Kelly, but this actually increases my anxiety. Did he manage to divert whoever was waiting for me? Or is he lying dead beneath a pay phone, the slug from a silenced pistol in his head?

The Taurus is parked sixty yards from the terminal. I can see it from the doors. Exiting the terminal with a group of LSU fraternity guys, I fall in with them until they stop near a Blazer thirty yards from the door, then break for the Taurus at a flat-out sprint. To my surprise, the wind cuts through my jacket with a cold bite. Maybe fall has come to Mississippi at last.

Laying Kelly's pistol on the seat beside me, I retrieve the keys, crank the engine, and force myself to drive normally as I leave the lot. In ten minutes I'm on Highway 61. Natchez lies eighty miles to the north, but much of the road is two-lane blacktop and heavily traveled by log trucks. The trip can be agonizingly slow during the day.

I reach under the seat for the cell phone, switch it on, and dial the Natchez *Examiner*. Caitlin has been handling the transportation of my out-of-town witnesses. Huey Moak and Lester Hinson are scheduled to arrive in Baton Rouge tonight, and we'd planned to have one of the Argus men pick them up.

"Penn?" Caitlin asks, after a minute of hold music.

"Yes. Remember, your phone's tapped."

"What's going on? I've been freaking out here."

"Have you asked any of the Argus guys to pick up the witnesses yet?"

"Not yet. I can call them now."

"Don't."

"Why not?"

"Just don't. Don't even mention it. I'll be there soon, and I'll handle it. Hang tight until then. Stay inside the newspaper building if you can."

"Penn, Kelly was acting a little strange before he left. Like I might not see him again."

You might not. "Things are pretty fluid right now. I'm on my way."

"Listen. An hour ago my receptionist told me I

589

had a call from the editor of the *Rocky Mountain News*. When I got to the phone, he told me he was sending a reporter down to cover your trial, and he wanted to know if the guy could use our office facilities."

"And?"

"He said the reporter's name was Bookbinder. Henry Bookbinder."

Bookbinder. Stone's dead partner. And the *Rocky Mountain News* is based in Denver. I want to scream with joy, but I just say, "Did he say when this reporter would arrive?"

"Only that he'd be here in time to cover the trial. And there's something else."

"What?"

"CNN, Court TV, and some others have been pressing Judge Franklin to allow the trial to be televised."

"Cameras aren't allowed in Mississippi courtrooms."

"I know, but this is a civil case. Apparently if both parties agree, the judge could allow it."

"But why would Leo agree? Portman would tear him a new one if he did."

"CNN and the other networks have been saying publicly that if Marston and Portman have nothing to hide, they should have no problem with cameras. It's a PR nightmare for Portman. It's extortion, basically. I assume you'd have no objection to cameras?"

"Of course not."

"Good, because I already told a CNN reporter that you didn't."

"That's fine. Listen, if that 'reporter' you mentioned shows up, keep him inside the building until I get there."

"I will."

"Thanks. I'll be there before you know it."

As I hang up the phone, I yell, "You tough old son of a bitch!" Though he is probably a thousand miles away right now, Dwight Stone is almost certainly alive. If he can reach Natchez by tomorrow morning without being killed, my slander trial will provide more fireworks than the city has seen in decades. And Leo Marston will be indicted for murder. Only now that prospect does not offer even a shadow of the satisfaction it would have two days ago. If I'm right about Leo being Jenny Doe's father, every judgment I ever made about Livy Marston was wrong. In my mind she has already been transformed from a privileged princess into a tragic figure, a lost girl trying to find her way.

I try to keep the Taurus under the speed limit. A state trooper has haunted this stretch of road for years, handing out tickets like confetti. As the hardwood forest drifts past, I lean back in the seat and force myself to ponder one of the connections that came to me last night in the darkness of the Denver motel. Sometime near dawn a remarkable and frightening idea struck me. A possible link between Del Payton and Leo Marston. Dwight Stone believes Ray Presley randomly chose Del Payton to be murdered. But if my theory of paternal incest is true, there could be a secret link joining the Payton and Marston families, one which Dwight Stone would have known nothing about.

Althea Payton.

Althea is a nurse now. She works in the hospital nursery. But where did she work in the 1960s? Could she have worked for a private physician? A pediatrician perhaps? Is it possible that she noticed some physical evidence of sexual abuse while handling Livy Marston and reported it to the doctor? If she had, what would have been the likely result? In the 1960s sexual abuse of children was grossly underreported, and became public only in the most egregious cases. A man as powerful as Leo Marston would have had little to fear from a doctor, especially if the evidence was equivocal. And even if it wasn't, would the doctor have the nerve to confront Leo? To bring in the police to investigate the district attorney?

Of course, Leo Marston would never have been to the pediatrician's office. He wouldn't have taken time out of his day to carry his daughter to the doctor. Maude would have done that. A pediatrician might have been more comfortable bringing certain suspicious symptoms to the mother's attention. But if he wasn't, a compassionate nurse certainly might have. Mother to mother. I can see Althea Payton doing that. Pulling Maude aside and pointing out a couple of things. In the interest of the child.

What would Leo have done if Maude had confronted him with such a thing? Denied it, of course. Deny, deny, deny. Then he would have demanded to know the source of Maude's suspicions. If she told him it was Althea, what then? Killing Althea would certainly silence her. But it was Del who had died, not his wife. Perhaps Leo had initially taken no action. But later, when the necessity arose to kill a black man to make an example for the Georgia carpet magnate, had Leo chosen Del Payton out of some perverse desire to strike back at the woman who had threatened him? A wild scenario perhaps. But Leo long ago demonstrated his penchant for holding grudges. Whatever the case, unraveling the truth of this low tragedy will be a nightmare for everyone involved. The idea of confronting Livy with my deductions leaves me numb.

A few miles before I reach town, I call Sam Jacobs at work, tell him my family might be in danger, and ask for his help. Jacobs is thirty-eight years old, with a wife and two kids, but by the time I arrive at the Prentiss Motel, he is parked outside with a .357 Magnum sitting on the front seat of his Hummer. When I see that, I know I am looking at the Jewish boy who discovered the list of Klansmen and White Citizens' Council members in his father's attic with me twenty-five years ago.

With Sam beside me, I inform the three remaining Argus security men that their services are no longer required. It's an awkward moment, but they say little and leave the motel with expressionless faces. I'm tempted to tell them to pass a message to their boss when they get back to Houston — that he should look forward to a multimillion-dollar lawsuit — but I don't want to do anything that might hurt Daniel Kelly in the future.

My parents are stunned by my action, but as soon as I explain what Kelly told me, my father gets on the phone and speaks to two patients of his — avid hunters — and they promise to arrive within the hour, loaded for bear. Dad then makes my day by informing me that while I was in Crested Butte, he finally persuaded Betty Lou Beckham to take the witness stand tomorrow and tell the jury that she saw Ray Presley in the Triton Battery parking lot only seconds after Del Payton died.

What we need now is a new place to stay, a secure location, and it's my mother who solves this problem. When our house burned, a friend of Mom's offered us rooms in her bed-and-breakfast, which occupies the slave quarters of her home, Aquitaine, a massive Greek Revival mansion completed in 1843. Not wanting to impose on her friend's hospitality, Mom declined. But these are special circumstances, and the fall Pilgrimage has just ended, so our staying there won't cost the chatelaine her peak season fees. One phone call secures us lodgings in the slave quarters of Aquitaine.

Since the fire destroyed most of our things, moving from the motel to the mansion is relatively painless. The two-story slave quarters was sited across the ornamental gardens from the main house, which occupies most of a city block on the north side of town, near Stanton Hall. Once we're settled in our rooms, I order out for pizza and spend the forty-minute wait playing with Annie in the garden. She dances around the rim of the central fountain like a gymnast, oblivious to the anxiety mounting in the adults as the hours tick down to tomorrow's trial. That she does not pick up on our feelings shows me just how far she has come in her journey from the hypersensitive state that followed Sarah's death.

After devouring my share of pizza, I deal with the messages that came in while I was in Crested Butte. Althea Payton called several times, but the most persistent caller was Ike Ransom. Dad says Ike is desperate to talk to me, and that he sounded both angry and afraid during their conservations. I call Althea and give her an encouraging update, editing the violence into a less frightening picture. Nevertheless, she tells me that Del Jr. wants to help me any way he can, and that she's going to send him over to "help keep the no-goods away" until the trial. In less than an hour, Del arrives carrying a sawed-off shotgun, and takes up a post on the balcony of the slave quarters, overlooking the street.

Which leaves me Ike.

I am not particularly anxious to talk to him after the way he acted at Ruby's funeral. Whatever the source of his hatred for Leo Marston, it has pushed him into unstable territory. Ike clearly has both a drug and alcohol problem, and since he is unwilling or unable to provide me with any facts that will help prove Marston guilty of murder in a court of law, I see no urgent need to call him.

I call Ray Presley instead. Dwight Stone's revelation that Marston gave up Presley to the Feds as part of his deal with J. Edgar Hoover was music to my "lawyer's ear." Presley considers Leo Marston his friend, and loyalty is the supreme virtue to men of Presley's ilk. But if Ray was to learn that the five years he spent in Parchman were courtesy of Leo Marston, his attitude toward the judge might change fast. But whether he will or not remains a mystery, because Presley doesn't answer his phone.

I am working up the courage to call Livy when the telephone rings in my room. Somehow Ike Ransom has discovered that we've moved to Aquitaine, and he wants to see me. He got my phone number from the main house. I start to beg off, but he stops me cold. He has, he says, what we've been looking for since day one. Hard evidence linking Leo Marston to Payton's murder. He will say no more, and he refuses to come to the B&B. He insists on a face-to-face meeting and says I must come alone. When I ask why, he tells me that no one can know he is the source for what he's about to tell me.

"Where do you want to meet?" I ask, recalling the feeling of being shot at in the warehouse by the river and not liking it too much.

"You're three blocks away from it," he replies.

"Where are you talking about?"

"The old pecan-shelling plant."

An image of a hulking brown brick building where I sold the pecans I collected as a boy comes into my mind. It is set right on the edge of the bluff, and as Ike said, it's only three blocks west of where I am now.

"What about the surveillance on me here?"

"Slip out the back alley on foot. They lookin' for that BMW. Or you could send your Jew buddy out first in the BMW, then come on in that Maxima your mama got."

It's nearly dark, and I want to refuse, largely out of fear. But Ike is offering something of which I have precious little: hard evidence. Dwight Stone's testimony could be powerful, but without his FBI files to back him up, it will be his word against Marston's (and Portman's too, if the FBI director decides to honor my subpoena). Hard evidence is worth a three-block trip.

"When?" I ask.

"Thirty minutes. The place is an equipment-storage yard now. Drive around to the left side of the building. The chain on the gate'll be cut."

"I'll be there."

I hang up and speak to Sam Jacobs on the balcony, and Sam declares himself ready to draw off the surveillance long enough to get me clear of Aquitaine.

The old pecan-shelling plant stands on prime real estate in Natchez's old warehouse district, a sort of no-man's-land between the town proper and a sleepy residential area filled with Victorian gems. It has an unobstructed view of the river, and one day will probably be the site of a luxury hotel. At the moment it is an eerily lighted compound surrounded by a high fence and razor wire, with the rigid arms of great cranes jutting against the night sky.

As Ike promised, the chained gate on the left side of the building has been cut open. I nose the Maxima through it without getting out, and negotiate my way through backhoes, draglines, and D-9 bulldozers parked like Patton's army marshaling for a campaign. I can't see the river, but forty yards to my left, the bluff drops away to a vast dark sky, leaving the impression that I'm driving along the edge of a mountain.

Out of the blackness to my right, a pink and blue light bar strobes like a carnival, then vanishes. I slow nearly to a stop, trying to place the location of Ike's cruiser.

There.

I turn right and idle toward the main building. As the black silhouette looms over me, the lights flash again. In their light I see that Ike has opened the old truck door of the plant and is parked in it. As I approach, he starts his engine and pulls forward, leaving me plenty of room to pull inside the building. I park the Maxima beside his cruiser and shut off the engine. Kelly's Browning is in the glove box, but I don't want to cause any kind of reflex reaction in Ike, especially if he's wired on speed.

Ike is standing by my passenger door, between his car and mine. I get out and walk around the trunk of the Maxima, extending my hand to shake his.

"What have you got, Ike?"

He holds out his hand, but instead of shaking he grabs my wrist and jerks me to my knees on the concrete floor. As I try to look up, something slams into the top of my skull. The blow drives every thought out of my head, leaving only white noise. My first coherent perception is of something cold and hard pressed against my hairline.

"That's a gun," he says. "Don't fucking move."

The terror generated by the gun barrel is absolute, paralyzing. If any muscle in my body is moving, it's the sphincter of my bladder. "Ike? What the hell are you doing?"

His breath is ragged above me, like a sick animal's.

"*Ike?*"

"Where the fuck you been?" he shouts, and the reek of cheap whiskey rolls over me like steam. "Answer me, goddamn it!"

"Ike, what's wrong? Let's talk face to face, man."

"I said, where the fuck have you been?"

"Colorado! I went back to see Stone."

"I knew it! You sneaky son of a bitch. You been holding out the whole time. What that motherfucker tell you?"

"He told me what we want to know. He told me what happened here in sixty-eight. I've got Marston nailed, man."

He twists around me and jabs the gun into my cervical spine. "What did Stone say happened?"

"He told me why Marston wanted Payton dead. It was a land deal . . . Marston stood to make a lot of money off some land, but he had to make an example of a black union worker first. He paid Presley to do it for him. Presley chose Payton."

"Bullshit!" Another fog of whiskey blows over me.

"What do you mean, bullshit?"

"Don't lie to me, goddamn it! *Don't you lie!*"

He jerks back the slide on the gun, and everything inside me goes into free fall. My thoughts, my courage, my blood pressure. "Ike, please . . . I've got a little girl, man. Just tell me what the problem is and —"

The gun barrel rakes around my neck, under my jaw, up my right cheek to my eye. All I can see now is the taut belly of Ike's brown uniform.

"Get up," he says coldly. "Get up!"

The gun barrel stays screwed into my eye socket as I rise, but my terror abates slightly. The prospect of dying on my knees was as debasing as it was frightening.

Ike's gun is shaking. As he pulls it out of my eye socket and lays the barrel against my forehead, I see his eyes, bloodshot and jerky, the eyes of a man in agony.

"You a goddamn liar," he says. "I shoulda known a white boy wouldn't go against his own in the end. You been dicking that Marston bitch all along. You in with 'em all the way." He shakes his head as though at his own stupidity. "Setting up to get the nigger. Like always."

"Ike, I have no idea what you're talking about. I'm setting up to get Leo Marston, and I'm going to use Ray Presley to do it. If I can find him. Dwight Stone and Ray Presley are going to send that bastard to the extermination chamber at Parchman."

But Ike isn't listening. At the word Presley, his eyes glaze over with blind rage. "That fucking Presley . . . he told you, didn't he?"

"Told me what? Talk to me, Ike! Something's been eating you up since we started this. What is it?"

He bites his lip and presses the gun harder against my forehead. Then suddenly he lets it drop to his side. "I didn't know what I was doing, man," he says in a desolate voice. "Hadn't been back in the World but three months. Couldn't get no kind of job. I applied with the police three times. They wouldn't even talk to me. Had all the *Negro* cops they needed, they said. Didn't have but three. Same with the sheriff. I'd done more police work in Saigon than them motherfuckers done their whole lives, and they wouldn't even give me a *chance.*"

I'm more confused than I've been since the start of this mess, but I'm not about to interrupt him.

"What else could I do, man?" he almost wails. "Wasn't gonna go on no welfare! I had to deal." He slaps at a mosquito on his sweating face. "Presley got me on a traffic stop. Just speeding, but he pulled his weapon and made me open my trunk. He found half a pound of white lady. Illegal search if I ever saw one, but you think that mattered back then? In them days he coulda sent me to Parchman for fifty years behind that much heroin."

A dark perception is blooming in the corner of my brain. A fetid, cloying orchid of a thought. "What did he want you to do, Ike?"

"Don't play that shit! You already know!"

The pain in his eyes is terrible to behold. I hold up both my hands. "I know what you tell me. That's all."

"What you *think* happened, man? Motherfucker put it to me right there on the side of the road. Said he had somebody needed killing. Said I'd been killing for Uncle for two years, what was one more? *I* knew what one more was. But what could I do, man? He had me. I didn't want to die on Parchman Farm. Presley took my dope and told me if I tried to back out, he'd plant it on me and bust me all over again."

"He wanted you to kill Del Payton?"

"What you think I been saying?"

The nausea of a roller coaster that hurtles in only one direction — down — sweeps over me as the whole sick plan falls together in my head.

"You asked Presley to get the C-4, didn't you?"

He stares at me with strangled emotion. "Presley wanted the car blown up. I didn't know nothing about dynamite, but I'd worked with C-4 in 'Nam. I told him if he could get me some plastic, I could do the job."

"Jesus, Ike. Did you know Del?"

"No. He was ten years older than me. Grew up out to Pine Ridge."

"Did you know about his civil rights work?"

"Hell, no. I thought he was dicking a white woman or something. Didn't matter, though. I was so fucked up, I didn't know nothing 'bout nothing."

"Ike, listen . . . what you did was terrible, but —"

"Don't you judge me!" he cries, the whites of his eyes making him look wild in the dark. "Don't you cast no stone! I been torturing myself thirty years. After I realized the work Del was doing, I just about went crazy. The whole town was marching for him. I wanted to scream out what I'd done, what Presley made me do. But I didn't have the guts. I couldn't face my own sin."

The diabolical irony of Ray Presley's plan leaves me cold. He actually blackmailed a black man into committing a civil rights murder. He and Marston must have laughed for weeks over that one. They've been laughing for thirty years.

"Does Stone know this? Or does he really believe Presley killed Payton?"

"Stone? 'Course he knows. He came to see me

602

back then. He had the whole thing dogged out."

"Why didn't he arrest you? Why didn't he tell me about you?"

Ike seems only partially aware of what I'm saying. "I don't know why. He was different, I guess."

"Why didn't you tell me all this at the start?"

"What could I tell you, man? I knew what I'd done. I knew about Presley. But that's all. I knew *what* happened, but I didn't know *why*. And that was the only way you were gonna get Marston."

"But how did you know Marston was involved? Did Presley tell you?"

"He didn't tell me shit. A year after it happened, somebody called me on the phone. Wouldn't say nothing. I was about to hang up when they started playing this tape. It was Marston and Presley, talking about Del being killed. Talking about *me*. I figured it was Stone. Had to be."

Stone must have called and played Ike Ransom the copy he'd made of the evidence tape he'd sent to J. Edgar Hoover. And his reason, I suspect, was a dark one. "Thirty years, Ike. Thirty *years*. Couldn't you figure a way to trade what you knew for immunity, or —"

"*Who was I gonna go to, man?*" Spittle flies from his mouth. "The FBI *already knew* what had gone down. And they didn't arrest nobody! A few years later I tried to find Stone, but the Bureau had fired his ass. Portman was a U.S. attorney, and I knew better than to trust that Yankee piece of shit. And Marston was on the state supreme court! What's a drunk nigger cop from Mississippi gonna do against people swingin' that kind of weight? You tell me."

"Then why tell me? Why try at all after thirty years?"

His broad shoulders sag as though under a great weight, and he speaks toward the floor. "I didn't have no choice. It ate at me so long . . . I thought it would get better over time, but it got worse. A few months back, I found myself going to church. Not wanting to . . . *needing* to. You know? Being raised Catholic, I guess. Don't matter if you stop goin'. You can give up on God, but it don't matter. 'Cause He don't give up on you."

The tortured paths this man has pushed himself down are beyond any imagining. "Ike, you came to me knowing you could go to jail for the rest of your life. That you could be executed. That means a lot. And I've figured a way to turn Presley against Marston. If you'll get on that witness stand to-morrow and tell the truth —"

"Is Stone gonna testify?"

"Yes."

"Is he here in town?"

This isn't the time to lie. "No. But he's on his way here. Some people tried to kill us last night. Portman's guys probably. We got split up."

Ike starts pacing back and forth, patting the Sig-Sauer against his leg. "But he's alive?"

"You can't let your decision be based on what Stone does. This thing's eating you alive because you know you did wrong. Terrible wrong. It's got nothing to do with you or me. You owe it to Althea Payton to tell the truth. You owe it to Del. You owe it to yourself, man."

"I don't owe nobody but God!" The Sig jerks up

again, aimed at my chest now. "You don't know how close it's been. At first I thought maybe you could nail Marston without me having to go down. But that was stupid. Crazy. The closer you got to the truth, the more I saw I was gonna have to pay the piper, no matter what. One night I got so drunk I thought about killing you, just to stop it all. That night you left the newspaper by yourself . . . I was right behind you."

My heart feels like a ball of lead.

"I couldn't do it, though. Part of me just wanted to pay, I guess. Father Tom says you got to. But I can't go to Parchman Farm. I done sent too many brothers there myself. I can't die in them cotton fields up there."

"You won't have to, Ike. CNN will be covering that trial tomorrow. You get on the stand and tell the story you just told me, you'll have Johnnie Cochran down here begging to defend you. What you did was wrong, but you're the least guilty of the three by far. I think Stone believed that too. You know what the right thing is. That's why you came to me in the first place."

He lets his gun fall again, then half turns from me and murmurs in the dark. "I started out all right. But I turned off somewhere. That day my shoulder got hurt, everything started going down."

He holsters his pistol and walks past me, toward the wide door, and looks out at the luminous clouds scudding over the river. Beyond him I can see a few stars, infinitely small on this first cool night. He turns back to face me, but since he's silhouetted in the door, I cannot see his features.

"I'll do it," he says. "Father Tom gonna think

605

I'm the best man he ever knew. But he gonna be the only one. Every black man, woman, and child in this country gonna curse my name."

He half turns again, and a dim shaft of light illuminates his face. In eight years as a prosecutor, I never saw a man look so lost.

Ike opens his mouth to say something, then flings an arm out as though to grab me, but he can't because he's flying backward, snatched like a puppet on a string. Before he hits the floor, a peal of thunder booms through the warehouse.

"Ike!"

He doesn't answer. He's lying facedown on the dirty floor, blood pumping from a fist-sized hole where his left shoulder blade used to be.

CHAPTER 37

I run to Ike, then drop to the cement floor as a second shot booms through the building. A third punches through the front and rear windshields of the Maxima, which is parked two feet to my left, and the concussion of the gun echoes around the old structure for three or four seconds.

The shooter is inside the building.

Inside, and probably at the front, shooting across the open floor. But he must not have a night-vision scope. He shot Ike as the deputy framed himself against the lighter background of the open loading door. Now that we're flat on the floor, his shots are far off the mark. Ike's face is less than six inches from mine, his eyes wide and glassy, like those of a wounded deer.

"Ike," I whisper. "Can you hear me?"

His eyelids blink once, slowly, but he doesn't speak. The man is dying before my eyes.

I need a gun.

Kelly's Browning is in the glove box of the Maxima, but I'm not about to try to reach it. If I rise off the ground, I will silhouette myself against the open door, just as Ike did. If I had walked to that door first, I would be dying now.

"Ike, I need your gun."

As I reach down to his holster, something cracks through the air less than a foot above us, and the report that follows seems trivial compared to that supersonic passage of metal. Fighting down panic, I try to wrest the Sig-Sauer from Ike's holster, but it won't budge. He must have snapped the strap when he holstered it. Unsnapping it by touch, I yank out the Sig and take the safety off. As I aim it across Ike's back, a bullet crashes into his body, knocking us both a foot across the cold floor.

He doesn't make a sound.

Then, like a rising wind, a wail of inhuman agony escapes his throat. I shove my arm across his waist and fire three quick rounds into the darkness at the front of the building. Something sharp pricks the skin of my forearm.

Bone splinters.

The last shot smashed Ike's pelvis. He screams again, the sound sickeningly reminiscent of those Sarah made when the narcotics began to lose their race to keep up with the pain of her bone lesions.

Who is shooting at us? An anonymous sniper, like the one who shot at me on the levee that night? The one Kelly killed? With a strange rush of clarity I realize that the levee sniper wasn't shooting only at me, as I'd thought at the time. What did Ike say that night? *How you know he was shooting at you?* Ike had known from the beginning that he carried knowledge people would kill him for. As I cower behind his body, a voice calls out from the other end of the building.

"Give it up! The nigger's dead!"

Before I can process these words, another

608

truncated wail bursts from Ike's lungs. *"Brrrraaaaaaah!"*

My instinct is to run for the door, run until my legs buckle beneath me. But that would be suicide. The moment I rise, I'll make myself a target. I could probably crawl out . . . but Ike isn't dead yet. I can't leave him. My next thought, born from rage, is to stand up and charge the darkness that shields the sniper, emptying Ike's automatic as I run.

With a defiant yell, I fire off two more rounds, then jump to my feet and grab Ike's legs. Two shots boom through the building as I drag him facedown and screaming behind his cruiser, but the bullets crack past without finding flesh or bone.

Kneeling beside him, I break the most fundamental rule of first-aid by turning him over onto his back. At this point it can't matter much. His eyes are still open. His jaw is moving, but no sounds come from his throat. I lean over his mouth.

"Brrr —" he groans.

I take one of his hands in mine and squeeze the cold flesh. "Ike? What are you saying?"

"Press me."

He must think I can stop the bleeding. "Where? Your shoulder?"

"Pressleee . . ."

Press lee? *The nigger's dead —*

Son of a bitch. No sniper hired by John Portman would talk that way. He wouldn't talk at all. The man at the other end of this building is Raymond Aucoin Presley. The trial is tomorrow, and Presley has no intention of being indicted for murder.

That's why he wasn't at his trailer when I called earlier. He's been following Ike around, laying for a shot.

"Ray!" I yell at the top of my voice. "Stop shooting! I need to talk to you!"

Both windshields of Ike's cruiser star into chaos as safety glass rattles across the floor.

"What you got to say I want to hear?" comes the voice I recognize so easily now. *"You want it in the head or the heart?"*

I will live or die by my actions in the next minute. "Listen to me, Ray! You want to hear this!"

"I want to hear you choke on your own blood!"

Every hair on my body is standing erect. Presley isn't nearly as far away as he was a moment ago. He's moving up for a kill shot. Crawling to the left side of the cruiser, I fire two quick rounds into the dark, then dart back to avoid return fire aimed at my muzzle flash.

"Not even close, boy."

The tire beside my head explodes into ragged strips of rubber as Presley's next shot reverberates through the building. When the echo dies, I call: "You want to know who sent you to Parchman, Ray? I think you'll be surprised."

He fires again, smashing up a divot of cement beside Ike's head.

"Parchman, Ray! Didn't you ever wonder who ratted you out?"

Silence. Then: *"Talk fast, boy, I'm getting close!"*

He is close. It takes every bit of nerve I possess to hold my ground. "It was Marston, Ray! Leo sent you up! Stone solved the murder, but Hoover didn't want Leo going down for it. Leo's old man had too much political clout. Hoover cut a deal to protect him, but he said you had to go down for shooting at Stone and Portman on the highway. It was Leo who gave you up!"

"That's bullshit!" For the first time the voice has come from more or less the same place.

"Stone said Marston didn't even hesitate! He fed the state police details of your drug business so they could catch you in the act. That's why Stone was at the bust!"

"You lying piece of shit! You're just trying to save your own ass!"

He's buying it. "Leo didn't give a shit about you, Ray. How else do you think they got you? You must have had a lot of time to think about it. Five years, man!"

More silence.

"Ray?"

No sound at all. Nothing but the slow ticking of the two cars, barely audible through the ringing in my ears. The son of a bitch is probably moving up to kill me, and if I don't move, I'm going to die. But if I break for the door, I'm framing myself for a shot. Shivering against Ike's body, I realize that I no longer hear his breathing. His eyes are still open, but they are fixed and dilated.

Ike the Spike is dead.

"Ray . . . ? Talk to me, Ray!"

Nothing.

The loading door beckons. But as I gather my legs beneath me, Ruby Flowers's voice sounds in my head, an echo from childhood. *"Broad is the gate that leads to destruction, but narrow the way*

611

that leads to salvation. . . . "

To my left — in what must be a corner of the old shelling plant — is a pool of darkness so black it could be the bottom of the Marianas Trench. My legs are tensed beneath me like steel springs. Gripping Ike's gun in my right hand, I launch myself low and hard toward that black hole. As the darkness envelops me, a stroke of lightning flashes in my brain, and I know no more.

Consciousness returns like blood to a sleeping limb.

Pain is the first sensation.

Then light.

The pain radiates from my forehead. The light is faint but real, thirty yards away, illuminating a parked police car. Not a police car. A sheriff's cruiser.

Ike's cruiser.

I roll over slowly and feel along the cold cement for Ike's gun. My right wrist bangs into something cold and immovable. I touch it with my hand and feel along it. A steel rail. It's one loading arm of a forklift. That's what I slammed into when I ran into the pool of darkness. A goddamn forklift.

The gun is underneath the fork.

Closing my hand around its butt, I get to my feet and walk toward Ike's car. Strangely, I am unafraid. Unafraid because I know I'm alone. If I wasn't, I would be dead. Ray finally believed what I was telling him, and once he did, his priorities changed.

At the edge of the darkness I look at my watch. Eight forty-five. I met Ike around eight. Ray started shooting about ten minutes after we started talking. I don't know how long the shooting lasted, but he's had at least twenty minutes to reach the target I offered up to him to save myself.

Ike's body lies behind his cruiser, where I dragged it in that last furious rush. His eyes are open but unseeing. I feel his carotid artery to be sure, then hold my hand over his mouth.

Nothing.

Climbing into the Maxima, I start the engine and dial Tuscany on the cell phone. While it rings, I floor the accelerator and make a wide squealing turn on the cement floor, then roar through the main loading door. The phone clicks as I hit Canal Street and nearly skid into the curb on the other side.

"Liv Marston," says a clipped voice. "If you're a reporter —"

"It's Penn."

"What do you want?" The voice hasn't warmed even one degree.

"I know you don't want to listen to me, but you've got to."

"Is it about the trial?"

"No. You've got to get out of the house."

"What?"

I hesitate before I reply. Some savage part of me wants to get Livy away and leave her father to face the retribution of his past. Poetic justice, if ever there was any. But I can't do it.

"Ray Presley's on his way to Tuscany. He's going to try to kill your father. He could already be at your house. Or on the grounds somewhere."

Silence.

"Did you hear me, Livy?"

"I heard you."

"Tell your father to call the police. They'll send an army out there to protect him."

"Are we done now?"

Are we done? "Did you understand what I just told you? Presley is coming there to *kill* your father."

"I hope he comes here."

"You what?"

A police car tears around the corner of Main and Canal, lights flashing, heading in the direction of the pecan-shelling plant. In fifteen minutes every cop and deputy in this town will be combing the downtown streets.

"You're playing in things you don't understand, Penn. I tried to tell you the other day. You were a fool to involve yourself in any of this."

"I understand more than you think. I know now why you did the things you did in the past. The choices you made."

"Such as?"

"I don't want to discuss it on the phone. It has to be face to face."

"We don't have anything to say to each other."

"I'm begging you, Livy. Meet me one last time. For the sake of whatever it is that's bound us together all these years. If you will, I think it will change both our lives. Maybe forever."

This time she hesitates. "It's not about the trial?"

"I don't give a damn what happens at the trial. Name a place. Anywhere, I don't care. I'll even come to Tuscany."

"No. Jewish Hill."

"Jewish Hill?" Yet another landmark from our past. "In the cemetery?"

"That's about as private as you can get."

"Isn't it locked at night?"

"Park at the foot of the hill. By the wall. It's not like we've never done it before."

"Do you still have the gun you had in the motel?"

"Yes."

"Bring it. And drive fast leaving the house."

"What time?"

"I'm five minutes from the cemetery. Leave now."

"All right."

Livy's borrowed Fiat is parked at the foot of Jewish Hill when I arrive, next to the low stone wall of the city cemetery. She got here first because I took a wide circle through town to avoid the police. I park behind the Fiat and shove Ike's pistol into my waistband, then get out and walk up to the Spyder.

Livy is not in the car.

To my left, across Cemetery Road, stands the dark silhouette of Weymouth Hall, an antebellum mansion that marks the two-hundred-foot drop to the river, its widow's walk silhouetted against the stars. To my right is the low wall and the nearly vertical slope of Jewish Hill. One mile south along the bluff, the police are taping off the pecan plant as a crime scene.

I climb the wall and push through the shrubbery, then dig my hands into the face of the hill and begin climbing. As I near the top, a ghostly figure appears at the edge, looking down at me.

It's Livy. Her hair is flying behind her, caught in the wind blowing up the bluff from the river. She's wearing a white blouse, a fitted jacket, and slacks tapered to the ankles. She bends and catches my hands, then pulls me up to the flat plateau of gravestones, statuary, and mausoleums.

"Did you call the police?" I ask.

She brushes a strand of hair from her eyes. "Daddy called some off-duty cops. They got there before I left."

"How did he react when you told him Presley might be coming to kill him?"

"What do you want, Penn?"

"It scared him to death, didn't it? Livy, your father gave the cops what they needed to send Presley to Parchman when we were kids."

"Really?" A hard smile tightens her mouth. "Good."

"What I don't understand is why my call didn't scare *you*."

She walks past me to the edge of the hill. The lights of Vidalia, Louisiana, a mile away, outline her like another marble angel among the stones. "Why are we here, Penn? What's the big mystery?"

"You are."

She turns back to me. "I'm the mystery?"

"You're the mystery of my life. But I understand you now."

Something flickers in her eyes. I can't tell if she's intrigued or afraid. "Do you? Enlighten me, then."

"I know who Jenny's father is."

Even in the dark I can tell she has gone rigid. She

turns away from me, then back, her chin held high. "How do you know? Did he tell you?"

"Tell me? God, no. He hates me. Why would he tell me?"

She shakes her head. "I can't believe this. I can't believe you know this. It's so pathetic."

"I know it's bad, Livy. I realize I can't ever understand what it was — what it is — to be in your position."

"How could you possibly know unless he told you? No one knows. *He* doesn't even know. Not as far as I —"

"Your father doesn't know about Jenny?"

She blinks. "My father? Of course he knows. But he doesn't know, you know . . . who the father is."

My mind reels, trying to parse the semantics. "Livy, who is Jenny's father?"

"You just said you knew."

"Pretend I don't."

Suspicion now. "If you don't know, I'm not telling you."

"Livy —"

"Who do you think it is?"

I take a step toward her, but she moves back, nearer the edge of the hill. As though she knows what I am about to say. As though she could fly from the edge of the hill if I dare speak the truth. "I think Jenny's father is your father."

She stares at me like she hasn't heard correctly. Then she closes her eyes and lowers her head into her hands.

"You don't have to say anything," I say softly. "You —"

"Shut up, Penn. Please just shut up. You might

say something even more asinine than you already have."

"What?"

She takes her hands away from her face. She is not crying. She is staring at me with what looks like morbid curiosity. "Did you actually think my father raped me?"

Her voice is strong, but that could be the strength of denial, not truth. "I still think so. What I can't figure out is how he forced you when you were eighteen."

A bitter laugh. "That's easy. He didn't. Christ. First you accuse my father of murder. Now incest? Could you possibly be more sick?" She holds her palms out to me. "Have I done something to deserve this?"

"I'll tell you what you did to deserve this. You told me you wanted a future together and then disappeared. You let your father try to destroy mine without lifting a finger to stop him, and went on with your life as though none of it ever happened."

"My God, Penn. We were just kids! Haven't you grown up yet? After twenty years?"

"Have you? You've been chasing me around like the lost love of your life, trying to relive our past, pulling me into bed every chance you got. Was all that heat manufactured to distract me from going after your father?"

At last she gives me an unguarded look. "No."

"If my incest idea is so off the mark, why did you treat that poor girl like you did? You gave Jenny up for adoption, which is understandable. But she had a pretty shitty life, and when she showed up at your door looking for a little information, maybe

618

an explanation, you treated her like dirt. And your father did worse."

"How *dare* you judge me. You don't know anything about it."

"You're right. Why is that?"

Her eyes flash in the dark. "You want an explanation? All right. Remember the week after graduation? The week you went touring battlefields with your dad?"

"I remember."

"I had two weeks before Radcliffe. The senior parties were still going on. Everybody was getting as drunk as they had been before graduation, maybe drunker. Someone from South Natchez threw a party on one of the sandbars past the paper mill. It was wild. Trucks driving all over the sand, people shooting guns, skinny-dipping. One car even went into the river. You were out of town, so guys were hitting on me all night. Ray Presley was there, watching me for Daddy, like he always did. At some point the police showed up. Ray put me in his truck and talked to one of the cops, got me past the roadblock."

She turns toward the river, and the wind carries much of her voice away. "I was as drunk as I'd ever been, and I decided to play a little game. Ray was always watching me, making me nervous, hanging around like some malevolent shadow. And I'd always heard these stories . . . how he'd killed people, been in prison, other stuff. Anyway, I started teasing him. I asked if he'd ever killed anybody, and he admitted that he had. I asked him what it was like, what prison was like, stuff like that. Then I told him I'd always heard this story about how he had the biggest thing in town. You know, his equipment. He kept driving, but I could see I was getting to him, he was gripping the wheel so hard. So I said, Hey, is it true or what? And he said, Only one way to find out. It was like a dare, you know? So I said, Okay, let's see it."

The knowledge of what's coming hits me like a blow to the solar plexus. "Livy . . ."

She holds up her hand; she means to tell this story no matter what. "So, he unbuckles his belt and takes it out. While he's driving. And it was. I mean, the stories were true. I know this sounds gross — Ray Presley, right? What a creep. But he was only thirty-five or so then. Younger than we are now. So, I took the dare further. I thought I'd drive him a little crazier, to get back at him for all the times he'd ogled me. It was the stupidest thing I ever did. He pulled off Lower Woodville Road, right into the woods. I knew then things were slipping out of control, but I wasn't sure how to get out of it. I figured, you know, just be calm, let him kiss me, touch him enough to get it over with and get out of there. The next thing I knew my dress was around my chest and he was raping me."

"You don't have to tell me this."

She turns to me, her eyes bright with pooled tears. "A little too real for you? I think I passed out the first time. I woke up later and it was happening again, outside the truck. I started screaming, so he stuffed my dress into my mouth. It was like being simultaneously strangled and bludgeoned to death from the inside. When it was over, we got back into the truck, but he wouldn't leave. He was completely freaked out. I think he thought my father

620

was going to kill him, so he just sat there, trying to figure out what to do. He sat there for twenty minutes with me screaming at him, trying to get out and run, going crazy. Then he did it *again*. I knew then that he was crazy. I mean, three times in an hour, that's just not normal for a thirty-five-year-old man."

The déjà vu is almost too powerful to endure. Livy and I once sat in the dark while she told me the story of being raped by a high school football player during a date. Twenty years later, only the context has changed.

"I'm sorry. I had no idea. I couldn't even have imagined that."

"But isn't it such a touching little story?" Her tears are rolling down her cheeks now. "Ray Presley, proud father of my first and only child."

I want to hold her, but I think she would probably hit me if I touched her.

"I couldn't believe I even conceived," she says, wiping her face. "But I did. And *you* think I should have welcomed Jenny with open arms." She modulates her voice into a hysterical exaggeration of a TV mom: *"Hello, sweetheart! Where have you been all my life? Give Mama a hug!"*

The delirium in her voice sends chills through me. "Jenny had nothing to do with what Presley did to you that night."

"She *is* that night to me! Don't you get that? Do you think I could ever look at her without reliving every second of those rapes?"

I shrug and stay silent. I am not a woman. I can't know. "When I told you Presley was coming to kill your father, you said you hoped he would come."

"I'd kill him in a minute," she says in a flat voice. "Like stepping on a cockroach."

"I knew it was something like this. Something dark."

"Dark? The whole thing is so *Sally Jessy Raphael* it makes me want to vomit."

"You didn't tell your father Presley had raped you?"

A shadow of shame crosses her face. "No. I'd started the whole thing, hadn't I? I suppose I could have lied and said he attacked me out of the blue, but my father is pretty hard to lie to. He's scary that way. He sees dishonesty in people."

"Maybe because he's so dishonest himself."

"Don't, Penn."

"But he knew you were pregnant. Eventually, I mean."

She nods. "My sister told him. She'd gotten pregnant three years before, and Daddy made her get an abortion. It really messed her up. Our great Catholic parents practically forcing her to terminate her pregnancy. You'd think that when I turned up pregnant, she would have done all she could to help me hide it. But she'd felt inferior to me her whole life. I was the special one, the adored one. She just had to tell them that I'd screwed up as badly as she had."

"Livy, why in God's name did you have the baby? Under the circumstances —"

"Under the circumstances, I wasn't thinking rationally, okay? After the rape I was so upset, I went to Radcliffe a week early. Two months later, when I found out for sure I was pregnant, I thought about terminating it. But then my sister blabbed, and the next thing I knew, my father was in Cambridge trying to force me to have an abortion. You know how he and I are. The simple fact that he tried to force me was enough to make me refuse, especially after all the lip service he'd paid to Catholic dogma. But more than that, the pregnancy gave me a chance I'd never had before. An absolute excuse to break the pattern laid out for me before I was born. I didn't know what I wanted, but I knew I didn't want to spend four years at Ole Miss in a sorority full of girls majoring in fashion merchandising and looking for husbands."

"Thanks for telling me in time to change my plans."

A momentary look of penitence. "I'm sorry about that. I never told you to go there."

"No. You just talked about how wonderful it would be if we were both there. What I can't believe is that you let your parents think I had gotten you pregnant. You did, didn't you? That's the root of all the pain that came after."

She takes a deep breath and sighs. "I suppose I did."

"Suppose, nothing. You didn't have the guts to admit you teased Ray Presley into raping you, but you didn't mind letting me take the blame for knocking you up."

"Penn, you don't understand. When Ray took me home that night, he threatened me. He said that if I told my father what had happened, he'd kill my mother."

"Your mother?"

"He knew I wouldn't care about myself. Ray said my father might kill him for hurting me, but

623

he'd thank him for killing my mother. And on some level . . . I felt like he might be right. Daddy was such a bastard to Mother back then."

A wave of shame rolls through me, shame for thinking Livy was so selfish and shallow that she would let my family pay for something that was someone else's fault without any excuse. But the shame passes quickly. Livy is twisting the truth even now.

"You're lying. I don't mean about the threat. I'm sure Presley threatened you. But you've *always* cared about yourself. More than anything else. And I don't think you would have bought Ray's threat, not for long. He was scared shitless of your father. He still is, in some ways. And when Leo decided to go after my father out of revenge, you could have spoken up. You could have said, Daddy, it wasn't Penn. But you didn't. You knew why he took that suit, and you never said a damn word to change his mind."

"It was too late by then. I was at Virginia and —"

"I flew up there to see you! And you said nothing. You're gutless, Livy. I never knew that about you until now."

"I suppose I am. About the big things."

"Just like your father. He wanted a man dead, but he didn't have the balls to do it himself. He was district attorney, and he arranged to have an innocent man killed for profit."

"That is such bullshit."

"You think so? You'll find out different tomorrow. Your father and Ray Presley set up one of the most heinous murders I've ever come across, and J. Edgar Hoover covered it up to keep your grandfather happy. To keep them pulling for Nixon in the sixty-eight election."

"What are you babbling about?"

"Never mind."

Her face has taken on a strange cast. "I met him once, you know. Hoover. When I was a little girl. Up in Jackson with my father."

"Oh, they were big buddies. And the root of their friendship was the murder of Del Payton."

She shakes her head as if I'm hopelessly insane.

"By sundown tomorrow your father will be indicted for murder, unless he can kill my witnesses. And he's trying hard, believe me."

"What are you talking about?"

"Your father and John Portman tried to kill me last night."

She shakes her head. "You're lying."

"When have you known me to lie, Livy? Ever? Your father killed for money and power in 1968, and he'll do it now to cover his ass. That's all he's ever been about. He's played every angle and skimmed every deal, from factory locations to backroom adoptions. Everything's money to him."

Livy has gone still. "What do you mean, backroom adoptions?"

"Come on. That can't be news to you. I saw a record of the private adoptions he handled over the years. He did about twenty of them, and yours was one. Jenny's, I mean. For big money too. Big for those days, anyway."

She reaches out and touches my arm. "Tell me what you're talking about."

"You really don't know? Remember those records you and Leo took out of his office last

625

week? The ones he tried to burn?"

"Yes."

"There was a scrap of paper in there, a record of income from adoptions. He pocketed thirty-five grand off of yours. One of the highest prices paid for any baby on the list. I guess he wanted top dollar, since the baby came from his gene pool."

The blood has drained from her face.

"Look at it, if you don't believe me. I've been carrying the list around in my wallet since the day Jenny told me her story. I thought it was a record of our child being given away."

"Let me see it."

I pull out my wallet and fish the scrap of yellow paper from the bill compartment. Livy snatches it away and holds it up in the blue glow of the street-light across the road, trying to read in the dark. Her face is in shadow, but after a few moments the paper starts to quiver in her hand.

"That son of a bitch," she murmurs. "That son of a *bitch*."

"You still think I'm lying?"

"That he would *profit* from my pain like that . . ."

"I doubt he gave it a second thought. Making money was his habit. Everything that passed through his hands had to turn a profit. You should know that better than anyone."

She looks up at last, her eyes empty of everything but desire for the truth. These are the eyes I knew in high school. "Do you really believe my father ordered Del Payton's death?"

"It's not a question of belief. I know."

"You can prove it?"

"If my witnesses reach the courtroom alive."

She folds the paper slowly. "I'm going to do something you may not believe. I'm going to do it because I don't believe my father killed Del Payton. I *can't* believe that. But if it should turn out that he did, I won't protect him."

"What are you talking about?"

"The papers you requested under discovery. Business records, all that?"

"Yes."

"You got sanitized versions. There's another set of files. One that nobody sees. Not the IRS, not anybody."

My heart jumps in my chest. "You realize that withholding those papers from the court —"

"Is a felony? I'm not telling you this to hear the Boy Scout oath repeated back to me. Before I tell you where those files are, I want a promise from you."

"What?"

"Any evidence of illegal activity that doesn't directly pertain to the death of Del Payton, you'll forget you ever saw."

"Livy —"

"That's nonnegotiable."

"All right. Agreed. Where are these files?"

She bites her bottom lip, still resisting the deeply bred urge to protect her family's secrets. "Ever since I was a little girl, Daddy kept his sensitive papers in a big safe under the floor of his study. He called it his potato bunk, whatever that means. If he's hiding anything from you, it's in there."

"How can I get a look in there? He's home tonight. Isn't he?"

"He's probably upstairs by now. Mother's been

flipping in and out for the past few days. He's probably up there feeding her Darvocet and Prozac cocktails."

"What about the off-duty cops he called?"

"They won't look twice at you if I drive you in."

She looks sincere. But it's anger that's driving her now. Her relationship with her father has always been one of extremes, love and hate commingling in proportions that change too fast to be assayed. To see the secret safe in Leo Marston's study, I'll have to go back to Tuscany. And at Tuscany, on this night, Leo could kill me and tell the police anything he wanted. He could even have one of his cops kill me. My only real protection would be the woman standing before me.

"Are you sure you want to do this?" I ask.

She folds the paper in half, then twice again, into a tiny rectangle which she slips between the buttons of her blouse and into her bra. Her eyes shine with utter resolution.

"I've never been more sure of anything in my life."

CHAPTER 38

The grounds of Tuscany are dark. I parked my mother's shot-up Maxima at a gas station a quarter mile up the road from Tuscany's gate, then got into Livy's Fiat for the ride to the estate. As we approached the gate, she took a remote control from her purse, touched a button, and the barred fence slid back into itself. That was twenty seconds ago. We should have seen the lights of the mansion well before now.

"Livy —"

"I know. I've never seen it like this. The flood-lights are always on."

"I told you he was scared of Presley."

"Look," she says, pointing at a dim light high in the trees. "They're on the third floor. Mother's room."

I close my hand around the butt of the gun in my waistband. Ike's gun.

A thin beam of light slices through the darkness and comes to rest on the windshield of Livy's car. I start to pull the gun, but then our headlights sweep across a black police uniform.

Livy slows to a stop.

The cop walks around to her window and shines his light onto her chest, sparing her the direct glare of the beam.

"Evening, Miss Marston. Everything okay?"

"Yes. My friend and I are going in for a drink. Have you seen anything suspicious?"

"No, ma'am. Not a thing."

"Why are all the lights off?"

"Your daddy said he didn't want nobody taking potshots through the windows."

"I see."

"Don't you worry. Billy and me are on the job."

"I feel so much better knowing that." She gives him a synthetic smile, then rolls up her window and drives on.

Tuscany materializes suddenly, like a spectral palace in the moonlight, ringed by towering oaks and dark magnolias. Livy pulls around to the back of the mansion and parks in a small garage.

"There's a new entrance here," she says. "To the pantry."

She unlocks the door, then takes my hand and leads me quickly through the enormous house: pantry, kitchen, breakfast room, parlor, living room. The interior is shrouded in darkness, but the sense of space, of high ceilings and broad doorways, communicates itself through the sound of our footsteps and the way the air moves. Livy stops me by putting her hand against my chest, then opens a door, peeks inside, and pulls me through.

Leo's private study looks as though it had been surgically removed from an English manor house, shipped to America, and meticulously reconstructed inside Tuscany. The paneling alone must be worth a hundred thousand dollars. Livy sets her purse on the desk and points to a Bokara rug on the floor before it.

"There."

There's a club chair sitting on the rug. As I start to move it, she takes my arm and looks into my eyes. "Remember your promise."

"Have you known your whole life that your father was a crook?"

She gives me a look of disdain. "My father made a science of walking the line between what's legal and what's not. So have a lot of other businessmen. That's the way you get rich."

"Like those adoptions?" I say softly. "Let's not forget why we're here."

"You're so damned self-righteous. You must have cut a few corners in a decade of practicing law."

"I was a prosecutor, Livy. I stayed on the right side of that line you're talking about."

"You never conveniently misplaced a piece of exculpatory evidence to keep it from the defense?"

"Never."

"I suppose you never cheated on your wife either."

"Sorry. Why don't we look at those files?"

She studies me a moment more, then drops her hand and pulls the club chair off the Bokara. I roll up the rug and prop it against Leo's desk.

Where the rug had lain, discolored floorboards outline a trapdoor three feet square. Livy goes to the desk and brings back a small metal handle with a hook on one end. Kneeling, she slips the hook into an aperture I cannot see and folds back the trapdoor, exposing the steel door of a floor safe.

She bends over the combination lock, thinks for a moment, then spins it left, right, and left again. "He hasn't changed the combination in years," she says, getting to her feet.

I crouch to turn the heavy handle of the safe, but the butt of Ike's gun digs into my stomach. After setting it on the desk beside Livy's purse, I get down on my knees, turn the handle, and pull open the heavy door.

Inside is a hoard of velvet-covered jewelry boxes, stock certificates, cash, gold coins, manila envelopes, and computer disks. Nine square feet of paydirt.

"How much time do we have?" I ask, reaching for the manila envelopes.

"Maybe five minutes. Maybe all night."

"Maybe you should go upstairs and talk to your parents. Then I could be sure —"

"I'm staying here."

The envelopes are thick and marked with handwritten labels. The handwriting is Leo's. After wading through the mountain of discovery material, I recognize it as easily as my own. One label reads: FEDTAX '94/NOT TO BE SHOWN AT AUDIT. Another: THIRD-PARTY HOLDINGS (LAND). A third reads: GRAND CAYMAN TRUST ACCOUNT.

"That's got nothing to do with Del Payton," Livy says over my shoulder.

Maybe not. But it could probably put Leo Marston in jail for a few years, and cost him a considerable portion of his fortune. Reluctantly I set these envelopes aside and continue searching. There are more offshore accounts, records of hidden shares in oil fields, a dozen other ventures. I am about to abandon the files for the computer disks when a label jumps out at me as though written in neon. It says only: EDGAR.

Inside this folder is a thick sheaf of personal letters, all signed *Yours, Edgar.* The first begins, *Dear Leo, In the matter of the Nixon funds, please be assured that I consider your work in this area to be exemplary, and also a direct favor to me. He has his idiosyncrasies, yes, but he is a sound man, and we understand each other. The possibility of a Muskie or McGovern in the White House cannot be contemplated for one moment —*

The woodwind *oomph* of a wine bottle being uncorked draws my gaze away from the safe. Livy has taken a bottle of red from Leo's cherrywood bar and opened it with a silver corkscrew.

"Pretend it's our lost bottle," she says in a cynical voice.

She takes two Waterford goblets from the bar and fills them to the rim, then lifts one to her lips. She drinks a long swallow and passes it to me. Her upper lip is stained red, but she doesn't wipe it. She simply watches me drink. I can't read anything in her expression. The wine is tart on my tongue, acidic. She takes back the glass, drains it, then sets it beside the bottle and lifts the second glass to her lips. Half the wine disappears in three swallows.

She is more upset than I thought.

I turn back to the safe and flip quickly through the Hoover letters, searching for any mention of Del Payton, John Portman, or Dwight Stone. Most of the letters date from the seventies, after the secret relationship was well established, and deal with political matters.

"Is there a computer in here?" I ask, glancing at the 3.5-inch floppies.

"There's a PowerBook in the bottom drawer of the desk."

I'm reaching for the disks when Livy's wineglass shatters on the floor beside me.

"Someone's coming!"

As quickly as I can, I slide the manila envelopes back into the safe — all but the Edgar file — and shut the steel door.

"The rug!" she hisses.

While I unroll the rug, Livy shuts the trapdoor and jumps clear. I slide the rug into place just as someone begins jerking at the doorknob.

"Who's in there?" says a muffled voice.

It's Leo.

Livy thumps the envelope in my hands. "If you want that file, you'd better do something with it. Quick."

Leo bangs on the door. "Who's in there?"

"It's me, Daddy. I'm coming."

Unbuckling my belt, I shove the envelope down the back of my pants, retuck my shirt over it, then zip up and rebuckle the belt. As I do this, Livy unbuttons the top three buttons of her blouse and musses her hair.

"Let's make it look real," she says, and pulls my face to hers. Her kiss is passionate, desperate even, fueled by anger and wine and God knows what else. In the few seconds that it lasts, it flushes my face and brings sweat to my skin. My senses are still buzzing when she walks to the door and unlocks it.

"What are you doing in here with the door

locked?" Leo asks.

"I'm not alone."

He pushes his six-foot-four-inch frame through the door and swings his head around to me. His hard features go slack with amazement.

"What the hell's going on here?"

"Penn and I were talking."

"Talking." Leo is still wearing a suit, though he has untied his necktie. "Button that blouse, Olivia."

Livy does not button the blouse. She steps away from her father, leaving no obstacle between him and me.

"I can't believe you brought this bastard into our house," he says, his eyes locked on mine. "I want an explanation."

"Make one up. Anything you like."

Her defiant tone draws Leo's gaze away from me for a moment. "Don't take that tone of voice with me, young lady."

"I'll take whatever tone I please."

Leo looks off balance. Livy is not playing the role of favorite daughter. "What's going on here?" he asks. "What's Cage been telling you?"

"What could he tell me? Have you been keeping things from me?"

"Of course not."

"No?" She reaches into her blouse and brings out the scrap of legal paper, which she unfolds and hands to him without a word.

Leo stares at it for several seconds, then looks up blankly. "What's this?"

"Think about it," she says, her arms folded over her chest.

His face shows only confusion. He looks like he might have had a couple of drinks since receiving the warning about Presley. "Why don't you save me the trouble?"

"The adoption," Livy says in a dead voice.

"Your adoption?"

"Yes."

"What about it?"

"You took money for it?"

Leo shrugs. "So?"

"Thirty-five thousand dollars?"

"That paid a full year of your tuition at UVA."

Her mouth falls open. "Paid . . . you sold my baby to pay my college tuition?"

" 'My' baby?" Leo's face softens as he senses the hurt in his daughter. "Honey, you didn't want that child. I tried to get you to terminate the pregnancy, but you were against it. Given that adoption was your choice, I don't see what's wrong with —"

"Selling your own flesh and blood?" Her eyes are blazing now. "Like you *needed* the fucking money?"

"Profanity doesn't become you, Olivia."

"Profanity? Try obscenity. Selling my misery for money. That's about as obscene as it gets. I was just another profit-loss entry, I guess. Offset the liability of college tuition with the asset of unwanted babies. What the hell, right?"

Leo reaches out to her. "Honey —"

"Don't even try to justify it," she says coldly, backing away.

His look of sympathy evaporates. "I don't have to justify anything. You made a mess, I cleaned it up. It was the only big one you ever made, but it damn sure ruined most of what came after." He swings back to me. "Thanks to this punk."

"Leave me out of this," I tell him. "You've had the wrong idea about me for twenty years."

"How so?"

Livy looks at me and shakes her head.

"Ask her."

"Livy?"

"I don't know what he's talking about."

Leo's eyes roam over the study, taking in the wine bottle on the bar, his bookshelves, and finally the desk, where his gaze settles on the Sig-Sauer lying beside Livy's purse. He is nearer the gun than I, and he knows I'm thinking that.

"It was you who said Ray Presley was coming here to kill me, wasn't it, Cage?"

"That's right. I was doing you a favor."

"I think you were lying." He stabs a finger in my direction. "I think you broke in here looking for some kind of evidence. And I think I'd be within my rights to blow your goddamn head off."

He picks up the Sig-Sauer, cycles the slide, and walks around the desk.

"Presley killed Ike Ransom tonight," I say quickly. "He tried to kill me, but I got clear by sending him after you. I told him you gave him up to the FBI as part of your deal with Hoover."

Something twitches in Leo's cheek. "You're still lying. You're using my daughter to try and get at me." He turns to Livy. "The trial's tomorrow, and he's desperate. He's using you."

A dark light shines in Livy's eyes. "The way you used me against him?"

Leo isn't much of an actor; his feigned surprise is almost comical.

"Once I got here," she says, "I realized why you'd asked me to come. What you wanted me to do. The sad thing is, I wanted to do it. I thought Penn could wipe away all the mistakes I'd made. I thought his wife's death was fate. That we were being given a second chance."

"That's only natural," Leo says in a soothing voice. "But he took advantage of you, honey. What did he ask you to do for him?"

"Nothing. He loves me. He always has." Her smile is full of irony and self-disgust. "And he has more integrity than both of us put together."

Leo snorts. "Spare me the wine and roses. Did you have to bring him here? Couldn't you have checked into a motel?"

"The way you always did?"

"Olivia —"

"Don't say anything. Just go back to your room. Go upstairs and take care of Mother. Better late than never."

Instead of walking to the door, Leo gives me the superior stare I've received in the private chambers of a dozen judges. "The trial's tomorrow," he says in a peremptory voice. "I'm going to give you one last opportunity to save face, and to help this town. Call your little tart at the newspaper and get her to print a public apology for the remarks you made about me. A full apology from you, and a retraction from the paper. If that's printed tomorrow I'll dismiss the suit."

His offer leaves me dumbfounded. There can be only one reason for it. He's running scared.

"I don't see your lips moving," Leo says. "You'd

better jump while you can. The offer's good for sixty seconds."

"Dwight Stone is alive," I think aloud. "And neither you nor Portman can find him."

His face remains impassive. "Fifty seconds."

A wicked elation flows through me. "You can stick that offer right up your ass. Tomorrow—"

All of us turn at the sound of the door.

Ray Presley is standing in the study, aiming a revolver at Leo's chest. It looks like a .357 Magnum. He's abandoned his pajamas in favor of Levis, Redwing boots, and a black western shirt. Only the John Deere cap remains the same. The vulpine eyes burn from beneath its bill just as they did the day I bought my father's .38 back from him.

"Evening, Judge," he says.

Presley looks like he's lost ten pounds since I saw him last. He's still ropy and tough, but he seems diminished somehow. Imagining him raping Livy is almost beyond me, he looks so much older than she now. Yet Livy has backed against the wall opposite me like a frightened girl, like she's trying to become her own shadow.

"I'm not armed, Ray," Leo says from behind his desk, but I see that he's holding Ike's Sig-Sauer behind him.

"Throw that Sig on the floor, Judge," Presley says like a chiding parent. "I saw it in your hand when I came in."

Marston knows better than to try to raise the gun and fire before Ray can pull his trigger. He tosses Ike's gun onto the floor at Presley's feet.

"I saw the boys outside too," Presley says, his

voice almost friendly. "You knew I was coming, didn't you?"

"Ray —"

"Anybody makes a move, it's their last," Presley says, glancing at me. "I hit what I aim at."

"Like Ike Ransom?" I say.

He smiles. "That nigger talk any before he died?"

"Enough."

"You lookin' to get killed too, college boy?"

"Fuck you, Ray."

The smile disappears. "I came here to kill one, but I can kill three just as easy and damn near as quick." He motions toward Livy and me. "You two come here. Stay right in front of me, backs to me."

I move slowly, gauging my chances of getting to Livy's purse — and gun — before Ray shoots me. Less than zero at this point. But if I can get closer . . .

Livy and I stand shoulder to shoulder, facing Leo across the desk, with Presley behind us. Presley's hand pats its way up my legs, around my waist, up my torso.

"Don't you touch me," Livy says in a voice that could freeze alcohol.

But he must have touched her, because she suddenly spins into his gun and slaps him hard enough to rock him back on his heels.

"Livy!" shouts Leo. "Don't be stupid!"

Presley's harsh laugh fills the room as Livy backs away from him, panting with outrage. If she grabs for her purse, I'll have to stop her. Presley might endure a slap with a laugh, but he'll recognize a lunge for a gun.

"Ray?" Leo says in a careful voice. "This boy's got nothing on us. He can't connect us to Del."

A snort from Presley. "He can't connect *you*. But he's got me nailed down tight as a tick. Don't make no never mind, though. This visit's got nothing to do with that dead nigger. This is about you and me, Judge."

Leo affects puzzlement. "I don't understand, Raymond."

Presley jerks up his gun at this use of his Christian name, what must once have been a gesture of friendship. "Yes, you do. You gave me up to the Feds while you kept raking in the money. You made me your goddamn scapegoat."

Marston's eyes flick toward me, not in anger, but with purpose in them. He's prodding me to think. Leo is first and foremost a survivor, and he intends to live through this. If that means a short-term alliance with me to neutralize the most immediate threat, he won't hesitate.

"Nobody in this room but me knows what five years of prison means," Presley says. "Five years I'll never get back. And I need them years now. You got to pay for 'em, Judge." He fingers the trigger of his gun, raises his aim to Leo's head. "And there ain't but one way to do it."

Marston remains calm. "Ray, you shot at those FBI boys on your own hook. Hoover demanded a price, and you were it. Cost of doing business, son. You understand that. You were sentenced to seven years, and I got you out in five. It cost me to do that. You want to kill me for it?"

Presley's chin quivers with rage, and the gun trembles in his hand. "It *cost* you? You could pass out half a million bucks and you wouldn't feel it. You'd make it back in a couple of months. But time? You don't never get that back. Make your peace with the Lord, Judge. And be quick."

"Ray!" I shout, trying to hold his attention. "If you shoot him, you'll spend every hour you have left behind bars."

Presley laughs. "If I stick around to get arrested. Which I ain't. Tomorrow night I'll be in Mexico, and nobody in this world can stop me getting there. I know ways in and out that the wets ain't even thought of."

"I can see why you'd want to shoot him," I go on. "I'd like to shoot him myself. But the way I figure it, you two are already square."

He gives me an uncertain look. "What do you mean?"

"I mean, I just found out what you did to him in seventy-eight."

"What you talking about?"

I nod at Livy. "Well, to her, I mean. That's the same as to him, isn't it? It damn sure gives him the right to shoot you, if anything gives a man that right."

"*Shut up,*" Livy hisses.

Presley starts to turn the gun on me, but he steadies himself and holds it on Marston.

"What's that, Cage?" Leo asks. "What are you talking about?"

"Tell him, Ray." Keep tapping on the pressure point.

Presley takes a step closer to Marston, but he doesn't fire. I think he *wants* Marston to know the truth before he dies.

"Do you know a girl named Jenny Doe?" I ask Leo.

"Please," Livy begs.

"I've met her," Leo says.

"Do you know who her father is?"

His eyes flash with anger. "You are, you pissant."

"Sorry, Judge. I never knew that girl existed, and I am most definitely not her father."

"Then who is?"

"The man holding the gun on you."

Leo blinks three times quickly. Livy has gone white. But Presley's face is a strange mix of wonder and defiance. He obviously knew nothing about Jenny Doe until this moment.

"You and me got a kid?" he says, his eyes on Livy.

"Olivia?" Leo says quietly.

"Tell him, Livy," I urge her.

"He raped me," she says simply. "When I was eighteen, Ray raped me three times one night and got me pregnant."

"That's a goddamn lie!" Presley bellows. "She give it to me, Judge. Teasing me with it all the time, prissing around like a bitch in heat, grabbing my privates. She told me she wanted it that night."

"Livy?" Leo says again.

The mere fact that he's asking tells me Leo believes Presley's story could be true. Livy knows this too. Her lips are pressed tightly together, her nostrils flared. She stares into the middle distance for a few moments, alone with her demons. Then she looks at her father with absolute sincerity.

"He raped me, Daddy. I should have told you when it happened, but I was too afraid. He told me he would kill Mother if I did. All these years I let you think Penn was the father. He wasn't. It was *him*."

Leo's face goes through a dozen different emotions, only a small number of them readable. But the one that finally settles in his features is rage. Pure, unalloyed rage. This is the natural reaction of any father, but there is more here. Ray Presley served Leo for more than thirty years, performing deeds too dirty for his master to soil his hands with. But whatever bond this forged between them, Presley was always a servant. A hired man. The realization that he transgressed this class boundary — trespassed into the very flesh of the Marston family line — probably offends Leo more than the act of rape itself. His jaw muscles are working with enough force to grind his teeth to nubs if he keeps it up, and his blue-gray eyes burn with a fearsome light.

"You *white-trash bastard*," he says, each word dripping with contempt. "You touched my little girl? I'll snap your neck like a stick."

Presley shakes his gun in front of him like a man waving a crucifix before a vampire.

"You're the one, goddamn it! Ratting me out after all I did for you? So I fucked your slut daughter. You think I was the first? She handed it out like candy in school, and God knows what she did after she left this town. Like father, like daughter, I guess."

To my surprise, Leo does not explode at this but instead seems to calm down. He drops his hands to his desk drawer. "How much will it take to buy you off, Ray? To make you go to Mexico and never come back?"

"More than you got, Judge."

"I've got a lot."

"That's the Lord's truth. But you ain't got enough to buy your life. Not this time."

Leo reaches into the drawer and feels around inside. His mouth goes slack.

Presley smiles darkly and takes a step forward. "What you lookin' for, Judge? You lose something?"

Leo freezes, his hand still in the drawer. His face has lost all color. It's the face of an animal, a predator backed into a corner by a larger one.

Presley reaches into his pocket with his left hand and removes the derringer Leo pulled on me the day Kelly backed him down. "You're too predictable, Judge." He points the derringer at Livy, who's standing to his left, and straightens the arm, pointing the .357 at Leo's head.

He means to shoot.

I have only one weapon to hand, the half-empty wine bottle on the bar behind me. Presley's attention is divided between what he perceives as the most immediate threats. He probably figures I won't even mind him shooting Leo. Visualizing the bottle as I saw it last, I reach back with my right hand, relaxing my fingers so that I won't knock it off the bar by mistake.

My fingertips touch cool glass.

I close my hand around the neck of the bottle. Now it's a matter of peripheral vision. If Presley would glance at Livy again, I could swing without him seeing the bottle until it's too late. Focusing on Livy, I concentrate the full power of my will on communicating to her what I need. Her eyes search mine, trying to read my thoughts. As she stares, I incline my head very slightly toward Ray.

Presley cocks the hammer of his .357, and Leo at last gives in to terror. "Ray, I'm begging you. Please don't do it."

Presley wrinkles his lips in disgust.

Livy says, "Our daughter looks just like you, Ray."

Presley's profile vanishes as he looks toward her, and in a single fluid motion I swing the bottle in a sweeping arc that terminates at the base of his skull. The impact of the heavy glass club slams him forward, and he falls over the front of the desk.

Somehow he still has both pistols in his hands. I leap forward and hammer at his head with both fists, thinking of Livy lying under him with her dress stuffed down her throat. As I flail away, I see Leo's huge hands take hold of Presley's IV-scarred wrists and pin them to the desktop like brittle sticks.

Presley pulls the trigger of the derringer.

Leo flinches as though stung by a hornet, but he looks less hurt than pissed off. He rakes a huge right hand down Presley's left wrist, stripping the derringer from the smaller hand and tossing it on the floor. With his other hand he yanks the .357 out of Presley's right, which is still pinned to the desk.

Presley tries to raise himself off the desk, but all my weight is on him.

Leo presses the .357 to Presley's forehead.

"Let him go, Cage."

I smack Presley once more for good measure,

then heave myself off him. Despite the blows to his head, he straightens up, like a punch-drunk boxer who can remember only one thing: *stay on your feet.*

Leo pulls open his jacket long enough to reveal a bloodstain on the right side of his shirt, but he doesn't examine the wound any more closely than that. "This creates a problem," he says, the anger gone from his voice. Already he is computing the calculus of how Ray's actions will affect tomorrow's trial. "Cage, you and I should try to —"

He stops at the sound of Livy's voice. I'm not sure, but I think she said, *"Ray?"* in the intimate voice of a lover. She must have, because Presley turns from the desk to the sound of her voice, his eyes glassy but still curious.

"I wanted you to see this," she tells him.

Then she brings up Ike's Sig-Sauer and shoots him in the chest.

Ray sits down on Leo's desk as though he has decided to have a think there. Then his eyes bulge as he looks down at the red river flowing from his upper chest with a depressingly regular rhythm.

Livy stands with the automatic held stiffly before her, smoke drifting from its barrel, exactly the way it looks in old westerns. She doesn't look the slightest bit upset. She seems, in fact, to be contemplating a second shot. Before she can fire again, I jump in front of her and grab her wrist. She doesn't resist as I pull the gun from her hand.

"Lock the door, Cage," Leo orders from behind his desk. "Hurry."

I obey without hesitation, though I'm not sure why.

"The guards will be here any second," he says. "*I* shot Ray. Do you understand? He broke in, tried to kill me, and I shot him." Leo's eyes are full of paternal concern. "Will you back me up?"

"Are you kidding? You can't lie about something like this. Not these days."

His eyes glow with hypnotic intensity. "Listen to me, Cage. We can tear each other to pieces at trial tomorrow. But if you've ever cared for my daughter, help me protect her now."

"You can't pull it off. Not nowadays. There are nitrate tests . . . a hundred things." I look at Ray, who, despite horrific blood loss, is still sitting on the desk. "Besides, he's *still alive.*"

Leo walks around his desk and takes the Sig-Sauer from my hand. Before I can ask what he means to do, he backs three feet away from Ray, aims at his head, and blows his brains out. Presley flips backward over the desk and lands with his head in the corner.

"Now he's dead," Leo says, giving me a look so matter-of-fact that it makes a psycho like Arthur Lee Hanratty look like a Cub Scout. "So much for your nitrate tests."

The study door shudders under a sudden barrage of rapping.

"Judge Marston!" shouts a male voice. "Judge! Are you all right?"

"Cage?" Leo asks calmly, the Sig-Sauer still in his hand. "Are we agreed?"

I look at Livy, who seems to be undergoing some sort of delayed shock reaction. Then at Ray Presley, the man who engineered the murder of Del Payton and the living death of Ike Ransom . . .

who killed Ike in the end and probably killed Ruby Flowers. Who raped the girl I loved at eighteen, dooming us to lose each other forever.

"Agreed," I say softly.

The off-duty cops are still rapping and yelling at the door. Leo crosses the study, opens it, and waves the officers in. Two uniforms step into the room, guns drawn.

"You're a little late, boys," Leo says, pointing at the body behind the desk. "He got past you."

The cops gape at the corpse on the floor. Without his John Deere cap Presley looks like a hundred-year-old man with three eyes.

"Goddamn," says one of the cops in an awed voice. "Ain't that Ray Presley?"

"I'll be damned if it ain't," says his partner. "You were right, Judge."

"It's a good thing I was ready for him," Leo says. "He got off a shot, hit me in the gristle. But I nailed him. You'd better call the chief, Billy, so we can get this mess straightened out. I've got to be in court tomorrow."

The cop called Billy starts around the desk to examine Ray more closely, but Leo says: "Why don't you use the hall phone?"

Billy stops. "Sure thing, Judge."

"When you're done talking to the chief, y'all come back and drag this piece of trash out of here for me."

Billy bites his lip. "Well . . . it's a crime scene, Judge. We can't move anything. You know that."

"It's more of a crime to have this bastard bleeding all over my Bokara rug."

"Um," says Billy's partner, the one who stopped

649

Livy and me outside. "Is your daughter okay?"

"She's fine," says Leo, though Livy is standing like a statue near the door. "A little squeamish. All the blood, you know."

An absurd laugh escapes my lips. Livy is about as squeamish as a fur trapper.

After Billy and his partner leave the study, Leo walks back behind his desk and sits in his chair. "Penn," he says, using my Christian name for the first time in two decades. "I was wrong to blame you all those years for what happened to Livy. I see that now."

"That's why you went after my father?" I ask, making sure. "Because of me?"

He nods. "I was wrong to do that too. It's a hard thing to accept after all this time. I guess Livy bears the ultimate responsibility." He gives me a fatherly look. "You call your girl at the newspaper and tell her to run that apology. We'll end this thing like gentlemen, and save the town a hell of a lot of misery."

"I might do that," I say quietly. "If you were a gentleman."

His eyes narrow.

"But since you're an amoral, hypocritical, heartless bastard, I won't. Tomorrow you're going to be indicted for capital murder in the death of Del Payton."

I turn away from him and walk toward the door.

"Goodbye," I say, touching Livy's hand. "Don't think twice about Presley. You did the world a favor. I'll tell it just the way your dad wants it." I squeeze her hand, then pause and kiss her lightly on the cheek.

She says nothing at first, but as I move away she says, "Penn, I can't let you take that file."

"What?" Leo says, his voice instantly alive with suspicion. "What file?"

"I showed him your safe. I was angry. Penn, please give me the envelope. I can't help you destroy my father. Not like that. Not after all that's happened."

I reach for the doorknob, wondering how far she'll go to stop me.

"She won't shoot you, Cage. But I will."

I don't know if he'd shoot me in the back or not. But I have a daughter waiting for me at home. And I will not bet our future on the honor of Leonidas Marston.

Turning to face him, I untuck my shirt, slip the Hoover file out of my pants, and toss it toward him. There's a flutter of papers as the letters scatter across the desk and floor. I start to leave, but then I bend down and lift the fallen wine bottle from the Bokara. It survived the impact with Presley's skull, though most of the wine has spilled out. Glancing back at Livy, I invert the bottle and pour the remaining wine onto the desk, splashing the red fluid across Hoover's personal missives to Leo.

"Pretend it's our lost bottle," I tell her. "You two were made for each other."

I reach for the brass knob, open the door, and walk out into the hall. The last thing I hear is Leo's voice floating after me:

"See you in court."

CHAPTER 39

An hour before jury selection in the slander trial of Penn Cage, the police blocked motor-vehicle access to the streets surrounding the Natchez courthouse. The television vans had already been let through, at least eight, despite the fact that only crews from CNN and the black-owned Jackson station would be allowed inside the courtroom.

Judge Franklin's decision to allow cameras in her court was a landmark in Mississippi jurisprudence, and she had carefully defended it in her pretrial order. Besides stating that *Marston* v. *Cage* was a civil case and that both parties to the suit had agreed to have the proceedings televised, Franklin observed that community interest in the Payton murder — which was the central issue of the trial — was at such a pitch that the "window into the court" provided by the news camera could go a long way toward fostering the perception of fair and impartial justice.

The police roadblocks did nothing to limit the crowds outside the courthouse. Caitlin's newspaper account of the deaths of Ike Ransom and Ray Presley had electrified the city. Black families laid out blankets beneath the oak trees on the north lawn, and endured without complaint the desultory showers that had fallen since dawn. The whites stood mostly on the south lawn, huddled under umbrellas with Calvinist stoicism. The division was not solely racial; there was intermingling at the edges of each crowd, but for the most part a natural segregation had occurred. Police officers milled through the throngs, watching for verbal altercations that could all too easily spark violence under the circumstances.

None of this concerned me as I entered the courthouse flanked by two sheriff's deputies. All I could think about was Dwight Stone. Except for the strange call Caitlin had received yesterday, saying that Stone's dead FBI partner would be at the trial, I'd heard nothing. This morning Caitlin picked up a story off the AP wire saying that four unidentified men had been found dead in the mountains near Crested Butte, Colorado. This buttressed my hope that Stone had at least survived our encounter by the river, but many hours had passed since then. I tried calling his daughter several times but had no luck. Dwight Stone seemed to have vanished from the face of the earth.

In a city with over six hundred antebellum buildings, more than sixty of which are mansions, one might expect the courtrooms to be marvels of architectural splendor, spacious and high-ceilinged, paneled with oak and smelling faintly of lemon oil. In fact, while the original Natchez courthouse was built in 1818, and has been expanded several times since, its second-floor courtrooms are small compared to those in Houston, and surprisingly functional in character.

The circuit court has seven rows of benches for spectators, with another six in an upstairs balcony at the rear, several of which have been co-opted today by the cameras of CNN and WLBT. Viewed from the rear door, the jury box stands against the right wall, with the door to the jury room in the far right corner. The witness box stands to the right of the judge's bench and, awkwardly, a little behind it, attached to the rear wall. The judge's bench is set on a dais at the center, with desks for the court reporter and circuit clerk extending forward into the room at right angles to the bench. The reporter sits on the right, the clerk and his deputy on the left. Beyond the clerk's desk on the left is a large, open space for the presentation of exhibits. The lawyers' tables stand just beyond the bar, not far separated from the clerk's and reporter's desks, with the podium beside the table on the right. The only touches of Southern atmosphere are the white capitals of the Doric columns visible through the windows behind the judge's bench, and the intertwining oak branches beyond them, which give an unexpected airiness to the otherwise close room. And then there is the clock on the wall. Symbolically enough, it has no hands, and I am reminded of Carson McCullers's dark and poignant novel. She would feel right at home in the midst of the strange and tragic case that has brought us here today.

Walking up the aisle toward my table to begin the voir dire phase of the trial, I receive one of the greatest shocks of my life. Seated at the plaintiff's table alongside Leo Marston and Blake Sims is

Livy Marston Sutter. She doesn't look up at me, but any fleeting hope that she might be here for moral support is quickly banished by her appearance. From her pulled-back hair to her tailored navy suit and Prada shoes, she is every inch a lawyer. Every movement precise, every glance measured, Livy radiates a self-assurance that draws the eyes of everyone in sight of her, producing in both men and women a desire for her attention and approval.

Blake Sims looks dowdy beside her. He wears the traditional uniform of the Ole Miss lawyer: blue blazer, white pinpoint button-down, striped tie, dress khakis, and cordovan wing tips. His face is pink and fleshy, the face of a student council president, with sandy blond hair and blue eyes. The more I think about Sims, the more obvious it becomes why Leo wants Livy here.

Leo himself sits facing the bench with imperious detachment. He is a head taller than Blake Sims, and his close-cropped silver hair and chiseled features give him the look of a wise but austere judge, which he was. Four decades spent roaming the corridors of power have served him well. His tailored English suit was made for the television cameras, and no one looking at him this morning would suspect that he executed a man last night.

Moving toward my table, I scan the faces of the spectators who have managed to get into the packed courtroom. This morning I arranged with the bailiff that my parents be allowed in, with Sam Jacobs escorting them, and also Althea and Georgia Payton, with Del Jr. All are seated in the second row on the right, behind my table. The first row was roped off for city officials, who have turned out in force. Mayor Warren and District Attorney Mackey shoot me glares whenever I look their way. Beyond them are many faces from my youth and, peppered among these, the characters who have populated my life for the past two weeks. Ex-police chief Willie Pinder. Reverend Nightingale. Some of the neighbors who helped search for Annie on the day of the fire. Charles Evers. What sobers me is my awareness of those who aren't here. Ruby. Ike. Ray Presley. Dwight Stone.

I shake hands with my father over the bar, then take my seat. As I begin reviewing the notes I made last night about questioning potential jurors, someone touches my shoulder. It's Caitlin Masters. For the first time since the cocktail party, she has abandoned her informal uniform of jeans and button-downs for a dress. A blue sleeveless one that emphasizes her lithe body. The effect is so profound that I simply stare at her.

"I do own dresses," she says, obviously pleased by my reaction.

"You look very nice. Any word from Stone?"

She bites her lip and shakes her head, then pats her pocket. "He has the number of the paper. They'll call me the second he or his daughter calls in."

"*If* he calls. Is Portman here?"

"They've got him in a room upstairs with five FBI agents." She reaches out and touches my forearm. "Hold on to your hat. They've got the governor up there too."

"The governor of what?"

"Mississippi. He's here as a character witness for Marston."

I feel my face flushing. "He's not on the witness list."

She gives me a "get real" look. "Do you think Judge Franklin is going to tell the governor to go back to Jackson without letting him take the stand?"

"Damn." I fight the urge to tear out a handful of my hair.

"Take it easy. African Americans hate the governor. Did you get any sleep?"

Sleep. Last night, after the police and the sheriff's department took turns grilling me for hours over the shootings at the pecan plant and at Tuscany, I met with Betty Lou Beckham and her husband. Mr. Beckham is totally against his wife testifying, but she promised my father she would, and she means to go through with it. Considering the embarrassment she will suffer when the circumstances that allowed her to witness the crime come to light, she is doing a brave thing indeed. After meeting the Beckhams I went to the Eola Hotel and woodshedded with Huey Moak and Lester Hinson, whom Kelly had delivered safely from Baton Rouge. When we finished, I spent the few hours before dawn trying to build a convincing case against Marston that did not rely on the testimony of Dwight Stone.

I failed.

"Hang on as long as you can," Caitlin says, squeezing my hand. "If Stone is alive, he'll be here."

"Do you think Portman would be here if he

thought there was any chance Stone would show? With TV cameras?"

"Don't second-guess yourself. You've got a murder to prove, and that's what you're good at. Pick your jury and forget the rest."

She gives my hand a final squeeze and walks back to the benches.

Judge Franklin enters the court wearing a black robe with a white lace collar, looking very different than she did the night she confiscated Leo's files from Tuscany. She's obviously had her hair done, and her makeup looks television-ready. She takes her seat on the bench, and the bailiff calls the court to order.

Blake Sims rises and informs the judge that Livy Marston Sutter has been retained as co-counsel, and with the court's permission will occupy the second chair at the plaintiff's table during the trial. Judge Franklin makes a show of asking if I have any objection, but she clearly expects me to go along. I could point out that Livy is not licensed in Mississippi, but with her considerable trial experience and Sims acting as lead counsel, I don't really have a leg to stand on.

Livy meets my eyes only once during the entire voir dire process, which turns out to be a surprise in itself. I had always assumed I would enjoy the advantage of a largely black jury. White professionals tend to use their jobs and influence to avoid jury duty, but this morning that tradition goes out the window. Not one white in the first group taken from the venire, or pool of potential jurors, tries to evade his civic responsibility. The usual excuses about job and health problems are not voiced, nor are distant blood relations to trial principals invoked. Every juror in the pool wants a front-row seat.

Blake Sims handles voir dire for Marston, pacing before the jury box in a rather annoying fashion while he questions the potential jurors about their backgrounds and what they've read in the newspapers. Most admit that they've read about the case (how could they have avoided it?) but claim they have formed no opinion as to the guilt or innocence of either party. Most of them are lying, of course. That's the way these things go. You can't keep human nature out of a human process.

As the voir dire progresses, I notice that Sims is avoiding direct questions about racial views. At first I thought this was circumspection; with cameras in the courtroom, he would want to avoid any hint of racial bias. But as he exercises his peremptory challenges, his strategy becomes clear. He has seen that he has a shot at a predominantly white jury, and he means to get it, even if it means breaking the law.

After Sims rejects the fourth black juror, I stand and make my first objection of the day, citing *Batson* v. *Kentucky* and the line of subsequent cases extending the prohibition against excluding potential jurors on the basis of race to civil cases. Judge Franklin immediately sustains my objection, and Livy finally turns in my direction. Her eyes hold nothing for me. They are merely the eyes of opposing counsel, acknowledging my small victory in a war that will see many more skirmishes before the issue is decided.

After this point the voir dire passes more quickly than any in my career. I judiciously exercise my peremptories, culling on the basis of instinct. When my mental radar picks up echoes of blue-collar or rural backgrounds combined with religious fundamentalism, I pull the trigger. I challenge some whites for cause after tripping them up on questions about prejudice, but most racists quickly figure out how to conceal their true beliefs. Nearly every potential juror admits knowing Leo Marston to some degree, so many that I cannot realistically disqualify them on this basis. By eleven-forty-five A.M., we have empaneled twelve jurors (seven white, five black) and two alternates. Judge Franklin recesses for lunch and instructs the lawyers to be ready for opening statements at one.

I eat a quick lunch with Caitlin in an empty conference room near the chancery court, gobbling deli sandwiches from Clara Nell's between calls to the newspaper to see whether they've heard anything from Stone or his daughter. They haven't. Then I hurry downstairs through a crowd of courthouse employees and rubbernecking lawyers to give my witnesses one last pep talk, paying particular attention to Betty Lou Beckham, who looks as though she might come apart at any moment. Admitting on the stand that she was fornicating in a car with a married man must be akin to donning a scarlet letter in the village square. If it wasn't for my father's influence, Betty Lou wouldn't be coming near this courthouse today. After holding her hand for a few minutes, I return to the crowded courtroom, sit at my table, and wait for one o'clock to tick around on the clock without hands.

Judge Franklin brings her court to order with a stern look, and Blake Sims rises from the plaintiff's table and walks to the podium to make his opening statement. Sims is the son of Leo Marston's former law partner (now deceased) and was raised in Greenville because of a divorce. He speaks with a cultured Delta accent rarely heard in Natchez, and though Greenville — the home of Hodding Carter's *Delta Democrat-Times* — was perhaps Mississippi's most liberal city during the civil rights era, Sims's accent might evoke some negative responses in the black jurors.

"Ladies and gentlemen of the jury," he begins. "My client needs no introduction. But allow me to say a few words about him. Leo Marston is one of the most distinguished figures in Mississippi jurisprudence. He is a former attorney general of Mississippi and former justice of the state supreme court. He is a friend and adviser to Mississippi congressmen, and has been for more than thirty years. He's a powerful business force for the city of Natchez, bringing industry and jobs to Adams County. He is also a pillar of the Catholic church, and a major supporter of charities in our area."

Sims leaves the podium and walks halfway to the jury box, testing Judge Franklin's formality. She makes no objection to his move. "With that in mind," he goes on, "I want to ask you a question. What is a man's name worth? The defendant in this case, Mr. Penn Cage, has signed an agreement stipulating to certain facts. First, that he uttered

661

the vile charges in question. Second, that he uttered them in the full knowledge that they would be published in a newspaper. And third, that my client's reputation has been severely damaged by his charges. That being the case, I won't waste your valuable time trying to prove damages. Mr. Cage has publicly called my client a murderer. What more malicious charge could anyone make against another human being? Child molestation perhaps." Sims slowly bobs his head as though weighing this issue.

"My client does not contest the fact that a tragic murder took place in May of 1968. Mr. Cage may even have evidence against the man who committed that crime. But what he does not have — what he cannot possibly have — is evidence that *Leo Marston* had anything whatever to do with that crime. Leo Marston was, in fact, the district attorney at that time. The chief law enforcement officer of the county. Mr. Cage may present some sort of *circumstantial* evidence, which he may try to weave into a web of deception to fool you good people. But my client and I know that you will not be fooled. Del Payton was a civil rights worker murdered to stop him from doing his noble work. And Leo Marston is demonstrably one of the most racially progressive leaders in this town, and has been since he was a young man."

Sims lists various pro–civil rights statements Leo made during the sixties, his friendships with black leaders, donations to black causes. He cites testimonial letters he will enter into evidence, attesting to Marston's contributions to Mississippi's economy: letters from John Stennis and Jim

Eastland (both deceased), Trent Lott, Mike Espy, and five former governors.

"What we have here," Sims concludes — giving me a theatrical look of disdain — "is an irresponsible and sensational attack carried out by a man who has had a personal vendetta against my client for more than twenty years. Before this trial is over, you will understand why. And I want you people to know something else. The money involved in this case is of secondary importance to my client. What he wants, and what he deserves, is the *vindication of his good name*." Sims fold his hands with the apparent probity of a deacon. "But if you good people should see fit to teach Mr. Cage a moral lesson about the price of such irresponsible action, so be it. We leave that to you. Thank you."

Sims is unable to conceal his self-satisfaction as he takes his seat, but if he was hoping for congratulations from his client or co-counsel, he is disappointed. Leo stares sullenly ahead like a truck driver in the eleventh hour of a drive, while Livy sits with the cool composure of a pinch hitter waiting to be called to the plate.

In the restless silence of the crowd, I rise from my table and walk slowly toward the jury box. Their faces are expectant, as they always are at the beginning of a trial. Before boredom has set in. Before resentment against vain attorneys who love to hear themselves talk has settled in their veins. I lay my hands on the rail and speak directly to them.

"Ladies and gentlemen, my name is Penn Cage. I am a writer. Before I wrote books, I was a prosecuting attorney. I spent every day of my life putting violent criminals behind bars. I put more than a few on death row.

"I was born and raised right here in Natchez, but like a lot of our young people, I had to move away to earn my living."

Several jurors nod their heads, probably those with adult children.

"I earned that living as a prosecutor in Houston, Texas. Now, if you were to go to Texas and ask about Penn Cage, you might find some people willing to speak ill of him. If you went to the penitentiary at Huntsville, you'd find a lot of them."

General laughter from the gallery.

"What you would *not* find is a single person who would describe me with the word Mr. Sims just used. *Irresponsible.* Because when you are prosecuting murderers and asking for the death penalty, irresponsibility is not a weakness you can afford. It's not a trait that my former boss, the district attorney of Harris County, would tolerate for one minute. Folks, you are looking at a man who says what he means, and means what he says."

From the rapt faces of the jury, I can see that I haven't lost the old touch. It's a good feeling, like climbing onto a horse after ten years away and feeling him respond without a moment's hesitation. It's a pity that I have no case.

"When I called Leo Marston a murderer," I say evenly, "I meant it. Together with a brutal and crooked cop named Ray Presley, Leo Marston engineered the death of a young father, army veteran, and civil rights worker named Delano Payton. And contrary to what Mr. Sims suggested — and what the citizens of our town have believed for thirty years — that murder had nothing to do with civil

664

rights. No, Leo Marston had Del Payton killed for *profit*." I glance back at Livy, but she refuses to look at me. "The same reason he does everything else. And despite what Mr. Sims told you, money is *never* of secondary importance to Leo Marston.

"Mr. Sims also mentioned the term 'circumstantial evidence' in a rather derogatory tone. After all the television lawyers we've seen, a misconception has grown up that circumstantial evidence is somehow inherently weak. But that is simply not true. Circumstantial evidence is merely *indirect* evidence. Let's say a woman is shot to death at midnight with a thirty-eight caliber pistol. When the police arrive, they learn from one neighbor that the woman and her husband were in the middle of a messy divorce, and from another that the husband sped away from the house at five past midnight. The next day the police discover that the husband has a thirty-eight revolver registered in his name. Everything I just told you is circumstantial evidence. But I think a pretty clear picture of what happened is emerging in your minds. I'm not saying it's conclusive evidence. I'm saying this is evidence that *cannot be ignored*."

More nods from the jury, especially from the women.

"Mr. Sims asked what a man's name is worth. I'll tell you." I turn and point at Leo, the man who acted with such shocking dispatch last night. His blue-gray eyes burn with the subzero cold of liquid nitrogen. "After this trial that man's name won't be worth the price of a cup of coffee. He ordered one of the most terrible crimes in the history of this city, and by so doing stained the name of Natchez,

Mississippi, for thirty years. And with the help of J. Edgar Hoover, he sabotaged the investigation that followed that crime. The cold-blooded details of this premeditated murder will sicken you, just as they did me. But you must hear them. For the time has come to remove the bloody stain from the name of our fair city. Thank you."

The jury seems a bit flabbergasted by the passion of my indictment, but it's been my experience that juries like passion — to a point. And in my present situation, passion is better than nothing.

When Blake Sims rises to present his case, he does just as he promised: he ignores the question of damage to Leo's reputation. He accomplishes this by a neat reversal, calling three character witnesses whose combined testimony is designed to canonize his client, making the image of Leo Marston as a cold-blooded murderer one that jurors will feel guilty for even entertaining.

The first is Governor Nunn Harkness, a Republican with a two-fisted, shoot-from-the-hip style that has won him two terms despite his methodical gutting of social programs. Playing to the balcony TV cameras, Harkness praises Leo to the skies, lauding his success in bringing industry and gaming to Mississippi, and lamenting that, while Marston is a bit too liberal on issues like affirmative action, he is morally beyond reproach. It's a pitch-perfect performance by a master, and the jury is visibly impressed. When Sims tenders the governor to me for cross-examination, I don't ask a single question. Best to get Nunn Harkness offstage as soon as possible.

Sims's second character witness is Thomas

O'Malley, bishop of the Catholic diocese of Jackson. Once the priest of St. Mary Cathedral in Natchez, O'Malley has moved up the hierarchy. For fifteen minutes he waxes poetic about the multitudes of poor children whose Christmases Leo Marston brightened with toys. Then he moves on to the church itself. To hear O'Malley tell it, Leo single-handedly restored the cathedral to its present splendor, donating over half a million dollars to the restoration effort. As the bishop speaks, I am reminded of Michael Corleone being honored by the pope in *The Godfather III*. I shudder to think what sins O'Malley must have heard Leo confess during his years as a priest in Natchez, but none of that will ever pass the bishop's lips. When Sims tenders O'Malley to me, I let him go without a word. Unless you're dealing with questions of sexual molestation or mismanagement of funds, a Catholic bishop is bulletproof.

Sims's third witness is another matter. As Bishop O'Malley leaves the courtroom, pausing in the aisle to shake the hands of a half dozen former parishioners, Sims calls FBI Director John Portman.

Portman enters the courtroom with two bodyguards, who take up posts at the door as their master walks up the aisle. Lean, tanned, perfectly coiffed, and attired in a dark blue suit, the FBI director is clearly accustomed to television. He ascends to the witness box with the air of a medical expert about to hold forth on matters beyond the understanding of a lay audience.

This time it is not Blake Sims but Livy who rises from the plaintiff's table and approaches the box.

Judge Franklin gives Sims a questioning look, but Sims says nothing.

"You will be handling this witness, Ms. Sutter?" asks Franklin, using Livy's legal surname.

"With the court's permission, Your Honor."

Franklin turns to me. "Any objection, counselor?"

"No, Your Honor."

Livy walks past the podium and up to the witness box. Though Portman is much older than she, both emanate a sense of confidence and ease to which lesser mortals should not begin to aspire.

"Mr. Portman, what is your current position?" she asks.

"I'm the director of the Federal Bureau of Investigation. The FBI."

"Do you know the plaintiff in this case?"

"I do. I've known Leo Marston for thirty years."

"How did you meet?"

Portman purses his lips like he's thinking back. "Leo was the district attorney in Natchez in 1968. I was serving here as an FBI field agent at that time, investigating the death of Delano Payton. Mr. Marston gave the Bureau valuable assistance during that investigation."

My heart lurches.

"Why do you think he did that?" Livy asks.

Portman opens his hands, palms upward, as though the answer were obvious. "Leo Marston believed in the necessity of civil rights legislation. At no small risk to himself, he worked to help us enforce that. The man was a hero."

Livy nods thoughtfully. "How did you first become aware of the charges made by Penn Cage against Leo Marston?"

"Leo contacted me in Washington by telephone on the day the charges were printed in the local newspaper. We spoke at length at that time, and several times subsequent."

So much for the phone records. Livy's strategy is all too clear. She plans to undercut what little documentary evidence I have before I can present it.

"What was the substance of those conversations?" she asks.

"Judge Marston expressed anxiety that this sensitive case was being dragged through the media, and that his reputation was being damaged."

"You called the Payton case a sensitive case. Why is that?"

Portman adopts a pose of paternal concern. "I'm afraid I can only speak indirectly to this issue. As I've stated to the press, our file on Delano Payton is sealed on the grounds of national security interest. It has been for thirty years. Earlier this week the Senate Intelligence Committee voted to maintain the sanctity of that file."

"Please tell us anything you can about the case."

Portman nods agreeably. "The Payton case involved a veteran of the U.S. Army, a man who served in Vietnam. J. Edgar Hoover, the FBI director at that time, felt that the details involving this man, if released during the Vietnam conflict, might damage national morale, particularly the morale of line troops in Vietnam, where racial problems had become an issue."

He has to be talking about Ike Ransom.

"But the Vietnam War has been over for more

than twenty years," Livy points out. "Why is the file still sealed?"

"As I said, I can't speak as fully to this issue as I would like. I'm sorry Mr. Cage has seen fit to exploit this case in his bid for publicity or revenge, or whatever it is."

Livy pretends to be intrigued by this aside. "Have you had experience with Mr. Cage in the past?"

"I had some dealings with him when he was an assistant district attorney in Houston, Texas. I found him to be highly partisan, and indeed an unstable sort of man for that type of job. He actually killed the brother of a man he tried for murder, and the facts of that incident were never satisfactorily explained. I think the citizens of Texas were well served when he left that job to pursue a career in which a vivid imagination is an asset, not a liability."

I feel like throwing my pen at Portman, just to break up the rhythm. He and Livy are like tennis pros giving an exhibition match, sleek and practiced, the volleys perfectly timed, every shot a winner.

"One final question," she says. "As one of the agents who originally investigated the Payton murder, what do you think of the allegation that Leo Marston was somehow involved in that crime?"

A superior smile touches Portman's lips. God, he's enjoying this. "I find the notion utterly preposterous. The fact that we are sitting here today discussing it is a travesty of justice."

"Thank you, Mr. Director. Your witness."

I would prefer to cross-examine Portman after I have presented my case, but I cannot let his slurs against me stand unchallenged. Nor can I be sure that Portman will even stick around Natchez after he leaves the stand. I rise but remain at my table.

"Mr. Portman, you and I were involved in a jurisdictional dispute over the extradition of a murderer from Texas to Los Angeles, California, where you were a U.S. attorney. Is that correct?"

"Broadly."

"Where was that murderer ultimately tried and convicted?"

"Houston, Texas."

"Thank you. You also stated that I killed the brother of a man I tried for murder. That trial ended in a conviction, did it not?"

"Yes."

"And wasn't the man I convicted also the subject of our jurisdictional dispute?"

"He was. But —"

"Was I charged in the shooting of his brother?"

"Not to my knowledge."

"Your Honor, I have further questions for this witness, but I would prefer to examine him during the presentation of my case."

Seeing Franklin gearing up to explain to me why the director of the FBI cannot be expected to sit around at my beck and call, I add, "I hope to recall Mr. Portman before the end of the day."

Judge Franklin turns to Portman with a solicitous smile. "Will that impose an undue hardship on you, Mr. Director?"

"I can be available until the end of the day, barring an unforeseen emergency."

"Very well. You are temporarily excused." Franklin turns to the defense table. "Mr. Sims, does the plaintiff intend to call further witnesses?"

Blake Sims leans across Leo's massive chest and holds a whispered conference with Livy. She listens, then shakes her head. They want this show to close as quickly as possible.

"Your Honor," says Sims. "Reserving the right to call rebuttal witnesses, the plaintiff rests."

Judge Franklin looks at her watch. "This phase of the trial has taken much less time than I anticipated. Let's take a ten-minute break, and then Mr. Cage will present his defense."

As the jurors file out, I turn and look for Caitlin. She's sitting with my parents. She slides along the bench, then comes up to the bar behind my table. I can tell by her face that she doesn't have good news.

"No word from Stone?"

"Nothing. I'm sorry. You'd better drag out the testimony of every witness you have."

"I hate to do that. Juries always sense it."

"I don't think you have a choice."

What a comfort. The ten-minute recess lasts about two minutes, and then I'm on my feet again, doing what I have done countless times in my life: presenting a murder case. I do not stall for time. I do not equivocate. I present it just as I'd planned.

My witnesses come and go like commentators in a documentary. Frank Jones admits he lied about being alone in the Triton parking lot; his ex-wife describes finding the soiled stockings in their car; Betty Lou tearfully places Ray Presley at the crime scene (earning points with the jury for testifying against her

672

own interest), then describes Presley's subsequent threats and brutal harassment; Huey Moak's expert testimony establishes that Payton's car was destroyed by C-4, proving the evidence "discovered" by Presley was planted; and Lester Hinson testifies that he sold C-4 to Ray Presley in April 1968. All this testimony runs like a Swiss watch.

And therein lies the problem.

Neither Blake Sims nor Livy rise once to cross-examine my witnesses. They don't even challenge Huey Moak's credentials. Every time I tender a witness, Sims waves his hand from the table and says, "No questions, Your Honor." Their strategy is simple. They'll happily let me prove Ray Presley guilty of murder. And they will probably let me draw connections between Presley and Ike Ransom, if I can. As long as I can't link Presley or Ransom to Leo Marston, I am fulfilling the scenario painted in Sims's opening statement. The Payton murder was a race crime, committed by a racist. In his closing argument Sims will probably laud my efforts to find justice in this terrible tragedy. But to suggest any nefarious link between such men and Leo Marston must indicate some secret malice toward Marston on my part.

My dilemma is simple. Either I begin the long, laborious task of building circumstantial links between Presley and Marston, which will last well into tomorrow and bore the jury to tears (not to mention sabotage my opportunity to cross-examine John Portman in this lifetime), or I can question Portman now, do what damage I can, and pray that Dwight Stone descends from the heavens like the deus ex machina of my dreams. Without Stone's testimony as a fulcrum, I can't force Portman to help my cause. But by forcing him to lie, I can set him up for a later fall on perjury charges. And for the director of the FBI, that could be a very long fall.

"Call John Portman," I say loudly.

"Bailiff," says Judge Franklin. "Call John Portman."

Portman returns to the courtroom wearing the same confidence with which he left it. He takes his seat in the witness box, shoots his cuffs, and gives me a serene smile.

"Director Portman," I begin, "in your earlier testimony you stated that Leo Marston rendered valuable assistance in the investigation of Del Payton's death. What was the nature of that assistance?"

He pretends to agonize over this question. "He provided certain information to us."

"In other words, he acted as a federal informant."

"Yes."

A couple of the white jury members frown.

"I'm going to ask you a direct question. Please answer yes or no. Did the FBI solve the murder of Delano Payton in 1968?"

Portman takes a deep breath but says nothing. We have come down to the nut-cutting, as we say in the South. If he lies now, he is laying himself open to perjury charges.

"Director Portman, I asked whether the Bureau learned the identity of Del Payton's murderer in 1968."

"Yes. We did."

674

A gasp goes up from the spectators.

"Order," snaps Judge Franklin.

"Why didn't the FBI arrest or charge anyone in connection with that murder?"

"For reasons of national security."

"Let me be sure I understand this. The FBI preserved the national security by protecting the identity of a man who had murdered a veteran of the Korean War?"

Portman shifts in his seat. "Director Hoover made that decision. Not me."

"Did you agree with his decision?"

"It wasn't my place to agree or disagree."

"You were just following orders."

"Yes."

"Like a good German," I remark, recalling Stone's phrase.

"I strongly resent that."

"Mr. Cage," Franklin warns. "Don't push me."

"Withdrawn. Director Portman, did you —"

The loud clearing of a throat behind me breaks my train of thought. I start to ignore it, but something tells me to turn.

Caitlin Masters is crouched at the bar behind my table, urgently beckoning me with her hand.

"Your Honor, I beg the court's indulgence."

I walk back behind my table and kneel so that Caitlin can whisper to me. Her lips touch the shell of my ear. "I just talked to Stone's daughter," she says. "She and Stone were both at the newspaper. Two of my people are bringing them over now. They'll be on the courthouse steps in two minutes."

Relief and elation flood through me.

675

"Mr. Cage?" Judge Franklin presses. "We're waiting."

I squeeze Caitlin's arm, then rise and walk back toward the witness box with a briskness Portman cannot fail to notice. Caitlin's news has galvanized me.

"Director Portman, was there only one man responsible for Payton's death? Or more than one?"

"More than one."

A murmur from the spectators.

"How many? Two? Three? Ten?"

Portman folds his arms across his stomach. "I decline to answer on grounds that it might damage the national security."

"But you did say more than one. So, a minimum of two. Was one of those conspirators a Natchez police officer named Ray Presley?"

He gives me the great stone face. "I decline to answer on grounds that it might damage the national security."

"Did you work the Payton case alone, Director?"

"I was part of a team."

"Did that team include a veteran agent named Dwight Stone?"

Portman's eyes track me as I move, trying to read the source of my newfound confidence. "Yes."

"Was the Payton murder your first major case as a field agent?"

"It was."

"Had Agent Stone wide experience in working civil rights cases for the Bureau?"

"Yes."

"Did you admire and respect Agent Stone?"

Portman hesitates. "At the time, yes."

"Did you, earlier this week, order the assassination of Agent Dwight Stone, who is now retired?"

"Objection!" shouts Blake Sims, with Livy close behind.

Franklin bangs her gavel in a vain attempt to silence the gallery. "Mr. Cage, you'd better be prepared to substantiate that statement."

"I intend to do just that, Your Honor." I turn back to Portman. "Did you also order the assassination of Sheriff's Deputy Ike Ransom, the man murdered at the old pecan-shelling plant last night?"

The spectators collectively suck in their breath as Portman turns to Judge Franklin for help.

Franklin looks hard at me, then says, "The witness will answer the question."

"I did not," Portman says in an indignant voice.

"Did you last week order the assassination of former Natchez police officer Ray Presley?"

"Mr. Cage," Franklin interrupts, "I'm losing my patience."

"One final question, Your Honor. Director Portman, if Special Agent Dwight Stone walks through that door back there and takes the stand, will you remain in Natchez to be recalled as a witness by me?"

He looks right through me. "I will."

"No more questions, Judge."

"Director Portman, you are excused," says Franklin.

Portman glances up at the TV cameras, then stands, shoots his cuffs again, and leaves the witness box. As he passes me on the way to the aisle, I say: "Call retired Special Agent Dwight Stone."

The hitch in Portman's walk is momentary, but for me it occurs in slow motion. His eyes flit instinctively to the main door, searching for his old enemy. Then they return to me, the fear in them tamped down, varnished over with the go-to-hell defiance of a man who has survived every threat to his monumental egotism.

"Call Dwight Stone," Judge Franklin orders.

The bailiff opens the back door. A tall, wiry man wearing a Denver Broncos windbreaker and leaning on the shoulder of a much younger woman limps through it with a cane in his left hand. Even from my table I can see the steely resolve in Stone's eyes. But he is not looking at me. As his daughter squeezes in beside Caitlin, he limps up the aisle using the cane, his eyes never leaving the face of John Portman, the man who threatened his daughter's life, and who tried to kill us two nights ago. I have a feeling that a lot of dead Koreans and Chinese saw the look that is on Stone's face right now. I would not want to be John Portman at this moment. But when I turn back to Portman, what I see unsettles me.

He looks surprised but unafraid.

CHAPTER 40

When Stone finishes his slow journey to the witness box, he pauses for a few deep breaths, then turns to Judge Franklin. "May I stand during my testimony, Your Honor?"

"Do you have a physical malady that prevents you from sitting?"

"I was shot two nights ago. In the left buttock."

Predictably, some spectators snicker in spite of Stone's obvious pain.

"You may stand," says Franklin, glaring at the crowd.

I move slowly toward the podium, running through memories of everything Stone told me two nights ago in Colorado. He lied to me then — by omission — leaving Ike Ransom completely out of his story. I need the truth today, the whole truth. Stone must be made aware that Ike the Spike no longer needs his protection. Instead of stopping at the podium, I adopt Livy's tactic and continue right up to the witness box. In a voice barely above a whisper, I say:

"Ike Ransom was shot to death last night."

As Judge Franklin orders me to speak at an audible level, Stone winks, and my heartbeat rushes ahead.

"Mr. Stone, were you ever an agent of the Federal Bureau of Investigation?"

"I was a field agent for sixteen years."

"Did your duties ever bring you to Natchez, Mississippi?"

"Yes."

"In what capacity?"

"In May of 1968, I was assigned to investigate the death of Delano Payton. I arrived here the day after he was murdered."

"Who gave you that assignment?"

"J. Edgar Hoover."

"Personally?"

"Yes."

"Did you succeed in that assignment? Did you solve the murder?"

"I did."

Even though Portman said the same thing during his testimony, the crowd buzzes in expectation. It's plain that Dwight Stone does not intend to hold anything back.

"Could you briefly describe how you went about doing that?"

"Objection," says Livy, rising to her feet. "Judge, this man is testifying to information that has been sealed to protect national security. His willingness to break the law or even to commit treason is no reason to allow him to divulge protected information in front of television cameras."

I try not to let my anxiety show on my face, but Livy may have just stopped this trial dead, at least until government officials are brought in to decide what Stone may and may not say.

Judge Franklin looks at me. "Ms. Sutter raises a

serious issue, Mr. Cage. You have argument on this point?"

I could argue for an hour, but I would probably lose. "Perhaps we should hear Mr. Stone on this point, Judge. He's an attorney himself."

Franklin gives Stone an inquisitive glance. "Mr. Stone?"

Stone shakes his head like a soldier pondering a heavily defended hill he has just been ordered to take. "Judge, the heart of my testimony goes to the justification of that national security classification. After sixteen years working for J. Edgar Hoover, I can tell you this. No man more readily abused such classifications for his own personal ends than Hoover. He sealed the Del Payton file *solely* to mask evidence of criminal activity. It had nothing to do with the national interest. If you allow my testimony, you'll know beyond a shadow of a doubt that you've done the right thing." He looks Franklin square in the eye. "Have the courage of your office, Judge."

She regards him thoughtfully. "My dilemma, Mr. Stone, is that once you've spoken, your words cannot be taken back."

Stone sighs. "With all respect, Judge, I'm going to tell my story regardless of your decision. I've been silent too long. I can tell it here on the stand, or outside on the steps."

Franklin tilts her head back, shocked by Stone's frank threat. "I have a third choice. I can have you jailed for contempt."

Stone doesn't even blink. "You can jail me, Judge. But you can't stop me from speaking. That is the one thing you cannot do."

Eunice Franklin studies Stone for a long time. What does she see in him? He is ten years her senior, but from another era altogether. Is he a veteran cop with a conscience? Or an unstable and dangerous has-been, as John Portman would portray him? Livy opens her mouth to argue further, but Franklin stops her with an upraised hand.

"No additional argument, Ms. Sutter. If Mr. Stone has the courage to risk jail, I will risk censure. If he strays into what I feel is dangerous territory, I'll stop him. Continue with your story, Mr. Stone."

"Under protest," Livy says in a cold voice.

"Noted. Mr. Cage?"

I turn to Stone with as much gratitude as I can bring to my eyes. "Mr. Stone, could you describe how you went about solving the Delano Payton murder?"

In clear and concise language, the former agent gives a chronological account of his investigation up to the point that he nailed Ray Presley. His story mirrors exactly the testimony given by my earlier witnesses, from Frank Jones to Lester Hinson, and he confirms that John Portman worked with him every step of the way. Their discovery that Lester Hinson had sold C-4 to Ray Presley, Stone says, prompted a "rather intense" meeting with Presley, during which Presley stated that he'd merely acted as a middleman in the deal, purchasing the plastic explosive for a young Natchez black man, an army veteran. This brings us just past the point at which Stone began lying to me in Colorado.

"What was that young black man's name, Mr. Stone?"

"Ike Ransom."

"Are you aware that a sheriff's deputy by that name was murdered last night?"

"Yes."

"Was he the same man you interviewed in 1968?"

"Yes."

"John Portman stated that the FBI file on Del Payton was sealed because of the involvement of a certain Vietnam veteran. Was Ike Ransom that man?"

"Yes."

"What did you do after Patrolman Ray Presley told you he'd bought the C-4 for Ike Ransom?"

"Portman and I interviewed Ransom at his apartment. Two minutes after we were inside, he confessed to the murder of Delano Payton."

Livy jumps to her feet, but her objection is drowned by the explosive reaction of the crowd. Judge Franklin bangs her gavel, but it takes some time for order to be restored. Even the jury is gaping at Stone.

"Your Honor," says Livy, "I object. This witness's testimony is hearsay."

Franklin nods and looks at me. Under the Mississippi rules of evidence, Livy is right. But all rules are proved by exceptions. As I come to my feet, I troll my memory for the details of exceptions under Mississippi law, which I scanned less than six hours ago in the office of the chancery judge, an old high school friend.

"Your Honor, this qualifies as a hearsay exception under Rule 804 (b)3. Deputy Ransom was on my witness list specifically to testify to this information. His murder last night has made that im-

683

possible. Since the declarant is unavailable due to death, Mr. Stone's statement should be admitted."

Franklin looks surprised by my knowledge of Mississippi law.

Livy says, "Your Honor, Mr. Cage's exception is —"

"Sidebar," Franklin cuts in. "Approach the bench."

Livy and I meet before Franklin and lean toward her.

"Judge," says Livy, "this is patent hearsay, and no exception should be made."

"Judge, Ike Ransom's confession was a statement made against interest. A murder confession so obviously subjected him to criminal liability that great weight must be accorded to it."

Franklin taps her pen on a notepad as she considers my argument. "Given the totality of the circumstances, I'm going to allow it."

"His entire statement?" I press.

"Let's see where it leads. I may stop him."

Livy starts to argue, then thinks better of it. She returns to her table as I approach Stone.

"Please continue, Mr. Stone."

He lifts his cane from the rail and leans heavily upon it. "Ike Ransom was a mess. Suicidal probably. He was living in squalor that would be difficult to believe by today's standards. There was drug paraphernalia in plain view. What we called 'heroin works' back then. He was literally dying to tell someone his story."

"What was his story?"

"He had recently separated from the army after

a tour in Vietnam. He'd served as a military policemen there, as I recall. He'd tried to find work with the local police department but was turned down. Desperate for money, he'd turned to drug dealing."

"He admitted this to you?"

"Yes. Two weeks before Del Payton was murdered, Ransom was stopped on a rural road by Patrolman Ray Presley. Presley discovered a large quantity of heroin in Ransom's trunk. He offered to overlook this if Ransom agreed to kill a man for him."

"Objection!" Blake Sims cries.

"On what grounds?" asks Judge Franklin.

But Livy has taken hold of Sims's jacket and pulled him back down to his seat.

"There's no objection," she says.

Franklin gives them an admonitory look. "Continue, Mr. Stone."

"Patrolman Presley also promised Ransom that if he carried out this murder, Presley would ensure that he was eventually hired by the police department. Presley had told the truth about Ike Ransom asking him to get the C-4. Ransom was afraid of dynamite, but he'd had experience with C-4 in Vietnam."

"Did you report Ransom's confession to Director Hoover?"

"I did."

"What was his reaction?"

"I would describe it as glee."

"Glee. Could you elaborate on that?"

"Mr. Hoover was being forced to aggressively pursue a civil rights agenda. This did not reconcile with his personal feelings. He particularly hated Martin Luther King and Robert Kennedy. My revelation that the murder of Del Payton — a crime which Robert Kennedy considered a civil rights murder — had in fact been carried out by a black man gave the director obvious enjoyment. He remarked that he would dearly enjoy telling Bobby Kennedy that Payton's death had been nothing but another 'shine killing.' Those were his words."

"Did Hoover in fact report this to Bobby Kennedy?"

"Not to my knowledge."

"What did he do?"

"He authorized me to wiretap the home of Ray Presley, and also the pay phones within a two-mile radius of his home."

"Did you learn anything from those wiretaps?"

"A few days later Presley called Leo Marston, the local district attorney, and asked for a private meeting."

"Objection!" cries Sims, to Livy's obvious displeasure.

It looks to me like Sims may be objecting on the order of his client. Leo's face has grown steadily redder during Stone's testimony.

"Grounds?" asks Judge Franklin.

When Sims hesitates, Franklin says, "I want no more frivolous interruptions of this testimony. You can object from now till doomsday, but Mr. Stone is going to tell his story. Is that clear?"

Sims sighs and takes his chair, while Leo sets his jaw and glares at Franklin.

Stone relates the story of wiretapping Tuscany,

and of Hoover taking personal control of the investigation because of its political sensitivity. "The meeting between Presley and Marston took place in the gazebo outside the Marston mansion. It became clear in the first ten minutes of that conversation that Ray Presley had arranged the death of Delano Payton at the specific request of the district attorney, Leo Marston."

Judge Franklin is so engrossed by Stone's testimony that it takes her several seconds to realize that the spectators are out of order. She furiously bangs her gavel.

"I'll clear this court!" she vows, pointing her gavel at the balcony for emphasis.

I would have expected Livy to leap to her feet at Stone's last statement, but she seems as engrossed in the story as Judge Franklin.

"How did that become clear, Mr. Stone?" I ask.

"Marston knew every detail of the murder, right down to Ike Ransom's request for the C-4."

"Did their conversation shed any light on the possible motive for this crime?"

"Yes." Stone lucidly lays out the pending land deal between Marston and Zebulon Hickson, the carpet magnate from Georgia. He explains Leo's secret ownership of the land, Hickson's concern with black labor problems, and his insistence that an "example" be made of a black union worker before committing to purchase Marston's property.

"Yes. Mr. Stone, I'm sure everyone in this courtroom is wondering why, since you solved the murder, no one was arrested for it. Can you explain that?"

"After Director Hoover had all the evidence and

reports in his possession — including the audio-tapes — he set up a meeting with Leo Marston at the Jackson field office of the FBI. After this meeting took place, I was instructed to stand down my Natchez detail and report to Tuscaloosa, Alabama, for other duties. I was told that no arrest would be made because that was in the best interests of the Bureau and the country."

"What did you make of that?"

Stone shakes his head. "I'd seen it before. Hoover liked having leverage over people. Particularly people in government. Leo Marston came from a powerful political family. His father had tremendous influence in both Mississippi and Washington. Over the next year, I learned that Hoover used the leverage of the Payton murder to force Leo's father to influence the 1968 presidential election by trying to swing Mississippi's electoral votes away from George Wallace to Richard Nixon, who was a protégé of Hoover's. It was also clear in 1968 that Leo himself was destined for higher office. Director Hoover and Leo Marston developed a mutually beneficial relationship that flourished from Payton's death in 1968 until Hoover's death in 1972."

Judge Franklin is shaking her head in amazement.

I can't believe that Livy or Sims did not object to Stone's last statements, but they probably assumed — rightly, I suspect — that Judge Franklin meant to hear him out no matter what.

"So," I summarize, trying to bring it all into perspective for the jury, "J. Edgar Hoover was willing to bury conclusive evidence of a civil rights murder in order to strengthen his own political influence. How did you react to this?"

"Not well."

"Please be specific."

"I began drinking. It affected my work. I cheated on my wife. She divorced me, took my daughter from me. I was eventually dismissed from the Bureau."

A fragment of Ike's confession in the pecan-shelling plant comes to me from the ether. "Did you ever make any attempt to right what you considered the terrible wrong that had been done in the Payton case?"

Surprise flashes in Stone's eyes. "Yes."

"How?"

"I had retained a copy of the incriminating tape. About a year after the murder, when I knew no official action would ever be taken against the killers, I called Ike Ransom. He'd been hired as a police officer by then, just as Presley had promised."

"What did you tell him?"

"Nothing. I played him my copy of the tape. Then I hung up."

"What did you think Ransom would do after hearing that tape?"

"I don't know. I suppose I hoped that he might take direct action."

"You hoped he would kill Presley and Marston?"

Stone's face remains impassive. "The thought entered my mind."

"Mr. Stone, when you described these events to me two days ago, you didn't mention Ike Ransom. Why?"

He looks at the rail, his eyes filled with something like grief. "I felt some sympathy for Ike Ransom, despite what he'd done."

"Sympathy for a murderer?"

"Ransom was a combat veteran. I was one myself. Del Payton too. Ransom had a bad time in Vietnam, I could tell that right off. When Presley caught him with that heroin, his choices narrowed down to nothing. Parchman prison or commit murder. That may not mitigate his act, but when I interviewed the man, he was paralyzed by remorse. He was the only one of the three who ever showed any, and to this day, I'm surprised he lived through those weeks." Stone rubs his free hand over the one holding the head of the cane, then expels a lungful of air. "Presley and Marston were *arrogant* about what they'd done. And why not? The system rewarded Marston for it."

I ask Stone to briefly explain the Presley angle of the Marston-Hoover deal (Marston's betrayal of Presley to the FBI), my goal being to show the jury that even last night's attempt by Presley to kill Marston had its roots in the Payton murder. When Stone finishes, Judge Franklin looks overwhelmed by the implications of the case.

"One last question, Mr. Stone. Why, knowing all that you did, did you wait so long to come forward with the truth?"

He looks past me, but I doubt he sees anything of the courtroom. "Cowardice," he says. "Plain and simple. Hoover used John Portman to threaten my family if I caused a scandal. After my ex-wife died, I thought about coming forward. But by then my daughter had graduated law school and against my advice joined the FBI. She was subject to the will of the Justice Department, of which John Portman was a major part. The murder had happened so long ago. I just tried to put it behind me."

"Did you succeed?"

"No. It's haunted me my whole life."

"Thank you, Mr. Stone. I tender the witness, subject to redirect."

Judge Franklin lays both hands on her desk and sighs. "I'm going to take a recess here. I'd like to think for a bit, and I'm sure Mr. Stone would like to rest his legs."

Livy stands abruptly. "I'd prefer to cross-examine now, Your Honor."

Franklin frowns and looks at me. "Mr. Cage?"

I should probably opt for the recess, to give Stone time to decompress. But something pushes me in the opposite direction. Something in me is driven to witness Livy's performance. How far is she willing to go to protect her father? How far, now that Stone's testimony has destroyed any remaining illusions she might have had about Leo's innocence?

"No objection, Your Honor."

"Proceed, Ms. Sutter."

Livy squeezes Leo's shoulder in a gesture that looks genuine. Then she approaches Stone at an oblique angle, walking slowly with a burgundy Montblanc pen in her hand, not looking at him but at the jury. Every man and woman in the box watches her with fascination.

"Mr. Stone, what year were you dismissed from the FBI?"

"1972."

"Were you summarily dismissed, or were efforts made to help you stop drinking?"

"I wasn't fired for drinking."

"Your record states that you were. But I'm interested. Why do you *think* you were fired?"

"For drawing my service weapon on Leo Marston in the lobby of the Watergate office complex."

Livy doesn't bat an eye. "There's no mention of such an incident in your record. Were there any witnesses to it?"

"My partner, Henry Bookbinder."

"Will he corroborate your story?"

"He would if he were alive."

"Any other witnesses?"

"Not that I know by name. Only Marston himself."

Leo actually smirks from his table. He loves seeing Livy perform this way. This is what he fantasized about before she ran off to Virginia and then Atlanta.

"Let's return to your dismissal," she says. "I admired the candor of your earlier testimony. Being honest about things like losing your wife and child must be very hard. I know, because I'm going through a divorce myself."

Livy wins instant points with the jury for this personal revelation, one with stratospheric value in the Natchez gossip market. Stone stands with a resigned frown on his face, like a soldier being court-martialed, one who knows something bad is coming and that he has no choice but to endure it.

"I wonder," Livy says with false spontaneity, "were you *completely* honest about your dismissal?"

Stone just waits.

"Do you know a woman named Catherine Neumaier?"

His face sags.

"Would you like some water?"

Stone's jaw clenches. He is clearly offended by Livy's feigned concern. "I did know Catherine Neumaier. She's dead now. Dead twenty-five years."

"Did Miss Neumaier have a profession?"

"She was a dancer."

"A dancer. She had no other profession?"

"Not to my knowledge."

"FBI records indicate that Miss Neumaier was a prostitute."

"I don't know anything about that."

"How did you meet Miss Neumaier?"

"I was working an organized crime task force. I was assigned to try to compromise her as an informant."

"Because she had ties to organized crime?"

"She danced in a club owned by Sam Giancana."

"The Mafia boss of Chicago?"

"Yes."

"Did Miss Neumaier become your informant?"

"Yes."

"Was she an alcoholic?"

"No."

"FBI records indicate that she was. Also that she took drugs."

Stone sighs. "She had a severe health problem. Lupus. She took pills to help her stay awake for work. Pills to help her sleep."

"Did you have a sexual relationship with Miss Neumaier?"

His eyes don't waver. "Yes."

"Wasn't it this relationship that caused the breakup of your marriage?"

"Yes."

"Were you reprimanded for unprofessional conduct because of this sexual relationship with Miss Neumaier?"

"Officially. And only after the fact. Unofficially, Hoover encouraged it from the start."

"You were encouraged by the director of the FBI to have an affair with a Mob prostitute? I find that difficult to believe."

Stone's eyes are burning now, all patience gone from his face. "Lady, the total tonnage of what you don't know about federal law enforcement would sink a damned oil tanker."

Livy is already smiling in triumph when Judge Franklin reprimands Stone for his language.

"Did you feel," she goes on, prodding a different nerve, "that John Portman had anything to do with your dismissal from the FBI?"

"I know he did."

"How do you know?"

"Portman had known since the Payton case that I didn't go along with what Hoover had done."

"Allegedly done."

"Keep telling yourself that."

"I'm warning you, Mr. Stone," Franklin cuts in.

"How did Mr. Portman influence your dismissal?" Livy asks.

"He reported all my conversations and movements to Hoover after the director took over the Payton case."

"Why would he do that?"

"Because he sensed that I wasn't going to toe the line. He sensed my sympathy for Del Payton and Ike Ransom. Hoover's standard procedure would have been to tell Portman to keep a close eye on me and report back. This was Portman's first major case. He would have kissed Hoover's — He'd have done whatever Hoover told him to without question."

"What else did Portman do?"

"Two days before I was fired, evidence pertaining to the Payton case was stolen from my apartment. Portman took that."

"I thought you told us that Director Hoover requested that all the Payton evidence be forwarded to Washington."

"I kept copies of certain things."

"Against direct orders?"

"Yes."

"Why do you think it was Portman who allegedly stole this material?"

"He left me a calling card."

"A business card?"

"No. A map."

Livy looks less certain here. "What kind of map?"

"My evidence was hidden behind a wall panel. After the theft the panel was purposefully left out of place. When I looked inside the wall, I found a map of Natchez, Mississippi. There'd been no map there before. That was Portman's calling card. That was the only place we'd ever served together. I suppose he thought it displayed a certain wit."

"How do you feel about Mr. Portman personally?"

"Since he sent four men to kill me last night, I don't feel too well disposed toward him."

"The jury will disregard that statement," Judge Franklin cuts in. "Confine yourself to the question, Mr. Stone."

"All right. I think John Portman is a rich, spineless bureaucrat who didn't get spanked enough when he was a kid."

Franklin turns red, but Livy is ecstatic. Stone is giving her exactly what she wants. Before Franklin can reprimand him, she turns to face the jury box.

"Mr. Stone, did you enter into a conspiracy with the author Penn Cage to ruin the careers of John Portman and Leo Marston?"

He blinks in surprise. "What? Absolutely not."

"But you see the symmetry of the suggestion?"

"I do not."

She turns back to him with a knowing smile. "Come, now. You're a smart man. I'm suggesting that you and Mr. Cage made a deal of sorts. Mr. Cage hated Leo Marston, you hated John Portman. Alone, neither of you could do much to destroy those men. But together —"

"Objection," I say at last.

Livy smiles. "I withdraw the question, Your Honor. And I have no further questions for this witness."

I can't understand why she's releasing Stone so soon until she says, "If this is Mr. Cage's final witness, I would very much like to call Mr. Cage at this time as a rebuttal witness."

Her suggestion stuns me. All I can think to say

is, "Ms. Sutter is out of order, Judge."

"Just a moment," says Franklin. "You are excused, Mr. Stone. But don't leave the courthouse."

Stone makes no move to leave the witness box. He looks down at Livy with contempt and says, "You're not worth a hangnail on Catherine Neumaier's little finger. Your father is a murderer, and you know it. But you stand there —"

"Mr. Stone!" snaps Franklin. "Leave the stand, or I'll be forced to hold you in contempt."

Stone looks away from Livy like a man looking away from a dead enemy, then limps off the stand with his soldier's bearing. As he passes me, he stops, shakes my hand, and leans close.

"I told you you didn't want me as a witness."

I squeeze his hand and whisper, "Bullshit. I wanted the truth, and you gave it to me. The question is, was the jury ready for it?"

As Stone passes the spectators' benches, his cane rapping on the hardwood floor, his daughter rises, takes his elbow, and helps him toward the doors.

"Ms. Sutter," says Judge Franklin. "This is an unusual request. Whose testimony are you calling Mr. Cage to rebut?"

"Mr. Stone's, Your Honor."

Franklin considers this for a few moments. "Mr. Cage, do you plan to call additional witnesses?"

I had planned to recall Portman, but now that Livy has undercut everything Stone said by making him look bent on revenge, I'm not sure what to do. And now she wants to question me? I suppose she is finally answering the question of how far she is willing to go.

"I have no more witnesses, Your Honor."

"Does the defense rest, then?"

A strange sense of sadness flows through me, not for myself but for Althea Payton, sitting out there in the benches. She nods at me as though to say, *At least we tried.* "Subject to calling rebuttal witnesses, the defense rests."

"Very well. Please take the stand, Mr. Cage."

Without looking at Livy, I mount the steps to the witness box and seat myself. Everyone in the room is watching me. My parents. The Paytons. Austin Mackey, who looks like he's in shock from the revelations he's heard in the past half hour. High in the back of the court, more faces watch from the balcony, and among them the larger gleaming eyes of the CNN and WLBT cameras.

One pair of eyes is not watching me. Livy Marston's, and it's a damn good thing. If she had the nerve to look me in the eye while playing out this obscene charade, I might decide to stand up and announce her sins to the world. But I won't do that. And she knows it. It's not in me to do something like that. But maybe it is in her.

"Mr. Cage," she says, facing the jury. "Did you and I have a romantic relationship when we attended the St. Stephens Preparatory School?"

"Yes."

"Was it a serious relationship?"

"Define serious."

"An extended relationship of a sexual nature."

She has guts, I'll give her that. "Yes."

"When did that relationship finally end?"

Two minutes ago. "Our freshman year of college."

"Did it end that year because my father, Leo

Marston, handled a malpractice suit against your father, Thomas Cage?"

"Yes."

"In the course of that lawsuit, did your father suffer a near-fatal heart attack?"

"Yes."

"Did you blame my father for that?"

"Yes."

"Did that lawsuit effectively end any chance of you and I getting married?"

"Yes."

At last she turns to me, but her eyes look opaque, as though she has closed them against all my feeling for her, steeling herself against mercy. "Did you blame my father for that as well?"

Does she want me to tell the truth? Does she want me to say, *No, I blame you? The whole goddamn thing happened because you got yourself pregnant by a stupid redneck murderer and couldn't deal with it?*

"For a long time, I did."

"And did you conspire with former Special Agent Dwight Stone to destroy my father and John Portman?"

"I did not."

She holds my eyes a moment longer, as though waiting for me to counterattack with everything I know about her.

I say nothing. What would it accomplish, besides convincing Livy that I'm willing to sink as low to destroy her father as she is to protect him? Would it convince the jury that Marston and Portman are guilty? If Stone's testimony didn't do that, the Marston family's dirty laundry certainly won't.

"No further questions," Livy says, turning away at last.

Judge Franklin looks at me as though I have fulfilled the assertion she made on the day we met in her office. I have a fool for a client. "Mr. Cage," she says, "I find myself in the curious position of asking if you would like to cross-examine yourself."

I almost laugh out loud. Here it is, my chance to say anything I want. And curiously enough, I have no inclination to say anything. Without Ike Ransom or Ray Presley to confirm Stone's story, I can add nothing that will sway the twelve people in the jury box.

"No questions, Your Honor."

"You're excused, Mr. Cage."

Excused. My parents are watching me with agony in their faces. Althea Payton nods, her lips tight. Caitlin's black veil of hair frames her porcelain face among all the others. She's looking at me with something like pity in her eyes. She thinks I'm unable to turn Livy's sword against her, not trapped in a situation where my conscience is forcing me to endure humiliation without fighting back. As I walk back to the defense table, I turn toward the jury. I do not give them my lawyer's look — full of confidence, certain of victory — but a simple human look, an unstated question.

Their faces are hard to read. Stone's testimony resonated with the black jurors, but even they cannot help but connect the simple dots Livy held up before them. I blamed Leo Marston for making my father ill and ruining my prospects with his daughter. Stone hated Portman for his dismissal from the FBI. Once the two of us were brought to-gether, a conspiracy was almost inevitable. Fac-tually, this theory has at least one major hole. But emotionally it makes sense. It plays. And some of the jury members are bound to buy into it.

As I reach the table, the door at the rear of the courtroom opens, and a young woman walks in. It's Jenny Doe. She looks toward the judge's bench, then pans her eyes until they settle on me. She waves at me.

I nod to her and take my seat just as Judge Franklin says: "Ms. Sutter? Does the plaintiff rest?"

Any lingering illusion that Blake Sims is leading Leo Marston's legal team crumbles into dust.

Livy nods. "The plaintiff rests, Your Honor."

As Franklin turns to me, someone pulls at my elbow. "Mr. Cage?"

It's Jenny, crouching at the bar behind my table.

"Mr. Cage?" says Judge Franklin. "Does the de-fense rest?"

Jenny grabs my arm above the elbow and jabs her thumb into a nerve. I jerk my elbow away.

"Mr. Cage?" says Franklin. "Is that young lady bothering you?"

"May I have a moment, Your Honor?"

"If you must."

I twist in my chair until I'm face to face with Jenny. "What the hell are you doing?"

Her eyes are glittering with excitement. "I have something for you," she whispers. "I think I have what you need to win your case."

"What are you talking about?"

"I tried to get in here this morning to watch the

701

trial, but it was too crowded. And it's a good thing for you. Because I went back to my apartment and watched it on TV. I didn't realize what I had until I heard that Mr. Stone talking about J. Edgar Hoover. I ran —"

"Mr. Cage," Judge Franklin presses. "I'm ready to give this case to the jury."

I hold up my hand. "Jenny, for God's sake, get to the point."

"It's the tapes."

I blink in bewilderment. "Tapes?"

She reaches into the pocket of her jeans and pulls out a black Maxell cassette tape. "This," she says. "It's one of the tapes I stole from Clayton Lacour's office. Remember? The mobbed-up lawyer who handled my adoption? When I stole all the files relating to Marston, I stole his phone tapes too. Lacour's conversations with Marston. Twelve tapes. And on this one he's talking about your case. About Del Payton. He never actually says the name, so I never realized what I had. But when that poor Beckham woman started saying the name Ray Presley, something zinged in my mind. I couldn't place it until Mr. Stone started talking about J. Edgar Hoover. I had to fast-forward through eight different tapes before I found it. I sprinted the three blocks over here."

"Jenny, what *is* it? What do they say?"

She shakes her head, her eyes brimming with secret joy. "Just get the judge to play it. You won't believe it."

I close my eyes, thinking furiously.

"Mr. Cage, I've had enough," says Judge Franklin. "Does the defense rest?"

I take the tape from Jenny, get to my feet, and lay my hands on the table. "No, Your Honor. I request a conference in chambers. Critical new evidence has just come to my attention. I believe it will be conclusive evidence, and —"

"Objection!" Livy cries, shaking her head. She has already seen the tape in my hand. She probably thinks it's Dwight Stone's recording of her father and Ray Presley talking in the gazebo of Tuscany. "No such evidence was disclosed to us!"

"Your Honor, I didn't know about it myself until a moment ago. The young lady behind me just brought it to my attention."

Livy looks at Jenny with dread in her face.

"Who is that person?" Franklin asks.

Livy closes her eyes.

"Her name is Jenny Doe, Judge. Who she is, is less important than what she has."

"What does she have?"

"A tape of Leo Marston discussing the Payton murder with a New Orleans attorney named Clayton Lacour."

Judge Franklin looks to Livy for an objection, but Livy is still standing with her eyes closed, as though she can no longer stand the schizophrenic nature of what she is being called upon to do today. Prodded by Leo, Blake Sims gets to his feet.

"Judge, I object to the introduction of this surprise evidence on the grounds of —"

Eunice Franklin stops him with an upraised hand. "I'll hear argument in my chambers." She stands in her black robe and looks down at me. "Mr. Cage, this had better not be desperation grandstanding."

"The tape will speak for itself," I assure her, praying that Jenny knows evidence when she hears it.

"Counsel in my chambers," says Franklin. She points at Jenny. "You too, young lady."

CHAPTER 41

We stand like human islands in Judge Franklin's chambers, an archipelago of attorneys situated around the mainland of her mahogany desk. Blake Sims to the left. I'm in the center with Jenny behind me. Livy stands to the right, apart and alone, reading the spines of the books in Franklin's shelves.

"Ms. Sutter, are you with us?"

Livy half turns to the judge but doesn't come close to eye contact with me or Jenny. "Yes, Your Honor."

The judge looks up at me, her eyes hard. "All right, Mr. Cage. What exactly is on this tape?"

Blake Sims is shaking his head, but he doesn't speak.

"I haven't heard it myself, Judge. But this woman claims that it refers directly to the murder of Del Payton, and I have reason to believe she's telling the truth."

Franklin transfers her glare to Jenny. "How did you come by this tape, young lady?"

"I worked for Clayton Lacour. The lawyer who made the tape. I went to work for him to try to find out the identities of my birth parents. I'm an adopted child, and I knew that Lacour had handled my adoption." Jenny glances at Livy, who is pointedly ignoring her. "While working for Lacour, I found out Leo Marston had been involved in my adoption. When I quit that job, I took all the files and tapes pertaining to Judge Marston with me."

"You mean you stole them?"

"Yes, ma'am."

Judge Franklin looks like she wants a cigarette or a drink, and probably both. "I don't understand. Why were there tapes at all?"

"Mr. Lacour taped most of his phone calls. He was connected with the Marcello family in New Orleans. You know, Mafia. He was seriously paranoid."

Franklin sighs and holds out her hand. "Let me have the tape."

I hand over the cassette. The judge studies it for a few moments, then speaks without looking up. "Did you learn who your birth parents were?"

"Yes, Your Honor."

"Who are they?"

Livy goes rigid beside the shelves.

"At least one of them is in this room right now, Judge. Do you want me to say more?"

Franklin shakes her head in amazement. "Not at this time." She looks up at me. "I don't know exactly what's going on behind this lawsuit, but I don't appreciate having my court used as an arena to play out private vendettas. Is that clear?"

"Absolutely, Your Honor."

"I want counsel back at their respective tables. You" — Franklin points at Jenny — "stay with me. I'm going to listen to this tape. Then I'll make my decision as to admissibility. If I walk back into that courtroom and announce that the tape will be played, I don't want to hear a single objection. If I don't mention the tape, the same holds true, and I will give this case to the jury. It's late, and there's too much craziness surrounding this trial to drag it into tomorrow if we don't have to." She claps her hands together. "Everybody out."

As I walk back to my table, Caitlin nods in encouragement from the bar. I take my seat and slide back within earshot of her.

"What do you have?" she whispers.

"I'm not sure. A tape of Marston and a New Orleans lawyer. Jenny says it will nail Marston."

"You haven't heard it?"

"No. Franklin's listening to it now. She's going to rule on admissibility."

"I'm praying here," Caitlin says. "I'm actually praying."

The wait is almost impossible to bear. Two minutes stretch to five, then ten. The spectators are silent at first, but as the minutes drag on, they begin to whisper. Without Franklin to intimidate them, the whisper grows to a hum, then a dull roar. It reminds me of students assembled in a gymnasium. Twice I look across the aisle to Marston's table, but Leo and Livy stare straight ahead, their faces set in stone. Only Blake Sims looks worried. Sims looks, in fact, like he would rather be getting a root canal than sitting at his client's table.

At last Judge Franklin's chamber door opens, silencing the court. Jenny Doe walks through first and heads for the spectators' benches, her head bowed. Franklin emerges carrying a cassette tape player, a cheap jam box with a silver antenna sticking up off of it.

At Marston's table, Blake Sims actually covers his eyes.

"*Yes,*" whispers Caitlin from behind me.

Judge Franklin takes the bench, sets the tape player before her, then turns to the jury box. "Members of the jury, I am about to play a tape recording of two voices having a telephone conversation. One, I am told, belongs to a lawyer in New Orleans. The other, I am convinced, belongs to the plaintiff in this case, Leo Marston. I have instructed counsel to make no objections to the playing of this tape. The supreme court might disagree with my decision, but this is not a murder trial, and I suspect that it will never see an appeals court."

A murmur of anticipation ripples through the crowd.

"The language on the tape is profane," Judge Franklin goes on, "as language spoken between men in private sometimes tends to be. I will play only that portion of the tape I believe relevant to this case. I want no displays of emotion. I want *absolute silence.* I will eject anyone who disobeys that order."

She rubs the bridge of her nose and sighs. Then another liver-spotted hand emerges from the black robe. It presses a button on the machine and turns the speakers toward the jury.

Static fills the courtroom. Then an unfamiliar male voice comes from the speakers, the New Orleans accent plain: Brooklyn with a little crawfish thrown in. This must be Clayton Lacour.

"... and this problem, Leo, it's, you know, one of those things you could earn a lot of gratitude by fixing."

"*I'm listening.*"

A collective intake of breath by the crowd as it recognizes the resonant voice of Leo Marston.

"Order!" demands Judge Franklin.

"*This goddamn new guy they got at the field office here,*" Lacour goes on, "*Hughes, his name is, he's not playing by the old rules. This is the new SAC I'm talkin' 'bout. He's stoppin' by for coffee at Carlos's office at the Town and Country, for God's sake, got surveillance on him around the clock. Uncle C is gettin' ulcers. You gotta help me out here, cher.*"

"*I'm not sure what you want.*"

"*What I want? It's not me, Leo. I'm just passing a message from the man.*"

"*From Marcello?*"

"*Yeah. Elvis was down here a few months ago, and he told Carlos you were tight with Hoover. He said —*"

"*Elvis?*"

"*Yeah. Presley. That, ah . . . what's his first name? Ray. Carlos's guys call him Elvis.*"

A pause on Marston's end. Then: "*I thought Frank Costello greased the skids with Hoover for Marcello.*"

"*Well, you didn't hear it from me, okay? But Carlos and Frank are on the outs just now. Not a good time for Carlos to call New York for a favor. So anyway, Elvis was down here, and he told the man you guys cooled out a nigger down there two or three years back, and Hoover let it slide for you —*"

A gasp from the jury box.

"*— said you call him Edgar, like he's your uncle or*

something." Lacour laughing now. *"Anyway, Carlos wants you to talk to the old queen and get this Harold Hughes off his back. This fucking guy don't know how it works down here."*

"Does Marcello understand how things work with Hoover?"

"What do you mean?"

"Hoover expects a quid pro quo."

"Hey, there's always a quid pro quo, right? That's business. But look, Elvis wasn't just talkin' shit about this nigger, was he?"

"No. Hoover grew up in Washington, D.C., when it was still a Southern town. This business you're talking about was in sixty-eight. Hoover would have traded twenty nigras for one electoral vote for Nixon. It was that close. You tell Marcello I'll speak to Edgar, but remember . . . quid pro quo. That goes for me as well."

"Hey, do I know you or don't I? Now, what about those gas leases where they're dredging down by Houma —."

Judge Franklin switches off the machine.

The silence is total. I'm not sure anyone in the courtroom is breathing. The jury appears to be in shock, particularly the black jurors, who are staring at Leo Marston as they might at a dangerous wild animal. Blake Sims gets to his feet to start listing objections, but Franklin stops him with a gesture.

A chilling screech of chair legs rips through the courtroom. As all heads turn toward the source of the sound — the plaintiff's table — Livy rises from her chair, puts her purse over her shoulder, and without looking at her father or anyone else walks around the table and down the aisle to the door at the back of the courtroom.

This act is probably more damning to her father than the tape. To me it suggests a chance for the possibility of redemption. At least she draws the line somewhere. I suppress the urge to go after her, even though I know that at this moment she might do something truly desperate. I must play my part in this grotesquerie to the end. As I turn back toward the bench, Austin Mackey stands and hurries after Livy. I'll have to wait to find out what he's up to.

"Mr. Sims," Judge Franklin says from the bench. "I know what you're going to say. First, that the voice on this tape is not Leo Marston's. Second, that if the voice *is* Marston's, it has been spliced together using some miracle of modern technology. Third, you want to request a continuance while your experts examine the tape."

Franklin drums her fingers on her desk. "Mr. Sims, that is not going to happen. I am not going to recall this jury three weeks from now just to hear your experts denounce the tape and Mr. Cage's experts argue that it's genuine. I've known Leo Marston for twenty-five years, and *I* believe the tape is genuine. Mr. Sims, I am giving this case to the jury."

Most of the heads in the jury box are nodding.

"Does the plaintiff rest?" Franklin asks.

"Under protest," Sims says weakly.

"Noted." Franklin turns to me. "Does the defense rest?"

"Your Honor, the defense rests."

Franklin is about to begin instructing the jury when Leo Marston rises from his chair and walks

711

toward the aisle as though to follow Livy out.

"Judge Marston?" Franklin says from the bench.

He gives the judge his broad back and starts down the aisle.

"Leo?" she calls.

Marston ignores her. He is nearly to the doors, his enormous shoulders rocking with purposeful motion.

"Bailiff," says Franklin, her voice quavering with what sounds like fear. "Please restrain Mr. Marston."

The bailiff, a middle-aged black man, stands in front of the door and lays a hand on the butt of his holstered gun. Leo looks prepared to make the poor man use it.

"You will stay to hear the verdict of this jury, Mr. Marston," Franklin says in a firmer voice. "Unless you're dismissing this suit."

Leonidas Marston finally stops and turns back to Judge Franklin, his face a mask of contempt. "I'm entitled to a jury of my peers," he says, his voice booming through the courtroom. "I won't be judged by that rabble sitting up there."

Franklin's face reddens to the point that I fear she might stroke out. "Leo, I'm holding you —"

"I'm dismissing the suit," he growls. Then he turns back to the door as though he could as easily dismiss the consequences of this proceeding from his life.

As the bailiff looks to Judge Franklin for guidance, the door behind him is yanked open and Austin Mackey walks through, followed by two large deputies. The deputies block the door while Mackey walks far enough up the aisle to make sure the TV cameras capture the full range of his limited charisma.

"Judge Franklin," he says in the deepest voice he can muster. "Regardless of the verdict of this jury, I am ordering the arrest of Leo Marston for the crime of capital murder."

Pandemonium erupts in the courtroom.

"Order!" Franklin shouts. "Quiet in this court!"

"The grand jury will be convened in two weeks," Mackey goes on, "and I intend to bring the case before them at that time."

Judge Franklin shakes her head and gives the district attorney a sarcastic smile. "Let me state for the record, Mr. Mackey, that you are a day late, and a dollar short. Since Mr. Cage has proved your case for you, I suggest you forward your salary for the month to him."

Mackey blushes from his neck to the top of his head, but he recovers quickly and turns back to the deputies blocking the door. "Place Mr. Marston under arrest. The charge is capital murder."

It must gall Mackey to have to get the deputies to make this arrest. But even with his overarching ambition, Mackey hasn't the nerve to try to arrest Leo Marston. It would be like a rabbit confronting a Bengal tiger. I half expect Leo to fight the deputies to the floor, but he allows himself to be quietly handcuffed.

"Judge Franklin," says Blake Sims. "I request that Judge Marston be taken out through a side door, to spare the embarrassment of a mob scene. He's done great service to this city and this state, no matter what else he might have done."

Technically, Leo is Mackey's prisoner now, but

this is Eunice Franklin's court. He defers to her.

Franklin stares at Leo, who is looking indifferently ahead, as though bored by the events around him. His problem has become one for the criminal courts, and he knows that particular jungle better than most.

"Take him out the front door," Franklin says.

As the deputies escort Marston out, Judge Franklin looks to the jury box. "Ladies and gentlemen, you have done your duty. I apologize for the incompleteness of the process. At least it only took one day. You are discharged." She turns to the gallery. "This court is dismissed."

A wild roar erupts from outside the building, undoubtedly prompted by the appearance of Leo Marston in handcuffs. I have no desire to be in that crowd of jubilant blacks and confused whites, people who still know nothing of the facts of this case, and who probably won't fully absorb them for several days. As the spectators rise from the benches in a rush, I am surrounded by people slapping my back and trying to shake my hand.

The first hand I take is my father's. His grip is firm and strong, his eyes filled with pride. "You did a fair job, son." He breaks into a smile.

My mother is in tears beside him. She reaches out and hugs me, while behind her Charles Evers and Willie Pinder give me brief salutes, then turn and move toward the door. As I stare after them, Caitlin materializes out of the crowd, smiling with relief.

"Well, I guess we won," she says. "Right?"

"You're damn right," Dad agrees.

"I'm thinking of Ruby," my mother says quietly.

714

"Me too," I tell her.

She takes my hand. "You had to do it. I see that now."

Before I can say anything else, Caitlin steps up to me, stands on tiptoe, and kisses me on the cheek. "I've been wanting to do that all day." She turns to my parents. "I hope you don't mind public displays of affection."

My mother surprises the hell out of me by saying, "That's quite all right."

I punch Caitlin's shoulder. "Can you win the Pulitzer if you're personally involved in the story you're covering?"

She waves her hand as though swatting a fly. "To hell with the Pulitzer. I'll take it if they offer it, but I'm not chasing it anymore."

My father grips my right shoulder and turns me in place. Judge Franklin is standing behind me in her black robe. She extends her hand and shakes mine. "That's the first time I've ever seen a slander case hijacked into a murder trial," she says.

"I couldn't figure any other way to do it. I apologize."

"Don't. Sometimes you have to go the long way around to get justice."

"I appreciate what you did. The hearsay exception . . . letting the tape in."

A hint of a smile comes to her lips. "The truth will out. Good-bye, Mr. Cage."

I nod thanks and turn back to Caitlin, who takes my hand, pulls it behind her back, and squeezes it tight.

Out of the swirl of my parents' friends, Althea Payton steps forward wearing a dark blue dress.

715

Behind her stands Del, looking very uncomfortable in a Sunday suit.

"I can finally get on with living," Althea says softly. Her liquid brown eyes meet mine, and for a moment there is no one in the courtroom but us. "I think you know what I'm talking about," she adds.

An image of Sarah flashes behind my eyes, but too much has happened today to let it in. "I do."

Del reaches over his mother's shoulder and shakes my hand. "Thanks, man."

I shake his hand, nod thanks, then prepare to accept the congratulations of all the others waiting behind him. But my thoughts are already far away. Somewhere outside this building Livy Marston is walking or driving alone, pondering the wreckage of her life. Her father is right where I hoped he would be, but Livy isn't. Despite all I have seen of her — the coldness and dishonesty and manipulation — part of me longs to be with her now. The bottle of wine we sank twenty years ago still waits at the bottom of that cold, clear pool, buried under mud and sand and time, but there all the same. And God help me, I wish I were going to her bed tonight.

But I'm not. I will not.

The past is dead.

EPILOGUE

I am standing in line for It's A Small World at Walt Disney World in Florida. Annie is in my arms, but this time we are not alone. Caitlin stands beside us, smiling as the line snakes toward the boats filled with parents and wide-eyed children. We are not a family, the three of us, not legally, but we are very happy together in this moment. Caitlin takes my hand as the line moves forward, not looking at me but simply being with me, with the comfort of familiar lovers.

I hardly ever think of Livy now, and when I do it is only with sadness for her, not for us. She flew back to Atlanta the day after the trial, but whether to conclude her divorce or to reconcile with her husband, I have no idea. Before she left, I had coffee with her at the Eola Hotel. In the awkward silence between us, I made three requests. First, that she inform Jenny Doe that her father was a boy who is now married and does not want his identity revealed. Second, that Livy provide funds for Jenny to attend the college of her choice, and establish a trust fund that will provide a livable income for the rest of Jenny's life. And third, that she make no fuss over Jenny using the Marston family name, should she elect to do so. I suspect that

Jenny will elect not to, but I want her to have the choice. The threat of what could happen should Livy not live up to these conditions did not need to be stated. My knowledge of the contents of Leo's secret safe could decimate her family fortune.

The remaining fallout from the trial happened quickly. Less than forty-eight hours after portions of Dwight Stone's testimony began running on CNN, John Portman was asked by the President to resign as director of the FBI. One week later it was announced that he had accepted a position with the DeTocqueville Trust, a conservative think-tank based in Alexandria, Virginia.

Four days after Portman's resignation, Special Agent Peter Lutjens's transfer to North Dakota was rescinded, and he resumed his duties in Washington, D.C. Dwight Stone's daughter also resumed her Bureau duties, but Stone has confided to me by telephone that she plans to resign soon. She seems to have some crazy idea about practicing country law with her father in Colorado.

Two weeks after Stone mounted the witness stand in Natchez, a grand jury indicted Leo Marston on capital murder charges. He is scheduled to go to trial in two days, with Austin Mackey prosecuting. The consensus of the Natchez legal community is that he will be found guilty and receive life imprisonment. When the masses finally turn on a tyrant, they turn viciously.

In the mayoral election, Wiley Warren defeated Shad Johnson by a percentage margin of 51–49. Shad did not win the votes of those "good whites" he needed to push him over the top, and the ill feeling stirred up by my pursuit of the Payton case may well have been the cause of that. Such is life. Wiley Warren has not been a bad mayor. And if Shad means business, he can stick around four more years and become a true citizen of the town. I may do that myself.

The cool November air has thinned the crowds at Disney World, and we've had our run of the park. Some popular rides have no lines at all. Yet the Fantasyland rides — Dumbo and Alice's Tea Party and It's A Small World — are always backed up at least to the end of the chute. Some parents have the stupefied looks of ride hypnosis, but most of the faces are alight with joy. The longing for that kind of innocence never quite fades.

As we near the magical grotto, the syrupy sweet chorus of "It's A Small World After All" envelops us, and I think again of Jenny Doe. As a foster child, she never set foot in a place like this. She never had the chance to believe it was real, or to return later and laugh about how corny it is. Jenny was not my child. But she could have been. She could have been. In the dreadful moment that she told me she thought she was, my fear had testified to the possibility. Our actions have consequences that last long after us, entwining the present with the future in ways we cannot begin to understand. I have resolved a simple thing: I will do those things which make me happy today, and which I can also live with ten years from now.

As Caitlin helps Annie into the flat-bottomed boat, she turns back and looks at me, her green eyes sparkling. My mind is a thousand miles away, and she knows it. She kisses me anyway, pulling me gently back to reality with a warm and promising gesture of love. Caitlin is not a substitute for the wife I lost. She is a different person. Her own person. Sarah will always be the secret sharer in my heart, and in Annie's too. But Annie no longer walks the streets of Disney World with haunted eyes, searching for a face she will never see in life again. And when I make love with Caitlin, holding her tenderly in the dark as Annie sleeps, I push not into the past but into the future.

As the little boat jerks forward off the rollers and settles into the water, I put my arms around Caitlin and Annie and hug them to me with all my strength and soul. Their laughter is like lamplight in the dark.

I can live with this.